P9-DMU-205

'Absolutely captivating' *Andrea Camilleri*

'Its complexity turns *Confessions* into a piece of writing that has the power to influence our view of the world – a quality belonging to the best of literature' *El Mundo*

'Jaume Cabré deserves to be recognised for what he is, one of the greatest of world literature' *Jordi Cevera*

'Hitting the jackpot with *Confessions*, Cabré's is a story of European history from the Inquisition to Auschwitz' *Le Figaro*

'A narrative that unfolds with such creativity and mastery ... perfection from an author who has reached the very highest level of excellence in his craft. This book has earned its place alongside the classics' *Joan Josep Isern*

'The complexity of the novel makes *Confessions* a work that is capable of influencing its readers' views of the world. This can only be found in the very, very best literature' Angel Basanta

'770 pages of a story where clashing eras and characters are viewed through a series of memories that are more or less exploded out of the brain of an Alzheimer's patient. And yet, it is impossible to abandon or lose the thread of this exciting novel. This is called A MASTERPIECE' *Marianna* magazine, France

'An exquisite swan song – an ode to a ruined humanity that has been swept away by history. You'll find yourself on the edge of an abyss – at the dawn of a new order. Most extraordinary. Most moving. Most of all something you will never forget' *La Quinzane Litterataire*

'An incredible text that speaks to all – the walls, the dead, the unborn. Outstanding' Marine Landrot, *Telerama*

'A work of art more than a novel' Karine Papillaud, *Le Point*

## ABOUT THE AUTHOR

Jaume Cabré is one of the most internationally celebrated contemporary Catalan writers. He is the author of a number of bestselling novels, with over a million copies sold throughout Europe, and has been awarded most of the Catalan literary awards, including the Premi d'Honor de les Lletres Catalanes. *Confessions* has been called a masterpiece of world literature by international reviewers, and awarded the Premio de la Crítica, Premi de la Crítica Serra d'Or, Premi de Narrativa Maria Àngels Anglada, Premi Joan Crexells de l'Ateneu Barcelonès, Premio La Tormenta en un Vaso (all 2012). *Confessions* has also been shortlisted for both the Prix Femina and the Prix Medicis in France (2013).

## ABOUT THE TRANSLATOR

Mara Faye Lethem has translated novels by David Trueba, Albert Sánchez Piñol, Javier Calvo, Patricio Pron, Marc Pastor and Pablo De Santis, among others. Her translations have appeared in *The Best American Non-Required Reading 2010*, *Granta*, *The Paris Review* and *McSweeney's*.

# Confessions

## JAUME CABRÉ

Translated from the Catalan by
Mara Faye Lethem

ARCADIA BOOKS

Arcadia Books Ltd
139 Highlever Road
London W10 6PH

*www.arcadiabooks.co.uk*

First published in the United Kingdom by Arcadia Books 2014
Originally published by Raval Edicions SLU, Proa, as *Jo Confesso* 2011
Copyright © Jaume Cabré 2011

English language translation copyright © Mara Faye Lethem 2014
Jaume Cabré asserted his moral right to be identified as the author of this work in
accordance with the Copyright, Designs and Patents Act, 1988.

All Rights Reserved. No part of this publication may be reproduced in any form or by
any means without the written permission of the publishers.

A catalogue record for this book is available from the British Library.

ISBN 978-1-910050-27-9

Typeset in Minion by MacGuru Ltd
Printed and bound in Australia by Griffin Press

The translation of this work has received a grant from Institut Ramon Llull, and
Arcadia Books is grateful for their help and support.

LLLL **Institut**
**ramon llull**
Catalan Language and Culture

This book is published in agreement with
Cristina Mora Literary & Film Agency

Arcadia Books supports English PEN *www.englishpen.org* and
The Book Trade Charity *www.btbs.org*

*Arcadia Books distributors are as follows:*

*in the UK and elsewhere in Europe*:
Macmillan Distribution Ltd
Brunel Road
Houndmills
Basingstoke
Hants RG21 6XS

*in the USA and Canada*:
Dufour Editions
PO Box 7
Chester Springs
PA 19425

*in Australia/New Zealand*:
NewSouth Books
University of New South Wales
Sydney NSW 2052

# Contents

*To Margarida*

# I

# A CAPITE …

I will be nothing.

Carles Camps Mundó

1

It wasn't until last night, walking along the wet streets of Vallcarca, that I finally comprehended that being born into my family had been an unforgivable mistake. Suddenly I understood that I had always been alone, never able to count on parents or a God I could entrust to search for solutions though, as I grew up, I got in the habit of delegating the weight of thought and the responsibility for my actions into vague beliefs and very wide readings. Yesterday, Tuesday night, caught in the downpour on my way home from Dalmau's house, I came to the conclusion that this burden was mine alone. And that my successes and my mistakes were my responsibility and only mine. It had taken me sixty years to see it. I hope you can understand me, understand that I feel abandoned, alone and absolutely bereft without you. Despite the distance that separates us, you are an example for me. Despite my panic, I refuse to cling to driftwood in order to stay afloat. Despite some insinuations, I remain without beliefs, without priests, without consensual codes that smooth out my road to who knows where. I feel old, and the hooded figure with the scythe calls me to follow him. I see that he has moved his black bishop and gestures politely for me to continue the game. He knows I have very few pawns left. Still, it is not tomorrow yet and I look for a piece to move. I am alone before this page, my last chance.

Don't trust me blindly. Memoirs written for a single reader are prone to falsehoods and I know that I'll tend to land on my feet, like cats do; but I'll make an effort not to invent much. It was all like this and worse. I know that I should have talked to you about this long ago; but it's difficult and right now I don't know where to begin.

It all started, really, more than five hundred years ago, when a tormented man decided to request entry into the monastery of Sant Pere del Burgal. If he hadn't, or if Father Prior Josep de Sant Bartomeu had held firm in his refusal, I wouldn't be explaining all this now. But I can't go back that far. I'll begin later on. Much later on.

'Your father … Look, Son. Father …'

No, no; I don't want to start there either. It's better to start with the study where I am writing now, in front of your impressive self-portrait. The study is my world, my life, my universe, where almost everything has a place, except love. I wasn't usually allowed in here when I ran through the flat in shorts or with my hands covered in chilblains during autumns and winters. I had to sneak in. I knew every nook and corner, and for a few years I had a secret fortress behind the sofa, which I had to dismantle after each incursion so Little Lola wouldn't discover it when she passed the floorcloth back there. But every time I entered lawfully I had to behave like a guest, with my hands behind my back as Father showed me the latest manuscript he'd found in a rundown shop in Berlin, look at this, and be careful with those hands, I don't want to have to scold you. Adrià leaned over the manuscript, very curious.

'It's in German, right?' – his hand reaching out as if by reflex.

'Psst! Watch those fingers! You're always touching everything …' He smacked his hand. 'What were you saying?'

'It's in German, right?'– rubbing his smarting hand.

'Yes.'

'I want to learn German.'

Fèlix Ardèvol looked proudly at his son and told him you can start studying it very soon, my boy.

In fact, it wasn't a manuscript but a packet of brownish folios: on the first page, in an overly ornate hand, it read *Der begrabene Leuchter. Eine Legende.*

'Who is Stefan Zweig?'

Father – a magnifying glass in his hand, distracted by a correction in the margin of the first paragraph – instead of answering a writer, my son, just said well, some guy who

killed himself in Brazil ten or twelve years ago. For a long
time the only thing I knew about Stefan Zweig was that he
was a guy who killed himself in Brazil ten or twelve, or thirteen, fourteen or fifteen years ago, until I was able to read the
manuscript and learn a little about who he was.

And then the visit ended and Adrià left the study with the
recommendation that he keep quiet: you could never run or
shout or chat inside the house because if Father wasn't studying a manuscript under a magnifying glass, he was reviewing
the inventory of medieval maps or thinking about where to
acquire new objects that would make his fingers tremble. The
only thing I was allowed to do that made noise, in my room,
was studying the violin. But I couldn't spend the entire day
practising arpeggio exercise number XXIII in *O livro dos exercícios da velocidade*. That exercise made me hate Trullols so
much, but it didn't make me hate the violin. No, I didn't hate
Trullols. But she could be very annoying, especially when she
insisted on exercise XXIII.

'I'm just saying we could change it up a bit.'

'Here,' and she would tap the score with the heel of the bow,
'you will find all the difficulties summed up on one page. It is
a simply genius exercise.'

'But I ...'

'For Friday I want number XXIII perfect. Even bar 27.'

Sometimes Trullols was thick like that. But, overall, she was
an acceptable woman. And sometimes, more than acceptable.

Bernat thought the same. I hadn't yet met Bernat when I did
*O livro dos exercícios da velocidade*. But we shared the same
opinion about Trullols. She must have been a great teacher
even though she doesn't appear in the history books, as far
as I know. I think I need to focus because I'm jumbling everything up. Yes, there are surely things you know, especially
when they're about you. But there are snippets of the soul that
I don't believe you do know because it's impossible to know a
person completely, no matter what.

Even though it was more spectacular, I didn't like the shop
as much as the study at home. Perhaps because those very few
times when I went in there, I always felt I was being watched.

The shop had one advantage, which was that I could gaze upon Cecília, who was gorgeous; I was deeply in love with her. She was a woman with galactic blonde hair, always well-coiffed, and with full lips of furious red. And she was always busy with her catalogues and her price lists, and writing labels, and helping the few customers that came in, with a smile that revealed her perfect teeth.

'Do you have musical instruments?'

The man hadn't even removed his hat. Standing in front of Cecília, he glanced around: lights, candelabra, cherry-wood chairs with very fine inlay work, *canapés en confident* from the early nineteenth century, vases of every size and period … He didn't even see me.

'Not many, but if you'll follow me …'

The not many instruments at the shop were a couple of violins and a viola that didn't sound very good but had gut strings that were miraculously unbroken. And a dented tuba, two magnificent flugelhorns and a trumpet, which the valley's governor had sounded desperately to warn the people in the other valleys that the Paneveggio forest was burning. Those in Pardàc asked for help from Siròr, San Martino and even from Welschnofen, which had suffered its own flames not long before, and from Moena and Soraga, where they had perhaps already noticed the alarming odour of that disaster in the Year of Our Lord 1690, when the earth was round for almost everyone and – if unknown ailments, godless savages and beasts of sea and land, ice storms or excessive rains didn't impede it – the boats that vanished to the west returned from the east, with their sailors more gaunt and haggard, their gazes lost out on the horizon and bad dreams gripping their nights. The summer of that Year of Our Lord 1690, every inhabitant of Pardàc, Moena, Siròr, and San Martino except the prostrate, ran to look with sleepy eyes at the disaster that was destroying their lives, some more than others. That dreadful fire they watched helplessly had already consumed loads of good wood. When the fire was put out with the help of some timely rains, Jachiam, the fourth and cleverest son of Mureda of Pardàc, travelled carefully through the devastated forest to search for serviceable logs in corners the flames hadn't reached. Halfway down to the Ós ravine, he squatted to move his bowels beneath a young fir tree that was now coal. But what he saw took away all desire to relieve himself: resinous wood wrapped in a rag that gave off the scent of camphor and some other strange substance. He very carefully unravelled the rags that hadn't been completely burned in the hellish fire that had demolished his future. What he discovered made him feel faint: the dirty green rag that hid the resinous kindling, with hems of an even dirtier yellow cord, was a piece of the doublet usually worn by Bulchanij Brocia, the fattest man in Moena. When he found two more piles of cloth, those ones well burned, he understood that Bulchanij – that monster – had followed through on his threat to ruin the Mureda family and, with them, the entire village of Pardàc.

'Bulchanij.'

'I don't speak to dogs.'

'Bulchanij.'

The sombre tone of voice made him turn reluctantly. Bulchanij of Moena had a prominent belly that, had he lived longer and eaten enough, would have been a very good spot to rest his arms.

'What the hell do you want?'

'Where's your doublet?'

'What the hell business is that of yours?'

'Why aren't you wearing it? Show it to me.'

'Piss off. What do you think, just because you're down on your luck everybody from Moena has to do what you say? Eh?' He pointed to him with hatred in his eyes. 'I'm not going to show it to you. Now get lost, you're blocking the damn sun.'

Jachiam, the fourth Mureda boy, with cold rage, unsheathed the bark-stripping knife he always carried in his belt. He rammed it into the belly of Bulchanij Brocia, the fattest man in Moena, as if he were the trunk of a maple tree. Bulchanij opened his mouth and his eyes widened as big as oranges, surprised less by the pain than by the fact that a piece of shit from Pardàc dared to touch him. When Jachiam Mureda pulled out his knife, which made a disgusting bloop

CONFESSIONS

gloop and was red with blood, Bulchanij collapsed into a
chair as if deflating from the wound.

Jachiam looked up and down the deserted road. Naively, he
set off running towards Pardàc. When he had passed the last
house in Moena, he realised that the hunchbacked woman from
the mill, who was loaded down with wet clothes and looked
at him mouth agape, might have seen everything. Instead of
lashing out at her gaze, he just increased his pace. Even though
he was the best at finding tonewoods, even though he was not
yet twenty, his life had just abruptly changed course.

His family reacted well, because they quickly sent people
to San Martino and Siròr, to explain with evidence that
Bulchanij was an arsonist who had burned the forest down
maliciously, but the people of Moena thought that there was
no need to come to any arrangement with the law and they
prepared, without any arbitrators, to hunt down villainous
Jachiam Mureda.

'Son,' said old man Mureda, his gaze even sadder than usual.
'You must flee.' And he held out a bag with half of the gold he'd
saved over thirty years of working the Paneveggio wood. And
none of Jachiam's siblings said a word about that decision. And,
somewhat ceremoniously, he said even though you are the best
tree tracker and the best at locating tonewood, Jachiam, my
dear son, the fourth of this ill-fated house, your life is worth
more than the best maple trunk we could ever sell. And this
way you will save yourself from the ruin that surely awaits us,
because Bulchanij of Moena has left us without wood.

'Father, I …'

'Run, flee, be quick about it, go through Welschnofen,
because they will surely be looking for you in Siròr. We will
spread the word that you are hiding in Siròr or Tonadich. It's
too dangerous for you to stay in the valleys. You'll have to
make a very, very long trip, far from Pardàc. Run, Son, and
may God keep you and protect you.'

'But Father, I don't want to leave. I want to work in the
forest.'

'They've burned it down. What could you work with, Son?'

'I don't know; but if I leave the valleys I'll die!'

'If you don't run away this very night, I'll kill you myself. Do you understand me now?'

'Father ...'

'No one from Moena will lay a hand on any son of mine.'

And Jachiam of the Muredas from Pardàc said goodbye to his father and kissed each of his siblings one by one: Agno, Jenn, Max and their wives. Hermes, Josef, Theodor and Micurà. Ilse, Eria and their husbands; and then, Katharina, Matilde, Gretchen and Bettina. They had all gathered to say goodbye to him in silence, and when he was already at the door, little Bettina said Jachiam, and he turned and saw how the girl held out her hand, and from it hung the medallion of Saint Maria dai Ciüf of Pardàc, the medallion that Mum had entrusted her with on her deathbed. Jachiam, in silence, looked at his brothers and sisters, and fixed his gaze on his father, who made a wordless gesture with his head. Then he went over to little Bettina and took the medallion and said Bettina, my sweet little one, I will wear this treasure until the day I die; and he didn't know how true what he was saying would be. And Bettina touched both of her hands to his cheeks, refusing to cry. Jachiam left the house with his eyes flooded; he murmured a brief prayer at his mother's grave and disappeared into the night, towards the endless snow, to change his life, change his history and his memories.

'Is that all you have?'

'This is an antiques shop,' responded Cecília with that stern attitude that made men feel ashamed. And with a hint of sarcasm, 'Why don't you try a luthier?'

I liked Cecília when she got mad. She was even prettier. Prettier than Mother even. Than Mother in that period.

From where I was I could see Mr Berenguer's office. I heard Cecília escorting the disappointed customer, who still wore his hat, to the door. As I heard the little bell ring and Cecília wish him well, Mr Berenguer looked up and winked at me.

'Adrià.'

'Yes.'

'When are they coming to pick you up?' he said, raising his voice.

I shrugged. I never knew exactly when I had to be one place or the other. My parents didn't want me home alone so they brought me to the shop whenever they were both out. Which was fine for me because I entertained myself looking at the most unimaginable objects, things that had already lived and now rested patiently waiting for a second or third or fourth opportunity. And I imagined their lives in different homes and it was very amusing.

Little Lola always ended up coming for me, rushing because she had to make dinner and hadn't even started. That was why I shrugged when Mr Berenguer asked me when they were picking me up.

'Come,' he told me, lifting up a blank piece of paper. 'Sit at the Tudor desk and draw for a bit.'

I've never liked drawing because I don't know how; I haven't a clue. That's why I've always admired your skill, which I find miraculous. Mr Berenguer told me to draw for a bit because it bothered him to see me there doing nothing, which wasn't true, because I spent the time thinking. But you can't say no to Mr Berenguer. Seated there at the Tudor desk, I did whatever I could to keep him quiet. I pulled Black Eagle out of my pocket and tried to draw him. Poor Black Eagle, if he could see himself on that paper … That was before Black Eagle had had a chance to meet Sheriff Carson, because I'd acquired him that very morning in a swap with Ramon Coll for a Weiss harmonica. If my father finds out, he'll kill me.

Mr Berenguer was very special; when he smiled he scared me a little and he treated Cecília like an inept maid, something I've never forgiven him for. But he was the one who knew the most about Father, my great mystery.

2

The *Santa Maria* reached Ostia on the foggy early morning of Thursday, September 2nd. His voyage from Barcelona was worse than any of the trips Aeneas took in search of his destiny and eternal glory. Neptune did not smile on him aboard the *Santa Maria* and he spent much of the journey feeding the fish. By the time he arrived, his skin colour had changed from the healthy tan typical of a peasant from the Plain of Vic to pale as a mystical apparition.

That seminarian had such excellent qualifications – he was studious, pious and polished, learned despite his age – that Monsignor Josep Torras i Bages had personally decided that he would be squandering his God-given gift of bountiful natural intelligence in Vic. They had a precious flower on their hands and it would wither in the humble vegetable patch that was Vic's seminary; it needed a lush garden in which to thrive.

'I don't want to go to Rome, Monsignor. I want to devote myself to study bec

'That's precisely why I'm sending you to Rome, dear boy. I know our seminary well enough to know that an intelligence like yours is wasting its time here.'

'But, Monsignor …'

'God has great designs for you. Your instructors have been insisting,' he said, shaking the document in his hands a bit theatrically.

Born at Can Ges in the village of Tona, into the bosom of an exemplary family, son of Andreu and Rosalia, at six years old he already possessed the academic preparation and the accordant resolve to commence his ecclesiastical studies, beginning with the first course in Latinity under

the direction of Pater Jacint Garrigós. His academic
progress was so noteworthy and immediate that when
he began to study Rhetoric, he had to lecture on the
celebrated 'Oratio Latina'. The Monsignor knows from
personal experience, since we have had the immense
pleasure of having you as a student in this seminary,
that this is one of the first literary acts with which
the instructors honour their most distinguished and
proven student orators. But that distinction exceeded his
eleven years and, above all, his still slight frame. While
the audience could hear the solemn rhetorician Fèlix
Ardèvol lecturing conscientiously in the language of
Virgil, a not small stool was required to allow the tiny
and circumspect speaker to be seen by the spectators
who included his thrilled parents and brother. Thus Fèlix
Ardèvol y Guiteres set off on the path of great academic
triumphs in Mathematics, Philosophy, Theology, reaching
the height of illustrious students of this seminary such as
the distinguished fathers Jaume Balmes y Urpià, Antoni
Maria Claret y Clarà, Jacint Verdaguer y Santaló, Jaume
Collell y Bancells, Professor Andreu Duran and Your
Grace, who honours us as bishop of our beloved diocese.

May our virtue of gratitude extend to our predecessors
as well. The Lord Our God calls on us to do so: 'Laudemos
viors gloriosos et parentes nostros in generatione sua'
(Eccles. 44:1) It is for this reason that we are convinced we
are correct in enthusiastically requesting that seminary
student Fèlix Ardèvol y Guiteres continue his Theology
studies at the Pontifical Gregorian University.

'You have no choice, my child.'
Fèlix Ardèvol didn't dare to say that he hated boats, he who
had been born on terra firma and had always lived far from
the sea. Since he hadn't known how to face up to the bishop,
he'd had to undertake that arduous voyage. In a corner of the
Ostia port, beside some half-rotted boxes infested with huge
rats, he vomited up his impotence and almost all his memories of the past. For a few seconds, he breathed heavily as he

stood up again, wiped his mouth with a handkerchief, briskly smoothed the cassock he'd worn on the trip and looked towards his splendid future. Despite the circumstances, like Aeneas, he had arrived in Rome.

'This is the best room in the residency.'

Surprised, Fèlix Ardèvol turned. In the doorway a short, somewhat plump student, who was sweating like a pig inside a Dominican habit, smiled kindly.

'Félix Morlin, from Liège,' said the stranger, taking a step into the cell.

'Fèlix Ardèvol. From Vic.'

'Oh! A namesake!' he shouted, laughing as he extended a hand.

They were fast friends. Morlin told him that he'd been given the most coveted room in the residence hall and asked him what his inside connection was. Ardèvol had to confess that he had none; that at reception, the fat, bald concierge had looked at his papers and said Ardevole?, cinquantaquattro, and he'd given him the key without even looking him in the eye. Morlin didn't believe him, but he laughed heartily.

Exactly a week later, before the school year began, Morlin introduced him to eight or ten students he knew in the second year; he advised him not to waste his time befriending students outside of the Gregorian or the Istituto Biblico; he showed him how to slip out unnoticed by the guard, urging him to have lay clothes prepared in case they had to stroll incognito. He was the guide for the new first-year students, showing them the unique buildings along the shortest route from the residence hall to the Pontifical Gregorian University. His Italian was tinged with a French accent but totally understandable. And he gave them a speech about the importance of knowing how to keep your distance from the Jesuits at the Gregorian, because, if you weren't careful, they would turn your brain on its ear. Just like that, plof!

The day before classes began, all the new and old students, who came from a thousand different places, gathered in the huge auditorium of the Palazzo Gabrielli-Borromeo at the

Gregorian's headquarters, and the Pater Decanus of the Pontifical Gregorian University of the Collegio Romano, Daniele D'Angelo, S.J., in perfect Latin, urged us to be aware of our great luck, of the great privilege you have to be able to study in any of the faculties of the Pontifical Gregorian University, etcetera, etcetera, etcetera. Here we have had the honour of welcoming illustrious students, and among them there have been a few holy fathers, the last of which was our sorely missed Pope Leo XIII. We will demand nothing more of you than effort, effort and effort. You come here to study, study, study and learn from the best specialists in Theology, Canonical Law, Spirituality, Church History, etcetera, etcetera, etcetera.

'Pater D'Angelo is called D'Angelodangelodangelo,' Morlin whispered in his ear, as if he were communicating worrisome news.

And when you have finished your studies, you will scatter all over the world, you will return to your countries, to your seminaries, to the institutes of your orders; those who are not yet will be ordained priests and will bear the fruit of what you were taught here. Etcetera, etcetera, etcetera and then fifteen minutes more of practical advice, perhaps not as practical as Morlin's, but necessary for everyday life. Fèlix Ardèvol thought that it could have been worse; sometimes the Orationes Latinae in Vic were more boring than that pragmatic instruction manual he was reciting for them.

The first months of the school year, until after Christmas, passed without incident. Fèlix Ardèvol particularly admired the brilliance of Pater Faluba, a half-Slovak, half-Hungarian Jesuit with infinite knowledge of the Bible, and the mental rigour of Pater Pierre Blanc, who was very haughty and taught the revelation and its transmission to the Church, and who, despite also having been born in Liège, had failed Morlin on the final exam in which his friend wrote about the approximations to Marian theology. Since he sat next to him in three subjects, he began to make friends with Drago Gradnik, a red-faced Slovenian giant who had come from the Ljubljana seminary and had a wide, powerful bull's neck that

looked as if it was about to burst out of his clerical collar. They
talked little, although his Latin was fluent. But both were shy
and tried to channel their energies in getting through the
numerous doors their studies opened for them. While Morlin
complained and widened his circle of contacts and friends,
Ardèvol locked himself up in cinquantaquattro, the best cell
in the residence hall, and he discovered new worlds in the
paleographic study of papyri and other biblical documents
that Pater Faluba brought them, written in Demotic, Coptic,
Greek or Aramaic. He taught them the art of loving objects.
A destroyed manuscript, he would repeat, is of no use to
science. If it must be restored, it must be restored no matter
the cost. And the role of the restorer is as important as the
role of the scientist who will interpret it. And he didn't say
etcetera, etcetera, etcetera, because he always knew what he
was talking about.

'Balderdash,' declared Morlin when he mentioned it to
him. 'Those people are happy with just a magnifying glass
in their hand and some tattered, mouldy papers on the table.'

'Me too.'

'What good are dead languages?' he now said in his
pompous Latin.

'Pater Faluba told us that men don't inhabit a country; we
inhabit a language. And that by rescuing ancient languages ...'

'Sciocchezze. Stupiditates. The only dead language that's
truly alive is Latin.'

They were on Via di Sant'Ignazio. Ardèvol was protected
by his cassock, and Morlin by his habit. For the first time,
Ardèvol looked at his friend strangely. He stopped and asked
him, perplexed, what he believed in. Morlin stopped as well
and told him that he had become a Dominican friar because
he had a deep yearning to help others and serve the church.
And that nothing would dissuade him from his path; but
that you had to serve the church in a practical way, not by
studying rotting papers, but by influencing people who influence the life of ... He stopped and then added: etcetera,
etcetera, etcetera, and the two friends both burst out laughing. Just then, Carolina passed them by for the first time, but

neither noticed her. And when I reached the house with Little Lola, I had to study the violin while she prepared supper and the rest of the flat grew dark. I didn't like that at all because some villain could always come out from behind some door and that was why I carried Black Eagle in my pocket, since at home, as Father had decided years ago, there were no medallions, scapulars, engravings or missals, and Adrià Ardèvol, poor boy, had need of invisible help. And one day, instead of studying the violin, I stayed in the dining room, fascinated, watching how the sun fled to the west, along Trespui, in the painting above the dining room sideboard, lighting up the Santa Maria de Gerri abbot with magical colour. Always the same light, which drew me in and made me think of impossible stories, and I didn't hear the door to the street open and I didn't hear anything until my father's deep voice frightened me out of my skin.

'What are you doing here, wasting time? Don't you have homework? Don't you have violin? Don't you have anything? Eh?'

And Adrià went to his room, with his heart still going boom-boom. He didn't envy children with parents who kissed them because he didn't think such a thing existed.

'Carson: let me introduce you to Black Eagle. Of the brave tribe of the Arapaho.'

'Hello.'

'How.'

Black Eagle gave Sheriff Carson a kiss, like the one Father hadn't given him, and Adrià put both of them, with their horses, on the bedside table so they could get to know each other.

'You seem down.'

'After three years of studying theology,' Ardèvol said, pensively, 'I still have yet to work out what really interests you. The doctrine of grace?'

'You haven't answered my question,' insisted Morlin.

'It wasn't a question. The credibility of the Christian revelation?'

Morlin didn't answer and Fèlix Ardèvol insisted, 'Why do you study at the Gregorian if theology doesn't …'

They were both far from the stream of students making the trip back from the university to the residence hall. In two years of Christology and Soteriology, Metaphysics I, Metaphysics II and Divine Revelation, and diatribes from the most demanding professors, especially Levinski in Divine Revelation, who thought that Fèlix Ardèvol wasn't progressing in that discipline according to expectations, Rome hadn't changed much. Despite the war that had thrown Europe into upheaval, the city wasn't an open wound; it had just got a bit poorer. Meanwhile, the students at the Pontifical University continued their studies, oblivious to the conflict and its dramas. Almost all of them. And growing in wisdom and virtue. Almost all of them.

'And you?'

'Theodicy and original sin no longer interest me. I don't want more justifications. It's hard for me to think that God allows evil.'

'I've been suspecting it for months.'

'You too?'

'No: I suspected that you're getting yourself in a muddle. Observe the world, like I do. I have a lot of fun in the Canonical Law Faculty. Legal relationships between the church and civil society; Church Sanctions; Temporal Goods of the church; Divine gift of the Institutes of consecrated life; the canonical Consuetudine …'

'What are you saying?'

'Speculative studies are a waste of time; the ones based on rules are a welcome rest.'

'No, no!' exclaimed Ardèvol. 'I like Aramaic; I love looking at manuscripts and understanding the morphological differences between Bohtan Neo-Aramaic and Jewish Barzani Neo-Aramaic. Or the reason behind Koy Sanja Surat and Mlahso.'

'You know what? I don't know what you're talking about. Do we study at the same university? In the same faculty? Are we both in Rome? Are we?'

'It doesn't matter. As long as I don't have to have Pater

Levinski as a professor, I want to learn everything there is to
know about Chaldean, Babylonian, Samaritan ...'

'What good will all that do you?'

'What good will it do you to know the difference between
ratified, consummated, legitimate, putative, valid and nulli-
fied marriage?'

They both started to laugh in the middle of Via del Semi-
nario. A woman dressed in dark clothes looked up, a bit
frightened to see those young chaplains making a commotion
and violating the most basic rules of modesty.

'Why are you down, Ardevole? Now it is a question.'

'What interests you, in your heart of hearts?'

'Everything.'

'And theology?'

'That's part of everything,' answered Morlin, lifting his
arms as if he were preparing to bless the facade of the Bibli-
oteca Casanatense and the twenty-odd people who, unawares,
were passing in front of it. Then he set off walking and Fèlix
Ardèvol had trouble keeping up.

'Look at the European war,' continued Morlin, pointing
energetically towards Africa. And in a softer voice, as if he
worried there were spies around, 'Italy has to remain neutral
because the Triple Alliance is only a defensive pact,' said Italy.

'The allies are going to win the war,' the Entente Cordiale
responded.

'I am not moved by interests beyond being true to my
word,' proclaimed Italy, with dignity.

'We promise you the unredeemed regions of Trentino,
Istria and Dalmatia.'

'I repeat,' insisted Italy with more dignity and rolling its
eyes, 'Italy's honourable position is that of neutrality.'

'All right: if you join today, not tomorrow, OK? If you join
today, you will have the whole unredeemed package: South
Tyrol, Trentino, Julian Venice, Istria, Fiume, Nice, Corsica,
Malta and Dalmatia.'

'Where do I sign?' answered Italy. And with shining
eyes, 'Long live the Entente! Death to the Central European
empires! And that's it, Fèlix, that's politics. On both sides.'

'And the great ideals?'

Now Félix Morlin stopped and looked up at the sky, preparing to emit a memorable phrase.

'International politics are not the great international ideals: they are the great international interests. And Italy understood it well: once you have got on the side of the good guys, who are us, launch the offensive in Trentino to destroy that divine blessing of forests, counter-attack, the battle of Caporetto with three hundred thousand dead, Piave, breaking the front in Vittorio Veneto, then the Padua armistice and the creation of the Kingdom of the Serbs, Croats and Slovenians – which is an invention that won't last more than a couple of months even if they call it Yugoslavia. And I predict that the unredeemed regions are the carrot that the allies will snatch away, leaving Italy frustrated. Since everyone is going to keep fighting, the war won't be entirely over. And just wait for the real enemy, who hasn't even woken up yet.'

'Who is it?'

'Bolshevik communism. If not now, in a few years.'

'How did you learn all that?'

'Reading the newspaper, listening to the right people. It's the art of effective contacts. And if you knew the sad role of the Vatican in these affairs …'

'And when do you study the spiritual effect of the sacraments on the soul or the doctrine of grace?'

'What I do is studying, too, dear Fèlix. It's preparing myself to serve the church well. The church needs theologians, politicians and even an enlightened few like you who look at the world through a magnifying glass. Why are you down?'

They walked in silence for a while, their heads bowed, each with his own thoughts. Suddenly, Morlin stopped short and said nooo!

'What?'

'I know what your problem is. I know why you're down.'

'Oh, really?'

'You're in love.'

Fèlix Ardèvol i Guiteres, fourth-year student at the Pontifical Gregorian University in Rome, winner of the special prize for his brilliant performance over the first two academic years, opened his mouth to protest, but then closed it again. He was seeing himself on the Monday after Easter, at the end of the Holy Week holidays – with nothing to do after preparing his dissertation on Vico, the verum et factum reciprocanture seu convertuntur and the impossibility of understanding everything, unlike Félix Morlin, the anti-Vico, who seemed to understand all of society's strange movements – when he crossed the Piazza di Pietra and saw her for the third time. Luminous. The pigeons, about thirty of them, created an obstacle between them. He approached her, and she, carrying a small package in her hand, smiled at him just as the world turned brighter, cleaner, purer and more generous. And he reasoned logically: beauty, so much beauty, cannot be the work of the devil. Beauty is divine, and so must be her angelic smile. And he remembered the second time he had seen her, when Carolina was helping her father unload the cart in front of the store. How could that sweet back be made to carry rough wooden boxes cruelly filled with apples? It was intolerable to him, and he rushed to her aid. They unloaded three boxes between the two of them, in silence, with the ironic complicity of the mule, who chewed on hay from his muzzle. Fèlix stared at the infinite landscape of her eyes, not wanting to lower his gaze towards her incipient cleavage, and Saverio Amato's entire store was silent because no one knew what to do when a father dell'università, un prete, a priest, a seminarian rolls up his holy cassock's sleeves and acts as a porter and observes their daughter with such a dark gaze. Three boxes of apples, a blessing from God in times of war; three delicious moments beside such beauty and then glancing around, realising that he was inside Signor Amato's store and saying buona sera and leaving without daring to look at her again. And her mother came out and put two red apples in his hand, whether he wanted them or not, which made him blush because it crossed his mind that they could be Carolina's lovely breasts. Or thinking of the first time he saw her, Carolina, Carolina, Carolina, the most beautiful name in the world, when she was still a nameless girl, who walked in front of him and just then twisted an ankle, and let out a shriek of pain, poor baby, and almost fell to the ground. He was with Drago Gradnik who, in the two years since he'd entered the Theology Faculty, had grown a few inches taller and six or seven butchers' pounds heavier and, for the last three days, lived only for Saint Anselm's ontological argument, as if there were nothing else in the world that proved God's existence, for example the beauty of that sweet, sweet creature. Drago Gradnik was unable to realise how terribly painful that twisted ankle must be, and Fèlix Ardèvol took the leg of the lovely Adalaisa, Beatrice, Laura, delicately by the ankle, to help her to rest on the ground, and as he touched her little leg, an electric current more intense than the voltaic arcs at the World's Fair ran down his spine and while he asked her if it hurt, signorina, he would have liked to pounce on her and have his way with her, and that was the first time in his life that he'd felt such an urgent, painful, implacable and terrifying sexual desire. Meanwhile, Drago Gradnik was looking the other way, thinking about Saint Anselm and other more rational ways to prove God's existence.

'Ti fa male?'

'Grazie, grazie mille, padre ...' said the sweet voice with the infinite eyes.

'If God has given us intelligence, I take that to mean that faith can be accompanied by reasoning. Don't you agree, Ardevole?'

'Come ti chiami (my precious nymph)?'

'Carolina, Father. Thank you.'

Carolina, what a lovely name; of course you have a beautiful name, my love.

'Ti fa ancora male, Carolina (sheer, absolute beauty)?' he repeated, distressed.

'Reason. Faith through reason. Is that heretical? Is it, Ardevole?'

He had had to leave her sitting on a bench, because the nymph, blushing intensely, assured him that her mother would soon come by. While the two students resumed their walk – as Drago Gradnik, in his nasal Latin, ventured that perhaps Saint Bernard isn't everything in life, that Teilhard de Chardin's conference seems to invite us to think – he found himself bringing a hand to his face and trying to smell what remained of the scent of the goddess Carolina's skin.

'Me, in love?' He looked at Morlin, who was watching him with a smirk.

'You show all the symptoms.'

'What do you know?'

'I've been through it.'

'And how did you get over it?' Ardèvol's tone is anxious.

'I didn't get over it. I got under it. Until the love ended and then I got out.'

'Don't shock me.'

'That's life. I'm a sinner and I repent.'

'Love is infinite, it never ends. I couldn't ...'

'My God, you've got it bad, Fèlix Ardevole!'

Ardevole didn't answer. Before him were some thirty pigeons, the Monday after Easter, in the Piazza di Pietra. The urgency of his yearning made him cut through the jungle of pigeons until he reached Carolina, who handed him the little package.

'Il gioiello dell'Africa,' said the nymph.

'And how do you know that I ...'

'You pass by here every day. Every day.'

In that moment, Matthew twenty-seven fifty-one, the veil of the temple was torn in two from top to bottom, the earth quaked, the rocks were split, and the graves were opened and the many bodies of saints who had fallen asleep were resurrected.

Mystery of God and the incarnate Word of God.

Mystery of the Virgin Mary and Mother of God.

Mystery of the Christian faith.

Mystery of the church, human and imperfect; divine and eternal.

Mystery of the love of a young woman who gives me a little package that I've kept on the table inside cinquantaquattro for two days. On the third day I only dared to unwrap the outermost layer of paper. It is a small closed box. My God. I'm on the edge of the abyss.

He waited until Saturday. Most of the students were in their rooms. A few had gone out for walks or were scattered among the various Roman libraries where they rummaged around, exasperated, for answers on the nature of evil and why God allows it, on the exasperating existence of the devil, on the correct reading of the Holy Scriptures or on the appearance of the neume in Gregorian and Ambrosian chants. Fèlix Ardèvol was alone in cinquantaquattro, no book on the table, nothing out of place because if something drove him nuts it was the infuriating chaotic profusion of objects that were relegated to junk, or objects out of place, or for his gaze to get stuck on things that weren't well displayed, or … He thought that maybe he was becoming obsessive. I think so; that it began in that period: Father was a man fixated on material order. I think that intellectual incoherence didn't bother him much. But a book on the table instead of put away on its shelf, or a paper forgotten atop a radiator, it was simply inexcusable and unforgivable. Nothing could ruin the view and he kept us all in line, especially me. I had to tidy up each and every day, all the toys I had played with except for Sheriff Carson and Black Eagle because they secretly slept with me and Father never found out about that.

He kept cinquantaquattro as clean as a whistle. And Fèlix Ardèvol, standing, looking out the window at the flow of cassocks entering and leaving the residence hall. And a horse and cart passing along the Via del Corso with some unconfessable and infuriating secrets inside its closed cabin. And the child dragging an iron bucket and making a gratuitous, infuriating racket. He was shaking with fear and that was why everything made him indignant. On the table lay an unexpected object, an object that did not yet have its place. The little green box that Carolina had given him with a gioiello dell'Africa inside. His fate. He had sworn to himself that before the bells struck twelve at Santa Maria he would have thrown out the little box or opened it. Or he would have killed himself. One of the three.

Because one thing is living to study, making a path in the thrilling world of paleography, in the universe of ancient manuscripts, learning languages that no one speaks any longer because centuries ago they were frozen into stale papyri that become their only window onto memory, distinguishing medieval paleography from ancient paleography, being happy that the world was so large that, when I got bored, I could start to investigate Sanskrit and the Asian languages, and if some day I have a child I would want ...

And why am I thinking about having a child? he thought, annoyed; no, he thought indignantly. And he looked at the little box again, alone on the tidy table in cinquantaquattro. Fèlix Ardèvol brushed an imaginary thread off his cassock, ran a finger along the skin chafed by his clerical collar and sat in front of the table. In three minutes they would ring the bells at Santa Maria. He took a deep breath and came to a resolution: for the moment, he wasn't going to kill himself. He picked up the little box with his hands, very carefully, like a boy carrying a nest he'd stolen from a tree to show his mother the greenish eggs or the helpless baby birds that I will feed, Mother, don't worry, I'll give them a lot of ants. Like the thirsty deer, oh, Lord. Somehow or another he knew that the steps he was taking were creating an aura of irreversibility in his soul. Two minutes. With trembling fingers he tried to untie the red ribbon, but each time the knot grew tighter and it wasn't because Carolina was inept but rather a question of his nerves. He stood up, irritable. One minute and a half. He went over to the wash-hand basin and grabbed his shaving razor. He opened it hurriedly. One minute and fifteen seconds. And he cruelly cut that ribbon, of the loveliest red colour he'd ever seen in his entire long life, because, at twenty-five, he felt old and tired and wished these things wouldn't happen to him, wished that they would happen to the other Félix, who seemed to be able to handle them without ... One minute! His mouth dry, his hands sweating, a drip running down his cheek and it wasn't a very hot day ... Ten seconds left before the bells of Santa Maria in Via Lata strike twelve noon. And while in Versailles a bunch of novices were saying that the war was over and as they signed the armistice, their tongues hanging out from the effort, they set into motion the mechanisms to make a splendid new war possible just a few years later, bloodier and more evil, a war which God should never have allowed, Fèlix Ardèvol i Guiteres opened the little green box. With hesitant gestures, he removed the pink cotton and, as the first bell rang, Angelus Domini nutiavit Mariae, he burst into tears.

It was relatively simple to leave the residence hall incognito. He had practised it many times with Morlin, Gradnik and two or three other trusted friends, and they'd always got away with it. Dressed in lay clothes, Rome opened many doors; or it opened other, different doors than it did for the cassocks. In normal attire they could enter all the museums that decorum kept them from entering with cassocks on. And they could have coffee in the Piazza Colonna and even further, watching people pass by, and two or three times Morlin took him, beloved disciple, to meet people whom, according to him, he had to meet. And he introduced him as Fèlix Ardevole, a wise man who knew eight languages and for whom manuscripts held no secrets, and the scholars opened up their safes and let him examine the original manuscript of *La mandragola*, which was lovely, or some trembling papyri related to the Maccabees. But today while Europe was making peace pacts, wise Fèlix Ardevole slipped out of the residence hall, unbeknownst to the hall authorities and, for the first time, without his friends. With a pullover and a hat that hid his clerical air. And he headed straight to Signor Amato's fruit shop to wait, and the hours passed, he with the little box in his pocket, watching the people circulate blithely and happily because they didn't have his fever. Including Carolina's mother, and her little sister. Everyone except his love. The gioiello, a crude medallion with a rudimentary engraving of a Romanesque Virgin beside a huge tree, some sort of fir. And on the back, the word 'Pardàc'. From Africa? Could it be a Coptic medallion? Why did I say my love when I have no right to ... and the fresh air became unbreathable. The bells began to chime, and Fèlix, who had yet to be informed, attributed it to a homage that all of Rome's churches were making to his furtive, clandestine and sinful love. And people stopped, surprised, perhaps searching for Abelard; but instead of pointing at him they asked themselves why in the world were all the bells in Rome chiming at three in the afternoon, which isn't a time they're usually rung, what must be going on? My God: what if the war was over?

Then Carolina Amato appeared. She had come out of her house with her short hair fluttering, crossed the street and gone directly to where Fèlix, who thought he was perfectly camouflaged, was waiting. And when she stood before him she looked at him with a radiant, but silent, smile. He swallowed hard, squeezed the little box in his pocket, opened his mouth and said nothing.

'Me too,' she replied. And after many chimes of the bells, 'Did you like it?'

'I don't know if I can accept it.'

'It's mine, the gioiello. My Uncle Sandro gave it to me when I was born. He brought it from Egypt himself. Now it's yours.'

'What will they say to you, at home?'

'It's mine and now it's yours: they won't say anything. It's my pledge.'

And she took his hand. From that moment on, the sky fell to earth and Abelard focused on the touch of Heloise's skin, which dragged him down an anonymous vicolo, filled with trash but smelling of love's roses, and into a house that had open doors and no one inside, while the bells chimed and a neighbour lady, from a window, shouted nuntio vobis gaudium magnum, Elisabetta, la guerra è finita! But the two lovers were about to begin an essential battle and couldn't hear her announcement.

# DE PUERITIA

A good warrior can't go around falling in love
with every squaw he comes across, even if they
make themselves up with war paint.

Black Eagle

Don't look at me like that. I know I make things up: but I'm still telling the truth. For example, my oldest memory in my childhood room, in History and Geography, is trying to make a house under the bed. It wasn't uncomfortable and it was truly fun because I saw the feet of people coming in and saying Adrià, Son, where are you or Adrià, snacktime. Where'd he go? I know, it was incredible fun. Yes, I was always bored like that, because my house wasn't designed for children and my family wasn't a family designed for children. My mother had no say and my father lived only for his buying and his selling, and the jealousy ate away at me when I saw him caress an engraving or a fine porcelain decanter. And Mother … well, Mother had always seemed to me like a woman on guard, alert, her eyes darting here and there; even though Little Lola was looking out for her. Now I realise that my father made her feel like a stranger at home. It was his house and he let her live there. When Father died, she was able to breathe and her expression was no longer uneasy, even though she avoided looking at me. And she changed. I wonder why. I also wonder why my parents married. I don't think they ever loved each other. There was never love at home. I was a mere circumstantial consequence of their lives.

It's strange: there are so many things I want to explain to you and yet I keep getting distracted and wasting time with reflections that would make Freud drool. Perhaps it's because my relationship with my father is to blame for everything. Perhaps because it was my fault he died.

One day, when I was a bit older, when I'd already secretly taken over the space between the back of the sofa and the wall in my father's study and turned it into a mansion for my cowboys and Indians, Father came in followed by a familiar voice that I still found somewhere between pleasant and blood-curdling. It was the first time I'd heard Mr Berenguer outside of the shop and he sounded different: and ever since then I didn't like his voice inside the shop or out of it. I remained stock still and put Sheriff Carson down on the floor. Black Eagle's brown horse, normally so silent, fell and made a small noise that startled me but the enemy didn't notice, and Father said I don't have to give you any explanations.

'I think you do.'

Mr Berenguer sat on the sofa, which moved a bit closer to the wall, and, heroically, I told myself better squashed than discovered. I heard Mr Berenguer tapping and my father's icy voice saying no smoking in this house. Then Mr Berenguer said that he demanded an explanation.

'You work for me.' My father's voice was sarcastic. 'Or am I wrong?'

'I got ten engravings, I got the people who sold them at a loss not to complain too much. I got the ten engravings across three borders and got them appraised myself and now you tell me that you've sold them without even consulting me. One of them was a Rembrandt, you know that?'

'We buy and sell; that's how we earn our living in this fucking life.'

That was the first time I'd heard the word fucking and I liked it; Father said it with two fs: ffucking life, I guess because he was angry. I knew that Mr Berenguer was smiling; I already knew how to decipher silences and was sure that Mr Berenguer was smiling.

'Oh, hello, Mr Berenguer.' It was Mother's voice. 'Fèlix, have you seen the boy?'

'No.'

Crisis was imminent. How could I get out from behind the sofa and disappear into some other part of the flat, pretending I hadn't heard a thing? I talked it over with Sheriff Carson and Black Eagle, but they were no help. Meanwhile, the men were in silence, surely waiting for my mother to leave the study and close the door.

'Goodbye.'

'Goodbye, madam.' Returning to the bitter tone of their discussion, 'I feel I've been cheated. I deserve a special commission.' Silence. 'I demand it.'

I couldn't care less about the commission. To stay calm, I translated the conversation into French in my head; so I must have been seven years old. Sometimes I did that to keep myself from worrying; when I was anxious I couldn't control my fidgeting and, in the silence of the study, if I moved around they would have heard me. Moi, j'exige ma commission. C'est mon droit. Vous travaillez pour moi, monsieur Berenguer. Oui, bien sûr, mais j'ai de la dignité, moi!

In the background, Mother, shouting Adrià, boy! Little Lola, have you seen him? Dieu sait où est mon petit Hadrien!

I don't remember too well, but I believe Mr Berenguer left even angrier than he'd arrived and that Father got rid of him with a through thick and thin, monsieur Berenguer, which I didn't know how to translate. How I wish Mother had even once called me mon petit Hadrien!

So I was able leave my hidey hole. The time it took my father to walk his visitor to the door was enough for me to erase my tracks. I had acquired great skill for camouflage and near ubiquity, in that life of a partisan I led at home.

'Here!' Mother had appeared on the balcony where I was watching the cars whose lights had just started to flick on, because life in that period, as I remember it, was endless dusk. 'Didn't you hear me?'

'What?' With the sheriff and the brown horse in one hand, I pretended I'd had my head in the clouds.

'You need to try on your school smock. How is it possible that you didn't hear me calling you?'

'Smock?'

'Mrs Angeleta let down the sleeves.' And with an authoritative gesture, 'Come on!'

In the sewing room, Mrs Angeleta, with a pin between her lips, looked at the hang of the new sleeves with a professional air.

'You grow too fast, lad.'

Mother had gone to say goodbye to Mr Berenguer and

Little Lola went into the ironing room to look for clean shirts while I put on the smock without sleeves, as I had done so many other times throughout my childhood.

'And you wear out the elbows too fast,' hammered home Mrs Angeleta, who was already a thousand years old, give or take.

The door to the flat closed. Father's footsteps headed off towards his study and Mrs Angeleta shook her snow-covered head.

'You have a lot of visitors lately.'

Little Lola was silent and acted as if she hadn't heard. Mrs Angeleta, as she pinned the sleeve to the smock, went on anyway.

'Sometimes I hear shouts.'

Little Lola grabbed the shirts and said nothing. Mrs Angeleta continued to prod. 'Lord knows what you talk about …'

'About ffucking life,' I said without thinking.

Little Lola's shirts fell to the floor, Mrs Angeleta pricked my arm and Black Eagle turned and surveyed the parched horizon with his eyes almost closed. He noticed the cloud of dust before anyone else. Even before Swift Rabbit.

'Three riders are approaching,' he said. No one made any comment. That cave-like room offered some respite from the harsh summer heat; but no one, no squaw, no child, no one had the energy to care about visitors or their intentions. Black Eagle made an imperceptible motion with his eyes. Three warriors started to walk towards their horses. He followed them closely while keeping one eye on the dust cloud. They were coming straight to the cave, without the slightest subterfuge. Like a bird distracting a predator and diverting it away from its nest with various techniques, he and his three men shifted to the west to distract the visitors. The two groups met close to the five holm oaks; the visitors were three white men, one with very blond hair and the other two with dark skin. One of them, the one with the theatrical moustache, nimbly got down from his saddle with his hands away from his body and smiled.

'You are Black Eagle,' he declared, keeping his hands away from his body in a sign of submission.

The great Arapaho chief of the Lands to the South of Yellow Fish's Shore of the Washita gave an imperceptible nod from up on his horse, without moving a hair, and then he asked whom he had the honour of receiving, and the man with the black moustache smiled again, made a jocular half bow and said I'm Sheriff Carson, from Rockland, a two-day ride from your lands.

'I know where you established your town, Rockland,' the legendary chief responded curtly. 'In Pawnee territory.' And he spat on the ground to show his contempt.

'These are my deputies,' – not entirely sure who the gob of spit was directed at. 'We are looking for a criminal on the lam.' And he, in turn, spat and found it wasn't half bad.

'What has he done to be treated as a criminal?' The Arapaho chief.

'Do you know him? Have you seen him?'

'I asked you what he did to be treated as a criminal.'

'He killed a mare.'

'And dishonoured two women,' added the blond.

'Yes, of course, that too,' accepted Sheriff Carson.

'And why are you looking for him here?'

'He's an Arapaho.'

'My people extend several days toward the west, toward the east and toward the cold and the heat. Why have you come to this spot?'

'You know who he is. We want you to deliver him to justice.'

'You are mistaken, Sheriff Carson. Your murderer is not an Arapaho.'

'Oh, no? And how do you know that?'

'An Arapaho would never kill a mare.'

Then the light turned on and Little Lola waved him off with one hand, ordering him out of the larder. In front of Adrià, Mother, with war paint on her face, without looking at him, without spitting on the ground, said Lola, have him wash his mouth out well. With soap and water. And if necessary, add a few drops of bleach.

Black Eagle withstood the torture bravely, without a single groan. When Little Lola had finished, as he dried himself with a towel, he looked her in the eyes and said Little Lola, do you know what dishonouring a woman means exactly?

When I was seven or eight years old I made some decisions about my life. One was very wise: leaving my education in my mother's hands. But it seems that things didn't go that way. And I found out because, that night, I wanted to know how my father would react to my slip and so I set up my espionage device in the dining room. It wasn't particularly complicated because my room shared a partition wall with the dining room. Officially, I had gone to sleep early, so my father, when he came home, wouldn't find me awake. It was the best way to save myself the sermon that would have been filled with pitfalls because if I told him, in self-defence, that the whole ffucking life thing was something I'd heard him say, then the topic of the conversation would have shifted from you've got a very dirty mouth that I'll now scrub with Lagarto soap to how the fuck do you know I said that about ffucking life, you bald-faced liar? Huh? Huh? Were you spying on me? And there was no way I was going to reveal my espionage cards, because over time, without even really trying, I was the only one in the house who controlled every corner, every conversation, the arguments and the inexplicable weeping, like that week Little Lola spent crying. When she emerged from her room, she had very skilfully hidden her pain, which much have been immense. It was years before I knew why she was crying, but at the time I learned that there was pain that could last a week and life scared me a little bit.

So I was able to listen in on the conversation between my parents by putting my ear to the bottom of a glass placed against the partition wall. Since Father's voice was weary, Mother summed up the matter by saying that I was very trying. Father didn't want to know the details and said it's already been decided.

'What's been decided?' Mother's frightened voice.

'I've enrolled him at the Jesuit school on Casp Street.'

'But, Fèlix ... If ...'

That day I learned that Father was the only one in charge.

And I mentally made note that I had to look up what Jesuits were in the *Britannica*. Father held Mother's gaze in silence and she made up her mind to press on, 'Why the Jesuits? You aren't a believer and ...'

'Quality education. We have to be efficient; we only have one child and we can't make a cock-up of it.'

Let's see: yes, they only had one child. Or no; but that wasn't the point anyway. So Father brought up the idea of the languages, which I'll admit I liked.

'What did you say?'

'Ten languages.'

'Our son isn't a monster.'

'But he can learn them.'

'And why ten?'

'Because Pater Levinski at the Gregorian knew nine. Our son has to do him one better.'

'Why?'

'Because he called me inept in front of the other students. Inept because my Aramaic was not progressing after an entire year with Faluba.'

'Don't make jokes: we are talking about our son's education.'

'I'm not joking: I am talking about my son's education.'

I know that it bothered my mother a lot that my father referred to me as *his* son in front of her. But Mother was thinking of other things because she started to say that she didn't want to turn me into a monster; and, with a skill I didn't know she had in her, she said do you hear me? I don't want *my* son to end up being a carnival monster who has to do Pater Luwowski one better.

'Levinski.'

'Levinski the monster.'

'A great theologian and Biblicist. A monster of erudition.'

'No: we have to discuss it calmly.'

I didn't understand that. That was exactly what they were doing: discussing my future calmly. And I was pleased because ffucking life hadn't come up at all.

'Catalan, Spanish, French, German, Italian, English, Latin, Greek, Aramaic, and Russian.'

'What are you listing?'

'The ten languages he has to know. He already knows the first three.'

'No, he just makes up the French.'

'But he does a pretty good job, he makes himself understood. My son can do anything he sets out to. And he has a particular talent for languages. He will learn ten.'

'He also needs time to play.'

'He's already big. But when it's time to go to university he has to know them.' And with a weary sigh, 'We'll talk about it some other time, OK?'

'He's seven years old, for the love of God!'

'I'm not demanding he learn Aramaic right now.' He drummed his fingers on the table with a conclusive gesture, 'He'll start with German.'

I liked that too, because I could almost figure out the *Britannica* on my own with a dictionary by my side, no problem: but German, on the other hand, I found pretty opaque. I was very excited about the world of declinations, the world of languages that change their word endings according to their function in the sentence. I didn't exactly put it that way, but almost: I was very pedantic.

'No, Fèlix. We can't make that mistake.'

I heard the small sound of someone spitting curtly.

'Yes?'

'What is Aramaic?' asked Sheriff Carson in a deep voice.

'I don't really know: we'll have to research it.'

I was a strange kid; I can admit that. I see myself now remembering how I listened to what would be my future, clinging to Sheriff Carson and the brave Arapaho chief and trying not to give myself away, and I think I wasn't strange, I was very strange.

'It isn't a mistake. The first day of school a teacher I've already got my eye on will come to teach him German.'

'No.'

'His name is Romeu and he's a very bright lad.'

That irked me. A teacher at home? My house was my house and I was the one who knew everything about what happened inside it: I didn't want awkward witnesses. No, I didn't like that Romeu chap, poking his nose around my house, saying oh, how lovely, a personal library at seven years old and that kind of crap grownups say when they come to the house. No way.

'And he will study three majors.'

'What?'

'Law and History.' Silence. 'And a third, which he can choose. But definitely Law, which is most useful for manoeuvring in this dog-eat-dog world.'

Tick, tick, tick, tick, tick, tick. My foot began to move of its own accord, tick, tick, tick, tick, tick. I hated law. You don't know how much I hated it. Without knowing exactly what it was, I hated it to death.

'Je n'en doute pas,' disait ma mère. 'Mais est-ce qu'il est un bon pédagogue, le tel Gomeu?'

'Bien sûr, j'ai reçu des informations confidentielles qui montrent qu'il est un individu parfaitement capable en langue allemagne. Allemande? Tedesque? Et en la pédagogie de cette langue. Je crois que ...'

I was already starting to calm down. My foot stopped moving in that out of control way and I heard Mother get up and say what about the violin? Will he have to give it up?

'No. But it will be secondary.'

'I don't agree.'

'Good night, dear,' said Father as he opened the newspaper and paged through it because that was what he always did at that time of the day.

So I was changing schools. What a drag. And how scary. Luckily Sheriff Carson and Black Eagle would go with me. The violin will be secondary? And why Aramaic so much later? That night it took me a while to get off to sleep.

I'm sure I'm mixing things up. I don't know if I was seven or eight or nine years old. But I had a gift for languages and my parents had realised that and wanted to make the most of it. I had started French because I spent a summer in Perpignan at Aunt Aurora's house and there, as soon as they got a little flustered, they'd switch from their guttural Catalan to French; and that's why when I speak French I add the hint of a Midi accent I've maintained my whole life with some pride. I don't remember how old I was. German came later; English I don't really recall. Later, I think. It's not that I wanted to learn them. It was that they learned me.

Now that I'm thinking about it in order to tell you, I see my childhood as one long and very boring Sunday afternoon, wandering aimlessly, looking for a way to slip off into the study, thinking that it would be more fun if I had a sibling, thinking that the point would come when reading was boring because I was already up to my eyeballs in Enid Blyton, thinking that the next day I had school, and that was worse. Not because I was afraid of school or the teachers and parents, but because of the children. It was the children at school that frightened me, because they looked at me like I was some kind of a freak.

'Little Lola.'

'What?'

'What can I do?'

Little Lola stopped drying her hands or applying lipstick and looked at me.

'Can I go with you?' Adrià, with a hopeful look.

'No, no, you'd be bored!'

'I'm bored here.'

'Turn on the radio.'

'It's a yawn.'

Then Little Lola grabbed her coat and left the room that always smelled of Little Lola and, in a whisper, so no one would hear it, she told me to ask Mother to take me to the cinema. And louder she said goodbye, see you later; she opened the door to the street, winked at me and left; yeah, she could have fun on Sunday afternoons, who knows how, but I was left condemned to wander the flat like a lost soul.

'Mother.'

'What.'

'No, nothing.'

Mother looked up from her magazine, finished the last sip of her coffee, and glanced at me over it.

'Tell me, Son.'

I was afraid to ask her to take me to the cinema. Very afraid and I still don't know why. My parents were too serious.

'I'm bored.'

'Read. If you'd like, we can study French.'

'Let's go to Tibidabo.'

'Oh, you should have said that this morning.'

We never went there, to Tibidabo, not any morning nor any Sunday afternoon. I had to go there in my imagination, when my friends told me what Tibidabo was like, that it was filled with mechanical devices, mysterious automatons and lookout points and dodgem cars and … I didn't know what exactly. But it was a place where parents took their children. My parents didn't take me to the zoo or to stroll along the breakwater. They were too staid. And they didn't love me. I think. Deep down I still wonder why they had me.

'Well, I want to go to Tibidabo!'

'What is all this shouting?' complained Father from his study. 'Don't make me punish you!'

'I don't want to study my French!'

'I said don't make me punish you!'

Black Eagle thought that it was all very unfair and he let me and Sheriff Carson know how he felt. And to keep from getting utterly bored, and especially to keep from getting punished, well, I started in on my arpeggio exercises on the violin, which had the advantage of being difficult and so it was hard to get them to come out sounding good. I was terrible at the violin until I met Bernat. I abandoned the exercise halfway through.

'Father, can I touch the Storioni?'

Father lifted his head. He was, as always, looking through the magnifying lamp at some very odd piece of paper.

'No,' he said. And pointing at something on top of the table, 'Look how beautiful.'

It was a very old manuscript with a brief text in an alphabet I didn't recognise.'

'What is it?'

'A fragment of the gospel of Mark.'

'But what language is it in?'

'Aramaic.'

Did you hear that, Black Eagle? Aramaic! Aramaic is a very ancient language, a language of papyrus and parchment scrolls.

'Can I learn it?'

'When the time is right.' He said it with satisfaction; that was very clear because, since I generally did things well, he could brag of having a clever son. Wanting to take advantage of his satisfaction, 'Can I play the Storioni?'

Fèlix Ardèvol looked at him in silence. He moved aside the magnifying lamp. Adrià tapped a foot on the floor. 'Just once. Come on, Father …'

Father's expression when he is angry is scary. Adrià held it for just a few seconds. He had to lower his eyes.

'Don't you understand the word no? Niet, nein, no, ez, non, ei, nem. Sound familiar?'

'Ei and nem?'

'Finnish and Hungarian.'

When Adrià left the study, he turned and angrily proffered a terrible threat.

'Well, then I won't study Aramaic.'

'You will do what I tell you to do,' warned Father with the coldness and calmness of one who knows that yes, he will always do what he says. And he returns to his manuscript, to his Aramaic, to his magnifying glass.

That day Adrià decided to lead a double life. He already had secret hiding places, but he decided to expand his clandestine world. He proposed a grand goal for himself: working out the combination of the safe and, when Father wasn't at home, studying with the Storioni: no one would notice. And putting it back in its case and into the safe in time to erase all trace of the crime. He went to study his arpeggios so no one would realise and he didn't say anything to either the Sheriff or the Arapaho chief, who were napping on the bedside table.

# 4

I always remembered Father as an old man. Mother, on the
other hand, was just Mother. It's a shame she didn't love me.
All that Adrià knew was that Grandfather Adrià raised her
like men used to do when they became widowers very young
and with a baby in their arms, looking from side to side to
see if someone will offer them a manual for fitting the child
into their life. Grandmother Vicenta died very young, when
Mother was six. She had a vague recollection of her; I merely
had the memory of the only two photos ever taken of her: her
wedding shot, in the Caria Studio, in which they were both
very young and attractive, but too dolled up for the occasion;
and another of Grandmother with Mother in her arms and a
broken smile, as if she knew she wouldn't see her First Communion, wondering why is it my lot to die so young and be
just a sepia photo for my grandson, who it seems is a child
prodigy but whom I will never meet. Mother grew up alone.
No one ever took her to Tibidabo and perhaps that's why it
never occurred to her that I was dying to know what the animated automatons were like, the ones that I'd heard moved
magically and looked like people once you put a coin into
them.

Mother grew up alone. In the 20s, when they killed on the
streets, Barcelona was sepia coloured and the dictatorship
of Primo de Rivera tinted the eyes of Barcelonians with the
colour of bitterness. So when Grandfather Adrià understood
that his daughter was growing up and he'd have to explain
things to her that he didn't know, since they had nothing to do
with paleography, he got Lola's daughter to come and live at
the house. Lola was Grandmother Vicenta's trusted woman,
who still took care of the house, from eight in the morning
to eight in the evening, as if her mistress hadn't died. Lola's

daughter, who was two and half years older than Mother, was also named Lola. They called the mother Big Lola. The poor woman died before seeing the republic established. On her deathbed she passed the baton to her daughter. She said take care of Carme as if she were your own life, and Little Lola never left Mother's side. Until she left the house. In my family, Lolas appeared and disappeared when there was a death.

With hope of a republic and the king's exile, with the proclamation of the Catalan Republic and the push and pull with the central government, Barcelona shifted from sepia to grey and people went along the street with their hands in their pockets if it were cold, but greeting each other, offering a cigarette and smiling at each other if necessary, because there was hope; they didn't know exactly what they were hoping for, but there was hope. Fèlix Ardèvol, disregarding both the sepia and the grey, came and went making trips with his valuable merchandise and with a single goal: increasing his wealth of objects, which gave meaning to his thirst for, more than collecting, harvesting. He didn't care whether the atmosphere was sepia or grey. He only had eyes for that which helped him accumulate his objects. He focused on Doctor Adrià Bosch, an eminent paleographer at the University of Barcelona who, according to his reputation, was a wise man who knew how to date things exactly and without hesitation. It was an advantageous relationship for them both and Fèlix Ardèvol became a frequent visitor to Doctor Bosch's office at the university, to the extent that some of the assistant professors began to look askance at him. Fèlix Ardèvol liked meeting with Doctor Bosch at his house more than at the university. Just because setting foot in that building made him uncomfortable. He could run into some former classmate from the Gregorian; there were also two philosophy professors, two canons, who had been with him at the seminary in Vic and who could be surprised to see him visiting the eminent palaeographer so assiduously and could good-naturedly ask him what do you do, Ardèvol? Or is it true you gave it all up for a woman? Is it true that you abandoned a brilliant future of Sanskrit and theology, all to chase a skirt? Is it true? There was so much talk

about it! If you only knew what they said about you, Ardèvol!
What ever happened to her, that famous little Italian woman?

When Fèlix Ardèvol told Doctor Bosch I want to talk to you
about your daughter, she'd been noticing Mr Fèlix Ardèvol
for six years, every time Grandfather Adrià received him
at home; she was usually the one to open the door. Shortly
before the civil war broke out, when she had turned seventeen, she began to realise that she liked that way Mr Ardèvol
had of removing his hat when he greeted her. And he always
said how are you, beautiful. She liked that a lot. How are
you, beautiful. To the point that she noticed the colour of Mr
Ardèvol's eyes. An intense brown. And his English lavender,
which gave off a scent that she fell in love with.

But there was a setback: three years of war; Barcelona was
no longer sepia nor grey, but the colour of fire, of anxiety, of
hunger, of bombardments and of death. Fèlix Ardèvol stayed
away for entire weeks, with silent trips, and the university
managed to stay open with the threat hovering over classroom ceilings. And when the calm returned, the heavy calm,
most of the senior professors who hadn't escaped into exile
were purged by Franco and the university began to speak
Spanish and to display ignorance without hang-ups. But
there were still islands, like the palaeography department,
which was considered insignificant by the victors. And Mr
Fèlix Ardèvol resumed his visits, now with more objects in
his hands. Between the two of them they classified and dated
them and certified their authenticity, and Fèlix sold merchandise all over the world. They shared the profits, so welcome
in that period of such hardship. And the professors who had
survived the brutal Francoist purges kept looking askance at
that dealer who went around the department as if he were a
senior professor. Around the department and around Doctor
Bosch's house.

During the war, Carme Bosch hadn't seen him much. But
as soon as it ended, Mr Ardèvol visited her father again and
the two men locked themselves up in the study and she went
on with her things and said Little Lola, I don't want to go out

to buy sandals now, and Little Lola knew that it was because Mr Ardèvol was in the house, talking to the master about old papers; and, hiding a smile, she said as you wish, Carme. Then her father, almost without consulting her about it, enrolled her in the recently re-established Librarians' School and the three years she spent there, in fact right by their house because they lived on Àngels Street, were the happiest of her life. There she met fellow students with whom she vowed to stay in touch even if their lives changed, they married and etcetera, and whom she never saw again, not even Pepita Masriera. And she started working at the university library, pushing carts of books, trying, without much luck, to adopt Mrs Canyameres' severe mien, and missing some of her schoolmates, especially Pepita Masriera. Two or three times she ran into Mr Ardèvol who, apparently coincidentally, was going to that library more often than ever and he would say to her how are you, beautiful,

'Intense brown isn't a colour.'

Little Lola looked at Carme ironically, waiting for an answer.

'OK. Nice brown. Like dark honey, like eucalyptus honey.'

'He's your father's age.'

'Come on! He's seven and a half years younger.'

'All right, I won't say another word.'

Mr Ardèvol, despite the purges, still looked distrustingly at both the new and old professors. They would no longer pester him about his love life, probably because they were unaware of it, but they would surely say you're skating on thin ice, my friend. What Fèlix Ardèvol wanted to avoid was having to give a lot of explanations to someone who looked at you with polite sarcasm and made clear with his silence that he hadn't asked you for any explanation. Until one day he said that's it: I'm not cut out to suffer and he went to the police headquarters on Via Laietana and said Professor Montells, palaeography.

'What's that you say?'

'Professor Montells, palaeography.'

'Montells, Palaeography,' the superintendent wrote down slowly. And his first name?

'Eloi. And his second last name …'

'Eloi Montells Palaeography, I've already got his full name.'

The office of Superintendent Plasencia was dirty olive greenish, with a rusty file cabinet and portraits of Franco and José Antonio on the flaking wall. Through the dirty windowpane he could see the traffic on the Via Laietana. But Mr Fèlix Ardèvol was all business. He was writing down the full name of Doctor Eloi Montells, whose second last name was Ciurana, assistant to the head of Palaeography, also educated at the Gregorian in another period, who gave Fèlix cutting looks every time he visited Doctor Bosch about his matters, which it was imperative Montells didn't stick his nose into.

'And how would you define him?'

'Pro-Catalan. Communist.'

The superintendent whistled and said my, my … and how could he have escaped our notice?

Mr Ardèvol didn't say anything because the question was rhetorical and it wasn't prudent to answer that he'd escaped their notice out of pure police inefficiency.

'This is the second professor you've denounced. It's odd.' He tapped the desk with a pencil, as if he wanted to send a message in Morse code. 'Because you aren't a professor, are you? Why do you do it?'

To clean up the landscape. To be able to move about without inquisitive looks.

'Out of patriotism. Long live Franco.'

There were more. There were three or four. And they were all pro-Catalan and communist. In vain, they all claimed unconditional support for the regime and exclaimed me, a communist? The longlivefrancos they offered up to the superintendent did them no good, because grist was needed for the mill that was the Model Prison, where they sent those untouchables who hadn't chosen to accept the Generalísimo's generous offers and stubbornly persisted in the error of their ways. Such convenient accusations cleared out the department, while Doctor Bosch had no clue and continued to provide information to that clever man who seemed to admire him so much.

For a little while after the professors were arrested, just in case, Fèlix Ardèvol stayed away from Doctor Bosch's university office, instead showing up at his house, much to Carme Bosch's delight.

'How are you, beautiful?'

The girl, who was prettier by the day, always answered with a smile and lowered her gaze. Her eyes had become one of Fèlix Ardèvol's most fascinating mysteries, which he was determined to get to the bottom of as soon as possible. Almost as fascinating as a handwritten manuscript by Goethe without an owner.

'Today I've brought you more work, and better paid,' he said when he entered Professor Bosch's study. And Grandfather Adrià prepared to offer his expert opinion and certify its authenticity, charge his fee and never ask but Fèlix, listen, where in God's name do you get all this stuff. And how do you manage to … Eh?

As he watched him pull out papers, Grandfather Adrià took a moment to clean his pince-nez eyeglasses. His task didn't begin until he had the manuscript on the table.

'Gothic chancery script,' said Doctor Bosch putting on his spectacles and looking greedily at the manuscript that Fèlix had placed on the table. He picked it up and looked it over carefully from every angle over a long while.

'It is incomplete,' he said, breaking the silence that was lasting too long.

'Is it from the fourteenth century?'

'Yes. I see that you are learning.'

By that period, Fèlix Ardèvol had already set up a network through much of Europe that searched for any paper or papyrus, loose or bundled parchments in the often disorganised and dusty shelves of archives, libraries, cultural institutes, town halls and parishes. Young Mr Berenguer, a true ferreter, spent his days visiting these spots and making a first evaluation, which he explained over the faulty phone lines of the period. Depending on the decision, he paid the owners as little as possible for the treasure, when he was unable to just

make off with it, and he brought it to Ardèvol, who did the
expert's report along with Doctor Bosch. Everyone came out
a winner, including the posterity of the manuscripts. But it
was best if everyone was kept in the dark. Everyone. Over ten
years he had found a lot of junk. A lot. But every once in a
while he happened upon a real gem, like a copy of the 1876
edition of *L'après-midi d'un faune* with illustrations by Manet,
inside of which there were manuscripts by Mallarmé himself,
surely the last things he had written. They'd been sleeping in
the attic of a wretched municipal library in Valvins. Or three
complete parchments in good shape from the corpus of the
chancery of John II, miraculously rescued from an inheritance
lot in an auction in Göteborg. Every year he'd get his hands
on three or four gems. And Ardèvol worked day and night for
those gems. Gradually, in the solitude of the huge flat he had
let in the Eixample district, the idea took shape of him setting
up an antiquarian's shop where everything that wasn't a true
gem would end up. That decision led to another: accepting
inheritance lots with other things beside manuscripts. Vases,
bongos, chippendale furniture, umbrella stands, weapons ...
anything that was made a long time ago and wasn't useful
in the slightest. That was how the first musical instrument
entered his home.

The years passed; Mr Ardèvol, my father, would visit Professor Bosch, my grandfather whom I knew as a small child.
And Carme, my mother, turned twenty-two and one day Mr
Fèlix Ardèvol said to his colleague I want to talk to you about
your daughter.

'What's wrong with her?' Doctor Bosch, a bit frightened,
taking off his pince-nez and looking at his friend.

'I want to marry her. If you have no objections.'

Doctor Bosch got up and went out into the dark hall, flustered, brandishing his pince-nez. A few steps behind, Ardèvol
watched him attentively. After some minutes of nervous
pacing he turned and looked at Ardèvol, without realising
that he had intense brown eyes.

'How old are you?'

'Forty-four.'

'And Carme must be eighteen or nineteen, at most.'

'Twenty-two and a half. Your daughter is over twenty-two.'

'Are you sure?'

Silence. Doctor Bosch put on his glasses as if he were about to examine his daughter's age. He looked at Ardèvol, opened his mouth, took off his glasses and, with a hazy look, said to himself, filled with admiration, as if before a Ptolemaic papyrus, Carme's twenty-two years old …

'She turned twenty-two months ago.'

At that moment the door to the flat opened and Carme came in, accompanied by Little Lola. She looked at the two silent men, planted in the middle of the hall. Little Lola disappeared with the shopping basket and Carme looked at them again as she took off her coat.

'Is something wrong?' she asked.

For a long time, despite his aloof nature, I was fascinated by my father and wanted to make him happy. Above all, I wanted him to admire me. Brusque, yes; irascible, that too; and he hardly loved me at all. But I admired him. Surely that's why I find it so hard to talk about him. So as not to justify him. So as not to condemn him.

One of the only times, if not the only, that my father admitted that I was right he said very good, I think you're right. I hold on to that memory like a treasure in a little chest. Because in general it was us, the others, who were always wrong. I understand why Mother watched life pass by from the balcony. But I was little and wanted to always be where the action was. And when Father gave me impossible objectives, at first I had no problem with it. Even though the main ones weren't achieved. I didn't study Law; I only had one major but, on the other hand, I've spent my entire life studying. I didn't collect ten or twelve languages so as to break Pater Levinski's record: I learned them relatively easily and because it appealed to me. And even though I still have outstanding debts with Father, I haven't sought to make him proud wherever he may be, which is nowhere because I inherited his scepticism about eternal life. Mother's plans, always relegated to a second plane, didn't turn out either. Well, that's not exactly true. I didn't find out until later that Mother had plans for me, because she kept them hidden from Father.

So I was an only child, carefully observed by parents eager for signs of intelligence. I could sum up my childhood thusly: the bar was set high. The bar was set high in everything, even for eating with my mouth closed and keeping my elbows off the table and not interrupting the adults' conversation, except when I exploded because there were days when I couldn't take

it any more and not even Carson and Black Eagle could calm
me down. That was why I liked to take advantage of the occasions when Little Lola had to run an errand in the Gothic
Quarter; I'd go along and wait for her in the shop, my eyes
wide as saucers.

As I grew up, I became more and more attracted to the
shop: because it filled me with a kind of apprehensive awe.
At home we just called it the shop, even though, more than
a shop, it was an entire world where you could dispense with
life beyond its walls. The shop's door stood on Palla Street, in
front of the ruinous facade of a church ignored as much by
the bishopric as by town hall. When you opened it, a little bell
rang, which I can still hear tinkling, letting Cecília or Mr Berenguer know. The rest, from that point on, was a feast for the
eyes and nose. Not for the touch, because Adrià was strictly
forbidden to touch anything, you're always touching everything, don't you dare touch a thing. And not a thing means
not a thing, boy, do you understand that, Adrià? And since
not a thing was not a thing, I wandered along the narrow
aisles, with my hands in my pockets, looking at a worm-eaten
polychrome angel, beside a golden washbasin that had been
Marie Antoinette's. And a gong from the Ming dynasty that
was worth a fortune, which Adrià wanted to sound before he
died.

'What's that for?'

Mr Berenguer looked at the Japanese dagger, then back at
me and he smiled, 'It's a Bushi kaiken dagger.'

Adrià was left with his mouth hanging open. Mr Berenguer
looked towards where Cecília was polishing bronze goblets,
leaned towards the boy, giving him a whiff of his dubious
breath, and said in a whisper, 'A short knife Japanese women
warriors use to kill themselves.' He looked him up and down
to see if he could make out a reaction. Since the boy seemed
unfazed, the man finished more curtly. 'Edo period, seventeenth century.'

Obviously Adrià had been impressed, but at eight years old
– which is what he must have been at the time – he already
knew how to mask his emotions, just as Mother did when

Father locked himself in the study and looked at his manuscripts with a magnifying glass and no one could make any
noise in the house because Father was reading in his study
and god only knows what time he'd emerge for dinner.

'No. Until he shows signs of life don't put the vegetables on
the stove.'

And Little Lola would head towards the kitchen, grumbling I'd show that guy what for, the whole house at the mercy
of his loupe. And, if Adrià were near that guy, I would hear
him reading:

A un vassalh aragones. / Be sabetz lo vassalh qui es, / El a
nom. N'Amfos de Barbastre. / Ar arujatz, senher, cal desastre
/ Li avenc per sa gilozia.

'What is it?'

'*La reprensió dels gelosos.* A short novel.'

'Is it Old Catalan?'

'No. Occitan.'

'They sound similar.'

'Very much so.'

'What does *gelós* mean?'

'It was written by Ramon Vidal de Besalú. Thirteenth
century.'

'Wow, that's old. What does *gelós* mean?'

'Folio 132 of the Provençal songbook from Karlsruhe. There
is another one in the National Library of Paris. This is mine.
It's yours.'

Adrià understood that as an invitation and extended his
hand. Father smacked my hand back and it really, really hurt.
He didn't even bother to say you're always touching everything. He went over the lines with his loupe and said life
brings me such joy, these days.

A Japanese dagger for female suicide, summed up Adrià.
And he continued his journey to the ceramic pots. He left the
engravings and manuscripts for last, because they inspired
such reverence in him.

'Let's see when you'll start helping us, we've a lot of work.'

Adrià looked about the deserted shop and smiled politely
at Cecília. 'When Father lets me,' he said.

She was going to say something, but she thought better of it and just stood with her mouth open for a few moments. Then her eyes gleamed and she said, come on, give me a kiss.

And I had to kiss her because it wasn't the time or the place to make a scene. The year before I had been deeply in love with her, but now the kissing stuff was starting to irk me. Even thought I was still very young, I had already begun the phase of serious kiss aversion, as if I were twelve or thirteen; I had always been precocious in the non-essential subjects. I must have been eight or nine then, and that anti-kissing fever lasted until … well, you already know until when. Or perhaps you don't know yet. By the way, what did that bit about 'I've remade my life' that you said to the encyclopaedia salesman mean?

For a few moments Adrià and Cecília watched the people who passed on the street without even glancing at the window display.

'There's always work,' said Cecília, who had read my thoughts. 'Tomorrow we are emptying a flat with a library: it's going to be pandemonium.'

She went back to her bronze. The scent of the Netol metal cleaner had gone to Adrià's head and he decided to get some distance. Why did they commit suicide, those Japanese women, he thought.

Now it seems that I was only there a few times, poking around the shop. Poking around is a figure of speech. I mostly felt bad about not being able to touch anything in the corner with musical instruments. Once, when I was older, I tried a violin, but when I glanced back I hit upon Mr Berenguer's silent gaze and I swear I was frightened. I never tried that again. I remember, over time, besides the flugelhorns, tubas and trumpets, at least a dozen violins, six cellos, two violas and three spinets, plus the Ming dynasty gong, an Ethiopian drum and some sort of immense, immobile snake that didn't give off any sound, which I later found out was called a serpent. I'm sure they must have sold and bought some, because the instruments would change but I remember that being the usual amount in the shop. And for a while some violinists from the Liceu would come in to make deals – usually unsuccessfully – to acquire some of those instruments. Father didn't want musicians, who are always short on cash, as clients; I want collectors: those who want the object so badly that if they can't buy it, they steal it; those are my clients.

'Why?'

'Because they pay the price I tell them and they leave contented. And some day they return, with their tongues hanging out, because they want more.'

Father knew a lot.

'Musicians want an instrument to play it. When they have it, they use it. The collector doesn't own it to play it: he might have ten instruments and just run his hand over them. Or his eyes. And he's happy. The collector doesn't play a note: he takes note.'

Father was very intelligent.

'A musician collector? That would be a windfall; but I don't know any.'

And then, in confidence, Adrià told Father that Herr Romeu was more boring than a Sunday afternoon and he looked at me in that way where his eyes went right through me and which, at sixty years old, still makes me anxious.

'What did you say?'

'That Herr Romeu …'

'No: more boring than what?'

'I don't know.'

'Yes you do.'

'Than a Sunday afternoon.'

'Very good.'

Father was always right. His silence made it seem as if he were putting my words into his pocket, for his collection. Once they were tucked away carefully, he returned to the conversation.

'Why is he boring?'

'All day long he makes me study declinations and endings that I already know by heart and makes me say this cheese is very good; where did you buy it? Or I live in Hannover and my name is Kurt. And where do you live? Do you like Berlin?'

'And what would you like to be able to say?'

'I don't know. I want to read some amusing story. I want to read Karl May in German.'

'Very well: I think you're right.'

I repeat: very well: I think you're right. And I'll take it even further: that was the only time in my life where he said I was right. If I were a fetishist, I would have framed the sentence, along with the time and date of its occurrence. And I would have made a black and white photo of it.

The next day I didn't have class because Herr Romeu had been fired. Adrià felt very important, as if people's fates were in his hands. It was a glorious Tuesday. That time I was glad that Father took a hard line with everyone. I must have been nine or ten, but I had a very highly developed sense of dignity. Or, better put, sense of mortification. Especially now that I look back, Adrià Ardèvol realised that not even when he was little had he ever been a little boy. He was caught up in every possible precociousness, the way others catch colds and infections. I even feel sorry for him. And that without knowing the details that I can now cobble together, such as that Father – after having opened the shop under very precarious circumstances, with Cecília who was learning to do her hair up very prettily – he received a visit from a customer who said he wanted to talk to him about some matter and Father had him enter the office and the stranger told him Mr Ardèvol, I haven't come here to buy anything, and Father looked him in the eye and grew alarmed.

'And would you mind telling me why you did come?'

'To tell you that your life is in danger.'

'Is that so?' A smile from Father. A slightly peeved smile.

'Yes.'

'Would you mind telling me why?'

'For example, because Doctor Montells has been released from prison.'

'I don't know what you are talking about.'

'And he has told us things.'

'And who are 'us'?'

'Let's just say that we are very angry with you because you denounced him as pro-Catalan and communist.'

'Me?'

'You.'

'I'm no grass. Anything else I can help you with?' he said, getting up.

The visitor did not rise from his chair. He made himself even more comfortable, rolling a cigarette with unusual skill. And then he lit it.

'No one smokes here.'

'I do.' He pointed to the hand with the cigarette. 'And we know that you denounced three other people. They all send greetings, from prison or from their homes. From now on, be very careful with corners: they are dangerous.'

He put out the cigarette on the wooden tabletop as if it were a vast ashtray, exhaled the smoke into Mr Ardèvol's face, got up and left the office. Fèlix Ardèvol watched a part of the tabletop sizzle without doing anything to impede it. As if it were his penitence.

That evening, at home, perhaps to rid himself of those bad feelings, Father had me come into his study and to reward me, to reward me especially for making demands on my teachers, that's what my son has to do, he showed me a folded piece of parchment, written on both sides, which was the founding charter of the Sant Pere del Burgal monastery, and he said look, Son (I wished he'd added, after the look, Son, a 'in whom I have placed all my hopes', now that we'd established a close alliance), this document was written more than a thousand years ago and now we are holding it in our hands … Hey, hey, hold your horses, I'll hold it. Isn't it lovely? It's from when the monastery was founded.'

'Where is it?'

'In Pallars. You know the Urgell in the dining room?'

'That monastery is Santa Maria de Gerri.'

'Yes, yes. Burgal is even further up. Some twenty kilometres more towards the cold.' About the parchment: 'Sant Pere del Burgal's founding charter. The Abbot Deligat asked Count Ramon de Tolosa for a precept of immunity for that monastery, which was tiny but survived for hundreds of years. It thrills me to think that I hold so much history in my hands.'

And I listened to what my father was telling me and it wasn't very hard at all for me to imagine that he was thinking the day was too luminous, too springlike to be Christmas. They had just buried the Right Reverend Father Prior Dom Josep de Sant Bartomeu in the modest, scant cemetery at Sant Pere where the life that burst forth in springtime from beneath the tender, damp grass into a thousand colourful buds was now held hostage by the ice. They had just buried the father prior and with him all possibility of the monastery keeping its doors open. Sant Pere del Burgal, before, when it still snowed abundantly, was an isolated, independent abbey; since the remote times of Abbot Deligat, it had undergone various transformations including moments of prosperity, with some thirty monks contemplating the magnificent panorama created each day by the waters of the Noguera River, with the Poses forest in the background, praising the Lord and giving thanks for his works and cursing the Devil for the cold that devastated their bodies and made the entire community's souls shrink. Sant Pere del Burgal had also gone through moments of hardship, without wheat for the mill, with barely six or seven old, sick monks to do the same tasks a monk always does from when he joins the monastery until he is transferred to its cemetery, as they'd done that day with the father prior. But now there was only one survivor whose memory went back that far.

There was a brief, feeble prayer for the dead, a rushed and dismayed benediction over the humble box. Then the improvised officiant, Brother Julià de Sau, gave the signal to the five peasants from Escaló who'd climbed up to help the monastery with that mournful event. There were no signs yet of the brothers who were to come from the Santa Maria de Gerri abbey to confirm the monastery's closing. They would arrive too late, as they always did when they were needed.

Brother Julià de Sau entered the small monastery of Sant Pere. He went into the church. With tears in his eyes, he used the hammer and chisel to make a hole in the stone of the high altar and pull out the tiny wooden lipsanotheca that held the saints' relics. He was overcome with dread because for the first time in his life he was alone. Alone. No other brothers. His footsteps echoed in the narrow corridor. He glanced at the tiny refectory. One of the benches was up against the wall, and had damaged the dirty plaster. He didn't bother to move it. A tear fell from his eye and he headed towards his cell. From there he contemplated the beloved landscape he knew like the back of his hand, tree by tree. Above his cot, the Sacred Chest that held the monastery's founding charter and that now would also hold the lipsanotheca containing the relics of unknown saints that had been with them for centuries of daily prayers and masses. And the community's chalice and paten. And the only two keys in Sant Pere del Burgal: one to the small church and one to the monastic area. So many years of canticles to the Lord reduced to a sturdy savin wood box that would become, from that moment on, the only testimony to the history of a closed monastery. On one end of his straw mattress lay the handkerchief to make a bundle with two pieces of clothing, some sort of rudimentary scarf and the book of hours. And the little bag with the fir cones and maple seed pods that reminded him of the other, old life he didn't miss much, when he was called Friar Miquel and he taught in the Dominican order; when, at the palace of His Excellency, the wife of the Wall-eyed Man of Salt stopped him near the kitchens and said here, Friar Miquel, pine and fir cones and maple seeds.

'And what would I want them for?'

'I have nothing more to offer you.'

'And why would you need to offer me anything?' said Friar Miquel impatiently.

The woman lowered her head and said in an almost inaudible whisper, His Excellency raped me and wants to kill me so my husband doesn't find out, because then *he* would kill me.

Stunned, Friar Miquel had to go into the hallway and sit down on the boxwood bench.

'What do you say?' asked the woman, who had followed him and stood before him.

The woman didn't add anything more because she'd already said it all.

'I don't believe you, you despicable liar. What you want is ...'

'When I've hung myself from a rotten beam will you believe me then?' Now she looked at him with frightening eyes.

'But child ...'

'I want you to hear my confession because I am going to kill myself.'

'I'm not a priest.'

'But you can ... I have no choice but to die. And since it's not my fault I think that God will forgive me. Isn't that right, Friar Miquel?'

'Suicide is a sin. Run away from here. Far away!'

'Where can I go, a woman alone?'

Friar Miquel would have liked to be far away, where the world ends, despite the dangers lurking at the wild limits of the universe.

In his cell at Sant Pere del Burgal, Brother Julià looked at his outstretched hand that held the seeds he'd been given by that desperate woman whom he hadn't known how to console. The next day they found her hanging from a rotten beam in the large hayloft. She swung by the rosary of the fifteen mysteries that hung around the waist of His Excellency's habit, which had been lost two days earlier. By order of His Excellency, the suicide victim was denied burial on sacred ground and the Wall-eyed Man of Salt was expelled from the palace for having allowed his wife to commit an act that cried out to heaven. It was the Wall-eyed Man of Salt himself who'd found her that morning, and he'd tried to break the rosary in the absurd hope that she was still breathing. When Friar Miquel found out, he cried bitterly and prayed, despite his superior's orders, for the salvation of that desperate woman's soul. He swore before God that he would never lose those seed pods and pine cones that reminded him of his cowardly silence. He looked at them again, twenty years later, in his open hand, now that life had thrown him a curve and he would become a monk at Santa Maria de Gerri. He put the seeds in the pocket of his Benedictine habit. He looked out the window. Perhaps they were already quite close, but he could no longer make out movements in the distance. He tied the handkerchief into an awkward bundle. That night no monk would sleep at the monastery of Burgal.

Holding tight to the Sacred Chest, he went into each and every one of the cells, Friar Marcel's, Friar Martí's, Friar Adrià's, Father Ramon's, Father Basili's, Father Josep de Sant Bartomeu's, and his humble cell, at the end of the narrow corridor, the cell that was closest to the tiny cloister and closest to the monastery's door, which he had been entrusted, if that's the word, to watch over since his arrival. Then he approached the reservoir, the modest chapterhouse, the kitchen and once again the refectory where the bench was still eating away at the wall's plaster. Then he went out into the cloister and he couldn't keep his grief from welling up, a burst of deep sobbing, because he didn't know how to accept that as the will of God. To calm himself down, to bid farewell forever to so many years of Benedictine life, he went into the monastic chapel. He got down on his knees before the altar, clinging to the Sacred Chest. For the last time in his life he looked at the paintings in the apse. The prophets and the archangels. Saint Peter and Saint Paul, Saint John and the other apostles and the Mother of God showing her devotion, along with the archangels, to severe Christ Pantocrator. And he felt guilty, guilty of the extinction of the little monastery of Sant Pere del Burgal. And with his free hand he beat on his chest and said confiteor, Domine. Confiteor, mea culpa. He put the Sacred Chest down on the floor and he knelt until he could kiss the ground that so many generations of monks had walked upon in their praise of the Almighty God who observed him impassively.

He stood, picked up the Sacred Chest again, looked at the holy paintings one last time and walked backwards to the door. Once he was outside the small church, he closed the two door leaves with a brisk motion, gave the key its final turn in the lock and placed it inside the Sacred Chest. Those beloved paintings wouldn't be seen again by human eyes until Jachiam of Pardàc opened the church up, almost three hundred years later, by simply pushing on a rotten worm-eaten door leaf with his flat hand.

And then Brother Julià de Sau thought of the day that his feet – eager and weary, still filled with fear – had reached the door of Sant Pere and he'd knocked with a closed fist. Fifteen monks then lived intra muros monasterii. My God, Glorious Lord, how he missed those days – despite not having any right to feel nostalgia for a time he hadn't experienced – when there was a job for each monk and a monk for each job. When he knocked on that door begging for admission, it had been years since he had left security behind and entered deep into the realm of fear, which is every fugitive's constant companion. And even more so when he suspects that he might be making a mistake, because Jesus speaks to us of love and kindness and I didn't fulfil his commandment. But he did, yes, because Father Nicolau Eimeric, the Inquisitor General, was his superior and it was all carried out in God's name and for the good of the Church and the true faith, and I couldn't, I couldn't because Jesus was so far from me; and who are you, Friar Miquel, silly lay friar, to ask where Jesus is? Our Lord God lies in blind, unconditional obedience. God is with me, Friar Miquel. And he who is not with me is against me. Look me in the eyes when I speak to you! He who is not with me is against me. And Friar Miquel chose to flee, he preferred uncertainty and perhaps hell to salvation with a bad conscience. And that was why he fled, taking off his Dominican habit and entering the kingdom of fear, and he travelled to the Holy Land searching for forgiveness for all his sins as if forgiveness were possible in this world or the next. If they had been sins. Dressed as a pilgrim he had seen much misfortune, he had dragged himself along compelled by regret, he had made promises that were difficult to keep, but he wasn't at peace because if you disobey the voice of salvation your soul will never find rest.

'Can't you keep your hands still?'

'But Father … I just want to touch the parchment. You said that it was mine, too.'

'With this finger. And carefully.'

Adrià brought a timid hand forward, with one finger extended, and touched the parchment. He felt as if he was already inside the monastery.

'OK, that's enough, you'll dirty it.'

'A little bit more, Father.'

'Don't you know what that's enough means?' shouted Father.

And I pulled away my hand as if the parchment had shocked me, and that was why, when the former friar returned from his journey in the Holy Land with his soul wizened, his body gaunt and his face tanned, his gaze hard as a diamond, he still felt the fires of hell inside him. He didn't dare go near his parents' house, if they were even still alive; he wandered the roads dressed as a pilgrim, begging for alms and spending them at inns on the most poisonous drinks they had on hand, as if he was in a hurry to disappear and not have to remember his memories. He also relapsed into sins of the flesh, obsessively, in a search for the oblivion and redemption that penitence hadn't afforded him. He was a true soul in purgatory. Then the kindly smile of Brother Julià de Carcassona, caretaker of the Benedictine abbey of La Grassa where he had asked for hospitage to spend a freezing winter's night, suddenly and unexpectedly illuminated his path. The night's rest became ten days of prayer at the abbey church, on his knees beside the wall furthest from the community's seats of honour. It was at Santa Maria de la Grassa where he first heard of Burgal, a cenobium so far from everything that they said that the rain reached it so weary that it barely dampened your skin. He held on to Brother Julià's smile, which may have sprung from happiness, like a deep secret treasure, and he set off on the road to the Santa Maria de Gerri abbey, as the monks at La Grassa had advised him to do. He brought with him a pouch filled with donated food and the secret, happy smile, and he headed towards the mountains that are snow-capped all year round, towards the world of perpetual silence where, perhaps, with a bit of luck, he could seek redemption. He went through valleys, over hills and waded, with his destroyed sandals, through the icy water of the rivers that had just been born of the snow. When he reached the Santa Maria de Gerri abbey, they confirmed that the priory of Sant Pere del Burgal was so secluded and remote that no one knew for sure if thoughts reached there in one piece. And what the father prior there decides with you, they assured him, will be approved by the father abbot here.

So, after a journey that lasted weeks, aged despite not having reached forty, he knocked hard on the door to the monastery of Sant Pere. It was a cold, dark dusk and the monks had finished evensong and were preparing for supper, if a bowl of hot water can be called supper. They took him in and asked him what he wanted. He begged for entrance into their tiny community; he didn't explain his pain to them, instead he spoke of his desire to serve the Holy Mother Church with a modest, anonymous job, as a lay brother, on the lowest rung, just attentive to the gaze of God Our Lord. Father Josep de Sant Bartomeu, who was already the prior, looked into his eyes and sensed the secret in his soul. Thirty days and thirty nights they had him at the door to the monastery, in a precarious shack. But what he was asking for was the shelter entailed in the habit, the refuge of living according to the holy Benedictine law that transforms people and bestows inner peace on those who practise it. Twenty-nine times he begged them to let him be just another monk and twenty-nine times the father prior, looking into his eyes, refused. Until that one rainy, happy Friday that was the thirtieth time he begged for entrance.

'Don't touch it, goddamn it, you're always touching everything!'

The alliance with Father was shaky if not already cracked.

'But I was just ...'

'No ifs, ands or buts. You want a smack? Eh? You want a smack?'

That Friday had been long ago. He entered the monastery of Burgal as a postulant and after three freezing winters he took his vows as a lay brother. He chose the name Julià in memory of a smile that had changed his life. He learned to calm his soul, to tranquilise his spirit and to love life. Despite the fact that often the Duke of Cardona's or Count Hug Roger's men passed through the valley and destroyed that which did not belong to them, there in the monastery at the mountain's peak, he was closer to God and his peace than to them. Tenaciously, he initiated himself in the path to the shores of wisdom. He didn't find happiness, but he attained complete serenity, which gradually brought him balance, and he learned to smile, in his way. More than one of the brothers came to think that humble Brother Julià was climbing the path to sainthood.

The high sun struggled uselessly to provide warmth. The brothers from Santa Maria de Gerri hadn't yet arrived; they must have stopped for the night at Soler. Despite the timid sun, it was bitterly cold at Burgal. The peasants from Escaló had arrived hours earlier with sad eyes and asked for no pay. He closed the door with the big key that for years he had kept close to him as the brother caretaker and that he would now have to hand over to the Abbot. Non sum dignus, he repeated, clutching the key that summed up the half millennium of uninterrupted monastic life at Burgal. He remained outside, alone, sitting beneath the walnut tree, with the Sacred Chest in his hands, waiting for the brothers from Gerri. Non sum dignus. And what if they want to spend the night at the monastery? Since Saint Benedict's rule specifically orders that no monk should live alone in any monastery, when the father prior felt himself growing weaker, he had sent word to the Abbot of Gerri so they could make arrangements. For eighteen months he and the father prior were the only monks at Burgal. The father said mass and he listened devoutly, they both attended hourly prayers, but they no longer sang them because the cheeping of the sparrows drowned out their worn, flat voices. The day before, mid-afternoon, after two days of high fevers, when the venerable father prior had died, he was left alone in life again. Non sum dignus.

Someone approached along the steep path from Escaló, since the one from Estaron was impassable in wintertime. Finally. He got up, dusted off his habit and walked a few steps down the path, gripping the Sacred Chest. He stopped: perhaps he should open the doors for them as a sign of hospitality? Beyond the instructions of the father prior on his deathbed, he didn't know how one closes up a cenobium with

so many years of history. The brothers from Gerri climbed
slowly, with a weary air. Three monks. He turned, with tears
in his eyes, to say goodbye to the monastery and started
down the path to save the brothers from climbing the final
stretch of the steep slope. Twenty-one years at Burgal, filled
with memories, died with that gesture. Farewell, Sant Pere,
farewell, ravines with the murmur of cold water. Farewell icy
mountains that have brought me serenity. Farewell, cloistered
brothers and centuries of chants and prayers.

'Brothers, may peace be with you on this day of the birth
of Our Lord.'

'May the Lord's peace be with you as well.'

'We've already buried him.'

One of the brothers pulled back his hood. A noble forehead, surely of a professed father – perhaps the ecclesiastical
administrator or the novice master – gave him a smile similar
to the one the other Brother Julià had given him long ago.
He didn't wear a habit beneath his cape but a knight's coat of
mail. He was accompanied by Friar Mateu and Friar Maur
from Gerri.

'Who is the dead man?' asked the knight.

'The father prior. The deceased is the father prior. Didn't
they tell you that? ...'

'What is his name? What was his name?'

'Josep de Sant Bartomeu.'

'Praise the Lord. So you are Friar Miquel de Susqueda.'

'Brother Julià is my name. I'm Brother Julià.'

'Friar Miquel. The Dominican heretic.'

'Supper is on the table.'

Little Lola had poked her head into the study. Father responded with a silent, peevish gesture as he continued to read
aloud the articles of the founding charter, which were incomprehensible on the first reading. As if in response to Little
Lola's demand, 'Now you read the rest.'

'But the writing is so strange ...'

'Read,' said Father, impatient and disappointed at having
such a wishy-washy son. And Adrià began to read, in
good mediaeval Latin, the words of Abbot Deligat, without

completely understanding them and still dreaming about the other story.

'Well … The name Friar Miquel belongs to my other life. And the Order of Saint Dominic is very far from my thoughts. I'm a new man, different.' He looked into his eyes, as the father prior had done. 'What do you want, brother?'

The man with the noble forehead fell to the ground on his knees and gave thanks to God with a brief, silent prayer. When he crossed himself devoutly, the three monks followed suit respectfully. The man stood up.

'It has taken me years to find you. A Holy Inquisitor ordered your execution for heresy.'

'You are making a mistake.'

'Gentlemen, brothers,' said one of the monks accompanying him, possibly Friar Mateu, very alarmed. 'We came to collect the key to Burgal and the monastery's Sacred Chest and to escort Friar Julià to Gerri.'

Friar Julià, suddenly remembering it, handed him the Sacred Chest he was still clinging to.

'It won't be necessary to escort him,' the man with the noble forehead said curtly. And then, addressing Brother Julià, 'I'm not making a mistake: it is imperative that you know who has condemned you.'

'My name is Julià de Sau and, as you can see, I am a Benedictine monk.'

'Friar Nicolau Eimeric condemns you. He ordered me to tell you his name.'

'You are confused.'

'He has been dead for some time, Friar Nicolau. But I am still alive and can finally rest my ravaged soul. In God's name.'

Before the horrified eyes of the two monks from Gerri, the last monk of Burgal, a new, different man, who had achieved spiritual serenity over years of effort, saw the dagger's glimmer just before it was sunk into his chest in the increasingly uncertain clarity of the weak sun on that winter's day. He had to swallow the old grudge in a single gulp. And, following the holy order, the noble knight, with the same dagger, cut off his tongue and put it inside an ivory box which was immediately dyed red. And in a strong, decisive voice, as he cleaned the iron blade with dried walnut leaves, he addressed the two frightened monks:

'This man has no right to sacred ground.'

He looked around him. Coldly. He pointed to the plot beyond the cloister.

'There. And without a cross. It is the Lord's will.'

Seeing that the two monks remained immobile, frozen with fear, the man with the noble forehead stood in front of them, practically stepping on Friar Julià's inert body, and shouted contemptuously, 'Bury this carrion!'

And Father, after reading Abbot Deligat's signature, folded it up carefully and said touching a vellum like this makes you imagine the period. Don't you think?

The inevitable consequence was me touching the parchment, now with five anxious fingers. Father's hard smack to the back of my neck was painful and very humiliating. As I struggled not to release a single tear, Father, indifferent, put the loupe aside and stored the manuscript in the safe.

'Come on, supper time,' he said, instead of sealing a pact with a son who knew how to read mediaeval Latin. Before reaching the dining room I had already had to wipe away two furtive tears.

## 6

Being born into that family had indeed been an unforgivable mistake. And the worst had yet to happen.

'Well, I liked Herr Romeu.'

Thinking that I was asleep, they were speaking a bit too loudly.

'You don't know what you're talking about.'

'Obviously. I'm useless. And a drudge!'

'I'm the one who makes sacrifices for Adrià!'

'And what do I do?' Mother's sarcastic, hurt voice, and then, lowering her tone, 'And don't shout.'

'You're the one shouting!'

'Don't I make sacrifices for the boy? Huh?'

Thick, solid silence. Father's brain cells scrambling to think.

'Of course, you do too.'

'Well, thanks for admitting it.'

'But that doesn't mean that you're right.'

I picked up Sheriff Carson because I sensed that I'd need some psychological support. I even called Black Eagle over just in case. And, without the slightest rustle, I opened the door to my room just a sliver. It wasn't the moment to make a dangerous excursion to the kitchen for a glass. Now I could hear them much better. Black Eagle congratulated me on the idea. Sheriff Carson was silent and chewed on what I thought was gum but turned out to be tobacco.

'Fine, he'll study violin, fine.'

'You make it sound like you're doing me a huge favour.'

'What are you talking about?'

'Fine, he'll study violin, fine.' I'll admit that my mother's imitation of Father was quite an exaggeration. But I liked it.

'Well, if you're going to act like that, forget the violin and have him devote his time to serious things.'

'If you take away the boy's violin, you'll hear it from me.'

'Don't threaten me.'

'Don't you, either.'

Silence. Carson spat on the floor and I made a mute gesture to scold him.

'The boy has to study real things.'

'And what are real things?'

'Latin, Greek, history, German and French. To start with.'

'The boy is only eleven years old, Fèlix!'

Eleven years old. I think that earlier I said eight or nine; time slips away from me in these pages too. Luckily Mother was keeping track. Do you know what happens? I don't have the time or the desire to correct all this; I write hurriedly, like when I was young, when everything I wrote I wrote hurriedly. But my urgency now is very different. Which doesn't mean I write quickly. And Mother repeated: 'The boy is eleven years old and already studies French at school.'

'"J'ai perdu la plume dans le jardin de ma tante" isn't French.'

'What is it? Hebrew?'

'He has to be able to read Racine.'

'My God.'

'God doesn't exist. And he could be much better at Latin. I mean, he's studying with the Jesuits!'

That affected me more directly. Neither Black Eagle nor Sheriff Carson said a peep. They had never gone to the Jesuit school on Casp Street. I didn't know if it was bad or good. But, according to Father, they weren't teaching me Latin well. He was right: we were working on the second declension and it was a total bore, because the other children didn't even understand the concept behind the genitive and the dative.

'Oh, now you want to pull him out of there?'

'What do you think about the French Lyceum?'

'No: the boy will stay at Casp. Fèlix, he's just a child! We can't be moving him from place to place as if he were your brother's livestock.'

'OK, forget I mentioned it. We always end up doing what you say,' lied Father.

'And sport?'

'None of that. They have plenty of playground breaks at the Jesuits', don't they?'

'And music.'

'Fine, fine. But the priorities come first. Adrià will be a great scholar and that's that. And I will find a substitute for Casals.'

Who was the substitute for Herr Romeu and in five pathetic classes had also got bogged down in vague explanations of German's elaborately complex syntax and couldn't find his way out.

'That's not necessary. Let him have a break.'

Two days later, in his study, with Mother sitting on the sofa I'd established my espionage base behind, Father had me come over and stand by his chair and explained my future in detail and listen well, because I'm not going to repeat this: that I was a clever lad, who had to take advantage of my intellectual ability, that if the Einsteins at school don't realise what I'm capable of, he would have to go in personally and explain it to them.

'I'm surprised that you weren't more insufferable,' you told me one day.

'Why? Because they told me I was intelligent? I already knew I was. Like when you're tall, or fat, or have dark hair. I never really cared much one way or the other. Like the masses and the religious sermons I had to sit through patiently, though they did affect Bernat. And then Father pulled a rabbit out of his hat: And now your real private German lessons with a real teacher will start. None of these Romeus, Casals and the like.'

'But I ...'

'And French tutoring.'

'But, Father, I want ...'

'You don't want anything. And I'm warning you,' he pointed at me as if with a pistol, 'you will learn Aramaic.'

I looked at Mother, searching for some sort of support, but she had her gaze lowered, as if she were very interested in the floor tiles. I had to defend myself all on my own and I shouted, 'I don't want to learn Aramaic!' Which was a lie. But I was looking at an avalanche of homework.

'Of course you do,' – in a low, cold, implacable voice.

'No.'

'Don't talk back to me.'

'I don't want to learn Aramaic. Or anything else!'

Father brought a hand to his forehead and, as if he had an awful migraine, he said, looking at the desk, in a very quiet voice, look at the sacrifices I'm making so that you can be the most brilliant student Barcelona has ever seen and this is how you thank me? Exaggerated shouting. 'With an "I don't want to learn Aramaic"?' And now shrieking, 'Eh?'

'I want to learn ...'

Silence. Mother looked up, hopeful. Carson, in my pocket, stirred curiously. I didn't know what I wanted to learn. I knew that I didn't want them to fill my head with too much too early, weigh it down. There were a few anxious seconds of reflection: in the end, I had to improvise:

' ... Well, I want to be a doctor.'

Silence. Confused looks between my parents.

'A doctor?'

For a few seconds Father visualised my future as a doctor. Mother did too, I think. I, who got dizzy just thinking about blood, thought I had blown it. Father, after a moment of indecision, brought his chair closer to the desk, preparing to return to his reading. 'No: you won't be a doctor and you won't be a monk. You will be a great humanist and that's that.'

'Father.'

'Come on, Son, I've got work to do. Go and make some noise with your violin.'

And Mother looking at the floor, still interested in the colourful tiles. Traitor.

Lawyer, doctor, architect, chemist, civil engineer, optical engineer, pharmacist, lawyer, manufacturer, textile engineer and banker were the foreseeable professions according to all the other parents of all the other children.

'You said lawyer more than once.'

'It's the only major that you can do with humanities. But children are more likely to think of studying to be a coal-merchant, painter, carpenter, lamplighter, bricklayer, aviator, shepherd, footballer, night watchman, mountain climber, gardener, train guard, parachute jumper, tram driver, fireman and the Pope in Rome.'

'But no father has ever said, Son, when you grow up you will be a humanist.'

'Never. I come from a very odd house. Yours was a bit like that too.'

'Well, yeah …' you said to me, like someone confessing an unforgivable defect who didn't want to go into detail.

The days passed and Mother said nothing, as if she were crouched, waiting for her turn. Which is to say I started German lessons again, but with a third tutor, Herr Oliveres, a young man who worked at the Jesuits' school but needed some extra money. I recognised Herr Oliveres right away, even though he taught the older children, because he always signed up, I suppose for the bit of money it brought, to watch over those in detention for tardiness on Thursday afternoons, and he spent the time reading. And he had a solid method of language instruction.

'Eins.'

'Ains.'

'Zwei.'

'Sbai.'

'Drei.'

'Drai.'

'Vier.'

'Fia.'

'Fünf.'

'Funf.'

'Nein: fünf.'

'Finf.'

'Nein: füüüünf.'

'Füüüünf.'

'Sehr gut!'

I put the time I'd wasted with Herr Romeu and Herr Casals behind me and I soon got the gist of German. I was fascinated by two things: that the vocabulary wasn't Latinate, which was completely new for me and, above all, that it had declensions, like Latin. Herr Oliveres was amazed and couldn't quite believe it. Soon I asked him for syntax homework and the man was flabbergasted, but I've always been interested in approaching languages through their intrinsic hard core. You can always ask for the time of day with a few gestures. And yes, I was enjoying learning another language.

'How are the German classes going?' Father asked me impatiently after the first lesson of the Oliveres period.

'Aaaalso, eigentlich gut,' I said, feigning disinterest. Out of the corner of my eye, not quite able to see him, I could tell that my father was smiling and I felt very proud of myself because I think that even though I never admitted it, at that age I lived to impress my father.

'Something you rarely achieved.'

'I didn't have time.'

Herr Oliveres turned out to be a cultured, timid man who spoke in a soft voice, who was always badly shaven, who wrote poems in secret and who smoked smelly tobacco but he was able to explain the language from the inside out. And he started me on the schwache Verben in the second lesson. And in the fifth he showed me, very cautiously, like someone sharing a dirty photo, one of Hölderlin's *Hymnen*. And Father wanted Herr Oliveres to give me a French test to see if I needed tutoring, and after the exam Monsieur Oliveres told Father I didn't need French tutoring because I was doing fine with what they taught me at school, and then, there was that hour in between … How is your English, Mr Oliveres?

Yes, being born into that family was a mistake for many different reasons. What pained me about Father was that he only knew me as his son. He still hadn't realised that I was a child. And my mother, looking down at the tiles, without acknowledging the contest Father and I were disputing. Or so I believed. Luckily I had Carson and Black Eagle. Those two almost always backed me up.

7

It was mid afternoon; Trullols was with a group of students who never seemed to finish and I was waiting. A boy, taller than me and with a bit of moustache fuzz and a few hairs on his legs, sat down beside me. Well, he was a lot taller than me. He held the violin as if he were hugging it and stared straight ahead, so as to not look at me, and Adrià said hello to him.

'Hello,' answered Bernat, without looking at him.

'You're with Trullols?'

'Uh-huh.'

'First year?'

'Third.'

'Me too. We'll be together. Can I see your violin?'

In that period, thanks to Father, I liked the object almost more than the music that came out of it. But Bernat looked at me suspiciously. For a few moments I thought he must have a Guarnerius and didn't want to show it to me. But since I opened my case and presented a very dark red student violin that produced a very conventional sound, he did the same with his. I imitated Mr Berenguer's demeanour: 'French, turn of the century.' And looking into his eyes, 'One of those dedicated to Madame d'Angoulême.'

'How do you know?' asked Bernat, impressed, perplexed, mouth agape.

From that day on Bernat admired me. For the stupidest possible reason: it's not hard at all to remember objects and know how to assess and classify them. You only have to have a father who's obsessed with such things. How do you know, eh?

'The varnish, the shape, the general air …'

'Violins are all the same.'

'Certainly not. Every violin has a story behind it. There's not only the luthier who created it, but every violinist who has played it. This violin isn't yours.'

'Of course it is!'

'No. It's the other way around. You'll see.'

My father had told me that, one day, with the Storioni in his hands. He offered it to me somewhat regretfully and said, without really knowing what he was saying, be very careful, because this object is unique. The Storioni in my hands felt as if it were alive. I thought I could feel a soft, inner pulse. And Father, his eyes gleaming, said imagine, this violin has been through experiences we know nothing about, it has been played in halls and homes that we will never see, and it has lived all the joys and pains of the violinists who have played it. The conversations it has heard, the music it's expressed … I am sure it could tell us many tender stories, he finally said, with an extraordinary dose of cynicism that at the time I was unable to capture.

'Let me play it, Father.'

'No. Not until you've finished your eighth year of violin study. Then it will be yours. Do you hear me? Yours.'

I swear that the Storioni, upon hearing those words, throbbed more intensely for a moment. I couldn't tell if it was out of joy or grief.

'Look, it's … how can I put it; look at it, it's a living thing. It even has a proper name, like you and I.'

Adrià looked at his father with a somewhat distant stance, as if calculating whether he was pulling his leg or not.

'A proper name?'

'Yes.'

'And what's it called?'

'Vial.'

'What does Vial mean?'

'What does Adrià mean?'

'Well … Hadrianus is the surname of a Roman family that came from Hadria, near the Adriatic.'

'That's not what I meant, for god's sake.'

'You asked me what my nam

'Yes, yes, yes ... Well, the violin is just named Vial and that's it.'

'Why is it named Vial?'

'Do you know what I've learned, Son?'

Adrià looked at him with disappointment because he was avoiding the question, he didn't know the answer or he didn't want to admit it. He was human and he tried to cover it up.

'What have you learned?'

'That this violin doesn't belong to me, but rather I belong to it. I am one of many who have owned it. Throughout its life, this Storioni has had various players at its service. And today it is mine, but I can only look at it. Which is why I wanted you to learn to play the violin, so you can continue the long chain in the life of this instrument. That is the only reason you must study the violin. That's the only reason, Adrià. You don't need to like music.'

My father – such elegance – twisting the story and making it look as if it had been his idea I study violin and not Mother's. What elegance my father had as he arranged others' fates. But I was trembling with emotion at that point despite having understood his instructions, which ended with that blood-curdling you don't need to like music.

'What year was it made?' I asked.

Father had me look through the right f-hole. Laurentius Storioni Cremonensis me fecit 1764.

'Let me hold it.'

'No. You think about all the history this violin has. But no touching.'

Jachiam Mureda let the two carts and the men follow him towards La Grassa, led by Blond of Cazilhac. He hid in a corner to relieve himself. A few moments of calm. Beyond the wooden carts that slowly headed off was the silhouette of the monastery and the wall destroyed by lightning. He had taken refuge in Carcassona three summers ago, fleeing the hatred of those in Moena, and fate was about to change the course of his life. He had got used to the sweet language of the Occitans. He had grown accustomed to not eating cheese every day; but what was hardest for him was not being surrounded by forests and not having mountains nearby; there were some, but always so far, far away that they didn't seem real. As he defecated he suddenly understood that it wasn't that he missed the landscape of Pardàc, but that he missed his father, Mureda of Pardàc, and all the Muredas: Agno, Jenn, Max, Hermes, Josef, Theodor, Micurà, Ilse, Erica, Katharina, Matilde, Gretchen and little Bettina who gave me the medallion of Saint Maria dai Ciüf, the patron saint of Pardàc's woodcutters, so I would never feel alone. And he began to cry with longing for his people and as he shat he took the medallion off his neck and looked at it: a proud Virgin Mary facing forward, holding a tiny baby and with a lush pine tree in the background that reminded him of the pine beside the Travignolo stream, in his Pardàc.

Repairing the wall had been complicated because first they'd had to knock down a good bit that was shaky. And in a few days he had built a magnificent scaffolding with his wood. The monastery's carpenter, Brother Gabriel, praised him for it. Brother Gabriel was a man with hands large as feet when it came to hacking and chopping, and thin as lips when it came time to gauge the wood's quality. They hit it off right away. The friar, a natural talker, wondered how he knew so much about the inner life of wood since he was just a carpenter, and Jachiam, finally free of his fear of vengeance, for the first time since he had run away said I'm not a carpenter, Brother Gabriel. I cut wood, I listen to wood. My trade is making the wood sing, choosing the trees and the parts of the trunk that will later be used by master luthiers to make a good instrument, such as a viola or a violin.

'And what are you doing working for a foreman, child of God?'

'Nothing. It's complicated.'

'You ran away from something.'

'Well, I don't know.'

'It's not my place to say this, but be careful you aren't running away from yourself.'

'No. I don't think so. Why?'

'Because those who run away from themselves find that the

shadow of their enemy is always on their heels and they can't
stop running, until finally they explode.'

'Is your father a violinist?' Bernat asked me.

'No.'

'Well, I … But the violin is mine,' he added.

'I'm not saying it's not yours. I'm saying that you are the
violin's.'

'You say strange things.'

They were silent. They heard Trullols raising her voice to
quiet a student who was zealously playing out of tune.

'How awful,' said Bernat.

'Yes.' Silence. 'What's your name?'

'Bernat Plensa. And you?'

'Adrià Ardèvol.'

'Are you a fan of Barça or Espanyol?'

'Barça. You?'

'Me too.'

'Do you collect any trading cards?'

'Of cars.'

'Wow. Do you have the Ferrari triple?'

'No. Nobody does.'

'You mean it doesn't exist?'

'That's what my father says.'

'Oh, boy, wow.' Desolate. 'Really?'

Both boys were silent thinking about Fangio's Ferrari,
which was composed of three cards that might not exist. That
gave them a gnawing feeling in their stomachs. And the two
men, also in silence, watched as the wall in La Grassa rose
up straight thanks to the solid scaffolding Jachiam had built.
After quite some time:

'And what wood do you use to make those instruments?'

'I don't make them, I never did. I offered the best wood.
Always the best. The masters in Cremona came to me for it
and they trusted that my father and I would have it prepared
for them. We sold them wood chopped during the January
full moon if they didn't want it to have resin and in midsum-
mer if they wanted a more bold, melodious wood. My father
taught me how to find the wood that sang best, from among

hundreds of trees. Yes; my father taught me, and his father –
who worked for the Amatis – taught him.'

'I don't know who they are.'

Then Jachiam of Pardàc told him about his parents and his
siblings and his wooded landscape in the Tyrolean Alps. And
about Pardàc, whom those further south call Predazzo. And
he felt relieved, as if he had confessed to the lay brother. But
he didn't feel guilty of any death, because Bulchanij of Moena
was a murdering swine who'd burned down the future out of
envy and he would carve open his belly ten thousand times if
he had the chance. Jachiam the unrepentant.

'What are you thinking about, Jachiam? I can see the
hatred in your face.'

'Nothing, I'm sad. Memories. My brothers and sisters.'

'You spoke of many brothers and sisters.'

'Yes. First we were eight boys and when they'd given up
hope of having a girl, they got six.'

'And how many are living?'

'All of them.'

'It's a miracle.'

'Depends on how you look at it. Theodor is lame, Hermes
can't think straight but he's got a big heart and Bettina, the
littlest, my dear sweet Bettina, is blind.'

'Your poor mother.'

'She's dead. She died giving birth to a boy who died too.'

Brother Gabriel was silent, perhaps in the memory of that
martyr. Then, to lighten up the conversation, 'You haven't told
me what wood you used for the instruments. Which one is it?'

'The fine instruments created by the master luthiers of
Cremona are made with a combination of woods.'

'You don't want to tell me.'

'No.'

'It doesn't matter: I'll work it out.'

'How?'

Brother Gabriel winked and went back to the monastery,
taking advantage of the fact that the bricklayers and their
mates, knackered after a day of sorting through stones and
bringing them up with the pulley, had come down from the

scaffolding to wait for nightfall, for the little food they had and for rest, preferably without many dreams.

'Someday I'll bring the Storioni to class.'

'Poor you. If you do, you'll find out what a good hard cuff is.'

'So what do we have it for?'

Father left the violin on the table and looked at me with his hands on his hips.

'What do we have it for, what do we have it for ...' he mimicked me.

'Yes.' Now I was peeved. 'What do we have it for if it's always in its case inside the safe and we can't even look at it?'

'I have it to have it. Do you understand?'

'No.'

'Ebony, a fir we don't have around here and maple.'

'Who told you?' asked Jachiam of Pardàc, impressed.

Brother Gabriel brought him to the monastery's sacristy. In one corner, protected by a sheath, there was a viola da gamba made of light wood.

'What's it doing here?'

'Resting.'

'In a monastery?'

Brother Gabriel made a vague gesture that said he wasn't in the mood to go into more details.

'But how did you work it out?'

'By smelling the wood.'

'Impossible. It's very dry and the varnish covers up the scent.'

That day, safe in the sacristy, Jachiam Mureda learned to distinguish woods by their odour and he thought what a shame, what a shame, not being able to share what he'd learned with his family, starting with his father, who was apt to die of sadness if he were to hear that anything had happened to him. And Agno, too, Jenn and Max who haven't lived at home for years now, Hermes the dim-witted, Josef, Theodor the lame, Micurà, Ilse and Erica, who are already married, Katharina, Matilde, Gretchen and little Bettina, my little blind one who gave me Mum's medallion, which is the bit of Pardàc that I always carry with me.

It wasn't until six weeks later, when they began to take down the scaffolding, that Brother Gabriel said that he knew something I think you'll find very interesting.

'What's that?'

He led him far away from the men who were dismantling the scaffolding and he whispered in his ear that he knew of an old, abandoned monastery, in the middle of nowhere, with a forest of fir trees beside it; that red fir that you like.

'A forest?'

'A fir grove. About twenty firs and a majestic maple tree. And the wood doesn't belong to anyone. No one has even touched it in five years.'

'Why doesn't it belong to anyone?'

'It's beside an abandoned monastery.' In a whisper: 'La Grassa and Santa Maria de Gerri won't miss a couple of trees.'

'Why are you telling me this?'

'Don't you want to go back with your family?'

'Of course. I want to go back to my father, who I hope is still alive. And I want to see Agno again, and Jenn and Max who no longer live at home, and Hermes the dim-witted ...'

'Yes, yes, yes, I know. And Josef and all the others, yes. And with a load of wood that will be of help to you all.'

Jachiam of Pardàc didn't return to Carcassona. From La Grassa, accompanied by Blond of Cazilhac with a couple of men and five mules laden with cart wheels and a bag filled with all his wages since his flight, he headed up through Ariège and the Salau pass, towards a dream.

They arrived at Sant Pere del Burgal seven or eight days later, at the end of the summer, along the Escaló trail, which, in the cold times of the great-grandparents of the great-grandparents of the great-great-grandparents, the envoy of death had travelled. On the peak was the monastery, whose walls showed signs of neglect. When he walked around the building he was shocked to find what he believed to be the equal of the finest part of the Paneveggio woods, before the fire. It was an awe-inspiring grove of ten or fifteen immense fir trees and in the centre, like a queen, rose a maple with a suitably large trunk. As his men rested after the wearisome trip, Jachiam blessed the memory of Brother Gabriel of La Grassa. He walked through the trees and touched them, and he made the wood sing like his father had taught him and he sniffed it like Brother Gabriel had. And he felt happy. Then, while his men were napping, he walked through the abandoned rooms until he reached the church's locked door. He pushed it with the palm of his hand and the rotten, worm-eaten wood of the door crumbled. Inside it was so dark that he just glanced in distractedly before going to take a nap himself.

They set up camp inside the walls of the isolated monastery, beneath a mouldy, half-rotten ceiling, and they bought provisions from the people of Escaló and Estaron, who didn't understand what those men were after in the ruins of Burgal. They devoted an entire moon to building sturdy carts for transport, further down near the river where the road was more level. Jachiam hugged all the living trunks after cutting off the lower branches. He tapped them with a flat hand and brought his ear close to listen carefully, to the sceptical silence and surprise of his men. By the time they had the carts built, Jachiam of Pardàc had decided which fir he would chop down along with the maple. He was convinced that it was a wood that had grown with exceptional regularity; despite years away from the trade, he knew that it would sing. And Jachiam spent many hours looking at the mysterious paintings in the apse of the little church, which must have contained stories that were new to him. Prophets and archangels, Saint Peter, the patron of the monastery, and Saint Paul, Saint John and the other apostles beside the Mother of God, praising the severe Pantocrator along with the archangels. And he felt no remorse.

And then they began to saw down the chosen fir. Yes: it was a tree with regular growth, marked by a cold that must be intense and, above all, constant. A tree with the same density in each growth despite the years. My God, what wood. And with the tree felled – again observed sceptically by the men helping him – he felt and he smelt, then tapped along the trunk until he found the good parts. He marked two areas in chalk, one twelve feet long and the other ten. Those spots were where the wood sang best. And he had them sawed knowing that it wasn't the new January moon, which is when many say the wood for a good violin should be chosen. The Muredas had realised that, unless the woodworms had got to it, a bit of resin would revive wood that had to travel a long way.

'I think you're pulling my leg,' said Bernat.

'Whatever you say.'

They were silent. But the out-of-tune student was so out of tune that it was worse when they were quiet. After quite some time, Adrià said, 'Whatever. But it's more fun to think that the violin is the one in charge, because it's alive.'

After a few days of rest, they began with the maple. It was immense, perhaps two centuries old. And its leaves were already yellowing in preparation for the first snowfall, which it would no longer be around for. He knew that the part closest to the stump was the best and they sawed close to ground level despite the complaints of his men, who found it laborious and didn't see the point. He had to promise them two more days of rest before setting off. They cut close to the ground. So close to the ground that Blond of Cazilhac, drawn by something, used his pick to make a hole down towards the roots.

'Come here, you have to see this,' he said, interrupting his daily visit to the magical paintings in the apse.

The men had almost completely uprooted the tree. Among the roots, there were bones, a skull and some human hairs with tatters of dark cloth ruined by the dampness.

'Who buries someone beneath a tree?' exclaimed one of the men.

'This is very old.'

'They didn't bury him beneath the tree,' said Blond of Cazilhac.

'They didn't?' Jachiam looked at him, puzzled.

'Don't you see? The tree comes out of the man, if it is a man. He nourished the tree with his blood and his flesh.'

Yes. It was as if the tree had been born from the skeleton's womb. And Adrià brought his face closer to his father's, so he would see him, so he would answer him.

'Father, I just want to see how it sounds. Let me play four scales. Just a tiny bit. Come on, Father! ...'

'No. And no means no. Full stop,' said Fèlix Ardèvol, eluding his son's gaze.

And do you know what I think? That this study, which is my world, is like a violin that, over the course of its life, has accommodated many different people: my father, me ..., you because you are here in your self-portrait, and who knows who else because the future is impossible to comprehend. So no; no means no, Adrià.

'Don't you know that no means yes?' Bernat would tell me, angrily, many years later.

'You see?' Father changed his tone. He had him turn the violin over and show him the back of the instrument. He pointed to a spot without touching it. 'This thin line ... who made it? How? Is it a blow? Was it done on purpose? When? Where?'

He took the instrument from me delicately and said to himself, as if in dreams, with this I'm happy. That's why I like ... He gestured with his head around the study, at all the miracles contained therein. And he carefully placed Vial into its case, and that into the dungeon of the safe.

Just then Trullols's classroom door opened. Bernat said, in a low voice the teacher couldn't hear, 'What claptrap: I don't belong to the violin. It's mine: my father bought it for me at Casa Parramon's. For a hundred and seventy-five pesetas.'

And he closed the case. I found it very unfriendly. So young and already mystery made him uncomfortable. There was no way he could be my friend. Ruled out. Kaputt. Then it turned out he also went to Casp, a year ahead of me. And his name was Bernat Plensa i Punsoda. I may have said that already. And he was so uptight, as if they'd bathed him in a vat of hair spray and forgot to rinse him off. And I had to admit, after sixteen minutes, that that unfriendly boy who refused to accept mystery, who would never be my friend, and who was named Bernat Plensa i Punsoda, had something about him that made a violin bought for one hundred and seventy-five pesetas at Casa Parramon sound with a delicacy I had never been able to achieve. And Trullols looked at him with satisfaction and I thought what a piece of shit my violin was. That was when I swore that I would make him shut up forever, him, the violin dedicated to Madame d'Angoulême and the hair spray he'd bathed in; and I think that it would have been much better for everyone if I'd never had that thought. For the moment, all I did was let it gradually ripen. It's hard to believe that the most unthinkable tragedies can be born of the most innocent things.

*Bernat, halfway up the stairs, felt his pocket and pulled out the vibrating mobile phone. Tecla. He hesitated for a few seconds, not sure whether to answer or not. He moved aside to let a hurrying neighbour get past him. He stood there like an idiot looking at the lit-up screen, as if he could see Tecla in it, cursing his name, and that gave him a guilty pleasure. He put the mobile back into his pocket and after a moment he could feel that it had stopped vibrating. Tecla must have been negotiating the last loose end with the voice mail operator. Maybe she was saying, and we each get the house in Llançà for six months a year. And the operator, who do you think you are, you've never set foot in there and when you have it was with that peeved face you are so fond of pulling just to make poor Bernat's life difficult! Who do you think you are? Bravo for the Orange operator, thought Bernat. He caught his breath at the landing on the main floor and, once he had, he rang the bell.*

*'Rrrrrrrrrrinnnnnng.'*

*It took so long for him to hear any reaction from inside the flat that he had time to think about Tecla, about Llorenç and about the very unpleasant conversation they'd had the night before. The murmur of dragging footsteps, the sudden clamour of the lock and the door began to move. Adrià, looking at him over narrow reading glasses, finished opening the door and turned on the light in the hallway. Its gleam reflected off his bald head.*

*'The bulb in the landing blew again,' he said in greeting.*

*Bernat hugged him and Adrià didn't hug him back. He took off his eyeglasses and said thank you for coming, as he waved him in.*

*'How are you?'*

*'Terrible. And you?'*

*'Terrible.'*

*'Would you like a drink?'*

*'No. Yes. I don't drink any more.'*

*'We don't drink any more, we don't fuck any more, we don't overeat any more, we don't go to the cinema any more, we don't*

ever like a book any more, now every woman is too young, we
can't get it up any more, we don't believe those who say they'll
save the country any more.'

'Quite a list.'

'How's Tecla doing?'

He had him enter the study. Bernat looked around with
open admiration, as he did every time he went in there. For
a few seconds his gaze stopped on the self-portrait, but he re-
frained from any comment.

'What did you ask me?' he said.

'How's Tecla?'

'Very well. Fabulous.'

'I'm glad to hear it.'

'Adrià.'

'What.'

'Come on, don't make fun.'

'Why?'

'Because I told you two days ago that we're separating, that
we're at each other's throats ...'

'Oh, Christ ...'

'Don't you remember?'

'No. I'm very absorbed and ...'

'You're an absent-minded scholar.'

Adrià grew quiet and, to break the silence, Bernat said we're
separating; at our age, and we're separating.

'I'm so sorry. But you're doing the right thing.'

'To tell you the truth, I couldn't care less. I'm tired of
everything.'

When he sat down, Bernat tapped his knees and, in a falsely
cheery tone, said come on, what was all the rush and urgency
about?

Adrià stared at him for a very long minute. Bernat held his
gaze until he realised that, even though he was looking at him,
Adrià was far, far away.

'What's wrong?' He paused. The other man was in the
clouds. 'Adrià?' A hint of panic. 'What's going on with you?'

Adrià swallowed hard and looked, somewhat anxiously,
towards his friend. Then he looked away. 'I'm ill.'

'Oh.'

Silence. Your whole life, our whole lives, thought Bernat, passing before your eyes when a loved one tells you they are ill. And Adrià was only half there. Bernat tried to forget for a few moments about Tecla, that bitch who was ruining his day, his week and his month, that shrew, and he said but what do you mean? What do you have?

'An expiration date.'

Silence. More long seconds of silence.

'But what is going on, for Christ's sake, are you dying, is it serious, is there anything I can do, I don't know, explain yourself, will you?'

If he hadn't been separated from Tecla, he never would have had that reaction. And Bernat was infinitely sorry for what he'd said but, on the other hand, from what he could see, it hadn't had much of an effect on Adrià because his response was a smile.

'Yes, there is something you can do for me. A favour.'

'Of course. But how are you? What do you have?'

'It's hard for me to explain. They have to put me in assisted living or something like that.'

'Shit, but you're fine. Look at you, all hale and hearty.'

'You have to do me a favour.'

He got up and disappeared into the flat. What patience I need lately, thought Bernat. First Tecla, and now Adrià, with his endless mysteries and his hypochondria.

Adrià came back with his hypochondria and a mystery in the shape of a large bundle of papers. He put it down on the little table, in front of Bernat.

'You need to make sure this doesn't get lost.'

'Let's see, let's see … How long have you been ill?'

'A while.'

'I didn't know anything about this.'

'I didn't know you and Tecla were separating either, even though I've suggested it to you more than once. And I always wanted to think that you'd worked it out. Can I continue?'

Men who are soulmates know how to fight and make up, and they know not to tell each other everything, just in case *the other could lend a helping hand. Adrià had told him that thirty-five years ago and Bernat remembered it perfectly. And he cursed life, which gives us so many deaths.*

'Forgive me, but I'm … Of course you can continue.'

'A few months ago they diagnosed me with a degenerative brain process. And now it seems it's speeding up.'

'Shit.'

'Yes.'

'You could have told me.'

'Would you have cured me?'

'I'm your friend.'

'That's why I called you.'

'Can you live alone?'

'Little Lola comes every day.'

'Caterina.'

'Yeah, that's right. And she stays until quite late. She leaves my supper prepared.'

*Adrià pointed to the stack of papers and said you aren't just my friend, you're also a writer.*

'A failed writer,' was Bernat's curt reply.

'According to you.'

'Yes, and you've certainly always been quick to remind me of it.'

'I've always criticised you, you know that, but I never said you failed.'

'But you've thought it.'

'You don't know what I have, inside here,' said Adrià, suddenly irritated, tapping his forehead with both hands.

'I haven't published in years.'

'But you haven't stopped writing. Isn't that right?'

*Silence. Adrià insisted,* 'Not long ago, in public, you said you were writing a novel. Yes or no?'

'Another failure. I've abandoned it.' *He breathed deeply and said,* 'Come on, what is it you want?'

*Adrià grabbed the pile of papers and examined them for a little while, as if it were the first time he had seen them. He looked at Bernat and passed the bundle to him. Now he got a good look at it: it was a thick pile of pages, written on both sides.*

'Only this side is good.'

'In green ink?'

'Uh huh.'

'And the other one?' He read the first page: 'The Problem of Evil.'

'Nothing. Nonsense. It's worthless,' said Adrià, uncomfortably.

Bernat looked through the pages in green, a bit disorientated, trying to get used to his friend's difficult handwriting.

'What is it?' he said finally, lifting his head.

'I don't know. My life. My life and other lies.'

'And since when … I didn't know this side of you.'

'I know. No one knows it.'

'Do you want me to tell you what I think of it?'

'No. Well, if you want to, sure. But … what I'm asking, begging, is that you type it into the computer.'

'You still haven't tried out the one I gave you.'

Adrià made a vague gesture in his defence: 'But I did classes with Llorenç.'

'That were of no help at all.' He looked at the bundle of pages. 'The part written in green doesn't have a title that I can see.'

'I don't know what to call it. Maybe you could help me with that.'

'Are you pleased with it?' asked Bernat, picking up the pile.

'It's not about whether I'm pleased with it or not. Besides, it's the first time that …'

'This is a surprise.'

'It was a surprise for me too; but I had to do it.'

Adrià leaned back in the armchair. Bernat continued leafing through the pile for a little while and then he placed it all on the small table.

'Tell me how you are. Can I do anything to …'

'No, thank you.'

'But how are you?'

'Right now, fine. But the process can't be stopped. In a few months …'

Adrià, hesitating over whether he should speak or not, looked forward, towards the wall where there was a photo of *the two friends with rucksacks on their backs, hair on their heads and no spare tires: in Bebenhausen, when they were young and still knew how to smile at the camera. And above it, in a place of honour, as if it were an altar, was the self-portrait. Then he spoke in a soft voice, 'In a few months I might not even be able to recognise you.'*

*'No.'*

*'Yes.'*

*'Shit.'*

*'Yes.'*

*'And how will you get along?'*

*'I'll tell you later, don't worry.'*

*'OK.' Bernat tapped the bundle of paper with a finger: 'And don't you worry about this. I hope I'll be able to understand your handwriting. Do you know what you want to do with it?'*

*Adrià rambled on for a while, almost without glancing at him. Bernat thought he looked like a penitent confessing. When he stopped speaking they were silent for some time, while the sky grew dark. Perhaps thinking about their lives, which hadn't been tranquil. And thinking about the things they hadn't said; and the insults and fights of the past; and the periods they'd gone without seeing each other. And thinking why does life always end with an unwanted death. And Bernat thinking I will do whatever you ask. And Adrià not knowing what he was thinking. And Bernat's phone started vibrating in his pocket and, at that moment, he found the sound irreverent.*

*'What is that?'*

*'Nothing, my mobile phone. We humans use the computer a good friend gives us. And we have mobile phones.'*

*'Fuck, then answer. Telephones are for answering.'*

*'No, it's probably Tecla. Let her wait.'*

*And they grew silent again, waiting for the vibration to stop, but it went on and on, becoming some sort of awkward guest in that silent conversation, and Bernat thought it has to be Tecla, what a nag. But finally the vibration died out. And their thoughts gradually returned, implanting themselves in the silence between the two men.*

## 8

'But we don't have a single manuscript!' exclaimed Bernat, as the two boys stood on the corner of Bruc and València Streets, in front of the conservatory before heading to one of their homes; which one would be decided along the way.

'I know what I'm talking about.'

'And our flat is small, compared to yours.'

'Yeah, but what about that marvellous terrace you guys have, eh?'

'What I want is a brother.'

'Me too.'

They walked in silence, now returning to Bernat's house before heading back towards Adrià's for the second time so they could put off the moment of separation. In silence they pined for the brother they didn't have and the mystery behind Roig, Rull, Soler and Pàmies having three, five or four or six siblings, while they had none.

'Yeah, but Rull's house is a huge mess, four in one room, with bunk beds. There's always shouting.'

'Fine, fine, that's true. But it's more fun.'

'I don't know. There is always some little kid pestering you.'

'Yeah.'

'Or some bigger kid.'

'Well, yeah.'

What Adrià was also trying to explain was that at Bernat's house his parents weren't so, I don't know, they aren't on top of you all day long.

'They are. You haven't practised your violin today, Bernat. And your homework? Don't you have homework? And look at how you've ruined your shoes, what a disaster, you're such an oaf. Like that, all day long.'

'You should see my house.'

'What.'

On the third trip between the two houses we came to the conclusion that it was impossible to decide which of the two boys was unhappier. But I knew that when I went over to Bernat's house, his mother would open the door and smile at me, she'd say hello, Adrià, and she'd tousle my hair a bit. My mother didn't even say how'd it go, Adrià, because it was always Little Lola who let me in and she'd just pinch my cheek, and the house was silent.

'You see? Your mother sings while she darns socks.'

'So?'

'Mine doesn't. There's no singing allowed in my house.'

'Come on.'

'Practically. I'm hapless.'

'Me too. But you get As and A+s.'

'That's no achievement. The classes are easy.'

'Nonsense.'

'Well: I have trouble with the violin.'

'I'm not talking about violin: I'm talking about school: grammar, geography, physics and chemistry, maths, natural sciences, boring old Latin; that's what I'm talking about. The violin is easy.'

I can't be sure of the dates, but you already know what I mean when I say we were very unhappy. Now as I listen to myself explaining it to you it sounds more like a teenage sadness than a childhood one. But I know I had that conversation with Bernat, walking along the streets that separated his house from mine, oblivious to the harsh traffic on València, Llúria, Bruc, Girona and Mallorca, the heart of the Eixample district, which was my world and, except for travels, has remained my world. I also know that Bernat had an electric train and I didn't. And he studied violin because he wanted to. And, above all, his parents would say to him Bernat, what do you want to be when you grow up?, and he could say I don't know yet.

'Think about it,' Mr Plensa would say, seeming like such a good egg.

'Yes, Father.'

And that was all they said, can you imagine? They would ask him what do you want to be when you grow up and my father one day said to me listen hard because I won't say it twice and now I'm going to tell you what you are going to be when you grow up. Father had planned my path to the tiniest detail of each curve. And Mother still had yet to put in her two penn'orth and I can't tell you which was worse. And I'm not complaining to you: I'm just writing. But the rope grew so taut that I didn't even feel comfortable talking to Bernat about it. Really. Because I hadn't been able to finish all my German homework for a few classes because Trullols had asked me to practise for an hour and a half if I wanted to get past the first stumbling blocks of the double stop chords, and I hated the double stop chord because when you want to play a single note, you get three, and when you want to do a double stop all you get is one and after a while you just want to smash the violin against the wall, because the fingering is so complicated and you put on a record where people like Iossif Robertovich Heifetz do it so perfectly it makes you dizzy, and I wanted to be Heifetz for three reasons: first, because I was sure his Trullevičius didn't say to him, no Jascha, the third finger has to slide with the hand, you can't leave it there in the middle of the fingerboard, for the love of God, Jascha Ardèvol! Second, because he always did it well; third, because I was sure he didn't have a father like mine, and fourth, because he believed that being a child prodigy was a serious illness he'd managed to survive and which I survived because I wasn't really a child prodigy, no matter what my father said.

'How.'

'What, Black Eagle.'

'You said three.'

'Three what?'

'Three reasons you wanted to be Jascha Heifetz.'

Sometimes I get mixed up. And now, as I write this, each day I get more and more mixed up. I don't know if I'll make it to the end.

What was clear, in my murky childhood, was my father's

immense pedagogical ability. One day, when Little Lola
wanted to stick up for me, he said but what the hell are
you saying! German, violin and because of that he can't do
English? Is that it? What is he, a total milksop? And you, who
are you to say … And why am I even talking about this with
you?

Little Lola flew out of the study in a rage. It had all started
when Father announced that I had to save Mondays for
English classes with Mr Prats, a young man who really knew
his stuff, and I was left with my mouth hanging open, because
I didn't know what to say, because I knew that I would love
studying English but I didn't want Father to … And I looked
at Mother as I finished my boiled veg in silence and Little Lola
took the empty plate to the kitchen. But Mother didn't say a
peep; she left me alone and then I said that I needed time for
the violin because the double stops …

'Excuses. The double stops … Look at how any normal violinist plays and don't tell me you can't be a normal violinist.'

'I need more time.'

'You'll make the time, you're young. Or quit the violin,
what do you want me to say.'

The next day there was a discussion between Mother and
Little Lola that I couldn't follow because I had no spy base
in the laundry room. And then, a few days later, Little Lola
confronted Father. That was when she flew out of the study
in a rage. But she was the only one in the house who could
stand up to him without fear of too much repercussion. And,
starting on the Monday before Christmas holidays, I could no
longer wile away my time with Bernat, on the streets.

'One.'

'Wan.'

'Two.'

'Tu.'

'Three.'

'Thrii.'

'Four.'

'Foa.'

'Four.'

'Fuoa …'

'Fffoouur.'

'Fffoooa.'

'It's all right!'

I was fascinated by English pronunciation, which was never what I expected from looking at the written words. And I was amazed by its morphological simplicity. And its subtle lexical relationship to German. And Mr Prats was extremely timid, to the extent that he didn't even look me in the eye when he had me read the first text, which I won't name in deference to good taste. Just to give you an idea, the plot was about whether my pencil was on top of or under the table, and the unexpected plot twist consisted of discovering that it was in my pocket.

'How are your English classes going?' my father asked me, impatiently, ten minutes after the first English class, at supper time.

'All right,' I said, adopting a disinterested pose. And it drove me crazy because, deep down, in spite of Father, I was already dying to know how you said one, two, three, four in Aramaic.

'Can I have two?' asked Bernat, always asking for more.

'Of course.'

Little Lola gave him two squares of chocolate; she hesitated for half a second and then gave me a second one, too. For the first time in my ffucking life, I didn't have to swipe it.

'And don't get any on the floor.'

The two boys went towards the bedroom and on the way Bernat said tell me, what is it, eh?

'A big secret.'

Once in the bedroom, I opened up my album of racing car collectors' cards to the centre page and, without looking at the album, watched his face. He opened his eyes wide as saucers.

'No!'

'Yes.'

'So, it exists.'

'Yes.'

It was the triple of Fangio at the wheel of the Ferrari. You heard me right, my beloved: the Fangio triple.

'Let me touch it.'

'Carefully, OK?'

But that's how Bernat was: when he liked something, he had to touch it. Like me. He was always that way. He still is. Like me. Adrià watched his friend's envy with satisfaction, as Bernat placed his fingertips on the Fangio triple and the fastest red Ferrari of all time, except for the future.

'We'd agreed it didn't exist ... How did you get it?'

'Contacts.'

That's how I was when I was little. I think I was trying to imitate Father. Or perhaps Mr Berenguer. In this case, the contacts were a very profitable Sunday morning at the second-hand stalls of the Sant Antoni market. You can find everything there; even quirks of fate; from Josephine Baker's underwear to a volume of poems dedicated to Jeroni Zanné by Josep Maria López-Picó. And the Fangio triple collectors' card that no other kid in Barcelona had, according to the rumours. When Father took me there, he always tried to keep me busy so he could exchange mysteries with a couple of men who always had a cigarette hanging from their lips, their hands in their pockets and a restless gaze. And he jotted down secrets in a little notebook that he then made vanish into a pocket.

After a heavy sigh, they closed the album. The two boys had to wait patiently, hidden away in the bedroom. They had to talk about something, and Bernat wanted to ask him about that thing he hadn't been able to get out of his head, but he knew he shouldn't because his parents had told him it's better if you don't go into that, Bernat. Still he ended up asking, 'Why don't you go to mass?'

'I have permission.'

'From who? From God?'

'No: from Father Anglada.'

'Wow. But why don't you go?'

'I'm not Christian.'

'Wow! ...' Confused silence. 'Can you be not Christian?'

'I suppose so. I'm not.'

'But what are you? Buddhist? Japanese? Communist? What?'

'I'm nothing.'

'Can you be nothing?'

I never knew how to answer that question when I was asked it as a child, because the wording troubled me. Can you be nothing? I will be nothing. Will I be like the zero that isn't a natural number nor a whole number nor a rational number nor a real number nor a complex number, but the neutral element in the addition of whole numbers? Not even that, I'm afraid: when I am no longer, I will no longer be necessary, if I am now.

'How. Now you've lost me.'

'Don't bother.'

'No, if it were up to me …'

'Then keep quiet, Black Eagle.'

'I believe in the Great Spirit of Manitou who covers the plains with bison, sends us rain and snow and moves the sun that warms us and makes it disappear so we can sleep, who blows the wind, guides the river along its bed, points the eagle's eye towards its prey and gives the warrior the courage to die for his people.'

'Hello? Where are you, Adrià?'

Adrià blinked and said here, with you, talking about God.

'Sometimes you're not here.'

'Me?'

'My parents say it's because you are wise.'

'Bollocks. I wish …'

'Don't even start.'

'They love you.'

'And yours don't?'

'No: they measure me. They calculate my IQ, they talk about sending me to a special school in Switzerland, they discuss making me do three school years in one.'

'Wow, how cool!' He looked at him out of the corner of his eye. 'No?'

'No. They argue over me, but they don't love me.'

'Bah. I don't think kisses …'

When Mother said Little Lola, go and get the aprons from Rosita's house, I knew that it was our time. Like two thieves, like the Lord when he comes for us, we went into the forbidden house. In strict silence, we slipped into Father's study, listening for the rustle from the back room where Mother and Mrs Angeleta were mending clothes. It took us a few minutes to get used to the darkness and heavy atmosphere in the study.

'I smell something strange,' said Bernat.

'Shhhh!' I whispered, somewhat melodramatically, because my main goal was impressing Bernat, now that we had become friends. And I told him that it wasn't a smell, it was the weight of the history the objects in the collection were laden with; he didn't understand me; I'm sure I wasn't entirely convinced that what I'd said was true, either.

When our eyes had grown used to the dark, the first thing Adrià did was look smugly at Bernat's amazed face. Bernat no longer smelled anything but instead felt the weight of the history the objects around him were laden with. Two tables, one covered with manuscripts and with a very strange lamp that was also … What is that? Oh, a loupe. Wow … and a ton of old books. At the back, a bookshelf filled with even older books; to the left a stretch of wall filled with tiny pictures.

'Are they valuable?'

'And how!'

'And how what?'

'A sketch by Vayreda,' Adrià proudly pointed at a small unfinished picture.

'Ah.'

'Do you know who Vayreda is?'

'No. Is it worth a lot?'

'A fortune. And this is an engraving by Rembrandt. It's not unique, because otherwise …'

'Aha.'

'Do you know who Rembrandt is?'

'No.'

'And this tiny one …'

'It's very lovely.'

'Yes. It is the most valuable one.'

Bernat moved closer to the pale yellow gardenias by Abraham Mignon, as if he wanted to smell them. Well, as if he wanted to smell their price tag.

'How much is it worth?'

'Thousands of pesetas.'

'No!' A few moments of meditation. 'How many thousands?'

'I don't know: but a lot.'

Better to leave it vague. It was a good start and now I just had to finish it off. So I turned him towards the glass cabinet and suddenly he reacted and said blimey, what's that?

'A Bushi Kaiken dagger,' said Adrià proudly.

Bernat opened the cabinet door, I nervously watched the door to the study; he grabbed the Bushi Kaiken dagger, like the one in the shop. He examined it very curiously and went over to the balcony to see it better, pulling it out of its sheath.

'Careful,' I said in a mysterious voice, since I didn't think he was sufficiently impressed.

'What does a booshikiken dagger mean?'

'The dagger that Japanese women warriors use to kill themselves.' In a soft voice, 'The instrument of their suicide.'

'And why do they have to kill themselves?' – without surprise, without shock, the stupid boy.

'Well ...' Using my imagination, I came up with this comment: 'If things don't go well for them; if they lose.' And to top it off: 'Edo Period, seventeenth century.'

'Wow.'

He looked at it closely, perhaps imagining the suicide of a Japanese Booshi warrior. Adrià grabbed the dagger, covered it with its sheath and, with exaggerated care in each movement, placed it back in the cabinet of precious objects. He closed it without making any noise. He had already decided he was going to really leave his friend flabbergasted. I had been hesitating up until then, but I saw Bernat making an effort not to get too carried away in the excitement and I lost all prudence. I put my hands to my lips, demanding absolute silence. Then I put on the yellowish light in the corner and I

turned the safe's combination: six, one, five, four, two, eight.
Father never locked it with the key. Just with the combination.
I opened the secret chamber of the treasures of Tutankha-
mun. Some old bundles of papers, two small closed boxes,
a lot of documents in envelopes, three wads of notes in one
corner and, on the lower shelf, a violin case with a dubious
stain on the top. I pulled it out very carefully. I opened the
case and our Storioni appeared, resplendent. More resplendent than ever before. I brought it over to the light and I put
the f-hole under his nose.

'Read that,' I ordered.

'Laurentius Storioni Cremonensis me fecit.' He looked up,
astounded. 'What does that mean?'

'Finish reading it,' I scolded, with the patience of a saint.

Bernat turned towards the violin's sound hole and looked
inside it again. The belly had to be at the right angle to read
one, seven, six, four.

'Seventeen sixty-four,' Adrià had to say.

'Ohh ... Let me touch it a little bit. Let me hear how it
sounds.'

'Sure, and my father will send us to the galleys. You can
only put one finger on it.'

'Why?'

'It's the most valuable object in this house, OK?'

'More than the yellow flowers by what's his name?'

'Much more. Much, much more.'

Bernat touched it with one finger, just to be on the safe side;
but I wasn't careful enough and he plucked the D; it sounded
sweet, velvety.

'It's a bit low.'

'Do you have perfect pitch?'

'What?'

'How do you know it's a bit low?'

'Because the D has to be a teensy bit higher, just a touch.'

'Boy, you make me so jealous!' Even though that afternoon
was all me about leaving Bernat with his mouth hanging
open, the exclamation came straight from my heart.

'Why?'

'Because you have perfect pitch.'

'What does that mean?'

'Forget about it.' And going back to the initial situation: 'Seventeen sixty-four, did you hear me?'

'Seventeen sixty-four …' He said it with sincere admiration and I was very pleased. He stroked it again, sensually, like he had when he said I've finished, Maria, my love. And she whispered I'm proud of you. Lorenzo stroked its skin and the instrument seemed to shiver, and Maria felt a bit jealous. He admired the rhythm of its curves with his hands. He placed it on the workshop table and moved away from it until he could no longer smell the intense scent of the miraculous fir and maple and he proudly contemplated the whole. Master Zosimo had taught him that a good violin, besides sounding good, had to be pleasing to the eye and faithful to the proportions that make it valuable. He felt satisfied. With a shadow of doubt, because he still didn't know the price he would have to pay for the wood. But yes, he was satisfied. It was the first violin that he had started and finished all by himself and he knew that it was a very good one.

Lorenzo Storioni smiled in relief. He also knew that the sound would take on the right colour with the varnishing process. He didn't know if he should show it to Master Zosimo first or go and offer it directly to Monsieur La Guitte, who they say is a bit fed up with the people of Cremona and will soon return to Paris. A feeling of loyalty to his teacher sent him to Zosimo Bergonzi's workshop with the still pale instrument under his arm, like a corpse in its provisional coffin. Three heads lifted up from their labours when they saw him come in. The maestro understood the smile of his young quasi disciple. He placed the cello he was polishing on a shelf and brought Lorenzo to the window that opened onto the street below, which had the best light for examining instruments. In silence, Lorenzo pulled the violin from its pinewood case and presented it to the master. The first thing that Zosimo Bergonzi did was caress its back and face. He understood that everything was going as he had foreseen when, a few months earlier, he had secretly presented his disciple Lorenzo with a gift of some exceptional wood so he could prove that he had truly learned his lessons.

'This is really a gift?' Lorenzo Storioni had said, shocked.

'More or less.'

'But this is part of the wood that …'

'Yes. That Jachiam of Pardàc brought. It is at its best moment now.'

'I want to know the price, Master Zosimo.'

'I told you not to worry about it. When you have made the first instrument I will tell you the price.'

That wood had never been free. The Year of Our Lord 1705, many years ago, long before young Storioni had been born, when the earth was increasingly round, Jachiam the unrepentant, of the Muredas of Pardàc, had arrived in Cremona with a cart loaded down with wood that was apparently worthless, saving them quite a few scares along the endless journey. Jachiam was a man over thirty, strong and with a gaze darkened by the determination with which he took on life. He left Blond with the load at a safe distance from Cremona and he headed quickly towards the city. When he reached a small wood of holm oaks, he entered it. He soon found a spot where he could empty his bowels comfortably. As he squatted he looked out in front of him distractedly, and saw some discarded cloth tatters. Those anonymous scraps of clothing reminded him of the accursed doublet of Bulchanij of Moena, and all the misfortune that fell upon the Muredas of Pardàc and which might now end with the stroke of luck he was working in his favour. He cried as he defecated, unable to contain his nervousness. When he was fully composed, after he'd relieved his body and carefully replaced his greasy clothes, he entered the city and went straight to Stradivari's workshop as he had done a few times as a lad. He asked to speak directly to Master Antonio. He told him that he knew he was about to have problems finding wood because of the fire in the Paneveggio fifteen years ago.

'I get it from other places.'

'I know. From the Slovenian forests. When you make an instrument you will find its sound is muffled.'

'That's all there is.'

'No, it's not. I have an alternative.'

Stradivari must really have been in a bind, because he followed the stranger to the outskirts of Cremona, where he
had hidden the cart. His most taciturn son, Omobono, and
a workshop apprentice named Bergonzi came with him. All
three of them examined the wood, cutting off pieces, chewing
them, looking at each other furtively, and Jachiam, Mureda's
son, watched them with satisfaction, sure of his work, as they
examined the pieces again and again. It was already getting
dark when Master Antonio challenged Jachiam: 'Where did
you get this wood?'

'From very far away. From the West, a very cold place.'

'How do I know you didn't steal it?'

'You have to trust me. My whole life is wood, I know how to
make it sing, I know how to smell it, I know how to choose it.'

'It is of very high quality and very well packed. Where did
you learn the trade?'

'I am the son of Mureda of Pardàc. Have someone sent to
ask my father.'

'Pardàc?'

'Down here you call it Predazzo.'

'Mureda of Predazzo is dead.'

Two unexpected tears of pain sprang from Jachiam's eyes.
My father is dead and won't see me return home with ten bags
of gold so he and and all my brothers and sisters won't ever
have to work again. Agno, Jenn, Max, Hermes the slow one,
Josef, Theodor who can't walk, Micurà, Ilse, Erica, Katharina,
Matilde, Gretchen and little Bettina, my little blind sweet-
heart who gave me the medallion of Santa Maria dai Ciüf that
our mother had given her when she died.

'Dead? My father?'

'From grief at the burning of his woods. From grief over
the death of his son.'

'Which son?'

'Jachiam, the best of the Muredas.'

'I am Jachiam.'

'Jachiam was drowned in the eddies of Forte Buso because

of the fire.' With an ironic look, 'If you are Mureda's son, you must remember that.'

'I am Jachiam, son of Mureda of Pardàc,' insisted Jachiam, son of Mureda of Pardàc, as Blond of Cazilhac listened with interest despite the fact that he sometimes missed a word because they spoke so quickly.

'I know that you are trying to trick me.'

'No. Look, Master.'

He pulled out the medallion around his neck and showed it to Master Stradivari.

'What is that?'

'Santa Maria dai Ciüf of Pardàc. The patron saint of the woodcutters. The patron saint of the Muredas. It belonged to my mother.'

Stradivari grabbed the medallion and studied it carefully. A stately Virgin Mary and a tree.

'A fir tree, Master.'

'A fir tree in the background.' He gave it back to him. 'That's your proof?'

'The proof is the wood I am offering you, Master Antonio. If you don't want it, I will offer it to Guarneri or someone else. I'm tired. I want to go home and see if my brothers and sisters are still alive. I want to see if Agno, Jenn, Max, Hermes the dull-witted, Josef, Theodor the lame, Micurà, Ilse, Erica, Katharina, Matilde, Gretchen and little Bettina who gave me the medallion are still alive.'

Antonio Stradivari, sensing the possibility that Guarneri would profit from this wood, was generous and paid very well for that load that would save him work when he was able to use it, after a few years of peaceful ageing in the warehouse. He had his future well protected. And that was why the violins he made twenty years later were his finest. He couldn't know that yet. But Omobono and Francesco, after the master's death, knew it full well. They still had quite a few planks of that mysterious wood that had come from the west and they used it sparingly. And when they both died, Carlo Bergonzi inherited the workshop, along with the secret stash of special wood. And Bergonzi passed on the secret to his two sons. Now, the younger of the Bergonzi boys, who had become Master Zosimo, was examining the first instrument that young Lorenzo had made in the light that came from the window overlooking the Cucciatta. He examined its interior: 'Laurentis Storioni Cremonensis me fecit, seventeen sixty-four.'

'Why did you underline Cremonensis?'

'Because of my pride in being from here.'

'That is a signature. You should do the same thing in every violin you make.'

'I will always be proud of having been born in Cremona, Master Zosimo.'

The master was satisfied and he returned the corpse to its maker, who placed it in the coffin.

'Don't ever say where you got your wood. And buy some from wherever you can for the coming years. At whatever price, if you want to have a future.'

'Yes, Master.'

'And don't screw up with the varnish.'

'I know how I have to do it, Master.'

'I know you know. But don't screw it up.'

'What do I owe you for the wood, Master?'

'Just one favour.'

'I'm at your service …'

'Keep away from my daughter. She is too young.'

'What?'

'You heard me. Don't make me repeat myself.' He extended his hand towards the case. 'Or give me back the violin and the wood that's left over.'

'Well, I …'

He grew as pale as his first violin. He didn't dare look the maestro in the eye and he left Zosimo Bergonzi's workshop in silence.

Lorenzo Storioni spent several weeks absorbed in the varnishing process as he began a new violin and considered the price Zosimo had demanded of him. When the sound was as it should be, Monsieur La Guitte, who was still wandering about Cremona, got the chance to have a look at that slightly darkened varnish that would become a distinctive mark of a Storioni. He passed it to a silent, scrawny boy who grabbed the bow and began to play. Lorenzo Storioni cried, over the sound and over Maria. The scrawny boy got an even better sound out of it than he'd been able to. Maria, I love you. He added a florin to the original price for each tear shed.

'A thousand florins, Monsieur La Guitte.'

La Guitte looked him in the eyes for ten very uncomfortable seconds. Out of the corner of his eye he watched the scrawny, taciturn boy, who lowered his lids in a sign of assent; and Storioni thought that surely he could have got more out of him and that he would still have to learn about that aspect of the trade.

'We can't see each other any more, my beloved Maria.'

'It's a fortune,' said La Guitte, reflecting his refusal in his facial expression.

'Your Lordship knows it is worth that.' And in an act of supreme bravery, Lorenzo grabbed the violin. 'If you don't want it, I have other buyers lined up for next week.'

'Why, Lorenzo, my love?'

'My client will want Stradivari or Guarneri ... You are still unknown. Storioni! Connais pas.'

'In ten years' time, everyone will want a Storioni in their home.' He placed the violin in its protective case.

'Your father has forbidden me from seeing you. That's why he gave me the wood.'

'Eight hundred,' he heard the Frenchman say.

'No! I love you. We love each other!'

'Nine hundred and fifty.'

'Yes, we love each other; but if your father doesn't want us to ... I can't ...'

'Nine hundred, because I'm in a rush.'

'Let's run away together, Lorenzo!'

'Sold. Nine hundred.'

'Run away? How can we run away from Cremona when I'm setting up my workshop here?'

It was true that he was in a rush. Monsieur La Guitte was anxious to leave with the new instruments he had bought and the only thing that kept him in Cremona were the attentions of dark, passionate Carina. He thought that one would be a good violin for Monsieur Leclair.

'Set it up in another city!'

'Far from Cremona? Never!'

'Lorenzo, you are a traitor! Lorenzo, you are a coward! You don't love me any more.'

'If next year I come back with a couple of commissions, we'll renegotiate the price in my favour,' warned La Guitte.

'I do love you, Maria. With all my heart. But if you can't understand ...'

'Agreed, Monsieur La Guitte.'

'There's another woman, isn't there? Traitor!'

'No! You know how your father is. He's got my hands and feet tied.'

'Coward!'

La Guitte paid without any further discussion. He was convinced that Leclair, in Paris, would pay five times more for it without batting an eyelash and he was pleased with the job he'd done. It was a shame that it would be the last week he'd get to sleep with sweet Carina.

Storioni was also pleased with his own work. And he also felt sad because he hadn't realised up until that point that selling an instrument meant never seeing it again. And making the instrument had also meant losing a love. Ciao, Maria. Coward. Ciao, beloved. There's nothing you can say. Ciao: I'll never forget you. You traded me for fine wood, Lorenzo: I hope you drop dead! Ciao, Maria, you don't know how sorry I am. I hope your wood rots, or burns up in a fire. But it went worse for Monsieur Jean-Marie Leclair of Paris or Leclair l'Aîné or Tonton Jean depending on who was addressing him, because, besides the inflated price they asked of him, he barely got the chance to hear that sweet, velvety D that Bernat had imprudently plucked.

That was one of the many times in life that I let myself get carried away by crazy impulse because I understood that I had to take advantage of Bernat's musical superiority for my own gain, but I also knew it would require something really spectacular. As I let my new friend stroke the top of the Storioni with his fingertips, I said if you teach me how to do vibrato, you can take it home with you one day.

'Whoa!'

Bernat smiled, but after a few seconds he grew serious, even disconsolate: 'That's impossible: vibrato isn't something you can teach; you have to find it.'

'You can teach it.'

'You have to find it.'

'I won't lend you the Storioni.'

'I'll teach you to do vibrato.'

'It has to be now.'

'OK. But then I'll take it with me.'

'Not today. I have to prepare it. Some day.'

Silence, mental calculation, avoiding my eyes, thinking of the magical sound and not trusting me.

'Some day is like saying never. When?'

'Next week. I swear.'

In my room, Ševcîk's scales and arpeggios were on the music stand, open to the page detailing the accursed exercise XXXIX, which was, according to Trullols, pure genius and the essence of what I had to learn in life, before or after tackling the double stop. They spent half an hour, in which Bernat drew out the sounds in a measured, sweet vibrato, and Adrià watched him, seeing how Bernat closed his eyes as he concentrated on the sound, thinking that to vibrate the sound I have to close my eyes, trying it, closing his eyes … but the sound came out stunted, snide, in a duck's voice. And he closed his eyes and squeezed them tight; but the sound escaped him.

'You know what? You're too anxious.'

'You're the one who's anxious.'

'Me? What are you talking about?'

'Yeah, because if you don't teach me right, forget about the Storioni. Not next week and not ever.'

It's called moral blackmail. But Bernat didn't know what more to do besides stop saying that vibrato couldn't be taught and had to be found. He had him check his hand position, and his sequence of hand movements.

'No, no, you're not making mayonnaise with the strings. Relax!'

Adrià didn't entirely know what relax meant; but he relaxed; he closed his eyes and he found the vibrato at the end of a long C on the second string. I will remember it my entire life because it seemed to me like I was starting to learn how to make the sound laugh and cry. If it weren't for the fact that Bernat was there and it wasn't allowed in my house, I would have roared with happiness.

Despite that epiphany I can still recall, despite the infinite appreciation I felt towards my brand-new friend, I didn't have it in me to tell him about the Arapaho chief or Carson the tobacco chewer, because it didn't look good that a boy of ten or twelve who went around acting like a child genius still played with Arapaho chiefs and sheriffs with hard hearts and full beards. I simply stood there with my mouth agape, remembering the sound *I* had made with *my* student violin. It was with the second string in first position: a C that Adrià made vibrate with his second finger. It was seven in the evening on some autumn or winter day of nineteen fifty-seven in Barcelona, in what will always be my flat on València Street, in the heart of the Eixample, at the centre of the world, and I thought I was touching heaven without realising how close I was to hell.

## 9

That Sunday, which was memorable because Father had
awoken in a good mood, my parents had invited Doctor
Prunés over. He was the best living palaeographer in the
world according to Father. They had invited him over for
coffee with his wife, who was the best wife of the best living
palaeographer in the world. And he winked at me and I
didn't understand anything even though I knew that the
wink referred to some essential subtext that I couldn't catch
because of lack of context. I think I already told you that I
was a real know-it-all, and I thought about things in almost
just that way.

They talked about the coffee, about the porcelain china that
was so fine it made the coffee even better, about manuscripts
and, every once in a while, they enlivened the conversation
with uncomfortable silences. And Father decided to put
an end to it. In a loud voice I could hear from my room, he
ordered, 'Come here, boy. Do you hear me?'

Of course Adrià could hear him. But he feared disaster.

'Boooy!'

'Yes?' as if from a long distance away.

'Come here.'

Adrià had no choice but to go there. Father's eyes were
gleaming from the cognac; Mr and Mrs Prunés were looking
sympathetically at the boy. And Mother was just serving more
coffee and washing her hands of the disaster.

'Yes. Hello, good day.'

The guests murmured an expectant good day and looked
towards Mr Ardèvol, their hopes raised. Father pointed to my
chest and ordered, 'Count in German.'

'Father ...'

'Do as I tell you.' Flashes of cognac in his eyes. Mother,

serving coffee and looking at the little porcelain cups that
were so fine they made the coffee even better.

'Eins, zwei, drei.'

'Slowly, slowly,' Father stopped me. 'Start again.'

'Eins, zwei, drei, vier, fünf, sechs, sieben, acht, neun, zehn.'
And I stopped.

'What else?' said Father, severely.

'Elf, zwölf, dreizehn, vierzehn.'

'Etcetera, etcetera, etcetera,' said Father as if he were Pater
D'Angelo. Switching to a curt, commanding tone: 'Now in
English.'

'That's enough, Fèlix,' said Mother, finally.

'I said in English.' And to Mother, severely, 'Isn't that right?'

I waited a few seconds, but Mother didn't respond.

'One, two, three, four, five, six, seven, eight, nine, ten.'

'Very good, lad,' said the best living palaeographer in the
world, enthusiastically. And his wife applauded silently until
Father interrupted us with a wait, wait, wait and he pointed
at me again.

'Now in Latin.'

'No ...' said the best living palaeographer in the world,
humbled by admiration.

I looked at Father, I looked at Mother, who was as uncomfortable as I was but kept her eyes glued on the coffee, and I said
unus una unum, duo duae duo, tres, tria, quattuor, quinque,
sex, septem, octo, novem, decem. And pleading, 'Father ...'

'Quiet,' said Father curtly. And he looked at Doctor Prunés
who said goodness gracious, sincerely impressed.

'He's so precious,' said Doctor Prunés's wife.

'Fèlix ...' said Mother.

'Father ...' I said.

'Quiet!' he said. And to the guests: 'That's nothing.' He
snapped his fingers in my direction and said curtly, 'Now in
Greek.'

'Heis mia hen, duo, treis tria, tettares tessares, pente, hex,
hepta, octo, ennea, deka.'

'Fan-tast-tic!' Now Mrs and Mrs Prunés clapped, captivated by the spectacle.

'How.'

'Not now, Black Eagle.'

Father pointed at me, gesturing from top to bottom, as if showing off a freshly caught sea bass, and said proudly, 'Twelve years old.' And to me, without looking at me, 'OK, you can leave.'

I locked myself in my bedroom, upset with Mother, who hadn't lifted a finger to save me from that ridiculous situation. I dove into Karl May to drown my sorrows. And Sunday afternoon slowly gave way to evening and night. Neither Black Eagle nor brave Carson dared to disturb my sorrow.

Until one day I found out Cecília's true nature. I was slow to realise it. When the bell on the shop door rang Adrià (who, as far as Mother was concerned, was practising with the school's second string handball team) was in the manuscript corner (doing homework as far as Mr Berenguer was concerned). He was actually illegally examining a thirteenth-century vellum manuscript written in Latin, which I barely understood a word of, but which filled me with strong emotions. The bell. I immediately thought that Father had unexpectedly returned from Germany and now there would be a big scene; prepare yourself, and you had the three-part lie so well set up. I looked towards the door: Mr Berenguer, putting on his coat, said something hurriedly to Cecília, who was the one who had just arrived. And then, with hat in hand, a very angry face and in a big hurry, he left without saying goodbye. Cecília remained standing there for a while, in the entrance, with her coat on, thinking. I didn't know whether to say hello, Cecília, or wait for her to see me. No, I should say something; but then she'll think it very strange that I hadn't shown myself earlier. And the manuscript. Better not; no, better to hide and to … or perhaps better if I wait to see what … I'd have to start thinking in French.

He decided to remain hidden when Cecília, sighing, went into the office as she removed her coat. I don't know why, but that day the air was heavy. And Cecília didn't emerge from the office. And suddenly I heard someone crying. Cecília was crying in the office and I wanted to vanish, because otherwise it was impossible for her not to know that I had heard her secretly crying. Grownups cry sometimes. And what if I went to console her? I felt bad because Cecília was highly respected in our home and even Mother, who usually had contempt for all the women Father saw often, spoke very well of her. And besides, hearing a grownup cry, as a lad, makes a big impression. So Adrià wanted to vanish. The woman made a phone call, turning the numbers violently. And I imagined her, irritated, irate, and I didn't understand that I was the one in danger because at some point they would close up the shop and I would be inside, walled up alive.

'You're a coward. No, no, let me speak: a coward. It's been five years of the same old song and dance, yes, Cecília, next month I'll tell her everything, I swear. Coward. Five years of excuses. Five years! I'm not a little girl.'

I agreed with that. The rest of it I didn't understand. And Black Eagle was at home, on the bedside table, having a peaceful nap.

'No, no, no! I'm talking now: we will never live together because you don't love me. No, you be quiet, it's my turn to talk. I said be quiet! Well, you can stick your sweet words up your arse. It's over. Do you hear me? What?'

Adrià, from beside the manuscript table, didn't know what was over nor whether it affected him; he didn't really get why grownups were always losing sleep because don't you love me, when he was starting to discover that the whole love thing was a drag, what with the kissing and all that.

'No. Don't say a word. What? Because I'll hang up when I'm good and ready. No, sir: quan a mi em roti.'

It was the first time I had ever heard that expression 'quan a mi em roti'. I could tell it meant when I feel like it, yet it contained the word burp. And it was strange that I'd heard it from the mouth of the most polite person in my world. 'Rotar', to burp, came from the Latin *ructare*, frequentative of *rugere*. Over time it became *ruptare* and continued evolving from there. Cecília hung up with such force that I thought she might have shattered the telephone. And she began working on labelling and cataloguing new material into two registry

books, serious, with her eyeglasses on and no apparent sign
of the collapse she'd had moments earlier. It wasn't hard for
me to leave through the small door and come in again from
the street, say hello Cecília and check whether there were any
traces of tears on that always impeccable face.

'What are you doing, cutie?' She smiled at me.

And I, mouth agape, because she looked like another
woman.

'What did you ask the Three Kings to bring you for Christmas?' she inquired.

I shrugged because in my house we never celebrated Epiphany because it was your parents and not the Three Kings who
brought presents and one shouldn't fall for primitive supersti-
tions: so, from the first time I ever heard of the Three Kings,
the excited wait for their gifts was more of a resigned wait for
the present or presents that my father had chosen and which
had no relationship to my achievement at school, which was
expected without question, or with whether I'd been nice
instead of naughty, which was also assumed. But at least I
was given gifts meant for a child, in contrast with the general
seriousness of our home.

'I asked for a ...' I remember that my father had informed
me that I would receive a lorry that made a siren noise and
that I'd best not make the noise inside the house, 'a lorry with
a siren.'

'Come on, give me a kiss,' said Cecília, waving me over.

Father returned from Bremen on the weekend with a Myce-
naean vase that spent many years in the store, and, from what
I understood, with many useful documents and a couple of
possible gems in the shape of first editions and handwritten
manuscripts, including one from the fourteenth century that
he said was now one of his prized jewels. Both at home and at
work, they told him he had received a couple of strange calls.
And, as if he couldn't care less about all that would happen in
a few days' time, he told me look, look, look how beautiful this
is, and he showed me some notebooks: it was a manuscript
of the last things Proust had written. From À la recherche.

A hotchpotch of tiny handwriting, paragraphs written in the margins, notes, arrows, little slips of paper attached with staples … Come on, read it.

'It's unintelligible.'

'Come on, boy! It's the end. The last pages; the last line: don't tell me you don't know how the *Recherche* ends.'

I didn't answer. Father, all on his own, realised that he had tightened the rope too much and he played it off in that way he was so good at: 'Don't tell me you still don't know French!'

'Oui, bien sûr: but I can't read his handwriting!'

That must not have been the right answer because Father, without any further comment, closed the notebook and put it away in the safe while he said under his breath I'll have to make some decisions because we are starting to have too many treasures in this house. And I understood that we were starting to have too many skeletons in this house.

## 10

'Your father ... How can I say this, my son? Father ...'

'What? What happened to him?'

'Well, he's gone to heaven.'

'But heaven doesn't exist!'

'Father is dead.'

I paid more attention to Mother's excessively pale face than to the news. It looked like she was the one who was dead. As pale as young Lorenzo Storioni's violin before it was varnished. And her eyes filled with anguish. I had never heard Mother's voice catch. Without looking at me, staring at a stain on the wall where the bed was, she was telling me I didn't kiss him as he left the house. Perhaps I could have saved him with a kiss. And I think she added he got what he deserved, in a softer voice. But I wasn't sure.

Since I didn't fully understand her, I locked myself in my messy bedroom, holding tight to the Red Cross lorry that the Three Kings had given me, and sat down on the bed. I started to cry silently, which was how I always did everything at home because if Father wasn't studying manuscripts, he was reading or he was dying.

I didn't ask Mother for details. I couldn't see my father dead because they told me he'd had an accident, that he'd been run over by a lorry on the Arrabassada road, which isn't on the way to the Athenaeum and well, you can't see him, there's no way. And I felt distressed because I had to find Bernat urgently before my world crumbled and they put me in prison.

'Boy, why did he take your violin?'

'Huh? What?'

'Why did your father take your violin?' repeated Little Lola.

Now it would all come out and I was dying of fright. I still had the pluck to lie, 'He asked me for it for some reason. I don't know why.' And I added desperately, 'Father was acting very strange.'

When I lie, which is often, I have the feeling that everyone can tell. The blood rushes to my face, I think I must be turning red, I look to either side searching for the hidden incoherence crouching inside the fiction I am creating … I see that I am in their hands and I'm always surprised that no one else has realised. Mother never catches on; but I'm sure Little Lola does. And yet she pretends she doesn't. Everything about lying is a mystery. Even now that I'm older, I still turn red when I lie and I hear the voice of Mrs Angeleta, who one day when I told her I hadn't stolen that square of chocolate, grabbed my hand and made me open it, revealing to Mother and Little Lola the ignominious chocolate stain. I closed it again, like a book, and she said you can catch a liar faster than a cripple, always remember that, Adrià. And I still remember it, at sixty. My memories are etched in marble, Mrs Angeleta, and marble they will become. But now the problem wasn't the stolen chocolate square. I made a sad face, which wasn't difficult because I was very sad and very afraid and I said I don't know anything about it, and I started to cry because Father was dead and …

Little Lola left the bedroom and I heard her talking to someone. Then a strange man – who gave off an intense odour of tobacco, spoke in Spanish, hadn't removed his coat, and had his hat in his hand – came into the bedroom and said to me what's your name.

'Adrià.'

'Why did your father take your violin.' Like that, like a weary interrogative.

'I don't know, I swear.'

The man showed me pieces of wood from my student violin.

'Do you recognise this?'

'Well, sure. It's my violin … it was my violin.'

'Did he ask you for it?'

'Yes,' I lied.

'Without any explanation?'

'No. Yes.'

'Does he play the violin?

'Who?'

'Your father.'

'No, of course not.'

I had to repress a mocking smile that came up at the mere thought of Father playing the violin. The man with the coat, hat and tobacco smell looked towards Mother and Little Lola, who nodded in silence. The man pointed, with his hat, to the Red Cross lorry in my hands and said that lorry is really nice. And he left the room. I was left alone with my lies and didn't understand a thing. From inside the ambulance lorry, Black Eagle shot me a commiserating look. I know that he thinks little of liars.

The funeral was dark, filled with serious gentlemen with their hats in their hands and ladies who covered their faces with thin veils. My cousins came from Tona and some vague Bosch second cousins from Amposta, and for the first time in my life I felt that I was the centre of attention, dressed in black with my hair well parted and very kempt because Little Lola had given me a double dose of hair spray and said I was very handsome. And she kissed me on the forehead the way Mother never did, and even less now, when she doesn't even look at me. They say that Father was in the dark box, but I wasn't able to check. Little Lola told me that he had been badly injured and it was better not to look at him. Poor Father, all day long immersed in books and strange objects and he somehow manages to die covered in wounds. Life is so idiotic. And what if the wounds had been caused by a Kaiken dagger in the shop? No: they told me that it had been an accident.

For a few days, we lived with the curtains drawn and I was entirely surrounded by whispers. Lola paid more attention to me and Mother spent hours sitting in the armchair where she took her coffee, in front of the empty armchair where Father took his coffee, before he died. But she didn't take any coffee because it wasn't coffee hour. It was complicated, all that, because I didn't know if I could sit in the other armchair

because Mother didn't see me and as many times as I said
hey, Mother, she grabbed my wrist but she looked at the wallpaper and she didn't say anything to me and then I thought
it doesn't matter and I didn't sit in Father's armchair and I
thought this is what grief is like. But I was grieving too and I
still looked all around. There were a few very anguished days
because I knew that Mother didn't see me. Then I got used
to it. I think that Mother hasn't looked at me since. She must
have guessed that it was all my fault and that was why she
didn't want to have anything more to do with me. Sometimes
she looks at me, but it's only to give me instructions. And she
left my life in the hands of Little Lola. For the moment.

Without any prior discussion, Mother showed up at the
house one day with a new student violin, a nice one with good
proportions and good sound. And she gave it to me almost
without saying a word and definitely without looking me in
the eyes. As if she were distracted and acting mechanically.
As if she were thinking about before or after but not about
what she was doing. It took me a long time to understand her.
And I returned to my violin studies, which had been interrupted many days before.

One day, while I was studying in my bedroom, I tuned the
bass-string with such fury that I snapped it. Then I snapped
two more strings and I went out into the sitting room and I
said Mother, you have to take me to Casa Beethoven. I have
no more E strings. She looked at me. Well: she looked towards
me, more or less, and she said nothing. Then I repeated that
I had to buy new strings and then Little Lola came out from
behind some curtain and said I'll take you, but you have to
tell me which strings they are because they all look the same
to me.

We went there on the metro. Little Lola explained that she
had been born in the Barceloneta and that often, when she
would walk with her girlfriends, they'd say let's go to Barcelona and in ten minutes they'd be at the lower end of the
Ramblas and they'd go up and down the Ramblas like silly
fools, laughing and covering their mouths with their hands
so the boys wouldn't see them laugh, which it seems is more

fun than going to the cinema, according to what Little Lola told me. And she told me that she'd never imagined that in that tiny, dark shop they sold violin strings. And I asked for a G, two Es and one Pirastro, and she said that was easy: you could have written that down on a piece of paper and I could have come by myself. Then I said no, that Mother always had me come with her just in case. Little Lola paid, we left Casa Beethoven, and as she bent down to kiss my cheek she looked down the Ramblas with nostalgia, but she didn't cover her mouth with her hand because she wasn't laughing like a silly fool. Then it occurred to me that perhaps I was also losing my mother.

A couple of weeks after the funeral, some other men who spoke Spanish came and Mother again turned pale like death and again the whispering between Mother and Little Lola and I felt left out and I screwed up my courage and I said to my mother, what is going on. It was the first time she really looked at me in many days. She said it's too big, my son, it's too big. It's best that … and then Little Lola came in and took me to school. I noticed that some of the other children were looking at me strangely, more than usual. And Riera came over to me at breaktime and he told me did they bury it too? And I said, what? And Riera, with a smug smile, said how disgusting, right, seeing a head by itself? And he insisted with the you buried it too, right? And I didn't understand anything and, just in case, I went to the sunny corner, with the lads who were trading collectors' cards, and from then on I avoided Riera.

It had always been hard for me to be just another kid like the others. Basically, I just wasn't. My problem, which was very serious and according to Pujol had no solution, was that I liked to study: I liked studying history and Latin and French and I liked going to the conservatory and when Trullols made me do mechanics, because I did scales and I imagined myself before a full theatre and then the mechanics came out with a better sound. Because the secret is in the sound. The hands are a cinch, they move on their own if you invest the hours. And sometimes I improvised. I liked all that and I also liked picking up the encyclopaedia Espasa and taking a trip through its entries. And then, at school, when Mr Badia asked a question about something, Pujol would point to me and say that I'd been chosen to answer all the questions. And then I would be embarrassed about answering the question because it seemed they were parading me around, as if they were Father. Esteban, who sat at the desk behind mine and was a right bastard, called me girl every time I answered a question correctly until one day I said to Mr Badia that no, I didn't remember what the square root of one hundred and forty-four was and I had to go to the toilet and throw up, and as I threw up Esteban came in. He saw me vomit and he told me look what a girl you are. But when my father died I saw that they looked at me somehow differently, as if I had gone up in their estimation. Despite everything, I think I envied all the children who didn't want to study and who, every once in a while, failed something. And in the conservatory it was different because you'd put the violin in your hand right away and try to get a good sound out of it, no, no, it sounds like a hoarse duck, listen to this. And Trullols grabbed *my* violin and got such a lovely sound out of it that even though she was quite old and too thin, I almost fell in love. It was a sound that seemed made of velvet and had the perfume of some flower I can't name, but I can still remember.

'I'll never be able to get that sound out of it. Even though I can do vibrato now.'

'These things take time.'

'Yes, but I never …'

'Never say never, Ardèvol.'

It is surely the most poorly expressed bit of musical and intellectual advice ever, but it has had more of an effect on me than any other throughout my life, either in Barcelona or in Germany. A month later the sound had ostensibly improved. It was a sound that still lacked perfume but was closer to velvet. But now that I think about it, I didn't go back right away, not to school and not to the conservatory. First I spent some days in Tona, with my cousins. And when I came back, I tried to understand how it had all happened.

On 7 January, Doctor Fèlix Ardèvol wasn't at home because he had an appointment with a Portuguese colleague who was in town.

'Where?'

Doctor Ardèvol told Adrià that when he returned he wanted to see his entire room tidied because the next day the holidays were ending and he looked at his wife.

'What did you say?' He used the severe tone of a professor, although he wasn't one, as he put on his hat. She swallowed hard like a student, although she wasn't one. But she repeated the question, 'Where are you meeting Pinheiro?'

Little Lola, who was entering the dining room, headed back towards the kitchen when she noticed the air was heavy. Fèlix Ardèvol let three or four seconds pass, which she found humiliating, and which gave Adrià time to look first at his father, then at his mother and to realise that something was going on.

'And why do you want to know?'

'Fine, fine … Forget I said anything.'

Mother left to another part of the flat without giving him the kiss she'd been saving for him. Before she got to the back, to Mrs Angeleta's territory, she heard him say we are meeting at the Athenaeum – and with heavy emphasis: 'if you don't mind.' And in a reproachful tone to punish her for that atypical slight prying, 'And I don't know when I'll be back.'

He went into his study and came out quickly. We heard the door to the flat, the sound it made as it opened and the bang when it closed with perhaps more force than usual. And then the silence. And Adrià trembling because his father had taken, oh my God, Father had taken the violin. The violin case with the student violin inside. Like an automaton, on the warpath, Adrià waited for the right moment and went into the study like a thief, like the Lord I will enter your house, and praying to the God who doesn't exist that his mother wouldn't happen to come in just then, he murmured six one five four two eight and he opened the safe: my violin wasn't there and I wanted to die. And then I tried to put everything back the way it was and then I locked myself in my bedroom to wait for Father to return, furious and saying who the hell is trying to trick me? Who has access to the safe, who? Who? Little Lola?

'But I …'

'Carme?'

'For the love of God, Fèlix.'

And then he would look at me and he would say Adrià? And I would have to start lying, as badly as ever, and Father would work it all out. And despite the fact that I was two steps away, he would shout at me as if he were calling me from Bruc Street and he would say come over here and since I wouldn't budge, he, shouting even more, would say I said come over here! And poor Adrià would go over with his head bowed and he would try to act innocent and all told it would be a very bitter bitter pill to swallow. But instead of that there was the telephone call and Mother coming into the bedroom and saying your father … How can I say this? … My son … Father … And he said, what? What happened to him? And she, well, he's gone to heaven. And it occurred to him to answer that heaven doesn't exist.

'Father is dead.'

Then the first feeling was relief, because if he was dead, he wasn't going to lay into me. And then I thought that it was a sin to think that. And also that even though there's no such thing as heaven, I can feel like a miserable sinner because I knew for a fact that Father's death had been my fault.

Mrs Carme Bosch d'Ardèvol had to do the painful, distressing official identification of the headless body that was Fèlix's: a birthmark on … yes, that birthmark. Yes, and the two moles. And he, a cold body that could no longer scold anyone, but unmistakably him, yes, my husband, Mr Fèlix Ardèvol i Guiteres, yes.

'Who did he say?'

'Pinheiro. From Coimbra. A professor in Coimbra, yes. Horacio Pinheiro.'

'Do you know him, Ma'am?'

'I've seen him a couple of times. When he comes to Barcelona he usually stays at the Hotel Colón.'

Commissioner Plasencia gestured to the man with the thin
moustache, who left silently. Then he looked at that widow
who'd been widowed so recently that she wasn't yet in mourning clothes because they'd come looking for her half an hour
earlier and they'd said you'd better come with us, and she,
but what's going on, and the two men I'm sorry madam but
we aren't authorised to speak about it, and she put on her red
coat with an elegant tug and told Little Lola you look after the
boy's tea, I'll be back soon, and now she was seated, with her
red coat, looking without seeing them, at the cracks in the
commissioner's desk and thinking this is impossible. And out
loud, pleading, she said can you tell me what is going on?

'Not a trace, Commissioner,' said the one with the thin
moustache.

Not at the Athenaeum, nor at the Hotel Colón or anywhere
in Barcelona, not a trace of Professor Pinheiro. In fact, when
they called Coimbra, they heard the very frightened voice of
Doctor Horacio da Costa Pinheiro who only managed to say
ho-ho-ho-how can it be that that that … Doctor Ardèvol, how
can … how … Oh, how awful. But Mr Ardèvol, but he, but he
… are you sure there isn't some mistake? Decapitated? And
how do you know that … But it can't be that … It's just not
possible.

'Your father … My son, Father has gone to heaven.'

Then I understood that it was my fault he had died. But
I couldn't tell that to anyone. And while Little Lola, Mother
and Mrs Angeleta looked for clothes for the deceased and occasionally broke out into tears, I felt miserable, a coward and
a killer. And many other things I don't remember.

The day after the burial, Mother, as she washed her hands
anxiously, sudden froze and said to Little Lola, give me Commissioner Plasencia's card. And Adrià heard her speaking on
the phone and she said we have a very valuable violin in the
house. The commissioner showed up at home and Mother
had called for Mr Berenguer so he could give them a hand.

'No one knows the combination to the safe?'

The commissioner turned to look at Mother, Mr Berenguer, Little Lola and me, who was watching from outside my father's study.

For a few minutes, Mr Berenguer asked for my mother's and my birthdates and tried the combination.

'No luck,' he said, annoyed. And from the hallway, I almost said six one five four two eight, but I couldn't because that would make me a murder suspect. And I wasn't suspected of that. I was guilty of it. I stayed quiet. It was very hard for me to stay quiet. The commissioner made a call on the study telephone and after a little while we watched a fat man, who sweated a lot because it seemed kneeling was a lot of work for him; even so he touched things very delicately and found, with a stethoscope and much silence, the mystery of the combination and jotted it down on a secret slip of paper. He opened the safe with a ceremonial gesture of satisfaction and he straightened up with difficulty as he made way for the others. Inside the safe was the Storioni, naked, without its case, looking at me ironically. Then it was Mr Berenguer's turn, and he picked it up with gloves on. He inspected it carefully beneath the beam from the desk lamp, lifted up his head and his right eyebrow and with a certain solemnity said to Mother, to the commissioner, to the fat man who wiped the sweat from his forehead, to Sheriff Carson, to Black Eagle, Arapaho chief, and to me, who was on the other side of the door:

'I can assure you that this is the violin that goes by the name of Vial and was built by Lorenzo Storioni. Without a shadow of a doubt.'

'With no case? Does he always put it away without a case?' – the commissioner who stank of tobacco.

'I don't think so,' – my mother – 'I think he kept it inside the case, in the safe.'

'And what sense does it make to grab the case, open it up, leave the violin in the safe, close it, ask your son for his student violin and put that into the good one's case? Huh?'

He looked around. He focused on me, who was on the threshold trying to conceal my fearful trembling. Le tremblement de la panique. For a few seconds his gaze indicated that he had guessed the why behind the mystery. I was already imagining myself speaking French for my entire ffucking life.

I don't know what happened, I don't know what my father wanted. I don't know why, if he had to go to the Athenaeum, they found him on the Arrabassada. I only know that I pushed him to his death and today, fifty years later, I still think the same thing.

And one day Mother ascended from the nadir and began to observe things with her eyes again. I noticed because at dinnertime – she, Little Lola and I – she looked at me for an instant and I thought she was going to say something and I was trembling all over because I was convinced she was about to say I know everything, I know it's your fault Father died and now I'm going to turn you in to the police, murderer, and I, but Mother, I just, I didn't mean to do it, I didn't … and Little Lola trying to keep the peace, because she was the one in charge of keeping the peace in a house where little was said and she did it with few words and measured gestures. Little Lola, I should have kept you by my side my entire life.

And Mother kept looking at me and I didn't know what to do. I think that my mother hated me since my father's death. Before his death she wasn't overly fond of me. It's strange: why have we always been so cold with each other in my family? I imagine, today, that it all comes from the way my father set up our lives. At that time, at dinner, it must have been April or May, Mother looked at me and didn't say anything. I didn't know what was worse: a mother who doesn't even look at you or a mother who accuses you. And then she launched her terrible accusation:

'How are your violin classes going?'

The truth is I didn't know how to answer; but I do remember that I was sweating on the inside.

'Fine. Same as ever.'

'I'm glad to hear it.' Now her eyes drilled into me. 'Are you happy, with Miss Trullols?'

'Yes. Very much so.'

'And with your new violin?'

'Come now …'

'What does come now mean? Are you happy or not?'

'Well, sure.'

'Well, sure or yes?'

'Yes.'

Silence. I looked down and Little Lola chose that moment to take away the empty bowl of green beans and acted as if she had a lot of work to do in the kitchen, the big coward.

'Adrià.'

I looked at her with bulging eyes. She observed me the way she used to in the past and said are you OK?

'Well, sure.'

'You're sad.'

'Well, sure.'

Now she would finish me off with a finger pointing at my black soul.

'I haven't been there for you, lately.'

'Doesn't matter.'

'Yes, it does matter.'

Little Lola returned with a dish of fried mackerel, which was the food I detested most in the world, and Mother, seeing it, sketched a sort of meagre smile and said how nice, mackerel.

And that was the end of the conversation and the accusation. That night I ate all the mackerel that was put on my plate, and afterward, the glass of milk, and when I was on my way to bed, I saw that Mother was rummaging around in Father's study and I think it was the first time she'd done that since his death. And I couldn't help sneaking a glance, because for me any excuse was a good one to have a look around in there. I brought Carson with me just in case. Mother was kneeling and looking through the safe. Now she knew the combination. Vial was leaning, outside of the safe. And she pulled out the bunch of papers and gave them an apathetic glance and started to pile them up neatly on the floor.

'What are you looking for?'

'Papers. From the store. From Tona.'

'I'll help you, if you'd like.'

'No, because I don't know what I'm looking for.'

And I was very pleased because Mother and I had started up a conversation; it was brief, but a conversation. And I had the evil thought of how nice that Father had died because now Mother and I could talk. I didn't want to think that, it just came into my mind. But it was true that Mother's eyes had begun to shine from that day on.

And then she pulled out three or four small boxes and put them on top of the table. I came closer. She opened one: there was a gold fountain pen with a gold nib.

'Wow,' I said, in admiration.

Mother closed the little box.

'Is it gold?'

'I don't know. I suppose so.'

'I've never seen it before.'

'Neither have I.'

Immediately, she chewed on her lips. She put away the box with the gold pen that she hadn't known was there and opened the other box, smaller and green. With trembling fingers, she pulled aside the pink cotton.

Over the years I have come to understand that my mother's life wasn't easy. That it must not have been a great idea to marry Father, despite the fact that he removed his hat so elegantly to greet her and said how are you, beautiful. That surely she would have been happier with another man who occasionally wasn't right, or made mistakes, or started laughing just because. All of us, in that house, were marked by Father's incorruptible seriousness, with its slight covering of acrimony. And, even though I spent the day observing and I was quite a clever lad, I have to admit that really the lights were on but no one was home. So, as a colophon to that night that I found extraordinary because I had got my mother back, I said can I study with Vial, Mother? And Mother froze in her tracks. For a few moments she stared at the wall and I thought here we go again, she's never going to look at me again. But she gave me a shy smile and said let me think it over. I think that that was when I realised that maybe things were starting to change. They changed, obviously, but not the way I would have liked. Of course, if that weren't the case, I wouldn't have met you.

Have you noticed that life is an inscrutable accident? Out of Father's millions of spermatazoa, only one fertilises the egg it reaches. That you were born; that I was born, those are vast random accidents. We could have been born millions of different beings who wouldn't have been either you or me. That we both like Brahms is also a coincidence. That your family has had so many deaths and so few survivors. All random. If the itinerary of our genes and then our lives had shifted along another of the millions of possible forks in the road, none of this would have been written and who knows who would read it. It's mind blowing.

After that night, things began to change. Mother spent many hours locked in the study, as if she were Father but without a loupe, combing through all the documents in the safe now that six one five four two eight was in the public domain. She had so little regard for Father's way of doing things that she didn't even change the combination to the safe, which I liked even though I couldn't say why. And she spent even more hours going through the papers and speaking to strange men, with eyeglasses that they would put on or take off depending on whether they were reading papers or looking at Mother, always speaking in a soft tone, everyone very serious, and neither I nor Carson nor even silent Black Eagle could catch much of anything. After a few weeks of murmuring, advice given almost in a whisper, recommendations, eyebrow raising and brief, convincing comments, Mother put away the whole lot of papers into the safe, six one five four two eight, and she put a few papers into a dark folder. And in that precise moment, she changed the combination to the safe. Then she put on her black coat over a black dress, she took in a deep breath, she picked up the dark folder and she showed up unexpectedly at the shop and Cecília said good day, Mrs Ardèvol. And she went directly to the office of Mr Ardèvol, she went in without asking for permission, she placed her hand, delicately, on the interrupter of the telephone that a startled Mr Berenguer was using and she cut off his call.

'What the hell …'

Mrs Ardèvol smiled and sat in front of Mr Berenguer, who had an irritated expression as he sat in Fèlix's grey desk chair. She put the dark folder down on the desk.

'Good day, Mr Berenguer.'

'I was talking to Frankfurt.' He smacked his open palm angrily against the desktop. 'It took me a long time to get a line, damn it!'

'That's what I wanted to avoid. You and I need to talk.'

And they talked about everything. It turns out that Mother knew much more than she was supposed to. And more or less half of the material in the shop is mine.

'Yours?'

'Personally. An inheritance from my father. Doctor Adrià Bosch.'

'Well, I knew nothing about this.'

'Neither did I until a few days ago. My husband was very good with such details. I have the documents to prove it.'

'And if they've been sold?'

'The profits belong to me.'

'But this is a business that'

'That's what I've come here to discuss. From now on I will run the shop.'

Mr Berenguer looked at her with his jaw dropped open. She smiled without pleasure and said I want to see the books. Now.

Mr Berenguer took a few seconds to react. He got up and went into Cecília's territory, and had a curt, quick and informative conversation with her, and when he returned, with a stack of accounting ledgers, he found that Mrs Ardèvol had sat down in Fèlix's grey desk chair and she granted him entrance into the office with a wave.

Mother came home trembling and, as soon as she closed the door, took off her black coat and, not finding the strength to hang it up, left it on the bench in the hall and went to her room. I heard her cry and I opted to stay out of things I didn't really understand. Then she spoke with Little Lola for a long time, in the kitchen and I saw how Little Lola put a hand over hers and gave her an encouraging look. It took me years to put together the pieces of that image, which I can still see, as if it were a painting by Hopper. My entire childhood in that house is etched into my brain like slides of Hopper's paintings, with the same mysterious, sticky loneliness. And I see myself in them like one of the people on an unmade bed, with a book abandoned on a bare chair, who looks out the window or sits beside a clean table, watching the blank wall. Because at home everything was resolved in whispers and the noise that could be heard most clearly, besides my violin portamento exercises, was when Mother put on her high-heeled shoes to go out. And while Hopper said that he painted to express what he couldn't put into words, I write with words because, even though I can see it, I'm unable to paint it. And I always see it like he did, through windows or doors that aren't quite closed. And what he didn't know, I have learned. And what I don't know, I invent and it's just as true. I know that you will understand me and forgive me.

Two days later, Mr Berenguer had taken his belongings back to his little office, beside the Japanese daggers, and Cecília barely concealed her satisfaction by feigning being above such details. It was Mother who spoke with Frankfurt, and that redistribution of pieces was what, attacking with the knights and the queen, I imagine, was what made Mr Berenguer decide, in what could be considered an unexpected and sudden attack, to bring out the big guns. The heavyweight antiquarians on Palla Street had declared war and everything was fair game.

Mother had always presented herself as long-suffering, submissive and discreet and she'd never raised her voice to anyone except me. But when Father died, she transformed and became an excellent organiser, with a relentless toughness that I never would have suspected. The shop soon shifted its focus towards high-quality objects no more than a century old, which increased turnover, and Mr Berenguer had to live through the humiliation of thanking his enemy for a raise he hadn't asked for and which was accompanied by a threatening you and I need to have a long conversation soon. Mother rolled up her sleeves again and then looked towards me, took a deep breath and I clearly understood that we were entering what would be a difficult period in my life.

At that time I didn't know anything about Mother's secret movements. I wouldn't know about them for some time because at home we only discussed things when there was no other option, delegating confidences to written notes to avoid full frontal eye contact. It took me a long time to find out that my mother was acting like a new Magdalena Giralt. She hadn't demanded her husband's head because they'd given it to her as soon as they'd found it. What she demanded was the head of her husband's murderer. Each Wednesday, whatever was going on at the shop or at home, she dressed in full black and went down to the police station on Llúria, where the case was being dealt with, and asked for Commissioner Plasencia, who led her into that smoke-filled office that made her dizzy, and she demanded justice for the death of her husband who had never loved her. And every time, after the greetings, she asked if there were any developments in the Ardèvol case and every time the commissioner, without inviting her to sit down, answered stiffly, no, madam. Remember that we agreed that we'd be in touch with you if that were the case.

'You can't decapitate a man without leaving a trace.'

'Are you calling us incompetent?'

'I am considering appealing to a higher authority.'

'Are you threatening me?'

'Take care, Commissioner.'

'Take care, madam. And we will let you know if there is any news.'

And when the black widow left the office, the commissioner opened and closed the top drawer of his desk angrily and Inspector Ocaña came in without asking permission and said not her again and the commissioner didn't deign to answer even though sometimes he wanted to burst out laughing at the strange accent that elegant woman had when she spoke Spanish. And that happened every Wednesday, every Wednesday, every Wednesday. Every Wednesday at the time the Caudillo held audience at the Palacio del Pardo. At the time that Pius XII held audience at the Vatican, Commissioner Plasencia received the black widow, he let her speak, and when she left, he took out his irritation on the top drawer of his desk, opening and slamming it shut.

When Mrs Ardèvol had had enough, she hired the services of the best detective in the world, according to the leaflet in his waiting room, which was so small that it gave her hives. The best detective in the world asked for a month up front, a month's time, and a month-long moratorium on her visits to the commissioner. Mrs Ardèvol paid, waited and abstained from visiting the commissioner. And in a month's time, after waiting in the oppressive waiting room, she was received for the second time by the best detective in the world.

'Have a seat, Mrs Ardèvol.'

The best detective in the world hadn't got up, but he waited for his client to sit down before getting comfortable in his chair. The desk was between them.

'What's new?' she asked, intrigued.

The best detective in the world drummed his fingers on the desk in reply, perhaps following some mental rhythm, perhaps not, because the thoughts of the best detectives in the world are indecipherable.

'And so ... what's new?' repeated my mother, peeved.

But the detective threatened with another minute of finger drumming. She cleared her throat with a cough and in a bitter voice, as if she were dealing with Mr Berenguer, said why did you have me come, Mr Ramis?

Ramis. The best detective in the world was named Ramis. I couldn't come up with his name until just now. Now that I'm explaining it all to you. Detective Ramis looked at his client and said I'm quitting the case.

'What?'

'You heard me. I'm quitting the case.'

'But you just took it on four days ago!'

'A month ago, madam.'

'I don't accept this decision. I've paid you and I have a right to …'

'If you read the contract,' he cut her off, 'you will see that section twelve of the appendix foresees the possibility of recision by either party.'

'And what is your reason?'

'I have too much work.'

Silence in his office. Silence in the entire place. Not a single typewriter typing up a report.

'I don't believe it.'

'Pardon?'

'You are lying to me. Why are you quitting?'

The best detective in the world got up, pulled an envelope out from under his leather desk pad and put it in front of my mother.

'I am returning my fees.'

Mrs Ardèvol got up abruptly, looked at the envelope with contempt and, without touching it, left stomping her heels. When she slammed the door hard on her way out, she was pleased to hear the ensuing clatter that told her that the door's central pane of glass had come out of its frame and was falling to the floor in pieces.

All that, along with more details that I can't recall right now, I learned much later. On the other hand, I remember that I already knew how to read quite complex texts in German and English; they said my aptitude was astounding. It had always seemed to me like the most normal thing in the world, but seeing what usually happens around me, I understand that I do have a gift. French was no problem, and reading Italian, although I put the accents in the wrong places, was almost second nature. And the Latin of *De bello Gallico*, besides of course Catalan and Spanish. I wanted to start either Russian or Aramaic, but Mother came into my room and said don't even think about it. That I was fine with the languages I knew, but that there were other things in life beside learning languages like a parrot.

'Mother, parrots

'I know what I'm talking about. And you know what I mean.'

'I don't understand.'

'Well, try harder!'

I tried harder. What scared me was the direction she wanted to give my life. It was clear that she wanted to erase the traces of Father in my education. So what she did was take the Storioni, which was in the safe protected by the new secret combination that only she knew, seven two eight zero six five, and offer it to me. Then she informed me that starting from the beginning of the month you will leave the conservatory and Miss Trullols and you will study under Joan Manlleu.

'What?'

'You heard me.'

'Who is Joan Manlleu?'

'The best. You will begin your new career as a virtuoso.'

'I don't want a caree

'You don't know what you want.'

Here, Mother was wrong; I knew that I wanted to be a … well, it's not that Father's programme completely satisfied me, spending all day studying what the world had written, closely following and thinking about culture. No, in fact it didn't satisfy me; but I liked to read and I liked to learn new languages and … Well, OK. I didn't know what I wanted. But I knew what I didn't want.

'I don't want a career as a virtuoso.'

'Master Manlleu has said you are good enough.'

'And how does he know that? Does he have magical powers?'

'He's heard you. A couple of times, when you were practising.'

It turned out that Mother had meticulously planned to get Joan Manlleu's approval before hiring him. She had invited him over for tea at my practice time and, discreetly, they had spoken little and listened. Master Manlleu quickly saw that he could ask for whatever he wanted and he did. Mother didn't bat an eyelash and hired him. In the rush, she overlooked asking Adrià for his approval.

'And what do I tell Trullols?'

'Miss Trullols already knows.'

'Oh, really? And what does she say?'

'That you are a diamond in the rough.'

'I don't want to. I don't know. I don't want to suffer. No. Definitely, categorically no and no.' One of the few times I yelled at her. 'Do you understand me, Mother? No!'

At the start of the next month, I began classes with Master Manlleu.

'You will be a great violinist and that's that,' Mother had said when I convinced her to leave the Storioni at home just in case and go around with the new Parramon. Adrià Ardèvol began the second educational reform with resignation. At some point he began to daydream about running away from home.

Between one thing and another, after Father's death, I didn't go to school for many days. I even spent a few very strange weeks in Tona, with my cousins, who were surprisingly silent and looked at me out of the corners of their eyes when they thought I didn't see. And at one point I caught Xevi and Quico discussing decapitations in low voices, but with such energy that their low voices found their way into every corner. And meanwhile Rosa, at breakfast, gave me the largest slice of bread before her brothers could grab it. And Aunt Leo tousled my hair dozens of times and I came to wonder why couldn't I stay in Tona forever close to my Aunt Leo, as if life were a never-ending summer far from Barcelona, there in that magical place where you can dirty your knees and no one will scold you for it. And Uncle Cinto, when he came home covered in dust from the threshing floor or dirty with mud or manure, looked down because men weren't allowed to cry, but it was clear that he was very affected by his brother's death. By his death and the circumstances surrounding his death.

When I returned home, and as the great Joan Manlleu's presence took shape in my life, I reintegrated myself in at school as a brand-new fatherless child. Brother Climent took me to class. He pinched my back hard with his fingers yellowed from snuff, which was his way of showing his affection, consideration and condolence, and once we were at the classroom he bade me enter with a magnanimous gesture, that it didn't matter that class had already begun, that the teacher had already been informed. I went into the classroom and forty-three pairs of eyes looked at me with curiosity and Mr Badia, who, judging by the sentence he was in the middle of, was explaining the subtle difference between the subject and the direct object, stopped his lecture and said come in,

Ardèvol, sit down. On the blackboard, Juan writes a letter to Pedro. I had to cross the entire room to reach my desk and I was very embarrassed, and I would have liked having Bernat in my class, but that was impossible because he was in second and even though I was still bored in first listening to that twaddle about direct and indirect objects that had already been explained to us in Latin and that, surprisingly, some of my classmates still didn't understand. Which is the direct object, Rull?

'Juan.' Pause. Mr Badia, undaunted. Rull, wary, sensing a trap, pondered deeply and lifted his head. 'Pedro?'

'No. Terrible. You didn't understand a thing.'

'Wait, no! Writes!'

'Sit down, it's hopeless.'

'I know! Wait, I know it: it's the letter. Right?'

When the idea of the direct object had been fully explained and we entered into the shadowy world of the indirect object, I realised that four or five kids had been staring at me for a while. From the layout of the desks I knew that they were Massan, Esteban, Riera, Torres, Escaiola, Pujol and maybe Borrell, because the nape of my neck was itchy. I guessed that they were looks of ... of admiration? More likely a strange mix of emotions.

'Look, kid ...' Borrell said to me at breaktime. 'Play with us.' And to avoid a disaster, 'But stay here in the middle to keep them from getting through, OK?'

'I don't like football.'

'You see?' said Esteban, who was also part of the group of ambassadors. 'Ardèvol likes the violin; I told you he's a poof.'

And they left quickly because the game had already started without the ambassadors. Borrell, resigned, gave me a few pats on the back and left in silence. I looked for Bernat among the muddle of students in first, second and third who, distributed into bands throughout the playground, played twelve different games and, in general, didn't mix up the balls. Poof, big *marica*. The Russians call girls named Maria Marika, and I'm sure Esteban doesn't know Russian.

'*Marica*?' Bernat looked out into the distance, as he

ruminated despite the noise of the over-excited footballers. 'No. That's Russian for Maria.'

'I already knew that.'

'Well, look it up in the dictionary. Am I supposed to explain everything to …'

'Do you know what it means or not?'

It was very cold those days and pretty much everyone had chafed hands and thighs, except for me and Bernat, who always wore gloves by express orders from Trullols because, with chilblains on your hands, playing the violin was insufferable torment. But chafed thighs weren't a problem.

The first days at school after Father's death were special. Particularly after Riera spoke openly about my father's head, which it turned out gave me a prestige that no one else could match. They even forgave me for my good marks and I became just another kid. And when the teachers asked a question, Pujol no longer said that I was the one chosen to answer all the questions, instead everyone played dumb and then Father Valero, to put an end to it said, Ardèvol, and I would finally answer. But it wasn't the same.

Even though he wouldn't admit that he didn't know what *marica* meant, Bernat was my point of reference, especially after Father's death. He kept me company and helped me feel more comfortable with life. The thing is that he was also a kind of special boy. He wasn't like the other boys at school either, who were normal, they fought, failed and, at least some in fifth and even fourth, knew how to smoke, and they did it hidden right inside the school. And the fact that he was in a different year and I didn't see him much at school made our friendship more clandestine and unofficial. But that day, sitting on my bed, his mouth agape, my friend's eyes were teary because what he'd just heard was too much for him. He looked at me with hatred and said that is a betrayal. And I said, no, Bernat, it was my mother's decision.

'And you can't go against it? Huh? Can't you say that you have to study with Trullols because otherwise …'

Otherwise, otherwise we won't go to class together, he

wanted to say; but he didn't dare because he didn't want to look like a little boy. His rebellious tears said more than any words could. It is so difficult to be a child pretending to be a man, but who couldn't care less about what it seemed men cared about, and realise that you couldn't care less but you have to play it off because if the others see that you do care, and quite a bit, then they'll laugh at you and say what a baby you are, Bernat, Adrià, what a little boy. Or if it was Esteban, he would say little girl, what a little girl. No, now he'd say marica, you big poof. Along with our moustache hairs, evidence was growing that life was really difficult. But it wasn't yet unbelievably difficult; I hadn't met you yet.

We had our tea in silence. Little Lola was already serving us each two squares of chocolate. We were silent for a good long while, chewing our bread, sitting on the bed, looking out at the future that was so complicated. And then we started our arpeggio exercises and I echoed what Bernat played even when it wasn't in the score and that was a way to make the exercise more fun. But we were sad.

'Look, look, look, look! …'

Bernat, his mouth agape, put the bow down on the music stand and went over to the window of Adrià's bedroom. The world had changed, the sadness was no longer so bad; his friend could do what he wanted with his violin teachers; his blood was returning to his veins. Bernat was looking towards the window of the room across the interior courtyard, with the light on and a thin curtain drawn. You could see the bare bust of a woman. Naked? Who is it? Who?

It was Little Lola. It was Lola's room. Little Lola naked. Wow. From the waist up. She was changing. She must be going out. Naked? And Adrià thought that … you couldn't see very well but the drawn curtain made it more arousing.

'That's the neighbour's house. I don't know her,' I replied, offhandedly, as I again began the anacrusis of the eighteenth bar so that Bernat would now echo me. 'Come on, let's see if we can get this right.'

Bernat didn't come back to the music stand until Lola was completely covered up. The exercise came out quite well, but

Adrià was hurt by his friend's enthusiasm and also because he didn't like having seen Lola ... A woman's breasts are ... It was the first time he had seen them, the curtain didn't ...

'Have you ever seen a naked lady?' asked Bernat when they finished the exercise.

'You just saw her, didn't you?'

'Well, that was seeing without really seeing. I mean really seeing. And the whole thing.'

'Can you imagine Trullols naked?'

I said it to divert his attention from Little Lola.

'Don't talk nonsense!'

I had imagined her a hundred times, not because she was good-looking. She was older, skinny and had long fingers. But she had a pretty voice, and she looked you in the eyes when she spoke to you. But when she played the violin, that was when I imagined her naked. But that was because the sound she made was so lovely, so ... I've always been one to mix things up like that. It's not something I'm proud of; it's more like contained resignation. As hard as I've tried, I've never been able to create watertight compartments and everything blends together like it's blending now as I write to you and my tears are the ink.

'Don't worry, Adrià,' Trullols told me. 'Manlleu is a great violinist.' She ruffled my hair with her hand. And as a farewell she made me play the slow tempo of Brahms's sonata number one and when I finished she kissed my forehead. That's how Trullols was. And I didn't realise that she'd said Manlleu was a great violinist and she hadn't said don't worry, Adrià; Manlleu is a great teacher. And Bernat looking all serious and pretending he wasn't about to cry. I did shed three or four tears. My God. It must have been because he felt so sad that, when they reached Bernat's house, Adrià said that he was giving him the Storioni, and Bernat said really? And Adrià, sure, so you remember me fondly. Really? repeated the other boy, incredulous. And Adrià, you can count on it. And your mother, what will she say? She won't even notice. She spends all day at the shop. And the next day Bernat went home with his heart beating boom, boom, boom like the bells of the

Concepción ringing out the noon mass, and that was when he said Mama, I have a surprise for you; and he opened up the case and Mrs Plensa smelled the unmistakable scent of old things and with extreme emotion she said where did you get this violin, Son? And he, playing it cool, answered by imitating Cassidy James when Dorothy asks him where that horse came from:

'It's a long story.'

And it was true. Europe smelled of burnt gunpowder and of walls turned to rubble; and Rome, even more so. He let a fast American Jeep past. It bounced along the gutted streets but didn't slow at the corners, and he continued at a good clip towards Santa Sabina. There, Morlin gave him a message: Ufficio della Giustizia e della Pace. The concierge, someone named Signor Falegnami. And be careful, he could be dangerous.

'Why dangerous?'

'Because he is not what he seems. But he's having problems.'

Fèlix Ardèvol didn't take long to find that vaguely Vatican office located on the outskirts of the Papal City, in the middle of Borgo. The man who opened the door, fat, tall, with a large nose and a restless gaze, asked him who he had come to see.

'I'm afraid I've come to see you. Signor Falegnami?'

'Why are you afraid? Do I scare you?'

'It's just an expression.' Fèlix Ardèvol wanted to smile. 'I understand you have something interesting to show me.'

'In the evening, the office closes at six,' he said, gesturing with his head towards the glass door, which gave off a sad light. 'Wait outside on the street.'

At six three men came out, one of whom wore a cassock, and Fèlix felt like he was on a secret romantic date. Like in Rome many years earlier, when he still had hopes and dreams and the apples in Signor Amato's fruit shop reminded him of earthly paradise. Then the man with the restless gaze stuck his head out and waved him in.

'Aren't we going to your house?'

'I live here.'

They had to go up a solemn staircase, almost in the dark,

the man panting from the effort, with footsteps echoing in that strange office. On the third floor, a long corridor, and suddenly, the man opened a door and turned on a wan light. They were greeted by an overwhelming stench of musty air.

'Go on in,' the man said.

A narrow bed, a dark wooden wardrobe, a bricked-up window and a sink. The man opened the wardrobe and pulled a violin case out from the back of it. He used the bed as a table. He opened the case. It was the first time Fèlix Ardèvol saw it.

'It's a Storioni,' said the man with the uneasy gaze.

A Storioni. That word didn't mean anything to Fèlix Ardèvol. He didn't know that Lorenzo Storioni, when he'd finished it, had stroked its skin and felt the instrument tremble and decided to show it to the good master Zosimo.

The man with the uneasy gaze turned on the table lamp and invited Fèlix to come closer to the instrument. Laurentius Storioni Cremonensis me fecit, he read aloud.

'And how do I know it's authentic.'

'I'm asking fifty thousand U.S. dollars.'

'That's no proof.'

'That's the price. I'm going through a rough patch and ...'

He had seen so many people who were going through rough patches. But the rough patches in thirty-eight and thirty-nine weren't the same as the ones at the end of the war. He gave the violin back to the man and felt an immense void in his soul; exactly the way he had when six or seven years earlier he had held Nicola Galliano's viola in his hands. He was increasingly able to get the object itself to tell him that it was valuable, pulsing with life in his hands. That could be an authentication of the object. But Mr Ardèvol, with that much money at stake, couldn't rely on intuitions and poetic heartbeats. He tried to be cold and made a quick calculation. He smiled, 'Tomorrow I will return with an answer.'

More than an answer it was a declaration of war. That night he had managed to get a meeting in his room at the Bramante with Father Morlin and that promising young man named Berenguer, who was a tall, thin lad: serious, meticulous and, it seemed, an expert in many things.

'Be careful, Ardevole,' insisted Father Morlin.

'I know how to get around in life, dear friend.'

'Appearances are one thing and reality another. Negotiate, earn your living, but don't humiliate him, it's dangerous.'

'I know what I'm doing. You've seen that already, haven't you?'

Father Morlin didn't insist, but he spent the rest of the meeting in silence. Berenguer, the promising young man, knew three luthiers in Rome but could only trust one of them, a man named Saverio Somethingorother. The other two …

'Bring him to me tomorrow, sir.'

'Please, no need for such formality with me, Mr Ardèvol.'

The next day, Mr Berenguer, Fèlix Ardèvol and Saverio Somethingorother knocked on the door of the room of the man with the frightened eyes. They entered with a collective smile, they stoically withstood the stench of the room, and Mr Saverio Somethingorother spent half an hour sniffing the violin and looking at it with a loupe and doing inexplicable things to it with instruments he carried in a doctor's satchel. And he played it.

'Father Morlin told me that you were trustworthy people,' said Falegnami impatiently.

'I am trustworthy. But I don't want to get taken for a ride.'

'The price is fair. It's what it's worth.'

'I will pay what it's worth, not what you tell me.'

Mr Falegnami picked up his small 'just in case' notebook and wrote something down in it. He closed the notebook and stared into impatient Ardèvol's eyes. Since there was no window, he looked at Dottor Somethingorother, who was lightly tapping the wood of the top and side, with a phonendoscope in his ears.

They went out of that wretched room and into the evening. Dr Somethingorother walked quickly, eyes forward, talking to himself. Fèlix Ardèvol looked at Mr Berenguer out of the corner of his eye, as the young man pretended to be completely disinterested. When they reached Via Crescenzio, Mr Berenguer shook his head and stopped. The other two followed suit.

'What's going on?'

'No: it's too dangerous.'

'It's an authentic Storioni,' said Saverio Somethingorother, fervidly. 'And I'll say something more.'

'Why do you say it's dangerous, Mr Berenguer?' Fèlix Ardèvol was beginning to like that somewhat stiff-looking young man.

'When a wild beast is cornered, it will do all it can to save itself. But later it can bite.'

'What more do you have to say, Signor Somethingorother?' asked Fèlix, turning coldly towards the luthier.

'I'll say something more.'

'Well, then say it.'

'This violin has a name. It's called Vial.'

'Excuse me?'

'It's Vial.'

'Now you've lost me.'

'That's its name. That's what it's called. There are instruments that have proper names.'

'Does that make it more valuable?'

'That's not the point, Signor Ardevole.'

'Of course that's the point. Does that mean it's even more valuable?'

'It's the first violin he ever made. Of course it's valuable.'

'That who made?'

'Lorenzo Storioni.'

'Where does its name come from?' asked Mr Berenguer, his curiosity piqued.

'Guillaume-François Vial, Jean-Marie Leclair's murderer.'

Signor Somethingorother made that gesture that reminded Fèlix of Saint Dominic preaching from the throne about the immensity of divine goodness. And Guillaume-François Vial took a step out of the darkness, so the person inside the carriage could see him. The coachman stopped the horses right before him. He opened the door and Monsieur Vial got into the coach.

'Good evening,' said La Guitte.

'You can give it to me, Monsieur La Guitte. My uncle has agreed to the price.'

La Guitte laughed to himself, proud of his nose. 'We are talking about five thousand florins,' he confirmed.

'We are talking about five thousand florins,' Monsieur Vial reassured him.

'Tomorrow you will have the famous Storioni's violin in your hands.'

'Don't try to deceive me, Monsieur La Guitte: Storioni isn't famous.'

'In Italy, in Naples and Florence … they speak of no one else.'

'And in Cremona?'

'The Bergonzis and the others aren't happy at all about the appearance of that new workshop. Everyone says that Storioni is the new Stradivari.'

They continued to talk half-heartedly on three or four more topics, for example, hopefully this will lower instrument prices, which are sky high. You can say that again. And they said goodbye to each other. Vial got out of La Guitte's coach convinced that this time it would come off.

'Mon cher tonton! …' he declared as he burst into the room early the next morning. Jean-Marie Leclair didn't even deign to look up; he was watching the flames in the fireplace. 'Mon cher tonton,' repeated Vial, with less enthusiasm.

Leclair half turned. Without looking him in the eyes he asked him if he had the violin with him. Leclair soon was running his fingers over the instrument. From a painting on the wall emerged a servant with a beak-like nose and a violin bow in his hand, and Leclair spent some time searching out all of that Storioni's possible sounds with fragments of three of his sonatas.

'It's very good,' he said when he had finished. 'How much did it cost you?'

'Ten thousand florins, plus a five-hundred coin reward that you'll give me for finding this jewel.'

With an authoritative wave, Leclair sent out the servants. He put a hand on his nephew's shoulder and smiled.

'You're a bastard. I don't know who you take after, you son of a rotten bitch. Your mother or your pathetic father. Thief, conman.'

'Why? I just …' Fencing with their eyes. 'Fine: I can forget about the reward.'

'You think that I would trust you, after so many years of you being such a thorn in my side?'

'So why did you entrust me to …'

'As a test, you stupid son of a sickly, mangy bitch. This time you won't escape prison.' After a few seconds, for emphasis: 'You don't know how I've been waiting for this moment.'

'You've always wanted my ruin, Tonton Jean. You envy me.'

Leclair looked at him in surprise. After a long pause: 'What do you think I could envy about you, you wretched, crappy fleabag?'

Vial, red as a tomato, was too enraged to be able to respond.

'It's better if we don't go into details,' he said just to say something.

Leclair looked at him with contempt.

'Why not go into details? Physique? Height? People skills? Friendliness? Talent? Moral stature?'

'This conversation is over, Tonton Jean.'

'It will end when I say so. Intelligence? Culture? Wealth? Health?'

Leclair grabbed the violin and improvised a pizzicato. He examined it with respect. 'The violin is very good, but I don't give a damn, you understand me? I only want to be able to send you to prison.'

'You're a bad uncle.'

'And you are a bastard who I've finally been able to unmask. Do you know what?' He smiled exaggeratedly, bringing his face very close to his nephew's. 'I'll keep the violin, but for the price La Guitte gives me.'

He pulled the little bell's rope taut and the servant with the beak-like nose entered through the door to the back of the room.

'Call the commissioner. He can come whenever he's ready.' To his nephew: 'Have a seat, we'll wait for Monsieur Béjart.'

They didn't have a chance to sit down. Instead Guillaume-François Vial walked in front of the fireplace, grabbed the poker and bashed in his beloved tonton's head. Jean-Marie

Leclair, known as l'Aîne, was unable to say another word. He collapsed without even a groan, the poker stuck in his head. Splattered blood stained the violin's wooden case. Vial, breathing heavily, wiped his clean hands on his uncle's coat and said you don't know how much I was looking forward to this moment, Tonton Jean. He looked around him, grabbed the violin, put it into the blood-spattered case and left the room through the balcony that led to the terrace. As he ran away, in the light of day, it occurred to him that he should make a not very friendly visit to La Guitte.

'As far as I know,' continued Signor Somethingorother, still standing in the middle of the street, 'it is a violin that has never been played regularly: like the Stradivarius Messiah, do you understand what I'm saying?'

'No,' said Ardèvol, impatient.

'I'm saying that that makes it even more valuable. The same year it was made, Guillaume-François Vial made off with it and its whereabouts have been unknown. Perhaps it has been played, but I have no record of it. And now we find it here. It is an instrument of incalculable value.'

'That is what I wanted to hear, caro dottore.'

'Is it really his first?' asked Mr Berenguer, his interest piqued.

'Yes.'

'I would forget about it, Mr Ardèvol. That's a lot of money.'

'Is it worth it?' asked Fèlix Ardèvol, looking at Somethingorother.

'I would pay it without hesitating. If you have the money. It has an incredibly lovely sound.'

'I don't give a damn about its sound.'

'And exceptional symbolic value.'

'That does matter to me.'

'And we are returning it right now to its owner.'

'But he gave it to me! I swear it, Papa!'

Mr Plensa put on his coat, shifted his eyes imperceptibly towards his wife, picked up the case and, with a forceful nod, ordered Bernat to follow him.

The silent funereal retinue that transported the scrawny

coffin was presided over by Bernat's black thoughts, as he cursed the moment when he'd flaunted the violin in front of his mother and showed her an authentic Storioni, and the dirty grass went straight to his father as soon as he arrived and said Joan, look what the boy has. And Mr Plensa looked at it; he examined it; and after a few seconds of silence he said blast it, where did you get this violin?

'It has a beautiful sound, Papa.'

'Yes, but I'm asking you where you got it.'

'Joan, please!'

'Come now, Bernat. This is no joking matter.' Impatiently, 'Where did you get it from.'

'Nowhere; I mean they gave it to me. Its owner gave it to me.'

'And who is this idiotic owner?'

'Adrià Ardèvol.'

'This violin belongs to the Ardèvols?'

Silence: his mother and father exchanged a quick glance. His father sighed, picked up the violin, put it into its case and said we are going to return it to its owner right now.

I was the one who opened the door for her. She was younger than my mother, very tall, with sweet eyes and lipstick. She gave me a friendly smile as soon as she saw me and I liked her right away. Well, more than liked her, exactly, I fell irresistibly and forever in love with her and was overcome with a desire to see her naked.

'Are you Adrià?'

How did she know my name? And that accent was truly strange.

'Who is it?' Little Lola, from the depths of the flat.

'I don't know,' I said and smiled at the apparition. She smiled at me and even winked, asking if my mother was home.

Little Lola came into the hall and, from the apparition's reaction, I assumed she had taken her for my mother.

'This is Little Lola,' I warned.

'Mrs Ardèvol?' she said with the voice of an angel.

'You're Italian!' I said.

'Very good! They told me you're a clever lad.'

'Who told you?'

Mother had been in the shop waging war and organising things since the crack of dawn, but the apparition said she didn't mind waiting as long as it took. Little Lola pointed brusquely to the bench and vanished. The angel sat down and looked at me, a very pretty golden cross glittering around her neck. She said come stai. And I answered bene with another charming smile, my violin case in my hand because I had class with Manlleu and he couldn't abide by tardiness.

'Ciao!' I said timidly as I opened the door to the stairwell. And my angel, without moving from the bench, blew me a kiss, which rebounded against my heart and gave me a jolt.

And her red lips soundlessly said ciao in such a way that I heard it perfectly inside my heart. I closed the door as gently as I could so that the miracle wouldn't disappear.

'Don't drag your bow, child! You are reproducing negroid, epileptic rhythms, more suited to a wind instrument!'

'What?'

'Look, look, look!'

Professor Manlleu snatched the violin from him and did a wildly exaggerated portamento, something I had never done. And, with the violin in position, he said to me that is crap. You understand me? Insanity, dementia, filth and rubbish!

And boy did I miss Trullols, and I was only ten minutes into my third class with Master Manlleu. Later, surely in an attempt to impress him with his dazzling talent, he explained that when he was his age, uff, at your age: I was a child prodigy. At your age I played Max Bruch and I learned it all on my own.

And he snatched the violin out of his hands again and began with the sooooooltiresolsiiila#faasooool. Tiresoltiiiietcetera, how lovely.

'That is a concert and not these lousy studies you've been studying.'

'Can I start with Max Bruch?'

'How can you start with Bruch when you're still not out of nappies, child?' He gave him back the violin and he drew very close to him and shouted so he could hear him loud and clear: 'Maybe, if you were me. But I'm one of a kind.' In a brusque voice: 'Exercise twenty-two. And don't harbour any illusions, Ardèvol: Bruch was mediocre and just happened to get lucky.' And he shook his head, pained by life: if only I could have devoted more time to composing …

Exercise twenty-two, dei portamenti, was designed to teach you how to do portamenti but Master Manlleu, when he heard the first portamento, was again shocked and again began to talk about his precocious genius and, this time, about the Bartók concerto that he knew backwards and forwards without the slightest hesitation at the age of fifteen.

'You must know that the good interpreter has a special memory in addition to his normal memory that allows him retain all of the soloist's notes and all of the orchestra's. If you can't do that, you're no good; you should deliver ice or light streetlamps. And then don't forget to put them out.'

So I opted to do the portamenti exercise without portamenti and that way we were able to keep the peace. And I would learn the portamenti at home. And Bruch was mediocre. In case I didn't have that clear, I received the last three minutes of my third class with Master Manlleu in the hall of his house, standing, my scarf around my neck, while he ranted against gypsy violinists, who play in bars and night clubs and do such harm to the young folk because they incite them to do unnecessary and exaggerated portamenti. It quickly becomes obvious that they are only playing to impress women. Those portamenti are only admissible for poofs. Until next Friday, child.

'Good night, Master Manlleu.'

'And remember, as if it were burned onto your brain, everything I've told you and will be telling you in each class. Not everyone has the privilege of studying with me.'

At least I already knew that the concept of poofs was closely linked to the violin. But when I'd looked marica up it didn't help at all because it wasn't in the dictionary and my question remained. Bruch must have been a mediocre poof. I guess.

In that period, Adrià Ardèvol was a saintly person, with endless saintly patience, and that was why the classes with Master Manlleu didn't seem as bad to him as they seem to me now when I describe them to you. I did my duty with him and I remember, minute by minute, the years I was under his yoke. And I particularly remember that after two or three sessions I began to turn a problem over in my mind, one that I've never been able to resolve: musical interpreters are required to be perfect. They can be miserable wretches, but their execution must be perfect. Like Master Manlleu, who seemed to have every possible defect but who played perfectly.

The problem was that listening to him and listening to Bernat I thought I could grasp a difference between Manlleu's perfection and Bernat's truth. And that made me a bit more interested in music. I don't understand why Bernat isn't satisfied with his talent and obsessively seeks out personal dissatisfaction, crashing up against self-confessed impotence, in book after book. We've both truly got a gift for finding dissatisfaction in life.

'But you don't make mistakes!' Bernat told me, shocked, fifty years ago, when I explained my doubts to him.

'But I need to know that I can make them.' Perplexed silence. 'Don't you understand?'

And that's why I stopped playing the violin. But that's another story. As Bernat and I walked to school, I explained all the ins and outs of my classes with Manlleu. And we took forever to get to school because in the middle of Aragó Street, amid the smoke from the locomotive engines that blackened the facades, Bernat tried to imitate, without a violin, what Manlleu had told me to do. The people passing by looked at us, and later, at home, he would try it and that was how he became, for free, some sort of second disciple of Wednesdays and Fridays with the great Manlleu.

'Thursday afternoon, you are both punished. This is the third time you've been late in fifteen days, young men.' The beadle with the blond moustache who stood guard at the entrance smiled, pleased to have caught us.

'But ...'

'No buts.' Shaking the loathsome notebook and pulling a pencil out of his smock. 'Name and class.'

And on Thursday afternoons in the Manlleu era, instead of being at home secretly rummaging through Father's papers, may he rest in peace, instead of being at Bernat's house, practising or having him over to my house to practise, we were forced to show up at the 2B classroom, where twelve or fifteen other scamps were purging their tardiness with a textbook open on their desks while Herr Oliveres or Mr Rodrigo watched over us with obvious boredom.

And when I got home, Mother interrogated me about my lessons with Manlleu and asked captious questions about the possibilities that I would very soon give a dazzling recital, you

hear me, Adrià? with top-notch works, as it seems Manlleu
had promised her.

'Like which ones?'

'The *Kreutzer Sonata*. Or Brahms,' she said one day.

'That's impossible, Mother!'

'Nothing's impossible,' she answered, as if she were Trullols saying never say never, Ardèvol. But even though it was
almost the same piece of advice, it didn't have any effect on
me.

'I don't know how to play as well as you think I do, Mother.'

'You will play perfectly.'

And, perfectly imitating Father's skill for avoiding being
contradicted, she left the room before I could tell her that I
hated the perfection demanded of musicians, blah, blah, blah
… and she headed towards Mrs Angeleta's dominions and I
felt a little sad because even though Mother was speaking to
me again, she barely looked me in the eye and she was more
interested in my progress report than in my irrepressible
desire to see a woman naked and the inexplicable stains on
my sheets, which, actually, I had no interest in making a topic
of conversation. And now how could I study i portamenti at
home without doing portamenti?

At home? As soon as I had reached the stairs I thought
again about my angel whom I had cruelly abandoned to her
fate, forced to by my Negroid rhythm classes with Manlleu. I
went up the stairs two by two thinking of the angel who must
have flown away as I dilly-dallied, thinking that she would
never forgive me, and I knocked impatiently and Lola opened
the door. I pushed her aside and looked towards the bench.
Her red smile welcomed me with another ciao dolcíssim and
I felt like the happiest violinist on earth.

And three hours after her miraculous apparition, Mother
arrived with a worried expression and when she saw the angel
in the hall, she looked at Little Lola, who had come out to
greet her, and she made that face she makes when she understands, because without allowing her much introduction, she
had her go into Father's study. Three minutes later the shouting began.

One thing is hearing a conversation clearly enough, and
another is understanding what it's about. The espionage
system that Adrià used to know what was cooking in Father's
study was complicated and, as he grew taller and heavier, it
had to become more sophisticated because I could no longer
fit behind the sofa. When I heard the first shouts I saw that I
had to somehow protect my angel from Mother's rage. From
the little dressing room, the door that opened onto the gallery
and the laundry room left me before a ground glass window
that was never opened but looked into Father's study. The
little natural light that reached the study entered through that
window. And by lying down under the window I could hear
the conversation. As if I were in there with them. At home
I was always everywhere. Almost. Mother, pale, finished
reading the letter and looked at the wall.

'How do I know this is true?'

'Because I inherited Can Casic in Tona.'

'Pardon?'

My angel, in reply, handed her another document in which
the notary Garolera of Vic certified to all effects the willing
of the house, the straw loft, the pond, the garden plot and the
three fields of Can Casic to Daniela Amato, born in Rome on
25th December of 1919, daughter of Carolina Amato and an
unknown father.

'Can Casic in Tona?' Vehemently: 'It didn't belong to Fèlix.'

'It did. And now it's mine.'

Mother tried to conceal the trembling in the hand that held
the document. She gave it back to its owner with a disdainful
gesture.

'I don't know where you are going with this. What do you
want?'

'The shop. I have a right to it.'

From her tone of voice, I could tell that my angel had said
it with a delicious smile, which made me want to cover her
in kisses. If I were in my mother's place, I would have given
her the shop and whatever else it took with the only condition being that she never lost that smile. But Mother, instead
of giving her anything, started laughing, pretending to laugh

heartily: a fake laugh that she had recently added to her repertoire. I started to be scared, because I still wasn't used to
that side of Mother, the heartless, anti-angel side; I had always
seen her either with her gaze lowered before Father or absent
and cold, when she was recently widowed and was planning
my future. But I had never seen her snap her fingers, demanding to see the document detailing ownership of Can Casic
again and saying, after a pause, I don't give a ffuck what this
paper says.

'It is a legal document. And I have a right to my part of the
shop. That is why I've come.'

'My solicitor will inform you of my refusal of all of your
proposals. All of them.'

'I am your husband's daughter.'

'That's like saying you are Raquel Meller's daughter. It's a
lie.'

My angel said no, Mrs Ardèvol: it is not a lie. She looked
around her, slowly, and she repeated it is not a lie: Fifteen
years ago I was in this study. He didn't invite me to take a seat
either.

'What a surprise, Carolina,' said Fèlix Ardèvol, his mouth
agape, completely disconcerted. Even his tone of voice had
cracked from the shock. The two women came in and he had
them go into the study before Little Lola, who was busy with
Carme's trousseau, noticed the inopportune visit.

The three of them were in the study, standing as hustle and
bustle reigned in the rest of the house, porters bringing up
Mother's furniture, Grandmother's dresser, the hall mirror
that Fèlix had agreed to put in the dressing room and people
coming and going, and Little Lola, who had only been there for
two hours but already knew every tile in Mr Ardèvol's house,
my God, what a grand flat the girl will have. And the study
door was closed, with those visitors she didn't find amusing in
the least, but she couldn't pry into Mr Fèlix's affairs.

'Are you busy?' asked the older woman.

'Quite.' He lifted his arms. 'Everything's topsy-turvy.'
Curtly: 'What do you want?'

'Your daughter, Fèlix.'

'Carolina, I ...'

Carolina had understood pretty much everything from the moment her seminarian with the clean gaze of a good man had shrugged so cowardly when she'd placed his palm on her belly.

'But we've only gone to bed together three or four times!' he had said, frightened, pale, scared, terrified, sweaty.

'Twelve times,' she replied gravely. 'And it only takes once.'

Silence. Hiding the fear. Looking at the future. Glancing at the exit doors. Looking the girl in the face and hearing her say, with her eyes glassy with emotion, aren't you excited, Fèlix?

'Oh, sure.'

'We're going to have a baby, Fèlix!'

'How great. I'm so happy.'

And the next day fleeing Rome, leaving his studies half completed. What he most regretted was not being able to hear the end of Pater Faluba's course.

'Fèlix Ardèvol?' Bishop Muñoz had said with his mouth hanging open. 'Fèlix Ardèvol i Guiteres?' He shook his head. 'That's not possible.'

He was sitting before the desk in his office and Father Ayats was standing, with a folder in his hand and that deferential bearing that so irked the monsignor. Through the palace's balcony rose the whine of a cart that must have been overloaded and the shriek of a woman scolding a child.

'Yes it is possible.' The episcopal secretary didn't stifle his smug tone. 'Unfortunately, he has done it. He got a woman pregnant and ...'

'Save me the details,' said the bishop.

Once he had informed him of every last facet, shocked Monsignor Muñoz went to pray because his soul was confused, as he mused over his luck that Monsignor Torras i Bages had been saved the shame of the behaviour of the student many said was the pearl of the bishopric, and Father Ayata lowered his eyes humbly because he had known for some time that Ardèvol was no pearl. Very clever, very philosophical, very this and very that, but an inveterate rogue.

'How did you know I'm marrying tomorrow?'

Carolina didn't answer. Her daughter couldn't stop looking at the face of that man who was her father, and she barely paid attention to the conversation. Carolina looked at Fèlix – fatter, not as charming, badly aged, with darker skin and crow's feet – and she hid a smile. 'Your daughter is named Daniela.'

Daniela. She looks just like her mother did when I met her.

'That day, right here,' said my angel, 'your husband signed Can Casic over to me under oath. And when you came back from Majorca the inheritance was formalised.'

The trip to Majorca, the days with her husband, who no longer removed his hat when he ran into her because they were together all day long and, so he couldn't say how are you, beautiful, either. Or he could say it but he didn't; at first her husband was very attentive to her every move and, gradually, more mindful of his own silent thoughts. I never understood what your father did, thinking all day without saying a word, Son. All day long thinking without a word. And every once in a while shouting or smacking whomever was closest because he must have thought about that Italian tart, and about missing her and giving her Can Casics.

'How did you know that my husband had died?'

My angel looked into my mother's eyes and, as if she hadn't heard her, 'He promised me. No, he swore to me that I would be in his will.'

'Then you must already know that you aren't.'

'He didn't think he would die so soon.'

'Farewell. And send your mother my regards.'

'She is dead too.'

Mother didn't say I'm sorry or anything like that. She opened the door to the study but my angel still stipulated, turning towards Mother as she left, 'A part of the business is mine and I won't stop fighting unt

'Farewell.'

The door to the street slammed, like the day Father left the house to be killed. Honestly, I hadn't understood much. Only a vague suspicion of I don't know what. In that period, I had the absolute ablative conquered but life, not so much. Mother went back to the study, locked the door behind her, rummaged through the safe for a little while, pulled out a small green box, moved aside the pink cotton and pulled out a chain from which hung a very pretty golden medallion. She put it back in the little box and she threw it in the bin. Then she sat on the sofa and she started to cry all the tears she hadn't cried since the day she was married, with that bittersweet weeping that produces stinging tears because they are made of a mix of rage and grief.

I was skilful. Accompanied by clever Black Eagle (fine, I was a big baby but I sometimes needed moral support), when everyone was sleeping, I slipped into Father's study and, feeling my way, I searched through the bin until I came upon the small cube-shaped box. I grabbed it and the valiant Arapaho kept me from doing anything rash. Following his instructions, I turned on the magnifying lamp, I opened the little box and I pulled out the medallion. I closed the little box again and I placed it silently at the bottom of the bin. Adrià turned off the lamp with the loupe and backed up, his booty in his hands, to his room. Once he was inside with the door closed, violating the unwritten law that the doors at home should never be shut but rather ajar, he turned on the lamp on his bedside table, silently expressed his gratitude to Black Eagle and looked at that medallion with an interest that made his heart beat like a runaway train. It was a fairly rudimentary Madonna, surely a reproduction of a Romanesque sculpture, vaguely resembling the Virgin of Montserrat, with a slight baby Jesus in her arms. It had a very curious background, an enormous, lush tree in the distance. On the flip side, where I hoped to find the solution to the mystery, was only the word Pardàc roughly engraved on the bottom. And that was all. I sniffed the medallion to see if it gave off the scent of angel, since – although I couldn't say why – I was convinced that it was closely linked to my great, only and forever Italian love.

## 14

Mother usually spent mornings at the shop. As soon as she entered she raised her eyebrows and didn't lower them again until she left. As soon as she entered she considered everyone an enemy to be distrusted. It seems that's a good method. First she attacked Mr Berenguer and came out the winner because her surprise attack had caught him with his guard down and he was unable to fight back. When he was very, very old, he explained it to me himself, I think with a hint of admiration towards his bosom enemy. I never would have thought that your mother knew what a promissory note was or the differences between ebony and cherry wood. But she knew that and she knew many things about the shady dealings that your father—

'Shady dealings?'

'More like murky.'

So Mother took the reins at the shop and began to say you do this and you do that, without having to look them in the eye.

'Mrs Ardèvol,' said Mr Berenguer one day, entering Mr Ardèvol's office, which he had tried, unsuccessfully, to convert into Mr Berenguer's office. And he said Mrs Ardèvol with his voice sullied by rage. She looked at him, with an eyebrow raised and in silence.

'I should think that I have some rights earned over so many years of working at the highest level. I am the expert in this shop; I travel, I buy and I know the buying and selling prices. I know how to negotiate prices and, if necessary, I know how to swindle. I am the one your husband always trusted! It's not fair that now I … I know how to do my job!'

'Well, then do it. But from now on I will be the one who says what your job is. For example: of the three console tables from Turin, buy two if they don't give you the third for free.'

'It's better to have all three. That way the prices will be m
'Two. I told Ottaviani that you would go there tomorrow.'
'Tomorrow?'

It wasn't that he minded travelling; in fact, he enjoyed it immensely. But going to Turin for a couple of days meant leaving the shop in the hands of that witch.

'Yes, tomorrow. Cecília will go and pick up the tickets this afternoon. And come back the day after tomorrow. And if you think you need to make a decision that isn't the one we've discussed, check with me by telephone.'

Things had changed in the shop. Mr Berenguer was so constantly surprised that he hadn't shut his mouth in weeks. And Cecília had spent that same time carefully trying to conceal her smugly innocent smile; she hid it pretty well, but not perfectly because she wanted Mr Berenguer to see that for once she had the whip hand. Vengeance is so sweet.

But Mr Berenguer didn't see it the same way and that morning, before Mrs Ardèvol arrived at the shop to put everything on its head, he stood in front of Cecília, with his hands on her desk and his body leaned towards her, and said what the hell are you laughing about, eh?

'Nothing. Just that finally someone is getting things in order and keeping you on a short lead.'

Mr Berenguer debated between smacking her and strangling her. She looked into his eyes and added that's what the hell I'm laughing about.

It was one of the few times that Mr Berenguer lost control. He went around the desk and grabbed Cecília's arm roughly, so hard that he sprained it, and she shrieked with pain. So when Mrs Ardèvol entered the shop, after the ten o'clock bells had rung, into a silence so thick it could only be cut with a straight razor, all sorts of bad things could happen.

'Good morning, Mrs Ardèvol.'

Cecília couldn't pay much attention to the boss because a customer came in with an urgent need to buy two chairs that matched the chest of drawers in the photo, you see, with these kind of legs, you see?

'Come to my office, Mr Berenguer.'

They prepared the trip to Turin in five minutes. Then, Mrs Ardèvol opened Mr Ardèvol's briefcase and pulled out a file, put it on the desk and, without looking at her victim, said now you'll have to explain why this, this and this don't add up. The buyer paid twenty and fifteen went into the till.

Mrs Ardèvol began to drum her fingers on the desk, deliberately imitating the best detective in the world. Then she looked at Mr Berenguer and passed him this, this and this, which were the accounts of about a hundred objects defrauded from the company. Mr Berenguer looked, with a disgusted face, at the first this and he'd had enough. How the hell had that woman been able …

'Cecília helped me,' said Mother as if she could read his thoughts, the way she did to me. 'I wouldn't have been able to on my own.'

Fucking cunts, both of them. That's what I get for working with women, damn it.

'When did you start this illegal practice that goes against the company's interests?'

Dignified silence, like Jesus before Pilate.

'The very beginning?'

Even more dignified silence, surpassing Jesus's.

'I will have to turn you in.'

'I did it with Mr Ardèvol's permission.'

'Come on now!'

'Do you doubt my word?'

'Of course! And why would my husband allow you to swindle us?'

'It's not swindling anyone: it's adjusting prices.'

'And why would my husband allow you to adjust prices?'

'Because he recognised that my salary was low considering all I do for the shop.'

'Why didn't he raise it?'

'You'll have to ask him that. Excuse me. But it's true.'

'Do you have any document proving that?'

'No. It was a verbal agreement.'

'Well, I will have to turn you in.'

'Do you know why Cecília gave you those receipts?'

'No.'

'Because she wants my ruin.'

'Why?' Mother, curious, leaning back in her chair with a questioning stance.

'It's a long story.'

'Go ahead. We have time. Your plane leaves in the mid-afternoon.'

Mr Berenguer sat down. Mrs Ardèvol placed her elbows on the desk and held up her chin with both hands. She looked him in the eye, inviting him to speak.

'Come on, Cecília, we don't have time.'

Cecília made that lewd smile she did when no one was watching and she let Mr Ardèvol grab her by the hand and take her into his office, here.

'Where is Berenguer?'

'In Sarrià. Emptying out the Pericas-Sala flat.'

'Didn't you send Cortés?'

'He doesn't trust the heirs. They want to hide things.'

'What sneaks. Take off your clothes.'

'The door is open.'

'More exciting. Take off your clothes.'

Cecília naked in the middle of the office, her eyes lowered and that innocent smile of hers. And I wasn't emptying out the Pericas-Sala flat because the inventory was very specific and if even a drawing-pin were missing I would have demanded it back. The nasty girl, sitting on top of this desk, doing things to your husband.

'You get better every day.'

'Someone could come in.'

'You just do your job. If someone comes in, I'll deal with them. Can you imagine?'

They started laughing like crazy as they knocked things over and made a mess, the inkwell fell to the floor and you can still make out the stain, see?

'I love you.'

'Me too. You'll come with me to Bordeaux.'

'What about the shop?'

'Mr Berenguer.'

'But he doesn't even know where the

'Don't stop what you're doing. You'll come to Bordeaux and we'll have a party every night.'

Then the little bell on the door sounded and in came a customer who was very interested in buying a Japanese weapon he'd looked at the week before. While Fèlix helped him, Cecília did what she could to tidy up her appearance.

'Can you help him, Cecília?'

'One moment, Mr Ardèvol.'

Without underwear, trying to erase the trail of lipstick smudged all over her face, Cecília emerged from the office bright red and waved for the customer to follow her while Fèlix watched the scene with amusement.

'And why are you telling me this, Mr Berenguer?'

'So you know everything. It went on for years.'

'I don't believe a word.'

'Well, there's more. And we are all tired of the song and dance.'

'Go ahead, I already told you, we've got time.'

'You are a coward. No, no, let me speak: a coward. It's been five years of the same old song and dance, yes, Cecília, next month I'll tell her everything, I swear. Coward. Coward. Five years of excuses. Five years! I'm not a little girl. ( …) No, no, no! I'm talking now: we will never live together because you don't love me. No, you be quiet, it's my turn to talk. I said be quiet! Well, you can stick your sweet words up your arse. It's over. Do you hear me? What? ( …) No. Don't say a word. What? Because I'll hang up when I'm good and ready. No, sir: quan a mi em roti.'

'I already told you that I don't believe a word. And I know of which I speak.'

'As you wish. I suppose I'll have to look for a new job.'

'No. Each month you'll pay me back a part of what you've stolen and you can continue working here.'

'I'd rather leave.'

'Then I will turn you in, Mr Berenguer.'

Mother pulled a sheet with some figures out of her briefcase. 'Your salary, from now on. And here is the amount you won't receive, as the repayment. I want you to give back every last red cent and from prison you won't be able to do that. So what do you say, Mr Berenguer? Yes or yes?'

Mr Berenguer opened and closed his mouth like a fish. And he still had to feel Mrs Ardèvol's breath on his face. She had sat up and leaned over the desk, to say, in a soft voice, if anything funny happens to me, you should know that I have all this information and instructions for the police in a notary's safe in Barcelona, on the twenty-first of March of nineteen fifty-eight; signed, Carme Bosch d'Ardèvol. Notary XXX bore witness. And after another silence she repeated yes or yes, Mr Berenguer?

And while she was at it, seizing the momentum, she requested an appointment with Barcelona's Civil Governor, the loathsome Acedo Colunga. In her role as General Moragues's widow, Mrs Carme Bosch d'Ardèvol went before the Governor's personal secretary and demanded justice.

'Justice for what, madam?'

'For my husband's murder.'

'I will have to look into it in order to know what you are referring to.'

'The form they had me fill out explained the reason behind my request to be seen. In detail.' Pause. 'Have you read it?'

The Governor's secretary looked at the papers he had in front of him. He read them carefully. The black widow, trying to even out her breathing, thought what am I doing here, wasting my breath over a man who ignored me from the very start and never loved me in his entire ffucking life.

'Very well,' said the secretary. 'And what do you want?'

'To speak with His Excellency the Civil Governor.'

'You are already speaking with me, which is the same thing.'

'I wish to speak with the Governor personally.'

'That's impossible. Forget about it.'

'But ...'

'You cannot do that.'

And she could not do it. When she left the governor's offices, her legs shaking with rage, she decided to let it go.

Perhaps she was more worried about the miraculous apparition of my guardian angel than the disdain of the Francoist authorities. Or the maddening insistence of various parties that Fèlix was an impossibly compulsive fornicator. Or, who knows, maybe she'd finally arrived at the conclusion that it wasn't worth her while demanding justice for a man who had been so unjust with her. Yes. Or no. Really I have no idea, because after Father, the biggest question mark in my life, before meeting you, has always been my mother. I can say that, only two days later, things shifted slightly and her plans changed, and that I can speak of first-hand without making any of it up.

'Rrrrrrrrinnnnnnng.'

I opened the door. Mother had just arrived from wreaking havoc in the shop and I think she was in the bathroom. The first thing that entered the house was the stench of Commissioner Plasencia's tobacco.

'Mrs Ardèvol?' He screwed up his face in what may have been an attempt at a smile. 'We've met, haven't we?' he said.

Mother had the Commissioner and his stench enter the study. Her heart went boom, boom, boom and mine went bam, boom, bom because I urgently assembled Black Eagle and Carson, without his horse, to avoid making any noise. Little Lola was in the gallery with the window, so I had to do something desperate and I slipped, like a thief, behind the sofa just as Mother and the policeman were sitting down and making noise with their chairs. It was the last time I used the sofa as a base for spying: my legs were too long. Mother went out to tell Little Lola not to let anyone disturb her even if the shop is on fire, you hear me, Little Lola? And she turned around and closed the door with the five of us inside.

'Commissioner.'

'It seems you've tried to discredit me to His Excellency the Civil Governor.'

'I'm not discrediting or criticising anyone. I am only demanding the information I am owed.'

'Well, now I will give you the information and let's see if you can make an effort to understand the situation.'

'Let's see,' she said sarcastically. And I applauded her in silence, as the best wife of the best palaeographer in the world had done.

'I am sorry to tell you that if we dig into your husband's life we will find unpleasant things. Do you want to hear them?'

'Of course.'

I suppose that Mother, after the appearance of my Italian angel (I lovingly touched the medallion I secretly wore around my neck), was prepared for anything. So she added, go ahead, Commissioner.

'I warn you that you'll say I'm making things up and you won't believe me.'

'Try me.'

'Very well.'

The Commissioner paused and then he began to tell her the truth and nothing but the truth. He explained that Mr Fèlix Ardèvol was a criminal who ran two brothels in Barcelona and had got involved in a shady affair of inducing a minor into prostitution. Do you know what a whore is, madam?

'Go on.'

'Il fait déjà beaucoup de temps que son mari mène une double vie, madame Agdevol. Deux prostíbuls (prostiboules?) with l'agreujant (agreujant?) de faire, de … de … d'utiliser des filles de quinze ou seize ans. Je suis désolé d'être obligé de parler de tout ça.'

My foot had calmed down, thankfully, because my French was awful that day and I could go back to the Commissioner's difficult, muttered Spanish. I think Carson winked at me when he saw that I managed to control my foot.

'Do you want me to continue, madam?'

'Please.'

'It seems that the father of one of these girls your husband prostituted took his revenge. Because before locking them up in the brothel, he tried them out personally. Do you understand me?' With some emphasis: 'He deflowered them.'

'How.'

'Yes.'

'That's two.'

'Yes: brothel and deflower.'

'It's awful and hard to believe. Put yourself in those girls' skins. Or the father of those girls'. Mind if I smoke?'

'Yes, I do, Commissioner.'

'If you'd like, we can investigate and find the desperate father who disappeared after taking justice into his own hands. But any movements on our part will make your husband's unwholesome life more public.'

Silence. My foot threatened to bouger encore une fois. Little sounds. The Commissioner was probably putting away the small cigar he'd been denied. Suddenly, Mother: 'Do you know what, Commissioner?'

'What?'

'You're completely right. I don't believe a word. You are making this up. Now I need to know why.'

'You see? You see? I warned you.' Raising his voice: 'Didn't I? Eh?'

'That's no argument.'

'If you aren't afraid of the consequences, I can keep pulling on loose ends. But only your husband knows what we'll find.'

'Farewell, Commissioner. I have to admit it was a good try.'

Mother spoke like Old Shatterhand, a bit cocksure. I liked it. Carson and Black Eagle were so gobsmacked that Black Eagle, that evening, asked me if I would call him Winnetou. I refused. Mother had said farewell and they hadn't even stood up yet! Since she had started cracking the whip in the shop she had got much better at setting a scene. Because Commissioner Plasencia could only stand up and mutter something incoherent. And I was left wondering whether what the Commissioner had said about Father, which I hadn't entirely understood, was true or not.

'How.'

'Yes. Brothel and what was the other one?'

'Depowder?' suggested Carson.

'I don't know. Something like that.'

'Well, let's look up brothel. In the Espasa dictionary.'

'Brothel: whorehouse, bawdyhouse, cathouse.'

'Wow. We'll have to look up whorehouse now. Here, in this volume.'

'Whorehouse: brothel, bawdyhouse, house of ill repute.'

Silence. All three of them were still confused.

'And bawdyhouse?'

'Bawdyhouse: whorehouse, cathouse, brothel. That's annoying. Place or house that serves as a den of iniquity.'

'Now cathouse.'

'Cathouse: whorehouse, brothel.'

'Jeez!'

'Hey, wait. House or place that lacks decorum and is filled with noise and confusion.'

So Father had cathouses, which are noisy public houses. And they had to kill him for that?

'What if we look up depowder?'

'How do you say depowder in Spanish?'

They were silent for a little while. Adrià was confused.

'How.'

'Yes.'

'That's all about sex, not noise.'

'Are you sure?'

'I'm sure. When a warrior reaches adulthood, the shaman explains the secrets of sex to him.'

'When I reach adulthood, nobody's going to explain any sex secrets to me.'

Slightly bitter silence. I heard someone spitting curtly.

'What is it, Carson?'

'I could you tell you a few things.'

'So, come on, tell me.'

'No. You aren't the right age for some things.'

Sheriff Carson was right. I was never the right age for anything. I was either too young or I'm too old.

## 15

'Put your hands in hot water. Take them out, take them out, don't let them get too soft. Walk. Don't get nervous. Relax. Walk. Take deep breaths. Stop. There. Very good. Think about the beginning. Imagine yourself entering the theatre and bowing to the audience. Very, very good. Now, bow. No, come on, not like that, please. You have to lean forwards, you have to submit to the audience. But, don't really submit. The audience has to think you are submitting to them; but if you reach the summit, where I am, you'll know that you are superior and that they should be kneeling before you. I said don't get nervous. Dry your hands; do you want to catch a cold? Pick up the violin. Stroke it, dominate it, think how you are in charge, that you order it to do what you want. Think about the first bars. That's it, without the bow, as if you were playing. Very good. Now you can do more scales.'

Master Manlleu, spent, left the dressing room and I was finally able to breathe. I was more relaxed doing scales, extracting the sound without gaffes, without shrillness, making the bow glide well, measuring the rosin, breathing. And then Adrià Ardèvol said never again, that this was torture, that he wasn't made for going out onto that display case that was the stage and presenting his merchandise in case someone wanted to buy it with a smattering of applause. From the theatre came the sounds of a very well-played Chopin prelude, and he imagined the hand of a lovely girl stroking the piano keys and he couldn't take it any more, he put the violin into the open case and went out and, through the curtain, he saw her; she was a girl, she was beyond lovely and he fell head over heels and urgently in love; at that moment he wanted to be the baby grand piano. When the sublime girl had finished and was taking an unbelievably cute bow, Adrià began to applaud frantically and a very impatient hand landed on his shoulder.

'What the hell are you doing here? You are about to go on stage!'

On the way to the dressing room, Master Manlleu cursed my lack of professionalism, which was that of a twelve- or thirteen-year-old boy not terribly excited for his first recital, and look at how we've worked for this, your mother and I; and here you are with your head in the clouds. In such a way that he left me suitably nervous. I greeted Professor Marí, who was already waiting at the stage exit (You see? Now that's a professional), and Professor Marí winked at me and said relax, you do it very well and it'll be even better up there. And that I shouldn't speed up in the introduction: that I was the boss and that she would follow me; don't rush. Like in the last rehearsal. And then Adrià felt Master Manlleu's breath on the back of his neck.

'Breathe. Don't look at the audience. Bow elegantly. Feet slightly apart. Look at the back of the theatre and begin even before Professor Marí is completely prepared. You are the one in charge.'

I had wanted to know who the girl who'd gone on before me was so I could say hi to her or give her a kiss, or hug her and smell her hair; but it seems that those who'd already finished exited on the other side, and I heard them say the young talent Adrià Ardèvol i Bosch with the collaboration of Professor Antònia Marí. So we had to go out on stage and I found that Bernat, who had sworn don't worry, really, Adrià, relax, I won't come, I swear, was in the front row, the big poof, and I thought I could see him trying to hide a mocking smile. He had even brought his parents, the little ... And Mother, accompanied by two men I had never seen before. And Master Manlleu, who joined the group and whispered something into Mother's ear. More than half of the theatre was filled with strangers. And I was overcome with an irrepressible need to piss. I told Professor Marí, into her ear, that I was going to go make a pee pee and she said, don't worry, they won't leave without hearing you.

Adrià Ardèvol didn't head to the bathroom. He went to the dressing room, put the violin in its case and left it there. When he ran towards the exit he found himself before Bernat, who watched him, frightened, and said, where do you think you're going? And he said home. And Bernat but you're crazy. And Adrià said you have to help me. Say that they took me to the hospital or something like that, and he left the Casal del Metge and was greeted by the night-time traffic on the Via Laietana and he noticed he was sweating profusely and then he headed home. And it wasn't until a long hour later that he found out that Bernat had been a good friend because he went back inside and told Mother that I didn't feel well and that they had taken me to the hospital.

'To what hospital, darling?'

'What do I know? Ask the taxi driver.'

And, in the middle of the hallway, Master Manlleu gave contradictory orders, completely losing it because the strangers who were with him could barely stifle their laughter, and Bernat was the crucial obstacle that kept them from seeing me run down the Via Laietana, when they stepped out onto the street.

An hour later they were already home, because Little Lola, the big dummy, sneaked on me when she saw me arriving in a panic and had called the Casal del Metge – because grownups always help each other out – and Mother made me go into the study and had Master Manlleu come in too and closed the door. It was terrible. Mother said what were you thinking. I said I didn't want to try it again. Mother: what were you thinking; Master Manlleu: lifting his arms and saying incredible, incredible. And me: no, I was fed up; that I wanted time to read; and Mother: no, you will study violin and when you are grown up you can decide; and me, well, I've already decided. And Mother: at thirteen you aren't able to decide; and me, indignant: thirteen and a half!; and Master Manlleu lifting his arms and saying incredible, incredible; and Mother, what was I thinking for the second or third time, and adding that with the money I'm spending on these classes and you acting like a ... and Master Manlleu who felt he was being alluded to, pointed out that they weren't actually expensive; and Mother: well, let me tell you, they are expensive, very expensive. And Master Manlleu, well, if they're so expensive then you can work it out with your son; it's not like he's Oistrakh. And my mother replied angrily, don't even start: you said that the boy had talent and that you would make a violinist out of him. Meanwhile I was calming down because they were hitting the ball back and forth between them and I didn't even have to translate the conversation into my French. And Little Lola, the sneaky pettegola, stuck her head in saying there was a very urgent call from the Casal del Metge, and Mother, saying as she left no one move I'll be right back, and Master Manlleu brought his face close to mine and said fucking coward, you had the sonata mastered, and I said I couldn't care less, I don't want to perform in public. And he: and what would Beethoven think about that? And I: Beethoven is dead and won't know. And he: incredulous. And I: poof. And there was a very thick silence the colour of a dirty smudge.

'What did you say?'

Both stock still, facing each other. Then Mother came back. Master Manlleu, his mouth hanging open, was still unable to react. Mother said that I was not allowed out except for going to school and violin class. Go to your room now and we'll discuss whether or not you'll have supper tonight. Go on. Master Manlleu still had his arm raised and his mouth open. Too slow for the rage Mother and I had inside of us.

I closed the door in an act of rebellion and Mother could complain if she wanted to. I opened the box of treasures where – except for Black Eagle and Carson, who roamed free – I kept my secrets. Now I remember there being a double trading card of a Maserati, some gorgeous glass marbles and my angel's medallion when it wasn't around my neck, which was my souvenir of my angel with her red smile saying ciao, Adriano. And Adrià imagined himself replying, ciao, angelo mio.

He arranged to meet him in the dusty rooms where the younger kids did their music theory classes, in the other building. When he went into the dark hallway, the excessive dust on the floor and the stillness muffled the shouts of his classmates running after the ball. Down the hall, in the far classroom, there was a light on.

'Look at him, the artist.'

Father Bartrina was an angular man, so tall and thin that his cassock was inevitably short on him and worn trousers peeked out at the bottom. Since he always had to lean over, it seemed that he was about to pounce on his interlocutor. Actually, he was kindly, and he had accepted that no student would ever be interested in music theory. But since he was the music teacher, he taught music theory and that was that. And the problem was maintaining a certain sense of authority because all of the students, without exception, even if they couldn't hit a note or had no idea how to write fa, would never be left back because of music. So he shrugged at life and just kept on, with that immense scratched blackboard with four red staves on which he wrote the absurd difference between a black (which in chalk was coloured white) and a white (a circle the colour of the blackboard). And he just kept passing every student, year after year.

'Hello.'

'I'm told you play the violin.'

'Yes.'

'And that you refused to go on stage at the Casal del Metge.'

'Yes.'

'Why?'

Adrian explained his theory about the perfection required of an interpreter.

'Forget about perfection. You have trac.'

'What?'

And Father Bartrina explained his theory about interpreters' trac, which he had got from an English music magazine: it was French for stage fright. No. It wasn't the same, I thought. But I had trouble getting him to understand that. It's not that I'm afraid: it's that I don't want to strive for perfection. I don't want to do a job that doesn't allow for error or hesitation.

'Error and hesitation are there, in the interpreter. But he

keeps them in the practice room. When he plays in front of an audience he has already overcome his hesitations. And that's that.'

'You're lying.'

'What?'

'Pardon. I do not agree. I love music too much to make it a slave to a misplaced finger.'

'How old are you?'

'Thirteen and a half.'

'You don't talk like a boy.'

Was he scolding me? I scrutinised his gaze and didn't find the answer.

'How come you never take communion?'

'I'm not baptised.'

'My God.'

'I'm not Catholic.'

'What are you?' Cautiously, as Adrià thought it over. 'Protestant? Jewish?'

'I'm not anything. We aren't anything at home.'

'We'll have to talk about that.'

'My parents were assured by the school that they wouldn't speak to me about those matters.'

'My God.' And to himself: 'I will have to investigate this.'

Then he began again with his accusatory tone: 'I've been told you get A+s in every subject.'

'Sure. There's no merit in that,' I said in my defence.

'Why not?'

'Because it's easy. And I have a good memory.'

'Do you?'

'Yes. I remember everything.'

'Can you play without a score?'

'Of course. If I've read it once.'

'Extraordinary.'

'No. Because I don't have perfect pitch. Plensa does.'

'Who?'

'Plensa in 4C. He plays the violin with me.'

'Plensa? That blond boy, slightly tall?'

'That's the one.'

'And he plays the violin?'

What could that man want. Why was he asking so many questions? What was he getting at? I nodded and thought that perhaps I was putting Bernat in a fix by revealing these secrets.

'And I've been told that you know languages.'

'No.'

'No?'

'Well … French … We study it in class.'

'For the last year; but they say that you already speak it.'

'It's that …' And now what do I tell him?

'And German.'

'Well, I …'

'And English.'

He said it as if rubbing salt in a wound after having caught me in fragranti, and Adrià got defensive. He had to admit that yes, English too.

'And that you taught yourself.'

'No,' I said with relief. 'That's a lie. I take lessons.'

'Well, I was told that …'

'No, it's Italian.' Contrite. 'That I'm teaching myself.'

'That's incredible.'

'No: it's very simple. Romance vocabulary. If you know Catalan, Spanish and French, it's a cinch, I mean it's very easy.'

Father Bartrina looked at me askance, as if trying to gauge whether that lad was pulling his leg. Adrià, to get on his good side: 'I'm sure my Italian pronunciation is bad.'

'Oh, really?'

'Yes. I never know where to put the tonic.'

After an incredibly long minute of silence: 'What do you want to do when you grow up?'

'I don't know. Read. Study. I don't know.'

Silence. Father Bartrina took a few steps towards the balcony. From the inner depths of his cassock he pulled out an immaculate white handkerchief and dried his lips, pensively. The traffic on Llúria Street was intense and, at points, overwhelming. Father Bartrina turned towards the boy, who was still standing in the middle of the room. Perhaps that was when he realised:

'Sit, sit.'

I sat at a desk, not knowing what the man wanted. He approached me and sat at the desk beside mine. He looked me in the eye.

'I play the piano.'

Silence. I had already figured that because in class he played the chords on the piano while we sol-faed drowsily. And that was also how he kept us from lowering our tone when we sang. It seemed he was having difficulties getting the words out. But he finally took the bull by the horns: 'We could rehearse the *Kreutzer* for the end of the school year, for the graduation event. What do you think? At the Palau de la Música! Wouldn't you enjoy playing in the Palau de la Música?'

I was silent. I imagined all the kids calling me a poof and me trying to be perfect up on stage. Utter hell.

'It's what you were supposed to play at the Casal del Metge. You must know it by heart, right?'

For the first time he sketched a smile, intent on inspiring me. Trying to convince me. So I would say yes. I was still silent, because I had come up with a great idea. It occurred to me that, as a musician, he could help me and I said Father Bartrina, do they call you a poof too?

Adrià Ardèvol i Bosch, of class 3A, was expelled for three days for unclear reasons they didn't even want to explain to Mother. The explanation given to his classmates was a sore throat. And to Bernat, well, when I asked him if he was a poof like me, the bloke flew into a rage.

'Are you a poof?'

'What do I know? Esteban says I am because I play the violin. So that means you're one too. And Father Bartrina, if playing the piano counts.'

'And Jascha Heifetz.'

'Yeah. I suppose so. And Pau Casals.'

'Yeah. But no one's said that to me.'

'Because they don't know you play the violin. Bartrina didn't know.'

Before reaching the conservatory, both friends stopped,

oblivious to the rapid traffic on Bruc Street. Bernat came up with an idea: 'Why don't you ask your mother?'

'Why don't you ask yours? Or your father, since you've got a father. Huh?'

'But I'm not the one who got expelled for calling someone a poof.'

'Why don't we ask Trullols?'

That day, Adrià had decided to attend Trullols's class to see if he could infuriate Master Manlleu once and for all. She was pleased to see him, checked his progress and didn't mention the incident at the Casal del Metge, although she'd surely heard about it. They didn't ask Trullols about the mysterious word poof; she complained that they were both out of tune just to annoy her and it wasn't true at all. What happened was that, to top it all off, we heard a younger boy playing before we came in, I think his name was Claret, he was visiting from somewhere, and he played the violin as if he were a man of twenty. And that, far from motivating me, made me feel small.

'Oh, not me. It makes me angry and I practise more.'

'You will be a great violinist, Bernat.'

'As will you.'

The conversations Bernat and I had weren't typical of boys our age. But a violin in your hands has the power to transform you.

That evening, Adrià lied to his mother. He had been expelled for three days because he had laughed at a teacher for not knowing something. Mother, who was thinking about the shop and the angelic machinations of Daniela the angel of my eyes, gave him a very half-hearted, utilitarian lecture. She said that you must know that God has blessed you with unique intelligence. Remember that it is not by your merit but by nature. And Adrià noticed that now that Father had died, Mother spoke of God again even though she jumbled him together with nature. Let see if it turns out God does exist and I'm here in the dark.

'All right, Mother. I won't do it again. Forgive me.'

'No: you have to ask for forgiveness from your teacher.'

'Yes, Mother.'

And she didn't ask who the teacher was, nor what exactly Adrià had said and what the teacher had answered. She was changed beyond all recognition. And as soon as they finished supper, she locked herself in Father's study, where she had some accounting books open on the incunabula table.

As Little Lola cleared the dishes and began to tidy up the kitchen, Adrià dragged his heels while pretending that he wanted to give her a hand, and when he was sure that Mother was good and busy in the study, he went into the kitchen, closed the door partway and, before shyness could make him change his mind, said Little Lola, can you explain why they call me a poof at school?

It took me a long time to fall asleep because the mere possibility of being able to demonstrate Bernat's ignorance –he who was the one who always knew everything that was beyond the realm of our studies – kept me up so late that I even heard the Concepció bells ringing out eleven and the night watchman's truncheon hitting the metal doors of Can Solà and echoing out through the entire neighbourhood, in those days when Franco ruled and the earth again became flat for us, when I was little and hadn't met you yet; in those days when Barcelona, as soon as night fell, was still a city that also went to sleep.

# ET IN ARCADIA EGO

When I was young, I fought to be myself;
now I am resigned to being how I am.

Josep Maria Morreres

# 16

Adrià Ardèvol had matured quite a lot. Time wasn't passing in vain. He now knew what poof meant and he had even discovered the meaning of theodicy. Black Eagle, the Arapaho chief, and valiant Sheriff Carson gathered desert dust on the shelf that held Salgari, Karl May, Zane Grey and Jules Verne. But he hadn't managed to escape his mother's implacable tutelage. My capacity for obedience had made me a technically good, yet soulless, violinist. Like a second-rate Bernat. Even my shameful flight from my first public recital was eventually accepted by Master Manlleu as a sign of my genius nature. Our relationship didn't change, except that, from then on, he considered it his right to insult me when he deemed it necessary. Master Manlleu and I never spoke about music. We only spoke about the violin repertoire, and about names like Wieniaswski, Nardini, Viotti, Ernst, Sarasate, Paganini and, above all, Manlleu, Manlleu and Manlleu, and I felt like saying to him but, sir, when will we play real music? But I knew that it would set off a tempest that could cause me real damage. We only spoke of repertoire, of his repertoire. Of hand position. Of feet position. Of what clothes you have to wear when you practise. And whether the foot position could be the Sarasate-Sauret position, the Wieniaswski-Wilhelmj position, the Ysaÿe-Joachim or, only for the chosen few, the Paganini-Manlleu position. And you have to try the Paganini-Manlleu position because I want you to be a chosen one even though, unfortunately, you were unable to be a child prodigy because I arrived in your life too late.

Resuming lessons with Master Manlleu after Adrià's escape from the recital, with a substantial raise from Mrs Ardèvol, had been extremely difficult because at first they were silent classes,

designed to show the offended silence of the genius who strove
to convert a boy confused by weak character into a semi-genius.
Gradually, the indications and the corrections led him back to
his usual loquacity until one day he said bring your Storioni.

'Why, sir?'

'I want to play it.'

'I have to ask my mother for permission.' Adrià had learned
the rules of prudence after so many disasters.

'She will let you if you tell her that it is my express wish.'

Mother said you're crazy, what are you thinking; take your
Parramon and get going. And Adrià insisted long enough
that she said no means no. That was when he let out that it
was Master Manlleu's express wish.

'You should have said that to begin with,' she said, serious.
Very serious, because mother and son had been at war for a
few years and any excuse was a good one, to the point that
one day Adrià said when I turn eighteen I'm going to leave
home. And she answered: with what money? And he: with my
hands; with my inheritance from Father; I don't know. And
she: well, you'd better find out before you leave.

And the next Friday I showed up with the Storioni. More
than playing it, the master wanted to compare it. He played
Wieniawski's tarantella with my Storioni; it sounded amazing.
And then, with his eyes gleaming, looking for my reaction, he
revealed a secret to me: a 1702 Guarnerius that had belonged
to Felix Mendelssohn. And he played the same tarantella,
which sounded amazing. With a triumphant look on his face
he told me that his Guarnerius sounded ten times better than
my Storioni. And he gave it back to me smugly.

'Master Manlleu, I don't want to be a violinist.'

'You keep quiet and practise.'

'No.'

'What will your adversaries say?'

'I have no adversaries.'

'Son,' he said, sitting in the listening chair. 'Everyone who
is studying violin at a level above you is your adversary. And
they will look for a way to sink you.'

And we went back to the vibrato, vibrato trill, and the hunt for harmonics, martelé and tremolo … and I was sadder with each passing day.

'Mother, I don't want to be a violinist.'

'Son: you are a violinist.'

'I want to give it up.'

Her response was to set up a recital for me in Paris. So I would realise what a spectacular life awaits you as a violinist, Son.

'At eight years old,' reflected Master Manlleu, 'I did my first recital. You've had to wait until seventeen. You'll never be able to catch up to me. But you must try to approach my greatness. And I'll help you to overcome the trac.'

'I don't want to be a violinist. I want to read. And I don't have trac.'

'Bernat, I don't want to be a violinist.'

'Don't say that, you'll make me angry. You play great and with seeming effortlessness. It's just trac.'

'I have no problem with playing the violin, but I don't want to be a violinist. I don't want to. And I don't have trac.'

'Whatever you do, don't give up your lessons.'

It wasn't that Bernat was interested in my mental health or my future. It was that Bernat was still following along with my lessons from Manlleu, second-hand. And he was making progress in his technique and, since he didn't have to deal with Manlleu, he didn't get bored of it or tire of the instrument or get heartburn. And meanwhile he was studying with Massià, who had been highly recommended by Trullols.

Many years later, as he faced the firing squad, Adrià Ardèvol was to realise that his aversion to a career as a soloist had sprung up as the only way to fight against his mother and Master Manlleu. And, when his voice was already beginning to crack because he couldn't control it, he said Master Manlleu, I want to play music.

'What?'

'I want to play Brahms, Bartók, Schumann. I hate Sarasate.'

Master Manlleu was silent for a few weeks, teaching lessons with mere gestures, until one Friday he put a stack of scores, a good six inches high, on top of the piano and said come now, let's return to the repertoire. It was the only time in his life that Master Manlleu acknowledged that Adrià was right. His father had done it only once, but he'd admitted it. Master Manlleu only said come now, let's return to the repertoire. And in revenge for having to acknowledge that I was right he wiped the dandruff off his dark trousers and said on the twentieth of next month, in the Debussy theatre in Paris. The *Kreutzer*, the César Franck, Brahms's third and just a brilliant performance of some Wieniaswski and Paganini for the encores. Happy now?

The spectre of my trac, because I had massive trac, skilfully disguised by the charming theory that my love for music kept me from etcetera. The spectre of my trac reappeared and Adrià began to sweat.

'Who will play the piano?'

'Some accompanist. I'll find one for you.'

'No. Someone who ... The piano won't accompany me: it should do what I do.'

'Nonsense: you are the leader. Yes or no? I will find an acceptable pianist for you. Three rehearsals. And now let's read. We'll begin with Brahms.'

And Adrià started to feel that perhaps knowing how to play the violin was a way to figure out life, figure out the mysteries of loneliness, the growing evidence that his desires never match up to his reality, his yearning to discover what he had made happen to his father.

The acceptable pianist was Master Castells, a good pianist, timid, able to hide beneath the keys at Master Manlleu's slightest bidding. Adrià realised very quickly that he formed part of the vast economic network of Mrs Ardèvol, who was shelling out a fortune for her son to play in Paris, in one of Pleyel's chamber halls with a seating capacity for one hundred, of which about forty were filled. The musicians travelled alone, to concentrate on their work. Mr Castells and Adrià, in third class. Master Manlleu, in first so he could focus on his multiple roles. The musicians fought insomnia by reading the concerto and Adrià was amused to see Master Castells singing and marking his entrance and he pretended to be playing and singing softly, humouring him; it was a brilliant system to get their entrances properly in sync. That was when the steward had to come in to make the beds and he turned right around thinking that it was a compartment filled with lunatics. When they had passed Lyon, after night-fall, Master Castells confessed that Master Manlleu had him under his thumb and he wanted to ask Adrià for a favour, could he ask Master Manlleu to let them take a walk alone before the concert because … I have to see my sister and Master Manlleu doesn't want us mixing work and pleasure, you know?

Paris was a contrivance designed by my mother to make me decide to continue studying the violin. But she didn't know that it would change my life. That was where I met you. Thanks to her contrivance. But it wasn't in the music hall, but before, during the semi-clandestine side trip I made with Mr Castells. To the Café Condé. He had to meet his sister there, and she brought a niece with her, who was you.

'Saga Voltes-Epstein.'

'Adrià Ardèvol-Bosch.'

'I draw.'

'I read.'

'Aren't you a violinist?'

'No.'

You laughed and the sky entered the Condé. Your aunt and uncle chattered, absorbed in their things, and they didn't notice.

'Don't come to the concert, please,' I implored. And for the first time I was honest and I said in a lower voice, I'm scared to death. And what I liked best about you was that you didn't come to the concert. That won me over. I don't think I ever told you that.

The concert went well. Adrià played normally, not nervous, knowing that he would never see the people in the audience again in his life. And Master Castells turned out to be an ex-cellent partner because on the couple of occasions when I hesitated he covered me very delicately. And Adrià thought that perhaps with him as a teacher he could make music.

We met thirty or forty years ago, Sara and I. The light of my life, and the person I weep most bitterly for. A girl with dark hair pulled back into two plaits, who spoke Catalan with a French accent she never lost, as if she were from the Roussillon. Sara Voltes-Epstein, who came into my life sporadically and whom I've always missed. The twentieth of September of the early nineteen-sixties. And after that brief encounter at the Café Condé we didn't see each other again for two years, and the next time was also random. And at a concert.

*Then Xènia stood before him and said, I'd love to.*

*Bernat looked into her dark eyes that matched the night. Xènia. He replied all right then, come up to my house. We can talk as long as we want. Xènia.*

*It had been a few months since Bernat and Tecla had parted ways in a meticulous and gruelling effort on both sides to ensure that it was a noisy, traumatic, useless, painful, angry break-up filled with petty details, particularly on her side, I don't understand how I ever was interested in a woman like that. Much less share my life with her, it's astounding. And Tecla explained that their last few months of living together were hell because Bernat spent all day looking in the mirror, no, no, you have to understand: he only cared about himself, as always; only his things were important at home; he was only worried about whether a concert went well, that the critics were more and more mediocre each day, how could they not mention our sublime interpretation; and whether the violin was tucked away in the safe or whether we should replace the safe because the violin is the most important thing in this house, you hear me Tecla?, and if you don't get that into your head, we'll regret it; and, above all, what hurt me was his absolute tactlessness and lack of love for Llorenç. I couldn't get past that. That was when I started to put my foot down. Until the blow-up and the sentencing a few months ago. He's a terrible egomaniac who thinks he's a great artist and he's just a good-for-nothing idiot who, in addition to playing the violin, is constantly playing on my nerves because he thinks he's the greatest writer in the world and he'll say here, read it and tell me what you think. And poor me if I give him a single but, because then he'll spend days trying to convince me that I was completely wrong and that he was the only one who knew anything about it.*

'I didn't know he wrote.'

'No one knows: not even his editor, really. He writes boring, pretentious crap … anyway. I still don't understand how I *could have ever been interested in a man like that. Much less spend my life with him!'*

'And why did you give up the piano?'

'I gave it up without realising I was. Partly ...'

'Bernat continued with the violin.'

'I gave up the piano because the priority in our house was Bernat's career, you understand? This was many years ago. Before Llorenç.'

'Typical.'

'Don't get all feminist on me: I'm telling you this as a friend; don't get me worked up, all right?'

'But do you really think that separating ... at our age?'

'So what? If you're too young, because you're too young. If you're old, because you're old. And we're not that old. I've got my whole life ahead of me. Well, I've got half my life ahead of me, all right?'

'You're very nervous.'

It was understandable: among other things, in that well-planned break-up process, Bernat had tried to get her to be the one to move out. Her reply was to grab his violin and throw it out the window. Four hours later she received word of her husband reporting her for serious damage to his assets and she had to go running to her lawyer, who had scolded her as if she were a little girl and warned her don't play around like that, Mrs Plensa, it's serious: if you want, I can handle the case; but you'll have to do what I tell you to.

'If I ever see that ruddy violin again, I'll throw it right out the window, just like I did before, I don't care if I end up in prison.'

'That's no way to talk. Do you want me to handle the case?'

'Of course: that's why I've come here.'

'Well, I have to say that it'd be better to fight, to hate each other and throw dishes. Dishes: not the violin. That was a serious mistake.'

'I wanted to hurt him.'

'And you did; but you chose an idiotic way to do it, excuse my frankness.'

And he explained their strategy.

'And now I'm telling you my problems because you're my best friend.'

'Don't worry, go ahead and cry, Tecla. It'll do you good. I do it all the time.'

'The judge was a woman and she ruled in her favour on everything. See how unjust justice can be. All she did was give her a fine for destroying the violin. A fine she hasn't paid and never will. Four months in Bagué's clinic and I still don't think it sounds the same.'

'Is it a good instrument?'

'Very good. A mirecourt from the late nineteenth century. A Thouvenel.'

'Why don't you insist she pays the fine?'

'I don't want to have anything more to do with Tecla. I hate her from the bottom of my heart. She's even prejudiced me against my son. And that is almost as unforgivable as destroying the violin.'

Silence.

'I meant the other way around.'

'I knew what you meant.'

Every once in a while, large cities have narrow streets, silent passageways that allow your footsteps to echo in the stillness of the night, and it seems like everything is going back to the way it was, when there were only a few of us and we all knew each other and greeted each other on the street. In the period when Barcelona, at night, also went to bed. Bernat and Xènia walked along the lonely Permanyer Alley, the child of another world, and for a few minutes all they heard were their own footsteps. Xènia wore heels. Dressed to the nines. She was dressed to the nines even though it was almost an improvised meeting. And her heels echoed in the night of her dark eyes; she's simply lovely.

'I feel your pain,' said Xènia when they got to Llúria and were greeted by the honk of a noisy taxi in a hurry. 'But you have to get it out of your head. It's better if you don't talk about it.'

'You were the one who asked me.'

'If only I'd known ...'

As Bernat opened the door to his flat he said right back where I started from, and then explained that he had grown up in the Born district and now, coincidentally, after his separation, he had moved back. And I like being back here because I have memories around every corner. You want whisky or something like that?

'I don't drink.'

'Neither do I. But I have some for guests.'

'I'll have some water.'

'The bitch didn't even give me the option of staying in my own home. I had to pull myself up by my bootstraps.' He opened his arms as if he wanted to show her the whole flat in one swoop. 'But I'm glad to be back in my old neighbourhood. This way.'

He pointed towards where she should go. He went ahead to turn on the light in the room. 'I think that people make a journey and then come back to where they started from. We always return to our roots. Unless we die first.'

It was a large room, surely meant to be a dining room. There was a sofa and an armchair in front of a small round table, two music stands with scores on them, a cabinet with three instruments and a table with a computer and a large pile of papers beside it. The opposite wall was covered with books and scores. As if they summed up Bernat's life.

Xènia opened her purse, pulled out the tape recorder and placed it in front of Bernat.

'You see? I've haven't got it all fixed up yet, but this is meant to be a living room.'

'It's quite comfortable.'

'Tecla, that bitch, didn't even let me take a stick of furniture. It's all from Ikea. At my age and shopping at Ikea. Hell's bells, are you recording?'

Xènia turned off the tape recorder. In a tone he hadn't heard the whole evening: 'Do you want to talk about your bitch of a wife or about your books? So I know whether to turn the tape recorder on or not.'

The silence was so deep they could have heard their own footsteps. But they weren't walking along a deserted narrow street. Bernat could make out his own heartbeat and he felt incredibly ridiculous. He waited for the sound of a motorbike going up Llúria to pass.

'Touché.'

'I don't speak French.'

Bernat vanished, embarrassed. He returned with a bottle of some water she'd never seen before. And two Ikea glasses.

'Water from the clouds of Tasmania. You'll like it.'

They spent half an hour talking about his short stories and his writing process. And that the third and fourth collections were the best. Novel? No, no: I like the short form. As he calmed down, he mentioned that he was embarrassed about the scene he'd made talking about his bitch of an ex-wife, but that it was still all going through his head and he couldn't believe that even after he'd paid a fortune to the lawyer they'd sided with Tecla on almost everything, and I'm still shaken up about it and I'm really sorry to have told you all that, but as you can see writers – all artists – are people too.

'I never doubted that.'

'Touché pour la seconde fois.'

'I told you I don't speak French. Can you tell me about your creative process?'

They spoke for a long time. Bernat explained how he started, many, many years ago, to write, in no particular rush. I take a long time to finish a book. Plasma took a good three years.

'Wow!'

'Yes. It wrote itself. How can I explain it …'

Silence. A couple of hours had passed and they'd finished off the Tasmanian cloud water. Xènia listened, rapt. The occasional car still went up Llúria. The place was comfortable; for the first time in many months, Bernat was comfortable at home, with someone who listened to him and didn't criticise him the way poor Adrià had always done.

Suddenly, he was overcome by the fatigue that followed the tension of so many hours of conversation. The years take their toll.

Xènia settled back in the Ikea armchair. She extended her hand as if she wanted to turn off the tape recorder, but she stopped halfway.

'Now I'd like to discuss … your double personality, as a musician and a writer.'

'Aren't you tired?'

'Yes. But this is something I've been wanting to do for some time, an interview so ... like this.'

'Thank you so much. But we can leave it for tomorrow. I'm ...'

He knew that he was spoiling the magic of the moment but there was nothing he could do about it. For a few minutes they were seated in silence, as she put away her things and both of them calculating whether it was a good moment to continue or if it was best to be prudent, until Bernat said I'm very sorry that I only offered you water.

'It was excellent.'

What I'd like to do is take you to bed.

'Should we meet tomorrow?'

'Tomorrow's not good for me. The day after.'

To the bedroom, right now.

'Very well. Come here, if that works for you.'

'All right.'

'And we'll talk about whatever.'

'Whatever.'

They grew silent. She smiled and he smiled back.

'Wait, I'll call you a cab.'

They were so close. Looking at each other, in silence, she with the serene night in her gaze. He, with the vague greyness of unconfessable secrets in his eyes. But despite everything, she left in the ruddy blooming taxi that always had to spoil everything. Before, Xènia had given him a furtive kiss on the cheek, near his lips. She'd had to stand on tiptoe to reach. She's so cute on tiptoes. Downstairs on the street he watched the taxi take Xènia out of his life, even just for a couple of days. He smiled. It had been two long years since he'd last smiled.

The second meeting was easier. Xènia took off her coat without asking permission, she put her recording devices down on the little table and patiently waited for Bernat, who had gone to the other end of the flat with his mobile, to finish an endless argument with someone who was probably his lawyer. He spoke in a low voice and with a kind of stifled rage.

*Xènia looked at some book spines. In one corner were the five books that Bernat Plensa had published; she hadn't read the first two. She pulled out the oldest one. On the first page was a dedication to my muse, my beloved Tecla, who was so supportive to me in the creation of these stories, Barcelona, 12 February 1977. Xènia couldn't help but smile. She put the book back in its place, beside its companions in the complete works of Bernat Plensa. On the desk, the computer was sleeping with the screen dark. She moved the mouse and the screen lit up. There was a text. A seventy-page document. Bernat Plensa was writing a novel and he had said no, no novels. She looked towards the hallway. She could hear Bernat's voice at the far end, still speaking softly. She sat in front of the computer and read* After buying the tickets, Bernat put them in his pocket. He gazed at the sign announcing the concert. The young man beside him, wearing a hat that hid his face and wrapped in a scarf, tapped his feet on the ground to ward off the cold, very interested in that night's programme. Another man, who was fat and stuffed into a slender coat, was trying to return his tickets because of some problem. They took a walk along Sant Pere Més Alt and they missed it. When they were back in front of the Palau de la Música, it was all over. The sign that read Prokofiev's Concerto for Violin and Orchestra No. 2 in G-Minor performed by Jascha Heifetz and the Barcelona Symphony Orchestra directed by Eduard Toldrà had an aggressive JEWS RAUS scrawled on it in tar and a swastika that dripped from each arm, and the atmosphere had become darker, people avoided eye contact and the earth had become even flatter. Then they told me that it had been a Falangist gang and that the couple of policemen who'd been sent from the headquarters on Via Laietana, right around the corner, had coincidentally been away from their post in front of the Palau having a coffee break and Adrià was overcome with an irrepressible desire to go live in Europe, further north, where they say people are clean and cultured and free, and lively and happy and have parents who love you and don't die because of something you did. What a crap country we were born into, he said looking at the smear that dripped hatred. Then the policemen arrived and said, all right, move it along, not in groups, come on, on your way, and Adrià and Bernat, like the rest of the onlookers, disappeared because you never know.

The auditorium of the Palau de la Música was full, but the silent was thick. We had trouble getting to our two empty seats, in the stalls, almost in the middle.

'Hello.'

'Hello,' said Adrià, timidly as he sat beside the lovely girl who smiled at him.

'Adrià? Adrià Ican'trememberwhat?'

Then I recognised you. You didn't have plaits in your hair and you looked like a real woman.

'Sara Voltes-Epstein! ...' I said, astonished. 'Are you here?'

'What does it look like?'

'No, I mean ...'

'Yes,' she said laughing and putting her hand over mine casually, setting off a fatal electric shock. 'I live in Barcelona now.'

'Well, how about that,' I said, looking from side to side. 'This is my friend Bernat. Sara.'

Bernat and Sara nodded politely to each other.

'How awful, eh, the thing with the sign ...' said Adrià, with his extraordinary ability to stick his foot in it. Sara made a vague expression and started looking at the programme. Without taking her eyes off of it, 'How did your concert go?'

'The one in Paris?' A bit embarrassed. 'Fine. Normal.'

'Do you still read?'

'Yes. And you, do you still draw?'

'Yes. I'm having an exhibition.'

'Where?'

'In the parish of ...' She smiled. 'No, no. I don't want you to come.'

I don't know if she meant it or if it was a joke. Adrià was so stiff that he didn't dare to look her in the eye. He just smiled timidly. The lights began to dim, the audience started to applaud and Master Toldrà came out on the stage *and Bernat's footsteps were heard coming from the other end of the flat. Then Xènia put the computer to sleep and stood up from the chair. She pretending she'd been reading book spines and when Bernat entered the study she made a bored face.*

*'Forgive me,' he said, brandishing the mobile.*

*'More problems?'*

*He furrowed his brow. It was clear he didn't want to talk about it. Or that he had learned he shouldn't discuss it with Xènia. They sat down and, for a few seconds, the silence was quite uncomfortable; perhaps that was why they both smiled without looking at each other.*

*'And how does it feel to be a musician writing literature?' asked Xènia, putting the tiny recorder in front of her on the small round table.*

*He looked at her without seeing her, thinking of the furtive kiss of the other night, so close to his lips.*

*'I don't know. It all happened gradually, inevitably.'*

*That was a real whopper. It all happened so bloody slowly, so gratuitously and capriciously and, yet, his anxiety did arrive all at once, because Bernat had been writing for years and for years Adrià had been telling him that what he wrote was completely uninteresting, it was grey, predictable, dispensable; definitely not an essential text. And if you don't like what I'm saying, stop asking me for my opinion.*

*'And that's it?' said Xènia, a bit peeved. 'It all happened gradually, inevitably? And full stop? Should I turn off the tape recorder?'*

*'Excuse me?'*

*'Where are you?'*

*'Here, with you.'*

*'No.'*

*'Well, it's post-concert trauma.'*

*'What's that?'*

*'I'm more than sixty years old, I am a professional violinist, I know that I do fine but playing with the orchestra doesn't do it for me. What I wanted was to be a writer, you understand?'*

*'You already are.'*

*'Not the way I wanted to be.'*

*'Are you writing something now?'*

*'No.'*

'No?'

'No. Why?'

'No reason. What do you mean by not the way you wanted to be?'

'That I'd like to captivate, enthral.'

'But with the violin ...'

'There are fifty of us playing. I'm not a soloist.'

'But sometimes you play chamber music.'

'Sometimes.'

'And why aren't you a soloist?'

'Not everyone who wants to be one can be. I don't have the skill or temperament for it. A writer is a soloist.'

'Is it an ego problem?'

Bernat Plensa picked up Xènia's recording device, examined it, found the button and turned it off. He placed it back down on the table while he said I am the epitome of mediocrity.

'You don't believe what that imbecile from

'That imbecile and all the others who've been kind enough to tell me that in the press.'

'You know that critics are just ...'

'Just what?'

'Big poofs.'

'I'm being serious.'

'Now I understand your hysterical side.'

'Wow: you don't pull your punches.'

'You want to be perfect. And since you can't ... you get cranky; or you demand that those around you be perfect.'

'Do you work for Tecla?'

'Tecla is a forbidden subject.'

'What's got into you?'

'I'm trying to get a reaction out of you,' replied Xènia. 'Because you have to answer my question.'

'What question?'

Bernat watched as Xènia turned on the recorder again and placed it gently on the little table.

'How does it feel to be a musician writing literature?' she repeated.

'I don't know. It all happens gradually. Inevitably.'

'You already said that.'

It's just that it happens so bloody slowly and yet his anxiety arrives all at once because Bernat had been writing for so many years and Adrià had been saying for so many years that what he wrote was of no interest, it was grey, predictable, unessential; it was definitely Adrià's fault.

'I am about to break off all ties with you. I don't like unbearable people. That's your first and last warning.'

For the first time since he had met her, he looked into her eyes and held Xènia's black gaze of serene night.

'I can't bear being unbearable. Forgive me.'

'Can we get back to work?'

'Go ahead. And thanks for the warning.'

'First and last.'

I love you, he thought. So he had to be perfect if he wanted to have those lovely eyes with him for a few more hours. I love you, he repeated.

'How does it feel to be a musician making literature?'

I am falling in love with your obstinacy.

'It feels ... I feel ... in two worlds ... and it bothers me that I don't know which is more important to me.'

'Does that matter?'

'I don't know. The thing is ...'

That evening they didn't call a cab. But two days later Bernat Plensa screwed up his courage and went to visit his friend. Caterina, with her coat already on and about to leave, opened the door for him and, before he could open his mouth, said in a low voice he's not well.

'Why?'

'I had to hide yesterday's newspaper from him.'

'Why?'

'Because if I don't notice, he reads the same paper three times.'

'Boy ...'

'He's such a hard worker, I hate to see him wasting his time rereading the newspaper, you know?'

'You did the right thing.'

'What are you two conspiring about?'

They turned. Adrià had just come out of his study and caught them speaking in low voices.

'Rrrrriiiiiiinnnnnnnnnnngggg.'

Caterina opened the door for Plàcida instead of answering, while Adrià had Bernat enter his study. The two women discussed their shift switch quietly and Caterina said loudly see you tomorrow, Adrià!

'How's it going?' asked Adrià.

'I've been typing it up when I have a moment. Slowly.'

'Do you understand everything?'

'Yeah,' he answered falteringly. 'I like it a lot.'

'Why do you say yeah like that?'

'Because you have the handwriting of a doctor, and it's tiny. I have to read every paragraph a couple of times to get it right.'

'Oh. Sorry …'

'No, no, no … I'm happy to do it. But I don't work on it every day, obviously.'

'I'm making a lot of work for you, aren't I?'

'No. Not at all.'

'Good evening, Adrià,' said a young woman, a smiling stranger, sticking her head into the study.

'Hello, good evening.'

'Who's that?' Bernat asked in a surprised whisper when the woman had left the study.

'Whatshername. Now they don't leave me alone for a second.'

'Whoa.'

'Yeah, you have no idea. This place is like the Ramblas with all the coming and going.'

'It's better that you're not alone, right?'

'Yes. And thank goodness for Little Lola, she takes care of organising everything.'

'Caterina.'

'What?'

'No, nothing.'

They were silent for a little while. Then Bernat asked him about what he was studying and he looked around him, touched the book on his reading table and made a vague expression that Bernat was unable to interpret. He got up and grabbed the book.

'Hey, poetry!'

'Huh?'

Bernat waved the book. 'You're reading poetry.'

'I always have.'

'Really? Not me.'

'And look how things turned out for you.'

Bernat laughed because it was impossible to get angry at Adrià now that he was ill. And then he repeated I can't do any more, I can't go any faster with your papers.

'Fine …'

'Do you want me to hire someone?'

'No!' Now the life came back into his appearance, his face and the colour of his hair. 'Definitely not! This can only be done by a friend. And I don't want …. I don't know … It's very personal and … Maybe once it's typed up I won't want it published.'

'Didn't you say I should give it to Bauça?'

'When the time comes, we'll discuss it.'

Silence came over the room. Someone was going through doors or making noise with something in some part of the house. Perhaps in the kitchen.

'Plàcida, that's it! Her name is Plàcida, this one.' Pleased with himself. 'You see? Despite what they say, I still have a good memory.'

'Ah!' said Bernat, remembering something. 'The backside of your manuscript pages, what you wrote in black ink, you know?, it's really interesting too.'

For a moment, Adrià hesitated.

'What is it?' he said, a bit frightened.

'A reflection on evil. Well: a study of the history of evil, I'd say. You called it 'The Problem of Evil'.'

'Oh, no. I'd forgotten. No: that's very … I don't know: soulless.'

'No. I think you should publish it too. If you want, I can type it up as well.'

'Poor thing. That's my failure as a thinker.' He was quiet for a few very long seconds. 'I didn't know how to say even half of what I had in my head.'

*He grabbed the volume of poems. He opened and closed it, uncomfortable. He put it back down on the table and finally said that's why I wrote on the other side, to kill it.*

*'Why didn't you throw it away?'*

*'I never throw away any papers.'*

*And a slow silence, as long as a Sunday afternoon, hovered over the study and the two friends. A silence almost devoid of meaning.*

## 17

Finishing secondary school was a relief. Bernat had already graduated the year before and he'd thrown his heart and soul into playing the violin while half-heartedly studying Liberal Arts. Adrià entered university thinking that everything would be easier from that point on. But he found many cracks and prickly bushes. And even just the low level of the students, who were frightened by Virgil and panicked over Ovid. And the policemen in the assembly rooms. And the revolution in the classrooms. For a while I was friends with a guy named Gensana who was very interested in literature but when he asked me what I wanted to devote myself to and I answered to the history of ideas and culture, he dropped his jaw in shock.

'Come on, Ardèvol, nobody says they want to be an historian of ideas.'

'I do.'

'You're the first I've ever heard. Jesus. The history of ideas and culture.' He looked at me suspiciously. 'You're having a laugh, right?'

'No: I want to know everything. What is known now and what was known before. And why it's known and why it's not yet known. Do you understand?'

'No.'

'And what do you want to be?'

'I don't know,' replied Gensana. He fluttered his hand vaguely over his forehead. 'I'm all batty. But I'll figure out something to do, you'll see.'

Three pretty laughing girls passed by them on the way to Greek class. Adrià looked at his watch and waved goodbye to Gensana, who was still trying to digest the bit about being an historian of ideas and culture. I followed the pretty laughing girls. Before entering the classroom I turned around. Gensana was still pondering Ardèvol's future. And a few months later, during a very cold autumn, Bernat, who was in his eighth year of violin, asked me to go with him to the Palau de la Música to hear Jascha Heifetz. Which was a one-of-a-kind opportunity and Master Massià had explained that despite Heifetz's reluctance to play in a fascist country, Master Toldrà's had finally managed to convince him. Adrià, who in most arenas had yet to lose his virginity, discussed it with Master Manlleu at the end of an exhausting lesson devoted to unison. After some seconds of reflection, Manlleu said that he had never known a colder, more arrogant, abominable, stupid, stuck-up, repulsive, detestable and haughty violinist than Jascha Heifetz.

'But does he play well, sir?'

Master Manlleu was looking at the score without seeing it. Violin in hand, he played an involuntary pizzicato and kept his eyes fixed straight ahead. After a very long pause: 'He plays to perfection.'

Perhaps he realised that what he'd said had come from too deep inside and wanted to temper it, 'Besides me, he is the best violinist alive.' Tap of the bow on the music stand. 'Come now, let's get back to it.'

Applause filled the hall. And it was warmer than usual, which was very noticeable because, in a dictatorship, people get used to saying things between the lines and between the applause, with indirect gestures, glancing at the man in the mackintosh with the pencil moustache who was most likely a secret agent, careful, look how he's barely clapping. And people had grown accustomed to understanding that language which, from fear, strove to fight against fear. I only sensed that, because I had no father, and Mother was absorbed by the shop and only turned her loupe on my violin progress, and Little Lola didn't want to talk about such things because during the war they had killed an anarchist cousin of hers and she refused to get into the thorny territory of street politics. They began to dim the lights, people clapped and Master Toldrà came out on stage and leisurely walked over to his music stand. In the penumbra, I saw Sara writing something in her programme and passing it to me and asking for my programme so she wouldn't be left without one. Some digits. A telephone number! I handed her mine, like an idiot, without jotting down my own phone number. The applause ended. I noticed that Bernat, wordless, in the seat to my other side, was observing my every move. Silence fell over the hall.

Toldrà played a *Coriolano* that I'd never heard before and really enjoyed. Then, when he came back out on stage, he brought Jascha Heifetz by the hand, probably to show his support or something like that. Heifetz made a cold, arrogant, abominable, stupid, stuck-up, repulsive, detestable and haughty nod of his head. He didn't have any interest in concealing his irritated, severe expression. He gave himself three long minutes to shake off his indignation while Master Toldrà stood, looking to either side, patiently waiting for the other man to say let's begin. And they began. I remember that my mouth hung open throughout the entire concert. And that I cried without the slightest embarrassment during the andante assai, compelled by the physical pleasure of the binary rhythm of the violin set on top of the triplets of the orchestral backdrop. And how the piece was left in the hands of the orchestra and, at the end, the horn and a humble pizzicato. True beauty. And Heifetz was a warm, humble, kind man devoted to the service of the beauty that captivated me. And Adrià thought he saw Heifetz's eyes gleaming suspiciously. Bernat, I know, held back a deep sob. And at intermission he rose and said I have to go meet him.

'They won't let you backstage.'

'I'm going to try.'

'Wait,' she said.

Sara got up and gestured for them to follow her. Bernat and I looked at each other quizzically. We went up the small stairs on the side and through a door. The guard inside gave us the sign for vade retro, but Sara, with a smile, pointed to Master Toldrà, who was talking to one of the musicians, and he, as if he had caught Sara's gesture, turned, saw us and said hello, princess, how are you? How's your mother?

And he came over to give her a kiss. He didn't even see

us. Master Toldrà explained that Heifetz was deeply offended by the graffiti that it seems was everywhere around the Palau and that he was cancelling his performance tomorrow and leaving the country. It's not the best moment to bother him, you understand?

When the concert was over and we were out on the street, we saw that it was true, that the tarred graffiti on the sign and on the walls, all over, suggested, in Spanish, that the Jews leave.

'If I were him, I would have done the concert tomorrow,' said Adrià, future historian of ideas, without knowing anything about the history of humanity. Sara whispered in his ear that she was in a rush and she also said call me, and Adrià barely reacted because his head was still filled with Heifetz and all he said was yes, yes, and thanks.

'I'm giving up the violin,' I said before the profaned sign, before an incredulous Bernat and before myself. All my life I've remembered myself saying I'm giving up the violin, at the exit, before the profaned sign before an incredulous Bernat and before myself, all my life I've remembered myself saying I'm giving up the violin.

'But ... but ...' Bernat pointed to the Palau as if he wanted to say what better argument cou

'I'm giving up the violin. I'll never be able to play like that.'

'Practise.'

'Bullshit. I'm giving it up. It's impossible. I'll finish seventh, take the exam and that's it. Enough. Assez. Schluss. Basta.'

'Who was that girl?'

'Which one?'

'That one!' He pointed at Sara's aura, which still lingered. 'The one who led us to Master Toldrà like Ariadna, that one! The one who said Adrià Ican'tememberwhat, my pet. The one who said call me ...'

Adrià looked at his friend with his mouth hanging open.

'What have I done to you this time?'

'What have you done to me? You're threatening to give up the violin.'

'Yes. It's final. But I'm not giving you up: I'm giving up the violin.'

When Heifetz finished the Prokofiev concert, he was transformed, to the point that he seemed taller and more powerful. And he played, I would almost say arrogantly, three Jewish dances and then I found him even taller and with an even more powerful aura. Then he gathered himself and gave us the gift of the Ciaccona of the Partita for Violin No. 2, which, apart from our attempts, I had only heard on a shellac 78 played by Ysaÿe. They were minutes of perfection. I have been to many concerts. But for me this was the foundation, the concert that opened up the path to beauty for me, the concert that closed the door to the violin for me, the concert that put an end to my brief career as a musician.

'You're a lousy bum,' was Bernat's opinion, who saw that he would have to face his eighth year all on his own, without my presence one year behind him. All alone with Master Massià. 'A lousy stinking bum.'

'Not if I learn how to be happy. I've seen the light: no more suffering and I'll enjoy music played by those who know how.'

'A lousy bum, and a coward to boot.'

'Yes. Probably. Now I can devote myself to my studies without added pressures.'

Right there in the street, as we walked home, the pedestrians caught in the cold wind coming down Jonqueres Street were witnesses to one of the three times I've seen my friend Bernat explode. It was terrible. He began to shout and to say German, English, Catalan, Spanish, French, Italian, Greek, Latin, counting on his fingers. You're nineteen and you can read one, two, three, four, five, six, seven, eight languages, and you're afraid of eighth-year violin, idiot? If I had your brain, for fuck's sake!

Then silent snowflakes started to fall. I had never seen it snow in Barcelona; I had never seen Bernat so indignant. I had never seen Bernat so helpless. I don't know if it was snowing for him or for me.

'Look,' I said.

'I don't give a shit about the snow. You're making a mistake.'

'You're afraid to face up to Massià without me.'

'Yeah, so?'

'You have what it takes to be a violinist. I don't.'

Bernat lowered his voice and said don't think that, I'm always at my limit. I smile when I play, but not because I'm happy. It's to ward off panic. But the violin is as treacherous as the horn: you can play a false note at any moment. Even still, I don't give up like you, like a little shit. I want to get to tenth and then I'll see whether I go on or not. Give it up after tenth.

'There will come a day when you'll smile with pleasure while you play the violin, Bernat.'

I realised I came off sounding like Jesus Christ with that prophecy, and if we examine how things turned out ... well, look, I don't know what to say.

'Give it up after tenth.'

'No. After the exams in June. For appearances. Because if you really make me angry, I'll stop right now and fuck appearances.'

And the snow continued to fall. We walked to my house in silence. He left me in front of the dark wooden door without even a good night or any slight gesture of affection.

I've fought with Bernat a few times in my life. This was the first serious fight, the first one that left scars. Christmas break that year took place in an unusually snowy landscape. At home, Mother was silent, Little Lola attentive to everything, and I was spending more and more hours in Father's study each day. I had earned the right to with the outstanding honours I'd received at the end of term, and the space drew me irresistibly further and further in. The day after Boxing Day I went for a walk along the white streets and I saw Bernat, who was living at the top of Bruc Street, skiing down Bruc with his violin on his back. He saw me but said nothing. I confess that I was overcome with jealousy because I immediately thought whose house is he going to go play at, the bastard, without saying anything to me. Nineteen- or twenty-year-old Adrià, in the throes of a fit of jealousy, started to chase after him, but he couldn't catch up to the skis and soon Bernat was just a tiny crèche figure, probably already at the Gran Via. How ridiculous, panting, exhaling through his scarf, watching his friend leave. I never found out where he went that day and I would give … I was about to say I would give half my life, but today that expression makes no sense. But what the hell, still today I would give half my life to know whose house he went to play at on that day during Christmas break when Barcelona was enveloped in several feet of unexpected snow.

That night, desperate, I went through the pockets of my coat, my jacket and my trousers, cursing because I couldn't find the concert programme.

'Sara Voltes-Epstein? No. Doesn't ring a bell. Try the Betlem parish, they do those sorts of activities there.'

I went to about twenty parishes, trudging through increasingly dirty snow, until I found her, in the neighbourhood of Poble Sec, in a very modest parish church, in an even more modest, and almost empty, room with three walls covered in extraordinary charcoal drawings. Six or seven portraits and some landscapes. I was impressed by the sadness of the gaze in one entitled *Uncle Haïm*. And a dog that was amazing. And a house by the sea that was called *Little Beach at Portlligat*. I've looked at those drawings so many times, Sara. That girl was a real artist, Sara. My mouth hung open for half an hour until I heard your voice at my neck, as if scolding me, your voice saying I told you not to come.

I turned with an excuse on my lips, but all that came out was a shy I just happened to be passing by and. With a smile she forgave me. And in a soft, timid voice you said, 'What do you think of them?'

## 18

'Mother.'

'What?' Without looking up from the papers she was going over on the manuscript table.

'Can you hear me?'

But she was avidly reading financial reports from Caturla, the man she had chosen to get the shop back on a sound footing. I knew that she wasn't paying attention, but it was now or never.

'I'm giving up the violin.'

'Fine.'

And she continued reading the reports from Caturla, which must have been enthralling. When Adrià left the study, with a cold sweat on his soul, he heard his mother's eyeglasses folding with a click-clack. She must have been watching him. Adrià turned. Yes, she was watching him, with her glasses in one hand and holding up a sheaf of reports in the other.

'What did you say?'

'That I'm giving up the violin. I'll finish seventh year, but then I'm done.'

'Don't even think it.'

'I've made up my mind.'

'You aren't old enough to make such a decision.'

'Of course I am.'

Mother put down Caturla's report and stood up. I'm sure she was wondering how Father would resolve this mutiny. To begin with, she used a low, private, threatening tone.

'You will take your seventh year examinations, then your eighth year examinations and then you will do two years of virtuosity and, when the time comes, you will go to the Julliard School or wherever Master Manlleu decides.'

'Mother: I don't want to devote my life to interpreting music.'

'Why not?'

'It doesn't make me happy.'

'We weren't born to be happy.'

'I was.'

'Master Manlleu says you have what it takes.'

'Master Manlleu despises me.'

'Master Manlleu tries to goad you because sometimes you're listless.'

'That is my decision. You are going to have to put up with it,' I dared to say.

That was a declaration of war. But there was no other way I could do it. I left Father's study without looking back.

'How.'

'Yes?'

'You can start painting my face with war paint. Black and white from the mouth to the ears and two yellow stripes from top to bottom.'

'Stop joking, I'm trembling.'

Adrià locked himself in his room, unwilling to give an inch. If that meant war, so be it.

Little Lola's voice was the only one heard in the house for many days. She was the only one who tried to give an appearance of normality. Mother, always at the shop, I at university, and dinners in silence, both of us looking at our plates, and Little Lola watching one of us and then the other. It was very difficult and so intense that, for a few days, the joy of having found you again was subdued by the violin crisis.

The storm was unleashed the day I had class with Master Manlleu. That morning, before vanishing into the shop, Mother spoke to me for the first time that entire week. Without looking at me, as if Father had just died: 'Bring the Storioni to class.'

I arrived at Master Manlleu's house with Vial and, as we went down the hallway to his studio, I heard his voice, now sweet, telling me we could look at some other repertoire that you like better. All right, lad?

'When I've finished seventh, I'm giving up the violin. Does everybody understand that? I have other priorities in my life.'

'You will regret this wrong decision for every day of your entire life' (Mother).

'Coward' (Manlleu).

'Don't leave me alone, mate' (Bernat).

'Negroid' (Manlleu).

'But you play better than I do!' (Bernat).

'Poof' (Manlleu).

'What about all the hours you've invested, what about that? Just flush them down the drain?' (Mother).

'Capricious gypsy' (Manlleu).

'And what is it you want to do?' (Mother).

'Study' (me).

'You can combine that with the violin, can't you?' (Bernat).

'Study what?' (Mother).

'Bastard' (Manlleu).

'Poof' (me).

'Watch it, or I'll walk out on you right now' (Manlleu).

'Do you even know what you want to study?' (Mother).

'How' (Black Eagle, the valiant Arapaho chief).

'Hey, I asked you what it is you want to study. Medicine?' (Mother)

'Ingrate' (Manlleu).

'Come on, Adrià, shit!' (Bernat).

'History' (me).

'Ha!' (Mother).

'What?' (me).

'You'll starve to death. And get bored' (Mother).

'History!?' (Manlleu).

'Yes' (Mother).

'But history …' (Manlleu).

'Ha, ha … Tell me about it' (Mother).

'Traitor!!' (Manlleu).

'And I also want to study philosophy' (me).

'Philosophy?' (Mother).

'Philosophy?' (Manlleu).

'Philosophy?' (Bernat).

'Even worse' (Mother).

'Why even worse?' (me)

'If you have to choose between two evils, become a lawyer' (Mother).

'No. I hate the normalisation of life with rules' (me).

'Smart arse' (Bernat).

'What you want is to contradict just for the sake of contradicting. That's your style, isn't it?' (Manlleu).

'I want to understand humanity by studying its cultural evolution' (me).

'A smart arse, that's what you are. Should we go to the cinema?' (Bernat).

'Sure, let's go. Where?' (me).

'To the Publi' (Bernat).

'I don't understand you, Son' (Mother).

'Irresponsible' (Manlleu).

'History, philosophy ... Don't you see they're useless?' (Manlleu).

'What do you know!' (me).

'Arrogant!' (Manlleu).

'And music? What use is it?' (me).

'You'll make a lot of money; look at it that way' (Manlleu).

'History, philosophy ... Don't you see they're useless?' (Bernat).

'Tu quoque?' (me).

'What?' (Bernat).

'Nothing' (me).

'Did you like the film?' (Bernat).

'Well, yeah' (me).

'Well, yeah or yes?' (Bernat).

'Yes' (me).

'It's useless!' (Mother).

'I like it' (me).

'And the shop? Would you like to work there?' (Mother).

'We'll discuss that later' (me).

'How' (Black Eagle, the valiant Arapaho chief).

'Not now, damn, don't be a drag' (me).

'And I want to study languages' (me).

'English is all you need' (Manlleu).

'What languages?' (Mother).

'I want to perfect my Latin and Greek. And start Hebrew, Aramaic and Sanskrit' (me).

'Whoa! What a disappointment …' (Mother).

'Latin, Greek and what else?' (Manlleu).

'Hebrew, Aramaic and Sanskrit' (me).

'You've got a screw loose, lad' (Manlleu).

'That depends' (me).

'The girls on aeroplanes speak English' (Manlleu).

'What?' (me).

'I can assure you that you have no need for Aramaic when flying to New York for a concert' (Manlleu).

'We speak different languages, Master Manlleu' (me).

'Abominable!' (Manlleu).

'Maybe you could stop insulting me' (me).

'Now I understand! I'm too difficult a role model for you' (Manlleu).

'No, no way!' (me).

'What does "no, no way" mean? Eh? What do you mean by "no, no way"?' (Manlleu).

'What is said cannot be unsaid' (me).

'Cold, arrogant, abominable, stupid, stuck-up, repulsive, detestable, haughty!' (Manlleu).

'Very well, as you wish' (me).

'What is said cannot be unsaid' (Manlleu).

'Bernat?' (me).

'What?' (Bernat).

'Want to go for a walk along the breakwater?' (me).

'Let's go' (Bernat).

'If your father could see you now!' (Mother).

I'm sorry, but the day that Mother said that, in the middle of the war, I couldn't help a booming, exaggerated laugh at the thought of a decapitated corpse seeing anything. I know that Little Lola, who was listening to everything from the kitchen, also stifled a smile. Mother, pale, realised too late what she'd said. We were all exhausted and we just left it at that. It was the seventh day of conflict.

'How' (Black Eagle, the valiant Arapaho chief).

'I'm tired' (me).

'All right. But you should know that you've begun a war of attrition, of trenches, like World War One; I just want you to keep in mind that you are fighting on three fronts' (Black Eagle, the valiant Arapaho chief).

'You're right. But I know that I don't aspire to be an elite musician' (me).

'And, above all, don't confuse tactics with strategy' (Black Eagle, the valiant Arapaho chief).

Sheriff Carson spat chaw on the ground and said keep it up, what the hell. If what you want is to spend your life reading, go ahead, you and your books. And tell the others where they can stuff it.

'Thank you, Carson' (me).

'Don't mention it' (Sheriff Carson).

It was the seventh day and we all went to sleep, worn out from so much tension and hoping an armistice would come. That night was the first of many in which I dreamt about Sara.

From a strategic point of view it was very good that the armies of the Triple Alliance fought amongst themselves: Turkey stood up to Germany in Master Manlleu's house. And that was good for the Entente, who had time to lick its wounds and begin to think about Sara constructively. The chronicles of the battle say that the old allies were bloodthirsty and cruel and that the screams could be heard echoing through the courtyard of Master Manlleu's house. She said everything that had been kept quiet for years and accused him of not being able to hold on to a boy who was very flighty but had an extraordinary intellectual ability.

'Don't exaggerate.'

'My son is extremely gifted. Didn't you know? Haven't we discussed it enough?'

'There has only ever been one extremely gifted person in this house, Mrs Ardèvol.'

'My son needs a guiding hand. Your ego, Mr Manlleu ...'

'Master Manlleu.'

'You see? Your ego keeps you from seeing reality. We have to rethink the financial agreement.'

'That's unfair. This is all your extremely gifted son's fault.'

'Don't try to be funny, it's lame.'

Then they moved straight into the insults (negroid, gypsy, coward, poof, cold, arrogant, abominable, stupid, stuck-up, repulsive, detestable and haughty on one hand. On the other, only pathetic.)

'What did you just say to me?'

'Pathetic.' And bringing her face very close to his: 'Pa-thet-ic!'

'The last straw. Insulting me! I'll take you to court.'

'It would be a pleasure to be able to set a few lawyers on you. Now I won't even pay you for next month. As far as I'm concerned ... As for me ... I'll speak with Yehudi Menuhin.'

And, it seems, they came to blows, he saying that Menuhin was greyness personified and that he'd charge her ten times more, while she headed towards the door, followed by an indignant Manlleu, who kept repeating do you know how Menuhin teaches? Do you know?

When she heard the whack of the door to Manlleu's house, after she herself had slammed it in rage, Carme Bosch knew that her dream of making Adrià into the finest violinist in the world was finished. What a shame, Little Lola. And I told Bernat that he would get used to it and I promised we could play together whenever he felt like it; at my house or his, whichever he preferred. Then I began to breathe and to be able to think about you without impediments.

## 19

Et in Arcadia ego. Although Poussin made the painting thinking that it was death speaking, death which is present everywhere, even in the corners of happiness, I have always preferred to believe that it is my own ego speaking: I have been in Arcadia, Adrià has his Arcadia. Adrià, so sad, bald, miserable, pot-bellied and cowardly, has lived in an Arcadia, because I have had several and the first, the personified one, is your presence, and I've lost it forever. I was expelled from it by an angel with a fiery sword, and Adrià headed out covering his naughty bits and thinking from now on I'll have to work to earn a living, alone, without you, my Sara. Another of my Arcadias – the one that is a place – is Tona, the ugliest and prettiest town in the world, where I spent fifteen summers frolicking on the edges of the fields of Can Casic, my body covered in the itchy spikes that came off the harvested piles where I hid from Xevi, Quico and Rosa, my inseparable companions during the eight weeks my summer out of Barcelona lasted, far from the tolling bells of the Concepció, the black and yellow taxis and anything that reminded me of school. Far from my parents; later, far from my mother, and far from the books that Adrià couldn't bring with him. And we scampered up to the castle, to look out at Can Ges, the large house, the gardens and, in the distance, the farms; the landscape looked like a nativity scene. And closer, the fields covered in harvested piles and Can Casic, the small house, the old gnawed haystack, also like in a nativity scene. And further on, the cork mountains, the Collsacabra to the northeast and the Montseny to the east. And we shouted and were the kings of the world, especially Xevi, who was six years older than me and beat me at everything, until he started helping his father with the cows and stopped playing with us. Quico also won all the time, but one day I beat him in a race to the white wall. All right: it was because he tripped; but I won fair and square. And Rosa was very pretty and, yes, she too beat me at everything. At Aunt Leo's house life was different. It was life without grumbling, without silences. People spoke and made eye contact. It was an immense house where Aunt Leo reigned without ever removing her neat, beige apron. Can Ges, the Ardèvol family home, is a vast house with more than thirteen rooms, open to every current in the summer and all the urban comforts in the winter, conveniently distanced from the cow barn and the horse stables, and whose southern face is adorned with a porch that was the best place in the world to read and also the best spot for practising the violin. My three cousins would casually come over to hear me, and I would practise repertoire instead of doing exercises, which is always more enjoyable, and one day a blackbird alighted on the porch's parapet, beside a potted geranium, and watched me as I played Leclair's Sonata No. 2 from his *Second livre de sonates*, which is very ornate and the blackbird seemed to really like and that Trullols had made me play one year in the opening concert at the conservatory on Bruc. And Tonton Leclair, when he wrote the last note, blew on the manuscript because he had run out of drying powder. Then he got up, satisfied, picked up his violin and played it without glancing at the score, think-ing of impossible continuations. And he clicked his tongue, proud of himself. And he sat back down. On the lower half of the last page, which was blank, in his most ceremonious hand, he wrote: 'I dedicate this sonata to my beloved nephew Guillaume-Francois, son of my beloved sister Annette, on the day of his birth. May his passage through this vale of tears be auspicious.' He read it over and had to blow again, cursing all the servants in the house, who were incapable of keeping his writing implements in proper order. Everyone knew what had to be done, at Can Ges. Everyone, including me now, was welcome there as long as they fulfilled their duties. And in the summer, I didn't have anything to do except eat bounti-fully, because these city lads are skinny as beanstalks, look at his colour when he gets here, poor thing. My cousins were older; Rosa, the youngest, was three years ahead of me. So I was sort of the spoiled baby they had to fatten up with real cow's milk and proper sausage. And bread smeared with oil. And bread drizzled with wine and sprinkled with sugar. And streaked bacon. What worried Uncle Cinto was that Adrià had the somewhat unhealthy habit of shutting himself up in his room for hours reading books without illustrations, only letters: and that, at seven, ten or twelve years old, was frankly distressing. But Aunt Leo would gently place her hand on his uncle's arm and he would change the subject, saying to Xevi that he'd have to come with him that afternoon because Prudenci was going to pay the cows a visit.

'I want to come too,' Rosa.

'No.'

'And me?'

'Yes.'

Rosa stormed off, affronted because Adrià, who was the littlest, could go with you and I can't.

'It's very unpleasant, my girl,' said Aunt Leo.

And I went to see how Prudenci jammed his fist and entire arm into Blanca's arsehole and then said something I didn't catch to my uncle and Xevi jotted it down on a piece of paper and Blanca chewed her cud, oblivious to the worries of the—

'Watch out, watch out, watch out, she's pissing!' shouted Adrià in excitement.

The men moved aside, still discussing their matters, but I stayed in the front row because watching a cow piss and shit from the stalls was one of the great spectacles life in Tona had to offer. Like watching Parrot, the mule at Can Casic, piss. That was really something to see, and that's why I think my aunt and uncle were being unfair with poor Rosa. And there were more things, like fishing for tadpoles in the stream beside the Matamonges gully. And returning with eight or ten victims that we kept in a glass bottle.

'Poor creatures.'

'No, Auntie, I'll feed them every day.'

'Poor creatures.'

'I'll give them bread, I promise.'

'Poor creatures.'

I wanted to see how they turned into frogs or, more often, into dead tadpoles because we never thought to change their water or about what they could eat inside the bottle. And the swallows' nests in the lean-to. And the sudden downpours. And the apotheosis of the threshing days at Can Casic, where the grain was no longer winnowed but separated by machines that made the haystack and filled the town and my memories with straw dust. Et in Arcadia ego, Adrià Ardèvol. No one can take those memories from me. And now I think that Aunt Leo and Uncle Cinto must have been made of solid stuff because they pretended nothing had happened after the fight between the two brothers. It was a long time ago. Adrià hadn't been born yet. And I knew about it because the summer I turned twenty, to avoid being alone with Mother in Barcelona, I decided to spend three or four weeks in Tona, if you'll have me. I was also feeling somewhat forlorn because Sara, who I was already dating while keeping it secret from both families, had had to go to Cadaqués with her parents and I was feeling so, so alone.

'What does if you'll have me mean? Don't ever say that again,' said my Aunt Leo, indignant. 'When are you coming?'

'Tomorrow.'

'Your cousins aren't here. Well, Xevi is, but he spends all day at the farm.'

'I reckoned.'

'Josep and Maria from Can Casic died this past winter.'

'Oh, no.'

'And Viola died of grief.' Silence on the other end of the line. As a consolation: 'They were very old, both of them. Josep walked in a right angle, poor thing. And the dog was also very old.'

'I'm so sorry.'

'Bring your violin.'

So I told Mother that Aunt Leo had invited me and I couldn't refuse. Mother didn't say yes or no. We were very distant and didn't speak much. I spent my days studying and reading, and she spent hers in the shop. And when I was at home, her gaze still accused me of capriciously throwing away a brilliant violin career.

'Did you hear me, Mother?'

It seems that, as always, in the shop, there were problems she didn't want to let me in on. And so, without looking at me, she just said bring them a little gift.

'Like what?'

'I don't know. Something small, you choose it.'

My first day in Tona, with my hands in my pockets, I went into town to find a little gift at Can Berdagué. And when I reached the main square I saw her sitting at the tables of El Racó, drinking tiger nut milk and smiling at me as if she were waiting for me. Well, she was waiting for me. At first I didn't recognise her; but then, wait, I know her, who is she, who is she, who is she. I knew that smile.

'Ciao,' she said.

Then I recognised her. She was no longer an angel, but she had the same angelic smile. Now she was a grown woman, simply lovely. She waved me over to sit by her side, and I obeyed.

'My Catalan is still very spotty.'

I asked her if we could speak in Italian. Then she asked me caro Adrià, sai chi sono, vero?

I didn't buy any gift for Aunt Leo at Can Berdagué. The first hour was spent with her drinking tiger nut milk and Adrià swallowing hard. She didn't stop talking and she explained everything to me that Adrià didn't know or pretended not to know because even though he was now twenty years old, at home such things weren't discussed. It was she, in Tona's main square, who told me that my angel and I were siblings.

I looked at her, stunned. It was the first time that anyone had put it into words. She could sense my confusion.

'É vero,' she insisted.

'This is like something out of a photo-novel,' I said, wanting to conceal my bewilderment.

She didn't bat an eyelash. She clarified that she was old enough to be my mother, but that she was my half-sister, and she showed me a birth certificate or something where my father recognised his paternity of some Daniela Amato, which was her according to her passport, which she also showed me. So she had been waiting for me, with the conversation and the documents at the ready. So what I half knew but no one had come out and said was true; I, only child par excellence, had an older, much older, sister. And I felt defrauded by Father, by Mother, by Little Lola and by so many secrets. And I think it hurt me that Sheriff Carson had never even ever insinuated it. A sister. I looked at her again: she was just as pretty as when she'd showed up at my house in angel form, but she was a forty-six year old woman who was my sister. We had never played over boring Sunday afternoons. She would have gone off laughing with Little Lola, and covering her mouth with her hand every time they'd caught a man looking at them.

'But you're my mother's age,' I said, just to say something.

'A bit younger.' I noticed an irritated tone in her reply.

Her name was Daniela. And she told me that her mother … and she explained a very beautiful love story, and I couldn't imagine Father in love and I kept very quiet and listened, listened to what she told me and tried to imagine it, and I don't know why she started to talk about the relationship between the two brothers, because Father, before beginning his studies at the seminary in Vic, had had to learn to winnow the wheat, to thresh properly and to touch Estrella's belly to see if she had finally got knocked up. Grandfather Ardèvol had taught both sons to tie the hampers tightly to the mule and to know that if the clouds were dark but came from Collsuspina they always blew past without a sprinkle. Uncle Cinto, who was the heir, put more care into things around the farm. And in the management of the land, the harvests, and the hired hands. Our father, on the other hand, was in the clouds whenever he could be, thinking and reading hidden in the corners, like you do. When they, somewhat desperately, sent Father to the seminary in Vic he was already, despite his lack of interest, half-trained to be a farmer. There he found his motivation and started to learn Latin, Greek and some lessons from the great teachers. Verdaguer's shadow was still fresh and ran through the hallways, and two out of three seminarians tried their hand at writing verse; but not our father: he wanted to study the philosophy and theology they offered him in instalments.

'And how do you know all this?'

'My mother explained it to me. Our father was quite talkative as a young man. Later, it seems he shut up like a closed umbrella, like a mummy.'

'What else?'

'They sent him to Rome because he was very clever. And he got my mother pregnant. And he fled Rome because he was a coward. And I was born.'

'Wow … like something out of a photo-novel,' I insisted.

Daniela, instead of getting annoyed, smiled encouragingly and continued with her story saying and your father had a fight with his brother.

'With Uncle Cinto?'

'You can shove the idea of marrying me off to that drip where the sun don't shine,' said Fèlix, pushing the photo back at him.

'But you won't have to lift a finger! The estate is a well-oiled machine. I've looked into it carefully. And you can devote yourself to your books, hell, what more do you want?'

'And why are you in such a hurry to marry me off?'

'Our parents asked me to; that if you ever left the path of priesthood … then you should marry; that I should have you marry.'

'But you're not married! Who are you to …'

'I will be. I have my eye on a …'

'As if they were cows.'

'You can't offend me. Mama knew it would be work to convince you.'

'I'll marry when I'm good and ready. If I ever do.'

'I can find you a better-looking one,' said Cinto, putting away the grey photo of the heiress of Can Puig.

Then our father asked, too curtly, if Cinto would buy out his share of the estate because he wanted to move to Barcelona. That was when the shouting began and the words thrown like rocks, to hurt. And both brothers looked at each other with hatred. It didn't come to blows. Fèlix Ardèvol got his share and they didn't have much to do with each other for a few years. Thanks to Leo's insistence, Father showed up when she and Cinto married. But then the brothers grew apart. One, buying up land in the area, raising livestock, making fodder, and the other, spending his share on mysterious trips to Europe.

'What do you mean by mysterious trips?'

Daniela slurped up the last of her tiger nut milk and said no more. Adrià went to pay and when he returned he said why don't we take a walk, and Tori, the waiter at El Racó, as he sullied the table with a cleaning rag, made a face as if to say damn, I wouldn't mind getting my paws on that French lady, no, I would not.

Still standing, in the square, Daniela stood in front of him and put on dark glasses that gave her a modern and inevitably foreign air. As if they shared a private secret, she came over to him and undid the top button on his shirt.

'Scusa,' she said.

And Tori thought bloody hell, how did that punk kid get a French lady like that. And he shook his head, astonished that the world moved so fast, as Daniela's gaze fell on the little chain with the medallion.

'I didn't know you were religious.'

'This isn't religious.'

'The Madonna of Pardàc is a Virgin Mary.'

'It's a keepsake.'

'From who?'

'I don't rightly know.'

Daniela stifled a smile, rubbed the medallion with her fingers and let it drop onto Adrià's chest. He hid it, angered by that invasion of his privacy. So he added it's none of your business.

'That depends.'

He didn't understand her. They walked in silence.

'It's a lovely medallion.'

Jachiam pulled it out, showed it to the jeweller and said it's gold. And the chain is too.

'You haven't stolen it?'

'No! Little Bettina, my blind sister, gave it to me so I would never feel lonely.'

'And so why do you want to sell it?'

'That surprises you?'

'Well … a family heirloom …'

'My family … Oh, how I miss the living and the dead. My mother, my father and all the Muredas: Agno, Jenn, Max, Hermes, Josef, Theodor, Micurà, Ilse, Erica, Katharina, Matilde, Gretchen and little blind Bettina … I miss the land-scape of Pardàc too.'

'Why don't you go back?'

'Because there are still people there who want to hurt me and my family has let me know that it wouldn't be prudent to …'

'Yeah …' said the goldsmith, lowering his head to get a better look at the medallion, not even slightly interested in the problems of the Muredas of Pardàc.

'I sent my siblings a lot of money, to help them.'

'Aha.'

He continued to examine it before giving it back to its owner.

'Pardàc is Predazzo?' he said, looking him in the eye, as if he had just thought of something.

'The people of the plains call it Predazzo, yes. But it's Pardàc … Don't you want to buy it?'

The jeweller shook his head.

'If you spend the winter with me, I'll teach you my trade and when the snows melt you can go wherever you like. But don't sell the medallion.'

And Jachiam learned the trade of smelting metals to turn them into rings, medallions and earrings and for a few months he buried his longing at that good man's house until one day, shaking his head, he said, as if picking up the thread of their first conversation: 'Whom did you entrust the money to?'

'What money?'

'The money you sent to your family.'

'A trustworthy man.'

'From Occitania?'

'Yes, why?'

'No, nothing, nothing …'

'What have you heard?'

'What was the man's name?'

'I called him Blond. His name was Blond of Cazilhac. He was very blond.'

'I don't think he got past …'

'What?'

'They killed him. And robbed him.'

'Who?'

'Mountain people.'

'From Moena?'

'I believe so.'

That morning, with the winter's wages in his pocket, Jachiam asked for the jeweller's blessing and rushed northward to find out what had happened to the Muredas's money and poor Blond. He walked rapidly, spurred on by rage and throwing all caution to the wind. On the fifth day he reached Moena and began bellowing in the main square. Come out, Brocias, he said, and a Brocia who heard him warned his cousin, and that cousin told another, and when they were ten men they went down to the square, snatched up Jachiam and brought him to the river. His panicked screams didn't reach Pardàc. The medallion of the Madonna dai Ciüf was kept, as a reward, by the Brocia who had seen him.

'Pardàc is in Trento,' said Adrià.

'But in my house,' replied Daniela, pensively, 'they always said that a sailor uncle I'd never met brought it back from Africa.'

They strolled to the cemetery and the chapel of Lourdes without saying anything, and it was a lovely day for walking. After half an hour of silence, sitting on the stone benches in the chapel's garden, Adrià, who now trusted her more, pointed to his chest and said do you want it?

'No. It's yours. Don't ever lose it.'

The sun's trajectory had shifted the shadows in the garden, and Adrià again asked what do you mean about Father's mysterious trips.

He had checked into a little hotel in the Borgo, five minutes from St. Peter's in the Vatican, on the edge of the Passetto. It was a discreet, modest and inexpensive hostel called Bramante that was run by a Roman matron who had spent many years rearing geese with an iron hand and who looked like a page pulled from the transition between Julius and Augustus. The first person he visited once he was set up in the narrow, damp room overlooking the Vicolo delle Palline was Father Morlin, whose initial reaction was to stand staring in the door to the cloister of the Santa Sabina monastery, struggling to remember who that man was who ... no!

'Fèlix Ardevole!' he shouted. 'Il mio omonimo! Vero?'

Fèlix Ardèvol nodded and submissively kissed the friar's hand, who was sweating beneath his heavy habit. Morlin, after looking him in the eyes, hesitated for a moment and instead of having him enter one of the visiting rooms, or stroll in the cloister, he sent him down an empty corridor, with the occasional worthless painting on its white walls. A very long corridor with few doors. Instinctively lowering his tone of voice, like in the old days, he said what do you want, and Fèlix Ardèvol replied I want contacts, only contacts. I want to establish a shop and I think you can help me to find top quality material.

They walked a few steps in silence. It was strange because despite the barrenness of the location, neither their footsteps nor their words echoed. Father Morlin must have known it was a discreet spot. When they had passed two paintings, he stopped in front of a very modest Annunciation, wiped his brow and looked him in the eye: 'While you are at war? How were you able to get out?'

'I can come and go pretty easily. I have my system. And I have contacts.'

Father Morlin's expression seemed to indicate that he didn't want to know any more details.

They talked for a long time. Fèlix Ardèvol's idea was crystal clear: in the last few years, many Germans, Austrians and Poles began to feel uncomfortable with Hitler's plans and searched for a change of scenery.

'You are looking for rich Jews.'

'People on the run always have great bargains for an antiquarian. Take me to those wanting to move to America. I'll take care of the rest.'

They reached the end of the corridor. A window overlooked a small austere cloister, decorated only with geraniums the colour of blood in some pots on the ground. Fèlix had trouble imagining a Dominican friar watering a row of geraniums. On the other side of the small cloister a similar window perfectly framed, as if on purpose, the distant dome of Saint Peter's. For a few seconds, Fèlix Ardèvol thought that he'd like to take the window and its view along with him. He returned to reality, convinced that Morlin had brought him there to show him the window.

'I need three or four addresses, of people in such circumstances.'

'And how do you know, dear Ardevole, that I could help you with this?'

'I have my sources: I devote many hours to my work and I know that you've been constantly widening your circle of contacts.'

Father Morlin took the blow but showed no outward reaction.

'And where does this sudden interest in others' objects come from?'

He was about to say because my work fascinates me; because when I find an object that I'm interested in, the world reduces to that object, whether it's a statuette, a painting, a document or a fabric. And the world is filled with objects that need no justification. There are objects that …

'I've become a collector.' He specified: 'I am a collector.'

'A collector of what?'

'A collector.' He opened his arms, like Saint Dominic preaching from the throne. 'I'm looking for beautiful things.'

And heavens did Father Morlin have information. If there was one person in the world able to know everything while barely ever leaving Santa Sabina, it was Father Fèlix Morlin, a friend to his friends and, according to what they say, a danger to his enemies. Ardevole was a friend and, therefore, they soon came to an agreement. First, Fèlix Ardèvol had to put up with a sermon about the frenzied times that were their lot and no one wants, and to make a good impression he added a you can say that again, you can say that again, and if you were watching from a distance, you'd think they were reciting the litanies of the rosary. And the frenzied times that Europe was experiencing were starting to force a lot of people to look towards America and, thanks to Father Morlin, Fèlix Ardèvol spent a few months travelling through Europe before the fire, trying to save the furniture from any likely earthquake. His first contact was Tiefer Graben, in Vienna's Innere Stadt district. It was a very nice house, not very wide but surely quite deep. He rang the bell and smiled sympathetically at the woman who had opened the door to him somewhat re-luctantly. With that first contact he was able to buy all of the house's furnishings, which, after setting aside the five most valuable objects, he resold for twice the price without leaving Vienna, almost without crossing the Ring. Such a spectacular success that it could have given him a swelled head, but Fèlix Ardèvol was an astute man, as well as intelligent. And so he proceeded with caution. In Nuremberg he bought a collection of seventeenth- and eighteenth-century painting: two Frago-nards, an evanescent Watteau and three Rigauds. And the Mignon with the yellow gardenias, I imagine, which he saved for himself. Pontegradella, near Ferrara, was where he first held a valuable musical instrument in his hands. It was a viola made by Nicola Galliano of Naples. As he considered buying it, he even lamented not having learned to play that type of instrument. He knew enough to stay silent until the seller, a viola player named Davide Fiordaliso who, according to what his sources had informed him, had been forced out of the Vienna Philharmonic because of the new race laws and was reduced to earning a living playing in a café in Ferrara, anx-iously told him due milioni in a very soft voice. He looked at Signor Arrau, who'd spent an hour examining the viola with a magnifying glass, and Arrau gave him the sign with his eyes that meant yes. Fèlix Ardèvol knew that what he had to do then was give the object back to its owner with an offended expression on his face and offer some absurdly low figure. He did it, but he was so reluctant to endanger his chances of possessing that viola, that afterwards he had to sit down and rethink his strategy. One thing was buying and selling with a cool head and the other was setting up the shop, if he ever did. He bought the viola for duecentomila lire. And he refused to have a coffee with the seller whose hands trembled violently, because in war they teach you not to look your victim in the eye. A Galliano. Signor Arrau told him that, although instruments weren't his strong suit, he'd venture that he could get three times that if he discreetly spread the word and wasn't in a rush to sell. And if he wished, he would introduce him to another Catalan, Signor Berenguer, a promising young man who had learned to appraise things with extraordinary precision and who, when the war ended in Spain, which had to happen someday, planned to return home.

On the advice of Father Morlin, who seemed to know it all, he rented a storage space in a village near Zurich and stockpiled the sofas, canapes, console tables, Fragonards, Chippendale chairs and Watteaus there. And the Galliano viola. He still couldn't even imagine that one day a string instrument, similar on the face of it, would be his end. But he had already made a clear distinction between the shop and his private collection comprised of the most select objects in his catalogue.

Every once in a while he returned to Rome, to the Bramante hostel, and met with Morlin. They talked about possible clients, they talked about the future, and Morlin let on that the war in Spain would never end because Europe was now undergoing a convulsive period and that meant things would be very uncomfortable. The world map had to be reworked and the fastest way to do that was with bombs and trenches, he said with a touch of nonchalant resignation.

'And how do you know all this?'

I was unable to ask any other question. Daniela and I had gone up the Barri path to the castle, as if we were walking with someone elderly who didn't want to tackle the other, much steeper, one.

'What a marvellous view,' she said.

In front of the castle's chapel, they looked out at the Plana, and Adrià thought about his Arcadia, but only fleetingly. 'How do you know so much about my father?'

'Because he's my father. What's the name of that mountain in the distance?'

'The Montseny.'

'Doesn't it all look like a nativity scene?'

What do you know about my crèches, the ones we never set up at home, I thought. But Daniela was right, Tona looked more like a nativity scene than ever and Adrià couldn't help but point downhill, 'Can Ges.'

'Yes. And Can Casic.'

They walked to the Torre dels Moros. Inside it was filled with piss and shit. Outside, there was the wind and the landscape. Adrià sat beside the precipice to get a good view of his landscape. Until then he hadn't formulated the right question: 'Why are you telling me all this?'

She sat beside him and without looking at him said that they were brother and sister, that they had to understand each other, that she was the owner of Can Casic.

'I already know that. My mother told me.'

'I'm planning on demolishing the house, the filth, the pond, the manure and the stench of rotten hay. And put up new houses there.'

'Don't even think it.'

'You'll get used to the idea.'

'Viola died of grief.'

'Who is Viola?'

'The bitch of Can Casic. Dark beige with a black snout and droopy ears.'

Surely Daniela didn't understand him, but she didn't say anything. Adrià stared at her for a few seconds in silence.

'Why are you telling me all this?'

'You need to know who our father was.'

'You hate him.'

'Our father is dead, Adrià.'

'But you hate him. Why have you come to Tona?'

'To talk to you without your mother around. To talk to you about the shop. When it's yours I would like to be involved as a partner.'

'But why are you telling this to me? Deal with my mother …'

'Your mother is impossible to deal with. And you know that full well.'

The sun had hidden behind Collsuspina some time ago and I felt an immense void inside of me. The light was gradually dimming and I thought I could hear the crickets starting. The pale moon awoke drowsily, rising early, over the Collsacabra. When the shop is mine, was that what she had said?

'It will eventually be yours, sooner or later.'

'Go to hell.'

I said that last bit in Catalan. From her slight smile I could tell she had understood me perfectly even though she didn't bat an eyelash.

'I still have more things to tell you about. By the way, what violin did you bring with you?'

'I'm not planning on practising much at all. In fact, I've stopped my lessons. I only brought it for Aunt Leo.'

Since it would soon be dark, they started the walk down. Along the steep path, in revenge, he took long strides, making light of the precipice, and she, despite her narrow skirt, followed him without any apparent problems. The moon was already at its height when they reached the level of the trees, near the cemetery.

'But which violin did you bring with you?'

'My student one. Why?'

'As far as I know,' continued Signor Somethingorother, still standing in the middle of the street, 'it is a violin that has never been played regularly: like the Stradivarius Messiah, do you understand what I'm saying?'

'No,' said Ardèvol, impatient.

'I'm saying that makes it even more valuable. Guillaume-François Vial made off with it the very same year it was made, and its whereabouts since then are unknown. Perhaps it has been played, but I have no record of it. And now we find it here. It is an instrument of incalculable value.'

'That is what I wanted to hear, caro dottore.'

'Is it really his first?' asked Mr Berenguer, his interest piqued.

'Yes.'

'I would forget about it, Mr Ardèvol. That's a lot of money.'

'Is it worth it?' asked Fèlix Ardèvol, looking at Something-orother.

'I would pay it without thinking twice. If you have the money. It has an incredibly lovely sound.'

'I don't give a damn about its sound.'

'And exceptional symbolic value.'

'That does matter to me.'

They said goodbye because it was starting to rain. They said goodbye after Signor Somethingorother got paid his expert's fee, right there on the street. The ravages of war, besides millions of dead and entire cities destroyed, had got people out of the habits of courtesy and they now settled things on any old street corner, deals that could seriously affect more than one life. They said goodbye when Fèlix Ardèvol said all right, that he would take Mr Berenguer's advice and that yes, fifty thousand dollars was too much money. And thank you both very much. And until we meet again, if we ever do. Mr Berenguer, before going round the corner, turned to observe Ardèvol. He pretended to be lighting a cigarette that he didn't have in his hand in order to get a better look. Fèlix Ardèvol felt the other man's gaze on the back of his neck but didn't turn.

'Who is Mr Falegnami?

He was back at the Santa Sabina monastery. They were back in the discreet corridor without an echo. Father Morlin checked his watch and sent Ardèvol, forcefully, out towards the street.

'Blast it, Morlin, it's raining!'

Father Morlin opened a huge umbrella, the size used by country folk, grabbed Ardèvol by the arm and they started walking in front of the monastery. They looked like a Dominican friar consoling and giving advice to a poor mortal with a heavy conscience, pacing in front of Santa Sabina's facade, as if they were speaking of infidelities, fits of lust, sinful feelings of envy or rage, and it's been many years since my last confession, Father, and for the passers-by it was an uplifting image.

'He's the concierge of the Ufficio della Giustizia e della Pace.'

'I already know that.' Two drenched strides. 'Who is he, come on. How is it that he has such a valuable violin?'

'So it really is incredibly valuable ...'

'You'll have your commission.'

'I know what he's asking.'

'I reckoned as much. But you don't know what I'm going to give him.'

'His name isn't Falegnami: it's Zimmermann.'

He looked at him out of the corner of his eye. After a few steps in silence, Father Morlin tested the waters: 'You don't know who he is, do you?'

'I'm convinced his real name isn't Zimmermann either.'

'It's best if you continue to call him Falegnami. You can offer him a quarter of what he asked you for. But don't make him feel choked because ...'

'Because he's dangerous.'

'Yes.'

An American army jeep passed quickly along the Corso and splashed the bottoms of their habit and trousers.

'Damn it to hell,' said Ardèvol, without raising his voice. Morlin shook his head with displeasure.

'My dear friend,' he said with a distant smile as if looking into the future, 'your character will be your undoing.'

'What do you mean?'

'That you should know that you aren't as strong as you think you are. And even less so in times like these.'

'Who is this Zimmermann?'

Félix Morlin took his friend by the arm. The whisper of the rain hitting the umbrella didn't drown out his voice.

Outside, the extreme cold had turned the downpour into a profuse, silent snowfall. Inside, as he looked into the iridescent colour of the wine in his raised glass, he said, I was born into a wealthy and very religious family, and the moral rectitude of my upbringing has helped me to assume the difficult task, by direct order from the Führer via the explicit instructions from Reichsführer Himmler, of becoming a stalwart defence against the enemy inside our fatherland. This wine is excellent, Doctor.

'Thank you,' said Doctor Voigt, a bit weary of so much talk. 'It is an honour for me to be able to taste it here, in my improvised home,' he thought to say. With each passing day he was more repulsed by these grotesque characters without the slightest manners.

'Improvised but comfortable,' said the Oberlagerführer.

A second little sip. Outside, the snow was already covering the earth's unmentionables with a modest thick sheet of cold. Rudolf Höss continued, 'For me, orders are sacred, no matter how difficult they may seem, since as an SS I must be willing to completely sacrifice my personality in the fulfilment of my duty to the fatherland.'

Blah, blah, blah, blah, blah.

'Of course, Obersturmbannführer Höss.'

And then Höss told him, loudly, about that pathetic episode with Soldier Bruno something or other, until, as if he were Dietmar Kehlmann at the Berliner Theater, he ended with the famous line take away this carrion. He had told it to about twenty people and, as far as Doctor Voigt knew, always concluded with the same shrill ending.

'My parents, who were fervent Catholics in a predominantly Lutheran, if not Calvinist, Germany, wanted me to be a priest. I spent quite some time considering it.'

Envious wretch.

'You would have made a good priest, Obersturbannführer Höss.'

'I imagine so.'

And conceited.

'I'm sure: everything you do, you do well.'

'What you've just made out to be a virtue, could also be my ruin. And especially now that Reichsführer Himmler is going to visit us.'

'Why?'

'Because as Oberlagerführer, I am responsible for all the failings of the system. For example, I only have two or three cans at the most left from the last shipment of Zyklon gas and the quartermaster hasn't even thought to tell me to make a new order. And so I'll have to ask for favours, get some lorries to come here that probably should be somewhere else, and stifle my craving to yell at the quartermaster because we are all working at our limit, here at Auschwitz.'

'I imagine that the experience of Dachau …'

'From a psychological point of view, the difference is vast. At Dachau we had prisoners.'

'From what I understand huge numbers of them died and still do.'

This doctor is an imbecile, thought Höss. Let's call a spade a spade.

'Yes, Doctor Voigt, but Dachau is a prison camp. Auschwitz-Birkenau is designed, created and calculated to exterminate rats. If it weren't for the fact that Jews aren't human, I would think we are living in hell, with one door that leads to a gas chamber and another place that's cremation ovens and their flames, or the open pits in the forest, where we burn the remaining units, because we can't keep up with all the material they send us. This is the first time I've talked about these things with someone not involved in the camp, Doctor.'

And who does this brainless piece of shit think he was then?

'It's good to vent every once in a while, Obersturmbann-führer Höss.'

It feels good to really get things off your chest, even if it's with a conceited, stupid doctor like this one, thought Höss.

'I'm counting on your professional secrecy, because the Reichsführer …'

'Naturally. You, who are a Christian … In short, a psychiatrist is like a confessor, the confessor you could have been.'

'My men have to be strong to carry out the task they have been entrusted with. The other day a soldier, more than thirty years old, not some teenager, burst into tears in one of the barracks in front of his comrades.'

'And what happened?'

'Bruno, Bruno, wake up!'

Although it's hard to believe, the Oberlagerführer, the Obersturmbannführer Rudolf Höss, was about to relate the entire scene again from start to finish as soon as he drank his second glass of wine. By the fourth or fifth, his eyes were glassy. Then he began to be incoherent and inadvertently let slip that he was fixated on a Jewish girl. The doctor was shocked but he concealed it, telling himself that it could be very interesting information to use in periods of hardship. So the next day he spoke with Gefreiter Hänsch and very politely asked him whom the Obersturmbannführer was referring to. It was simple: his maid. And he jotted it down in his 'just in case' notebook.

A few days later, he had to once again tend to the odious task of selecting merchandise. Shielded, Doctor Voigt observed the soldiers, who tried to forcefully convince the women to let their children be taken away. He saw the selection that Doctor Budden made, the ten girls and boys that he had ordered, and then he noticed an old woman who was coughing and weeping. He went over to her.

'What's this?'

He touched the case with his hand, but the old shrew stepped back; who did that contemptible hag think she was, he thought. The old woman clung to the case in such a way that it was impossible to get it from her. Sturmbannführer Voigt pulled out his pistol, aimed it at the back of the woman's worn, grey neck and fired; the weak pac! was barely heard amid the general wailing. And the disgusting crone splattered blood on the violin case. The doctor ordered Emmanuel to clean it off and bring it to his office at once; meanwhile he headed off as he put away his weapon, followed by many terrified eyes.

'Here's the thing you asked for,' said Emmanuel, a few minutes later. And he put the case down on the desk. It was a fine one; that was what had caught Doctor Voigt's eye. A fine case doesn't usually hide a bad instrument. A person who spends money on a case has already spent plenty on the instrument. And if the instrument is good, you hold on to it for dear life, even if you are headed to Auschwitz.

'Break the lock.'

'How, commander?'

'Use your imagination.' Suddenly startled: 'But don't shoot it!'

The assistant opened it with a non-standard issue knife, a detail which Voigt wrote down in his 'just in case' notebook. He waved him off and, somewhat excited, opened the violin case. There was an instrument inside, yes; but at first glance he could already see it was nothing … No, wait a minute. He picked it up and read the label inside: Laurentius Storioni Cremonensis me fecit 1764. Would you look at that.

Höss, that idiot clodhopper, had him come in at three, wrinkled his nose and dared to tell him that, as a temporary guest to the Lager, you have no right to make a scene by executing a unit in the reception and selection area, Doctor Voigt.

'She refused to obey me.'

'What was she carrying?'

'A violin.'

'Can I see it?'

'It's nothing valuable, Obersturmbannführer.'

'Doesn't matter, but I still want to see it.'

'Trust me, it's of no interest.'

'That's an order.'

Doctor Voigt opened the door to the pharmacy's cabinet and said, with a soft voice and a fawning smile, 'As you wish, Obersturmbannführer.'

As he examined it and checked its scars, Rudolf Höss said I don't know any musician who can tell me what it's worth.

'Must I remind you that I am the one who found it, Obersturmbannführer?'

Rudolf Höss lifted his head, surprised by Doctor Voigt's excessively curt tone. He let a few seconds pass so the other man would have a chance to realise that he had realised what there was to realise, although he wasn't altogether sure what that was.

'Didn't you say it wasn't worth anything?'

'It's not. But I like it.'

'Well, I'm going to keep it, Doctor Voigt. In compensation for …'

He didn't know in compensation for what. So he let it trail off with a dot dot dot as he put the instrument back in its case and closed it.

'How disgusting.' He extended his arms to look at it. 'That's blood, right?'

He leaned back against the wall.

'Because of your little whim, I'll have to change the case.'

'I'll do it, because I'm keeping it.'

'You are mistaken, my friend: I'm keeping it.'

'You are not keeping it, Obersturmbannführer.'

Rudolf Höss grabbed the case by the handle, as if he was preparing to come to blows. Now he clearly saw that the instrument was valuable. From the Doctor Commander's boldness, it must be very valuable. He smiled, but he had to stop smiling when he heard the words of Doctor Voigt, who brought his breath and his thickset nose close to Höss's face: 'You can't keep it because I will report you.'

'On what grounds?' Höss, perplexed.

'Six hundred and fifteen thousand, four hundred and twenty-eight.'

'What?'

'Elisaveta Meireva.'

'What?'

'Unit number six hundred and fifteen thousand, four hundred and twenty-eight. Six, one, five, four, two, eight, Elisaveta Meireva. Your maid. Reichsführer Himmler will condemn you to death when he finds out you've had sexual relations with a Jewess.'

Red as a tomato, Höss put the violin down on the desk with a thud.

'All your talk about confessional secrets, you bastard.'

'I'm no priest.'

The violin remained with Doctor Voigt, who was just passing through Auschwitz, supervising with an iron hand

the experiments of Doctor Budden, that stuck-up Obersturmführer who must have swallowed a broomstick one day and
had yet to shit it out. And also the experiments of three more
deputy doctors; what he had conceived as the most in-depth
investigation ever attempted on the limits of pain. As for
Höss, he spent a few days nervously clenching his arse cheeks
together, wondering whether that artful poof of a bandit,
Aribert Voigt, was, in addition to being an artful poof of a
pirate, also a blabbermouth.

'Five thousand dollars, Mr Falegnami.'

The man with the frightened, increasingly glassy eyes
stared into Fèlix Ardèvol's.

'Are you pulling my leg?'

'No. Look, you know what? I'll take it for three thousand,
Mr Zimmermann.'

'You've gone mad.'

'No. Either you give it to me for that price or ... Well, the
authorities will be very interested in knowing that Doctor
Aribert Voigt, Sturmbannführer Voigt, is alive, hidden a
kilometre away from the Vatican City, probably with the
complicity of someone high up in the Vatican. And that he's
trying to sell a violin nicked from Auschwitz.'

Mr Falegnami had pulled out a feminine little parlour
gun and aimed it at him nervously. Fèlix Ardèvol didn't even
flinch. He pretending to be stifling a smile and shook his head
as if he were very displeased, 'You are alone. How will you get
rid of my corpse?'

'It will be a pleasure to face that challenge.'

'You'll still be left with an even bigger one: if I don't walk
out of here on my own two feet, the people waiting for me
on the street already have their instructions.' He pointed to
the gun, sternly. 'And now I'll take it for two thousand. Don't
you know that you are one of the Allies' ten most wanted?'
He improvised that part in the tone of someone scolding an
unruly child.

Doctor Voigt watched as Ardèvol pulled out a wad of notes
and put them on the table. He lowered the gun, with his eyes
wide, incredulous: 'That's not even fifteen hundred!'

'Don't make me lose my patience, Sturmbannführer Voigt.'

That was Fèlix Ardèvol's doctorate in buying and selling. A half an hour later he was out on the street with the violin, striding quickly with his heart beating fast and the satisfaction of a job well done.

'You just broke with the most sacred of diplomatic relations.'

'Excuse me?'

'You acted like an elephant in a Bohemian glassware shop.'

'I don't know what you are talking about?'

Friar Fèlix Morlin, with indignation in his face and voice, spat out, 'I'm in no position to judge people. Mr Falegnami was under my protection.'

'But he is a savage son of a bitch.'

'He was under my protection!'

'Why do you protect murderers?'

Félix Morlin closed the door in the face of Fèlix Ardèvol, who didn't really understand his reaction.

As he left Santa Sabina, he put on his hat and raised the lapels of his coat. He didn't know that he would never again see that Dominican who was full of surprises.

'I don't know what to say.'

'There are more things I can tell you about our father.'

It was already dark. They had to walk along dark streets and be careful not to trip on the hardened wheel tracks sculpted in the road's mud. Daniela gave him kiss on the forehead in front of Can Ges and for a few seconds Adrià was reminded of the angel she'd once been, now without wings or any special aura. Then he realised that all the shops were closed and Aunt Leo wouldn't be getting any little gift.

## 20

It was a face filled with tragic wrinkles. But I was impressed by his clear direct gaze, which made me feel as if he were accusing me of something. Or, depending on how you looked at it, as if he were begging for my forgiveness. I sensed many misfortunes in it before Sara told me anything. And all the misfortunes were contained in strokes made in charcoal on thick white paper.

'This is the drawing that most impressed me,' I told her. 'I would have liked to meet him.'

I realised that Sara hadn't said anything; she just stood in front of the charcoal of the Cadaqués landscape. We contemplated it in silence. The entire house was silent. Sara's huge flat, which we had entered furtively, today my parents aren't here and neither is anyone else. A rich home. Like mine. Like a thief, like the day of the Lord, I will come like a thief in the night.

I didn't dare to ask her why we had to go there on a day when no one was home. Adrià was thrilled to see the surroundings of that girl who got deeper into his bones with each passing day, with her melancholy smile and delicate gestures he'd never seen before in anyone else. And Sara's room was larger than mine, twice as large. And very pretty: with wallpaper with geese and a farmhouse that wasn't like Can Ges in Tona: it was prettier, neater, without flies or odours; more like a picture book; the wallpaper of a little girl who hadn't changed it even now that she was … I don't know how old you are, Sara.

'Nineteen. And you are twenty-three.'

'How do you know that I'm twenty-three?'

'I can tell by your face.'

And she put a new drawing on top of the one of Cadaqués. 'You draw really well. Let me see that portrait again.'

She put the drawing of Uncle Haïm on top of the pile. His gaze, his wrinkles, his sad aura.

'Did you say it was your uncle?'

'Yes. He's dead now.'

'When did he die?'

'Actually, he's my mother's uncle. I didn't get to know him. Well, I was very young when …'

'And how …'

'A photo.'

'Why did you draw his portrait?'

'To keep his story alive.'

They queued up to enter the showers. Gavriloff, who during the entire trajectory in the cattle wagon had warmed two girls who had no one to hold their hands, turned towards Doctor Epstein and said they are taking us to our death, and Doctor Epstein answered, in a murmur so other people wouldn't hear, that that was impossible, that he was crazy.

'No, they're the ones who are crazy, Doctor. When will you see!'

'Everyone inside. That's it, men on this side. Of course the children can go with the women.'

'No, no; leave your clothes neatly folded and remember the number of the hook, for when you get out of the shower, all right?'

'Where are you from?' asked Uncle Haïm looking into the eyes of the man giving the instructions.

'We're not allowed to speak to you.'

'Who are you? You are Jews, too, aren't you?'

'We aren't allowed, for fuck's sake. Don't make things difficult for me.' And shouting, 'Remember your hook number!'

When all the naked men were advancing slowly towards the showers, where there were already a group of naked women, an SS officer with a pencil moustache and a dry cough entered the dressing room and said is there a doctor in here? Doctor Haïm Epstein took a step towards the showers, but Gavriloff, beside him, said don't be an idiot, Doctor; that gives you a chance.

'Shut up.'

Then Gavriloff turned and pointed to Haïm Epstein's pale

back and said er ist ein Arzt, mein Oberleutnant; and Herr
Epstein cursed his companion in misfortune, who continued
towards the showers with his eyes slightly happy and softly
whistling a csárdás by Rózsavölgyi.

'Are you a doctor?' asked the officer, planted before Epstein.

'Yes,' he said, resigned and, most of all, tired. And he was
only fifty years old.

'Get dressed.'

Epstein dressed slowly while the rest of the men went into
the showers, shepherded by prisoners with grey, worn gazes.

The officer paced impatiently while that Jew put on his
clothes. And he began to cough, perhaps to cover up the
muffled screams of horror that emerged from the shower area.

'What is that? What's going on?'

'Come on, that's enough,' the officer said nervously, when
he saw the other pulling up his trousers over his open shirt.

He took him outside, into the inclement cold of Oświęcim,
and he had him go inside a guard post, pulling out the two
sentries who were loitering there.

'Listen to my chest,' he ordered, putting a stethoscope in
his hands.

Epstein was slow to understand what he wanted. The other
man was already unbuttoning his shirt. He unhurriedly put
the stethoscope in his ears and felt, for the first time since
Drancy, invested with some sort of authority.

'Sit down,' he ordered, now a doctor.

The officer sat down on the guard post stool. Haïm listened
to his torso carefully and, from what he heard, he imagined
the depleted cavities secreting mucous. He had him change
position and listened to his chest and his back. He had him
stand up again, just for the fun of ordering around an SS
officer. For a few moments he thought that while he was listening to his chest they wouldn't send him to those showers
with the horrifying screams. Gavriloff had been right.

He wasn't able to completely hide his satisfaction as he
looked into his patient's eyes and told him that he would have
to undergo a more thorough examination.

'What do you mean?'

'Genital exploration, tactile examination of the kidney area.'

'Fine, fine, fine …'

'Do you feel unexplained pains here?' he asked pressing hard on his kidney with fingers of steel.

'Watch it, fuck!'

Doctor Epstein shook his head, pretending he was concerned.

'What is it?'

'You have tuberculosis.'

'Are you positive?'

'Without a shadow of a doubt. The illness is quite far along.'

'Well, they've been ignoring me here. Is it serious?'

'Very much so.'

'What do I have to do?' he said, ripping the stethoscope from his hands.

'I would have you sent to a sanatorium. It's the only thing that can be done.' And pointing to his yellow fingers, 'And no more tobacco, for God's sake.'

The officer called the sentries and told them to take that man to the showers, but one of the sentries gave him the sign that they'd finished for the day, that that had been the last turn. Then he put on his coat and shouted, as he went down to the buildings accompanied by his persistent cough, 'Take him to barracks twenty-six.'

And that saved his life. But he'd often said that saving his life was a worse punishment than death.

'I never imagined it was so horrific.'

'Well, you haven't heard it all.'

'Tell me.'

'No. I can't.'

'Come on.'

'Come here, I'll show you the paintings in the parlour.'

Sara showed him the paintings in the parlour, she showed him family photos, she responded patiently about who each person was, but when it was time to think about leaving because someone might be coming home, she said you'll have to go. You know what? I'll walk you part of the way.

And that was how I didn't meet your family.

## 21

No art was cultivated and developed by the Sophists as systematically as rhetoric. Sara. In rhetoric, the Sophists saw a perfect instrument to control men. Sara, why didn't you want to have children? Thanks to the Sophists and their rhetoric, public speeches became literary, since man began to see them as works of art worthy of being preserved in writing. Sara. From that point on, oratory training became essential to the career of a statesman, but the rhetoric included, in its realm of influence, all prose and particularly historiography. Sara, you are a mystery to me. Thus man can understand that in the fourth century the dominant position in literature was held by prose and not poetry. Strange. But logical.

'Where have you been, man, I can never find you anywhere.'

Adrià looked up from the Nestle opened to chapter fifteen, to Isocrates and new education, where he was immersed. As if he had trouble focusing his eyes, he took a few seconds to recognise the face that entered the cone of light given off by the green lampshade in the university library. Someone hushed them and Bernat had to lower his voice as he sat in the chair in front of him and said Adrià hasn't been here for a month; no, he's out; I don't know where he went; Adrià? He spends the whole day out. Really, man ... Not even in your own house does anyone know where you are!

'Here I am, studying.'

'That's twaddle; I spend hours here.'

'You?'

'Yes. Making friends with pretty girls.'

It was hard to emerge from the fourth century before Christ, especially if Bernat was there to scold him.

'How's it going?'

'Who's this girl that they say's been stuck to you like a leech?'

'Who says that?'

'Everyone. Gensana described her to me and everything: dark, straight hair, thin, dark eyes, an art student.'

'Well, then you already know everything …'

'Is it the one from the Palau de la Música? The one who called you Adrià Ican'trememberwhat?'

'You should be happy for me, shouldn't you?'

'Bloody hell, now you're in love.'

'Will you please be quiet!?'

'Sorry.' To Bernat: 'Should we leave?'

They strolled through the cloister and Adrià told someone for the first time that he was definitively, absolutely, devotedly, unconditionally in love with you, Sara. And don't say a word about it at my house.

'Oh, so it's even a secret from Little Lola.'

'I hope so.'

'But some day …'

'We'll see about that when that day comes.'

'In such circumstances, it's hard for me to imagine that you could do a favour for your former best friend who's now been demoted to mere acquaintance because your world revolves around that luscious girl named … what was her name?'

'Mireia.'

'Liar. Her name is Saga Voltes-Epstein.'

'Then why did you ask? And her name is Sara.'

'So why do you have to lie to me? And hide from me? Huh? It's me, Bernat, what the hell?'

'Don't get like that, for god's sake'

'I get like this because it seems like you don't care a whit about your life before Sara.'

Bernat extended his hand to him and Adrià, a bit surprised, shook it.

'Pleased to meet you, Mr Ardèvol. My name is Bernat Plensa i Punsoda and until a few months ago I was your best friend. Will you grant me audience?'

'My goodness.'

'What.'

'You are a bit soft in the head.'

'No. I'm angry: friends come first. And that's that.'

'The two things aren't mutually exclusive.'

'That's where you're wrong.'

We cannot look for a philosophical system in Isocrates. Isocrates takes what he can use from wherever he finds it. Pure syncretism and no systematic philosophy. Sara. Bernat stood in front of him to keep him from continuing, and stared: 'What are you thinking about?'

'I don't know. I'm very ...'

'It sucks to see a pal in love.'

'I don't know if I'm in love.'

'What the hell, didn't you say you were definitively, absolutely, devotedly, unconditionally in love? Bloody hell, it's only been a minute since you made that declaration.'

'But deep down I don't know if I am. I've never felt a ... a ... um, I don't know how to say it.'

'I can tell you that you are.'

'That I am what?'

'That you are in love.'

'How would you know, you've never been in love.'

'What do you know?'

They sat down on a bench in a corner of the cloister and Adrià thought that Isocrates was interested in the Sophists, but only in specific questions: for example, Xenophanes and his idea of cultural progress (I'll have to read Xenophanes). And his interest in Philip of Macedonia was the result of his discovery of the importance of personality in history. Strange.

'Bernat.'

Bernat, pretending that he didn't hear, looked the other way. Adrià insisted, 'Bernat.'

'What.'

'What's wrong?'

'I'm angry.'

'Why?'

'Because in June I have my ninth-year exam and I'm not ready.'

'I'll come to hear you.'

'Oh, you mean you won't be too busy with that girl who's got such a monopoly on you lately?'

'And come over if you want, or I'll come over to your house and we can practise.'

'I don't want to distract you from wooing the Mireia of your dreams.'

Definitively, Isocrates's Athens school, more than a philosophy, offered that which in Rome was called *humanitas* and which we would today call 'general culture', all that which Plato, and his Academy, left out. Oh, bloody hell. I'd like to peep in on them through a keyhole. And see Sara and her family.

'I swear that I'll come to hear you play. And if you want, she'll come too.'

'No. Only friends.'

'You're a bastard.'

'How.'

'What?'

'You can bet on it.'

'On what?'

'On that you're in love.'

'And what do you know?'

The Arapaho chief adopted a dignified silence. Did that child think that he was going to reveal his experiences and his feelings? Carson spat on the ground and took up where he'd left off: 'You can see it a mile off. Even your mother must have noticed.'

'Mother only has eyes for the shop.'

'Trust me.'

Isocrates. Xenophanes. Sara. Bernat. Syncretism. Violin exam. Sara. Philip of Macedonia. Sara. Sara. Sara.

Sara. Days, weeks, months of being by your side and respecting that ancestral silence you were often enveloped in. You were a girl with a sad but marvellously serene gaze. And I had increasingly more strength to study knowing that afterwards I would see you and I would melt looking into your eyes. We always met on the street, eating a hot dog in Sant Jaume Square or strolling through the gardens in Ciutadella

Park, in our joyful secrecy; never at your house or at my house unless we were absolutely sure that no one was there because our secret had to be a secret from both families. I didn't know exactly why; but you did. And I let myself be carried along by days and days of unremitting happiness without asking questions.

# 22

Adrià was thinking that he'd like to be able to write something like the *Griechische Geistesgeschichte*. That was an impossible model: thinking and writing like Nestle. And he thought many more things, because those were intense, lively, heroic, once-in-a-lifetime, epic, magnificent, superb months of discovery. Months of thinking of and living for Sara, which multiplied his desire and energy for studying and more studying, abstracted from the daily police charges against anything that sounded like student, which was a synonym for communist, mason, pro-Catalan and Jew, the four great scourges that Francoism strove to eliminate with truncheon blows and shots. None of that blackness existed for you and me, we spent our days studying, looking towards the future, looking into each other's eyes, and saying I love you Sara, I love you, Sara, I love you, Sara.

'How.'

'What?'

'You're repeating yourself.'

'I love you, Sara.'

'Me too, Adrià.'

Nunc et semper. Adrià sighed with satisfaction. Was he satisfied? I often asked myself if life satisfied me. In those months, waiting for Sara, I had to admit that yes, I was satisfied, that I was eager to live because in a matter of minutes, a thin woman with dark, straight hair, dark eyes, an arts student, would come round the bakery corner, wearing a plaid skirt that was really cute on her, and with a soothing smile and she'd say hello, Adrià, and we would hesitate over kissing because I knew that there on the street everyone would stare, they'd stare and point at us and say look at you two, growing up and leaving the nest, secretly in love … The day was grey and cloudy, but he was radiant. It was ten past eight, and that was strange. She is as punctual as I am. And I've been waiting ten minutes. She's sick. A sore throat. She got flattened by a hit and run taxi. A flowerpot fell on her from a sixth-floor flat, my God, I'll have to go to every hospital in Barcelona. Ah, here she is! No: it was a thin woman, with dark, straight hair, but with light eyes and lipstick and twenty years older, who passed by the tram stop and probably wasn't named Sara. He struggled to think of other things. He lifted his head. The plane trees on the Gran Via sprouted with new leaves, but the passing cars couldn't care less. Not me! The cycle of life! Spring ... Follas novas. He looked at his watch again. Unthinkable, twenty minutes late. Three or four more trams passed and he couldn't help being overcome by a strange premonition. Sara. ¿Qué pasa ó redor de min? ¿Qué me pasa que eu non sei? Despite the premonition, Adrià Ardèvol waited two hours on a stone bench on the Gran Via, beside the tramvia stop, his eyes glued to the bakery corner, not thinking about the *Griechische Geistesgeschichte* because his head was filled with the thousand horrible things that could have befallen Sara. He didn't know what to do. Sara, the daughter of the good king, is sick; doctors come to see her, doctors and other people. It doesn't make any sense to keep waiting. But he doesn't know what else to do. He didn't know what to do with his life now that Sara didn't show up. His legs carried him to Sara's house, despite his beloved's strict orders against it: but he had to be there when the ambulance carried her off. The doors were closed and the doorman was inside, distributing the post in the letter boxes. A short woman was vacuuming the central carpet. The doorman finished his work and opened the doors. The sound of the vacuum was like an insult. Dressed in some sort of ridiculous apron, the doorman looked up at the sky to see if it had made up its mind to rain or if the weather would hold out. Or perhaps he was waiting for the ambulance ... Daughter, my daughter, what is it that ails you? Mother, my mother, I think you know full well. He wasn't sure which balcony was hers ... The doorman noticed that boy loitering, watching the building; he shot him a suspicious look. Adrià pretended to be waiting for a taxi; maybe the one that had mowed her down. He began to take a few steps down the street. Teño medo dunha cousa que vive e que non se ve. Teño medo á desgracia traidora que ven, e que nunca se sabe ónde ven. Sara, ónde estás.

'Sara Voltes?'

'Who shall I say is calling?' A confident, elegant, well-dressed lady's voice.

'No, uh. The parish of ... The drawings, the show of drawings at ...'

When you make up a lie, you have to think it over before you start talking, bloody hell. You can't take the first step and stand there with your mouth open and nothing coming out, you idiot. Ridiculous. Dreadfully ridiculous. So, it was logical that the elegant, confident lady's voice said I think you've got the wrong number and hung up delicately, politely, softly, and I cursed myself because I hadn't been up to the task. It must have been her mother. Poison you have given me, Mother, you want to kill me. Daughter, my daughter, now you must confess. Adrià hung up. At the back of the flat, Little Lola was going through the closets because she was changing the sheets. On the large table in Father's study, Adrià had a heap of books, but he could only focus on the useless telephone, which was unable to tell him where Sara was.

Fine Arts! He had never been there. He didn't know where it was, if it even existed. We had always met in neutral territory, at your indication, waiting for the day when the sun sparkled on the horizon. When I got out of the metro at the Jaume I stop, it had started to rain and I had no umbrella because I never carried an umbrella in Barcelona and I was only able to make the ridiculous gesture of raising my jacket lapels. I stood in the square of the Verònica, in front of that strange neo-classical building, which I never knew existed before that day. No sign of Sara inside nor outside; not in any hallway or classroom or studio. I went to the Llotja building, which retained the name of its former function as a fish market but there they knew nothing of fish or fine arts. At that point I was completely soaked; but then I thought to go to the Massana School and there, at the entrance, protected by a dark umbrella, I saw her chatting and laughing with a boy. She wore the pumpkin-coloured scarf that was so pretty on her. And unexpectedly she kissed the boy's cheek and she had to get on her tiptoes to do it, and Adrià felt the brutal stab of jealousy for the first time, and an unbearable tightness in his chest. And then the boy went into the school and she turned and started to walk towards me. My heart wanted to leap out and into someone else's body because the happiness I had felt a few hours ago faded into tears of disappointment. She didn't say hello; she didn't notice me; she wasn't Sara. She was a thin girl, with straight, dark hair but light eyes and, most of all, not Sara. And I, dripping with rain, was once again the happiest man in the universe.

'No, uh … I'm a classmate of hers in art school who …'
    'She's out of town.'
    'Excuse me?'
    'She's out of town.'
    Was it her father? I didn't know if she had an older brother, or if there was another uncle besides the memory of Uncle Haïm who lived with them.
    'But … what do you mean by out of town?'
    'Sara has moved to Paris.'
    The happiest man in the universe, when he hung up the phone, watched as his eyes, all on their own, against his will, began to cry disconsolately. He didn't understand anything; how could it be that Sara … , but she didn't tell me anything. From one day to the next, Sara. On Friday, when we saw each other, we made a date to meet at the tram stop! The forty-seven, yes, as we always did since … And what is she doing, in Paris? Huh? Why did she run away? What did I do to her?
    Adrià, for ten days, rain or shine, every morning, went to the tram stop at eight, hoping for a miracle and that Sara hadn't moved to Paris, but that really she was back here; or that it was just a test to see if you really loved me; or I don't know but something, anything and let's see if she shows up

before five trams pass. Until the eleventh day when, as soon as he reached the tram stop, he told himself that he was sick and tired of watching trams pass that they would never get on together. And he never again set foot on that tram stop, Sara. Never again.

In the conservatory, lying left and right, I managed to get the address of Master Castells, who had been a teacher there some time back. I imagined that, since they were relatives, he would have Sara's address in Paris. If she was in Paris. If she was even alive. The doorbell to Master Castell's flat went do-fa. My impatience led me to press do-fa, do-fa, do-fa and I pulled my finger away, frightened by how little control I had over my feelings. Or no: more likely because I didn't want Master Castells to get angry and say now I won't tell it to you, because of your poor manners. No one opened the door to offer me Sara's address and wish me luck.

'Do-fa, do-fa, do-fa.'

Nothing. After a few moments of insistence, Adrià looked round without knowing what he should do. Then I rang the neighbours' bell across the landing, which made an impersonal, ugly sound, like the one at my house. Very quickly, as if they had been waiting for some time, a fat woman opened the door, dressed in a sky-blue smock and a flowered kitchen apron. The evil eye. Hands on her hips, defiantly. 'What?' she said.

'Do you know if …' pointing behind me, towards Master Castells's door.

'The pianist?'

'Exactly.'

'Thank God he died, it's been …' She looked back and shouted, 'How long has it been, Taio?'

'Six months, twelve days and three hours!' said a hoarse voice from a distance.

'Six months, twelve days and …' Shouting into the flat, 'How many hours?'

'Three!' the hoarse voice.

'And three hours,' repeated the woman to Adrià. 'And

thank God for the peace and quiet, now we can listen to the
radio without interruptions. I don't know how he made that
pianola play every day, every day, all day long.' As if remembering something, 'What did you want from him?'

'Did he have …'

'Family?'

'Uh huh.'

'No. He lived alone.' Into the flat: 'He didn't have any relatives, did he?'

'No, just that damned bloody piano!' Taio's hoarse voice.

'And in Paris?'

'In Paris?'

'Yes. Relatives in Paris …'

'I have no idea.' Incredulous: 'That man, relatives in Paris?'

'Yes.'

'No.' As a general conclusion: 'For us he's dead and gone.'

When she left him alone on the landing with that flickering light bulb, Adrià knew that many doors were closing to
him. He went back home and then the thirty days of desert
and penitence began. At night he dreamt that he went to Paris
and stood in the middle of the street calling her name, but the
din of the traffic drowned out his desperate cries and he woke
up sweaty and crying, not understanding the world that, until
recently, had seemed so placid. He didn't leave the house for
a few weeks. He played the Storioni and was able to get a sad
sound out of it; but he felt his fingers lazy. And he wanted to
reread Nestle but couldn't. Even Euripides's voyage from rhetoric to truth, which had enthralled him on his first reading,
now said nothing to him. Euripides was Sara. He was right
about one thing, that Euripides: human reason cannot win
out over the irrational powers of the emotional mind. I cannot
study, I cannot think. I have to cry. Come, please, Bernat.

Bernat had never seen his friend in such a state. He was impressed to learn that heartache could be so profound. And he
wanted to help him, although he didn't have much experience
in binding hearts and he told him look at it this way, Adrià.

'How?'

'Well, if she just left like this, without any explanation …'

'What?'

'Well, she's a bi

'Don't even think about insulting her. Got it?'

'Very well, as you wish.' He looked around the study, opening his arms. 'But don't you see how she left you? And without even a sad piece of paper that says Adrià, lad, I found somebody better-looking? Bloody hell. Don't you see that that's not right?'

'Better-looking and more intelligent, yes, that's what I thought.'

'There are plenty better-looking than you, but more intelligent …'

Silence. Every once in a while, Adrià shook his head to show he didn't understand any of it.

'Let's go to her parents' house and say: Mr and Mrs Voltes-Epstein, what the hell is going on? What are you hiding from me? Where is Saga, etcetera. What do you think?'

Both of us in Father's study, which is now mine. Adrià stood up and approached the wall where years later your self-portrait would hang. He leaned against it as if he wanted to tickle the future. He shook his head: Bernat's idea wasn't very well thought out.

'Do you want me to entertain you with the Ciaccona?' attempted Bernat.

'Yes. Play it on Vial.'

Bernat did so, very well. Despite his pain and anguish, Adrià listened to his friend's version attentively and came to the conclusion that it was correctly played, but that, sometimes, Bernat had a problem: he didn't get deep into the soul of things. He had something about him that didn't allow him to be truthful. And there I was, wallowing in pain and unable to keep myself from analysing the aesthetic object.

'Are you feeling better?' he asked when he finished.

'Yes.'

'Did you like it?'

'No.'

I should have kept it to myself, I know. But I'm unable to. I'm like Mother in that way.

'What do you mean by no?' Even his tone of voice had changed, it was more shrill, more on guard, more gobsmacked …

'Doesn't matter, forget about it.'

'No, I'm very interested.'

'Fine, all right.'

Little Lola was at the back of the flat. Mother, in the shop. Adrià dropped onto the sofa. Standing in front of him, the Storioni in his hand, Bernat waited for the verdict and Adrià said welllll technically it's a perfect version, or almost perfect; but you don't get to the heart of things; it seems like you're afraid of the truth.

'You're insane. What is truth?'

And Jesus, instead of replying, remained silent as Pilate left the room impatiently. But since I'm not sure what the truth is, I was forced to reply.

'I don't know. I recognise it when I hear it. And I don't recognise it in you. I recognise it in music and in poetry. And in prose. And in painting. But only every once in a while.'

'Ffucking envy.'

'Yes. I can admit I envy your ability to play that.'

'Sure. Now you're trying to smooth things over.'

'But I don't envy how you play.'

'Bloody hell, don't pull your punches.'

'Your goal is to trap that truth and figure out how to express it.'

'Whoa.'

'At least you have a goal. I have none.'

So the friendly evening in which Bernat came over to comfort his afflicted friend ended in a bitter fight in hushed voices over aesthetic truth and you can go fuck off, you hear me, fuck off. Now I understand why Saga Voltes-Epstein split. And Bernat left, slamming the door. And a few seconds later, Little Lola peeked into the study and said what happened?

'No, Bernat was in a big rush, you know how he always is.'

Little Lola looked at Adrià, who was carefully examining the violin to keep from gazing idly into his pain. Little Lola was about to say something, but she stopped herself. Then

Adrià realised that she was still standing there, as if wanting to chat.

'What?' I said, with an expression that showed I didn't have the slightest desire to converse.

'Nothing. Do you know what? I'm going to make dinner because Mother should be coming soon.'

She left and I started to clean the rosin off the violin and I felt sad to the marrow of my bones.

## 23

'You're mad as a hatter, my boy.'

Mother sat down in her armchair where she takes her coffee. Adrià had outlined the conversation in the worst possible way. Sometimes I wonder why she didn't tell me to buzz off more often. Because instead of starting by saying Mother, I've decided to continue my studies in Tübingen and her answering in Germany? Aren't you doing fine here, my son? Instead of that, I started by saying, Mother, I have to tell you something.

'What?' Frightened, she sat in her armchair where she takes her coffee; frightened because we had lived together for years without any need to tell each other things, but, above all, without the need to say Mother, I have to tell you something.

'Well, a while back I spoke with a woman named Daniela Amato.'

'Whom did you say you spoke with?'

'With my half-sister.'

Mother leapt up as if she'd sat on a pin. I had her against me for the rest of the conversation: fool, worse than a fool, you don't know anything about getting what you want.

'You have no half-sister.'

'The fact that you've hidden it from me doesn't mean I don't have one. Daniela Amato, from Rome. I have her phone number and address.'

'What are you conspiring?'

'Oh, please. Why?'

'Don't trust that thief.'

'She told me that she wants to be a partner in the shop.'

'You know she stole Can Casic from you?'

'If I understood correctly, Father gave it to her; she didn't steal anything from me.'

'She's like a vampire. She'll want the shop for herself.'

'No. She wants to be a part of it.'

'Why do you think she wants it?'

'I don't know. Because it was Father's?'

'Well, now it's mine and my answer is no to any offer that comes from that tart. Fuck her.'

Wow: we'd got off on a good foot. She hadn't said ffuck because she'd used it as a verb and not an adjective, like the previous time I had heard her say it. I like Mother's linguistic refinement. Still standing, she paced around the dining room, silent, thinking whether or not she should continue with the cursing. She decided not to: 'Is that all you wanted to tell me?'

'No. I also wanted to tell you that I'm leaving home.'

Mother sat back down in the armchair where she took her coffee.

'You're mad as a hatter, my boy.' Silence. Nervous hands. 'You've got everything here. What have I done?'

'Nothing. What makes you ask that?'

She wrung her hands nervously. Then she took a deep breath to calm down and placed both hands flat on her skirt.

'And the shop? Don't you ever plan on taking it over?'

'It doesn't appeal to me.'

'That's a lie. It's your favourite place.'

'No. I like the things in the shop. But the work ...'

She looked at me with what I took for resentment.

'What you want is to contradict me. As always.'

Why didn't we ever love each other, Mother and I? It's a mystery to me. All my life I've envied normal children, who can say mum, oh, I hurt my knee so bad, and whose mother would frighten away the pain with a mere kiss. My mother didn't have that power. When I dared to tell her that I'd hurt my knee, instead of trying for the miracle, she sent me to Little Lola while she waited, impatiently, for my intellectual gift to begin to make some other sort of miracles.

'Aren't you happy here?'

'I've decided to continue my studies in Tübingen.'

'In Germany? Aren't you fine here?'

'I want to study under Wilhelm Nestle.'

To be precise, I had no idea if Nestle still taught at Tübingen. Actually, I didn't even know if he was still alive. In fact, at the time of our conversation, he had been dead for a little over eight years. And yes: he had taught classes in Tübingen, and that was why I had decided I wanted to study in Tübingen.

'Who is he?'

'A historian of philosophy. And I also want to meet Coșeriu.'

That time I wasn't lying. They said he was unbearable but a genius.

'Who is he?'

'A linguist. One of the great philologists of our century.'

'These studies won't make you happy, my son.'

Let's see: if I look at it with perspective, I'd have to say she was right. Nothing has ever made me happy except you, and you are the one who has made me suffer most. I have been close to much happiness; I have had some joy. I have enjoyed moments of peace and immense gratitude towards the world and towards some people. I have been close to beautiful things and concepts. And sometimes I feel the itch to possess valuable objects, which made me understand Father's anxiousness. But since I was the age I was, I smiled smugly and said no one ever said I had to be happy. And I was silent, satisfied.

'Look at how stupid you are.'

I looked at her, disarmed. Because with six words she had made me feel completely unpresentable. And then I attacked viciously, 'You made me how I am. I want to study, whether it makes me happy or not.'

Adrià Ardèvol was that much of a smart arse. If I could start my life over again now, the first thing I would search for would be happiness; and I would try, if possible, to shield it and keep it close throughout my entire life, without any other aspirations. If a child of mine had answered me the way I answered my mother, he would have got a slap. But I have no children. All my life I've only ever been a son. Why, Sara, why didn't you ever want to have children?

'What you want is to get far away from me.'

'No,' I lied. 'Why would I want that?'

'What you want is to run away.'

'Come now!' I lied again. 'Why would I want to run away?'

'Why don't you tell me?'

I would never tell her, even if I were drunk, about Sara, my desire to merge, to start afresh, to search Paris from top to bottom, about the two visits I had made to the Voltes-Epstein house until, on the third, her father and mother told me, very politely, that their daughter had, voluntarily, gone to Paris because, in her words, she wanted to get away from you, who were hurting her so much. So you can understand that you are not welcome in this house.

'But I ...'

'Don't insist, young man. We have nothing against you,' he lied, 'but you must understand that our duty is to defend our daughter.'

Desperate, I didn't understand a thing. Mr Voltes got up and indicated for me to do the same. Slowly, I obeyed him. I couldn't help the tears because I'm the crying type; they burned like drops of sulphuric acid cleaving my humiliated cheeks.

'There must be some misunderstanding.'

'It doesn't seem that way,' said Sara's mother, in guttural Catalan. She was tall, with hair that had been dark and was now slightly greyed and dark eyes, as if she were a photo of Sara thirty years on. 'Sara doesn't want to have anything to do with you. Not a single thing.'

I started to leave the room, forced out by Mr Voltes's gesture. I stopped, 'She didn't leave anything in writing, any note, for me?'

'No.'

I left that house that I had visited secretly when Sara loved me, without saying goodbye to her ever-so-polite but ever-so-inflexible parents. I left stifling my sobs. The door closed silently behind me and for a few seconds I remained on the landing, as if that was somehow a way to be closer to Sara. Then I burst into unbridled tears.

'I don't want to run away, nor do I have any reason to.' I paused to add emphasis. 'Do you understand, Mother?'

I had lied to Mother for the third time and I swear I heard a rooster crow.

'I understood you perfectly.' Looking into my eyes: 'Listen, Adrià.'

It was the first time she called me Adrià and not son. The first time in my life. The twelfth of April, nineteen sixty- or seventy-something.

'Yes?'

'You don't have to work if you don't want to. Devote your time to the violin and to reading your books. And when I'm dead, hire a manager for the shop.'

'Don't talk about dying. And I'm finished with the violin.'

'Where do you say you want to go?'

'To Tübingen.'

'Where is that?'

'In Germany.'

'And what's there that you're missing out on?'

'Coşeriu.'

'Who is that?'

'Don't you spend all your time at the library, chasing girls? System, norm, speech.'

'Come on, who is he?'

'A Romanian linguist I want to study under.'

'Now that you mention it, his name rings a bell.'

He grew silent, sulky. But he couldn't help himself: 'Aren't you studying here? Aren't you half finished, with A+s in everything, bloody hell?'

I didn't mention my wanting to study under Nestle because when Bernat and I had met up at the university bar, surrounded by shouting, pushing, hurrying and white coffees, I already knew that Wilhelm Nestle had been dead for some time. It would have been like faking a quote in a footnote.

After two days and no news, he came over to the house to practise for his exam, as if I were his teacher. Adrià opened the door and Bernat pointed an accusatory finger in greeting: 'Don't you realise that in Tübingen they teach classes in German?'

'Wenn du willst, kannst du mit dem Storioni spielen,' replied Adrià with an icy smile, as he ushered him inside.

'I don't know what you just said, but all right.'

And as he put rosin on the bow, just a smidge, concentrating so as to not saturate the instrument, he grumbled that it would have been nice to have been consulted.

'Why?'

'Come on, we're supposed to be friends.'

'That's why I told you now.'

'Best friends, you twat! You could have told me that you were considering the crazy idea of spending a few weeks in Tübingen; what do you think, best pal of mine? Haven't you ever heard of that?'

'You would have told me to forget about it. And we've already had this conversation.'

'Not exactly in these terms.'

'You want to always have me around.'

Bernat, in response, left the scores on the table and started to play the first movement of the Beethoven concerto. Ignoring the introduction, I was his out of tune orchestra, following the piano reduction, even imitating the timbre of some instruments. I ended up exhausted, but thrilled and happy because Bernat had played impeccably, beyond perfect. As if he wanted to make it clear that he hadn't liked my last comment. When he finished, I respected the silence that reigned.

'What?'

'Good.'

'That's all?'

'Very good. Different.'

'Different?'

'Different. If I heard it right, you were inside the music.'

They grew silent. He sat down and wiped away the sweat. He looked me in the eye: 'What you want is to run away. I don't know from what, but you want to run away. I hope it's not from me.'

I looked at the other scores he had with him.

'I think it's a good idea for you to play the Massià pieces. Who will accompany you on the piano?'

'Haven't you thought that you might get awfully bored studying those things you want to study, about ideas and all that?'

'Massià deserves it. And they are lovely. The one I like best is Allegro spiritoso.'

'And why study with a linguist, if what you want is cultural history?'

'Watch it with the Ciaccona, it's treacherous.'

'Don't go, you bastard.'

'Yes,' he said. 'From Fine Arts.'

'And what is it?'

The icy, distrusting figure of Mrs Voltes-Epstein terrified him. He swallowed hard and said she is missing some paperwork for the enrolment transfer and that's why we need her address.

'There is nothing missing.'

'Yes there is. The recidivism policy.'

'And what's that?' She sounded truly curious.

'Nothing. A slight detail. But it has to be signed.' He looked at the papers and casually let drop, 'She has to sign it.'

'Leave me the papers and …'

'No, no. I'm not authorised to do that. Perhaps if you give me the name of the school in Paris where she has transferred her enrolment …'

'No.'

'They don't have it in Fine Arts.' He corrected himself. 'We don't have it.'

'Who are you?'

'Pardon?'

'My daughter hasn't transferred any enrolment. Who are you?'

'And she slammed the door in my face. Bam!'

'She saw right through you.'

'Yup.'

'Shit.'

'Yup.'

'Thanks, Bernat.'

'I'm sorry … I'm sure you could have done it much better.'

'No, no. You did the best you could.'

'It makes me so angry, you know.'

After a while of heavy silence, Adrià said I'm sorry but I think I'm going to cry a little bit.

Bernat's examination ended with our Ciaccona from the second suite. I had heard him play it so many times … and I always had things to tell him, as if I were the virtuoso and he the disciple. He began studying it after we heard Heifetz play it at the Palau de la Música. Fine. Perfect. But once again without soul, perhaps because he was nervous about the exam. Soulless, as if the last rehearsal at my house a mere twenty-four hours before had been a mirage. Bernat's creative breath went flat when he was in front of an audience; he lacked that bit of God, which he tried to replace with determination and practice, and the result was good but too predictable. That was it: my best friend was too bloody predictable, even in his attacks.

He finished the exam dripping with sweat, surely thinking that he had pulled it off. The three judges, who'd had vinegary looks on their faces throughout the two-hour audition, deliberated for a few seconds and unanimously decided to give him an excellent, with personal congratulations from each of them. And Trullols, who was in the audience, waited until Bernat's mother had hugged him, and all that stuff that mothers who aren't mine do, and she gave him a kiss on the cheek, excited, the way some teachers get excited, and I heard her prophesise, you're the best student I've ever had; you have a brilliant future ahead of you.

'Extraordinary,' said Adrià.

Bernat stopped loosening his bow and looked at his friend. He put it away in the case and closed it, in silence. Adrià insisted: impressive, lad; congratulations.

'Yesterday I told you that you were my friend. That you are my friend.'

'Yes. You recently said best friend.'

'Exactly. You don't lie to your best friend.'

'Pardon?'

'I played competently and that's it. I have no élan.'

'You played well today.'

'You would have done it better than me.'

'What are you saying! I haven't picked up a violin in two years!'

'If my bloody best friend is unable to tell me the truth and he'd rather just act like everyone else ...'

'What are you saying?'

'Don't ever lie to me again, Adrià.' He wiped the sweat from his brow. 'Your comments are very irritating and you're making me angry.'

'Well, I ...'

'But I know that you are the only one who says the truth.' He winked. 'Auf Wiedersehen.'

When I had the train ticket in my hands, I understood that going to Tübingen to study was much more than thinking of the future. It was ending my childhood; distancing myself from my Arcadia. Yes, yes: I was a lonely, unhappy child with parents who were unresponsive to anything beyond my intelligence, and who didn't know how to ask me if I wanted to go to Tibidabo to see the automatons that moved like people when you inserted a coin. But being a child means having the ability to smell the flower that gleams amidst the toxic mud. And it means knowing how to be happy with that five-axle lorry that was a cardboard hatbox. Buying the ticket to Stuttgart, I knew that my age of innocence was over.

# IV

## PALIMPSESTUS

There isn't a single organisation that can
protect itself from a grain of sand.

Michel Tournier

## 24

Long ago, when the earth was flat and those reckless travellers who reached the end of the world hit up against the cold fog or hurled themselves off a dark cliff, there was a holy man who decided to devote his life to the Lord Our God. He was a Catalan named Nicolau Eimeric, and he became a well-known professor of Sacred Theology for the Order of Preachers at the monastery of Girona. His religious zeal led him to firmly command the Inquisition against evil heresy in the lands of Catalonia and the kingdoms of Valencia. Nicolau Eimeric had been born in Baden-Baden on 25 November, 1900; he had been promoted rapidly to SS Obersturmbannführer and, after a glorious first period as Oberlagerführer of Auschwitz, in 1944 he again took up the reins on the Hungarian problem. In a legal document, he condemned as perversely heretical the book *Philosophica amoris* by the obstinate Ramon Llull, a Catalan native from the kingdom of the Majorcas. He likewise declared perversely heretical all those in Valencia, Alcoi, Barcelona or Saragossa, Alcanyís, Montpeller or any other location who read, disseminated, taught, copied or thought about the pestiferous heretical doctrine of Ramon Llull, which came not from Christ but from the devil. And thus he signed it this day, 13 July, 1367, in the city of Girona.

'Proceed. I am beginning to have a fever and I don't want to go to bed until …'

'You can go untroubled, Your Excellency.'

Friar Nicolau wiped the sweat from his brow, half from the heat and half from fever, and watched Friar Miquel de Susqueda, his young secretary, finish the condemning document in his neat hand. Then he went out onto the street scorched by a blazing sun, barely catching his breath before he immersed himself in the slightly less hot shade of the chapel of

Santa Àgueda. He got down on his knees in the middle of the
room and, humbly bowing his head before the divine sacrar-
ium, said oh, Lord, give me strength, don't let my human
feebleness weaken me; don't let the calumnies, rumours, envy
and lies unsettle my courage. Now it is the King himself who
dares to criticise my proceedings to benefit the true and only
faith, Lord. Give me strength to never stop serving you in my
mission of strict vigilance over the truth. After saying an amen
that was almost a fleeting thought, he remained kneeling to
allow the strangely scorching sun to sink until it caressed the
western mountains; with his mind blank, in prayer position,
in direct communication with the Lord of the Truth.

When the light entering through the window began to
wane, Friar Nicolau left the chapel with the same energy
he'd entered with. Outside, he eagerly breathed in the scent
of thyme and dried grass that emanated from the earth, still
warm from the hottest day in the memory of several generations. He again wiped the sweat from his brow, which was
now burning, and he headed towards the grey stone building
at the end of the narrow street. At the entrance, he had to
control his impatience because just then a woman, always the
same one, accompanied by the Wall-eyed Man of Salt, who
acted as her husband, walked slowly into the palace, loaded
down with a sack of turnips bigger than she was.

'Must you use this door?' said Friar Miquel in irritation, as
he came out to receive her.

'The garden entrance is flooded, Your Excellency.'

In a curt voice, Friar Nicolau Eimeric asked if everything
was prepared and, continuing his long strides towards the
room, thought oh, Lord, all my energies, day and night, are
focused on the defence of Your Truth. Give me strength, for
at the end of the light it will be you who shall judge me and
not men.

I am a dead man, thought Josep Xarom. He hadn't been able
to hold the black gaze of the Inquisitor devil who had swept
into the room, formulated his question in shouts and now
waited impatiently for an answer.

'What hosts?' said Doctor Xarom after a long pause, his voice drowned in panic.

The Inquisitor got up, wiped the sweat from his brow for the third time since he'd entered the interrogation room and repeated the question of how much did you pay Jaume Malla for the consecrated hosts that he gave you.

'I know nothing about this. I have never met any Jaume Malla. I do not know what hosts are.'

'That means that you consider yourself a Jew.'

'Well … I am Jewish, yes, Your Excellency. You already know that. My family and all the families in the Jewish Quarter are under the King's protection.'

'In these four walls, the only protection is God's. Never forget that.'

Most High Adonai, where are you now, thought the venerable Doctor Josep Xarom, knowing that it was a sin to distrust the Most High.

During an hour that dragged on, Friar Nicolau, with the patience of a saint, ignoring his headache and the heating up of his internal humours, tried to discover the secret of the nefarious crime this abominable creature had committed with the consecrated hosts, which was detailed in the meticulous and providential report, but Josep Xarom just kept repeating things he'd already said: that he was named Josep Xarom, that he had been born in the Jewish Quarter, where he had lived all this time, that he had learned the arts of medicine, that he helped babies into the world both in and out of the Jewish Quarter and that his life was the practice of that profession and nothing more.

'And attending synagogue on your Sabbath day.'

'The King has not forbidden that.'

'The King cannot speak of the foundations of the soul. You are accused of practising nefarious crimes with consecrated hosts. What can you say in your defence?'

'Who is my accuser?'

'There is no need for you to know that.'

'Yes, there is. This is a calumny and, depending on its

source, I can demonstrate the reasons that would move someone to

'Are you insinuating that a good Christian could lie?' shocked, astounded, Friar Nicolau.

'Yes, Your Excellency. Undoubtedly.'

'That worsens your situation because if you insult a Christian you insult the Lord God Jesus Christ whose blood is on your hands.'

My Highest and Most Merciful Lord, you are the one and only God, Adonai.

Inquisitor General Nicolau Eimeric, without even looking at him – such was the disdain he provoked in him – ran his palm over his forehead with concern and told the men holding the stubborn man to torture him and bring him to me here in an hour with the declaration signed.

'Which torture, Your Excellency?' asked Friar Miquel.

'The rack, for one credo in unum deum. And hooks if need be, for a couple of ourfathers.'

'Your Excellency ...'

'And if that doesn't refresh his memory, repeat as necessary.'

He approached Friar Miquel de Susqueda, who had lowered his gaze some time earlier, and almost in a whisper ordered him to let this Jaume Malla know that if he sells or gives hosts to any Jew, he will hear from me.

'We don't know who he is, this Jaume Malla.' Taking a deep breath. 'He may not even exist.'

But the holy man did not hear him because he was focused on his terrible headache and offering it up to God as penance.

Doctor Josep Xarom of Girona – on the rack and with butcher's hooks in his flesh, ripping tendons – confessed that yes, yes, yes, for Almighty God, I did it, I bought them from this man you say, yes, yes, but stop, for the love of God.

'And what did you do with them?' Friar Miquel de Susqueda, sitting before the rack, trying not to look at the blood that dripped from it.

'I don't know. Whatever you say but, please, don't turn it any more, I ...'

'Watch out, if he faints on us, the declaration is over.'

'So? He's already confessed.'

'Very well: then you talk to Friar Nicolau, yes, you, the redhead, and you tell him that the prisoner merely slept through the torture, and I can assure you that he himself will put us on the rack, accused of putting sticks in the wheels of divine justice. Both of us.' Exasperated: 'Don't you know His Excellency?'

'Sir, but if we …'

'Yes. And I'll be the notary for the record of your torture. Look lively, come now.'

'Let's see: grab him by the hair, like this. All right, let's have it: what did you do with the consecrated hosts? Do you hear me? Hey! Xarom, fucking hell!'

'I will not tolerate such language in a building of the Holy Inquisition,' said Friar Miquel, indignant. 'Behave like good Christians.'

The light had completely disappeared and the room was now lit by a torch whose flame trembled like Xarom's soul, as he listened, in a semi-conscious state, to the conclusions of the high tribunal read by the powerful voice of Nicolau Eimeric, condemning him, in the presence of the attendant witnesses, to death purified by flame, on the eve of Saint James the Apostle's Day, since he refused to repent with a conversion that would have saved him, if not from the death of his body, at least from the death of his soul. Friar Nicolau, after signing the sentence, warned Friar Miquel: 'You must cut out the prisoner's tongue first. Remember that.'

'Wouldn't a gag be sufficient, Your Excellency?'

'You must cut out the prisoner's tongue first,' insisted Friar Nicolau with saintly patience. 'And I will not tolerate any leniency.'

'But Your Excellency …'

'They know all the tricks, they bite the gag, they … And I want the heretics to be mute from the moment they are brought to the bonfire. Even before it's lit because, if they still have the ability to speak, their blasphemies and vituperation can gravely wound the piety of those who attend the event.'

'That has never happened here ...'

'It has in Lleida. And while I hold this post, I will not allow it.' He looked at him with eyes so black they hurt, and in a softer voice; 'Never, I will never allow it.' Raising his tone: 'Look me in the eyes when I speak to you, Friar Miquel! Never.'

He stood up and left the room quickly without looking at the secretaries, or the prisoner or the rest of those in attendance because he was invited for dinner at the episcopal palace, he was running late and was terribly uncomfortable in the intense heat of the day, what with his headache and fevers.

Outside, the extreme cold had turned the downpour into a profuse, silent snowfall. Inside, as he looked into the iridescent colour of the wine in his raised glass, he said, I was born into a wealthy and very religious family, and the moral rectitude of my upbringing has helped me to assume the difficult task, by direct order from the Führer via the explicit instructions from Reichsführer Himmler, of becoming a stalwart defence against the enemy inside out fatherland. This wine is excellent, Doctor.

'Thank you. It is an honour for me to be able to taste it here, in my improvised home.'

'Improvised but comfortable.'

A second little sip. Outside, the snow was already covering the earth's unmentionables with a modest thick sheet of cold. The wine was warming. Obersturmbannführer Rudolf Höss, who had been born in Girona during the rainy autumn of 1320, in that remote period when the earth was flat and reckless travellers' eyes grew wide when they insisted, enflamed by curiosity and fantasy, on seeing the end of the world, was especially proud to be sharing that wine in a tête à tête with the prestigious and well-situated Doctor Voigt and he was anxious to mention it, oh so casually, to one of his colleagues. And life is beautiful. Especially now that the earth is flat again and that they, with the help of the Führer's serene gaze, were showing humanity who held the strength, power, truth and the future and teaching humanity how the unfailing attainment of the ideal was incompatible with any form of compassion. The strength of the Reich was limitless and turned the actions of all the Eimerics in history into child's play. With the wine's assistance, he came up with a sublime phrase: 'For me, orders are sacred, no matter how difficult they may seem, since as an SS I must be willing to completely sacrifice my personality in the fulfilment of my duty to the fatherland. That is why, in 1334, when I turned fourteen, I entered the monastery of the Dominican friar preachers in my city of Girona and I have devoted my entire life to making the Truth shine. They call me cruel, King Pedro hates me, envies me and would like to annihilate me, but I remain impassive because against the faith I defend neither my king nor my father. I do not recognise my mother and I do not respect my lineage since above all I serve only the Truth. You will only ever find the Truth coming from my mouth, Your Grace.'

The Bishop himself filled Friar Nicolau's glass. He took a taste without realising what he was drinking because, enraged, he continued his speech and said I have suffered exile, I was deposed from my post as Inquisitor by order of King Pedro, I was chosen Vicar General of the Dominican order here in Girona, but what you don't know is that the accursed king pressured Holy Father Urbà, who ended up not accepting my appointment.

'I didn't know that.'

The Bishop, seated in a comfortable chair but with his back very straight and his entire being alert, silently contemplated how the Inquisitor General wiped the sweat from his brow with his habit sleeve. After two good ourfathers: 'Are you feeling well, Your Excellency?'

'Yes.'

The Bishop was silent and took a sip of wine.

'Nevertheless, Your Excellency, you are now Vicar General again.'

'My constancy and faith in God and his holy mercy made them restore my post and dignity as Inquisitor General.'

'All for the good.'

'Yes, but now the King threatens me with new exile and I've been warned that he wants to have me killed.'

The Bishop thought it over for quite some time. In the end,

His Grace lifted a timid finger and said King Pedro maintains that your obsession with condemning the work of Llull ...

'Llull?' shouted Eimeric. 'Have you read anything by Llull, Your Grace?'

'Well, I ... Well ... ummm, yes.'

'And?'

Eimeric stared with that black gaze of his, the one that penetrated souls. His Grace swallowed hard: 'I don't know what to say. I ... What I read ... Anyway, I didn't know that ...' He ended up capitulating: 'I'm no theologian.'

'I'm no engineer, but I've managed to get the crematoria in Birkenau to function twenty-four hours a day without breaking down. And I've got my men who supervise the Sonderkommando's rat squads not to go mad.'

'How did you do it, dear Oberlagerführer Höss?'

'I don't know. By preaching the Truth. Showing all the hungry souls that there is only one evangelical doctrine, and that my sacred mission is to keep errors and evil from rotting the essence of the church. Therefore I work to eliminate all heresies and the most efficient way to do so is by eliminating the heretics, both the new and the relapsed.'

'Nevertheless, the King ...'

'The Inquisitor General Major and the Vicar of the Order, when he came from Rome, understood it very well. He knew of King Pedro's animosity towards my personage and he appreciated that, despite everything, I continued in my condemnation of the entire works, book by book, of the abominable and dangerous Ramon Llull. He didn't argue with any of the procedures we'd begun during these years and, in an emotive celebration of the holy mass, when it came time for the sermon, he put forth my humble personage as an example of conduct for all, from the first to the last Oberlagerführer. Whatever the King of Valencia and Catalonia and Aragon and the Majorcas may say. And then I considered myself a happy man because I was faithful to the most sacred of vows that I had taken and could take in my life. The problem, however, was that woman.'

'There is something that ...' The Bishop, after hesitating,

lifted a finger cautiously. 'Careful: I am not saying that they
don't deserve to die.' He looked at the colour of the wine in his
glass and it seemed red as a flame. 'Can't we ...'

'Can't we what?' Eimeric, impatient.

'Must they necessarily die by fire?'

'General practice throughout the Christian church con-
firms that yes, they must die by fire, Your Grace.'

'It's a horrific death.'

'I'm being eaten up by fevers right now and don't complain,
as I continue to work ceaselessly for the good of the Blessed
Mother Church.'

'I insist that death by fire is horrific.'

'But deserved!' exploded His Excellency. 'More horrific is
the blasphemy and stubbornness in error. Or don't you agree,
Your Grace?' – as I looked at the empty cloister, lost in my
thoughts. And I realised that I was alone. I looked around me.
Where had Kornelia gone?

The group of tourists waited, patient and disciplined, in a
corner of the Bebenhausen cloister, except for Kornelia who
... Now I saw her: she was strolling contemplatively, alone,
right through the middle of the cloister, always unpredictable. I watched her with a certain gluttony and it seemed she
knew my eyes were upon her. She stopped, her back to me,
and turned towards the group who were waiting for there to
be enough people to begin the visit. I waved to her, but she
either didn't notice or pretended not to see me. Kornelia. A
chaffinch stopped at the fountain before me, drank a sip of
water and gave a lovely trill. Adrià shivered.

On the eve of Saint James's Day, at dusk, Josep Xarom's
only consolation was being spared Friar Nicolau's gaze, as
the defender of the Church lay in his bed burning up with
a stubborn fever. Yet the relative tepidness of Friar Miquel
de Susqueda, notary and assistant to the Inquisitor General,
didn't spare him any pain, any suffering, any horror. In
the languidly encroaching dusk of Saint James's Day Eve,
scorched by days of inclement sun, two women and a man
led three mules loaded down with pack saddles and hampers
filled with memories and five children sleeping on top. They

fled the Jewish Quarter and headed to the bank of the River Ter, on the heels of the two families who'd left the previous day. They left behind sixteen generations of Xaroms and Meirs in their beloved Girona, that noble and ungrateful city. The smoke of the iniquity that had devoured poor Josep still rose, Josep who was victim of a fit of envy by an anonymous informer. Dolça Xarom, the only child who awoke in time to have a last look at the proud walls of the cathedral silhouetted against the stars, cried silently, on muleback, over the death of so many things in one single night. A spark of confidence awaited the group at Estartit, in the form of a boat rented by poor Josep Xarom and Massot Bonsenyor a few days earlier, when they saw trouble brewing, when they sensed it without knowing exactly where it would come from, or how and when it would drop on them.

The boat took advantage of a warm western wind to get some distance from the nightmare. The next evening it stopped in Ciutadella, on Minorca, where six more people embarked, and three days later it arrived in Palermo, Sicily, where they rested for half a week from the seasickness brought on by the roughness of the Tyrrhenian Sea. Once they had recovered, taking advantage of favourable winds, they crossed the Ionian Sea and docked at the Albanian port of Durrës, where the six families embarked, fleeing from tears towards some place where no one would be offended by their whisperings on the Sabbath. Since they were warmly welcomed by the Jewish community in Durrës, they established themselves there.

Dolça Xarom, the fleeing girl, had children there, and grandchildren and great-grandchildren, and at eighty years old, still stubbornly recalled the silent streets of Girona's Jewish Quarter and the hulking Christian cathedral, silhouetted against the stars and blurred by tears. Despite the nostalgia, the Xarom Meir family lived and prospered over twelve generations in Durrës and time was so insistent that a moment came when the memory of the ancestor burned by the ungodly goyim shattered and was almost erased in the memory of the children of the children of the children, just

like the distant name of their beloved Girona. One fine day
in the Year of the Patriarchs 5420, the nefarious Year of the
Christians 1660, Emanuel Meir was drawn by the commercial
boom to the Black Sea. Emanuel Meir, eighth great-great-
grandson of Dolça the fleeing girl, moved to bustling Varna,
in Bulgaria on the Black Sea, in the period when the Sublime
Porte ruled there. My parents, who were fervent Catholics in
predominantly Lutheran Germany, wanted me to be a priest.
And I spent quite some time considering it.

'You would have made a good priest, Obersturbannführer
Höss.'

'I imagine so.'

'I'm sure: everything you do, you do well.'

Obersturmbannführer Höss puffed up with the well-de-
served praise. He wanted to dig deeper into it, with a more
solemn air: 'What you just made out to be a virtue, could also
be my ruin. And especially now that Reichsführer Himmler
is going to visit us.'

'Why?'

'Because as Oberlagerführer, I am responsible for all the
failings of the system. For example, I only have two or three
cans at the most left from the last shipment of Zyklon gas and
the quartermaster hasn't even thought to tell me to make an
order. And so I'll have to ask for favours, get some lorries to
come that probably should be somewhere else, and stifle my
craving to yell at the quartermaster because we are all working
at our limit, here at Oświęcem. Pardon at Auschwitz.'

'I imagine that the experience of Dachau ...'

'From a psychological point of view, the difference is vast.
At Dachau we had prisoners.'

'From what I understand huge numbers of them died and
still do.'

'Yes, Doctor Voigt, but Dachau is a prison camp. Auschwitz-
Birkenau is designed, created and calculated to exterminate
rats. If it weren't for the fact that Jews aren't human, I would
think we are living in hell, with one door that leads to a gas
chamber and another place that's cremation ovens and their
flames, or the open pits in the forest, where we burn the

remaining units, because we can't keep up with all the material they send us. This is the first time I talk about these things with someone not involved in the camp, Doctor.'

'It's good to vent every once in a while, Obersturmbannführer Höss.'

'I'm counting on your professional secrecy, because the Reichsführer ...'

'Naturally. You, who are a Christian ... In short, a psychiatrist is like a confessor, the confessor you could have been.'

For a few moments, since he was letting it all out, Oberlagerführer Höss considered mentioning something about that woman, but, despite strong temptation, he managed not to bring it up. He realised it was a close call. He would have to be more careful with the wine. He expanded on the fact that my men have to be strong to carry out the task they have been entrusted with. The other day a soldier, more than thirty years old, not some teenager, burst into tears in one of the barracks in front of his comrades.

Doctor Voigt glanced at this guest and hid his surprise; he let the other man gulp down another glass of wine and waited a few seconds before asking the question the other man was anxiously expecting: 'And what happened?'

'Bruno, Bruno, wake up!'

But Bruno didn't wake up, he was howling and his agony bled from his mouth and eyes, and Rottenführer Mathäus had the superior officers called in, because he didn't know what to do, and three minutes later the Oberlagerführer himself, Obersturmbannführer Rudolf Höss, showed up just in the moment when the soldier Bruno Lübke had pulled out his pistol and stuck it into his mouth, still howling. An SS soldier! Every inch an SS!

'Stand at attention, soldier!' shouted Obersturmbannführer Höss. But since the soldier was howling and sticking the barrel down his throat, his superior made a motion to stop him and Bruno Lübke pulled the trigger with the hope that he would go straight to hell and thus escape Birkenau, the ash they had to breathe in and the gaze of that little girl, who was identical to his Ursula, whom he'd pushed into the gas chamber that very afternoon and seen again when a Jewish rat from the Sonderkommando shaved off her hair and put her in the pile in front of the crematoria.

Höss disdainfully contemplated the soldier – that cowardly jackal – laid out on the ground in a puddle of pale blood. He took advantage of the occasion to improvise a speech in front of the shocked soldiers, and he told them that there is no greater inner consolation and spiritual joy than having the absolute certainty that your actions are carried out in the name of God and with the intention of preserving the holy Catholic and apostolic faith from its many enemies who will never rest until they annihilate it, Friar Miquel. And if some day you falter and discuss in public whether or not the amputation of the confessed prisoners' tongues is appropriate, as much as I recognise your services to me, I can assure you that I will report you to the higher courts, for lassitude and weakness unworthy of an officer of the Holy Inquisition Tribunal.

'I spoke thus out of mercy, Your Excellency.'

'You confuse weakness with mercy.' Friar Nicolau Eimeric began to shake with repressed rage. 'If you continue to insist, you will be guilty of very serious insubordination.'

Friar Miquel lowered his head, trembling in fear. His soul shrank when he heard his superior add, you are starting to seem suspect of lassitude, not only for weakness, but for collusion with heretics.

'For the love of God, Your Excellency!'

'Don't take God's name in vain. And be warned that weakness makes you a traitor and enemy of the Truth.'

Friar Nicolau covered his face with his hands and prayed fervidly for a little while. From the depths of his reflection came a cavernous voice that said we are the only eye attentive to sin, we are the guardians of the orthodoxy, Friar Miquel, we have and we are the truth, and as harsh as the punishment we inflict on the heretic may seem, be it to his body or to his writings, as was the case with the abominable Llull whom I lament not having been able to send to the stake, remember that we are applying the law and justice, which is not exactly a fault, but rather of great merit. In addition, I remind you that we are only responsible before God and not before men. While those who hunger and thirst to be just men are happy, Friar Miquel, those who apply justice are much more so, especially if you remember that our mission was explicitly designed by our beloved Führer, who knows that he can trust in the integrity, patriotism and firmness of spirit of his SS. Or is there any doubt about the Führer's plans? He looked at each man, dominantly, defiantly, as he walked inaudibly among them. Or do any of you doubt the decision-making ability of our Reichsführer Himmler? What will you say to him when he arrives the day after tomorrow? Eh? And after a dramatic pause of a full five seconds: Take away this carrion!

He drank a couple more glasses of wine, or perhaps four or five, and he explained more things that he doesn't entirely remember, carried away by the euphoria the evocation of that heroic scene instilled in him.

Rudolf Höss emerged from Doctor Voigt's quarters quite reassured and slightly dizzy. What worried him was not the hell of Birkenau, but human weakness. No matter how many solemn vows those men and women had made, they weren't able to withstand having death so close. They didn't have souls of steel and that was why they made so many mistakes, and there was no worse way to do things than having to repeat them because of … Disgusting, really. Luckily he hadn't even insinuated the existence of that woman. And I realised that, without wanting to, he watched Kornelia out of the corner of his eye to see if she smiled at the other visitors or … I don't want to be a jealous chap, I thought. But it's just that she … Now! Finally there are ten people and the tour can start. The guide entered the cloister and said Bebenhausen monastery, which we will now visit, was founded by Rudolf I of Tübingen in 1180 and secularised in 1806. I searched out Kornelia with my eyes, and found her beside a very handsome boy, who was smiling at her. And she looked at me, finally, and it was cold at Bebenhausen. What does secularised mean? asked a short, bald man.

That night Rudolf and Hedwig Höss didn't sleep together in

their marriage bed. He had too much on his mind and the conversation with Doctor Voigt kept coming back to him. Had he
spoken too much? Had the third or fourth or seventh glass of
wine made him say things that should never have come out of
his mouth? His obsession with perfect order crumbled in the
face of the enormous blunders his subordinates had made in
recent weeks, and he could absolutely not allow Reichsführer
Himmler to think that he was failing him, because it all began
when I entered the Order of Preachers, guided by my absolute
faith in the Führer's instructions. During our novitiate, led
by the kindly hand of Friar Anselm Copons, we learned to
harden our hearts to human misery, because all SS must know
how to completely sacrifice their personality to the absolute
service of the Führer. And the basic mission of the preacher
friars is precisely that of eradicating internal dangers. For
the true faith, the presence of a heretic is a thousand times
more dangerous than that of an infidel. The heretic has fed
on the teachings of the church and lives within it, but at the
same time, with his pestilent, poisonous nature, corrupts the
holy elements of the sacred institution. In order to solve the
problem once and for all, in 1941 the decision was taken to
make the Holy Inquisition look like so much child's play and
programme the extermination of all Jews without exception.
And if horror was necessary, let it be infinite horror. And if
cruelty was necessary, let it be absolute cruelty, because now it
was history that was picking up the baton. Naturally only true
heroes with iron hearts and steel wills could achieve such a
difficult objective, could carry out such a valiant deed. And I,
as a faithful and disciplined friar preacher, got down to work.
Until 1944, only a handful of doctors and I knew the final
orders of the Reichsführer: start with the sick and the children and, solely for economic motives, make use of those who
could work. I got down to my task with the absolute intention
of being faithful to my oath as an SS. That is why the church
doesn't consider the Jews infidels, but heretics that live among
us insistent in their heresy, which began when they crucified Our Lord Jesus and continues in every place and every
moment, in their obstinacy at renouncing their false beliefs,

in perpetuating human sacrifices with Christian babies and in inventing abominable acts against the holy sacraments, like the aforementioned case of the consecrated hosts, profaned by the perfidious Josep Xarom. That is why the orders given to each Schutzhaftlagerführer in all of the camps dependent on Auschwitz were so severe: the road was narrow, it depended on the capacity of the crematory ovens, the crop was too abundant, thousands and thousands of rats, and the solution was in our hands. Reality, which never comes close to pure ideal, is that Crematorium I and II have the capacity to incinerate two thousand units in twenty-four hours and, to avoid breakdowns, I cannot go above that figure.

'And the other two?' asked Doctor Voigt before the fourth glass of wine.

'The third and fourth are my cross to bear: they don't get up to even one thousand five hundred units a day. The models chosen have sorely disappointed me. If the superiors paid attention to those in the know ...' And don't take it as a criticism of our leaders, Doctor, he said during dinner, or perhaps with the fifth glass. There is so much work that we are snowed under, and any sort of feeling at all akin to compassion must not only be ripped from the minds of the SS, but also severely punished, for the good of the fatherland.

'And what do you do with the ... the residue?'

'The ash is loaded onto lorries and dumped in the Vistula. The river drags off tonnes of ash each day, towards the sea, which is death, as the Latin classics taught us in the unforgettable lessons of Friar Anselm Copons, during our novitiate, in Girona.'

'What?'

'I am only the substitute for the notary, Your Excellency. I ...'

'What did you just read, wretch?'

'Well ... that Josep Xarom cursed you shortly before the flames ...'

'Didn't you cut out his tongue?'

'Friar Miquel forbade it. By the authority invested in him by ...'

'Friar Miquel? Friar Miquel de Susqueda?' Dramatic pause of the length of half a hailmary. 'Bring that carrion here before me.'

Reichsführer Heinrich Himmler, who arrived from Berlin, was understanding. He is a wise man, who realised what pressure Rudolf Höss's men were under and elegantly – what elegance – ignored the insufficiencies that had me so mortified. He approved the daily elimination figure, although I saw in his noble forehead a shadow of concern, because, it seems, finishing off the Jewish problem is urgent and we are only halfway through the process. He didn't discuss any plans with me and, in an emotional act with the Lager staff, he offered up my humble personage as an example of how each officer, from the first to the last, should conduct themselves on the Inquisition's high tribunal. I could well consider myself a happy man because I was faithful to the most sacred vows I had taken in my life. The problem, however, was that woman.

Wednesday, when Frau Hedwig Höss had gone out with the group of women to buy provisions in town, Obersturmbannführer Höss waited for her to arrive at his home under the supervision of her guard, with those eyes, with that sweet face, with those hands that were so perfect that she looks like a real human being. He pretended to have a lot of work piled up on his desk and he watched her as she swept the floor, which, although she did it twice a day, was always covered in a fine layer of ash.

'Your Excellency ... I didn't know you were here.'

'No bother, continue.'

Finally, after days of tension, sidelong glances, demonical obsessive imaginings that were increasingly powerful and insuperable, the demon of the flesh possessed Friar Nicolau Eimeric's iron will. And despite the sacred habits he wore, he said enough is enough and he clasped that woman from behind, with his hands pressed against those tempting breasts, and he sank his venerable chin into her nape that promised a thousand delights. The woman, terrified, dropped the bundle of firewood and remained rigid, stiff, not knowing what to do, against the wall in the dark hallway, not sure whether she should scream, whether she should run off or whether, on the other hand, she should lend an invaluable service to the church.

'Lift your dress,' said Eimeric as he untied the rosary of fifteen beads that was wrapped around his habit.

Prisoner number 615428, from shipment A27 from Bulgaria in January of 1944, saved from the gas chamber at the last minute because someone decided she would do for domestic labours, didn't dare to look into the eyes of that Nazi officer, horrifically afraid, and she thought not again, no, Lord, merciful almighty God. Obersturmbannführer Höss, understanding, without growing irritated, repeated his order. When she didn't react, he pushed her towards the armchair, with more impatience than brutality. He tore off her clothes and caressed her eyes, her face, her oh so sweet gaze. When he penetrated her, enraptured by that savage beauty born of weakness and destruction, he knew that number 615428 had got under his skin forever. 615428 had to be the best-kept secret of his life. He got up quickly, once again in control of the situation, fixed his habit, told the woman get dressed, six, one, five, four, two, eight. Quickly. Then he made it clear that nothing had happened and he swore to her that if she said anything about it to anyone, he would imprison the Wall-eyed Man of Salt, her husband, as well as her son and her mother, and he would accuse her of witchcraft, because you are nothing more than a witch who tried to seduce me with your evil powers.

The operation was repeated over the course of a few days. Prisoner 615428 had to get down on her knees, naked, and the Obersturmbannführer Höss penetrated her, and His Excellency Nicolau Eimeric reminded her, panting, that if you speak a word of this to that wretch, the Wall-eyed Man of Salt, it will be you sent to burn at the stake as a witch, you've got me under your spell, and 615428 couldn't say yes or no because she could only weep in horror.

'Have you seen the rosary I wear around my waist?' said His Excellency. 'If you've stolen it, you'll pay.'

Until stupid Doctor Voigt took an interest in that violin and crossed the line that no Inquisitor General could ever allow anyone to cross. Despite that, Voigt won the match and Oberlagerführer Eimeric had to put the instrument down on the table with a thud.

'All your talk about confessional secrets, you bastard.'

'I'm no priest.'

Sturmbannführer Voigt picked up the violin with eager hands and Rudolf Höss slammed the door excessively hard on his way out and rushed towards the chapel of his inquisitorial headquarters and remained on his knees for two hours, crying at his weakness in the face of the temptations of the flesh, until the new chief secretary, worried because he hadn't shown up for the first advance review, found him in that edifying state of holy devotion and piety. Friar Nicolau stood up, informed the secretary not to expect him until the following day and headed to the registry office.

'Prisoner number 615428.'

'One moment, Obersturmbannführer. Yes. Shipment A27 from Bulgaria on 13 January of this year.'

'What is her name?'

'Elisaveta Meireva. She's one of the few that has a file.'

'What does it say?'

Gefreiter Hänsch checked in the file cabinet and pulled it out and read Elisaveta Meireva, eighteen years old, daughter of Lazar Meirev and Sara Meireva of Varna. It doesn't say anything more. Is there some problem, Obersturmbannführer?

Elisaveta, sweet, with fairy eyes, witch eyes, lips of fresh moss; it was a shame she was so skinny.

'Any complaints, Obersturmbannführer?'

'No, no ... But begin urgent proceedings to have her sent back to the general population.'

'She still has sixteen days in the Kommando of domestic service in

'That's an order, Gefreiter.'

'I can't ...'

'Do you know what an order from a superior is, Gefreiter? And stand up when I speak to you.'

'Yes, Obersturmbannführer!'
'Then, proceed!'

'Ego te absolvo a peccatis tuis, in nomine Patris et Filii et Spiritus Sancti, Obersturmbannführer.'

'Amen,' replied Friar Nicolau as he humbly kissed the gold-filled cross on the venerable father confessor's stole, with his soul blessedly relieved by the sacrament of confession.

'You Catholics have it good, with confession,' said Kornelia, in the middle of the cloister, with her arms outstretched, taking in the springtime sun.

'I'm not Catholic. I'm not religious. Are you?'

Kornelia shrugged. When she didn't have a proper answer, she shrugged and kept quiet. Adrià understood that the subject made her uncomfortable.

'Seen from outside,' I said, 'I like Lutherans better: the Grace of God liberates us without intermediaries.'

'I don't like talking about that stuff,' said Kornelia, very tense.

'Why?'

'Because it makes me think about death, I guess. What do I know!' She grabbed him by the arm and they left the Bebenhausen monastery. 'Come on, we'll miss the bus.'

On the bus, Adrià, looking out at the landscape without seeing it, began to think about Sara, as he always did when he lowered his guard. He found it humiliating to realise that her facial features were beginning to fade in his memory. Her eyes were dark, but were they black or dark brown? Sara, what colour were your eyes? Sara, why did you leave? And Kornelia's hand took his and Adrià smiled sadly. And that afternoon they wandered through the cafés of Tübingen, first to have some beers and then, when they'd had their fill, they ordered very hot tea, and then dinner at the Deutsches Haus because, apart from studying and going to concerts, Adrià didn't know what else to do in Tübingen. Read Hölderlin. Listen to Coşeriu rant about what a blockhead Chomsky was, and against generativism and all that crap.

When they got off the bus in front of the Brechtbau,

Kornelia whispered in his ear don't come to the house this evening.

'Why not?'

'Because I'm busy.'

They parted without a kiss and Adrià felt something like vertigo in the very centre of his soul. And it was all your fault because you had left me without any reason to live, and we'd only been dating for a few months, Sara, but I lived in the clouds with you and you are the best thing that could ever happen to me, until you ran away, and Adrià, once he was in Tübingen, far from his painful memory, spent four months studying desperately, trying in vain to sign up for some course with Coşeriu but secretly auditing it, and going to all the conferences, seminars, talks and open meetings offered at the Brechtbau – which had just moved to a new building – and everywhere else but especially the Burse. And when winter came suddenly, the electric heater in his room wasn't always enough, but he continued studying to keep from thinking about Sara, because you left without saying a word, and when the sadness was too strong, he went out to stroll along the banks of the Neckar, with his nose frozen, and he would reach the Hölderlin Tower and he would think that if he didn't do something he would lose his mind over this love. And one day the snow began to melt, gradually, it was becoming green again, and he wished he weren't so sad, so that he could appreciate the nuances of the shades of green. And since he had no intention of returning to his distant mother's home that summer, he decided to change his life, laugh a little, drink beer with the others who lived with him in the pension, frequent the department's Clubhaus, laugh for laughter's sake, and go to the cinema to see boring and incredible stories, instead of dying over love. And with a hitherto unknown restlessness he started to look at the students with different eyes, now that they were beginning to remove their anoraks and hats, and he realised how pleasurable that was, and it helped to slightly fade the memory of runaway Sara's face and yet it didn't erase the questions I've asked myself throughout my entire life, like what did you mean when you told me I ran away crying, saying not again, it can't be. But in History of Aesthetics I, Adrià sat behind a girl with wavy black hair, whose gaze made him a bit dizzy, a girl named Kornelia Brendel who was from Offenbach. He noticed her because she seemed unattainable. And he smiled at her and she smiled back, and soon they had a coffee at the department bar and she swore you don't have the slightest accent, I thought you were German, really. And from coffee they moved to strolling together through that park bursting with spring, and Kornelia was the first woman I went to bed with, Sara, and I hugged her close pretending that ... Mea culpa, Sara. And I started to love her even though sometimes she said things I didn't completely understand. And I knew how to hold her gaze. I liked Kornelia. And we were together like that for a few months. I clung desperately to her. Which was why I became anxious when, as the second winter began, when we returned from our visit to the Bebenhausen monastery, she told me don't come to my house this evening.

'Why not?'

'Because I'll be busy.'

They parted without a kiss and Adrià felt something like vertigo in the very centre of his soul, because he didn't know whether you could say to a woman hey, hey, what do you mean you'll be busy? Or whether he had to be prudent and think she's old enough not to have to explain herself to you. Or shouldn't she, actually? Isn't she your girlfriend? Kornelia Brendel, do you take Adrià Ardèvol i Bosch as your boyfriend? Can Kornelia Brendel have secrets?

Adrià let Kornelia go off down Wilhelmstrasse without asking for any explanation because, deep down, he had his secrets from Kornelia: he still hadn't told her anything about Sara, for example. That was all very well and good in theory, but two minutes later he was sorry he'd let her go without raising any objections. He didn't see her in Greek or in Philosophy of the Experience. Nor in the open seminar in Moral Philosophy that she'd said she didn't want to miss. And very ashamed of myself, I headed towards Jakobsgasse and I stood, slightly hidden and even more ashamed of myself, on the corner with Schmiedtorstrasse, as if I were waiting for the 12. And after ten or twelve 12s had passed, I was still standing there, so cold my feet were like ice about to crack, trying to find out what Kornelia's secret was.

At five in the afternoon, when I was frozen from the heart down, Kornelia appeared with her secret. She was wearing the same coat as always, so pretty, so Kornelia. The secret was a tall, blond, handsome, laughing boy whom she'd met in the cloister at Bebenhausen and who was now kissing her before they both entered the building. He kissed her much better than I knew how to. That's where the problems began. Not because I had spied on her, but because she realised it when she drew the curtain in the living room and saw Adrià on the corner in front of her house, frozen, looking at her incredulously, with his eyes wide, waiting for the 12. That night I cried on the street and when I got home I found a letter from Bernat; it had been months since I'd heard from him and in the letter he assured me that he was bursting with happiness, that her name was Tecla and that he was coming to see me whether I liked it or not.

Since I'd been in Tübingen, my relationship with Bernat had cooled somewhat. I don't write letters: well, I didn't when I was young. The first sign of life from him was a suicidal postcard sent from Palma, with the text in full view of the Francoist military censors, which said I am playing the cornet for the colonel of the regiment and playing with myself when they don't let us go out or playing on everyone's nerves when I practise the violin. I hate life, soldiers, the regime and the rock they all crawled out from under. And how are you? There was no indication as to where he could send a reply and Adrià wrote back to Bernat's parents' house. I think I told him about Kornelia but very sketchily. But that summer I travelled down to Barcelona and, with the money that Mother had put in my own account, I paid a small fortune to Toti Dalmau, who was already a doctor, and he sent me for a few check-ups at the Military Hospital and I came out of them with a certificate stating that I had serious cardio-respiratory problems that kept me from serving my homeland. Adrià, for a cause he considered just, had moved the strings of corruption. And I don't regret it. No dictatorship has the right to demand a year and a half or two of my life, amen.

## 25

He wanted to bring Tecla. I told him that I only had one bed in my flat and blah, blah, blah, which was ridiculous because they could have easily gone to a hostel. And then it turned out that Tecla couldn't come because she had too much work, which, he later confessed to me, meant that Tecla's parents wouldn't allow her to go on such a long trip with that boyfriend of hers, who was too tall, with hair too long and a gaze too melancholy. I was glad he didn't show up with her because otherwise we wouldn't have been able to really talk, which meant that Adrià would have felt so envious that he wouldn't have been able to breathe and he would have said what are you doing with a woman, you should always put friends first; you know what I mean, loser? Friends! And I would have said that out of ffucking envy and desperation at seeing my cardiac problems with Kornelia take the same path as the ones I had with you, my love. With one advantage: I knew Kornelia's secret. Her secrets. And yet … I was still asking myself why you had run away to Paris. So he came alone, with a student violin, and with a lot of things he wanted to talk about. It seemed he had grown a bit. He was now a good half a head taller than me. And he was starting to look at the world with a little less impatience. Sometimes he even smiled for no reason, just because, just because of life.

'Are you in love?'

Then his smile widened. Yes, he was in love. Hopelessly in love. Unlike me, who was hopelessly confused by Kornelia, who went off with some other guy the minute I turned my back because she was at that age, the age of experiences. I envied Bernat's serene smile. But there was a detail that worried me. When he set himself up in my room, on the foldout bed, he opened his violin case. Serious violinists don't just carry a violin in their cases; they have half their lives in there: two or three bows, rosin for the strings, a photo or two, scores in a side pocket, sets of strings and their only review, from some local magazine. Bernat had his student violin, a bow and that's it. And a folder. And the first thing he opened was the folder. There was a clumsily stapled text inside, which he held out to me. Here, read.

'What is it?'

'A short story. I'm a writer.'

The way he said I'm a writer bothered me. In fact, it's bothered me all my life. With his usual lack of tact, he wanted me to read it right then and there. I took it, looked at the title and the length, and said I'll have to read it leisurely.

'Of course, of course. I'll go out and take a walk.'

'No. I'll read it tonight, when I usually read. Tell me about Tecla.'

He told me that she was like this and like that, that she had delicious dimples in her cheeks, that he'd met her at the conservatory of the Liceu; she played the piano and he was the concertmaster for the Schumann quintet.

'The funny thing is that she plays the piano and her name is Tecla.' Tecla means key.

'She'll get over it. Does she play well?'

Since if it were up to him we would stay there all day, I grabbed my anorak and said follow me and I took him to the Deutsches Haus, which was full as always, and I checked out of the corner of my eye for Kornelia and one of her experiences, which meant I wasn't entirely attentive to the conversation with Bernat, who, after ordering the same thing I had, just in case, started to say I miss you but I don't want to study abroad in Europe and …

'You're making a mistake.'

'I prefer to make an inner voyage. That's why I've started writing.'

'That's balderdash. You have to travel. Find teachers who will invigorate you, get your blood flowing.'

'That's disgusting.'

'No: it's Sauerkraut.'

'What?'

'Pickled cabbage. You get used to it.'

No sign of Kornelia, yet. Halfway into my sausage I was more calm, and barely thinking about her at all.

'I want to pack in the violin,' he said, I think to provoke me.

'I forbid you.'

'Are you expecting someone?'

'No, why?'

'No, it's just that you're … Well, it looks like you're expecting someone.'

'Why do you say you want to give up the violin?'

'Why did you give it up?'

'You already know that. I don't know how to play.'

'Neither do I. I don't know if you remember: I lack soul.'

'You'll find it studying abroad. Study under Kremer, or that kid, Perlman. Or have Stern hear you play. Hell, Europe is filled with great teachers that we've never even heard of. Light a fire under yourself, burn the candle at both ends. Or go to America.'

'I don't have a future as a soloist.'

'Nonsense.'

'Shut up, you don't understand. I can't do more than I'm doing.'

'All right. Then you can be a good orchestral violinist.'

'I still want to take on the world.'

'You decide: take the risk or play it safe. And you can take on the world sitting at your music stand.'

'No. I'm losing my excitement.'

'And when you play chamber music? Aren't you happy?'

Here Bernat hesitated, looking towards one wall. I left him with his hesitation because just then Kornelia came in with a new experience on her arm and I wanted to disappear but I followed her with my eyes. She pretended not to see me and they sat down behind me. I felt a horrific emptiness at my back.

'Maybe.'

'What?'

Bernat looked at me, puzzled. Patiently: 'Maybe when I play chamber I'm something like happy.'

I couldn't give two shits about Bernat's chamber music that evening. My priority was the emptiness, the itching at my back. And I turned, pretending I was looking for the blonde waitress. Kornelia was laughing as she checked the list of sausages on the plastic-coated menu. The experience had an amazing moustache that was completely odious and out of place. Diametrically opposed to the tall, blond secret of ten days earlier.

'What's wrong with you?'

'Me? What do you mean?'

'I don't know. You're like …'

Then Adrià smiled at the waitress who was passing by and asked her for a bit of bread and looked at Bernat and said go on, go on, forgive me, I was just …

'Well, maybe when I play chamber music I'm …'

'You see? And if you do Beethoven's entire series with Tecla?'

The itching at my back was growing so intense that I didn't think about whether I was making sense or not.

'Yes, I can do it. And why? Who would ask us to do it in a hall? Or record it on a dozen LPs? Huh?'

'You're asking for a lot … Just being able to play it … Excuse me for a moment.'

I got up and went to the bathroom. When I passed Kornelia and her experience, I looked at her, she lifted her head, saw me and said hello and continued reading the sausage menu. Hello. As if it were the most normal thing in the world, after having sworn eternal love or practically, and having slept with you, she picks up an experience and when you run into her she says hello and keeps reading the sausage menu. I was about to say you should try my Bratwurst, it's very good, miss. As I walked to the bathroom I heard the experience, in a superstrong Bavarian accent, say who is that guy with the Bratwurst? I missed Kornelia's response because I went into the bathroom to make way for some waitresses with full trays.

We had to get over the spiked fence to be able to stroll in the cemetery at night. It was very cold, but we could both use the walk because we'd drunk all the beer we could get our hands on, him thinking about chamber music and me meeting new experiences. I told him about my Hebrew classes and the philosophy I alternated with my philology studies and my decision to spend my whole life studying and if I can teach in the university, fantastic: otherwise, I'll be a private scholar.

'And how will you earn a living? That is if you have to at all.'

'I can always have dinner over at your house.'

'How many languages do you speak?'

'Don't give up the violin.'

'I'm about to.'

'So why did you bring it with you?'

'To do finger practice. On Sunday I'm playing at Tecla's house.'

'That's good, right?'

'Oh, sure. Thrilling. But I have to impress her parents.'

'What are you going to play?'

'César Franck.'

For a minute, both of us, I'm sure of it, were reminiscing about the beginning of Franck's sonata, that elegant dialogue between the two instruments that was merely the introduction to great pleasures.

'I regret having given up the violin,' I said.

'Now you say it, you big poof.'

'I say it because I don't want you to be regretting it a few months from now and cursing my name because I didn't warn you.'

'I think I want to be a writer.'

'I think it's fine if you write. But you don't have to give up

'Do you mind not being so condescending, for fuck's sake?'

'Go to hell.'

'Have you heard anything from Sara?'

We started to walk in silence to the end of the path, to the grave of Franz Grübbe. I was realising that I'd been wrong not to tell him about Kornelia and my suffering. In those days I was already concerned about the image others had of me.

Bernat repeated his question with his eyes and didn't insist. The cold was cutting and made my eyes water.

'Why don't we go back?' I said.

'Who is this Grübbe?'

Adrià looked pensively at the thick cross. Franz Grübbe, 1918–1943. Lothar Grübbe, with a trembling, indignant hand, pushed away a bramble that someone had put there as an insult. The bramble scratched him and he couldn't think of Schubert's wild rose because his thoughts had been abducted by his ill fate for some time. Lovingly, he put a bouquet of roses on his grave, white like his son's soul.

'You are tempting fate,' said Herta who, nevertheless, had wanted to accompany him. Those flowers are screaming.

'I have nothing to lose.' He stood up. 'Just the opposite: I have won the prize of a heroic, brave martyr for a son.'

He looked around him. His breath emerged in a thick cloud. He knew that the white roses, besides being a rebellious scream, would already be frozen come evening. But it had been almost a month since they had buried Franz, and he'd promised Anna he would bring him flowers on the sixteenth of each month until the day he could no longer walk. It was the least he could do for their son, the hero, the brave martyr.

'Is he somebody important, this Grübbe?'

'Huh?'

'Why did you stop here?'

'Franz Grübbe, nineteen eighteen, nineteen forty-three.'

'Who is he?'

'I have no idea.'

'Shit, it's so cold. Is it always like this in Tübingen?'

Lothar Grübbe had lived silent and sulking since Hitler had taken power and he showed his silent sulkiness to his neighbours, who pretended not to see Lothar Grübbe sulking as they said that man is looking for trouble; and he, sulking, spoke to his Anna as he strolled, alone, through the park, saying it's not possible that no one is rebelling, it just can't be. And when Franz went back to the university, where he wasted his time studying laws that would be abolished by the New Order, the world came crashing down around Lothar because his Franz, with his eyes bright with excitement, said Papa, following the indications and wishes of the Führer, I just asked to sign up with the SS and it's very likely that they'll accept me because I've been able to prove that we are unsullied for five or six generations. And Lothar, perplexed, disconcerted, said what have they done to you, my son, why …

'Father: We are Entering a New Era Made of Power, Energy, Light and Future. Etcetera, Father. And I want you to be happy for me.'

Lothar cried in front of his excited son, who scolded him for such weakness. That night he explained it to his Anna and he said forgive me, Anna, it's my fault, it's my fault for having let him study so far from home; they have infected him with fascism, my beloved Anna. And Lothar Grübbe had much time to cry because, one bad day, young Franz, who was again far from home, didn't want to see his father's reproachful gaze and so he just sent him an enthusiastic telegram that said The Third Company of the Waffen-SS of Who Knows Which One, Papa, Is Being Sent To The Southern Front, Stop. Finally I Can Offer My Life To My Führer, Stop. Don't Cry For Me In That Case. Stop. I Will Have Eternal Life in Valhalla. Stop. And Lothar cried and decided that it had to be kept secret and that night he didn't tell Anna that he had received a Telegram from Franz, Loaded With Detestable Capitals.

Drago Gradnik had to lean his immense trunk forward in order to hear the anaemic little voice of the employee at the Jesenice post office, near the Sava Dolinka River, which was running very high due to the spring thaw.

'What did you say?'

'This letter will not reach its destination.'

'Why?' thundering voice.

The little old man who worked in the post office put on his glasses and read out loud: Fèlix Ardèvol, 283 València ulica, Barcelona, Španija. And he held the letter out to the giant.

'It will get lost along the way, captain. All the letters in this sack are going to Ljubljana and no further.'

'I'm a sergeant.'

'I don't care: it will get lost anyway. We are at war. Or didn't you know?'

Gradnik, who didn't usually do such things, pointed threateningly at the civil servant and, using the deepest and most unpleasant voice in his repertoire, said you lick a fifty-para stamp, stick it on the envelope, mark it, put the letter in the sack I'm taking and let it go. Do you understand me?

Even though they were calling him from outside, Gradnik waited for the offended man to follow, in silence, that useless old partisan's orders. And when he'd finished, he placed the envelope into the sack of scant correspondence headed to Ljubljana. The giant sergeant picked it up and went out onto the sunny street. Ten impatient men shouted at him from the lorry, which, seeing him come out, had turned on its engine. In the lorry's trailer there were six or seven similar sacks and Vlado Vladić lying down, smoking and looking at his watch and saying, shit, all you had to do was pick up the sack, sergeant.

The lorry with the postal sacks and some fifteen partisans didn't get a chance to leave. A strange Citroën stopped in front of it and out came three partisans who explained the situation to their comrades: that Palm Sunday, the day that Croatia and Slovenia commemorate Jesus's triumphant entrance into Jerusalem on the back of a donkey, three companies of the SS Division Reich decided to emulate the Son of God and triumphantly enter Slovenia but on wheels, while the Luftwaffe destroyed the centre of Belgrad and the royal government, with the king on the first line of fire, running as fast as his legs could carry him, comrades. It is time to give our lives for freedom. You will go to Kranjska Gora to halt the Waffen-SS division. And Drago Gradnik thought the hour of my death has come, blessed be the Lord. I will die in Kranjska Gora trying to halt an unstoppable division of the Waffen-SS. And, as had been the case throughout his entire life, he didn't bemoan his fate. From the moment that he'd hung up his cassock and gone to see the local commando of partisans in order to offer himself to his country, he knew that he was making a mistake. But he couldn't do anything else because there was evil right before him, be it Pavelić's Ustaše or the devil's SS, and theology had to be set aside for these sad emergencies. They reached Kranjska Gora without running

into any devils and pretty much everyone was thinking that
perhaps the information was erroneous; but when they went
out on the Borovška highway, a commander with no stars,
with a Croatian accent and a twenty-day beard, told them that
the moment of truth had arrived; it is a battle to the death
against Nazism: you are the army of partisans for freedom
and against fascism. Show no mercy on the enemy just as no
enemy has or ever will with us. Drago Gradnik wanted to add
forever and ever amen. But he held himself back, because the
commander without stars was clearly explaining how each
defensive den had to act. Gradnik had time to think that, for
the first time in his life, he would have to kill.

'Come on, up into the hills, fast as you can. And good luck!'

The bulk of the force, with machine guns, hand grenades
and mortars, took the safe positions. The shooters had to go
up to the peaks, like eagles. The dozen marksmen spread out
nimbly – except for Father Gradnik who was wheezing like
a whale – to the defence positions, each with his rifle and
only thirteen magazines. And if you run out of bullets, use
rocks; and if they get close to you, strangle them: but don't
let them get into the town. Good aim got you a Nagant with
a telescopic sight. And it also meant watching, following, observing, relating to those you had to end up killing.

When he was about to die, drowned in his own panting, a
hand helped him up the last step. It was Vlado Vladić, who
was already flat on the ground, aiming at the deserted bend in
the highway and who said sergeant, we have to stay in shape.
From the top of the hill they heard scared golden orioles
flying over them, as if they wanted to reveal their location to
the Germans. A few minutes passed in silence, as he caught
his breath.

'What did you do, before the war, sergeant?' asked the
Serbian partisan in terrible Slovenian.

'I was a baker.'

'That's twaddle. You were a priest.'

'Why'd you ask me, if you already knew?'

'I want to confess, Father.'

'We are at war. I am not a priest.'

'Yes you are.'

'No. I have sinned against hope. I am the one who should confess. I hung up my

He was suddenly silent: around the deserted bend came a small tank followed by two, four, eight, ten, twelve, holy shit, my God. Twenty or thirty or a thousand armoured cars filled with soldiers. And behind them, at least three or four companies on foot. The golden orioles continued their racket, indifferent to the hatred and the fear.

'When the fighting starts, Father, you go for the lieutenant on the right and I'll go for the one on the left. Don't let him out of your sight.'

'The one that's taller and thin?'

'Uh-huh. Do what I do.'

Which was court death, thought Gradnik, his heart tied up in knots.

After the last vehicle, the young SS-Obersturmführer Franz Grübbe, at the head of his section, looked out at the hills to the left, over which flew some birds he had never seen before. He looked up, not so much to make out any enemies, but rather imagining the Moment Of Glory When All of Europe Will Be Led By Our Visionary Führer And Germany Becomes The Model Of Ideal Society That Inferior Races Must Strive To Imitate. And on the hill to the left, almost at the first houses of Kranjska Gora, one hundred partisans hidden in the landscape were waiting for the signal from their Croatian commander. And the signal was the first shot from the machine guns at the vehicles. And Drago Gradnik – born in Ljubljana on the thirtieth of August of eighteen ninety-five, who was a student at the Jesuit school in his city, who'd decided to devote his life to God and, inflamed with devotion, entered Vienna's diocesan seminary and who, based on his intellectual ability, was chosen to study theology at the Pontificia Università Gregoriana and Biblical exegesis at the Pontifico Istituto Biblico, since he was destined to carry out great projects within the Holy Church – had that repulsive SS officer in his Nagant's sight for a minute that stretched on forever while Grübbe looked up with victor's pride and led that company?, section?, patrol? that had to be halted.

And the fighting began. For a few moments it looked as if the soldiers were surprised to find a resistance outpost so far from Ljubljana. Gradnik coldly following the movements of his victim in his telescopic sight and thinking if you pull the trigger, Drago, you will no longer have the right to set foot in paradise. You are coexisting with the man you have to kill. Sweat tried to cloud his vision but he refused to be blinded. He was determined and he had to keep his victim in the sight. All the soldiers had their weapons loaded, but they didn't know exactly where to aim. It was the armoured cars and their occupants that would get the worst of it.

'Now, Father!'

They both fired at once. Gradnik's officer was facing him, with his rifle ready, still looking around unsure as to where to shoot. The SS officer leaned against the terraced wall behind him and, suddenly, dropped his rifle, immobile, indifferent to all that was going on around him, with his face abruptly red with blood. Young SS-Obersturmführer Franz Grübbe didn't have time to think about The Glory Of Combat or The New Order or The Glorious Tomorrow that he was offering the survivors with his death, because they had blown off half of his head and he could no long think about strange birds or where the shots were coming from. Then Gradnik realised that he didn't care if paradise was closed to him because he had to do what he was doing. He loaded the Nagant. With its telescopic sight he swept the enemy lines. An SS sergeant shouted at the soldiers to reorganise themselves. He aimed at his neck so he would stop shouting and he fired. And, coldly, without losing his nerve, he reloaded and took down some more lower-ranking officers.

Before the sun set, the Waffen-SS column had withdrawn, leaving behind the dead and the destroyed vehicles. The partisans came down, like vultures, to rummage among the corpses. Every once in a while the icy crack of an ununiformed commander's pistol sounded out, finishing off the wounded, a hardened curl on their lips.

Following strict orders, all the surviving partisans had to examine the corpses and gather up weapons, ammunition, boots and leather jackets. Drago Gradnik, as if compelled by some mysterious force, went over to confront his first kill. He was a young man with a kind face and eyes covered in blood, who stared straight ahead, still leaning against the wall, his helmet destroyed and his face red. He hadn't given him any choice. Forgive me, Son, he said to him. And then he saw Vlado Vladić, with two other comrades, collecting identification tags; they did that whenever they could to make it harder for the enemies to identify their dead. When Vladić got to Gradnik's victim, he tore off his tag without a second thought. Gradnik suddenly sprang to life: 'Wait! Give it to me!'

'Father, we have to …'

'I said give it to me!'

Vladić shrugged and passed the tag to him.

'Your first kill, eh?'

And he continued his task. Drago Gradnik looked at the tag. Franz Grübbe. His first kill was named Franz Grübbe, and he was a young SS-Obersturmführer, probably blond with blue eyes. For a few moments he imagined visiting the dead man's widow or parents, to comfort them and tell them, on his knees, it was me, I did it, confiteor. And he put the tag inside his pocket.

I shrugged, still in front of the grave, and repeated let's go back, it's freezing. And Bernat, whatever you want, you're in charge, you've always been the one in charge of my life.

'Screw you.'

Since we were stiff with cold, jumping over the cemetery fence and into the world earned me a rip in my trousers. And we left the dead alone and cold and in the dark with their never-ending stories.

I didn't read his story; Bernat fell asleep the minute his head hit the pillow because he was bone tired from his trip. I preferred to think about the culture clash during the decline of the Roman Empire as I waited to drift off to sleep, imagining whether that was possible in contemporary Europe. But suddenly Kornelia and Sara came into my happy thoughts and I felt deeply sad. And you don't have the balls to explain it to your best friend.

In the end the Bebenhausen option won out because Adrià was having a very historic day and

'No: you have a historic life. Everything is history to you.'

'Actually it's more that the history of any thing explains the present state of that thing. And today I am having a historic day and we are going to Bebenhausen because according to you I've always been the one in charge.'

It was unbelievably cold. The trees on Wilhelmstrasse in front of the faculty – poor things, naked of leaves – put up with it patiently, knowing that better times would come.

'I couldn't live like this. My hands would freeze and I wouldn't be able to play …'

'Since you're giving up the violin anyway, you can just stay here.'

'Have I told you what Tecla's like?'

'Yes.' He broke into a run. 'Come on, that's our bus.'

Inside the bus was just as cold as outside, but people unbuttoned their coat collars. Bernat started to say she has dimples in her cheeks that look like—

'That look like two navels, you already told me.'

'Hey, if you don't want me to …'

'Do you have a photo?'

'Oh, bother, no. I didn't even think of that.'

In fact, Bernat didn't have any photo of Tecla because he hadn't yet taken a photo of her, because he didn't yet have a camera and because Tecla didn't have one to lend him, but that's all right because I never grow tired of describing her.

'I, on the other hand, do grow tired.'

'You're so peevish, I don't know why I even talk to you.'

Adrià opened the briefcase that was his constant companion and pulled out a sheaf of papers and showed it to him.

'Because I read your ravings.'

'Wow, you've already read it?'

'Not yet.'

Adrià read the title and didn't turn the page. Bernat was

watching him out of the corner of his eye. Neither of them realised that the straight highway was entering a valley where the fir forests on both sides were dusted with snow. Two endless minutes passed during which Bernat thought that if it took him that long to read the title, then … Maybe it was evoking things for him; perhaps he's transported like I was when I wrote the first page. But Adrià looked at the five words of the title and thought I don't know why I can't just go to Kornelia and tell her, let's forget about this and it's over. And you acted like a real slut, you know?, and from now on I'll focus on missing Sara; and he knew that what he was thinking was a lie because when Kornelia was in front of him he melted, he would open his mouth and do whatever she told him to, even if it meant leaving because she was waiting for a new experience, my God, why am I so pussy-whipped?

'Do you like it? It's good, right?'

Adrià returned to his world. He stood up with a start.

'Hey, we're here!'

They got off at the stop on the side of the highway. Before them rose the frozen town of Bebenhausen. A woman with white hair had got off with them and gave them a smile. Adrià suddenly thought to ask her if she would take a photo of them with this camera, you see, madam? She puts her basket down, takes the camera and says sure, what button do I press?

'Right here. Thank you very much, madam.'

The two friends posed in front of the town, which was covered in a thin layer of ice that made it very uninviting. The woman snapped the shot and said there you go. Adrià took back the camera and picked up the basket. He silently indicated for her to go ahead, that he would carry it for her. All three of them started to walk up a ramp that led to the houses.

'Watch out,' said the woman, 'the frozen asphalt is treacherous.'

'What did she say?' asked Bernat, all ears.

Just then he slipped as he took a step, falling on his arse in the middle of the ramp.

'That,' replied Adrià, bursting into laughter.

Bernat got up, humiliated, mumbled a swear word and had

to put on a good face. When they reached the top of the ramp, Adrià gave the woman back her basket.

'Tourists?'

'Students.'

He shook her hand and said Adrià Ardèvol. Pleased to meet you.

'Herta,' said the woman. And she headed off, with the basket in one hand and not slipping for anything in the world.

The cold was more intense than in Tübingen. It was obscenely cold. The cloister was tranquil and silent as they waited for the guided tour at ten on the dot. The other visitors were waiting in the vestibule, more sheltered. They stepped on the still virgin ice of the night's freeze.

'What a beautiful thing,' said Bernat in admiration.

'I like this place a lot. I've come six or seven times, in spring, summer, autumn … It's relaxing.'

Bernat sighed in satisfaction, and said how can you not be a believer when you look at the beauty and peace of this cloister.

'The people who lived here worshipped a vengeful and vindictive god.'

'Have some respect.'

'It pains me to say it, Bernat; I'm not kidding.'

When they were silent, all that was heard was the ice cracking beneath their feet. No bird had any interest in freezing. Bernat took in a deep breath and expelled a thick cloud, as if he were a locomotive. Adrià returned to the conversation: 'The Christian God is vindictive and vengeful. If you make a mistake and you don't repent, he punishes you with eternal hell. I find that reaction so disproportionate that I just don't want to have anything to do with that God.'

'But …'

'But what.'

'Well, he is the God of love.'

'No way: you'll burn in hell forever because you didn't go to mass or you stole from a neighbour. I don't see the love anywhere.'

'You aren't looking at the whole picture.'

'I'm not saying I am: I'm no expert.' He stopped short. 'But there are other things that bother me more.'

'Like what?'

'Evil.'

'What?'

'Evil. Why does your God allow it? He doesn't keep evil from happening: all he does is punish the evildoer with eternal flames. Why doesn't he prevent it? Do you have an answer?'

'No ... Well ... God respects human freedom.'

'That's what the clever priests lead you to believe; they don't have the answers to why God does nothing in the face of evil, either.'

'Evil will be punished.'

'Yeah, sure: after it's done the damage.'

'Bloody hell, Adrià; I don't what to say to you. I don't have arguments, you know that ... I just believe.'

'Forgive me; I don't want to ... But you're the one who brought up the subject.'

He opened a door and a small group of explorers, captained by the guide, prepared to start their visit.

'Bebenhausen monastery, which we will now visit, was founded by Rudolf I of Tübingen in eleven eighty and was secularised in eighteen oh six.'

'What does secularised mean?' (a woman in thick plastic-framed eyeglasses and a garnet overcoat).

'That just means that it stopped being used as a monastery.'

Then the guide started to soft-soap them elegantly because they were cultured people who preferred twelfth- and thirteenth-century architecture to a glass of schnapps or a beer. And he went on to say that during several periods of the twentieth century the monastery was used as a meeting place for various local and regional political groups until a recent agreement with the federal government. It will be completely restored so that visitors can see a faithful reproduction of how it looked when it was a monastery and a large community of Cistercian monks lived here. This summer the construction will begin. Now, please follow me, we will enter what was the monastery's church. Be careful on the stairs. Watch out. Hold on here, madam, because if you break your leg you'll miss my wonderful explanations. And ninety per cent of the group smiled.

The frozen visitors entered the church, taking the stairs very carefully. Once inside, Bernat realised that Adrià was not among the nine ice-cold visitors. As the white-haired guide said this church, which still retains many late Gothic elements like this vault over our heads, Bernat left the church and returned to the cloister. He saw Adrià sitting on a stone that was white with snow, his back to him, reading … yes, reading his pages! He watched him anxiously. He was quite sorry not to have a camera because he wouldn't have hesitated to immortalise the moment in which Adrià, his spiritual and intellectual mentor, the person he most trusted and most distrusted in the world, was absorbed in the fiction that he had created from absolute nothingness. For a few moments he felt important and no longer noticed the cold. He went back into the church. The group was now beneath a window that was damaged but the guide didn't know how, and then one of the frozen visitors asked how many monks lived here, in the times of splendour.

'In the fifteenth century, up to a hundred,' answered guide.

Like the number of pages in my story, thought Bernat. And he imagined that his friend must now be on page sixteen, when Elisa says the only thing I can do is run away from home.

'But where will you go, child?' Amadeu asked in fright.

'Don't call me a child,' Elisa got angry, pushing her hair off her shoulders abruptly.

When she was angry, Elisa would get dimples on her cheeks that looked like tiny navels and Amadeu saw them, he looked at them and lost his bearings and all ability to speak.

'Excuse me?'

'You can't stay here by yourself. You have to follow the group.'

'No problem,' said Bernat lifting his arms in a show of

innocence and leaving his characters to Adrià's thorough
reading. And he went to the back of the group that was now
going down the steps and be very careful with the stairs, they
are very treacherous at these temperatures. Adrià was still in
the cloister, reading, oblivious to the cold wind, and for a few
moments Bernat was the happiest man in the world.

He chose to pay again and repeat the itinerary with a new
group of cold-looking visitors. In the cloister, immobile,
Adrià was still reading, his head bowed. And what if he was
frozen? thought Bernat, terrified. He didn't realise that what
worried him most about Adrià freezing was that he wouldn't
have finished reading his story. But he looked at him out of the
corner of his eye as he heard the guide who, now in German,
said Bebenhausen monastery, which we will now visit, was
founded by Rudolf I of Tübingen in eleven eighty and was
secularised in eighteen oh six.
    'What does secularised mean?' (a young man, tall and thin,
encased in an electric blue anorak).
    'That just means that it stopped being used as a monastery.'
Then the guide started to soft-soap them elegantly because
they were cultured people who preferred twelfth- and thirteenth-century architecture to a glass of schnapps or a beer.
And he went on to say that during several periods of the
twentieth century the monastery was used as a meeting place
for various local and regional political groups until a recent
agreement with the federal government. It will be completely
restored so that visitors can see a faithful reproduction of how
it looked when it was a monastery and a large community of
Cistercian monks lived here. This summer the construction
will begin. Now, please follow me, we will enter what was the
monastery's church. Be careful on the stairs. Watch out. Hold
on here, madam, because if you break your leg you'll miss
my wonderful explanations. And ninety per cent of the group
smiled. Bernat heard the man starting to say this church,
which still retains many late Gothic elements like this vault
over our heads; but he heard it from the doorway because
he was furtively going back, towards the cloister, and he hid

behind a column. Page forty or forty-five, calculated Bernat. And Adrià was reading, struggling to keep Sara and Kornelia from turning into Elisa and he didn't want to move from there despite the cold. Forty or forty-five, at the point where Elisa goes up the slope of Cantó on her bicycle, her hair fluttering behind her; now that I think about it, if she's pedalling up, her hair can't be fluttering because she can barely move the bicycle. I'll have to revise that. If it were downhill, maybe. Well, I'll change it to the descent of Cantó and let those locks fly. He must be enjoying it; he doesn't even notice the cold. Making sure that his footsteps weren't heard, he returned to the group that was just then lifting its head like a single person to gaze upon the coffered ceiling, which is a wonder of marquetry, and a woman with hair the colour of straw said wunderbar and looked at Bernat as if demanding to know his aesthetic stance. Bernat, who was bursting with emotion, nodded three or four times, but he didn't dare say wunderbar because they'd be able tell that he wasn't German and had no clue what it meant. At least not until Adrià had told him what he thought, and then he would jump and shriek, wild with joy. The woman with hair the colour of straw was satisfied with Bernat's ambiguous gesture and said wunderbar, but now in a softer voice, as if only to herself.

On the fourth visit, the guide, who had been looking at Bernat suspiciously for some time, came over to him and looked him in the eyes, as if he wanted to figure out whether that mute and solitary tourist was pulling his leg or whether he was an enthusiastic victim of the charms of the Bebenhausen monastery, or perhaps of his wonderful explanations. Bernat looked enthusiastically at the leaflet that he'd nervously wrinkled, and the guide shook his head, clicked his tongue and said the Bebenhausen monastery, which we will now visit, was founded by Rudolf I of Tübingen in eleven eighty and was secularised in eighteen oh six.

'Wunderbar. What does secularised mean?' (a young, pretty woman, wrapped up like an Eskimo and her nose red with cold).

When they left the cloister after having admired the coffered ceiling, Bernat, hidden among the blocks of ice that were the visitors, saw that Adrià must be on page eighty and Elisa had already emptied the pond and let the twelve red fish die in the moving scene where she decides to punish the feelings and not the bodies of the two boys by depriving them of their fish. And that was the setup for the unexpected ending, of which he was particularly, and humbly, proud.

There were no more groups. Bernat remained in the cloister, staring openly at Adrià, who in that moment turned page one hundred and three, folded the papers and contemplated the icy boxwood hedges he had before him. Suddenly he got up and then I saw Bernat, who was watching me with a strange expression as if I were a ghost and said I thought you had frozen. We left in silence and Bernat timidly asked me if I wanted to do the guided tour, and I told him there was no need, that I already knew it by heart.

'Me too,' he replied.

Once we were outside I said that I needed a very hot cup of tea, urgently.

'Well, what do you think?'

Adrià looked at his friend, puzzled. Bernat pointed with his chin to the packet of pages Adrià carried in his gloved hand. Eight or ten or a thousand agonizing seconds passed. Then Adrià, without looking Bernat in the eye, said it's very, very bad. It lacks soul; I didn't believe a single emotion. I don't know why, but I think it's terrible. I don't know who Amadeu is; and the worst of it is that I don't give a rat's arse. And Elisa, well, it goes without saying.'

'You're kidding.' Bernat, pale like Mother when she told me that Father had gone to heaven.

'No. I wonder why you insist on writing when with music ...'

'What a son of a bitch you are.'

'Then why did you let me read it?'

The next day they took the bus to Stuttgart Station because

something was going on with the train in Tübingen, each looking out at the landscape, Bernat draped in a stubborn hostile silence and with the same brooding expression he'd had since their educational visit to the Bebenhausen monastery.

'One day you told me that a close friend doesn't lie to you. Remember that, Bernat. So stop acting offended, bollocks.'

He said it in a loud, clear voice because speaking Catalan in a bus travelling from Tübingen to Stuttgart gave him a rare feeling of isolation and impunity.

'Pardon? Are you speaking to me?'

'Yes. And you added that if my bloody best friend can't tell me the truth and just acts like everybody else, oh, great, Bernat, what a load of ... It's missing the magical spark. And you shouldn't lie to me. Don't ever lie to me again, Adrià. Or our friendship will be over. Do you remember those words? Those are your words. And you went on: you said I know that you're the only one who tells me the truth.' He looked at him aslant. 'And I won't ever stop doing that, Bernat.' With my eyes straight ahead, I added: 'If I'm strong enough.'

They let the bus advance a few foggy, damp kilometres.

'I play music because I don't know how to write,' Bernat said while looking out the window.

'Now that's good!' shouted Adrià. And the woman in the seat in front of them looked back, as if they'd asked for her opinion. She shifted her gaze towards the sad grey, rainy landscape that was bringing them closer to Stuttgart: loud Mediterranean people; they must be Turks. Long silence until the taller of the two Turkish boys relaxed his expression and looked at his companion out of the corner of his eye: 'Now that's good? What do you mean?'

'Real art comes from some frustration. It doesn't come out of happiness.'

'Well, if that's the case, I'm a bona fide artist.'

'Hey, you are in love, don't forget.'

'You're right. But only my heart works,' pointed out Kemal Bernat. 'The rest is shite.'

'I'll switch places with you right now.' Ismaïl Adrià meant it.

'Fine. But we can't. We are condemned to envy each other.'

'What must that lady in front of us be thinking?'

Kemal watched her as she obstinately contemplated the landscape that was now urban but equally grey and rainy. Kemal was relieved to give up his brooding since, although he was quite offended, it was a lot of work to maintain. Like someone distilling a great thought: 'I don't know. But I'm convinced her name is Ursula.'

Ursula looked at him. She opened and closed her purse, perhaps to cover up her discomfiture, thought Kemal.

'And she has a son our age,' added Ismaïl.

As it headed uphill, the cart began to moan and the cart driver cracked the whip hard against the horses' backs. The slope was too steep to take with twenty men on board, but a bet was a bet.

'You can start digging in your pockets, sergeant!' said the cart driver.

'We're not at the top yet.'

The soldiers, who wanted to taste the pleasure of seeing the sergeant lose a bet, held their breath as if that could help the poor beasts make it up the slope to where the houses of Vet began. It was a slow, agonising ascent, and when they finally reached the top, the driver laughed and said Allah is great, and so am I! And my mules too! What do you think, sergeant?

The sergeant handed the cart driver a coin and Kemal and Ismaïl stifled a smile. To shake off the humiliation, the subordinate shouted orders: 'Everyone down. Have the Armenian assassins get ready!'

The cart driver lit a small cigar, satisfied, as he watched the soldiers, armed to the teeth, get down off the cart and head to the first house in Vet, ready for anything.

'Adrià?'

'Yes.'

'Where are you?'

'Huh?'

Adrià looked forward. Ursula was adjusting her jacket and looked out on the landscape again, apparently uninterested in the young Turks and their concerns.

'Maybe her name is Barbara.'

'Huh?' He made an effort to return to the bus. 'Yes. Or Ulrike.'

'If I'd known, I wouldn't have come to see you.'

'If you'd known what?'

'That you wouldn't like my story.'

'Rewrite it. But put yourself inside Amadeu.'

'Elisa is the protagonist.'

'Are you sure?'

Silence from the young Turks. After a short while: 'Well, have a look at that. You tell it from Amadeu's point of view and ...'

'All right, all right, all right. I'll rewrite it. Happy?'

On the platform, Bernat and Adrià hugged each other and Frau Ursula thought goodness, these Turks, here, in the light of day, and she continued towards the B sector of the platform, which was considerably further on.

Bernat, still with his arms around me, said thank you, son of a bitch, I really mean it.

'You really mean the son of a bitch or the thank you?

'Really what you said about dissatisfaction.'

'Come back whenever you want, Bernat.'

They had to run along the platform because they didn't realise they were supposed to be waiting at sector C. Frau Ursula was already seated when she saw them pass by and she thought Holy Mother of God, how scandalous.

Bernat, panting, got into the train car. After almost a minute I saw that he was still standing, talking to someone, gesturing, adjusting his rucksack and showing his ticket. Now I don't know if I should get on and help him or let him figure it out for himself so he doesn't get cross with me. Bernat leaned over to look through the window and I flashed him a smile. He sat with a weary gesture and looked at him again. When you say goodbye to a dear friend at the station, you have to leave when he's got into the train carriage. But Adrià was lingering. He smiled back at him. They had to look away. They both looked at their watches at the same time. Three minutes. I screwed up my courage and waved goodbye;

he barely shifted in his seat, and I left without looking back. Right there in the station I bought the *Frankfurter Allgemeine* and, as I waited for the bus to take me back, I paged through it, wanting to focus on something that wasn't Bernat's bitter-sweet lightning-fast visit to Tübingen. On page 12, a headline on a single column of a brief article. 'Psychiatrist murdered in Bamberg.' Bamberg? Baviara. My God, why would anyone want to kill a psychiatrist?

'Herr Aribert Voigt?'

'Yes, that's me.'

'I don't have an appointment. I'm very sorry.'

'That's fine, come in.'

Doctor Voigt politely let death in. The newcomer sat in the sober chair in the waiting room and the doctor went into his examining room saying I will see you shortly. From the waiting room the rustle of papers and file cabinets being opened and closed could be heard. Finally, the doctor poked his head out into the waiting room and asked death to come in. The newcomer sat where the doctor had indicated, while Voigt sat in his own chair.

'How can I help you?'

'I've come to kill you.'

Before Doctor Voigt had time to do anything, the new-comer had stood up and was pointing a Star at his temple. The doctor lowered his head with the pressure of the pistol's barrel.

'There's nothing you can do, Doctor. You know death comes when it comes. Without an appointment.'

'What are you, a poet?' without moving his head that was inches away from the desk, starting to sweat.

'Signor Falegnami, Herr Zimmermann, Doctor Voigt … I am killing you in the name of the victims of your inhuman experiments at Auschwitz.'

'And what if I tell you that you've got the wrong person?'

'I'd laugh my head off. Better not to try it.'

'I'll pay you double.'

'I'm not killing you for money.'

Silence, the doctor's sweat is already dripping off the tip of his nose, as if he were in the sauna with Brigitte. Death felt he had to clarify: 'I kill for money. But not you. Voigt, Budden and Höss. We were too late for Höss. Your own victims are killing you and Budden.'

'Forgive me.'

'Now that's hilarious.'

'I can give you information on Budden.'

'Oh, we've got a traitor. Give it to me.'

'In exchange for my life.'

'In exchange for nothing.'

Doctor Voigt stifled a sob. He struggled to pull himself together but was unable. He closed his eyes and began to cry with rage against his will.

'Come on! Do it already!' he shouted.

'Are you in a hurry? Because I'm not.'

'What do you want?'

'Let's do an experiment. Like one of the ones you did on your mice. Or your children.'

'No.'

'Yes.'

'Who's there?' he wanted to lift his head, but the pistol didn't allow him to.

'Friends, don't worry.' Clicking his tongue impatiently, 'Come on, let's have that information on Budden.'

'I don't have any.'

'Oy! You want to save him?'

'I don't give a shit about Budden. I regret what I've done.'

'Lift your head,' said death, grabbing his chin and roughly forcing his head up. 'What do you remember?'

Before him, dark, silent shadows, like in an exhibit in a parish centre, held up a panel with photos: men with their eyes destroyed, a weepy boy with his knees opened like pomegranates, a woman they performed a caesarean section on without anaesthesia. And a couple more he didn't recognise.

Doctor Voigt started crying again and shouting help and save me. He didn't stop until the shot sounded out.

'Psychiatrist murdered in Bamberg'. 'Doctor Aribert Voigt

was killed with a shot to the head in his office in the Bavarian city of Bamberg'. I had been in Tübingen for a couple of years. Nineteen seventy-two or seventy-three, I'm not sure. What I do know is that during those long frozen months I suffered over Kornelia. I couldn't have known anything about Voigt yet because I hadn't read the letter in Aramaic and I didn't know as many things as I know now, nor did I want to write you any letters. I had exams in a couple of weeks. And every day I met another of Kornelia's secrets. Perhaps I didn't read that, Sara. But it was in that period when someone killed a psychiatrist in Bamberg and I was unable to imagine that he was more closely linked to my life than Kornelia and her secrets were. Life is so strange, Sara.

## 26

I accuse myself of not having shed enough tears when my mother died. I was focused on the run-in I'd had with Coşeriu, my idol, who took down Chomsky, my idol, curiously without quoting Bloomfield. I already knew that he was doing it to provoke us, but on the day he mocked *Language and Mind* Adrià Ardèvol, who was a bit fed up with life and things like that, and was starting to have little patience, said – in a low voice and in Catalan – that's quite enough, Herr Professor, that's quite enough, there's no need to repeat it. And then Coşeriu looked at me across the desk with the most terrifying gaze in his repertoire and the other eleven students were silent.

'What's quite enough?' he challenged me, in German.

I, cowardly, remained quiet. I was petrified by his gaze and the possibility that he would tear me apart in front of that group. And he had one day congratulated me because he'd caught me reading *Mitul reintegrării* and he'd said that Eliade is a good thinker; you do well to read him.

'Come to see me in my office after class,' he told me quietly in Romanian. And he continued the lesson as if nothing had happened.

Curiously, when he went into Coşeriu's office, Adrià Ardèvol's legs weren't trembling. It had been exactly one week since he'd broken up with Augusta, who had succeeded Kornelia, who hadn't given him a chance to break up with her because, without giving any explanation, she had gone off with an experience almost seven feet tall, a basketball player who had just been signed by an important club in Stuttgart. His relationship with Augusta had been more measured and calm, but Adrià decided to distance himself after a couple of fights over stupid things. Stupiditates. And now he was in a bad mood and so humiliated by his fear of Coşeriu's gaze, and that was enough to keep my legs from trembling.

'Sit down.'

It was funny because Coşeriu spoke in Romanian and Ardèvol answered in Catalan, following the line of mutual provocation that had started on the third day of class when Coşeriu said what's going on here, why doesn't anyone ask any questions, and Ardèvol, who had one on the tip of his tongue, asked his first question about linguistic immanence and the rest of the class was the response to Ardèvol's question multiplied by ten and which I hold on to like a treasure, because it was a generous gift from a genius but thorny professor.

It was funny because they, each in their own language, understood each other perfectly. It was funny because they knew that they both thought of the professor's course as a version of the Last Supper at Santa Maria delle Grazie, Jesus and the twelve apostles, all hanging on the teacher's words and slightest gesture, except for Judas, who was doing his own thing.

'And who is Judas?'

'You are, of course. What are you studying?'

'This and that. History, philosophy, some philology and linguistics, some theology, Greek, Hebrew ... One foot in the Brechtbau and one in the Burse.'

Silence. After a little while, Adrià confessed I feel very ... very unhappy because I wanted to study everything.

'Everything?'

'Everything.'

'Yeah. I think I understand you. What is your academic situation?'

'If all goes well, I'll receive my doctorate in September.'

'What is your dissertation on?'

'On Vico.'

'Vico?'

'Vico.'

'I like it.'

'Well ... I ... I keep adding bits, smoothing ... I don't know how to decide when it's finished.'

'When they give you the deadline you'll know how to

decide when it's finished.' He lifted a hand as he usually did when he was going to say something important. 'I like that you're dusting off Vico. And do more doctorates, trust me.'

'If I can stay longer in Tübingen, I will.'

But I couldn't stay longer in Tübingen because when I got to my flat the trembling telegram from Little Lola was waiting for me, which told me Adrià, boy, my son. Stop. Your mother is dead. Stop. And I didn't cry. I imagined my life without Mother and I saw that it would be quite the same as it had been up until then and I responded don't cry, Little Lola, please, stop. What happened? She wasn't ill, was she?

I was a little embarrassed to ask that about my mother: I hadn't spoken with her in months. Every once in a while, there'd be a call and a very brief, unvarnished conversation, how's everything going, how are you, don't work so hard, come on, take care of yourself. What is it about the shop, I thought, that absorbs the thoughts of those who devote themselves to it.

She was ill, Son, for some weeks, but she had forbidden us from telling you; only if she got worse, then … and we didn't have time because it all happened very quickly. She was so young. Yes, she died this very morning; come immediately, for the love of God, Adrià, my son. Stop.

I missed two of Coşeriu's lectures and I presided over the burial, which the deceased had decided would be religious, beside an aged and saddened Aunt Leo and beside Xevi, Quico, their wives and Rosa, who told me that her husband hadn't been able to come because / please, Rosa, there's no need for you to apologise. Cecília, who was, as always, perfectly put together, pinched my cheek as if I were eight years old and still carried Sheriff Carson in my pocket. And Mr Berenguer's eyes sparkled, I thought it was from grief and confusion, but I later learned it was from pure joy. And I grabbed Little Lola, who was at the back, with some women I didn't know, and I took her by the arm to the family pew and then she burst into tears and in that moment I started to feel sorry for the deceased. There were a lot of strangers, a lot. I was surprised to find that Mother even had that many acquaintances. And my prayer with litanies was Mother, you died without telling me why you and Father were so distanced from me; you died without telling me why you were so distanced from each other; you died without telling me why you never wanted to continue with any serious investigation into Father's death; you died without telling me, oh, Mother, why you never really loved me. And I came up with that prayer because I hadn't yet read her will.

Adrià hadn't set foot in the flat in months. Now it seemed quieter than ever. It was difficult for me to enter my parents' room. Always half in penumbra; the bed was unmade, with the mattress lifted; the wardrobe, the dressing table, the mirror, everything exactly as it had been my entire life, but without Father and his bad humour, and without Mother and her silences.

Little Lola, seated at the kitchen table, looked at the void, still wearing dark mourning clothes. Without asking her opinion, Adrià rummaged through the cabinets until he managed to gather the implements to make tea. Little Lola was so dispirited that she didn't get up or say leave that, boy, tell me what you want and I'll prepare it for you. No, Little Lola looked at the wall and the infinity beyond the wall.

'Drink, it'll do you good.'

Little Lola grasped the mug instinctively and took a slurp. I left the kitchen in silence, Little Lola's grief weighing on me, taking the place of my lack of sorrow over Mother's death. Adrià was sad, sure, but he wasn't eaten up with pain and that made him feel bad; just like with his father's death when he'd let fears and, above all, guilt fill him, now he felt himself outside of that other unexpected death, as if he had no link to it. In the dining room, he opened the balcony's blinds to let the daylight in. The Urgell on the wall over the buffet received the light from the balcony naturally, almost as if it were the light inside the painting. The bell gable of the monastery of Santa Maria de Gerri de la Sal glittered under the late afternoon sun, almost reddish. The three-storey gable, the gable with the five bells which he had observed endless times and which had helped him daydream during the long, boring Sunday afternoons. Right in the middle of the bridge he stopped, impressed, to look upon it. He had never seen a gable like that one and now he understood what he'd been told about that monastery, that it was an institution that until recently had been rich and powerful thanks to the salt mines. To contemplate it freely, he had to lift his hood and his wide, noble forehead was illuminated like the bell gable by that sun that was setting behind Trespui. At that hour of the late afternoon the monks must be starting their frugal dinner, he calculated.

The pilgrim was received, after making sure he wasn't one of the count's spies, with Benedictine hospitality, simple, without any fuss, but practical. He went directly into the refectory, where the community was silently eating a spare meal while they listened, in quite imperfect Latin, to the exemplary life of Saint Ot, Bishop of Urgell who, they had just learned, was buried right there at the Santa Maria monastery. The sadness on the face of the thirty-odd monks perhaps reflected a longing for those happier days.

First thing the next morning, still dark, two monks began the trip north that would take them, in a couple of days' time, to Sant Pere del Burgal, where they had to collect the Sacred Chest, oh infinite grief, because the little monastery way up high over the same river as the Santa Maria was left without monks on account of death.

'What is the reason for your trip?' he asked the father prior of La Sal, after the light meal, to be polite, strolling through the cloister that provided very little shelter from the cold northern air that came down the channel created by the Noguera.

'I am searching for one of your brothers.'

'From this community?'

'Yes, Father. I have a personal message, from his family.'

'And who is it? I'll have him come down.'

'Friar Miquel de Susqueda.'

'We have no monk with that name, sir.'

Noticing the other man's shudder, he waved one hand as if in apology and said this spring is turning out to be quite chilly, sir.

'Friar Miquel de Susqueda, who once belonged to the order of Saint Dominic.'

'I can assure you that he doesn't live there, sir. And what sort of message did you have for him?'

Noble Friar Nicolau Eimeric, Inquisitor General of the Kingdom of Aragon, Valencia and the Majorcas and the principality of Catalonia, was lying on his deathbed in his monastery in Girona, watched over by twins, two lay brothers, who were keeping down his fever with a wet cloth and whispered prayers. The sick man straightened up when he heard the door opening. He noticed that he had trouble focusing his weak gaze.

'Ramon de Nolla?' Apprehensively, 'Is that you?'

'Yes, Your Excellency,' said the knight, as he bowed in reverence before the bed.

'Leave us alone.'

'But, Your Excellency!' protested the two brothers in unison.

'I said leave us alone,' he spat with a still frightful energy, but without shouting because he no longer had the strength. The two lay brothers, contrite, left the room without saying another word. Eimeric, sitting up in bed, looked at the knight: 'You have the chance to complete your penitence.'

'Praised be the Lord!'

'You have to become the executing arm of the Holy Tribunal.'

'You know that I will do whatever you order if that will earn me my pardon.'

'If you fulfil the penitence I give you, God will forgive you and your soul will be cleansed. You shall no longer live in inner torment.'

'That is all I wish for, Your Excellency.'

'My former personal secretary in the tribunal.'

'Who is he and where does he live?'

'His name is Friar Miquel de Susqueda. He was condemned to death in absentia for high treason to the Holy Tribunal. This was many years ago, but none of my agents have succeeded in finding him. Which is why I've now chosen a man of war such as yourself.'

He began to cough, surely induced by the eagerness with which he spoke. One of the nurse brothers opened the door, but Ramon de Nolla didn't think twice about slamming it in his face. Friar Nicolau explained that the fugitive wasn't hiding in Susqueda, that he had been seen in Cardona, and an agent of the tribunal had even assured him that he'd joined the order of Saint Benedict but they didn't know in which monastery. And he explained more details of his holy mission. And it doesn't matter if I've died; it doesn't matter how many years have passed; but when you see him, tell him I am your punishment, stick a dagger in his heart, cut off his tongue and bring it to me. And if I am dead, leave it on my grave, let it rot there as is the Lord Our God's will.'

'And then my soul will be free of all guilt?'

'Amen.'

'It is a personal message, Father Prior,' the visitor had insisted, when they had arrived in silence to the end of the cold cloister at Santa Maria.

Out of Benedictine courtesy, since he was no danger, the noble knight was received by the father abbot, to whom he repeated I am looking for a brother of yours, Father Abbot.

'Who?'

'Friar Miquel de Susqueda, Father Abbot.'

'We have no brother by that name. Why are you looking for him?'

'It is a personal matter, Father Abbot. A family matter. And very important.'

'Well, you have made the trip in vain.'

'Before joining the order of Saint Benedict as a monk, he was a Dominican friar for some years.'

'Ah, I know of whom you speak,' said the abbot, cutting him off. 'Yes … He is part of the community of Sant Pere del Burgal, near Escaló. Brother Julià de Sau was a Dominican friar long ago.'

'Blessed be the Lord!' exclaimed Ramon de Nolla.

'You may not find him alive.'

'What do you mean?' said the noble knight, alarmed.

'There were two monks at Sant Pere and yesterday we found

out that one has died. I don't know if it was the father prior or Brother Julià. The emissaries weren't entirely sure.'

'Then … How can I …'

'And you'll have to wait for better weather.'

'Yes, Father Abbot. But how can I know if the surviving brother is the one I am searching for?'

'I just sent two brothers to collect the Holy Chest and the surviving monk. When they return you will know.'

Silence, each man thinking his own thoughts. And the father abbot: 'How sad. A monastery closing its doors after almost six hundred years of praising the Lord with the chanting of the hours each and every day.'

'How sad, Father Abbot. I will head off on the path to see if I can catch up with your monks.'

'There's no need: wait for them. Two or three days.'

'No, Father Abbot. I have no time to wait.'

'As you wish, sir: they will get you there safely.'

With both hands he took the painting off the dining room wall and brought it over to the weaker light of the balcony. *Santa Maria de Gerri,* by Modest Urgell. Many families had a cheap reproduction of the last supper in their home; theirs was presided over by an Urgell. With the painting in his hand, he went into the kitchen and said Little Lola, don't say no: keep this painting.

Little Lola, who was still seated at the kitchen table thinking about the wall, looked towards Adrià.

'What?'

'It's for you.'

'You don't know what you're saying, boy. Your parents …'

'That doesn't matter: now I'm in charge. I'm giving it to you.'

'I can't accept it.'

'Why?'

'It's too valuable. I can't.'

'No: you are afraid that Mother wouldn't like it.'

'Either way. I can't accept it.'

And I stood there with the rejected Urgell in my hands.

I brought it back to the spot where I had always seen it and the dining room returned to being what it had always been. I went around the flat; I went into Father and Mother's study to rummage through drawers without any clear objective. And after rummaging through the drawers, Adrià began to think. After a few hours of stillness, he got up and went towards the laundry room.

'Little Lola.'

'What.'

'I have to go back to Germany. I have at least six or seven months before I can come back.'

'Don't worry.'

'I'm not worried: stay, please: this is your home.'

'No.'

'It's more your home than mine. I'm, as long as I have the study …'

'I came here thirty-one years ago to take care of your mother. If she's dead, my work here is done.'

'Little Lola, stay.'

Five days later I was able to read the will. In fact, it was the notary, Cases, who read it to me, Little Lola and Aunt Leo. And when, in his thin, rasping voice, the man announced it is my wish that the painting entitled *Santa Maria de Gerri*, by Modest Urgell, which is personal property of the family, be given without any compensation to my loyal friend Dolors Carrió, whom we have always called Little Lola, as a tiny show of appreciation for the support that she has offered me throughout my life, I started to laugh, Little Lola burst into tears and Aunt Leo looked at us, puzzled. The rest of the will was more complicated except for a personal letter in an envelope with a seal that the countertenor put into my hands and which began dear Adrià, my beloved son, something she had never said to me in my ffucking life.

Dear Adrià, my beloved son.

That was the end of my mother's sentimental expansiveness. All the rest was instructions about the shop. About my moral obligation to take care of it. And she explained in full detail the unusual relationship she maintained with

Mr Berenguer, imprisoned by a salary in order to return the amount of an old embezzlement, which was still in effect for one more year. And your father had all his hopes tied up in the shop and now that I'm no longer around you can't just wash your hands of it. But since I know that you always have and will do whatever you want to, I'm not convinced that you will heed me, roll up your sleeves, go into the shop and put everyone in their place the way I did after your father's death. I don't want to speak ill of him, but he was a romantic: I had to bring order to the shop; I had to rationalise it. I turned it into a good business that you and I have been able to live off of, and I've only added a couple of salaries, as you know. I'll be very sorry if you don't want to keep the shop; but since I won't be able to see you, well, what can I do? And then she gave me some very precise instructions as to how to deal with Mr Berenguer and she asked me to follow them to the letter. And then she went back to the personal arena and said but I am writing you these lines today, on the twentieth of January of nineteen seventy-five because the doctor told me that I probably won't live much longer. I gave instructions for them not to disturb your studies until the time came. But I am writing to you because I want you to know, besides what I've already said, two more things. First: I have gone back to the church. When I married your father I was a wishy-washy girl, very susceptible to influence, who didn't know exactly what she wanted out of life, and when your father told me that the most likely thing was that God didn't exist, I said ah, well, all right. But later I missed having him in my life, especially when my father died and Fèlix died, and with the loneliness I've felt not knowing what to do with you.

'What do you mean what to do with me? Love me.'

'I did love you, Son.'

'From a distance.'

'We've never been very affectionate in this house; that doesn't mean we're bad people.'

'Mother: love me, look me in the eyes, ask me what I want to do.'

'And your father's death ruined everything.'

'You could have tried.'

'I've never been able to forgive you for giving up the violin.'

'I've never forgiven you for forcing me to be the best.'

'You are.'

'No. I'm intelligent and, you could even say, gifted. But I can't do it all. I don't have any obligation to be the best. You and Father made a mistake with me.'

'Not your father.'

'I am finishing my doctorate and I don't plan on studying law. And I haven't learned Russian.'

'For the moment.'

'Fine. For the moment.'

'Let's not argue, I'm dead.'

'All right. And what was the other thing you wanted me to know? By the way: does God exist, Mother?'

'I'm dying with many regrets. The main one is not knowing who killed your father and why.'

'What did you do to try to find that out?'

'I now know that you were spying on me from behind the sofa. You know things that I didn't know you knew.'

'Not really. I only really learned what a brothel is, but not who killed my father.'

'Hey, hey, here comes the black widow!' said Inspector Ocaña, frightened, poking his head into the Commissioner's office.

'Are you sure?'

'Didn't you get rid of her for good?'

'Pain in my arse.'

Comissioner Plasencia stuck the rest of his sandwich into the drawer, stood up and looked out the window at the traffic on Llúria Street. When he heard the female presence at the door, he turned.

'What a surprise.'

'Good afternoon.'

'It's been days since ...'

'Yes. It's that ... I had them investigate and ...'

On the table, inside a cold ashtray, a small half-smoked, snuffed-out cigar was stinking up the room.

'And what?'

'Aribert Voigt, Commissioner. Revenge over some business dealings, Commissioner. Or you could call it, personal revenge; but it has nothing to do with brothels or raped girls. I don't know why you made up that deplorable story.'

'I always follow orders.'

'I don't, Commissioner. And I plan on taking you to court for obstruction of

'Don't make me laugh!' the policeman cut her off, rudely. 'Luckily, Spain is no democracy. Here we good guys are in charge.'

'You will soon receive the citation. If the guilt lies higher up, we will follow the loose ends and uncover it.'

'What loose ends?'

'Someone let that murderer act with impunity. And someone let him leave without detaining him.'

'Don't be naive. You won't find any loose ends, because there are none.'

The commissioner took the cigar from the ashtray, lit a match and began smoking. A thick bluish cloud momentarily concealed his face.

'And why didn't you go to court, Mother?'

Commissioner Plasencia sat down, still spewing smoke from his nose and mouth. Mother preferred to remain standing before him.

'There are loose ends!' said Mother.

'Ma'am, I have work to do,' responded the commissioner, remembering his half-eaten sandwich.

'A Nazi who lives without a care in the world. If he's still alive.'

'Names. Without names, it's all just smoke and mirrors.'

'A Nazi. Aribert Voigt. I'm giving you a name!'

'Farewell, madam.'

'On the evening of the crime my husband told me he was going to the Athenaeum to see someone named Pinheiro …'

'Mother, why didn't you take it to court?'

'… but that wasn't true, he wasn't meeting up with Pinheiro. A commissioner had called him.'

'Names. Ma'am. There are lots of commissioners in Barcelona.'

'And it was a trap. Aribert Voigt was acting under the protection of the Spanish police.'

'What you're saying could get you sent to prison.'

'Mother, why didn't you take it to court?'

'And the man lost control. He wanted to hurt my husband. He wanted to scare him, I think. But he ended up killing him and destroying him.'

'Ma'am, don't talk nonsense.'

'Instead of arresting him, they kicked him out of the country. Isn't that how it went, Commissioner Plasencia?'

'Ma'am, you've read too many novels.'

'I can assure you that is not the case.'

'If you don't stop badgering me and getting in the way of the police, you are going to have a very bad time of it. You, your little girlfriend and your son. Even if you flee to the ends of the earth.'

'Mother, did I hear that right?'

'Hear what right?'

'The part about your little girlfriend.'

The commissioner pulled back to observe the effect his words had had. And he drove them home: 'It wouldn't be difficult to spread information in the circles you frequent. Farewell, Mrs Ardèvol. And don't ever come back.' And he opened the half-empty drawer, with the remains of his thwarted sandwich, and he closed it angrily, this time in front of the black widow.

'Yes, yes, all right, Mother. But how did you know that all that about the brothels and the rapes was a lie?'

Mother, even though she was dead, grew silent. I was fretfully awaiting a response. After an eternity: 'I just know it.'

'That's not enough for me.'

'Fine.' Dramatic pause, I suppose to gather courage. 'Early on in our marriage, after we conceived you, your father was diagnosed with total sexual impotence. From that point on, he was completely unable to have erections. That made him bitter for the rest of his life. And it embittered us. Doctors and pitiful

visits to understanding ladies, none of it did any good. Your
father wasn't perfect, but he couldn't rape anyone, not even a
child, because he ended up hating sex and everything related
to it. I guess that's why he took refuge in his sacred objects.'

'If that was the case, why didn't you take them to court?
Did they blackmail you?'

'Yes.'

'About your lover?'

'No.'

And Mother's letter ended with a series of more general
recommendations and a timid sentimental effusion at the end
when it said goodbye, my beloved son. The last sentence, I will
watch over you from heaven, has always seemed to contain a
slight threat.

'Oh, boy ...' said Mr Berenguer, stretched out in the office
chair, wiping non-existent specks from his impeccable trouser
leg. 'So you've decided to roll up your sleeves and get to work.'

He was sitting in Mother's office, with the smug air of
someone who's reconquered valuable territory, and the
sudden appearance of lamebrained Ardèvol Jr, who's always
got his head in the clouds, distracted him from his thoughts.
He was surprised to see the lad entering his office without
knocking. That was why he said oh boy.

'What do you want to talk about?'

Everything, Adrià wanted to talk about everything. But
first, he cleverly laid the groundwork for them to clearly understand each other: 'The first thing I want to do is extricate
you from the shop.'

'What?'

'You heard me.'

'Do you know about the deal I have with your mother?'

'She's dead. And yes, I'm familiar with it.'

'I don't believe you do: I signed a contract obliging me to
work at the shop. I still have a year left in the galleys.'

'I'm releasing you from it: I want to see the back of you.'

'I don't know what it is with your family, but you've all got
a real nasty streak ...'

'Don't start lecturing me, Mr Berenguer.'

'Lectures, no; but some information, yes. Do you know that your father was a predator?'

'More or less. And that you were the hyena who tried to pinch the remains of the gnu from him.'

Mr Berenguer smiled widely, revealing a gold incisor.

'Your father was a merciless predator when it came to making a profit from a sale. And I say sale, but it was often a blatant requisition.'

'Fine, a requisition. But you will gather up your things today. You are no longer welcome in the shop.'

'My, oh my …' A strange smile tried to conceal his surprise at the words of the Ardèvol pup. 'And you call me a hyena? Who are you to …'

'I am the son of the king of the jungle, Mr Berenguer.'

'You're as much of a bastard as your mother was.'

'Farewell, Mr Berenguer. Tomorrow the new manager will call on you, if necessary, in the company of a lawyer who will be fully informed about everything.'

'You do know that your fortune is built on extortion?'

'Are you still here?'

Luckily for me, Mr Berenguer thought that I was solid as a rock, like my mother; he mistook my resigned fatalism for some sort of deep indifference and that disarmed him and strengthened me. He gathered, in silence, all that he must have only very shortly before placed in a drawer of my mother's desk and left the office. I saw him rummaging through various nooks and crannies until I noticed that Cecília, pretending to be working with the catalogues, was glancing curiously at the hyena's movements. She soon understood what was going on, and a lipsticked smile grew wide on her face.

Mr Berenguer slammed the door to the street, trying to crack the glass, but he didn't pull it off. The two new employees didn't seem to understand anything. Mr Berenguer, after working there for thirty years, had barely taken an hour to disappear from the shop. I thought he had disappeared from my life as well. And I locked Mother and Father's office with a key. Instead of demanding information and searching out signs of the king of the jungle's prowess, I began to cry. The next morning, instead of demanding information and searching out signs, I put the shop in the hands of the manager and went back to Tübingen because I didn't want to miss any more of Coşeriu's classes. Information and signs.

## 27

During my last months in Tübingen I began to long for that city, along with the landscape of Baden-Württemberg and the Black Forest and all of it, which was so lovely; because Adrià was going through the same thing that happened to Bernat: he was happier longing after something that was out of his reach than looking at what he held in his hands. He was thinking more about how the heck will I be able to live so far from this landscape when I return to Barcelona, how? And this was while still finishing his dissertation on Vico, which had somehow become some sort of atomic pile where he'd deposited all of his thoughts and which I knew would provide me with an unceasing series of intellectual reflections that would accompany me throughout my life. That could explain, my dear, why I didn't want to get distracted by information and signs that could disrupt my life and my studies. And I tried not to think about it much until I got used to not thinking about it at all.

'It's … No, not brilliant: it's profound; it's admirable. And your German, it's perfect,' Coşeriu told him the day after his dissertation defence. 'Above all, don't stop studying. And if you choose linguistics, let me know.'

What Adrià didn't know was that Coşeriu had barely slept over the course of two days and one night while reading one of the committee members' copies. I found out a few years later, from Doctor Kamenek himself. But that day Adrià was only able to stand there, alone, in the corridor, watching Coşeriu head off, unable to completely grasp that the man had hugged him and told him that he admired him; no: that he admired what he had written. Coşeriu recognising that

'What's wrong with you, Ardèvol?'

He had been standing in the corridor for five minutes and he hadn't seen Kamenek approaching from behind.

'Me? What?'

'Are you feeling OK?'

'Me? Yes … Yes, yes. I was …'

He made a vague gesture with his hands to indicate that he didn't really know. Afterwards, Kamenek asked him if he had decided whether he was going to stay in Tübingen and continue studying, and he responded that he had many binding commitments, which wasn't true, because he couldn't care less about the shop and the only thing he was longing for was Father's study and he was also starting to long for the possibility of longing for Tübingen's cold landscape. And he also wanted to be closer to the memory of Sara: I now recognised myself as a castrated man, without you. All those things were beginning to lead him to comprehend that he would never achieve happiness. That surely no one could. Happiness was always just out of reach, but unreachable; surely it was unreachable for everyone. Despite the joys that life sometimes brought, like that day when Bernat called him as if they hadn't been officially at odds for more or less six months and said can you hear me? He's finally dead, the rotten bastard! Everyone here is pulling the champagne out of the fridge. And then he said now is the moment for Spain to reconsider and free all its people and ask for all the historical forgiveness necessary.

'Ay.'

'What? Aren't I right?'

'Yes. But it sounds like you don't know Spain very well.'

'You'll see, you'll see.' And with the same momentum: 'Ah, and I am about to give you a surprise announcement.'

'Are you pregnant?'

'No, it's not a joke. You'll see. Wait a few days.'

And he hung up because a call to Germany cost an arm and a leg and he was calling from a phone booth, euphoric, thinking Franco's dead, the ogre is dead, the wolf is dead, the vermin is dead and with it its venom. There are moments when even good people can be happy over someone's death.

Bernat wasn't lying to him: in addition to his confirming the dictator's death, which was front page news the next day, five days later Adrià received a laconic, urgent letter that read

Dear Know-It-All: you remember when you said it'sveryvery bad.Itlackssoul;Ididn'tbelieveasingleemotion.Idon'tknowwhy ,butIthinkit'sterrible.Idon'tknowwhoAmadeuis;andtheworst ofitisthatIdon'tgivearat'sarse.AndElisa,well,itgoeswithoutsay ing. Do you remember? Well, that story without believable emotions just won the Blanes Prize. Awarded by an intelligent jury. I'm happy. YourfriendBernat.

WowI'mthrilled, answered Adrià. Butdon'tforgetthatif youhaven'trewrittenit,it'sstilljustasbad.YourfriendAdrià. And Bernat responded with an urgent telegram that read Gotakealongwalkoffashortpierstop. YourfriendBernatstop.

When I went back to Barcelona, they offered me a class in Aesthetic and Cultural History at the University of Barcelona and I said yes, without thinking it over, even though I had no need to work. There was something pleasing about it, after so many years of living abroad, to find work in my neigh-bourhood, a ten-minute walk from my house. And the first day that I went to the department to discuss the details of my joining the staff, I met Laura there. The first day! Blonde, on the short side, friendly, smiling and, I didn't yet know, sad on the inside. She had registered for her fifth year and was asking for some professor, I think it was Cerdà, who it turned out was her advisor for a thesis on Coşeriu. And blue eyes. And a pleasant voice. Nervous, not very well-groomed hands. And some very interesting cologne or perfume – I've never been clear on the difference. And Adrià was smiling at her, and she said hello, do you work here? And he said: I'm not sure. And she said: I wish you would!

'You should never have come back.'

'Why?'

'Your future is in Germany.'

'And weren't you the one who didn't want me to go? How's the violin going?'

'I'm going to try out for a spot in the Barcelona Symphony Orchestra.'

'That's great, right?'

'Yeah, sure. I'll be a civil servant.'

'No: you will be a violinist in a good orchestra with plenty of room for improvement.'

'If I make it.' A few seconds of hesitation. 'And I'm marrying Tecla. Will you be my best man?'

'Of course. When are you getting married?'

Meanwhile, things were happening. I had to start wearing reading glasses and my hair began to desert me without any explanation. I was living alone in a vast flat in the Eixample, surrounded by the boxes of books that had arrived from Germany that I never had the energy to classify and put away in their proper place, for various reasons including that I didn't have the shelf space. And I was unable to convince Little Lola to stay.

'Goodbye, Adrià, my son.'

'I'm so sorry, Little Lola.'

'I want to live my own life.'

'I can understand that. But this is still your home.'

'Find yourself a maid, trust me.'

'No, no. If you don't ... Impossible.'

Would I cry over Little Lola's departure? No. What I did do was to buy myself a good upright piano and put it in my parents' bedroom, which I was turning into my own. The hallway, which was very wide, had grown accustomed to the obstacles of unpacked boxes of books.

'But ... Forgive me for asking, all right?'

'Go ahead.'

'Do you have a home?'

'Of course. Even though I haven't lived there in a thousand years, I have a little flat in the Barceloneta. I've had it repainted.'

'Little Lola.'

'What?'

'Don't get offended, but I ... I wanted to give you something. In appreciation.'

'I've been paid for each and every one of the days I've lived in this house.'

'I don't mean that. I mean ...'

'Well, you don't need to say it.'

Lola took me by the arm and led me to the dining room; she showed me the bare wall where the painting by Modest Urgell used to hang.

'Your mother gave me a gift I don't deserve.'

'What more can I do for you …'

'Deal with these books, you can't live like this.'

'Come on, Little Lola. What more can I do for you?'

'Let me leave in peace; I mean it.'

I hugged her and I realised that … it's shocking, Sara, but I think I loved Little Lola more than I loved my own mother.

Little Lola moved out of the house; the tramcars no longer circulated noisily up Llúria because the city council, at the end of the dictatorship, had opted for direct pollution and replaced them with buses without removing the tracks, which caused many a motorbike accident. And I shut myself up in the house, to continue studying and to forget you. Installed in my parents' room and sleeping on the same bed where I'd been born on the thirtieth of April nineteen forty-six at six thirty-seven in the morning.

Bernat and Tecla married, deeply in love, with excitement in their eyes; and I was the best man. During the wedding reception, still dressed as bride and groom, they played Brahms's first sonata for us, just like that, bravely and without scores. And I was so jealous … Bernat and Tecla had their whole lives ahead of them and I joyfully envied my friend's happiness. I longed after Sara and her inexplicable flight, deeply envying Bernat again, and I wished them all the good fortune in the world for their life together. They left on their honeymoon – smiling and expansive – and began – gradually, consistently, day by day – sowing the seeds of their unhappiness.

For a few months, as I got used to the classes, the students' lack of interest in cultural history, the wild landscape of the Eixample, devoid of forests, I studied piano with a woman who was nothing like the memory I had of Trullols, but who was very efficient. But I still had too much free time.

'hàd.'

'hadh.'

'trēn.'

'trén.'

'tlāt.'

'tláth.'

*'arba.'*

'árba.'

*'arba.'*

'árba.'

**'arba!'**

**'arba!'**

'Raba taua!'

Aramaic classes helped mitigate the problem. Professor
Gombreny complained at first about my pronunciation, until
she stopped mentioning it, I don't know if it was because I'd
improved or she was just fed up.

Since Wednesdays dragged, Adrià signed up for a Sanskrit
class that opened up a whole new world to me, especially
because it was a pleasure to hear Doctor Figueres cautiously
venturing etymologies and establishing webs of connection
between the different Indo-European languages. I was also
doing slalom through the hallways to avoid the boxes of
books. I had pinpointed their exact locations and didn't even
crash into them in the dark. And when I was tired of reading,
I would play my Storioni for hours until I was drenched
in sweat like Bernat on the day of his exam. And the days
passed quickly and I only thought of you as I was making
my dinner, because then I had to let down my guard. And I
went to bed with a touch of sadness and, mostly, with the unanswered question of why, Sara. I only had to meet with the
shop manager twice, a very dynamic man who quickly took
care of the situation. The second time he told me that Cecília
was about to retire and, even though I'd had few dealings
with her, I was sad about it. I know it sounds hard to believe,
but Cecília had pinched my cheek and mussed my hair more
times than my mother.

The first time I felt a tickle in my fingers was when Morral,
an old bookseller at the Sant Antoni market, an acquaintance

of Father's, told me I think you might be interested in coming to see something, sir.

Adrià, who was going through a pile of books from the 'A Tot Vent' collection, from its beginnings to the outbreak of the Civil War, some with dedications from unknown people to other unknown people that he found highly amusing, lifted his head in surprise.

'Beg your pardon?'

The bookseller had stood up and gestured with his head for Adrià to follow him. He poked the man at the stall beside him, to let him know that he would be away for a while and could he keep an eye on his books, for the love of God. In five silent minutes they reached a narrow house with a dark stairwell on Comte Borrell Street that he remembered having visited with his father. On the first floor, Morral pulled a key out of his pocket and opened a door. The flat was dark. He switched on a weak bulb whose light didn't reach the floor and, with four strides through a very narrow hallway, he stood in a room filled with a huge cabinet with many wide but shallow drawers, like the ones illustrators use to store their drawings. The first thing I thought was how could they have got it through such a narrow hallway. The light in the room was brighter than the one in the hallway. Then Adrià realised that there was a table in the middle, with a lamp that Morral also turned on. He opened up one of the drawers and pulled out a bunch of pages and placed them beneath the beam of light on the small table. Then I felt the palpitations, the tickle in my insides and my fingertips. Both of us gathered over the gem. Before me were some sheets of rough paper. I had to put on my glasses because I didn't want to miss a single detail. It took me some time to get used to the strange handwriting on that manuscript. I read aloud *Discours de la méthode. Pour bien conduire sa raison, & chercher la vérité dans les sciences.* And that was it. I didn't dare to touch the paper. All I said was no.

'Yes.'

'It can't be.'

'You're interested, right?'

'Where in hell did you get it from?'

Rather than answering me, Morral turned the first page. And after a little while he said I'm sure you are interested.

'What do you know.'

'You are like your father: I know you are interested.'

Adrià had the original manuscript of *Discours de la méthode* before him, written before 1637, which is when it was published along with *Dioptrique*, *Les Météores* and *Géométrie*.

'Complete?' he asked.

'Complete. Well ... it's missing ... nothing, a couple of pages.'

'And how do I know that it's not a scam?'

'When you find out the price you'll know that it's not a scam.'

'No: I understand that it will be very expensive. How do I know you aren't cheating me?'

The man dug around in a briefcase that leaned against one of the table legs, pulled out some sheets of paper and extended them to Adrià.

The first eight or ten years of the 'A Tot Vent' collection would have to wait. Adrià Ardèvol spent the afternoon examining the packet and checking it against the certificate of authenticity and asking himself how in the hell that gem had surfaced and deciding that perhaps it was better not to ask too many questions.

I didn't ask a single question that wasn't related to the pages' authenticity and I ended up paying a fortune after a month of hesitation and discreet consultations. That was the first manuscript I acquired myself, of the twenty in my collection. At home, procured by my father, I already had twenty loose pages of the *Recherche*, the entire manuscript of Joyce's *The Dead*, some pages by Zweig, that guy who committed suicide in Brazil, and the manuscript of the consecration of the monastery of Sant Pere del Burgal by Abbot Deligat. From that day on I understood that I was possessed by the same demon as my father had been. The tickle in my belly, the itching in my fingers, the dry mouth ... all over my doubts on the authenticity, the value of the manuscript, the fear of missing the chance to possess it, the fear of paying too much, the fear of offering too little and seeing it vanish from my life ...

The *Discours de la méthode* was my grain of sand.

The first grain of sand is a speck in your eye; then it becomes a
nuisance on your fingers, a burning in your stomach, a small
protuberance in your pocket and, with a bit of bad luck, it
ends up transforming into a weight on your conscience.
Everything – all lives and stories – begins thus, beloved Sara,
with a harmless grain of sand that goes unnoticed.

I entered the shop as if it were a temple. Or a labyrinth.
Or hell. I hadn't set foot in there since I'd expelled Mr Berenguer into the outer shadows. The same bell sounded when
you opened the door. That same bell my whole life. He was
received by Cecília's affable eyes, still behind the counter, as if
she had never shifted from that spot. As if she were an object
displayed for sale to any collector with enough capital. Still
well dressed and coiffed. Without moving, as if she had been
waiting for him for hours, she demanded a kiss, like when he
was ten years old. She asked him how are you feeling, Son,
and he said fine, fine. And you?

'Waiting for you.'

Adrià looked from side to side. In the back some girl he
didn't recognise was patiently cleaning copper objects.

'He hasn't arrived yet,' she said. And she took his hand to
pull him closer and she couldn't resist running her fingers
through his hair, like Little Lola. 'It's getting thinner.'

'Yes.'

'You look more like your father with each passing day.'

'Really?'

'Do you have a girlfriend?'

'Sort of.'

She opened and closed a drawer. Silence. Perhaps she was
wondering if she should have asked that question.

'Why don't you have a look around?'

'May I?'

'You're the boss,' she said, opening her arms. For a few moments, Adrià thought she was offering herself to him.

I took my last stroll through the shop's universe. The objects were different, but the atmosphere and scent were the same. There he saw Father hunting through documents, Mr Berenguer thinking big ideas, looking towards the door to the street, Cecília all made up and coiffed, younger, smiling at a customer who was trying to get an unwarranted discount on the price of a splendid Chippendale desk, Father calling Mr Berenguer to his office, closing the door and speaking for a long time about matters Adrià knew nothing about, and some that he did. I went back to Cecília's side; she was on the phone. When she hung up, I stood in front of her. 'When are you retiring?'

'Christmas. You don't want to take over the shop, do you?'

'I don't know,' I lied. 'I have work at the university.'

'The two things aren't incompatible.'

I had the feeling that she was going to tell me something, but just then Mr Sagrera came in, apologising for the delay, greeting Cecília and waving me towards the office, all at once. We closed ourselves in there and the manager told me how things were and what the shop's current value was. And even though you haven't asked my opinion, I feel I must tell you that this is a profitable business with a future. The only obstacle was Mr Berenguer and you've already cleared that slate. He leaned back in his chair to give more weight to his words: 'A profitable business with a future.'

'I want to sell it. I don't want to be a shopkeeper.'

'What's wrong with that?'

'Mr Sagrera …'

'You're the one in charge. Is that your final word?'

What do I know if it's the final word? What do I know about what I want to do?

'Yes, Mr Sagrera, it's the final word.'

Then, Mr Sagrera got up, went over to the safe and opened it. I was surprised that he had a key and I didn't. He pulled out an envelope.

'From your mother.'

'For me?'

'She told me to give it to you if you came by the shop.'

'But I don't want …'

'If you came by the shop: not if you decided to run it.'

It was a sealed envelope. I opened it in front of Mr Sagrera. The letter didn't begin with my beloved son. It didn't have any preface; it didn't even say hey, Adrià, how's it going. It was a list of instructions, cold but pragmatic, with advice that I understood would be very useful to me.

Despite my intentions, after a few days or a few weeks, I can't remember which, I went to a clandestine auction. Morral, the bookseller from the Sant Antoni market, had given me the address with a mysterious air. Perhaps such mystery wasn't necessary, because apparently there was no protective filter. You rang the bell, they opened the door and you went into a garage in an industrial area of Hospitalet. There was a table with a display case, as if we were in a jewellery shop, well illuminated, where the objects for auction were placed. As soon as I began to examine them, the tickle returned and I was quickly covered in that sweat, my constant companion when I'm about to acquire something. And that thick, dry tongue. I think it's the same thing a gambler feels in front of a machine. I was actually the one who bought a large part of the things that I've always told you belonged to my father. For example, the fifty-ducat coin from the sixteenth century that is now worth millions. I bought it there. It cost me a pretty penny. Later, in other auctions and frenetic exchanges, leaping into the void, face to face with another fanatical collector, the five gold florins minted in Perpignan in the period of James III of Majorca. What a pleasure to hold them and make them clink in my hand. With those coins in my hand I felt like when Father lectured me about Vial and the different musicians it had had over its lifetime, serving it, trying to get a good sound out of it, respecting it, venerating it. Or the thirteen magnificent Louis d'ors that, in my hand, make the same noise that soothed Guillaume-François Vial as an old man. Despite the

danger inherent in living with that Storioni, he'd grown fond
of it and didn't want to be separated from it until he heard
that Monsieur La Guitte had spread the rumour that a violin
made by the famous Lorenzo Storioni could be linked to the
murder, years back, of Monsieur Leclair. Then his prized
violin began to burn in his hands and transformed from a
cherished possession into a nightmare. He decided to get
rid of it, somewhere far from Paris. When he was returning
from Antwerp, where he had been able to sell it most satis-
factorily along with its case stained with the odious blood of
Tonton Jean, the violin had metamorphosed into a soothing
goat leather purse filled with Louis d'ors. It made such a lovely
sound, that purse. He had even thought that the purse was his
future, his hidey hole, his triumph against the vulgarity and
vanity of Tonton Jean. Now that no one could link him to the
violin, which had been acquired by Heer Arcan of Antwerp.
And that was the sound of the Louis d'ors when he jangled
them together.

'Would you like to come to Rome?'

Laura looked at him in surprise. They were in the faculty's cloister, surrounded by students, he with his hands in
his pockets, she with a full briefcase, looking like a public
defender about to go into court to settle a difficult case, and
I, staring into her blue gaze. Laura was no longer a student
anxious for knowledge. She was a professor who was quite
beloved by the students. She still had the blue gaze and the
sadness inside. And Adrià contemplated her, filled with uncertainty, as images of you, Sara, mixed in his mind with
images of this woman who, from what he had seen, didn't
have much luck with the boyfriends she chose.

'Excuse me?'

'I have to go there for work … Five days at most. We could
be here on Monday and you wouldn't miss any classes.'

In fact, Adrià was improvising. Days earlier he had realised that he didn't know how to approach that blue gaze. He
wanted to take the step but he didn't know how. And I was
afraid to make up my mind because I thought that if I did I

would finally get you out of my mind. And then he had come up with the most presentable plan; the blue gaze smiled and Adrià wondered if Laura was ever not smiling. And he was very surprised when she said all right, sure.

'Sure what?'

'I'll go to Rome with you.' She looked at him, alarmed. 'That's what you meant, right?'

They both laughed and he thought you are getting involved again and you have no idea what Laura is like, besides blue.

During the take-off and the landing, she took his hand for the first time, smiled timidly and confessed I'm afraid of flying, and he said why didn't you tell me. And she shrugged as if to say look, this is how it played out, and he interpreted that to mean that it was worth it to her to swallow her fear and go with Ardèvol to Rome. I felt very proud of my rallying power, beloved Sara, even though she was just a young professor with her whole future ahead of her.

Rome was no bowl of cherries; it was a bedlam of vehicles atop an immense city, captained by suicidal taxi drivers like the one who took them in record time from the hotel to the Via del Corso, which was crucified by traffic. The Amato greengrocer's was a well-lit oasis of appetising boxes of fruit that made the passers-by turn their heads. He introduced himself to a man with a thick beard who was taking care of a demanding customer; he gave him a card with some instructions and pointed up the street, towards the Piazza del Popolo.

'Do you mind telling me what we're doing?'

'You'll know soon enough.'

'Fine: I would like to understand what I'm doing here.'

'Keeping me company.'

'Why?'

'Because I'm scared.'

'Fantastic.' She had to run to keep up with Adrià's strides. 'Then maybe you could explain to me what's going on. Don't you think?'

'Look, we're here.'

It was three doors further on. He pressed one of the bells

and soon the sound of a lock indicated that the door was open, as if they were expecting them. Up in the flat, with her hand on the open door, my angel – my former angel – was waiting, with a slightly distant smile. Adrià kissed her, pointed to her casually, informing Laura that, 'This is my half-sister. This is Mrs Daniela Amato.'

And to Daniela I said, 'This is my lawyer,' referring to Laura.

Laura reacted well. Actually, she was fantastic. She didn't bat an eyelash. The two women looked at each other for a few seconds, as if making calculations on the force they would have to exert. Daniela had us go into a very nice living room, where there was a Sheraton sideboard I was sure I'd seen in the shop; on top of the sideboard was a photo of Father quite young and a very pretty girl, who looked a bit like Daniela. I supposed it was the legendary Carolina Amato, Father's Roman love, la figlia del fruttivendolo Amato. In the photo she was a young woman, with an intense gaze and smooth skin. It was strange, because that young woman's daughter was right in front of me, and she was in her fifties and no longer bothered to try to conceal her wrinkles. My half-sister was still an elegant, beautiful woman. Before we began to speak, a lanky teenager with thick brows came in with a tray of coffee.

'My son Tito,' announced Daniela.

'Piacere di conoscerti,' I said, extending my hand.

'Don't bother,' he responded in Catalan as he put the tray down delicately on the coffee table. 'My father is from Vilafranca.'

And then Laura began to shoot me murderous glances because she must have thought that I'd gone too far, expecting her, in the role of my lawyer, to chat with the Italian branch of my family, whom she couldn't care less about. I smiled at her and put my hand over hers, to reassure her; it worked, as I had never got it to work with anyone else, before or since. Poor Laura: I have the feeling I owe her a thousand explanations and I'm afraid I'm too late.

The coffee was wonderful. And the sale conditions for the

shop were too. Laura just kept quiet; I said the price, Daniela looked at Laura a couple of times and saw that she was slowly and discreetly shaking her head, very professional. Even still, she tried to bargain: 'I don't agree with your offer.'

'Excuse me,' interjected Laura, and I looked at her in surprise. In a weary tone: 'This is the only offer that Mr Ardèvol will be making.'

She looked at her watch, as if she were in a big rush, and then she grew silent and serious. It took Adrià a few seconds to react and he said that the offer also included his right to rescue certain objects from the shop before you take over. Daniela carefully read the list I presented to her as I looked at Laura. I winked at her and she didn't wink back, serious in her role as lawyer.

'And the Urgell in the house?' Daniela lifted her head.

'That belongs to the family: it's not part of the shop.'

'And the violin?'

'That too. It's all in writing.'

Laura lifted a hand as if she wanted to have a word and, with a studied weary air, looking at Daniela, she said you know that we are talking about a shop filled with intangibles.

Ay, Laura.

'What?' Daniela.

It's best if you keep quiet.

'That one thing is the object and quite another its value.'

Why did I ever ask you to come with me to Rome, Laura?

'Bravo. So?'

'The price goes up with each passing day.'

Please don't start.

'And?'

'That the price you two agree on is one thing.' Laura said that without even glancing at me, as if I weren't there. While I thought shut up and don't mess things up, bloody hell, she said but regardless of the price you come to, you will never even approximate its true value.

'I'd be very curious to hear what you think the true value of the shop is, madam.'

I would be, too, Laura. But stop mucking things up, all right?

'No one knows that. X number of pesetas is the official price. To arrive at the true value, we would have to add the weight of history.'

Silence. As if we were digesting those wise words. Laura wiped her hair off her forehead, putting it behind one ear and, in a confident tone that I had never heard from her before, leaning towards Daniela, she said we aren't exactly talking about apples and bananas, Mrs Amato.

We continued in silence. I knew that Tito was behind the door, because a shadow with thick eyebrows gave him away. Soon I was imagining that the boy had inherited the fever for objects, the one that Father had, the one that Mother had acquired, the one that I have, the one that Daniela has ... Touched by the family obsession. The silence was so thick that it seemed we were all attempting to gauge the weight of history.

'Deal. The lawyers will dot the i's,' decided Daniela, exhaling. Then she looked at Laura with a hint of irony and said we can discuss the millions of lires of history, madam, when we are in the mood.

We didn't say a word until we were seated, one in front of the other. It was forty-five minutes of silence that was impossible to evaluate because that blonde, blue girl had completely disorientated him. Once they were seated, after ordering and waiting, also in silence, for them to bring the first course, Laura picked up a forkful of spaghetti that immediately began to unravel.

'You are a bastard,' she said, leaning over her plate before starting to suck on the sole remaining long strand of spaghetti.

'Me?'

'I'm talking to you, yes.'

'Why?'

'I'm not your lawyer, not that you needed one.' She abandoned the fork on the plate. 'By the way, I take it you sell antiques.'

'Uh-huh.'

'Why didn't you talk to me about it before?'

'All you had to do was keep quiet.'

'No one deigned to give me the manual for this trip.'

'Forgive me: it's my fault.'

'Yeah.'

'But you did very well.'

'Well, I wanted to ruin everything and run away, because you're a son of a bitch.'

'You're right.'

Laura was able to fish out another strand of spaghetti and, instead of her words bothering me, all I could think was that, at that rate, she would never finish her first course. I wanted to give her explanations I hadn't given her before: 'Mother gave me instructions for selling the shop to Daniela; step by step. She even indicated how I had to look at her and what gestures I had to make.'

'So you were acting.'

'To a certain extent. But you surpassed me.'

Both of them looked at their plates, until Adrià put down his fork and covered his full mouth with his napkin.

'The value of the weight of history!' he said, bursting into laughter.

The dinner continued with long rifts of silence. They tried to avoid eye contact.

'So your mother wrote you a book of instructions.'

'Yes.'

'And you were following it.'

'Yes.'

'You seemed … I don't know: different.'

'Different in what way?'

'Different from how you usually are.'

'How am I, usually?'

'Absent. You're always somewhere else.'

They nibbled on olives in silence, not knowing what to say to each other, as they waited for their dessert. Until Adrià said he didn't know she was so far-sighted and perceptive.

'Who?'

'My mother.'

Laura placed her fork on the table and looked him in the eye.

'Do you know I feel used?' she insisted. 'Did you get that, after everything I've said?'

I looked at her carefully and I saw that her blue gaze was damp. Poor Laura: she was saying the great truth of her life and I still didn't want to recognise it.

'Forgive me. I couldn't do it alone.'

That night Laura and I made love, very tenderly and cautiously, as if we were afraid of hurting each other. She curiously examined the medallion that Adrià wore around his neck, but she didn't mention it. And then she cried: it was the first time that smiling Laura showed me her perennial dose of sadness. And she didn't explain her heartaches. I was silent as well.

After strolling through the Vatican museums and silently admiring the Moses at San Pietro in Vincoli for over an hour, the patriarch took a step forward, with the tablets of the law in his hand and, when approaching his people and seeing that they were worshipping a golden calf and dancing around it, he angrily grabbed the stone tablets where Jahweh had engraved in divine script the points of the agreement, the new alliance with his people, and he threw them to the ground, smashing them to bits. While Aaron knelt and picked up a jagged piece, not too big and not too small, and saved it as a souvenir, Moses raised his voice and said you good-for-nothings, what are you doing adoring false gods the second I turn my back, bloody hell, what ingrates! And the people of God said forgive us, Moses, we won't do it again. And he replied I am not the one who has to forgive you, but rather God the merciful against whom you have sinned by worshipping false gods. Just for that you deserve to be stoned to death. All of you. And when they went out beneath the blazing Roman midday sun, thinking of stones and smashed tablets, it occurred to me, out of the blue, that, a century earlier, in the Hijri year of twelve hundred and ninety, a crying baby had been born in the small village of al-Hisw, with her face illuminated like the moon, and her mother, upon seeing her, said this daughter of mine is a blessing from Allah the Merciful; she is beautiful like the moon and splendorous as the sun, and her father, Azizzadeh the merchant, seeing his wife's delicate state, told her, hiding his anxiousness, what name should we give her, my wife, and she responded she will be called Amani, and the people of al-Hisw will know her as Amani the lovely; and she was left drained by her words; and her husband Azizzadeh, with bitter tears in his dark eyes, after making sure that everything was in order, gave a white coin and a basket of dates to the midwife; looked, worried, at his wife, and a black cloud crossed through his thoughts. The mother's cracked voice still said Azizzadeh: if I die, take good care of the golden jewel in my memory.

'You aren't going to die.'

'Listen to me. And when lovely Amani's first monthly blood comes, give it to her and tell her it is from me. To remember me by, my husband. To remember her mother who didn't have enough strength to.' And she began to cough. 'Promise me you will,' she insisted.

'I promise, my wife.'

The midwife came back into the room and said she needs to rest. Azizzadeh shook his head and went back to the shop because he had to supervise the unloading of the delivery of pistachios and walnuts that had just arrived from Lebanon. But even if it had been engraved on tablets like the law of the infidel sons of Mūsa who call themselves the chosen people, Azizzadeh would never have believed the sad end lovely Amani would meet in fifteen years' time, praise be the merciful Lord.

'What are you thinking about?'

'Pardon me?'

'You see, see how you're always somewhere else?'

They took the train back to Barcelona and arrived on Wednesday: Laura missed two classes for the first time in her life and without prior notice. Dr Bastardes, who must have sensed many things, didn't reproach her for it. And I, after the Roman operation, already knew that I would be able to devote my life to studying what I wished and teaching a few classes, just enough to maintain a presence in the academic world. It seemed that, apart from my romantic problems, the sky was clear. Even though I hadn't come across any juicy manuscripts lately.

Adrià had got a weight off his shoulders, with the help of his aloof mother who had considered his inability to handle practical matters and had watched over her son from the other side, the way every mother in the world except mine does. Just thinking of it gets me emotional and calculating that perhaps in some moment Mother did love me. Now I know for sure that Father once admired me; but I am convinced that he never loved me. I was one more object in his magnificent collection. And that one more object returned from Rome to his house with the intention of putting it in order, since he had been living too long stumbling into the unopened boxes of books that had come from Germany. He turned on the light and there was light. And he called Bernat to come over and help him to plan this ideal order, as if Bernat were Plato and he Pericles, and the flat in the Eixample the bustling city of Athens. And thus the two wise men decided that into the study would go the manuscripts, the incunabula that he would buy, the delicate objects, the books of the fathers, the records, the scores and the most commonly used dictionaries, and they divided the waters from below from those above and the firmament was made with its clouds, separate from the sea waters. In his parents' bedroom, which he had managed to make his own, they found a place for the poetry and music books, and they separated the lower waters so that there was a dry place, and they gave that dry spot the name earth, and they called the waters ocean seas. In his childhood bedroom, beside Sheriff Carson and valiant Black Eagle, who kept constant watch from the bedside table, they emptied out, without a second glance, all the shelves of books that had accompanied him as a child and there they put the history books, from the birth of memory to the present day. And geography as

well, and the earth began to have trees and seeds that germi-
nated and sprouted grasses and flowers.

'Who are these cowboys?'

'Don't touch them!'

He didn't dare to tell him that it was none of his business.
That would have seemed unfair. He just said, nothing, I'll get
rid of them some other day.

'How.'

'What.'

'You're ashamed of us.'

'I'm very busy right now.'

I heard the Sheriff, from behind the Arapaho chief, spitting contemptuously onto the ground and choosing not to say
anything.

The three long hallways in the flat were devoted to literary
prose, arranged by language. With some endless new shelving
that he ordered from Planas. In the hallway to the bedroom,
Romance languages. In the one beyond the front hall, Slavic
and Nordic languages, and in the wide back hall, Germanic
and Anglo-Saxon.

'But how can you read in crazy language like this?' asked
Bernat suddenly, brandishing Пешчаницат, by Danilo Kiš.

'With patience. If you know Russian, Serbian isn't that
difficult.'

'If you know Russian …' grumbled Bernat, offended. He
put the book in its place and muttered through his teeth,
'Sure, then it's a piece of cake.'

'We can put literary essays and literature and art theory in
the dining room.'

'Either take out the glassware or take out the buffet.' He
pointed at the walls without mentioning the white stain
above the buffet. Adrià lowered his eyes and said I'll give all
the glassware to the shop. They'll sell it and be happy. That'll
give me three good walls. And he created the fish and the
marine creatures and all the monsters of the sea. And the
empty spot left on the wall by the absence of the monastery
of Santa Maria de Gerri by Modest Urgell now had company:
Wellek, Warren, Kayser, Berlin, Steiner, Eco, Benjamin,

Indgarden, Grye, Canetti, Lewis, Fuster, Johnson, Calvino, Mira, Todorov, Magris and other joys.

'How many languages do you know?'

'I'm not sure. Doesn't matter. Once you know a few, you can always read more than you think you can.'

'Yeah, sure, I was just about to say that,' said Bernat, a bit peeved. After a little while, as they removed a piece of furniture, 'You never told me you were studying Russian.'

'You never told me you were practising Bartók's second.'

'And how do you know?'

'Contacts. In the laundry room I'll put

'Don't touch anything in the laundry room.' Bernat, the voice of reason. 'You'll have to have someone come in to dust, iron and do things like that. And she'll need her own space.'

'I'll do that myself.'

'Bullshit. Hire someone.'

'I know how to make omelettes, boiled rice, fried eggs, macaroni and other pastas and whatever I need. Potato frittata. Salads. Vegetables and potatoes.'

'I'm talking about things of a higher order: ironing, sewing, cleaning. And making cannelloni and baked capon.'

What a drag. But finally he listened to Bernat and hired a woman who was still young and active, named Caterina. She came on Mondays, stayed for lunch and did the whole house leaving no stone unturned. And she ironed. And sewed. A ray of sunshine in so much darkness.

'It's best if you don't go into the study. All right?'

'As you wish,' she said, going in and giving it the once-over with her expert eye. 'But I must say this place is a breeding ground for dust.'

'Let's not exaggerate ...'

'A breeding ground for dust filled with those little silver bugs that nest in books.'

'Don't exaggerate, Little Lola.'

'Caterina. I'll just dust the old books.'

'Don't even think about it.'

'Well, then let me at least sweep and clean the floor,' Caterina, trying to save some aspects of the negotiation.

'Fine. But don't touch anything on top of the table.'

'I wouldn't think of it,' she lied.

Despite Adrià's initial good intentions, he eventually took over the walls without wardrobes and Caterina ended up having to live with fine art books and encyclopedias. Visibly wrinkling her nose did her no good.

'Can't you see there's no other space for them?' begged Adrià.

'Well, it's not exactly a small flat. What do you want so many books for?'

'To eat them.'

'A waste of a lovely flat, you can't even see the walls.'

Caterina inspected the laundry room and said I'll have to get used to working with books around.

'Don't worry, Little Lola. They stay still and quiet during the day.'

'Caterina,' said Caterina looking at him askance because she wasn't sure if he was pulling her leg or if he was mad as a hatter.

'And all this stuff you brought from Germany, what is it?' asked Bernat one day, suspiciously opening the top of a cardboard box with his fingertips.

'Basically, philology and philosophy. And some novels. Böll, Grass, Faulkner, Mann, Llor, Capmany, Roth and things like that.'

'Where do you want to put them?'

'Philosophy, in the front hall. With mathematics and astronomy. And philology and linguistics, in Little Lola's room. The novels, each in the corresponding hallway.'

'Well, let's get to it.'

'What orchestra do you want to play Bartók with?'

'With mine. I want to ask for an audition.'

'Wow, that's great, don't you think?'

'We'll see if they'll listen to reason.'

'If they'll listen to the violin, you mean.'

'Yes. You're going to have to order more shelves.'

He ordered them, and Planas was happy as a clam because Adrià's orders showed no signs of letting up. And on the fourth day of creation Caterina won an important victory because she got permission from the Lord to dust all the books in the flat except for the ones in the study. And she decided that she would also come on Thursday mornings for a modest supplement, that way she could guarantee that once a year she'd have dusted all the books. And Adrià said as you wish, Little Lola: you know more about these things than I do.

'Caterina.'

'And since there is still space there, in the guest room, religion, theology, ethnology and the Greco-Roman world.'

And it was the moment when the Lord parted the waters and let the earth dry and created the ocean seas.

'You'll have to … What do you like better, cats or dogs?'

'No, no, neither.' Curtly, 'Neither.'

'You don't want them to shit on you. Right?'

'No, it's not that.'

'Yeah, sure, if you say so …' Sarcastic tone from Bernat as he placed a pile of books on the floor. 'But it would do you good to have a pet.'

'I don't want anything to die on me. Understood?' he said as he filled up the second row in front of the bathroom with prose in Slavic languages. And the domestic animals were created and the wild animals populated the earth and he saw that it was good.

And, seated on the dark floor of hallway one, they reviewed their melancholy: 'Boy, Karl May. I have a lot of his, too.'

'Look: Salgari. God, no: twelve Salgaris.'

'And Verne. I had this one with engravings by Doré.'

'Where is it now?'

'Who knows.'

'And Enid Blyton. Not the strongest prose. But I read them thirty times over.'

'What are you going to do with the Tintins?'

'I don't want to throw anything out. But I don't where to put it all.'

'You still have a lot of room.'

And the Lord said yes, I have a lot of room, but I want to

keep buying books. And my problem is where do I put the karlmays and julesvernes, you know? And the other said I understand. And they saw that in the bathroom there was a space between the little closet and the ceiling, and Planas, enthused, made a sturdy double shelf and all the books he had read as a kid went to rest there.

'That's not going to fall?'

'If it falls, I will personally come and hold it up for the rest of time.'

'Like Atlas.'

'What?'

'Like a caryatid.'

'Well, I don't know. But I can assure you that it won't fall down. You can shit with no worries. Pardon me. I mean, don't worry, it won't fall.'

'And in the small toilet, the magazines.'

'Sounds good,' said Bernat as he moved twenty kilos of ancient history through the Romance prose hallway to Adrià's childhood bedroom.

'And in the kitchen, cookbooks.'

'You need a bibliography to fry to an egg?'

'They're Mother's books; I don't want to throw them out.'

And as he said I will make man in my image and likeness, he thought of Sara. Of Laura. No, Sara. No, Laura. I don't know: but he thought of her.

And on the seventh day, Adrià and Bernat rested and they invited Tecla over to see their creation and after the visit they sat in the armchairs in the study. Tecla, who was already pregnant with Llorenç, was impressed by all their work and said to her husband let's see if some day you decide to tidy things up in our house. And they drank tea from Can Múrria that was delicious. And Bernat straightened up suddenly, as if he had been pricked with a pin: 'Where's the Storioni?'

'In the safe.'

'Take it out. It needs air. And you have to play it so its voice doesn't fade out.'

'I do play it. I'm trying to get my level back up. I play it obsessively and I'm starting to fall in love with that instrument.'

'That Storioni is easy to love,' said Bernat in a whisper.

'Is it true you play the piano too?' Tecla, curious.

'At a very basic level.' As if excusing himself: 'If you live alone, you have a lot of time for yourself.'

Seven two eight zero six five. Vial was the only occupant of the safe. When he pulled it out, it seemed it had grown pale from so long in the dungeon.

'Poor thing. Why don't you put it with the incunabula, in the cabinet?'

'Good idea. But the insurers ...'

'Screw them.'

'Who's going to steal it?'

Adrià passed it, with a gesture that strove for solemnity, to his friend. Play something, he said to him. And Bernat tuned it, the D string was slightly flat, and he played Beethoven's two fantasies in such a way that we could sense the orchestra. I still think that he played extraordinarily, as if having lived far away from me had matured him, and I thought that when Tecla wasn't there I would say kid, why don't you stop writing about stuff you know nothing about and devote yourself to what you do so well, eh?

'Don't start,' responded Bernat when I posed that question to him eight days later. And the Lord contemplated his work and said it was very good, because he had the universe at home and more or less in universal decimal classification. And he said to the books grow and multiply and go forth throughout the house.

'I've never seen such a large flat,' said Laura in admiration, still wearing her coat.

'Here, take that off.'

'Or such a dark one.'

'I always forget to open the blinds. Wait.'

He showed her the most presentable part of the flat and when they went into the study, he couldn't help but do so with possessive pride.

'Wow, is that a violin?'

Adrià pulled it out of the cabinet and put it in her hands. It was obvious that she didn't know what to do with it. Then he put it under the loupe and turned on the light.

'Read what's in here.'

'Laurentius Storioni Cremonensis …' with difficulty, but with longing, 'me fecit seventeen sixty-four. Wow.' She looked up, amazed. 'It must have cost a shitload, I mean an arm and a leg.'

'I guess. I don't know.'

'You don't know?' With her mouth agape she gave him back the instrument, as if it were burning her hand.

'I don't want to know.'

'You are strange, Adrià.'

'Yes.'

They were quiet for a little while, not knowing what to say to each other. I like that girl. But every time I court her, I think of you, Sara, and I wonder what made our eternal love suffer so many encumbrances. At that moment I still couldn't understand it.

'Do you play the violin?'

'Yeah. A little.'

'Come on, play me something.'

'Uhh …'

I supposed that Laura didn't know much about music. In fact, I was wrong: she didn't know a thing. But since I didn't yet know that, I played for her, from memory and with some invention, the *Meditation from Thaïs*, which is very effective. With my eyes closed because I couldn't remember all of the fingering and I needed all my concentration. And when Adrià opened his eyes, Laura was disconsolate, crying blue tears, and looking at me as if I were a god or a monster and I asked her what's wrong, Laura, and she replied I don't know, I think I got emotional because I felt something here and she made some circles with her hand on her stomach; and I answered that's the sound of the violin, it's magnificent. And then she couldn't hold back a sob and until then I hadn't realised that she wore a very discreet bit of makeup on her eyes because the mascara had smudged a little and she looked very, very sweet. But this time I hadn't used her, like in Rome. She came because that morning I had said would you like to come to the inauguration of my flat? And she, who was just getting out of Greek class, I think, said you've moved? And I, no. And she, are you having a party? And I, no, but I'm inaugurating a new order in the house and …

'Will there be many people?'

'Tons.'

'Who?'

'Well, you and I.'

And she came. And after the unrestrained sobbing, she was pensive for a while, sitting on the sofa behind which I had spent hours spying with Sheriff Carson and his valiant friend.

Black Eagle kept watch from the bedside table in history and geography. When we went in there, she picked him up and looked at him; the valiant Arapaho chief didn't complain and she turned to tell me something, but Adrià pretended he hadn't realised and asked her some silly question. I kissed her. We kissed each other. It was tender. And then I walked her home, convinced that I was making a mistake with that girl and that, probably, I was hurting her. But I still didn't know why.

Or I did know. Because in Laura's blue eyes I was searching for your fugitive dark eyes, and that is something that no woman can forgive.

The stairwell was narrow and dark. The further up he went the worse he felt. It seemed like a toy, like a dark doll's house. Up to the first door on the third floor. The doorbell, imitating a bell tower, went ding and then dong. And after that there was silence. Children's shouts were heard on the narrow, sunless street of that end of the Barceloneta. When he was already thinking he had made a mistake, he perceived a muffled sound on the other side of the door and it opened delicately, silently. I never told you this, Sara, but that was, surely, the most important day of my life. Holding onto the door, worse for the wear, older, but still just as neat and well-groomed as ever, she looked silently into my eyes for a few seconds, as if asking me what I was doing there. Finally she reacted, opening the door the rest of the way and moving aside to let me in. She waited until it was closed to say you'll be bald soon.

We went into a tiny area that was the dining room and the living room. On one wall, majestic, hung the Urgell of the Sant Maria de Gerri monastery, receiving the dusky light of a sun that was setting behind Trespui. Adrià, like someone apologising, said I knew you were sick and ...

'How did you know?'

'From a doctor friend. How are you feeling?'

'Surprised to see you here.'

'No, I mean how is your health?'

'I'm dying. Would you like some tea?'

'Yes.'

She disappeared down the hallway. The kitchen was right there. Adrià looked at the painting and had the feeling he was re-encountering an old friend who, despite the years, hadn't aged a bit; he took in a breath and smelled the springtime aroma of that landscape; he could even make out the murmur of the river and the cold Ramon de Nolla felt when he arrived there in search of his victim. He stood there, observing it, until he felt Little Lola's presence behind him. She was carrying a tray with two teacups. Adrià noticed the simplicity of that flat, which was so tiny that it could have fit quite easily inside his study.

'Why didn't you stay with me?'

'I'm fine. This has been my house before and after living by your mother's side. I have no complaints. Do you hear me? I have no complaints. I'm over seventy, older than your parents; and I've lived the life I wanted to live.'

They sat down at the table. A slurp of tea. Adrià was comfortable in silence. After a short while: 'It's not true that I'm going bald.'

'You can't see yourself from the back. You look like a Franciscan friar.'

Adrià smiled. She was the same old Little Lola. And she was still the only person in the world he had never seen wrinkle her nose in displeasure.

'This tea is very nice.'

'I got your book. It's slow going.'

'I know, but I wanted you to have it.'

'What have you been doing, besides writing and reading?'

'Playing the violin. Hours and hours, and days and months.'

'Of all things! Why did you give it up, then?'

'I was drowning. I had to choose between the violin or me. And I chose me.'

'Are you happy?'

'No. Are you?'

'Yes. Quite. Not entirely.'

'Is there anything I can do for you?'

'Yes. Why are you so anxious?'

'It's that … I can't stop thinking that if you sold the painting you could buy a larger flat.'

'You don't understand anything, boy.'

They were silent. She looked at the Urgell with a gaze that was obviously used to contemplating that landscape and to feeling, without realising it, the cold that had got into the bones of fleeing Friar Miquel de Susqueda as he searched along the road from Burgal for a refuge from the threat of divine justice. They were silent for perhaps five minutes, drinking tea, each of them remembering moments in their lives. And finally Adrià Ardèvol looked into her eyes and he said Little Lola, I love you very much; you are a very good person. She finished her last sip of tea, bowed her head, remained quiet for a long time and then began to explain that what he'd just said wasn't true because your mother told me Little Lola, you have to help me.

'What do you need, Carme?' a bit frightened by the other woman's tone.

'Do you know this girl?'

She put a photo of a pretty girl, with dark eyes and hair, on the kitchen table in front of her. 'Have you ever seen her?'

'No. Who is she?'

'A girl who's trying to dupe Adrià.'

Carme sat beside Little Lola and took her hand.

'You have to do me a favour,' she said.

She asked me to follow you, you and Sara, to confirm what the private investigator she had hired had told her. Yes: you were holding hands at the 47 stop on the Gran Via.

'They love each other, Carme,' she told her.

'That's dangerous,' insisted Carme.

'Your mother knew that girl wanted to hoodwink you.'

'My God,' said Adrià. 'What does hoodwink me even mean?'

Perplexed, Little Lola looked at Carme and repeated the question, 'What do you mean by she wants to hoodwink him? Can't you see that they love each other? Don't you see, Carme?'

Now they were in Mr Ardèvol's study, standing, and Carme said I've looked into that girl's family: her last name is Voltes-Epstein.'

'And?'

'They're Jews.'

'Ah.' Pause. 'So?'

'I don't have anything against the Jews, it's not that. But Fèlix … Ay, girl, I don't how to explain it …'

'Try.'

Carme took a few steps, opened the door to make sure that Adrià hadn't arrived yet, when she knew perfectly well he hadn't, closed the door and said, in a softer voice, that Fèlix had some dealings with some of their relatives and ...

'And what?'

'Well, they ended badly. Let's just say they ended very badly.'

'Fèlix is dead, Carme.'

'This girl has wormed her way into our life to make a mess of things. I'm convinced she's after the shop.' Almost in a murmur: 'Adrià couldn't care less.'

'Carme ...'

'He's very vulnerable. Since he lives in the clouds, it's easy for her to get him to do what she wants.'

'I'm sure that girl doesn't even know the shop exists.'

'Believe it. They've been sizing us up.'

'You can't know that for sure.'

'Yes. A few weeks ago she was in there with a woman who I suppose is her mother.'

Before making up her mind to ask, they glanced around, as many customers did, but leisurely, as if they wanted to evaluate the whole place, the whole business. Carme spotted them from the office and immediately recognised the girl who was secretly dating Adrià: then the pieces fell into place and she understood that all that secrecy was a subterfuge for the girl's murky intentions. Cecília waited on them; Carme, later, found out that they were foreigners, probably French, judging by the way they said humbrella stand and mihrohr, because they had asked for a humbrella stand and two mihrohrs, because it seemed that none of the objects in particular had caught their eye, as if they were just having a look around the shop. Do you understand me, Mrs Ardèvol? That same night Carme Bosch called the Espelleta Agency, asked for the owner and gave him a new assignment because she wasn't willing to let them use her son's feelings for unconfessable interests. Yes, if possible, with the same detective.

'But how ... Mother ... Sara and I saw each other in secret!'

'Well, um …' Little Lola, lowering her head and looking at the oilcloth that covered the table.

'How did she come to suspect that …'

'Master Manlleu. When you told him that you were giving up the violin.'

'What did you say?' Unkempt, bushy white eyebrows like storm clouds over the bulging eyes of appalled, indignant Master Manlleu.

'When this term ends, I will take my exam and give up the violin. Forever.'

'This is that lassie who's filling your head up with nonsense.'

'What lassie?'

'Don't play dumb. Have you ever seen two people holding hands through the entire Bruckner's fourth? Have you?'

'Well, but …'

'You can see it a mile away, you two idiots, there in the stalls, all lovey-dovey like two sugary-sweet negroid lovebirds.'

'That doesn't have anything to do with my decision to

'It has a lot to do with your decision to. This shrew is a bad influence. And you have to nip it in the bud.'

And since I stood there, shocked stiff by his audacity, he took the chance to drive his point home: 'You must marry the violin.'

'Excuse me, Master. It's my life.'

'Whatever you say, know-it-all. But I warn you that you will not give up the violin.'

Adrià Ardèvol closed his violin case more noisily than necessary. He stood up and looked the genius in the face. He was now a few inches taller than him.

'I'm giving up the violin, Master Manlleu; whether you like it or not. And I'm telling Mother today too.'

'Ah! So you had the delicacy to tell me first.'

'Yes.'

'You are not going to give up the violin. In a couple of months you'll be begging me to take you back and I'll tell you sorry, lad: my schedule is full. And you'll have to deal with it.' He looked at him with fire in his eyes. 'Weren't you leaving?'

And then he wasted no time in telling your mother that

there was a girl in the mix and Carme got it into her head that
it was all Sara's fault and she became her enemy.

'My God.'

'And because … What I told you about the Epstein family,
that …'

'My God.'

'I told her not to do it, but she wrote a letter to Sara's
mother.'

'What did she tell her? Did you read it?'

'She made things up; I guess they were ugly things about
you.' Long silence, much interest in the oilcloth. 'I didn't read
it.'

She glanced towards Adrià, whose eyes were wide, perplexed and teary, and then she went back to staring at the
oilcloth.

'Your mother wanted to get that girl out of your life. And
out of the shop.'

'That girl is named Sara.'

'Yes, sorry, Sara.'

'My God.'

The shouts from the children on the street began to fade.
And the light, outside, grew weaker. A thousand years later,
when the dining room was already half-dark, Adrià, who was
playing with his teacup, looked at Little Lola.

'Why didn't you tell me?'

'Out of loyalty to your mother. Really, Adrià: I'm so sorry.'

What I was sorrier about is that I left Little Lola's house
very hurt, almost without saying goodbye, almost without
saying Little Lola, I'm so sorry you're ill. I gave her a dry peck
on the cheek and I never saw her alive again.

Huitième arrondissement; quarante-huit rue Laborde. A pretty sad apartment building with the facade darkened by all sorts of smoke. I pressed the button and the door opened with a sharp, premonitory sound. On the mailboxes I checked that I had to go up to the sixième étage. I preferred to walk instead of taking the lift, to use up some of all my accumulated energy, which could lead to panic. When I got there, I spent a good couple of minutes calming my heartbeat and breathing. And I pushed the bell, which said bzsbzsbzsbzs, as if it wanted to maintain the mystery. The landing was quite dark and no one opened the door. Some delicate footsteps? Yes? The door opened.

'Hello.'

When you saw me, you mouth dropped open and your face froze. You don't know how my heart leapt to see you again after so many years, Sara. You were older; I don't mean old, but older and just as lovely. More serenely beautiful. And then I thought that no one had any right to steal our youth from us the way they had. Behind you, on a console table, was a bouquet of flowers that were very pretty but of a colour I found sad.

'Sara.'

She remained in silence. She had obviously recognised me, but she wasn't expecting me. I hadn't come at a good time; I wasn't well received. I'll leave, I'll come back some other time, I love you, I wanted to, I want to talk to you about … Sara.

'What do you want?'

Like the encyclopaedia vendor who knows he has half a minute to pass on the message that will keep the sceptical customer from slamming the door in his face, Adrià opened his mouth and wasted thirteen seconds before saying they tricked us, they tricked you; you ran away because they told you horrible things about me. Lies. And horrible things about my father. Those were true.

'And the letter that you sent me saying that I was a stinking Jewess who could stick my shitty, snotty family where the sun don't shine, what about that?'

'I never sent you any such letter! Don't you know me?'

'No.'

The encyclopaedia is a useful tool for any family with cultural interests such as yours, ma'am.

'Sara. I came to tell you that it was all staged by my mother.'

'Good timing. How long ago was all that?'

'Many years! But I only found out about it five days ago! The time it took me to find you! You're the one who vanished!'

A work of these characteristics is always useful, for your husband and for your children. Do you have children, ma'am? Do you have a husband? Are you married, Sara?

'I thought that you had run away because of some problems of yours, and no one would ever tell me where you were. Not even your parents ...'

In twenty-two easy payment instalments. And you can enjoy these two volumes from the very first day.

'Your family hated my father for ...'

'I already know all that.'

You can keep this volume to examine, ma'am. I'll come back, I don't know when, next year, but don't get mad.

'I didn't know anything about it.'

'The letter you wrote me ... You gave it to my mother personally.' Now the hand that held the door grew tense, as if it were about to slam it in my face any minute now. 'Coward!'

'I didn't write you any letter. It was all a lie! I didn't give anything to your mother. You didn't even let me meet her!'

Desperate attack before the retreat: don't make me think, ma'am, that you aren't a cultured woman who's interested in the world's problems!

'Show it to me! Don't you know my handwriting? Couldn't you see that they were tricking you?'

'Show it to me ...' she said sarcastically. 'I tore it up in little pieces and I burned it: it was a hateful letter.'

My God, what murderous rage. What can I do, what can I do?

'Our mothers manipulated us.'

'I am doing this for my son's own good; I'm protecting his future,' said Mrs Ardèvol.

'And I'm protecting my daughter's,' Mrs Voltes-Epstein's icy reply. 'I have no interest in her having anything to do with your son.' A curt smile. 'Knowing whose son he is was enough to put me off him.'

'Well, then we've nothing more to discuss: can you get your daughter away from here for a while?'

'Don't give me orders.'

'Fine. I implore you to give this letter from my son to your daughter.'

She handed her a sealed envelope. Rachel Epstein hesitated for a few seconds, but she took it.

'You can read it.'

'Don't tell me what I can and cannot do.'

They parted coldly; they had understood each other perfectly. And Mrs Voltes-Epstein opened the letter before giving it to Sara, you can bet she did, Adrià.

'I didn't write you any letter …'

Silence. Standing in the landing of the flat on rue Laborde of the huitième arrondissement. A neighbour lady came down the stairs with a ridiculous little dog and made a lacklustre gesture in greeting to Sara, who replied with a distracted nod.

'Why didn't you tell me? Why didn't you call? Why didn't you want to fight with me?'

'I ran off running and said not again, no, it can't be.'

'Again?'

Now your eyes were teary, burdened with the weight of your mysterious history.

'I had already had a bad experience. Before I met you.'

'My God. I'm innocent, Sara. I also suffered when you ran away. I only found out why five days ago.'

'And how did you find me?'

'Through the same agency that spied on us. I love you. I haven't stopped missing you every day that has passed. I asked your parents for an explanation, but they didn't want to tell me where you were nor why you had left. It was horrible.'

And they were still in the landing of the flat in the huitième arrondissement, with the door open, illuminating Adrià's figure, and she wasn't letting him in.

'I love you. They wanted to destroy our love. Do you understand me?'

'They did destroy it.'

'I don't understand how you believed everything they told you.'

'I was very young.'

'You were already twenty!'

'I was only twenty, Adrià.' Hesitant, ' ...They told me what I had to do and I did it.'

'And me?'

'Yes, fine. But it was horrible. Your family ...'

'What.'

'Your father ... did things.'

'I'm not my father. It's not my fault I'm my father's son.'

'It was very difficult for me to see it that way.'

She wanted to close the door, and with a confident smile, he says let's forget about the encyclopaedia, ma'am, and he pulls out his last recourse: the encyclopaedic dictionary, a single volume work to help your children with their homework. Surely, the way this ffucking life is, you've got heaps of kids.

'And why didn't you call me back then?'

'I had remade my life. I have to close the door, Adrià.'

'What do you mean I had remade my life? Did you marry?'

'That's enough, Adrià.'

And she closed the door. The last image he saw was the sad flowers. There on the landing, crossing out the name of the thwarted customer and cursing that job, which was comprised of many failures and only the occasional triumph.

With the door closed, I was left alone with the darkness of my soul. I didn't have the heart to stroll around the city of la lumière; I didn't care about anything. Adrià Ardèvol went back to the hotel, stretched out on the bed and cried. For a few moments he wondered if it would be better to break the mirror on the wardrobe that reflected his grief back to him or throw himself off the balcony. He decided to make a call, with his eyes damp, with desperation on his lips.

'Hello.'

'Hi.'

'Hi, where are you? I called your house and ...'

'I'm in Paris.'

'Ah.'

'Yes.'

'And you didn't need a lawyer this time?'

'No.'

'What's wrong?'

Adrià let a few seconds pass; now he realised that he was mixing oil and water.

'Adrià, what's wrong?' And since the silence went on too long, she tried to break it: 'Do you have a French half-sister?'

'No, nothing, nothing's wrong. I think I miss you a little bit.'

'Good. When do you come back?'

'I'll get on the train tomorrow morning.'

'Are you going to tell me what you're doing there, in Paris?'

'No.'

'Ah, very well,' terribly offended tone from Laura.

'Fine ...' condescending tone from Adrià. 'I came to consult the original of *Della pubblica felicità.*'

'What's that?'

'The last book Muratori wrote.'

'Ah.'

'Interesting. There are interesting changes between the manuscript and the published edition, as I feared.'

'Ah.'

'What's wrong?'

'No, nothing. You are a liar.'

'Yes.'

And Laura hung up.

He turned on the television to get her reproachful tone out of his head.

It was a Belgian channel, in Flemish. I left it on to check my level of Dutch. And I heard the news. I understood it perfectly because the horrifying images helped, but Adrià never could have imagined all that had anything to do with him. Everything implicates me. I think I am guilty of the unappealing direction that humanity has taken.

The facts, as explained by witnesses in the local press and as they later reached the Belgian press, are as follows. Turu Mbulaka (Thomas Lubanga Dyilo, Matongué, Kinshasa, resident of Yumbu-Yumbu) had been admitted to the Bebenbeleke hospital that day, the twelfth, complaining of strong abdominal pains. Doctor Müss had diagnosed him with peritonitis, put his trust in God and performed an emergency operation on him in the hospital's precarious operating theatre. He had to make it very clear that no bodyguard, armed or unarmed, could enter the operating theatre; nor could any of the patient's three wives or his firstborn, and that in order to operate on him he had to remove his sunglasses. And he treated him urgently not because he was the tribal chief of the region but because his life was in danger. Turu Mbulaka roared for everyone to let the doctor do his ffucking job, that he was in horrible pain and he didn't want to faint because a man who loses consciousness from pain lowers his guard and could be defeated by his enemies.

The anaesthesia, administered by the only anaesthesiologist in that hospital, lowered Turu Mbulaka's guard at thirteen hours and three minutes. The operation lasted exactly an hour and the patient was taken to the general ward two hours later (there is no ICU at Bebenbeleke), when the effects of the anaesthesia had already started to wear off and he could unreservedly say that his belly was killing him, what the hell did you do to me in there? Doctor Müss completely ignored his patient's threatening comment – he had heard so many over the years – and he forbade the bodyguards from being in the ward. They could wait on the green bench right outside the door, what Mr Turu Mbulaka needed was rest. The chief's wives had brought clean sheets, fans for the heat and a television that ran on batteries, which they placed at the foot of his bed. And a lot of food that the patient couldn't even taste for five days.

Doctor Müss had a busy end of his day, with the ordinary visits to the dispensary. Each day his age weighed more heavily on him, but he pretended not to notice and worked with maximum efficiency. He ordered the nurses, except the one on duty, to go rest even though they hadn't finished their shift; he usually asked them to do that when he wanted them to be well-rested for the following day that threatened to be really tough. That was about when he was visited by an unknown foreigner with whom he spent more than an hour discussing who knows what behind closed doors. It was starting to grow dark and through the window entered the cackling of a very anxious hen. When the moon peeked out over Moloa, a muffled crack was heard. It could have been a shot. The two bodyguards both got up from the green bench where they were smoking, as if moved by some precise mechanism. They drew their weapons and looked at each other with puzzlement. The sound had come from the other side. What should we do, should we both go, you stay, I'll go. Come on, go, you go, I'll hold the fort here, OK?

'Peel this mango for me,' Tutu Mbulaka had shouted to his third wife seconds before the shot was heard, if it was a shot.

'The doctor said that …' practically nothing had been heard in the ward, not the possible shot nor the conversation, because the chief's television was making such a racket. There was a game show contestant who didn't know the answer to a question, provoking much laughter from the studio audience.

'What does the doctor know? He wants to make me suffer.' He looked at the TV and made a disdainful gesture: 'Bunch of imbeciles,' he said to the unlucky contestant. And to his third wife, 'Peel me the mango, come on.'

Just as Turu Mbulaka was taking the first bite of the forbidden fruit, the tragedy unfolded: an armed man entered the half-light of the ward and let off a series of shots in Turu Mbulaka's direction, blowing up the mango and filling the poor patient so full of holes that the horrific surgical wound became anecdotal. With precision, the assassin shot his three

defenceless wives; then he looked, aiming, over the whole
ward, probably searching for his firstborn, before he left the
room. The twenty resting patients were resignedly waiting
for the final shots, but the breath of death passed over them.
The assassin – who according to some wore a yellow bandanna, according to others a blue one, but in both cases had
his face covered – disappeared nimbly into the night. Some
maintained that they'd heard a car's engine; others wanted
to have nothing to do with the whole thing and still trembled just thinking about it, and the Kinshasa press explained
that the assassin or assassins had killed Turu Mbulaka's two
incompetent bodyguards, one in the hospital halls, the other
on a green bench that was left sticky with blood. And they
had also killed a Congolese nurse and the doctor at the Bebenbeleke hospital, Doctor Müss, who, alerted by the noise,
had gone into the general ward and must have got in the assassins' way. Or perhaps he had even tried to foil the attack,
with his typical disdain in the face of danger, alleging that
he'd just operated on that man. Or maybe they had simply
shot him in the head before he could open his mouth. No,
according to some witnesses, he was shot in the mouth. No,
in the chest. In the head. Each patient defended a different
version of each chapter of the tragedy, even if they'd seen
nothing; the colour of the assassin's bandanna, I swear it was
green; or maybe yellow, but I swear. Likewise, a couple of
the recovering patients, among them some young children,
had got hit by some of the shots that were directed at tribal
chief Turu Mbulaka. That was about it for the description
of the surprising attack in an area where there are few European interests in play. And the VRT dedicated eighty-six
seconds to it because former president Giscard d'Estaing,
when the news broke that his hands were dirty with the diamonds of Emperor Bokassa, had begun an African tour and
visited the Kwilu region and had taken a detour to get to
Bebenbeleke, which was starting to be well-known despite
its reticent founder, who lived only for his work. Giscard had
been photographed with Doctor Müss, always with his head
bowed, always thinking of the things he had to do. And with

the Bebenbeleke nurses and with some lad with bright white teeth who smiled, without rhyme or reason, pulling a face behind the official group. That hadn't been long ago. And Adrià turned off the television because that news was the straw that broke the camel's back.

The French press as well as the Belgian revealed various facts over the course of the next two days, with details of the massacre in the Bebenbeleke hospital: in an attempt on the life of tribal chief Turu Mbulaka, a respected, hated, slandered, acclaimed and feared figure throughout the entire region, seven people had died: five from the chief's entourage, a nurse and the hospital's director, Doctor Eugen Müss, known for his thirty years of labour on behalf of the sick in that corner of the world, of Beleke and Kikongo. The continuity of the hospital he himself had founded in the 1950s was called into question ... and just like that, as if it were a last minute, trivial addition, the news report's final phrases said that in response to the beastly attack against Turu Mbulaka there had been riots in Yumbu-Yumbu that had caused a dozen deaths between supporters and detractors of this highly controversial figure, half warlord, half despot, direct product of the decolonialisation process led by Belgium.

Three hundred and forty-three kilometres north of the hotel where Adrià was spending his hours dreaming that Sara would come see him and ask him to start over, and he would say how did you know I was in this hotel, and she, well because I got in touch with the detective you used to find out where I was; but since she didn't come he didn't go down for breakfast or for dinner, and he didn't shave or anything, because he just wanted to die and so he couldn't stop crying; three hundred and forty-three kilometres from Adrià's pain, the trembling hands that held a copy of the *Gazet van Antwerpen* dropped it. The newspaper fell onto the table, beside a cup of lime blossom tea. In front of the television that was broadcasting the same news. The man pushed aside the newspaper, which fell to the floor, and looked at his hands. They were trembling uncontrollably. He covered his face and he started to cry in a way he hadn't for the last thirty years. Hell is always ready to enter any nook of our souls.

In the evening, the second channel of the VRT mentioned it, although it focused more on the personality of the hospital's founder. And they announced that at ten pm they would show the documentary the VRT had made of him a couple of years earlier, about his refusal to accept the King Baudouin Prize because it didn't come with a grant for the upkeep of the Bebenbeleke hospital. And because he was unwilling to travel to Brussels to receive any award because he was needed at the hospital more than anywhere else.

At ten that night, a trembling hand pressed the button to turn on the ramshackle television set. An aggrieved sigh was heard. On the screen were the opening credits of *60 Minutes* and immediately afterwards images, obviously shot clandestinely, of Doctor Müss walking along the hospital's porch, passing a green bench without the slightest trace of blood, and saying to someone that there was no need to do any feature story about anything; that he had a lot of work in that hospital and couldn't get distracted.

'A feature story could be very beneficial for you,' the voice of Randy Oosterhoff, slightly agitated as he walked backwards focusing the hidden camera on the doctor.

'If you'd like to make a donation, the hospital would be very grateful.' He pointed behind him, 'We have a vaccination session today and it makes for a very difficult day.'

'We can wait.'

'Please.'

Then came the title: *Bebenbeleke*. And next, views of the hospital's precarious facilities, the nurses hard at work, barely lifting their heads, bustling about, imbued with that almost inhuman dedication to their tasks. And in the background, Doctor Müss. A voice was explaining that Doctor Müss, originally from a village in the Baltic, had set himself up thirty years ago in Bebenbeleke on a wing and a prayer and had, stone by stone, built that hospital that now meets, albeit insufficiently, the health needs of the vast Kwilu region.

The man with the trembling hand got up and went over to

turn off the television. He knew that documentary by heart. He sighed.

They had shown it for the first time two years ago. He, who watched little television, happened to have it on at that moment. He could perfectly remember that what caught his eye was that dynamic, very journalistic introduction, with Doctor Müss walking towards some emergency, telling the journalists that he didn't have time to devote to things that weren't ...

'I know him,' the man with the trembling hands had said.

He watched the documentary assiduously. The name Bebenbeleke didn't ring a bell with him, nor did Beleke or Kikongo. It was the face, the doctor's face ... A face associated with pain, with his great, singular pain, but he didn't know how. And he was overcome with the excruciating memory of his women and girls, of little Trude, my lost Truu, of Amelietje accusing him with her eyes of not having done anything, he who had to save them all, and his mother-in-law who kept coughing as she gripped her violin, and my Berta with Juliet in her arms, and all the horror in the world. And what did seeing that doctor's face have to do with all that pain. Towards the end of the documentary, which he forced himself to watch, he found out that, in that region of endemic politic instability, Bebenbeleke was the only hospital for hundreds of kilometres. Bebenbeleke. And a doctor with a face that hurt him. Then, as the end credits were running, he remembered where and how he had met Doctor Müss; Brother Müss, the Trappist monk with the sweet gaze.

The alarm went off when the father prior received the report on Brother Robert, in a whisper, from a worried nurse brother who said I don't know what to do, forty-nine kilos, Father, and he's thin as a rail, and he's lost the gleam in his eyes. I ...

'He's never had any gleam in his eyes,' the father prior rashly remarked, quickly thinking that he should be more charitable towards a brother in the community.

'I just don't know what more I can do. He barely tastes the meat and fish soup for the ill. It goes to waste.'

'And his vow of obedience?'

'He tries, but can't. It's as if he's lost the will to live. Or as if he was in a rush to … God forgive me if I must say what I think.'

'You must, brother. You are obliged by obedience.'

'Brother Robert,' the nurse brother spoke openly, after running a handkerchief over his sweaty bald head in an attempt to contain the tremble in his voice, 'wants to die. And what's more, Father …'

As he made the handkerchief disappear into the folds of his habit, he explained the secret that the father prior didn't yet know because the Reverend Father Maarten – the abbot who had signed Brother Robert's entrance into the novitiate of the Cistercian Community of the Strict Observance in Achel, right beside the cool, limpid waters of the Tongelreep, which seemed like the perfect place to sooth the torments of a soul punished by the sins of others and its own weakness – had wanted to take it to his grave. The abbey of Saint Benedict in Achel was an idyllic spot where Matthias Alpaerts, the future Brother Robert, could learn to work the soil and breathe air that was pure except for cow manure, and where he could learn to make cheese, to work copper and to sweep the dusty corners of the cloister or any other room they told him needed sweeping, surrounded by the strict silence that accompany twenty-fours of each day for those Trappist monks, his new brothers. It wasn't at all difficult for him to get up each day at three in the morning, the coldest hour of the night, and walk, his feet stiff with a cold his sandals didn't fend off, to pray the Matins that brought them hope of a new day and, perhaps, of a new hope. And then, upon returning to his cell, he read the lectio divina, which sometimes was the hour of torment because all his experiences came flooding back into his mind without any pity for his destroyed soul and God fell silent each day, as he had when they were in hell. Which was why the bell that called to the Lauds prayer sounded to him like a sign of hope, and then, during the convent mass at six, he stared as much as modesty allowed at his lively, devout brothers and prayed with them in unison saying never again, Lord, never again. Perhaps it was when he began his four straight hours of farm work that he was closest to happiness. He murmured his terrible secrets to the cows as he milked them and they replied with intense looks filled with pity and understanding. Soon he learned to make cheese with herbs, which was so aromatic, and he dreamed of delivering it to the thousands of congregants and telling them the body of the Lord, he who wasn't able to distribute communion since he had begged them to respect his wish to not receive even minor orders because he was no one and he only wanted a corner to pray on his knees for the rest of his life, as Friar Miquel de Susqueda, another fugitive, had when asking to be admitted into Sant Pere del Burgal a few centuries earlier. Four hours amid the cow manure, hauling bales of grass, interrupting his work to pray the Terce, after washing his hands and face to get rid of the odour and not offend the other brothers, he would enter the church as if it were a shelter against evil, and pray the Sext with his brothers at midday. More than once the superiors had forbidden him from washing the dishes each day, since that was a task that every member of the community without exception had to take part in, and he had to repress, out of holy obedience, his desire to serve and at two in the afternoon they returned to the refuge of the church to pray the None and there were still two hours of work that weren't devoted to the cows, but rather to mending terraced walls and burning weeds while Brother Paulus milked the cows, and still he had to wash up again because it wasn't like the brothers who worked in the library, who at most had to rinse their dusty fingers when they finished their labours and perhaps envied the brothers who did physical exercise instead of being indoors wearing down their eyesight and memory. The second lectio divina, the afternoon one, was the long prelude that culminated at six with the Vespers. Dinner time, during which he only pretended to eat, gave way to the Complin: everyone in the church, in the dark, with only the faithful flame of the two candles that illuminated the image of the Madonna of Achel. And when the bells of the Saint Benedict monastery rang out eight o'clock, he got into bed, like his brothers, with the hope that the next day would be exactly the same as that one, and the day after that as well, forever and ever.

The father prior looked at the nurse brother with his mouth agape. Why did the reverend father abbot have to be away just then? Why did the General Chapter have to be celebrated precisely on the same day that Brother Robert had fallen into some sort of prostration that the nurse brother's limited knowledge was unable to pull him out of? Why, God of the Universe? Why did I accept the post as prior?

'But he's alive, isn't he?'

'Yes. Catatonic. I think. If you say get up, he gets up; if you say sit, he sits. If you say speak, he starts to cry, Father.'

'That's not catatonic.'

'Look, Father: I can handle wounds, scrapes, dislocated or broken bones, flu and colds and stomach aches: but these spiritual ailments ...'

'And what is your recommendation, brother?'

'I, Father, would ...'

'Yes, what do you recommend I do?'

'Have him seen by a real doctor.'

'Doctor Geel wouldn't know what to do with him.'

'I'm talking about a real doctor.'

Luckily, Father Abbot Manfred, at the third meeting of the General Chapter, commented worriedly in front of the other Brother Abbots on what the Prior had told him over the telephone, in a frightened, distant voice. The Father Abbot of Mariawald told him that, if he considered it opportune, they had a doctor monk at their monastery who, despite his extreme humility and completely reluctantly, had acquired a reputation even beyond the monastery. For ailments of both the body and the spirit. That Brother Eugen Müss was at his disposition.

For the first time in ten years, since the sixteenth of April of the Year of Our Lord nineteen fifty when he had managed to enter the abbey of Saint Benedict of Achel and had become Brother Robert, Matthias Alpaerts was going beyond the lands of the abbey. His hands, opened on his legs, trembled excessively. With tiny frightened eyes he looked through the dirty window of the Citroën Stromberg that bounced along the dusty road leading away from his refuge and brought him to the world of the tempests he had wanted to flee forever. The nurse brother occasionally looked at him out of the corner of his eye. He realised that and tried to distract himself by staring at the nape of the silent chauffeur's neck. The trip to Heimbach took four and a half hours, during which the nurse brother, in order to break the stubborn silence, had time to mumble, along with the hoarse noise of the car's ailing carburettor, the Terce, Sext and None, and they reached the gates of Mariawald when the bells, so different than those at Achel, Lord, were calling the community to their Vespers.

It was the next day, after Lauds, when they told him to wait, seated on a hard bench, in a corner of the wide, well-lit corridor. The German words, scant and respectful, of the nurse brother had echoed in his ears like cruel orders. The nurse monk, Brother Müss's assistant, accompanied by the nurse brother from Achel, disappeared behind a door. They must want a report first. They left him alone, with all his fears, and then Brother Müss had him enter the silent office and they sat with a table between them and he begged him, in quite good Dutch, to explain his torment to him, and Brother Robert scrutinised his eyes and found that his gaze was sweet and then the pain exploded and he started to say because imagine that you are at home having lunch, with your wife, mother-in-law and three little daughters, your mother-in-law with a bit of a chest cold, the new blue-and-white chequered tablecloth, because it's your eldest's birthday, little Amelietje. And after saying that Brother Robert didn't stop talking for an entire hour without taking a breath, without asking for a glass of water, without lifting his gaze from the polished table and without noticing Brother Eugen Müss's sad expression. And when he had explained the whole story, he added that that was why he went through life with his head bowed, crying over my cowardice and searching for some way to make amends for my evil until I had the idea of hiding there where the memory could never reach me. I had to return to speaking with God and I sought out entrance into a Carthusian monastery, where they counselled me that what I was attempting was not a good idea. From that day on I lied and at the other two places where I knocked on the door I didn't mention the reasons for my pain or express it. In each new interview, I learned what I had to say and what I had to keep quiet, so that when I knocked on the door of Saint Benedict's Abbey in Achel I already knew that no one would put up obstacles to my belated vocation and I begged, if obedience didn't demand otherwise, that they let me live there and fulfil the humblest tasks in the monastery. Ever since that day I again began speaking, a bit, with God and I have learned to get the cows to listen to me.

Doctor Müss took his hand. They were like that, in silence, for perhaps ten or twenty minutes; and then Brother Robert began to breathe somewhat more calmly and he said after years of silence at the monastery, the memory came back to blow up inside my head.

'You have to be prepared for it to blow up every once in a while, Brother Robert.'

'I can't bear it.'

'Yes, you can; with God's help.'

'God doesn't exist.'

'You are a Trappist monk, Brother Robert. Are you trying to shock me?'

'I ask for forgiveness from God, but I don't understand his designs. Why, if God is love ...'

'What will maintain you, as a man, is knowing that you would never have caused any evil such as the one that corrodes your spirit. Like the one that was inflicted on you.'

'Not on me: on Truu, Amelia, little Julietje, my Berta and my coughing mother-in-law.'

'You are right: but they also did harm to you. The heroic man is he who gives back good when he has been done wrong.'

'If I had here in front of me those responsible for ...' He sobbed. 'I don't know what I would do, Father. I swear I don't believe I'd be capable of forgiving them ...'

Brother Eugen Müss was writing something on a small

sheet of paper. Brother Robert looked into his eyes and the other gazed back, like that moment when Doctor Müss told the journalist that he had no time to waste and, without knowing it, looked towards the lens of the hidden camera with that same gaze. And then Matthias Alpaerts understood that he had to go to Bebenbeleke, wherever it was, to re-encounter that gaze that had been able to calm him because the memories had once again blown up inside his head a few days earlier.

The first thing you find, when you arrive in Bebenbeleke, is that there is no town with that name. That's just the name of the hospital, which is in the middle of nowhere, many miles north of Kikwit, many miles south of Yumbu-Yumbu, and a good distance from Kikongo and Beleke. The hospital is surrounded by cabins that some patients had built in the shelter of the hospital and that, unofficially, serve as lodgings for the relatives of the ill when they require a stay of several days and that, gradually, generated new cabins, some of which began to be inhabited by people with little or no relationship to the hospital and, over the years, would make up the town of Bebenbeleke. Doctor Müss had no problem with it. And the hens that lived tranquilly around the hospital and, even though they weren't allowed, often also inside it. Bebenbeleke is a town made of pain, because half a kilometre from the hospital, towards Djilo, after the white rock, there is the cemetery for patients who were unable to recover. The indicator of Doctor Müss's failures.

'I left the order after a few months,' said Matthias Alpaerts. I went in thinking it was the remedy and I left convinced that it was the best remedy. But within the monastery or outside of it, the memories remained fresh.

Doctor Müss had him sit on the green bench, still untainted by blood, beside the entrance and he took his hand the way he had thirty years earlier in the consultation room at the Mariawald Abbey.

'Thank you for wanting to help me, Brother Müss,' said Matthias Alpaerts.

'I'm sorry I couldn't have helped more.'

'You helped me a lot, Brother Müss. Now I am prepared and, when the memories explode, I am better able to defend myself against them.'

'Does it happen often?'

'More than I'd like, Brother Müss. Because …'

'Don't call me brother; I'm no longer a monk,' interrupted Doctor Müss. 'Shortly after our meeting I asked for dispensation from Rome.'

The silence of former Brother Robert was eloquent, and former Brother Müss had to break it and reply that he had abandoned the order out of a desire for penitence and, God forgive me, firmly thinking that I could be more useful doing good among the needy than locking myself up to pray the hours.

'I understand.'

'I have nothing against monastic life: it was about my temperament and my superiors understood that.'

'You are a saint, out here in this desert.'

'This is no desert. And I'm no saint. I am a doctor, a former monk, and I just practise medicine. And I try to heal the wounds of evil.'

'What stalks me is evil.'

'I know. But I can only fight against evils.'

'I want to stay and help you.'

'You are too old. You are over seventy, aren't you?'

'It doesn't matter. I can be helpful.'

'Impossible.'

Doctor Müss's tone had suddenly turned curt with that reply. As if the other man had deeply offended him. Matthias Alpaerts's hands began to tremble and he hid them in his pockets so the doctor wouldn't notice.

'How long have they been trembling like that?' Doctor Müss pointed to his hidden hands and Matthias stifled an expression of displeasure. He held out his hands in front of him; they were trembling excessively.

'When the memories explode inside me. Sometimes I think it's not possible for them to shake so much against my will.'

'You won't be useful to me, with that trembling.'

Matthias Alpaerts looked him in the eye; the commentary was, at the very least, cruel.

'I can be useful in many different ways,' he said, offended. 'Digging the garden, for example. In the Achel monastery I learned to work the land.'

'Brother Robert ... Matthias ... Don't insist. You have to return home.'

'I have no home. Here I can be useful.'

'No.'

'I don't accept your refusal.'

Then Brother Müss took Matthias Alpaerts by one arm and brought him to dinner. Like every evening, there was only a sticky mass of millet, which the doctor heated up on a little burner. They sat down right there in the office, using the doctor's desk as a dining room table. And Doctor Müss opened up a small cabinet to pull out two plates and Matthias watched him hide something, perhaps a dirty rag, behind some plastic cups. As they ate without appetite, the doctor explained why he couldn't possibly stay there to help him as an improvised nurse nor as a gardener nor as a cook nor as a farmhand who didn't know how to bear fruits without sweating blood.

At midnight, when everyone was sleeping, Matthias Alpaerts's hands didn't tremble as he went into Doctor Müss's office. He opened the small cabinet near the window and, with the help of a small torch, he found what he was looking for. He examined the rag in the scant, uncertain light. For a very long minute he hesitated because he didn't quite recognise it. All his trembling was focused on his heart, which struggled to escape through his throat. When he heard a cock crow, he made up his mind and put the rag back in its place. He felt an itching in his fingers, the same itching that Fèlix Ardèvol felt or that I was starting to feel when an object of my desires was slipping out of my grasp. Itching and trembling in the tips of his fingers. Even though Matthias Alpaerts's illness was different from ours.

He left before the sun came up, with the van that came from Kikongo and brought medicines and foodstuffs, and a sprinkling of hope for the ill in that extensive area that dipped its feet in the Kwilu.

3

I came back from Paris with my head bowed and my tail between my legs. In that period Adrià Ardèvol was teaching a course on the history of contemporary thought to a numerous audience of relatively sceptical students despite his reputation as a surly-sage-who-does-his-own-thing-and-doesn't-go-out-for-coffee-ever-and-wants-nothing-to-do-with-faculty-meetings-because-he's-above-good-and-evil that he had started to have among his colleagues at the Universitat de Barcelona. And the relative prestige of having published, almost secretly, *La revolució francesa* and *Marx?*, two fairly provocative little books that had started to earn him admirers and detractors. The days in Paris had devastated him and he had no desire to talk about Adorno because he couldn't care less about anything.

I hadn't thought about you again, Little Lola, because my head was filled with Sara. Not until some obscure relative called to tell me my cousin is dead and she left some addresses of people she wanted to be notified. She added the information of the place and time and we exchanged various words of courtesy and condolence.

At the funeral there were about twenty people. I vaguely remembered three or four faces, but I couldn't greet anyone, not even the obscure cousin. Dolors Carrió i Solegibert 'Little Lola' (1910–1982), born and died in the Barceloneta, mother's friend, a good woman, who screwed me over because Little Lola's only real family was Mother. And she was probably her lover. I wasn't able to say goodbye to you with the affection that, despite everything, you deserved.

'Hey, hey, but that was what, twenty years ago, that you broke up?'

'Come on, not twenty! And we didn't break up: they broke us up.'

'She must already have grandchildren.'

'Why do you think I've never looked for another woman?'

'The truth is I have no idea.'

'I'll explain it to you: every day, well, almost every day, when I go to sleep, you know what I think?'

'No.'

'I think now the bell is going to ring, ding dong.'

'Your bell goes rsrsrsrsrsrsrsrsrs.'

'All right: rsrsrsrsrsrsrsrs, and I open it and it's Sara saying that she left because of something or another and asking do you want me in your life again, Adrià.'

'Hey, hey, kid, don't cry. And now you don't have to think about her any more. You see? In a way it's better, don't you think?'

Bernat felt uncomfortable in the face of Adrià's rare expansiveness.

He pointed to the cabinet and Adrià shrugged, which Bernat interpreted as go ahead. He pulled out Vial and he played him a couple of Telemann's fantasies, at the end of which I felt better, thank you, Bernat, my dear friend.

'If you want to cry more, go ahead and cry, eh?'

'Thanks for giving me permission,' smiled Adrià.

'You are delicate, fragile.'

'It devastated me that my two mothers conspired against our love and we just fell right into their trap.'

'All right. The two mothers are dead and you can keep on …'

'I can keep on what?'

'I don't know. I meant …'

'I envy your emotional stability.'

'Don't be fooled.'

'Yes, yes. You and Tecla, wham bam.'

'I can't get Llorenç to understand anything.'

'How old is he?'

'He's the soul of contradiction.'

'He doesn't want to study violin?'

'How did you know?'

'I've heard that old song and dance somewhere before.'

Adrià was pensive for a while. He shook his head: I think
life is a botched job, he said, in conclusion. And, like someone
who takes up the bottle, he went to the Sant Antoni market on
Sunday to relax and he contrived a way to bump into Morral
at his stand, who signalled for Adrià to follow him. This time
they were the first ten pages of the Goncourt brothers' manuscript of *Renée Mauperin*, written in a uniform hand – with a
few corrections in the margin – that Morral assured me was
Jules's.

'Are you knowledgeable about literature?'

'I sell things: books, trading cards, manuscripts and
Bazooka chewing gum, you know what I mean?'

'But where in the hell do you get it from?'

'The chewing gum?'

Sly Morral didn't tell me his methods. His silence ensured
his safety and guaranteed that his mediation was always
necessary.

I bought the Goncourt pages. And, in the following few
weeks, as if they'd been waiting for me, manuscripts and
loose pages appeared by Orwell, Huxley and Pavese. Adrià
bought them all, despite his theoretical reticence to buying
for buying's sake. But he couldn't let the eighth of February of
he wasn't sure which year of *Il mestiere di vivere* slip through
his hands, a loose page that spoke of Guttoso's wife, and of
the hope of living with a woman who waits for you, who will
sleep beside you and keep you warm and be your companion and make you feel alive, my Sara, which I don't have and
never will. How could I say no to that page? And I'm sure that
Morral noticed my trembling and, depending on its intensity, upped the price. I am convinced that it is very difficult to
resist possessing the original pages of texts that have moved
you deeply. The paper with the handwriting, the gesture, the
ink, which is the material element that incarnates the spiritual
idea which will eventually become the work of art or the work
of universal thought; the text enters the reader and transforms him. It is impossible to say no to that miracle. Which
is why I didn't think it over long when Morral, as an intermediary, introduced me to a man whose name I never knew,

who was selling two poems by Ungaretti at ridiculous prices: *Soldati* and *San Martino del Carso*, the poem that speaks of a town reduced to ruins by war and not by the passing of time. È il mio cuore il paese più straziato. And mine as well, dear Ungaretti. What melancholy, what grief, what joy to own the piece of paper the author used to convert his first intuition into a work of art. And I paid what he asked, almost without haggling, and then Adrià heard a curt spitting on the ground and he looked around.

'What, Carson.'

'How. I have something to say, too.'

'Go ahead.'

'We have a problem,' they both said at the same time.

'What's that?'

'Don't you realise?'

'I don't want to realise.'

'Have you looked at how much you've spent on manuscripts these last few years?'

'I love Sara and she left because our mothers tricked her.'

'You can't do anything about that. She has remade her life.'

'Another whisky, please. Make it a double.'

'Do you know how much you've spent?'

'No.'

The buzzing of an office calculator. I don't know if it was the valiant Arapaho chief or the coarse cowboy who was using it. A few seconds of silence until they told me the scandalous amount of money that

'All right, all right, I'll stop. That's it. Are you happy now?'

'Look, doctor,' said Morral another day. 'A Nietzsche.'

'A Nietzsche?'

'Five pages of *Die Geburt der Tragödie*. I don't know what that means, by the way.'

'The birth of tragedy.'

'That's what I suspected,' Morral, with a toothpick in his mouth because it was after lunch.

Instead of sounding like a foreboding title to me, I looked at the five pages carefully for about an hour, and then Adrià lifted his head and exclaimed but where in the hell do you get these things from? For the first time, Morral answered the question:

'Contacts.'

'Sure. Contacts ...'

'Yes. Contacts. If there are buyers, the manuscripts sprout up like mushrooms. Especially if you can guarantee the authenticity of the merchandise the way we can.'

'Who is this we?'

'Are you interested or not?'

'How much?'

'This much.'

'That much?'

'That much.'

'Bloody hell.'

But the tingling, the itching in the fingers and in the intellect.

'Nietzsche. The first five pages of *Die Geburt der Tragödie*, which means the rupture of tragedy.'

'The birth.'

'That's what I meant.'

'Where do you get so many first pages?'

'The entire manuscript would be unattainable.'

'You mean that someone chops them up to ...' Horrified, 'And what if I want more? What if I want the whole book?'

'First we'd have to hear the price. But I think it's best to start with what we have on hand. Are you interested?'

'Indeed!'

'You already know the price.'

'That much less this much.'

'No. That much.'

'Well, then less this much.'

'We could start to negotiate there.'

'How.'

'Not now, goddamn it!'

'Excuse me?'

'No, no, talking to myself. Do we have a deal?'

Adrià Ardèvol paid that much less this much and he left with the first five pages of the Nietzsche as well as the pressing need to talk to Morral again about acquiring the complete manuscript, if they even really had it. And he thought that perhaps it was the moment to ask Mr Sagrera how much money he had left to know whether Carson and Black Eagle's hand wringing was founded or not. But Sagrera would tell him that he had to invest: that keeping it in the savings account was a shame.

'I don't know what I can do with it.'

'Buy flats.'

'Flats?'

'Yes. And paint. I mean paintings.'

'But … I buy manuscripts.'

'What's that?'

He would show him the collection. Mr Sagrera would examine them with his nose wrinkled and, after deep reflection, would conclude that it was very risky.

'Why?'

'They are fragile. They could get gnawed on by rats or those silvery insects.'

'I don't have rats. Little Lola deals with the silverfish.'

'How.'

'What?'

'Caterina.'

'Yes, thanks.'

'I insist: if you buy a flat, you are buying something solid that will never go down in price.'

As if wanting to spare himself that conversation, Adrià Ardèvol didn't talk to Mr Sagrera about flats or rats. Nor about the money spent on silverfish food.

A few nights later I cried again, but not over love. Or yes: it was over love. In the letter box at home there was a notification from someone named Calaf, a notary in Barcelona, a man I'd never met, and I soon thought of problems with the sale of the shop, some sort of problems with the family, because I've always distrusted notaries even though I am now acting as a notary of a life that belongs to me increasingly less and less. Where was I: oh, yes, the notary Calaf, a stranger who kept me waiting for half and hour with no explanation in a very drab little room. Thirty minutes later he came into the drab little room, making no apologies for his delay. He didn't look me in the eyes, he stroked a small thick white beard and asked me to show him my ID card. He gave it back to me with an expression I interpreted as one of displeasure, of disappointment.

'Mrs Maria Dolors Carrió has named you to receive a part of her estate.'

Me, inheriting something from Little Lola? She was a millionaire and she'd worked as a maid her whole life and, moreover, in a family like mine? My God.

'And what am I to inherit?'

The notary looked at me somewhat aslant; surely he didn't like me at all: but my heart was still upset about Paris, with that I remade my life, Adrià, and the closing door, and I couldn't give a hoot about what the entire association of notaries thought of me. The notary again stroked his little beard, shook his head and read the writing before him, in an exceedingly nasal voice: 'A painting by someone named Modest Urgell, dated eighteen ninety-nine.'

Little Lola, you are even more stubborn than I am.

Once the formalities were over and the taxes paid, Adrià once again hung the Urgell, the painting of the Santa Maria de Gerri monastery, on the wall that he hadn't wanted to cover with any other painting or any bookshelves. The light of the sun setting over Trespui still illuminated it with a certain sadness. Adrià pulled out a chair from the dining room table and sat in it. He was there for a long time, looking at the painting, as if he wanted to watch the sun's slow movement. When he returned from the monastery of Santa Maria de Gerri, he burst into tears.

## 33

The university, the classes, being able to live inside the world of books … His great joy was discovering an unexpected book in his home library. And the solitude didn't weigh on him because all his time was occupied. The two books he had published had been harshly reviewed by their few readers. A vitriolic comment on the second book appeared in *El Correo Catalán* and Adrià clipped it out and saved it in a file. Deep down he was proud of having provoked strong emotions. Anyway, he contemplated it all with indifference because his real pains were others and also because he knew that he was just getting started. Every once in a while, I played my beloved Storioni, mostly so its voice wouldn't fade out; and also to learn the stories that had left scars on its skin. Sometimes I even went back to Mrs Trullols's technical exercises and I missed her a little bit. What must have happened to everyone and everything. What must have become of Trullols …

'She died,' said Bernat one day, now that they were seeing each other again occasionally. 'And you should get married,' he added as if were Grandfather Ardèvol arranging nuptials in Tona.

'Did she die a long time ago?'

'It's not good for you to be alone.'

'I'm fine on my own. I spend the day reading and studying. And playing the violin and the piano. Every once in a while I buy myself a treat at Can Múrria, some cheese, foie gras or wine. What more could I want? Little Lola takes care of the mundane things.'

'Caterina.'

'Yes, Caterina.'

'Amazing.'

'It's what I wanted to do.'

'And fucking?'

Fucking, bah. It was the heart. That was why he had fallen hopelessly in love with twenty-three students and two faculty colleagues, but he hadn't made much progress because … well, except for with Laura who, well, who …

'What did Trullols die of?'

Bernat got up and gestured to the cabinet. Adrià raised one hand to say help yourself. And Bernat played a diabolical csárdás that made even the manuscripts dance and then a sweet little waltz, slightly sugary but very well played.

'It sounds marvellous,' said Adrià admiringly. And grabbing Vial, a bit jealous: 'Some day when you are playing in chamber, you should borrow it.'

'Too much responsibility.'

'So? What did you want, that was so urgent?'

Bernat wanted me to read a story he had written and I sensed we would have more problems.

'I can't stop writing. Even though you always tell me I should give it up.'

'Well done.'

'But I'm afraid that you're right.'

'About what?'

'That what I write has no soul.'

'Why doesn't it?'

'If I knew that …'

'Maybe it's because it's not your medium of expression.'

Then Bernat took the violin from me and played Sarasate's *Caprice basque*, with six or seven flagrant errors. And when he finished he said you see, the violin isn't my medium of expression.

'You made those mistakes on purpose. I know you, kid.'

'I could never be a soloist.'

'You don't need to be. You are a musician, you play the violin, you earn a living doing it. What more do you want, for Christ's sake?'

'I want to earn appreciation and admiration, not a living. And playing as assistant concertmaster I'll never leave a lasting impression.'

'The orchestra leaves a lasting impression.'

'I want to be a soloist.'

'You can't! You just said so yourself.'

'That's why I want to write: a writer is always a soloist.'

'I don't think that should be the great motivation for creating literature.'

'It's my motivation.'

So I had to keep the story, which was actually a story collection, and I read it and after a few days I told him that perhaps the third one is the best, the one about the travelling salesman.

'And that's it?'

'Well. Yes.'

'You didn't find any soul or any such shite?'

'No soul or any such shite. But you already know that!'

'You're just bitter because they rip apart what you write. Even though I like it, eh?'

From that declaration of principles, and for a long time after, Bernat didn't pester Adrià with his writing again. He had published three books of short stories that hadn't shaken up the Catalan literary world and probably hadn't shaken up a single reader either. And instead of being happy with the orchestra he sought out a way to be a tad bitter. And here I am giving lessons on how to attain happiness. As if I were some sort of a specialist. As if happiness were a required course.

The class had been pretty regular, leaning towards good. He had talked about music in the time of Leibniz. He had transported them to Leibniz's Hannover and he had played music by Buxtehude for them, specifically the variation for spinet of the aria 'La Capricciosa' (BuxWV 250) and he asked them to see if they could remember a later work (not much later, eh?) of a more famous musician. Silence. Adrià stood up, rewound the cassette and let them listen to another minute of Trevor Pinnock's spinet.

'Do you know what work I am referring to?' Silence. 'No?' he asked.

Some students looked out of the window. Others stared at

their notes. One girl shook her head. To help them, he spoke of Lübeck in that period and again said no? And then he drastically lowered the bar and said come on: if you can't tell me the work, at least tell me the composer. Then a student he'd barely noticed before, sitting in one of the middle rows, without raising his hand said Johann Sebastian Bach?, like that, with a question mark, and Adrià said bravo! And the work has a similar structure. A theme, the one I played twice for you, that is reminiscent of the development of a variation … Do you know what? For next Wednesday's class try to find out the work I'm talking about. And try to listen to it a couple of times.

'And if we can't guess which one it is?' The girl who had shaken her head before.

'It is number 998 in his catalogue. Happy now? Any more hints?'

Despite the bar lowering I had to do, I would have liked the classes of that period to have each lasted five hours. I would have also liked it if the students were always deeply interested in everything and posed questions that forced me to ask for more time so I could have my reply prepared for the next class. But Adrià had to settle for what he had. The students went down the tiered seats to the exit door. All except the one who'd guessed the right answer, who remained seated on the bench. Adrià, as he removed the cassette, said I don't think I've noticed you before. Since the other didn't respond, he looked up and realised that the young man was smiling in silence.

'What's your name?'

'I'm not one of your students.'

'Then what are you doing here?'

'Listening to you. Don't you recognise me?'

He got up and came down, without a briefcase or notes, to the professor's dais. Adrià had already put all the papers into his briefcase and now added the cassette tape.

'No. Should I recognise you?'

'Well … Technically, you are my uncle.'

'I'm your uncle?'

'Tito Carbonell,' he said, extending his hand. 'We saw each other in Rome, at my mother's house, when you sold her the shop.'

Now he remembered him: a silent teenager with thick eyebrows, who snooped behind the doors, and had become a handsome young man of confident gestures.

Adrià asked how is your mother, he said well, she sends her regards, and soon the conversation languished. Then came the question, 'Why did you come to this class?'

'I wanted to know you better before making my offer.'

'What offer?'

Tito made sure that no one else was in the classroom and then he said I want to buy the Storioni.

Adrià looked at him in surprise. He was slow to react.

'It's not for sale,' he finally said.

'When you hear the offer, you'll put it up for sale.'

'I don't want to sell it. I'm not listening to offers.'

'Two hundred thousand pesetas.'

'I said it's not for sale.'

'Two hundred thousand pesetas is a lot of money.'

'Not even if you offered me twice that.' He brought his face close to the young man's. 'It-is-not-for-sale.' He straightened up. 'Do you understand?'

'Perfectly. Two million pesetas.'

'Do you even listen when people speak to you?'

'With two million clams you can lead a comfortable life, without having to teach people who have no fucking clue about music.'

'Tito, is that what you said your name was?'

'Yes.'

'Tito: no.'

He picked up his briefcase and prepared to leave. Tito Carbonell didn't budge. Perhaps Adrià was expecting him to prevent him from leaving. Seeing that his path was clear, he turned around.

'Why are you so interested in it?'

'For the shop.'

'Aha. And why doesn't your mother make me the offer?'

'She isn't involved in these things.'

'Aha. What you mean is that she doesn't know anything about it.'

'Call it what you wish, Professor Ardèvol.'

'How old are you?'

'Twenty-six,' he lied, although I didn't know that until much later.

'And you are conspiring outside the shop?'

'Two million one hundred thousand pesetas, final offer.'

'Your mother should be informed about this.'

'Two and a half million.'

'You don't listen when people talk to you, do you?'

'I'd like to know why you don't want to sell it ...'

Adrià opened his mouth and closed it again. He didn't know how to respond. He didn't know why he didn't want to sell Vial, that violin that had rubbed elbows with so much tragedy but which I had grown accustomed to playing, more and more hours each day. Perhaps because of the things that Father had told me about it; perhaps because of the stories I imagined when I touched its wood ... Sara, sometimes, just running a finger over the violin's skin, I am transported to the period when that wood was a tree that never even imagined it would one day take the shape of a violin, of a Storioni, of Vial. It's not an excuse, but Vial was some sort of window onto the imagination. If Sara were here, if I saw her every day ... perhaps everything would be different ... obviously if ... if only I had sold it to Tito then, even for twenty lousy pesetas. But I still couldn't even suspect that then.

'Eh?' said Tito Carbonell, impatiently. 'Why don't you want to sell it?'

'I'm afraid that is none of your business.'

I left the classroom with a cold sensation on the nape of my neck, as if I were waiting for the treacherous shot any minute. Tito Carbonell didn't shoot me in the back and I felt the thrill of having survived.

## 34

It had been a couple of millennia since the Creation of the World according to the Decimal System, when he'd distributed the books throughout the house, although he hadn't made real inroads into his father's study. Adrià had devoted the third drawer of the manuscript table to some of his father's unclassifiable documents, conveniently separated into envelopes, which had no relationship to the shop nor space in the registry system, because Mr Ardèvol kept another separate one for the valuable documents that he kept for himself, which was his way of starting to enjoy the objects that he had tracked over days or sometimes years. In the library everything was organised. Almost everything. All that was left to classify were the unclassifiable documents; they were all gathered, relegated to the third drawer with the sincere promise that he would take a look at them when he had some time. A few years passed in which it seems Adrià didn't have the time.

Among the various papers in the third drawer, there was some correspondence. It was strange that a man as meticulous as Father had considered his correspondence as unclassifiable material and hadn't left a copy of the letters he wrote; he had only kept the ones he received. They were in a couple of old folders filled to bursting. There were replies from someone named Morlin to demands from Father that I assume were professional. There were five very strange letters, written in impeccable Latin, filled with hard to understand allusions, from a priest named Gradnik. He was from Ljubljana, and went on and on about the unbearable crisis of faith that had gripped him for years. From what he said he had been a fellow student with Father at the Gregoriana and he urgently asked for his opinion on theological questions. The last letter had a different tone. It was dated in the year

1941 from Jesenice and began by saying it is very likely that
this letter won't reach you, but I can't stop writing to you; you
are the only one who has always answered me, even when I
was most alone, serving as rector and sexton in the snow and
ice of a little town near Kamnik whose name I have tried to
forget. This may be my last letter because it is very likely that
I will die any minute now. I hung up my cassock a year ago.
There is no woman involved. It's all due to the fact that I lost
my faith. I've lost it drop by drop; it just slipped through my
fingers. I'm the one responsible: confiteor. Since the last time
I wrote to you, and after your words of encouragement that
inspired me tremendously, I can tell you more objectively.
Gradually, I realised that what I was doing made no sense.
You had to choose between a love that was impossible to resist
and the life of a priest. I have yet to come across any woman
who makes me swoon. All my problems are mental. It has
been a year since my big decision. Today, with all of Europe
at war, I know that I was right. Nothing makes sense, God
doesn't exist and man must defend himself as best he can
from the ravages of time. Look, dear friend: I am so sure of
this step I've taken, completed only a few weeks ago: I have
enlisted in the people's army. In short, I traded my cassock for
a rifle. I am more useful trying to save my people from Evil.
My doubts have vanished, dear Ardèvol. I have been talking
for years about Evil, the Archfiend, the Devil … and I was
unable to understand the nature of Evil. I tried to examine
the evil of guilt, the evil of grief, metaphysical evil, physical
evil, absolute evil and relative evil and, above all, the efficient
cause of evil. And after so much studying, after going over it
again and again, it turned out that I had to hear the confession of the lay sisters in my parish, confessing to the horrible
sin of not having been strict enough in their fasting from
midnight to taking Communion. My God, my gut was telling
me it can't be, it can't be, Drago: you are losing your reason
for being, if what you want is to be useful to humanity. I realised everything when a mother told me how can God allow
my little daughter to die in such pain, Father; why didn't God
intervene to stop it? And I had no reply and I found myself

giving her a sermon on the efficient cause of Evil, until I grew silent, ashamed, and I asked for her forgiveness and I told her I didn't know. I told her I don't know, Andreja, forgive me but I don't know. Perhaps this will make you laugh, dear Fèlix Ardèvol, you who write me long letters defending the selfish cynicism your life has become, according to you. I was once choked with doubts because I was defenceless in the face of my tears; but no longer. I know where Evil is. Absolute Evil, even. Its name is Himmler. Its name is Hitler. Its name is Pavelić. It is Luburić and his macabre invention in Jasenovac. Its name is Schutzstaffel and Abwehr. The war highlights the most beastly part of human nature. But Evil existed before the war and doesn't depend on any entelechy, but rather on people. That is why my inseparable companion for the last few weeks has been a rifle with a telescopic sight because the commander's decided that I'm a good shot. We will soon enter combat. Then I will blow Evil up bit by bit with every bullet and it doesn't upset me to think about that. As long as it is a Nazi, an Ustaša or, simply, and may God forgive me, an enemy soldier in my sights. Evil uses Fear and absolute Cruelty. I suppose to ensure that we are filled with rage, the commanders tell us horrifying things about the enemy and we all are eager to find ourselves face to face with him. One day I will kill a man and I hope to not feel sorry about it at all. I've joined a group filled with Serbians who live in Croatian towns but have had to flee from the Ustaša; there are four of us Slovenians and some of the many Croatians who believe in freedom. I still don't have any military rank, some people call me sergeant because I'm easy to spot: I'm as tall and stocky as ever. And the Slovenians call me Father because one day I got drunk and must have talked too much; I deserve it. I am ready to kill before being killed. I don't feel any sort of remorse; I don't worry about what I'm doing. I'll probably die in some skirmish now. I hear that the German army is advancing towards the south. We all know that any military operation inevitably leaves behind a trail of dead, on our side as well. Here at war we avoid making friends: we are all one because we all depend on each other, and I cry over the death of the man who yesterday ate breakfast by my side but whose name I didn't get the chance to ask. All right, I'll take off my mask: I'm terrified of killing someone. I don't know if I'll be able to. But Evil is specific people. I hope to be brave and I hope I'll be able to pull the trigger without my heart trembling too much.

I am writing to you from a Slovenian town called Jesenice. I will put a stamp on it as if we weren't at war. And I will take it in our lorry, which is filled with bags of mail today because until the conflict really starts, they want to keep us busy doing useful things. But I will entrust this letter to Jančar, who is the only person capable of getting it to you. May the God I no longer believe in assist him. Please answer to the sub-post office in Maribor, as always. If they don't kill me, I'll be anxiously awaiting your reply. I feel so alone, dear Fèlix Ardèvol. Death is cold and I shiver more and more. Your friend, Drago Gradnik, former priest, former theologian, who has renounced a brilliant career in the episcopal curia of Ljubljana and perhaps even in Rome. Your friend who is now a partisan rifleman on the front lines and who is impatient to blow off the head of the roots of Evil.

There were also replies from eight or ten antiquarians, collectors and vintage dealers from all over Europe to specific requests from Father. And a couple of letters from Doctor Wuang of Shanghai, which assured, in shaky English, that the happy manuscript (without further references) had never been in his hands and that he wished him a long happy life and prosperity in business and increasing happy wealth in his personal relationships, both familial and romantic. I felt Doctor Wuang was referring to me. And many other documents of all sorts.

One boring, rainy afternoon, when I'd finished grading exams and had no desire to think about the philosophy of language, I decided to be bored at home, without reading, mouth agape. The theatrical offerings were slim; I wasn't in the mood for a musical, and it had been so many years since I'd set foot in a cinema that I wasn't sure they were still making colour films. So I yawned and thought that it was a good moment to finally organise Father's papers. So, after having placed the *Tetralogia* on the record player, I got to it. The first thing I pulled out was one of the letters from Morlin, who lived in Rome and appeared to be a priest, even though I didn't know that yet. That was when I felt a desire to clarify certain moments in Father's life. For no particular reason, not thinking that it would clarify his death, but because every time I looked into his personal papers I found some small surprise that stirred something in me. Perhaps that is why I've been tirelessly writing to you for so many weeks, in a way I've never done before in my life. It is clear that the hound on my heels will soon catch up to me. Perhaps that's why I am putting together scraps of memory that, when the moment comes, will be very difficult to organise into anything presentable. In short, I continued with the selection. During a couple of hours, with the introduction still on in the background (we were at the point when Wotan and Loge, enraged, steal the ring and the Nibelung utters the terrible curse that will befall those who put it on their finger), I organised the correspondence and some drawings, which I assumed Father had made, of various objects. And I found, after a good long hour and a half – at the point where Brünnhilde disobeys Wotan and helps poor Sieglinde escape – a text in Hebrew on two yellowed pages of a size not commonly used any more, written in ink by a hand I recognised as my father's. In it I was hoping to find one of the thousand things that had aroused his curiosity and, when I began to read it, I thought that it was my rusty Hebrew that was hampering a comfortable reading of the text. After five fruitless minutes, with various useless dictionary consultations, the surprise came. It wasn't written in Hebrew, but in Aramaic camouflaged in the Hebrew alphabet. It was strange to read because I'm more used to Aramaic in the Syriac alphabet. But it was all just a question of making an effort. About a minute later I had figured out two things: first that Doctor Gombreny did her job because my Aramaic was decent; and second, that it wasn't a copy of an ancient text but rather a letter that my father had written to me. To me! My father who, in life, had perhaps addressed me directly only fifty times, and almost always to say bloody hell what are you shouting for, had written a text to his ignored son. And I learned that Father's Aramaic was much better than mine. Then, when I had almost read the whole thing, Siegfried, Sieglinde's enterprising son, with that cruelty heroes have, kills the Nibelung Mime, who had raised him, to keep him from betraying him. The forest of the heroes, the text in Aramaic, it all enjoined blood. I was surrounded by blood. Adrià, immersed in the text, without seeing it, thinking about the terrible things he had read, let the record spin on the platter for a long half hour before turning it over. As if the characters were repeating their movements ad infinitum, accompanied only by the slight crackling of the needle. He was stunned, like Siegfried, by the revelation. Because the letter read My beloved son Adrià. I am writing you this secret with the uncertain hope that some day, many years from now, you will know what happened. Most likely this letter will be lost among the papers and consumed by the voracious silverfish who always haunt those who keep libraries of old books. If you are reading this it's because you've saved my papers, and you have done what I set out for you: you have learned Hebrew and Aramaic. And if you have learned Hebrew and Aramaic, Son, then you are the type of scholar I imagined you would become. And I will have won out over your mother, who wants to turn you into an effete violinist. (Actually, in Aramaic it said effete rebec player, but my father's nasty swipe was clear.) I want you to know that if you are reading this it is because I was unable to return home to destroy it. I don't know if my death will be officially ruled an accident, but I want you to know I was murdered and that my killer is named Aribert Voigt, a former Nazi doctor who took part in brutalities which I will spare you here. He wanted to get back the Storioni violin, which was underhandedly taken from him at one point. I am leaving home, so that his rage won't harm you, like the bird who pretends to be wounded in order to lead the predator far from its nest. Don't look for my killer. By the time you read this he'll probably have been dead for a long time. Don't look for the violin, either; it's not worth it. Don't search for what I have found in many of the objects I've collected: the satisfaction of possessing something rare. Don't search for it, because it ends up eating away at you;

it's endless anguish and it makes you do things that you later regret. If your mother is alive, spare her this story that I am explaining to you. Farewell. And beneath that was some sort of postscript that made me unhappy. A postscript that said Aribert Voigt killed me. I took Vial out of his bloody clutches. I know that he has been released and that, inevitably, he will come looking for me. Voigt is evil. I am also evil, but Voigt is absolute evil. If I die violently, don't believe them when they say it was an accident. Voigt. I don't want you to avenge me, Son. You can't do it, obviously; because when you read this, if you ever do, Voigt will have been rotting in hell for many years already. If they killed me, that will mean that Vial, our Storioni, will have disappeared from the house. If for any reason there is public talk of Voigt or our violin, you should know that I found out who the instrument belonged to before Voigt confiscated it: Netje de Boeck, a Belgian woman, was the owner. I profoundly hope that Voigt meets a bad end and that someone, I don't know whom, ensures that he never sleeps easily until the end of his days. But I don't want it to be you, because I don't want to taint you with my business matters. You've tainted me, Father, indeed, thought Adrià, because I've inherited the family illness, you passed it on to me: that itching of desire in my fingers when I hold certain objects. And the text in Aramaic ended with a laconic farewell, Son. They were probably the last words he ever wrote. And not one said I love you, my son. Perhaps he didn't love me.

The record player spun in silence, accompanying Adrià's perplexity. Although he was a little bit surprised that he hadn't been the least surprised by his father's confirmation of his moral profile. A long while passed before he began to ask himself questions, for example, why didn't he want it known that he was killed by a Nazi like this Voigt. Was it that he didn't want other stories to come to light? Sadly, I think that was the reason. Do you know how I felt, Sara? I felt stupid. I had always thought that I'd designed my life my own way, defying everyone's plans, and now it turns out that I'd ended up doing what my authoritarian father had intended from the very beginning. I put on the start of the *Götterdämmerung* to go along with that strange feeling, and the three Norns, Erda's daughters, gathered beside Brünnhilde's rock to weave the rope of destiny, as my father had patiently done with mine, without asking me or my mother what we thought of it. But a rope of destiny that Father had prepared had been unexpectedly cut and confirmed my deepest fears: it made me guilty of his atrocious death.

'Hey! You said three days!' I had never heard Bernat so indignant. 'I've only had it for three hours!'

'I'm sorry, forgive me, I swear. Now. It has to be now or they'll kill me, I swear.'

'Your word means nothing. I taught you vibrato!'

'Vibrato isn't something you can teach; you have to find it,' I responded, desperate. At twelve years old I wasn't very skilled at arguing. And I continued, very frightened: 'They are going to find us out and my father will put me in jail. And you too. I'll explain everything later, I swear.'

They both hung up the phone at the same time. He had to explain something to Little Lola or Mother about Bernat having my violin homework.

'Stay on the pavement.'

'Of course,' he said, offended.

They met in front of the Solà family bakery. They opened their cases and made the switch, on the ground, on the corner of València and Llúria, ignoring the racket made by the tramvia struggling to make its way up the street. Bernat gave him back the Storioni and he gave back the violin of Madame d'Angoulême and explained that his father had all of a sudden gone into the study and had left the door open. And from his room Adrià had panicked, watching his father open the safe and pull out the case and close the safe without checking that the violin inside the case was the violin that should have been in the case, and I, I swear to you, I didn't know what to do, because if I tell him that you have it, he'd throw me off the balcony, you know, and I don't know what will happen, but ...

Bernat looked at him coldly. 'You just made all that up.'

'No, really! I put my student violin in the case so he wouldn't suspect anything if he opened it ...'

'I wasn't born yesterday you know.'

'I swear!' Adrià, desperate.

'You're a lily liver who can't keep his word.'

I didn't know what to say. I looked impotently at my furious friend, who was now several inches taller than me. He looked like some sort of vengeful giant. But I was more afraid of my father. The giant opened his mouth again: 'And you think that when he comes back and opens the safe and sees the Storioni he won't start asking questions?'

'And what do you want me to do? Huh?'

'Let's run away. To America.'

I liked Bernat for his sudden solidarity. Both of us running away to America, how cool. They didn't run away to America, and Adrià didn't have time to ask him, hey, Bernat, how is it to play the Storioni, can you tell the difference, is an old violin worth it? He didn't even find out if his parents had noticed anything or … He only said he's going to kill me, I swear he's going to kill me, give it back to me. Bernat left in silence, with an expression that made it clear he didn't believe his weird story that was just starting to get really complicated.

The day of the Lord will come like a thief in the night. Six one five four two eight. Adrià placed the Storioni in the safe, closed it, erased all traces of his furtive steps and left the study. In his room, Carson and Black Eagle were playing it cool and looking the other way, surely overwhelmed by the circumstances. And he sat there with an empty violin case and, to make things even more difficult, Little Lola stuck her head in twice to ask, on Mother's request, are you studying today or what? and the second time he said I have a callus on my finger, it hurts … see? I can't play.

'Let's see that finger?' said Mother, entering unexpectedly just as he was gluing the three trading cards he'd bought at the Sant Antoni market on Sunday into his album.

'I don't see anything,' she said, very crudely.

'But I can feel it, and it hurts.'

Mother looked to either side, as if she was having trouble believing I wasn't pulling her leg, and she left in silence. Luckily she hadn't opened the case. Now I just had to wait for my father's cosmic bollocking.

Mea culpa. It was my fault that he died. Even though he would have died by Voigt's hand anyway. The taxi had left him alone at kilometre three and he had returned to Barcelona. At that point of the winter, the day faded very early. Alone on the highway. A trap, an ambush. Didn't you see it, Father? Perhaps you thought it was a joke in poor taste and nothing more. Fèlix Ardèvol looked down on Barcelona for the last time. The sound of an engine. A car was coming down from Tibidabo with its lights on. It stopped in front of him and Signor Falegnami got out, thinner, balder, with the same big nose and his eyes gleaming. He was escorted by two muscular men and the chauffeur. All with disgusted faces. Falegnami demanded the violin with a curt gesture. Ardèvol gave it to him and Falegnami got into the car to open the case. He came out of the vehicle with the violin in his hand: 'Do you think I'm an idiot?'

'Now what?' I can imagine my father more irritated than scared.

'Where is the Storioni?'

'Oh, bollocks. You have it there!'

In reply, Voigt lifted the violin and broke it against a rock on the side of the highway.

'What are you doing?' Father, frightened.

Voigt put the busted violin in front of his face. The top had broken off in pieces and you could read the instrument's signature: Casa Parramon on Carme Street. Father must have been the one who was confused.

'That's impossible! I took it out of the safe myself!'

'Well, then you must have been robbed some time ago, imbecile!'

I want to imagine that a smile crossed his lips when he said, well, if that's the case, Signor Falegnami, then I have no idea who has that marvellous instrument.

Voigt lifted an eyebrow and one of the men punched Father in the stomach: he doubled over, panting.

'Start remembering, Ardèvol.'

And since Father had no way of knowing that Vial was in the hands of Bernat Plensa i Punsoda, Mrs Trullols's favourite student at Barcelona's Municipal Conservatory, he couldn't start remembering. Just in case, he said I swear I don't know.

Voigt pulled out the very portable, ladylike pistol from his pocket.

'I think we are going to have fun,' he said. Referring to the little pistol, 'Remember this?'

'Of course. And you won't get the violin.'

Another punch to the stomach, but it was worth it. Doubled over again. Panting again, his mouth and eyes open wide. And then, what do I know? The harried winter dusk had given way to night and to impunity, and there they ended up destroying my father in some way I can't even imagine.

'How.'

'Christ, where were you?'

'Even if your father had given them Vial, they would have killed him anyway.'

'Black Eagle is right,' added Carson. 'He was already a dead man, if you'll allow me the expression.' He spat curtly on the ground. 'And he knew it when he left the house.'

'Why didn't he check the violin?'

'He was too upset to realise that he wasn't carrying Vial with him.'

'Thank you, my friends. But I don't think that's any consolation.'

Voigt tortured my father, respecting the gentleman's promise he had made to Morlin in Damascus to not harm a single hair on his head because Father was as bald as a hardboiled egg. It couldn't have gone any other way. Just as Brünnhilde inadvertently sent Siegfried to his death, revealing his weak point to his enemies, I, by switching the violins, brought death upon my father who didn't love me. To maintain the memory of shameless Siegfried Ardèvol, whom she was unable to love, Brünnhilde swore that the violin would remain forever in that house. He swore it for his father, yes. But today I have to admit that I also swore it because of the itching I felt in my fingers at the mere thought of it leaving my possession. Aribert Voigt. Siegfried. Brünnhilde. My God. Confiteor.

## 35

'Rsrsrsrsrsrsrsrs.'

Adrià was in the toilet, reading *Le forme del contenuto*, and perfectly heard the rsrsrsrsrsrsrsrs. And he thought it must be the boy from Can Múrria, always arriving at just the right moment. He took long enough that he heard rsrsrsrsrsrsrsrs again and he told himself he had to change the bell to something more modern. Perhaps a ding dong, which is always more cheerful.

'Rsrsrsrsrsrsrsrsrsrs.'

'I'm coming, goddamn it,' he grumbled.

With the Eco beneath his arm, he opened the door and found you, my love, on the landing, standing, serious, with a fairly small suitcase; you looked at me with your dark eyes and for a long minute we both stood there, she on the landing, he inside the flat holding the door, shocked. And at the end of that endless minute all I could think of to say is what do you want, Sara. I can't even believe it: all I could think of to say was what do you want, Sara.

'Can I come in?'

You can come into my life, you can do whatever you want, beloved Sara.

But she only came into my house. And she put her little suitcase down. And we were about to repeat another minute of standing face to face, but now in the hall. Then Sara said I'd love a cup of coffee. And I realised that she was carrying a yellow rose in her hand.

Goethe had already said it. Characters who try to fulfill their youthful desires in adulthood are doomed to fail. It is too late for characters who didn't know or didn't recognise happiness at the right moment, no matter how hard they try. Love re-found in adulthood can at best only be a tender repetition of happy moments. Edward and Ottilie went into the dining room to have some coffee. She put the rose down on the table, just like that, elegantly abandoned.

'It's good, this coffee.'

'Yes. It's from Múrria's.'

'Can Múrria still exists?'

'Sure.'

'What are you thinking about?'

'I don't want ...' The truth is, Sara, I don't know what to say. So I just went straight to the heart of the matter. 'Have you come to stay?'

The Sara character who had come from Paris is not the same character who was twenty years old in Barcelona, because people undergo metamorphosis. And characters do, too. Goethe explained it to me, but Adrià was Edward and Sara was Ottilie. They had run out of time; that was also their parents' fault. Attractio electiva duplex works when it works.

'On one condition. And forgive me.' Ottilie looking at the ground.

'What is it.' Edward on the defensive.

'That you give back what your father stole. Forgive me.'

'What he stole?'

'Yes. Your father took advantage of many people to extort them. Before, during and after the war.'

'But I ...'

'How do you think he set up his business?'

'I sold the shop,' I said.

'Really?' Sara was surprised. I even thought that she was secretly disappointed.

'I don't want to be a shopkeeper and I never approved of my father's methods.'

Silence. Sara took a small sip of coffee and looked him in the eye. She searched him with her gaze and Adrià felt he had to respond, 'Listen: I sold an antiques shop. I don't know what my father had acquired fraudulently. I can assure you that it wasn't most of the objects. And I have broken ties with that history,' I lied.

Sara was silent for ten minutes. Thinking, looking straight

ahead but ignoring Adrià's presence; and I was afraid that perhaps she was giving me conditions that were impossible to meet so that she had an excuse to run away again. The yellow rose lay on the table, attentive to our conversation. I looked her in the eye, but it wasn't that she was avoiding my gaze, it was that she was immersed in her reflections and it was as if I wasn't there at all. It was a new behaviour I was unfamiliar with in you, Sara, and which I've only seen again on very special occasions.

'Fine,' she said, a thousand years later. 'We can give it a try.' And she took another little sip of coffee. I was so nervous that I drank three cups in a row, insuring I wouldn't sleep a wink that night. Now she did look me in the eye, in that way that hurts so badly, and she said it looks like you are scared stiff.

'Yes.'

Adrià took her by the hand and brought her to the study, to the flat file that held the manuscripts.

'This is a new piece of furniture,' you commented.

'You have a good memory.'

Adrià opened the first two drawers and I pulled out my manuscripts, my gems that make my fingers tremble: my Descartes, Goncourts ... and I said all this is mine, Sara: I bought it with my money, because I like to collect it and have it and buy it and I don't know what. It's mine, I bought it, it wasn't extorted from anyone.

I said it with all those words knowing that I was probably lying. Suddenly a grave, dark silence fell. I didn't dare to look at her. But since the silence persisted, I glanced towards her. She was silently crying.

'What's wrong?'

'Forgive me. I didn't come here to judge you.'

'All right ... But I also want to make things clear.'

She wiped her nose delicately and I didn't know how to say well, who knows where Morral gets them from, and how.

I opened the bottom drawer, which held the pages from the *Recherche*, Zweig and the parchment of Sant Pere del Burgal's consecration. When I was about to tell her that those manuscripts were Father's and probably the fruit of extor– she closed the drawer and repeated forgive me, I'm not the one to judge you. And I kept quiet as a church mouse.

You sat down, a bit befuddled, before the desk, where there was a book open, I think it was *Masse und Macht*, by Canetti.

'The Storioni was bought legally,' I lied again, pointing to the instrument cabinet.

She looked at me, weepy, wanting to believe me.

'All right,' you said.

'And I'm not my father.'

You smiled feebly and you said forgive me, forgive me, forgive me for coming into your house like this.

'Our house, if you want.'

'I don't know if you have any … If you have … I don't know, any ties that …' She took a deep breath. 'If there is another woman. I wouldn't want to ruin anything that …'

'I went to Paris to find you. Don't you remember?'

'Yes, but …'

'There is no woman,' I lied for the third time, like Saint Peter.

On that basis, we took up our relationship again. I know that it was imprudent on my part, but I wanted to hold on to her any way I could. Then she looked around. Her eyes went towards the stretch of wall with the paintings. She went over to them. She held up her hand and, like I did when I was little, she touched lightly, with two fingers, Abraham Mignon's miniature depicting a bouquet of lush yellow gardenias in a ceramic pot. And didn't tell her you're always touching everything, I just smiled, happily. She turned around, sighed and said everything is exactly the same. Just the way I remembered it every single day. She stood before me and she looked at me, suddenly serene, and said why did you come looking for me?

'To tell you the truth. Because I couldn't stand you living so long thinking that I'd insulted you.'

'I …'

'And because I love you. And why have you come?'

'I don't know. Because I love you too. Maybe I came because … No, nothing.'

'You can tell me.' I took both of her hands in mine to encourage her to speak.

'Weellll ... to compensate for my weakness as a twenty-year-old.'

'I can't judge you either. Things happened the way they did.'

'And also ...'

'What?'

'Also because I haven't been able to get your gaze out of my head, you there on the landing of my house.' She smiled, remembering. 'Do you know what you looked like?' she asked.

'An encyclopaedia salesman.'

She burst into laughter, your laugh, Sara! And she said yes, yes, that's exactly it. But she quickly contained herself and said I came back because I love you, yes. If you want it. And I stopped thinking about how much I had lied that morning. I couldn't even tell you that, there in the huitième arrondissement, you with your hand on the door as if you were prepared to slam it in my face at any moment, I was panicked; I never told you that. I covered it up like a good encyclopaedia salesman. In the deepest depths of my heart, I went to Paris, to your house, to quarante-huit rue Laborde, to be able to hear you say that you wanted nothing to do with me and thus be able to close a chapter without feeling guilty and have a good reason to cry. But Sara, after saying no in Paris, showed up in Barcelona and said I'd love a cup of coffee.

*Adrià in a wheelchair, looking into the study from the doorway. In his hands he gripped a dirty rag that he hadn't let anyone take from him. Adrià looking into the study. A long minute, excruciatingly long for everyone. He took a deep breath and he said whenever you wish; it had been a brief second for him. Jònatan's firm hand grabbed the wheelchair with poorly masked impatience and turned it towards the door to the street. Adrià pointed to Xevi and said Xevi. He pointed at Bernat, whose eyes were teary, and he said Bernat, he pointed at Xènia and said Tecla. And when he pointed at Caterina and said Little Lola, for the first time in her life Caterina didn't correct him.*

*'He will be well taken care of, don't worry,' said one of the survivors.*

*The retinue went downstairs in silence, looking out of the corners of their eyes at the light on the lift that held Adrià, the wheelchair and Jònatan. Once they were downstairs it occurred to Bernat that, when Jònatan wheeled him out of the lift and his friend saw them all again, Adrià might not recognise them. It was a like a flash of fear.*

*Ten days earlier the alarm had been sounded. It was sounded by Caterina when Adrià got lost inside his own house. In Slavic literature, looking around him, scared.*

*'Where do you want to go?'*

*'I don't know. Where am I?'*

*'At home.'*

*'At whose home?'*

*'Your home. Do you know who I am?'*

*'Yes.'*

*'Who am I?'*

*'That one.' Long pause. Frightened. 'Right? Or a direct object! Or the subject! The subject, right?'*

*That same week he had been rummaging around in the fridge, increasingly worried and grumbling, and Jònatan, the* nurse on the night shift that week, asked him what he was looking for, at that time of the night.

'My socks? What do you think I'm looking for?'

Jònatan had told that to Plàcida, who had let Caterina know. And Plàcida added that Adrià had asked her to put a book on to boil. He's completely lost it, hasn't he?

And now, in Slavic literature, Caterina insisted do you know who I am, Adrià?, and he: a direct object. So, frightened, she called Doctor Dalmau and Bernat. And Doctor Dalmau, frightened, called the nursing home to speak with Doctor Valls, and he said I think the time has come. There were a few days of exhaustive check-ups, of tests and analyses and of looking askance at the results. And of silences. The indirect object, really now! And finally, Doctor Dalmau called Bernat and the cousins from Vic together. Bernat offered his home and made sure there was plenty of Tasmanian water. Doctor Dalmau explained the steps they had to take.

'But he's a man who …' Xevi, indignant with fate, was still resisting: 'He speaks seven or eight languages!'

'Thirteen,' corrected Bernat.

'Thirteen? Every time I turn my head he's learned a new one.' His eyes light up. 'You see, doctor? Thirteen languages! I'm a farmer, I'm older and I only know one and a half. Isn't this unfair? Isn't it?'

'Catalan, French, Spanish, Germany, Italian, English, Russian, Aramaic, Latin, Greek, Dutch, Romanian and Hebrew,' ticked off Bernat. 'And he could easily read six or seven more.'

'You see, doctor?' An indisputable medical argument from Xevi Ardèvol, desperately opening up another defence front.

'Your cousin was one of a kind,' the doctor politely cut him off. 'I know because I followed him carefully. If you'll allow me to say so, I consider myself his friend. But it's over. His brain is drying up.'

'What a shame, what a shame, what a shame …'

After resisting in vain for a few more minutes, they agreed that the best they could do was put Adrià's life in order and accept the orders he himself had established when his head was *still clear. Bernat thought how sad to have to decide things for when you are no longer here; to have to write I give my flat in Barcelona to my cousins Xavier, Francesc and Rosa Ardèvol in three equal parts. As for my library, I would like, when I can no longer make use of it, for Bernat Plensa to decide either to keep it or donate it to the universities of Tübingen and Barcelona, according to their respective interests. It should be him, if he's willing, since he was the one who helped me to set it up long ago, when we worked together to create the world.*

'I don't understand a thing.' Xevi, perplexed, the day we met with the lawyer.

'It's one of Adrià's jokes. I'm afraid only I can understand it,' clarified Bernat.

*'And I wish for Mrs Caterina Fargues to be remunerated with an amount equal to two years' salary. I also authorise Bernat Plensa to keep whatever he would like of those things not specified in this will, which, more than a will, seems like an instruction manual. And Bernat should decide what to do with the rest of the things, including valuable objects such as the coin and manuscript collection, unless he considers it best to donate them to the aforementioned universities. I recommend following the criteria expressed by Professor Johannes Kamenek of Tübingen. As for the self-portrait of Sara Voltes-Epstein, it should be delivered to her brother Max Voltes-Epstein. And I wish the painting by Modest Urgell of the Santa Maria de Gerri monastery that hangs in the dining room to be given to Friar Julià of the neighbouring monastery of Sant Pere del Burgal, who is responsible for everything.*

'What?' Xevi, Rosa and Quico, all three at once.

Bernat opened his mouth and closed it. The lawyer read it to himself again and said yes, yes: it says Friar Julià of Sant Pere del Burgal.

'Who the hell is he,' said Quico from Tona, suspicious.

'And what does it mean that he should be held accountable? Accountable for what?'

'No, no: it says responsible.'

'Responsible for what?'

'For everything,' said the lawyer, after consulting the paper.

'We'll find out,' said Bernat. And he gestured to the lawyer to continue.

'And if he can't be located or he refuses it, I wish it to be offered to Mrs Laura Baylina of Uppsala. If she doesn't accept it, I delegate Mr Bernat Plensa to find the best solution. And the aforementioned Bernat Plensa should deliver to the editor, as we agreed, the book I gave him.'

'A new book?' Xevi.

'Yes. I'm already taking care of it, don't worry.'

'You mean to say that he was still in good health, when he wrote that?'

'We have to assume so,' said the lawyer. 'We can't ask him to explain things now.'

'Who is Mrs Ofupsala?' asked Rosa. 'Does she exist?'

'Don't worry: I'll find her. She exists.'

'And finally, a small reflection dedicated to you and whomever has joined you. They tell me that I won't miss my books or music, which I find hard to believe. They tell me that I won't recognise you: don't be too cruel with me. They tell me that I won't suffer over that. So, please don't you all suffer. And be indulgent with my decline, which will be gradual but constant.'

'Very well,' said the lawyer after reading what Adrià Ardèvol had entitled 'Practical Instructions For The Final Stretch Of My Life'.

'There is still a little bit,' Rosa dared to say, pointing to the page.

'Yes, sorry: it is a closing comment of farewell.'

'And what does it say?'

'It says that as for the spiritual instructions, I have collected them all separately.'

'Where?'

'In the book he wrote,' said Bernat. 'I'll take care of it, don't worry.'

Bernat opened up, trying not to make a sound. Like a thief. He felt along the wall until he found the switch. He flipped it, but the light didn't come on. Shit. He pulled a torch out of his briefcase and felt even more like a thief. There in the hall was the fuse-box or whatever it's called now. He flipped the switch and

the hall light came on as well as another one at the back of the
flat, perhaps the one in the Germanic and Asian prose corridor.
He stood there for a few seconds, contemplating the silence of
that house. He went towards the kitchen. The refrigerator was
unplugged, with the door open and no socks inside. And the
freezer, also empty. He walked through Slavic and Nordic prose,
led by the light that was on in fine arts and encylopaedias,
Sara's studio, which had been Little Lola's room before that.
The easel was still set up, as if Adrià hadn't stopped believing
that one day Sara would come back and start drawing, dirty-
ing her fingers with charcoal. And a mountain of huge folders
with sketches. Framed and placed on some sort of an altar were
In Arcadia Hadriani and Sant Pere del Burgal: A Dream, the
two landscapes that Sara had given Adrià and which, since
he'd left no specific instructions for them, Bernat had decided
he would send to Max Voltes-Epstein. He left the light on. He
glanced at religion and the classical world, and went back
through Romance languages and peeked into poetry; there he
switched on the light. Everything was in order. Then he went
to literary essays and turned on the light: the dining room was
the same as ever. The sun, at the monastery of Santa Maria de
Gerri, continued to come from Trespui. He pulled a camera out
of his jacket pocket. He had to move aside a couple of chairs to
stand before the painting by Modest Urgell. He took a couple of
photos with flash and a couple without. He left literary essays
and went into the study. Everything was just as they had left
it. He sat in a chair and began to think about all the time he
had spent in there, always with Adrià by his side, discussing
mostly music and literature, but also politics and life. As young
men and as boys, dreaming of the secret mysteries there. He
turned on the light beside the reading chair. He also turned on
the light beside the sofa and the light on the ceiling. There where
Sara's self-portrait had hung for years was now a blank spot
that made him feel sort of dizzy. He took off his jacket, rubbed
his face with the palms of his hands, the way Adrià used to, and
said let's get to it. He went behind the desk and knelt. He tried
six, one, five, four, two, eight. It didn't open. He tried seven,
two, eight, zero, six, five, and the safe opened silently. There

was nothing inside. Yes, there were some envelopes. He grabbed them and placed them on the desk to look at more comfortably. He opened one. He went through it page by page: a list of characters. He was there: Bernat Plensa, Sara Voltes-Epstein, Me, Little Lola, Aunt Leo ... the people ... well, the characters with the date of their birth and in some cases death. More papers: some sort of diagram with a lot of lines through it as if it'd been rejected. Another list with more characters. And that was it. If that was all, Adrià had written in a torrent, going from one place to another as dictated by his remaining fading memory. Bernat put it all back into the envelope and placed the envelope in his briefcase. He lowered his head and struggled to keep from crying. He breathed in and out slowly a few times until he was calmer. He opened up the other envelope. A few photos: one of Sara taking a picture of herself in the mirror. So pretty. Not even now did he want to admit that he had always been a little bit in love with her. The other photo was Adrià working, writing at that same desk where Bernat was now sitting. My friend, Adrià. And a few more photos: an illustration with sketches of a very young girl's face. And also several photos of Vial, from the back and from the front. He put the photos back into the envelope, with an expression of bitter disgust, thinking about lost Vial. He looked inside the safe. Nothing more; he closed it but didn't move the wheel. He paid a visit to history and geography. On the bedside table, Carson and Black Eagle kept faithful watch for no one. He picked them up, with their horses and everything, and put them into his briefcase. He went back to the study and sat in the armchair that Adrià usually used for reading. For almost an hour he stared into the void, reminiscing and longing for it all and allowing the occasional tear to slip down his cheek.

After a long time, Bernat Plensa i Punsoda finally snapped out of it. He looked around him and was no longer able to hold back a sob that came from deep inside. He covered his face with his hands. When he was calmer he got up from the reading chair; he took a last look over the whole study as he put on his jacket. Adéu, ciao, à bientôt, adiós, tschüss, vale, dag, bye, αντίο, Пока́, la revedere, viszlát, head aega, lehitraot, tchau, maa as-salama, puix beixlama, my friend.

## 36

You came into my life sweetly, like the first time, and I didn't think about Edward or Ottilie or about my lies again, but rather about your silent and comforting presence. Adrià told her take possession of the house; take possession of me. And he had her choose between two rooms to set up her drawing studio, and her books, and her clothes and your life, if you want to, my beloved Sara; but I didn't know that in order to store all of Sara's life it would take many more cupboards than Adrià could possibly offer her.

'This will work very well. It's larger than my studio in Paris,' you said, looking into Little Lola's room from the doorway.

'It has light and it's mostly quiet. Since it's interior.'

'Thank you,' she said, turning towards me.

'You don't have to thank me. Thank you.'

Then she sprang into the room. In the corner by the window there was, hanging on the wall, the little painting of the yellow gardenias by Mignon welcoming her.

'But how …'

'You like that one, don't you?'

'How did you know?'

'But do you like it or not?'

'It is my favourite object in this house.'

'Well, from now on it's yours.'

Her way of saying thank you was to stand in front of the gardenias and stare intensely at them for a good long while.

The next action was almost liturgical for me: adding the name Sara Voltes-Epstein to the mailbox in the lobby. And after ten years of living alone, as I wrote or read, I again heard footsteps, or a teaspoon hitting a glass, or warm music coming from her studio, and I thought that we could be happy to-gether. But Adrià didn't come up with a solution for the other open front; when you leave a file folder half open you can run into many problems. He already knew that full well; but his excitement was more intense than his prudence.

What was hardest for Adrià, in the new situation, was accepting the off-limits areas that Sara imposed on their lives. He realised it at her surprise when Adrià invited her to meet Aunt Leo and his cousins in Tona.

'It's better not to mix our families,' responded Sara.

'Why?'

'I don't want any unpleasantness.'

'I want to introduce you to Aunt Leo, and my cousins, if we can find them. I don't want to introduce you to any unpleasantness.'

'I don't want problems.'

'You won't have any. Why would you?'

When her luggage arrived with the half-finished drawings and completed works, and the easels and the charcoal and the coloured pencils, she made an official inauguration of her studio, giving me a pencil drawing of Mignon's gardenias that I hung up and still have on my wall, there where the original used to hang. And you got down to work because you were behind on the illustrations a couple of French publishers had commissioned from you for some children's stories. Days of silence and calm, you drawing, me reading or writing. Meeting up in the hallway, visiting each other every once in a while, having coffee mid-morning in the kitchen, looking into each other's eyes and not saying anything to avoid bursting the fragility of that unexpectedly recovered happiness.

It took a lot of work, but when Sara had the most urgent job finished, they ended up going to Tona in a second-hand Seat Six Hundred that Adrià had bought when he had finally passed his licence exam on the seventh try. They had to change a tyre in La Garriga: in Aiguafreda Sara made him stop in front of a florist's shop, went in and emerged with a lovely small bouquet that she placed on the back seat without comment. And on the slope of Sant Antoni, in Centelles, the radiator water started to boil; but apart from that, everything went smoothly.

'It's the most beautiful town in the world,' Adrià told her, excited, when the Six Hundred was getting to Quatre Carreteres.

'The most beautiful town in the world is pretty ugly,' responded Sara when they stopped on Sant Andreu Street and Adrià put on the hand brake too abruptly.

'You have to look at it through my eyes. Et in Arcadia ego.'

They got out of the car and he told her look at the castle, my love. Up here, up high. Isn't it lovely?

'Well ... I don't know what to tell you ...'

He could tell that she was nervous, but he didn't know what to do to ...

'You have to look at it through my eyes. You see that ugly house and the other one with geraniums?'

'Yes ...'

'This is where Can Casic was.'

And he said it as if he could see it; as if he could reach out and touch Josep with the smoking cigarette at his lips, hunched over, sharpening knives on the threshing floor, beside the haystack that was consumed like an apple core.

'You see?' said Adrià. And he pointed towards the stable of the mule who was always called Estrella and wore shoes that clicked like high heels against the manure-covered stones when she swatted away flies, and he even heard Viola barking furiously, pulling her chain taut because the silent, nameless white cat was getting too close, boasting haughtily of her freedom.

'For Pete's sake, kids, go play somewhere else, for Pete's sake.'

And they all ran to hide behind the white rock and life was an exciting adventure, different from fingering flat major arpeggios; with the scent of manure and the sound of Maria's clogs when she went into the pigsty, and the tanned gang of reapers in late July with their sickles and scythes. And the dog at Can Casic was also always named Viola and she envied the kids because they weren't tied down with a rope that measured exactly eight ells.

'For Pete's sake is a euphemism for for heaven's sake, which is a euphemism for for Christ's sake.'

'Hey, look at Adrià. He says for Christ's sake!'

'Yeah, but nobody ever understands him,' grumbled Xevi as they sledded down from the stone border to the street filled with wheel tracks from the cart and piles of shit from Bastús, the street sweeper's mule.

'You say things nobody understands,' challenged Xevi once they had reached the bottom.

'Sorry. Sometimes I think out loud.'

'No, I don't ...'

And he didn't smack the dust off of his trousers because everything was permitted in Tona, far from his parents, and no one got angry if you grazed your knees.

'Can Casic, Sara ...' he summed up, standing on the same street where Bastús used to piss and which was now paved; and it didn't even occur to him that Bastús was no longer a mule but a diesel Iveco with a trailer, a lovely thing that doesn't chew even a sprig of straw, is all clean and doesn't smell of manure.

And then, with the flowers in your hands, you got on tiptoe and gave me an unexpected kiss, and I thought et in Arcadia ego, et in Arcadia ego, et in Arcadia ego, devoutly, as if it were a litany. And don't be afraid, Sara, you are safe here, at my side. You go ahead and draw and I'll love you and together we will learn to build our Arcadia. Before knocking on the door of Can Ges you handed me the bouquet.

On the way home, Adrià convinced Sara that she had to get her licence; that she would surely be a better student than he'd been.

'All right.' After a kilometre in silence. 'You know, I liked your Aunt Leo. How old is she?'

Laus Deo. He had noticed about an hour into their visit to Can Ges that Sara had lowered her guard and was smiling inside.

'I don't know. Over eighty.'

'She's very fit. And I don't know where she gets her energy. She doesn't stop.'

'She's always been like that. But she keeps everyone in line.'

'She wouldn't take no for an answer about the jar of olives.'

'That's Aunt Leo.' And with the momentum: 'Why don't we go to your house one day?'

'Don't even think about it.' Her tone was curt and definitive.

'Why not, Sara?'

'They don't accept you.'

'Aunt Leo accepted you immediately.'

'Your mother, if she were alive, wouldn't have ever let me set foot in your house.'

'Our house.'

'Our house. Aunt Leo, fine, I'm sure I'll be fond of her in no time. But that doesn't count. What counts is your mother.'

'She's dead. She's been dead for ten years!'

Silence until Figueró. To break it, Adrià tightened the thumbscrews and said Sara.

'What.'

'What did they tell you about me?'

Silence. The train, on the other shore of the Congost, went up towards Ripoll. And we were about to hurl ourselves head-long into a conversation.

'Who?'

'At your house. To make you run away.'

'Nothing.'

'And what did it say in that famous letter I supposedly wrote to you?'

In front of them was a Danone lorry that was moving quite slowly. And Adrià still had to think three times before passing. The lorry or the conversation. He stopped and in-sisted: eh, Sara? What lies did they tell you? What did they say about me?

'Don't ask me again.'

'Why?'

'Never again.'

Now came a nice straight stretch. He put on his turn signal but didn't dare pass.

'I have a right to know what ...'

'And I have a right to close that chapter.'

'Can I ask your mother?'

'It's better if you never see her again.'

'Bollocks.'

Let someone else pass. Adrià was unable to pass a slow lorry loaded down with yogurts, mostly because his eyes were misty and had no windscreen wipers.

'I'm sorry, but it's better that way. For both of us.'

'I won't insist. I don't think I'll insist ... But I would like to be able to say hello to your parents. And your brother.'

'My mother is like yours. I don't want to force her. She has too many scars.'

Voilà: near Molí de Blancafort, the lorry turned towards La Garriga and Adrià felt as if he'd passed it himself. Sara continued: 'You and I have to do our own thing. If you want us to live together, you can't open that box. Like Pandora.'

'It's like we live inside the story of Bluebeard. With gardens filled with fruit but a locked room we aren't allowed to enter.'

'Something like that, yes. Like the forbidden apple tree. Are you up to the challenge?'

'Yes, Sara,' I lied for the umpteenth time. I just didn't want you to run away again.

In the department office there are three desks for four professors. Adrià had no desk because he had given it up on the first day: the thought of working anywhere that wasn't his home seemed impossible. He only had a place to leave his briefcase and a little cabinet. And yes, he needed a desk and he realised he'd been too hasty when relinquishing it. Which is why, when Llopis wasn't there, he usually sat at his desk.

He went in, ready for anything. But Llopis was there, correcting some galleys or something like that. And Laura looked up from her spot. Adrià just stood there. No one said anything. Llopis looked up discreetly, glanced at both of them, said he was going to get a coffee and prudently disappeared from the battlefield. I sat in Llopis's chair, face to face with Laura and her typewriter.

'I need to explain something to you.'

'You, giving explanations?'

Laura's sarcastic tone didn't bode well for a comfortable conversation.

'Do you want to talk?'

'Well … It's been a few months since you've answered my calls, you avoid me here, if I run into you, you say not now, not now …'

Both were silent.

'I should be thanking you for being so kind as to show up here today,' she added in the same hurt tone.

Oblique, uncomfortable looks. Then Laura moved her Olivetti aside, as if it were an obstacle between them, and, like someone rolling up her sleeves, preparing for anything, she said, 'There's another woman, isn't there?'

'No.'

If there's one thing I've never understood about myself, it is my inability to take the bull by the horns. At most, I grab it by the tail and then I'm doomed to receive one of its fatal kicks. I'll never learn; because I said no, no, no, bollocks, Laura, there's no one else … It's me who, well, it's just that I'd rather not …

'Pathetic.'

'Don't insult me,' said Adrià.

'Pathetic isn't an insult.' She got up, a bit out of control. 'Tell the truth, for fuck's sake. Tell me you don't love me!'

'I don't love you,' said Adrià just as Parera opened the door and Laura burst into tears. When she said what a son of a bitch you are, what a son of a bitch you are, what a son of a bitch you are, Parera had already closed the door, leaving them alone again.

'You used me like a tissue.'

'Yes. Forgive me.'

'Go to hell.'

Adrià left the office. At the railing of the cloister, Parera was making time, smoking a peace cigarette, perhaps taking sides without knowing the details. He passed by her and didn't dare to say thank you or anything.

At home, Sara looked at him strangely, as if the argument and the unpleasantness had got stuck to his face or his clothes,

but you didn't say anything; I am sure you understood everything, but you had the sense not to put it on the table and
when you said I have to tell you something, Adrià already saw
a new storm brewing; but instead of making it clear that you
knew everything, you said I think we should switch bakeries:
this bread is like chewing gum. What do you think?

Until one day Sara got a call and was speaking softly into the
dining room telephone and when I poked my head in I saw
that she was silently crying, her hand still on the receiver after
hanging up.

'What's going on?' No reply. 'Sara?'

She looked at him, absent. She took her hand off of the telephone, as if it were burning hot.

'Mama is dead.'

My God. I don't know how it happened, but I remembered
the day that Father had said we are starting to have too many
treasures in this house and I had understood that we were
starting to have too many skeletons in this house. Now I was
an adult, but I still had trouble accepting that life was made
up of one death after another.

'I didn't know that ...'

She looked at me through her tears.

'She wasn't sick: it was sudden. Ma pauvre maman ...'

It made me furious. I don't know how to say it, Sara, but
it made me furious that people died around me. It made me
furious even though, with the passing of time, things hadn't
improved much. Surely I can't accept life. That's why I rebelled
uselessly and dangerously and was unfaithful to you. Like a
thief, like the Lord, I entered the temple. I sat on a discreet
bench at the back of the synagogue. And I saw your father
again, who I hadn't seen since the day of that awful conversation, when you had disappeared without a trace and I could
only cling to desperation. Adrià was also able to enjoy watching the back of Max's neck; he was a head taller than his sister,
more or less Bernat's height. And Sara, squeezed between the
two men and other family members that I won't ever meet
because you don't want me to, because I am my father's son

and the blood of his sins will flow through his children and his children's children for seven generations. I would like to have a child with you, Sara, I thought. With no conditions, I thought. But I still didn't dare to tell you that. When you told me it's best if you don't come to the funeral, then Adrià grasped the magnitude of the aversion the Epsteins had to the memory of Mr Fèlix Ardèvol.

Meanwhile, the distance with Laura grew even though I always thought poor Laura, it was all my fault. And I was relieved when, in the middle of the cloister, she told me I am going to Uppsala to finish my thesis. And maybe I'll stay there forever.

Boom. Her blue gaze on mine like an accusation.

'I wish you the best of luck; you deserve it.'

'Bastard.'

'Good luck, really, Laura.'

And I didn't see her for at least a year or even think about her, because Mrs Voltes-Epstein's death slipped in. You don't know how it pains me to have to call your mother Mrs Voltes-Epstein. And one day, a few months after the funeral, I made a date with Mr Voltes in a café near the university. It's something I've never told you, my dear. I didn't dare. Why did I do it? Because I am not my father. Because I am guilty of many things. But, even though sometimes it seems that I am, I am in no way guilty of being my father's son.

They didn't shake hands. They both sort of nodded in greeting. They both sat in silence. They both struggled not to look each other in the eye.

'I'm very sorry about your wife's death.'

Mr Voltes thanked him for his comment with a nod of approval. They ordered two teas and waited for the waitress to walk away so they could continue in silence.

'What do you want?' asked Mr Voltes after a long while.

'I guess to be accepted. I would like to come to the commemoration for Uncle Haïm.'

Mr Voltes glanced at him in surprise. Adrià couldn't get the day she had said I'm going to Cadaqués out of his head.

'I'll go with you.'

'Impossible.'

Disappointment; again, she put up a wall.

'But tomorrow isn't Yom Kippur, it's not Hanukkah, it's no one's bar mitzvah.'

'It's the anniversary of Uncle Haïm's death.'

'Ah.'

The Voltes-Epsteins squeaked by with their fulfilment of the Sabbath precepts in the synagogue on Avenir Street, but they weren't religious. And when they celebrated Rosh Hashanah and Sukkot it was to say we are Jews in a land of goyim. And we always will be. But not out of ... My father isn't Jewish, Sara told me one day. But it's as if he were: he went into exile in '39. And he doesn't believe in anything; he always says that he just tries not to do harm.

Now Mr Voltes was sitting before Adrià, stirring in sugar with a little spoon. He looked Adrià in the eye and Adrià felt he should react and he said Mr Voltes, I really love your daughter. And he stopped stirring the sugar and he put the little spoon down silently on the saucer.

'Didn't Sara ever tell you about him?'

'About Uncle Haïm?'

'Yes.'

'A little bit.'

'Which little bit?'

'No, that ... That a Nazi pulled him out of the gas chamber so he could give him a check-up.'

'Uncle Haïm committed suicide in nineteen fifty-three and we always wondered why, when he had survived everything, why, when he was saved and back with his family ... with what was left of his family ... and to commemorate that why, we want to be alone.' And Adrià, with the arrogance that comes with being told an unexpected confidence, replied that perhaps Uncle Haïm had committed suicide because he couldn't bear having survived; because he felt guilty about not having died.

'Look at you, you know everything, eh? Is that what he told you? Did you ever meet him?'

Why don't I know how to keep my mouth shut, bloody hell.

'Forgive me. I didn't mean to offend you.'

Mr Voltes picked up the little spoon and stirred his tea some more, surely to help him think. When Adrià thought that the meeting was over, Mr Voltes continued, in a monotonous tone, as if reciting a prayer, as if what he said was part of the commemorative ceremony for Haïm's death:

'Uncle Haïm was a cultured man, a well-known doctor who, when he came back from Auschwitz after the war, couldn't look us in the eye. And he came to our home, because we were his only family. He was a bachelor. His brother, Sara's grandfather, had died in a goods train in nineteen forty-three. A train that Vichy France had organised to help with the world's ethnic cleansing. His brother. And his sister-in-law couldn't bear the shame and died in the Drancy detention camp before starting the voyage. And he, much later, returned to Paris, to the only family he had left, which was his niece. He never wanted to practise medicine again. And when we married, we forced him to come and live with us. When Sara was three years old, Uncle Haïm said to Rachel that he was going down to drink a pastis at the Auberge, he lifted Sara in his arms, kissed her, kissed Max, who was just arriving from nursery school, pulled his hat down and left the house whistling the andante of Beethoven's seventh. Half an hour later we found out that he jumped into the Seine from the Pont-Neuf.'

'I'm so sorry, Mr Voltes.'

'And we commemorate it. We commemorate all of our family members who died in the Shoah. And we do it on that day because it is the only date of death that we have out of the fourteen close relatives we know were eliminated without even a shred of compassion in the name of a new world.'

Mr Voltes drank a sip of tea and stared straight ahead, looking towards Adrià but not seeing him, perhaps only seeing the memory of Uncle Haïm.

They were silent for a long time and Mr Voltes got up.

'I have to go.'

'As you wish. Thank you for seeing me.'

He had parked right in front of the café. He opened the

door to his car, hesitated for a few seconds and then offered, 'I can drop you off somewhere.'

'No, I …'

'Get on in.'

It was an order. He got on in. They circled around aimlessly, through the thick traffic of the Eixample. He pressed a button and a violin and piano sonata by Enescu began to play softly. I don't know if it was the second or the third. And suddenly, stopped at a red light, he continued with the story that must have been continuing inside his head:

'After being saved from the showers because he was a doctor, he spent two days in barracks twenty-six, where sixty silent, skinny people with lost gazes slept, and when they went out to work, they left him alone with a Romanian kapo who looked at him suspiciously from a distance, as if wondering what to do with that newcomer who still looked healthy. On the third day, a Hauptsturmbannführer who was clearly drunk solved that by peeking into the empty barracks and seeing Doctor Epstein sitting on his bunk trying to become invisible.

'What's he doing here?'

'Orders of Strumbannführer Barber.'

'You!'

You was him. He turned slowly and looked the officer in the eye.

'Stand up when I speak to you!'

You stood up because a Hauptsturmbannführer was speaking.

'All right. I'll take him.'

'But, sir,' said the kapo, red as a beet. 'Strumbannführer Barber …'

'Tell Strumbannführer Barber that I've taken him.'

'But, sir! …'

'Screw Strumbannführer Barber. You understand me now?'

'Yes, sir.'

'Come on, You, come, we're going to have some fun.'

The fun was very good, incredibly good. Very intense. He found out that it was Sunday when the officer told him that he had some friends over and he brought him to the officers' houses and then he stuck him in some sort of cellar where there were eight or ten pairs of eyes that looked at him in fear and he asked what the hell is going on?, and they didn't understand him, because they were Hungarian women and he only knew how to say köszönöm and no one even smiled. And then they suddenly opened the door to the basement, which it turns out wasn't a basement because it was at the level of a long, narrow courtyard, and an Unterscharführer with a red nose bellowed a few inches from You's ear and said when I say go, start running to the far wall. Last one there is a poof! Go!

The eight or ten women and You began to run, like gladiators in the circus. Behind them they heard the laughter of excited people. The women and You reached the far wall. There was just one elderly woman who had only made it halfway. Then some sort of trumpet sounded and shots were heard. The elderly Hungarian woman fell to the floor, drilled through by half a dozen bullets, punished for having been in last place, poor anyóka, poor öreganyó; for not having reached the finish line, that'll teach the lousy hag. You turned in horror. From a raised gallery, three officers loaded their rifles and a fourth, also armed, was waiting for a clearly drunk woman to light his cigar. The men fervently argued and one of them brusquely ordered the red-nosed subordinate, who in turn shouted it at them, saying that now what they had to do was return to the shelter, slowly, that their job wasn't over, and the nine Hungarian women and You turned, weepy, trying not to step on the old woman's corpse, and they watched in horror as an officer aimed at them as they approached the basement and they waited for the shot and another officer realised the intentions of the one who was aiming and slapped his hand just as he was shooting at a very thin girl, and the shot diverted to a few inches from You's head.

'And now run to the wall again.' To Haïm, pushing him: 'You stand here, damn it!'

He looked at his team of hares with some sort of solidarity and pride and shouted: 'The bastard who doesn't run in zigzags, won't make it. Go!'

They were so drunk that they could only kill three women. You reached the other side, alive, and guilty of not having acted as a shield for any of the three women who lay on the ground. One of them was badly hurt, and Doctor You saw right away that the entry hole in her neck had cut her jugular; as if wanting to prove him right, the woman remained immobile as the puddle of blood that was her bed widened. Mea culpa.

And more things that he only told me and I wasn't brave enough to tell Rachel and the children. That he couldn't take it any more and he shouted at the Nazis that they were miserable wretches, and the least drunk among them started laughing and aimed at the youngest of the surviving women and said ffucking shut your trap or I'll start picking them off one by one. You shut up. And when they went back to the basement, one of the hunters started to vomit and another told him you see?, you see?, that's what you get for mixing so many sweet liquors, blockhead. And it seemed they had to stop their fun and games and the basement was left in the dark, and only the moans of horror kept them company. And outside, an exchange of cross shouts and vexed orders that You couldn't understand. And it turns out that the next day the camp's evacuation began because the Russians were approaching faster than they had foreseen and, in the confusion, no one remembered the six or seven hares in basement. Long live the Red Army, said You in Russian, when he realised the situation; and one of the women understood him and explained it to the other hares. And the moans stopped to give way to hope. And so, You's life was saved. But I often think that surviving was a worse punishment than death. Do you understand me, Ardèvol? That is why I am a Jew, not by birth, as far as I know, but by choice, as are many Catalans who feel we are slaves in our land and we have tasted the diaspora just for being Catalan. And from that day on I knew that I am also a Jew, Sara. Jewish not by blood, but by intellect, by people, by history. A Jew without God and trying not to do harm, like Mr Voltes, because trying to do good is, I think, too pretentious. I didn't pull it off either.

'It would be better if you didn't tell my daughter about this conversation,' were the last words Mr Voltes said to me as I got out of the car. And that is why I never told you anything about it, until writing it today, Sara. I was unfaithful to you with that secret as well. But I am very sorry that I never saw Mr Voltes alive again.

If I'm not mistaken, that was about the time that you bought the wine pitcher with the long spout.

And when we had only been living together for a couple of months Morral called me and said I have the original of *El coronel no tiene quien le escriba.*

'No.'

'Yes.'

'Guaranteed?'

'Mr Ardèvol, don't insult me.'

And I said, putting on a normal voice with no hint of emotion in it, I'm going out for a minute, Sara. And from the depths of her studio Sara's voice emerged from the tale of the laughing frog and said where are you going?

'To the Athenaeum' (I swear it just came out).

'Ah' (what did she know, poveretta).

'Yes, I'll be back shortly' (maestro dell'inganno).

'It's your night to cook' (innocente e angelica).

'Yes, yes, don't worry. I'll be back soon' (traditore).

'Is something wrong?' (compassionevole).

'No, what could be wrong' (bugiardo, menzognero, impostore).

Adrià ran away and didn't realise that, when he closed the door, he had slammed it, like his father had many years earlier, when he went to meet his death.

In the little flat where Morral carried out his transactions I was able to examine the splendid, extraordinary manuscript. The final part was typed, but Morral assured me that that was often the case with García Márquez manuscripts. What a delicacy.

'How much?'

'That much.'

'Come on!'

'As you wish.'

'This much.'

'Don't make me laugh. And I have to be frank with you, Doctor Ardèvol. I acquired it at, let's just say, a certain risk, and risk is costly.'

'You mean it's stolen?'

'Such words ... I can assure you that these papers haven't left any trail.'

'Then this much.'

'No: that much.'

'Deal.'

These transactions were never paid by cheque. I had to wait, impatient, until the next day; and that night I dreamt that García Márquez himself came to my house to reproach me for the theft and I pretended not to know what he was talking about and he chased me around the flat with a huge knife and I ...

'What's wrong with you?' asked Sara, turning on the light.

It was past four in the morning and Adrià had sat up in his parents' bed, which was now ours. He was panting as if he'd just run a race.

'Nothing, nothing ... Just a dream.'

'Tell me about it.'

'I can't remember.'

I lay back down. I waited for her to turn off the light and I said García Márquez was chasing me around the house and wanted to kill me with a knife this big.

Silence. No: a slight tremble in the bed. Until Sara exploded with laughter. Then I felt her hand running lovingly over my bald head the way my mother's never had. And I felt dirty and a sinner because I was lying to her.

The next day, we were quiet at breakfast, still waking up. Until Sara burst into explosive laughter again.

'And now what's wrong with you?'

'Even your ogres are intellectuals.'

'Well, I was really scared. Oh, today I have to go to the university' (impostore).

'But it's Tuesday' (angelica).

'I know, yeah ... But Parera wants something and asked me to ... pff ...' (spregevole).

'Well, have patience' (innocente).

One lie after another, and I was headed to La Caixa bank, I withdrew that much and went to Can Morral, with the anguished premonition that the flat had caught fire that night, or he'd changed his mind, or he'd found a more generous bidder ... or he'd been arrested.

No. The colonel was still waiting patiently for me. I picked him up tenderly. Now it was mine and I didn't have to suffer any more. Mine.

'Mr Morral.'

'Yes?'

'And the complete Nietzsche manuscript?'

'Aha.'

'What's the price?'

'If you're asking just to ask, I'll keep it to myself, and don't take it the wrong way.'

'I'm asking because I want to buy, if I can.'

'In ten days from now call me and I will tell you an amount, if it hasn't been sold yet.'

'What!?'

'Oh, what do you think? You're the only one in the world?'

'But I want it.'

'Ten days.'

At home, I couldn't show you my treasure. That was my clandestine side, to compensate for your secrets. I hid the manuscript at the bottom of a drawer. I wanted to buy a folder that showed each and every page, both sides, of the entire work. But I had to do it in secret. And to top it all off, Black Eagle.

'Come on, what, say it.'

'Now you've crossed the forbidden river.'

'What?'

'You keep spending money on trinkets, without saying a word to your squaw.'

'It's as if you were cheating on her,' added Carson. 'There's no way this ends well.'

'I can't do it any other way.'

'We are about to break ties with the white friend who has sheltered us our whole lives.'

'Or about to spill the beans to Sara.'

'You'd regret it: I'd throw you both off the balcony.'

'The brave warrior doesn't fear the threats from the pale-face liar and coward. Besides, you don't have the courage to do it.'

'I'm with you,' were Carson's two cents. 'Sick people don't think things through. They're trapped by their vice.'

'I swear that the Nietzsche manuscript will be my last acquisition.'

'I'll believe that when I see it.' Carson.

'I wonder why you hide it from your squaw,' Black Eagle. 'You buy it with your gold. I don't see any Jew pillaged by the cruel white man with the sticks that spit fire, and it's not stolen.'

'Some of them are, friend,' corrected Carson.

'But the paleface squaw doesn't need to know that.'

I left them discussing strategy, unable to tell them that I lacked the courage to go to Sara and tell her that this compulsion was stronger than I was. I want to possess the things that catch my eye. I want them and I would kill to have them.

'Sic?' – Carson.

'No. But nearly.' To Sara, 'I think I'm feeling poorly.'

'Get in bed, poor Adrià, I'll check your temperature' (compassionevole e innocente).

I spent two days with an intense fever at the end of which I came to some sort of a pact with myself (a pact that Carson and Black Eagle refused to sign) allowing me, for the good of our relationship, to keep quiet the details of Vial's specific history, which I only knew fragments of; and to not mention which objects in the house I suspected were the fruits of Father's cruel predation. Or the fact that with the shop I sold and, therefore, cashed in on many of Father's sins … something which I suppose you already imagined. I didn't have the courage to tell you that I lied to you that day you came from Paris with a yellow flower in your hand and said you'd love a cup of coffee.

## 37

'The style reminds me of Hemingway,' declared Mireia Gràcia.

Bernat lowered his head, humbly comforted by the comment. Momentarily, he stopped thinking that he had only managed to gather three people at Pols de Llibres.

'I don't recommend you do a presentation,' Bauçà had told him.

'Why?'

'There are too many events going on at the same time: no one will come to ours.'

'That's what you think. Or do you hold some of your authors in higher esteem than others?'

Bauçà decided not to respond the way he would have liked, instead saying, with a weary expression he was unable to conceal: 'Fine: you tell me what day is good for you and who you want to present it.' And to Bernat's smile: 'But if no one comes, don't blame me.'

On the invitation it read Heribert Bauçà and the author are pleased to invite you to the presentation of *Plasma*, Bernat Plensa's latest book of stories, at the Pols de Llibres bookshop. In addition to the author and the editor, Professor Mireia Gràcia will speak about the book. Afterwards, cava will be served.

Adrià put the invitation down on the table and for a few moments he imagined what Mireia Gràcia could say about that book. That it was subpar? That Plensa still hadn't learnt how to communicate emotions? That it was a waste of paper and trees?

'I won't get upset this time,' said Bernat when he suggested that Adrià present his book.

'And how can I believe that?'

'Because you're going to like it. And if you don't, well, I've grown: soon I'll be forty and I'm beginning to understand that I shouldn't get angry with you over these things. All right? Will you present the book for me? It's next month at Pols de Llibres. It's a landmark bookshop and …'

'Bernat. No.'

'Come on, at least read it first, yeah?' Offended, shocked, entranced.

'I'm very busy. Of course I will read it, but I can't tell you when. Don't do this to me.'

Bernat stood there with his mouth open, unable to understand what Adrià had told him, and then I said all right, come on, I'll read it now. And if I don't like it, I'll let you know and, obviously, I won't present it for you.

'Now that's a friend. Thank you. You're going to like it.' He pointed with his finger extended, as if he were Dirty Harry: 'And you're going to want to present it.'

Bernat was convinced that this time he would, that this time he would say Bernat, you've surprised me: I see the strength of Hemingway, the talent of Borges, the art of Rulfo and the irony of Calders, and Bernat was the happiest person in the world until three days later when I called him and I told him same as ever, I don't believe the characters and I couldn't care less about what happens to them.

'Excuse me?'

'Literature isn't a game. Or if it is just a game, it doesn't interest me. Do you understand?'

'What about the last story?'

'That's the best one. But in the land of the blind …'

'You're cruel. You like to devastate me.'

'You told me you were forty now and you weren't going to get angry if …'

'I'm not forty yet! And you have a really unpleasant way of saying you don't like something, that …'

'I only have my way.'

'Can't you just say I don't like it and leave it at that?'

'I used to do that. You don't remember now but when I would say I just don't like it, then you would say: that's it? And then I'd have to justify why I don't like it, trying to be honest with you because I don't want to lose you as a friend and then I tell you that you have no talent for creating characters: they are mere names. They all speak the same; none of them have any desire to capture my interest. Not a single one of these characters is necessary.'

'What the bloody hell do you mean by that? Without Biel, there's no story, in "Rats".'

'You are being stubborn. That whole story is unnecessary. It didn't transform me, it didn't enrich me, it didn't do anything for me!'

And now stupid Mireia was saying that Plensa had the strength of Hemingway and, before she could start comparing him to Borges and Calders, Adrià hid behind a display case. He didn't want Bernat to see him there, in that cold bookshop, with seventeen empty folding chairs and three occupied ones, although one man looked like he was there by mistake.

You are a coward, he thought. And he also thought that, just like he enjoyed always looking at the world and ideas through their history, if he studied the history of his friendship with Bernat, he would inevitably reach this impossible point: Bernat would be happy if he focused his capacity for happiness on the violin. He fled the bookshop without a sound and walked around the block thinking about what to do. How come not even Tecla was there? Or his son?

'Why in hell aren't you coming? It's my book!'

Tecla finished her bowl of milk and waited for Llorenç to go to his room to look for his school rucksack. In a softer voice, she said: 'If I had to go to every one of your concerts and every one of your presentations …'

'It's not as though I do one every week. It's been six years since the last one.'

Silence.

'You don't want to support my career.'

'I want to put things in their place.'

'You don't want to come.'

'I can't.'

'You don't love me.'

'You aren't the centre of the universe.'

'I know that.'

'You don't know that. You don't realise. You are always asking for things, demanding things.'

'I don't understand where this is coming from.'

'You always think that everyone is at your service. That you are the important one in this house.'

'Well …'

She looked at him defiantly. He was about to say of course I am the most important person in the family; but a sixth or seventh sense helped him catch it in time. He was left with his mouth hanging open.

'No, go ahead, say it,' prodded Tecla.

Bernat closed his mouth. Looking him in the eye, she said we have our life too: you take for granted that we can always go where you say and that we always have to read what you write and like it; no, and be excited about it.'

'You're exaggerating.'

'Why did you ask Llorenç to read it in ten days?'

'Is it wrong to ask my son to read a book?'

'He's nine years old, for the love of God.'

'So?'

'Do you know what he told me, last night?'

The boy was in bed, and he turned on the light on his bedside table just as his mother was tiptoeing out of the room.

'Mama.'

'Aren't you sleeping?'

'No.'

'What's wrong?'

Tecla sat by his bed. Llorenç opened the drawer on the bedside table and pulled out a book. She recognised it.

'I started reading it but I don't understand a thing.'

'It's not for children. Why are you reading it?'

'Dad told me that I had to finish it before Sunday. That it's a short book.'

She grabbed the book.

'Ignore him.'

She opened it up and flipped through it absentmindedly.

'He'll ask me questions.'

She gave him back the book: 'Hold onto it. But you don't
have to read it.'

'Are you sure?'

'I'm sure.'

'And what if he asks me questions?'

'I'll tell him not to ask you any.'

'Why can't I ask my son questions!' Bernat, indignant,
hitting his cup against the saucer. 'Aren't I his father?'

'Your ego knows no bounds.'

Llorenç poked his head into the kitchen, with his anorak
on and his rucksack on his back.

'Daddy's coming. You can start down, Son.'

Bernat got up, threw his napkin onto the table and left the
kitchen.

Adrià was now back in front of the bookshop after walking
around the block. And he still didn't know what to do. Just
then they turned off one of the lights in the display window.
He reacted in time, moving a few metres away. Mireia Gràcia
came flying out and even though she went right past him,
she didn't notice him because she was looking at her watch.
When Bauçà, Bernat and two or three other people came out,
he came walking over quickly, as if he were running very late.

'Hey! … Don't tell me it's over!' Adrià's face and tone were
disappointed.

'Hello, Ardèvol.'

Adrià waved at Bauçà. The other people headed off in their
various directions. Then Bauçà said that he was leaving.

'You don't want to go out to eat with us?' Bernat.

Bauçà said no, you go ahead, that he was running late for
dinner, and he'd left his two friends alone.

'Well? How did it go?'

'Well. Quite well. Mireia Gràcia was very persuasive. Very
… good, yeah. And there was a good crowd. Good. Right?'

'I'm glad to hear it. I would have liked to be there but …'

'Don't worry, laddie … They even asked me questions.'

'Where's Tecla?'

They started walking amid a silence that spoke volumes. When they reached the corner, Bernat stopped short and looked Adrià in the eye: 'I have the feeling that it's my writing against the world: against you, against Tecla, against my son, against my editor.'

'Where'd you get that come from?'

'No one gives a shit about what I write.'

'Bloody hell, but you just told me that …'

'And now I'm telling you that no one gives a shit about what I write.'

'Do you give a shit?'

Bernat looked at him warily. Was he pulling his leg? 'It's my whole life.'

'I don't believe you. You put up too many filters.'

'Some day I hope to understand you.'

'If you wrote the way you play the violin, you would be great.'

'Isn't that a stupid thing to say? I'm bored by the violin.'

'You don't want to be happy.'

'It's not necessary, according to what you once told me.'

'Fine. But if I knew how to play like you … I would do …'

'Nothing, bullshit, you'd do.'

'What's wrong? Did you have another fight with Tecla?'

'She didn't want to come.'

That was more delicate. What do I say now?

'Do you want to come over?'

'Why don't we go out to eat?'

'It's just that …'

'Sara's expecting you.'

'Well, I told her that … Yes, she's expecting me.'

This is the story of Bernat Plensa: we have been friends for many years. For many years he's envied me because he doesn't really know me; for many years I've admired him for how he plays the violin. And every once in a while we have monumental fights as if we were desperate lovers. I love him and I can't stop telling him that he is a clumsy, bad writer. And since he started giving me his work to read, he has published various very bad collections of stories. Despite his intellectual ability, he can't accept that no one likes them, perhaps not because everyone is always completely wrong but because what he writes is completely uninteresting. Completely. It's always the same between us. And his wife … I don't know for sure, but I imagine that living with Bernat must be difficult. He is assistant concertmaster in the Barcelona Symphony Orchestra. And he plays chamber music with a group of his colleagues. What more does he want? most of us mortals would ask. But not him. Surely, like all mortals, he can't see the happiness around him because he is blinded by what's out of his reach. Bernat is too human. And today I couldn't go out for dinner with him because Sara is sad.

Bernat Plensa i Punsoda, a very fine musician who insists in seeking out his own unhappiness in literature. There is no vaccine for that. And Alí Bahr watched the group of children who played in the shade, in the shelter of the wall that separated White Donkey's garden from the road that led from al-Hisw to distant Bi'r Durb. Alí Bahr had just turned twenty and didn't know that one of the girls, the one that was shrieking as a snot-nosed kid with grazed knees chased her, was Amani, who in a few years would be known throughout the plain as Amani the lovely. He whipped the donkey because in a couple of hours he had to be home. To save his energy, he picked up a rock from the middle of the path, not too big and not too small, and threw it forward, hard and furiously, as if to indicate the route to the donkey.

The life of *Plasma* by Bernat Plensa can be summed up as: no repercussion, not a single review, not a single sale. Luckily, neither Bauçà, nor Adrià nor Tecla said see, I told you so. And Sara, when I explained it to her, said you are a coward: you should have been there, in the audience. And I: it was humiliating. And she: no, he would have felt comforted by the presence of a friend. And life went on: 'They're conspiring against me. They want me to disappear; they want me to cease to exist.'

'Who?'

'Them.'

'One day you'll have to introduce me.'

'I'm not kidding.'

'Bernat, no one is ganging up on you.'

'Yeah, because they don't even know I exist.'

'Tell that to the people applauding at the end of your concerts.'

'It's not the same thing and we've discussed this a thousand times.'

Sara listened to them in silence. Suddenly, Bernat looked at her and, in an ever so slightly accusatory tone, asked her what did you think of the book?, which is the question, the only question I think an author cannot ask with impunity because he runs the risk that someone will answer it.

Sara smiled politely and Bernat lifted his eyebrows to make clear that the question was still hanging in the air imprudently.

'I haven't read it,' replied Sara, holding his gaze. And, making a concession that surprised me, added: 'Yet.'

Bernat was left with his mouth agape. You will never learn, Bernat, thought Adrià. And that day he understood that Bernat was hopeless and would trip on the same rock as many times as necessary over the course of his entire life. Meanwhile, Bernat, without realising what he was doing, drank half a glass of a marvellous Ribera del Duero.

'I swear I'm going to give up writing,' he proclaimed, putting the glass to one side, and I am convinced he said it with the hopes of making Sara feel guilty of neglect.

'Focus on your music,' you said with that smile that still captivates me. 'You'll be better off.'

And you took a swig from the long spout of the wine flagon. Drinking Ribera del Duero from a flagon. Bernat watched you, mouth agape, but said nothing. He was too depressed. Surely the only reason he didn't start crying was because Adrià was there. One can cry more easily in front of a woman, even if she is drinking good wine from a flagon. In front of a man, it's not as appealing. But that evening he had his first big fight with Tecla: Llorenç, with his eyes wide, from the bed, was witness to his father's outbursts and felt like the unhappiest boy in the world.

'I'm not asking for that much, bloody hell!' reflected Bernat. 'Just that you deign to read me. That's all I'm asking for.' Raising his voice, too much: 'Is that too much to ask? Is it? Is it?'

Then came the attack from behind. Llorenç, furious, bare-foot, in pyjamas, came into the dining room and leapt on his father just as he was saying I don't feel that you are with me on my artistic journey. Tecla was looking at the wall as if she were watching her own piano career that had slipped through her fingers because of the pregnancy while she felt totally of-fended, you understand? Totally and deeply offended, as if the only thing we have to do in life is adore you. And then the attack from behind: Llorenç let his fists fly on his father, turning Bernat's back into a veritable punching bag.

'Bloody hell. Cut it out!'

'Don't scold my mother.'

'Go to bed,' ordered Tecla, with a head gesture that, ac-cording to her, was supportive. 'I'll be there in a minute.'

Llorenç let loose a couple more punches. Bernat opened his eyes and thought everyone is against me; no one wants me to write.

'Don't mix things up,' said Adrià when he told him about it as they headed down Llúria, Bernat to rehearsal with his violin, and he to a History of Ideas II class.

'What am I mixing up! Not even my son will let me complain!'

Sara, my beloved: I am talking about many years ago, the period in which you filled my life. We have all grown older and you have left me alone for a second time. If you could hear me, I'm sure you would shake your head, worried to hear that Bernat is still the same, writing things of no interest to anyone. Sometimes it makes me cross that a musician with the ability to evoke that sound from his instrument and to create dense atmospheres is unable, not to write genius prose, but to realise that the characters and stories he writes don't interest us at all. In short, for us, what Bernat writes also had no repercussion, not a single review, not a single sale. And that's enough talk about Bernat, I'll end up embittered and I have other headaches to deal with before my time comes.

Around that same time … I think I said it not long ago. What importance does exact chronology have after all the chaos I've shown up to this point? Anyway, Little Lola started to grumble about every little thing and to complain that the Indian ink, the charcoal and the colours that Saga used were soiling everything.

'Her name is Sara.'

'She says Saga.'

'Well, her name is Sara. Besides, the charcoal and all the rest are in her studio.'

'Trust me. The other day she was copying the painting in the dining room, not that I can understand the point of painting things without any colour. And of course, leaving the rags for me to try and get clean again.'

'Little Lola.'

'Caterina. And the bathroom towels. Since her hands are always black … It must be some Frog custom.'

'Caterina.'

'What.'

'You have to let artists do their thing, that's all.'

'You give them an inch,' she said, making a gesture with her fingers; but I interrupted her before she got to the mile.

'Sara is the lady of the house and she is in charge.'

I know that I offended her with that declaration. But I let her and her indignation leave the study in silence, leaving me alone with those intuitions that would one day begin to shed some light on the grievance that would eventually become *La voluntat estètica*, the essay I am most pleased with having written.

'Did you draw the Urgell in the dining room?'

'Yes.'

'Can I see it?'

'I haven't …'

'Let me see it.'

You hesitated but finally gave in. I can still see you, a bit nervous, opening that huge folder where you kept your hesitations, which you carried around with you everywhere. You

put the drawing on the table. The sun wasn't hiding behind
Trespui, but the three-story gable on the bell tower of Santa
Maria de Gerri seemed to come alive with just the strokes of
Sara's charcoal. You were able to sense the wrinkles of age and
the years with all their scars. You draw so well, my beloved,
that there were centuries of history in the white, black and
thousands of greys smudged by your fingertips. The landscape and the church, and the beginning of the bank of the
Noguera. It was all so enchanting that I didn't miss the dark,
sad, magical colours Modest Urgell had used.

'Do you like it?'

'A *lot*.'

'A lott?'

'A loottt.'

'It's yours,' she said in satisfaction.

'Really?'

'You spend so many hours looking at the Urgell ...'

'Me? Really?'

'Don't you?'

'I don't know ... I hadn't even realised.'

'This is a homage to your hours of observation. What are
you searching for in it?'

'I don't really know. I do it instinctively. I like to.'

'I didn't ask what you found there, I asked you what you're
searching for.'

'I think about the monastery of Santa Maria de Gerri. But
mostly I think about the little monastery of Sant Pere del
Burgal, which is nearby and I've never visited. Do you remember that parchment by Abbot Deligat that I showed you?
It was the founding charter of the monastery in Burgal, from
so many years ago that I feel the thrill of history when I touch
the parchment. And I think about the monks pacing through
it over the centuries. And praying to a God who doesn't exist
for centuries. And the salt mines of Gerri. And the mysteries enshrined way up at Burgal. And the peasants dying of
hunger and illness, and the days passing slowly but implac-
ably, and the months and the years, and it thrills me.'

'I've never heard you string that many words together.'

'I love you.'

'What else are you searching for in it?'

'I don't know; I really don't know what I look for in it. It's hard to put into words.'

'Well, then what do you find in it?'

'Strange stories. Strange people. The desire to live and see things.'

'Why don't we go see it in the flesh?'

We went to Gerri de la Sal in the Six Hundred, which threw in the towel at the port of Comiols. A very chatty mechanic from Isona changed some part of the cylinder head, can't remember which, and insinuated that we should get a new car soon to avoid problems. We lost a day with those mundane misfortunes and we reached Gerri at night. The next day, from the inn, I saw the painting by Urgell in the flesh and I almost choked with emotion. And we spent the day looking at it, taking photographs of it, drawing it and watching the ghosts go in and out, ghosts of monks, peasants and salt miners until I sensed the two spirits of the monks who went to Sant Pere del Burgal to collect the key to close up that isolated, small monastery after hundreds of years of uninterrupted monastic life.

And the next day the convalescent Six Hundred took us twenty kilometres further north, to Escaló, and from there, on foot, along a goat path that climbed the sunny Barraonse slope, the only passable route to reach the ruins of Sant Pere del Burgal, the monastery of my dreams. Sara didn't let me carry the large rucksack with her notebook and pencils and charcoals inside: it was her burden.

A bit further on, I picked up a stone from the middle of the path, not too big and not too small, and Adrià contemplated it pensively and the image of Amani the lovely and her sad story came into his head.

'What is it about that rock?'

'Nothing, nothing,' said Adrià, putting it into his rucksack.

'You know what impression I get from you?' you said, breathing a bit heavily from the climb.

'Huh?'

'That's just it. You don't say what impression, you say huh.'

'Now you've lost me.' Adrià, who was leading, stopped, looked at the green valley, listened to the Noguera's distant murmur and turned towards Sara. She also stopped, a smile on her face.

'You are always thinking.'

'Yes.'

'But you are always thinking about something far from here. You are always somewhere else.'

'Boy ... I'm sorry.'

'No. That's how you are. I'm special too.'

Adrià went over to her and kissed her on the forehead, with such tenderness, Sara, that I still get emotional when I remember it. You don't know how much I love you and how much you have transformed me. You are a masterpiece and I hope you understand what I mean.

'You, special?'

'I'm a weird woman. Full of complexes and secrets.'

'Complexes ... you hide them well. Secrets ... that one's easy to fix: tell them to me.'

Now Sara looked down the path to avoid meeting his eyes.

'I'm a complicated woman.'

'You don't have to tell me anything you don't want to.'

Adrià started to continue heading up, but he stopped and turned: 'I'd just like you to tell me one thing.'

'What's that?'

I know it's hard to believe, but I asked her what did my mother and your mother tell you about me. What did they tell you that you believed.

Your radiant face grew dark and I thought shit, now I've put my foot in it. You waited a few seconds and, with your voice a bit hoarse, you said I begged you not to ask me that. I begged you ...

Annoyed, you picked up a stone and threw it down the slope.

'I don't want to relive those words. I don't want you to know them; I want to spare you them because you have every

right to be ignorant of them. And I have every right to forget
them.' You adjusted your rucksack with an elegant gesture.
'It's Bluebeard's locked room, remember.'

Sara said it so rotundly that I had the impression that she'd
never stopped thinking about it. We had been living together
for some time and I always had the question on the tip of my
tongue: always.

'All right,' said Adrià. 'I won't ever ask you again.'

They began their descent again. There was still a steeper
stretch before I finally reached, at the age of thirty-nine, the
ruins of Sant Pere del Burgal that I had dreamed of so often,
and Brother Julià de Sau, who as a Dominican had been called
Friar Miquel, came out to receive us with the key in his hands.
With the Sacred Chest in his hands. With death in his hands.

'Brothers, may the peace of the Lord be with you,' he told
us.

'And may the peace of the Lord also be with you,' I replied.

'What did you say?' asked Sara, surprised.

# V

## VITA CONDITA

**WRITTEN IN PENCIL IN THE SEALED RAILWAY-CAR**

here in this carload
i am eve
with abel my son
if you see my other son
cain son of man
tell him that i*

Dan Pagis

---

* Dan Pagis, *Variable Directions,* trans. Stephen Mitchell (San Francisco: North Point Press, 1989).

## 38

'Once you've had a taste of artistic beauty, your life changes. Once you've heard the Monteverdi choir sing, your life changes. Once you've seen a Vermeer up close, your life changes; once you've read Proust, you are never the same again. What I don't know is why.'

'Write it.'

'We are random chance.'

'What?'

'It would be easier for us to never have been and yet we are.'

'...'

'Generation after generation of frenetic dances of millions of spermatozoa chasing eggs, random conceptions, deaths, annihilations ... and now you and I are here, one in front of the other as if it couldn't have been any other way. As if there were only the possibility of a single family tree.'

'Well. It's logical, isn't it?'

'No. It's ffucking random.'

'Come on ...'

'And what's more, the fact that you can play the violin so well, that's even more ffucking random.'

'Fine. But ...' Silence. 'What you're saying is a bit dizzying, don't you think?'

'Yes. And then we try to survive the chaos with art's order.'

'You should write about this, don't you think?' ventured Bernat, taking a sip of tea.

'Does the power of art reside in the artwork or rather in the effect it has on someone? What do you think?'

'That you should write about this,' insisted Sara after a few days. 'That way you'll understand it better.'

'Why am I paralysed by Homer? Why does Brahms's clarinet quintet leave me short of breath?'

'Write about it,' said Bernat immediately. 'And you'll be doing me a favour, because I want to know as well.'

'How is it that I am unable to kneel before anyone and yet when I hear Beethoven's *Pastoral* I have no problem bowing down to it?'

'The *Pastoral* is trite.'

'Not on your life. Do you know where Beethoven came from? From Haydn's one hundred and four symphonies.'

'And Mozart's forty-one.'

'That's true. But Beethoven was only able to do nine. Because almost every one of the nine exists on a different level of moral complexity.'

'Moral?'

'Moral.'

'Write about it.'

'We can't understand an artwork if we don't look at its evolution.' He brushed his teeth and rinsed out his mouth. As he dried himself off with a towel, he shouted through the open bathroom door: 'But the artist's touch of genius is always needed, that's precisely what makes it evolve.'

'The power resides in the person, then,' Sara replied, from bed, without stifling a yawn.

'I don't know. Van der Weyden, Monet, Picasso, Barceló. It's a dynamic line that starts in the caves of the Valltorta gorge and has yet to end because humanity still exists.'

'Write about it.' It look Bernat a few days to finish his tea and then he put the cup down delicately on the saucer. 'Don't you think you should?'

'Is it beauty?'

'What?'

'Is it beauty's fault? What does beauty mean?'

'I don't know. But I recognise it when I see it. Why don't you write about it?' repeated Bernat, looking him in the eye.

'Man destroys man, and he also composes *Paradise Lost*.'

'It's a mystery, you're right. You should write about it.'

'The music of Franz Schubert transports me to a better future. Schubert is able to say many things with very few elements. He has an inexhaustible melodic strength, filled with elegance and charm as well as energy and truth. Schubert is artistic truth and we have to cling to it to save ourselves. It amazes me that he was a sickly, syphilitic, skint man. Where does his power come from? What is this power he wields over us? I bow down before Schubert's art.'

'Bravo, Herr Obersturmführer. I suspected that you were a sensitive soul.'

Doctor Budden took a drag on his cigarette and exhaled a thin column of smoke as he went over the beginning of opus 100 in his head and then sang it with incredible precision.

'I wish I had your ear, Herr Obersturmführer.'

'It's not much of an achievement. I studied piano.'

'I envy you.'

'You shouldn't. Between all the hours devoted to studying medicine and music, I feel like I missed out on many things in life.'

'Now you'll make them up, wholesale, if you'll allow me the expression,' said Oberlagerführer Höss waving his open arms. 'And you're in the prime of your life.'

'Yes, of course. Perhaps too suddenly.'

Silence from both men, as if they were keeping tabs on each other. Until the doctor made up his mind and, stubbing out his cigarette in the ashtray and leaning over the desk, said in a lower voice: 'Why did you want to see me, Obersturmbannführer?'

Then Oberlagerführer Höss, in the same low tone, as if he distrusted the walls of his own house, said I wanted to talk to you about your superior.

'Voigt?'

'Uh-huh.'

Silence. They must have been calculating risks. Höss ventured a what do you think of him, between us.

'Well, I …'

'I require … I demand sincerity. That is an order, dear Obersturmführer.'

'Well, between us … he's a blockhead.'

Hearing that, Rudolf Höss leaned back smugly in his chair. Staring into his eyes, he told Doctor Budden that he was laying the groundwork for Voigt the blockhead to be sent to some front.

'And who would run the ...'

'You, naturally.'

Wait a second. That's ... And why not me?

Everything had been said. A new alliance without intermediaries between God and his people. The Schubert trio still played beneath the conversation. To break the awkwardness, Doctor Budden said did you know that Schubert composed this marvellous piece just months before he died?

'Write about it. Really, Adrià.'

But it was all left momentarily up in the air because Laura returned from Uppsala and life at the university and particularly in the department office became somewhat uncomfortable again. She came back with a happier gaze, he said are you well? And Laura smiled and headed to classroom fifteen without answering. Adrià took that as a yes, that she was well. And pretty: she had come back prettier. Sitting at the sublet desk – that semester, from Parera – Adrià had trouble getting back to those papers that dealt with the subject of beauty. He didn't know why, but they distracted him and they'd made him late for class for the first time in his life. Laura's beauty, Sara's beauty, Tecla's beauty ... did they enter into these ruminations? Hmm, did they?

'I'd say yes,' Bernat answered cautiously. 'A woman's beauty is an irrefutable fact. Isn't it?'

'Vivancos would say that's a sexist approach.'

'I don't know about that.' Confused silence from Bernat. 'Before it was a petit-bourgeois idea and now it's sexist reasoning.' In a softer voice so no judge would hear him: 'But I like women. They are beautiful: that I know for sure.'

'Yeah. But I don't know if I should talk about it.'

'By the way, who is that good-looking Laura you mentioned?'

'Huh?'

'The Laura that you cite.'

'No, I was thinking of Petrarch.'

'And that's going to be a book?' asked Bernat, pointing to

the papers resting atop the manuscript table, as if they needed careful examination under Father's loupe.

'I don't know. At this point it's thirty pages and I'm enjoying feeling my way around in the dark.'

'How is Sara?'

'Well. She calms me.'

'I'm asking how she is: not how she affects you.'

'She's very busy. Actes Sud commissioned her to illustrate a series of ten books.'

'But how is she?'

'Fine. Why?'

'Sometimes she looks sad.'

'There are some things that can't be solved even with a bit of love.'

Ten or twelve days later the inevitable happened. I was talking to Parera and suddenly she said, listen, what is your wife's name? And just then Laura came into the office, loaded down with dossiers and ideas, and she heard perfectly as Parera said listen, what is your wife's name? And I lowered my eyes in resignation and said Sara, her name is Sara. Laura put the things down on her chaotic desk and sat down.

'She's pretty,' continued Parera, as if twisting the knife into my heart. Or perhaps into Laura's.

'Uh-huh.'

'And have you been married long?'

'No. In fact, we're not ...'

'Yeah, I mean living together.'

'No, not long.'

The interrogation ended there, not because the KGB inspector ran out of questions, but because she had to go to class. Eulaleyvna Parerova left the office, before closing the door, said take good care of her, these days things are ...

And she closed it gently, not feeling the need to specify exactly how things are. And then Laura stood up, put a hand at one end of the dossiers, papers, books, notes and journals on her always cramped desk and slid everything onto the floor, in the middle of the office. A tremendous clamour. Adrià looked at her, contrite. She sat down without glancing at him. Then the office telephone rang. Laura didn't pick it up, and, I swear, there is nothing that makes me more nervous than a telephone ringing with no one picking it up. I went over to my desk and answered it.

'Hello. Yes, one moment. It's for you, Laura.'

I stood there with the receiver in my hand; she staring out into the void without any intention of picking up the one on her desk. I brought it back to my ear.

'She's stepped out.'

Then Laura picked up the phone and said, yes, yes, go ahead. I hung up and she said hey, pretty lady, what are you up to! And she laughed with a crystal-clear laugh. I grabbed my papers on art and aesthetics that still had no title and I fled.

'I'll have to think about it,' said Doctor Budden, as he stood up and straightened his impeccable Obersturmführer uniform, 'because tomorrow there are new units arriving.' He looked at Oberlagerführer Höss and smiled and, knowing that he wouldn't understand him, said, 'Art is inexplicable.' He pointed to his host: 'At best, we can say that it is a display of love from the artist to humanity. Don't you think?'

He left the Oberlagerführer's house, knowing that he was still slowly digesting his words. From outside he heard, faintly, swaddled in the cold, the finale of the Trio opus 100 by angelic Schubert. Without that music, life would be terrible, he should have told his host.

Things began to sour for me when I had practically finished writing *La voluntat estètica*. The galleys, the translation to German that spurred me on to make additions to the original, Kamenek's comments on my translation, which also inspired me to add nuance and rewrite, all of it left me considerably agitated. I was afraid that the book I was publishing would satisfy me. I've told you many times, Sara: it is the book of mine that I like best. And following the imperatives of my discontented soul, which has caused you such suffering, in those days when Sara brought serenity into my life and Laura pretended she didn't even know me, Adrià Ardèvol's obsession was devoting hours to his Storioni, as good a way as any to hide his anxiety. He revisited the most difficult moments with Trullols and the most unpleasant with Master Manlleu. And a few months later he invited Bernat to do the sonatas of Jean-Marie Leclair's opus 3 and opus 4.

'Why Leclair?'

'I don't know. I like him. And I've studied him.'

'He's not as easy as he seems.'

'But do you want to give it a try, or not?'

During a couple of months, on Friday afternoons, the house filled with the music of the two friends' violins. And during the week, Adrià, after writing, would study repertoire. As he did thirty years earlier.

'Thirty?'

'Or twenty. But there's no way I can catch up to you now.'

'I should hope not. It's all I've been doing.'

'I envy you.'

'Don't mock me.'

'I envy you. I wish I could play the way you do.'

Deep down, Adrià wanted distance from *La voluntat estètica*. He wanted to return to the works of art that had provoked the book's reflections.

'Yes, but why Leclair? Why not Shostakovich?'

'That's beyond me. Why do you think I envy you?'

And both violins, now a Storioni and a Thouvenel, began to fill the house with longing, as if life could start anew, as if wanting to give them a fresh start. Mine would be having parents that were more parents, more different, more … And … I don't know exactly. And you? Eh?

'What?' Bernat, with his bow too taut and trying to look the other way.

'Are you happy?'

Bernat began sonata number 2 and I found myself forced to follow along. But when we finished (with three heinous errors on my part and only one rebuke from Bernat), I resumed my attack:

'Hey.'

'What.'

'Are you happy?'

'No. Are you?'

'Nope.'

I played the second sonata, number 1, even worse. But we were able to reach the end without interruption.

'How are things going with Tecla?'

'Fine. And with Sara?'

'Fine.'

Silence. After a long while:

'Well … Tecla … I don't know, but she's always getting mad at me.'

'Because you live in another world.'

'Look who's talking.'

'Yeah, but I'm not married to Tecla.'

Then we tried some études-caprices by Wieniawski from his opus 18. Poor Bernat, as first violin, ended up drenched in sweat, and I felt pleased despite the three curt rebukes he gave me, as if he were me criticising his writing in Tübingen. And I envied him, a lot. And I couldn't help but tell him that I would trade my writing for his musical ability.

'And I accept the swap. I'm thrilled to accept it, eh?'

The most worrisome part of it was that we didn't burst into laughter. We just looked at the clock because it was getting late.

The night was short as the doctor had predicted because the first units of material began arriving at seven in the morning, when it was still dark.

'This one,' said Budden to Oberscharführer Barabbas. 'And those two.' And he went back to the laboratory because he'd been given an exorbitant amount of work. Also for a darker reason, because deep down it angered him to see that line of women and children advancing in an orderly fashion, like sheep, without a shred of dignity that would lead them to revolt.

'No, leave her be!' said an older woman with a package in her arms, a violin case of some sort, as if it were an infant.

Doctor Budden washed his hands of the argument. As he headed off, he saw Doctor Voigt emerge from the officer's canteen and head over to the scuffle. Konrad Budden didn't even bother to conceal his disdainful look towards his superior officer, who was always attracted to conflict. He went into his office, still calm. He had time to hear the crack of a Luger firing.

'Where are you from?' he said in a harsh voice without looking up from the papers. Finally he had to lift his eyes because the mute little girl just stared at him in confusion. She was wringing a dirty napkin in her hands and Doctor Budden was starting to get nervous. He raised his voice, 'Would you mind keeping still?'

The girl stopped, but her perplexed expression remained. The doctor sighed, took in a breath and gathered his patience. Just then the telephone on his desk rang.

'Yes? / Yes, Heil Hitler. / Who?' Confused. / 'Put her on. (...)' 'Heil Hitler. Hallo.' Impatient. 'Ja, bitte? / What's going on?' Annoyed. / 'Who is this Lothar?' Peeved. / 'Ah!' Scandalised. 'Abject Franz's father? / And what do you want? / Who arrested him? / But why? / Girl ... Here I really ... / I'm very busy right now. You want to expose us all? / He must have done something. / Look, Herta: someone's got to pay the piper.'

And he looked the girl with the dirty napkin up and down:
'Holländisch?' he asked her. And into the telephone: 'I don't know about you, but I'm working. I have too much work to waste time on such nonsense. Heil Hitler!'

And he hung up. He stared at the girl, waiting for a reply.

The girl nodded. As if holländisch was the first word she had understood. Doctor Budden, in a softer voice, so no one would see that he wasn't using German, asked her in his cousins' Dutch what town she was from and she answered Antwerp. She wanted to say that she was Flemish, that she lived on Arenberg Street, and where was her father, that he'd been taken away. But she stood there with her mouth hanging open, observing that man who was now smiling at her.

'You just have to do what I tell you to.'

'It hurts me here.' And she pointed to the back of her neck.

'That's nothing. Now, listen to me.'

She looked at him, curious. The doctor insisted, 'You have to do what I say. You understand?'

The girl shook her head.

'Then I'll have to rip off your nose. Did you understand me now?'

And he looked patiently at the horrified girl, who frantically nodded her head.

'How old are you?'

'Seven and a half,' she replied, exaggerating to make herself seem older.

'Name?'

'Amelia Alpaerts. Twenty-two Arenberg Street, third apartment.'

'Fine, fine.'

'Antwerp.'

'I said that's fine!' Irritated. 'And stop messing with that damned handkerchief if you don't want me to take it away from you.'

The girl lowered her gaze and instinctively put her hands behind her back, hiding the blue-and-white chequered napkin, perhaps to protect it. She couldn't hold back a tear.

'Mama,' she implored, also in a soft voice.

Doctor Budden snapped his fingers and one of the twins who were holding up the back wall came forward and grabbed the girl brusquely.

'Get her prepped,' said the doctor.

'Mama!' shouted the girl.

'Next!' answered the doctor without looking up from the file he had on the desk.

'Holländisch?' heard the girl with the blue-and-white chequered napkin as they made her enter a room that smelled very strongly of medicine and I didn't know what to do: I didn't give any justification or explanation, because Laura didn't demand one of me. She could have calmly said you are a fucking liar because you told me that there was no other woman; she could have said why didn't you just tell me; she could have said you're a coward; she could have said you never stopped using me; she could have said many things. But no:

life went on like always in the office. For a few months I barely went in there. A couple of times we passed each other in the cloister or we saw each other in the bar. I had become a transparent person. It was hard to get used to. And forgive me, Sara, for not having told you any of this before.

Doctor Konrad Budden, after a very intense month, took off his glasses and rubbed his eyes. He was exhausted. When he heard a heel stomp in front of his desk he lifted his head. Oberscharführer Barabbas stood firm, rigid, always ready, awaiting orders. With a weary gesture, the doctor pointed to the stuffed file with the name of Doctor Aribert Voigt clearly visible, and the other man picked it up. When the subordinate stamped his heels hard, the doctor shook, as if he had stomped on his head. Barabbas left the office with the detailed report explaining that, unfortunately, the patellar tendon regeneration experiment, which consisted in exposing the tendon, slicing it, applying Doctor Bauer's salve and observing whether it would regenerate without the aid of any suture, hadn't succeeded as they had foreseen, neither in adults nor in children. They had expected it wouldn't be effective on the elderly, but they'd hoped that in the case of growing organisms the regeneration following the application of the Bauer salve could be spectacular. That failure put an end to the possibility of triumphantly offering this miraculous medication to humanity. What a shame, because if it had worked, the benefits for Bauer, Voigt and him would have been, not only triumphant, but unimaginable.

It had never been so hard for him to finalise an experiment before. After months of seeing moaning little guinea pigs – like the boy with that dark skin, or the albino who said Tève, Tève, Tève, cornered in his bed, refusing to get out of it until they finally had to finish him off right there, or that bloody girl with the dirty rag that was unable to stand up without crutches and, when they didn't sedate her, bellowed with pain to fuck with all the staff as if they didn't have enough with the responsibility of some of the experiments and brutal pressure of their blockhead superior, who it seems had friends in high places because not even Höss himself was able to get him sent off to some front so he would stop being such a nuisance – had to accept that it was useless to expect a more positive response on the cartilage treated with the Bauer salve. Twenty-six guinea pigs, boys and girls, and no restored tissue, revealed the conclusions he very reluctantly gave Professor Bauer. And one fine day Doctor Voigt left on a postal plane, without saying a word. That was very strange, because he hadn't left any instructions for how to continue the experiments. Doctor Budden understood it later on that day, when he began to receive word of the alarming advance of the Red Army and the inefficiency of the German lines of defence. And as the primary medical authority in the camp, he decided that it was time to mop up everything with bleach. First, with the help of Barabbas, he spent five straight hours burning papers and photographs, destroying any documentary evidence that could lead to the suspicion that anyone at Birkenau had experimented on little girls who clung desperately to dirty rags. Not a trace of the pain inflicted because it was too impossible to be believed. All burned, Barabbas, and the simpleton still kept saying what a shame, so many hours and so much work going up in smoke. And neither of them thought of all the people who had also gone up in smoke, right there, two hundred metres from the laboratory. And the copies sent by the research department must be in some part of the Health Ministry, but who would go looking for them when the only important thing then was saving their hides.

Under the cover of night, his hands still blackened by smoke, he went into the guinea pigs' bedroom with loyal Barabbas. Each child was in his or her bunk. He administered the injection into each of their hearts without any explanation. Except for that one boy who asked what the injection was, and he told him it was to calm the pain in his knees. The others probably died knowing they were finally dying. The girl with the dark, dirty rag was the only one who received him wide awake, with those accusatory eyes. She also asked why. But she asked in a different way. She asked why and she looked him straight in the eye. Weeks of pain had stripped her of her fear and, sitting up in her bunk, she opened her shirt so Barabbas could find the perfect spot to inject her. But she stared at Doctor Budden and asked him why. This time it was he who, unwillingly, had to look away. Why. Waarom. She said it until her lips darkened, tinted by death. A seven-year-old girl who doesn't despair in the face of death is a very desperate, very devastated girl. There is no other way to explain such composure. Waarom.

After leaving everything prepared to flee the Lager in the morning with several unassigned officers, for the first time in many months, Doctor Budden didn't sleep well. It was the fault of the waarom. And those thin, darkening lips. And Oberscharführer Barabbas smiling and giving him an injection, without taking off his uniform, and smiling with his lips blackened by a death that never quite came because the dream continued.

In the morning, without making much noise and before Oberlagerführer Rudolf Höss realised, some twenty officers and subordinates, among them Budden and Barabbas, took off, headed anywhere that was far from Birkenau.

Both Barabbas and Doctor Budden were lucky because, taking advantage of the confusion, they were able to get far enough away from their work and the Red Army that they were able to pass themselves off to the British as soldiers coming from the Ukrainian front, anxious to see the war end so they could finally get home to their wives and children, if they were still alive. Doctor Budden had transformed into Tilbert Haensch, yes, from Stuttgart, Captain, and he had no documents to prove it because with the surrender, you know. I want to go back home, Captain.

'Where do you live, Doctor Konrad Budden?' asked the officer in charge of the interrogations, as soon as the other man had abandoned his claim.

Doctor Budden looked at him, mouth agape. All he could think of to say was what?, with a very shocked expression.

'Where do you live,' insisted the British lieutenant, with that horrific accent.

'What did you call me? What did you call me?'

'Doctor Budden.'

'But …'

'You've never set foot on the front, Doctor Budden. Much less the Eastern front.'

'Why do you call me doctor?'

The British officer opened the folder he had on the desk in front of him. The army file. Their fucking obsession with archiving and controlling everything. He was a bit younger, but it was him, with that gaze that didn't gaze but rather punctured. Herr Doktor Konrad Budden, surgeon of the graduating class of 1938. Oh, and professional level piano studies. Wow, doctor.

'That is a mistake.'

'Yes, Doctor. A big mistake.'

It wasn't until the third of the five years in prison they'd given him – because by some last-minute miracle no one had linked him to Auschwitz-Birkenau – that Doctor Budden started to cry. He was one of the few prisoners that had yet to receive a single visitor, because his parents had died in the bombing of Stuttgart and he hadn't wanted to let any other relatives know where he was. Particularly not those in Bebenhausen. He didn't need visitors. He spent the day staring at the wall, especially when he began to suffer several days of insomnia. Like a sip of sour milk, the faces came back to him, the faces of each and every one of the patients who had passed before him when he was under Doctor Voigt's orders in the medical research office at Birkenau. And he took it upon himself to try to remember as many as possible, the faces, the moans, the tears and the frightened screams, and he spent hours sitting, immobile, in front of the bare table.

'What's that?'

'Your cousin Herta Landau still wants to visit you.'

'I said I don't want any visitors.'

'She's in front of the prison on hunger strike. Until you agree to see her.'

'I don't want to see anyone.'

'This time you'll be forced to. We don't want scandals

on the street. And your name has begun to appear in the newspapers.'

'You can't force me.'

'Of course we can. You two, take him by the arms and let's put an end to this little scene that madwoman has staged, for once and ffucking all.'

They put Doctor Budden in a visiting room. They made him sit in front of three austere Australian soldiers. The doctor had to wait five endless minutes until the door opened and an aged Herta came in, walking slowly towards the table. Budden lowered his gaze. The woman stood before him; they were only separated by a few feet of table. She didn't sit down. She only said on behalf of Lothar and me. Then Budden looked up and Herta Landau, who had leaned towards him, spat in his face. Without adding anything further, she turned around and left, her motions a bit more animated, as if she had shook off a few years. Doctor Budden didn't move to wipe his face. He stared into space for a little while until he heard a harsh voice saying take him out of here and he thought he heard take away this carrion. And alone again in his cell, the memory of the patients' faces came back to him, like a sip of sour milk in his mouth. Each and every one of the patients. From the thirteen that had been the subjects of the sudden decompression experiments, and the many that had received grafts and died of infections, to the group of children chosen to prove the possible beneficial effects of the Bauer salve. The face he saw most often was the little Flemish girl who asked him waarom without understanding why so much pain. Then he got into the habit, as if it were a liturgical act, of sitting at the bare table and unfolding a dirty rag with one poorly cut, fraying side, and on which a blue-and-white chequered pattern could barely be made out; and he would stare at it, without blinking, until he couldn't stand to any more. And the void he felt inside was so intense that he was still unable to cry.

After a few months of repeating more or less the same gestures each day, morning and afternoon, over the third year of his imprisonment, his conscience became more porous: in addition to the moans, shrieks, sobs and panicked tears, he started to remember the smells of each face. And the time came when he could no longer sleep at night, like the five Latvian subjects whom they were able to keep awake for twenty-two days until they died of exhaustion, with their eyes destroyed by looking at so much light. And one night he began to shed tears. Konrad hadn't cried since he was sixteen, when he'd asked Sigrid out on a date and she'd responded with a look of total disdain. The tears emerged slowly, as if they were too thick, or perhaps indecisive after remaining hidden for such a long time. And an hour later they were still streaming down slowly. And when, outside of the cell, the rosy fingers of dawn tinted the dark sky, he broke out into an endless sob as his soul said waarom, how can it be, warum, how can it be that I never thought to cry in the presence of those sad, wide eyes, warum, mein Gott.

'Works of art are of an infinite solitude, said Rilke.'

The thirty-seven students looked at him in silence. Professor Adrià Ardèvol got up, left the dais and began to deliberately ascend a few of the terraced rows of chairs. No comments?, he asked.

No: no one had any comments. My students have no comment when I prod them with that bit about works of art being an infinite solitude. And if I tell them that artwork is the enigma that no reasoning can master?

'Artwork is the enigma that no reasoning can master.'

Now his walking had led him to the middle of the classroom. Some heads turned to look at him. Ten years after Franco's death, students had lost the impetus that made them participate in everything, chaotically, uselessly but passionately.

'The hidden reality of things and of life can only be deciphered, approximately, with the help of art, even if it is incomprehensible.' He looked at them, turning to take them all in with his gaze. 'In the enigmatic poem echoes the voice of unresolved conflict.'

She raised her hand. The girl with the short hair. She had raised her hand! Perhaps she would ask him if all that about the incomprehensible was going to be on the exam the next day; perhaps she would ask him for permission to use the toilet. Perhaps she would ask him if through art we can grasp all that which man had to renounce in order to build an objective world.

He pointed to the girl with the short hair and said yes, go ahead.

'Your reprehensible name will always be remembered as one of those that contributed to the horror that vilified humanity.' He said it in English with a Manchester accent and a formulaic tone, not worrying if he'd been understood. With a dirty finger he pointed to a place on the document. Budden raised his eyebrows.

'Here must sign you,' said the sergeant impatiently, in a terrible German he seemed to be making up as he went along. And he tapped several times with his dirty finger to show exactly where.

Budden did so and returned the document.

'You are free.'

Free. Once he was out of prison, he fled for a second time, again without any clear destination. Yet he stopped in a frozen village on the Baltic coast, in the shelter of a humble Carthusian monastery, and he spent the winter contemplating the fireplace of the silent house where they'd taken him in. He did just enough odd jobs around the house and the town to survive. He spoke little because he didn't want to be recognised as an educated person and he worked hard to toughen up his pianist and surgeon's hands. In the house that took him in they didn't speak much either because the married couple who lived there were grieving over the death of their only son Eugen on the Russian front during damn Hitler's damn war. The winter was long for Budden, who had been put into the mourned son's room in exchange for all the work he could do; he stayed there for two long years, during which he spoke to no one, except when strictly necessary, as if he were one of the monks in the neighbouring Carthusian monastery; strolling alone, letting himself be whipped by the cutting wind off the Gulf of Finland, crying when no one could see him, not allowing the images that tormented him to vanish unjustly because in remembrance there is penitence. At the end of that two-year-long winter, he headed to the Carthusian monastery of Usedom and, on his knees, asked the brother doorman for someone to hear his confession. After some hesitation at his unusual request, they assigned him a father confessor, an old man who was accustomed to silence, with a grey gaze and a vaguely Lithuanian accent whenever he strung together more than three words. Beginning when the Terce rang out, Budden didn't leave out a single detail, with his head bowed and his voice monotonous. He could feel the poor monk's shocked eyes piercing the back of his neck. The monk only interrupted him once, after the first hour of confession.

'Are you Catholic, my son?' he asked him.

Throughout the other four hours of the confession, he didn't say a peep. There was one point where Budden thought that the man was crying silently. When the bells rang to call the monks to the Vespers prayers, the confessor said ego te absolvo a peccatis tuis with a trembling voice, and he made a shaky sign of the cross as he mumbled the rest of the formula. And then there was silence, even with the echo of the bell; but the penitent hadn't moved.

'And the penance, Father?'

'Go in the name of ...' He didn't dare to take God's name in vain; he coughed uncomfortably and continued. 'There is no penance that could ... No penance that ... Repent, my son; repent, my son. Repent ... Do you know what I think, deep down?'

Budden lifted his head, distressed but also surprised. The confessor had leaned his head sweetly to one side and was engaged by a crack in the wood.

'What do you think, Father? ...'

Budden stared at the crack in the wood; he had trouble seeing it because the light was starting to fade. Father? he said. Father? And it seemed that he was that Lithuanian boy who moaned and said Tėve, Tėve!, from the bunk bed at the back. The confessor was dead and he could no longer help him, no matter how much he begged. And he began to pray for the first time in many years, some sort of invented prayer pleading for relief he didn't deserve.

'Honestly, poems or a song ... they don't make me think all that.'

Adrià was thrilled because the girl hadn't asked if that was going to be on the exam. His eyes were even shining.

'All right. What do they make you think?'

'Nothing.'

Some laughter. The girl turned, a bit bothered by the laughing.

'Quiet,' said Adrià. He looked at the girl with the short hair, encouraging her to continue.

'Well ...' she said. 'They don't make me think. They make me feel things I can't describe.' In a softer voice, 'Sometimes ...' even softer voice, 'they make me cry.'

Now no one laughed. The three or four seconds of silence that followed were the most important moment of that course. The beadle ruined it by opening the door and announcing the end of the class.

'Art is my salvation, but it can't save humanity,' responded Professor Ardèvol to the beadle, who closed the door, ashamed by that professor who was off his rocker.

'Art is my salvation, but it can't save humanity,' he repeated to Sara as they breakfasted in the dining room, in front of the Urgell that seemed it was also awakening to the new day.

'No: humanity is hopeless.'

'Don't be sad, my love.'

'I can't stop being sad.'

'Why?'

'Because I think that ...'

Silence. She took a sip of tea. The doorbell rang and Adrià went to answer it.

'Watch out, move aside.'

Caterina came in and ran to the bathroom with a dripping umbrella.

'It's raining?'

'You wouldn't even notice lightning and snow,' she said from the bathroom.

'You're always exaggerating.'

'Exaggerating? You couldn't find water in the sea!'

I went back to the dining room. Sara was finishing her breakfast. Adrià put a hand over hers to keep her from getting up.

'Why can't you stop being sad?'

She was silent. She wiped her mouth with a blue-and-white chequered napkin and folded it slowly. I was waiting, standing, as I heard the usual noises Caterina made at the other end of the flat.

'Because I think that if I stop … I am sinning against the memory of my people. Of my uncle. Of … I have so many dead.'

I sat down without taking my hand off hers.

'I love you,' I told you. And you looked at me sadly, serenely and beautifully. 'Let's have a baby,' I finally dared to say.

You shook your head no, as if you didn't dare to say it out loud.

'Why not?'

You lifted your eyebrows and said oof.

'It's life against death, don't you think?'

'I don't have the heart.' You shook your head while you said no, no, no, no, no.

For a long time I wondered why you gave so many nos in response to having a child. One of my deepest regrets is not having watched a girl who looked like you grow up and to whom no one would say be still, damn it, or I'll rip off your nose, because she would never have to nervously wring a blue- and white-checked napkin. Or a boy who wouldn't have to beg Tëve, Tëve in panic.

After that confession he'd paid so dearly for on the frozen island of Usedom, Budden left the chair in front of the fireplace, he left behind that icy town on the Baltic shore having robbed his trusting hosts of an ID card from their beloved Eugen Müss to save himself problems with the Allied forces of occupation, and he began his third flight, as if he were afraid that the poor confessor, from his grave, could accuse him before his grieving brothers of any number of deserved sins. Deep down it wasn't the Carthusians and their silence that he was afraid of. He wasn't afraid of the penance they hadn't imposed on him; he wasn't afraid of death; he didn't deserve suicide because he knew that he had to make amends for his evil. And he knew full well that he deserved eternal hellfire and he didn't feel he had the right to avoid it. But he still had work to do before going to hell. 'You have to see, my son,' the confessor had told him before absolution and death, in the only, brief comments he had made during the long, eternal confession, 'how you can make amends for the evil you have done.' And in a lower voice, he had added: 'If amends are possible …' After a few seconds of doubt, he continued: 'May divine mercy, which is infinite, forgive me, but even if you try to make amends for the evil, I don't think there is a place for you in paradise.' During his flight, Eugen Müss thought about making amends for his evil. He'd had it easier the other times, because in his first flight they'd only had to destroy archives; he had to destroy the corpus delicti; the little corpses delicti. My God.

In three monasteries, two Czech and one Hungarian, they turned him away with kind words. The fourth, after a long period as a postulant, accepted him. He was luckier than that poor friar who was fleeing from fear, who begged to be admitted as just another monk twenty-nine times and the father prior at Sant Pere del Burgal, looking into his eyes, refused him. Until one rainy, happy Friday that was the thirtieth time he begged to be admitted. Müss wasn't fleeing from fear: he was fleeing from Doctor Budden.

Father Klaus, who was then the master of the novitiates, also kept a hand in with the aspirants. His interpretation was that the still young man had spiritual thirst, an eagerness for prayer and penance that the Cistercian life could offer him. So he accepted him as a postulant at the Mariawald monastery.

The life of prayer brought him close to the presence of God, always with the fear and certainty that he wasn't worthy of breathing. One day, after eight months, Father Albert collapsed in a heap as he was walking through the cloister in front of him, when he headed to the chapterhouse where the father abbot was waiting to speak with them about some changes to their schedule. Brother Eugen Müss didn't calculate his reaction well and when he saw Father Albert on the ground he said it's a heart attack and he gave precise instructions to those who rushed over to help him. Father Albert survived, but the surprised brothers discovered that Novice Müss not only had medical knowledge but was, in fact, a doctor.

'Why have you hidden this from us?'

Silence. He looked at the ground. I wanted to start a new life. I didn't think it was important information.

'I am the one who decides what is important and what is superfluous.'

He was unable to hold either the father abbot's gaze or Father Albert's, when he went to visit him in his convalescence. What's more, Müss was convinced that Father Albert, as he thanked him for his response that had saved his life, guessed his secret.

Müss's reputation as a doctor grew over the following months. When it came time for him to take the first vows and change his first name from Eugen, which wasn't his anyway, to Arnold – this time according to the Rule, as a sign of renunciation – he had already cured a bout of collective food poisoning effectively and selflessly, and his reputation was firmly established. So when Brother Robert had his crisis, very far to the West, in another monastery in another country, his Abbot decided to recommend Brother Arnold Müss as a medical expert. And that was where his despair began again.

'In the end, I can't help but refer to that bit about how there can be no poetry after Auschwitz.'

'Who said that?'

'Adorno.'

'I agree.'

'I don't: there is poetry after Auschwitz.'

'No, but I mean … that there shouldn't be.'

'No. After Auschwitz, after the many pogroms, after the extermination of the Cathars, of whom not one remains, after the massacres in every period, everywhere around the world … Cruelty has been present for so many centuries that the history of humanity would be the history of the impossibility of poetry 'after'. And yet it hasn't been that, because who can explain Auschwitz?'

'Those who have lived through it. Those who created it. Scholars.'

'Yes. All that will be evidence; and they've made museums to remember it. But something is missing: the truth of the lived experience. That cannot be conveyed in a scholarly work.'

Bernat closed the bound pages and looked at his friend and said and?

'It can only be conveyed through art; literary artifice, which is the closest thing to lived experience.'

'Bloody hell.'

'Yes. Poetry is needed after Auschwitz more than ever.'

'It's a good ending.'

'Yes, I think so. Or I don't know. But I think it is one of the reasons for the persistence of aesthetic will in humanity.'

'When will it be published? I can't wait.'

A few months later, *La voluntat estètica* appeared, simultaneously in Catalan and in German, translated by me and meticulously revised by the patient Saint Johannes Kamenek. One of the few things I'm proud of, my dear. And stories and landscapes emerged and I stored them away in my memory. And one day, behind your back and behind mine, I went to visit Morral again.

'How much?'

'That much.'

'That much?'

'Yes. Are you interested, Doctor?'

'If it were this much, yes.'

'That's a leap! This much.'

'This much.'

'All right, fine: this much.'

That time it was the hand-written score of *Allegro de concert* by Granados. For a few days, I avoided the gazes of Sheriff Carson and the valiant Arapaho Chief Black Eagle.

## 39

Franz-Paul Decker announced a ten-minute break because it seems that management was calling him in over something very urgent, because management was always more urgent than anything else, even the second rehearsal of Bruckner's fourth. Bernat began speaking with that quiet, shy French horn, whom Decker had made repeat the awakening of the first day in the Bewegt, nicht zu schnell, to show the entire orchestra how good a good French horn sounds. And he, the third time the director was having him display his talents, hit a false note that the French horn fears worse than death. And everyone laughed a bit. Decker and the French horn did as well, but Bernat felt a little anxious. That boy had joined the orchestra recently, and always kept to his corner, timid, eyes down, short and blond, a bit plump. It seemed his name was Romain Gunzbourg.

'Bernat Plensa.'

'Enchanté. First violins, right?'

'Yes. So? How's it going for you, in the orchestra? Besides the fancy stuff the maestro's been making you do.'

It was going well for him. He was Parisian, he was enjoying getting to know Barcelona, but he was anxious to visit the Chopin route in Majorca.

'I'll take you,' offered Bernat, the way he always did, almost without thinking. I had told him a thousand times, bloody hell, Bernat, think before you speak. Or just say it disingenuously, but don't commit yourself to …

'I gave my word and … Besides, he's a lad who's here alone, and I feel kind of sorry for …'

'And now you're going to have trouble with Tecla, can't you see that?'

'Don't exaggerate. Why would there be trouble?'

And Bernat went home after the rehearsal and said hey, Tecla, I'm going to Valldemossa for a couple of days, with a French horn.

'What?'

Tecla was coming out of the kitchen, wiping her hands on her apron, smelling of chopped onions.

'Tomorrow I'm going to show Gunzbourg where Chopin stayed.'

'Who in the hell is Gunzbourg?'

'A French horn, I already told you.'

'What?'

'From the orchestra. Since we have two days of …'

'Just like that, without letting me know?'

'I'm letting you know.'

'And what about Llorenç's birthday?'

'Oh, it slipped my mind. Shit. Well … It's that …'

Bernat took Gunzbourg to Valldemossa, they got drunk in a musical pub, Gunzbourg turned out to be excellent at improvising on the piano and Bernat, thanks to the Menorcan gin, sang a couple of standards in the voice of Mahalia Jackson.

'Why do you play the French horn?' The question he'd been wanting to ask him from the first time he saw him pull the instrument out of its case.

'Someone's got to play it,' he answered as they walked back to the hotel, with the sun emerging along the ruddy horizon.

'But you, the piano …'

'Let it go.'

The final result was that they forged a nice friendship and Tecla pouted for twenty days and added another offence to his curriculum. That was when Sara realised that Bernat never realised that Tecla was pouting until her pouting had solidified in the form of a crisis about to explode.

'Why is Bernat like that?' you asked me one day.

'I don't know. Maybe to show the world something or other.'

'Isn't he a bit old to be showing the world something or other?'

'Bernat? Even on his deathbed, he'll still be thinking that he has to show the world something or other.'

'Poor Tecla. She's always in the right when she complains.'

'He lives in his own world. He's not a bad kid.'

'That's easy to say. But then she's the one who ends up looking like a whinger.'

'Don't you get mad at me now,' Adrià, slightly peeved.

'He's a difficult man.'

'I'm sorry, Tecla, but I'd promised him! Bloody hell, you're making too big a deal of it. Don't be so dramatic, for god's sake! It was just a couple of days in Majorca, for god's sake! Bloody hell!'

'And Llorenç? He's your son! He's not the French horn's son.'

'What is he now, nine or ten?'

'Eleven.'

'That's it: eleven. He's not a baby any more.'

'Would you like me to tell you whether he's still a baby or not?'

'Go ahead.'

Mother and son each took a bite of birthday cake in silence. Llorenç said Mama, what about Dad? And she replied that he had work in Majorca. And they continued eating cake in silence.

'It's good, isn't it?'

'Yeah. It sucks that Dad's not here.'

'So get going on the gift you owe him.'

'But you already gave him some …'

'Right now!' screamed Tecla, almost about to cry with rage.

Bernat bought a very lovely book for Llorenç, which he gazed at for a good long while without daring to tear the wrapping paper. Llorenç looked at his father, he looked at his mother's frayed nerves and he didn't know that he was sad over things he couldn't comprehend.

'Thanks, Dad, it's really nice,' he said, without having torn the wrapping paper. The next morning, when he woke him up to go to school, the boy was sleeping with the wrapped book in his arms.

'Rsrsrsrsrsrrsrsrs.'

Caterina went to answer the door and found a very well-dressed young man, with the smile of a salesman selling those new water filters, very expressive grey eyes and a small briefcase in his hand. She stared at him without letting go of the door. He understood the silence as a question and said, yes, Mr Ardèvol, please.

'He's not here.'

'What do you mean?' Confused. 'But he told me that ...' He checked his watch, a bit lost. 'That's strange ... And the lady of the house?'

'She's not here either.'

'Boy. In that case ...'

Caterina made a gesture that said I'm very sorry but there's nothing we can do. But the nice young man, who was also quite attractive, pointed to her with one finger and said for what I've come to do, maybe they don't even need to be here.

'What do you mean?'

'I've come for the appraisal.'

'The what?'

'The appraisal. Didn't they mention it to you?'

'No. What appraisal?'

'So, they haven't told you anything about it?' Desolate, the clever young man.

'No.'

'The appraisal of the violin.' Gesturing inside, 'Posso?'

'No!' Caterina thought it over for a few seconds. 'It's just that I don't know anything about this. They didn't tell me anything.'

The clever young man had got both feet onto the doorsill by degrees and now widened his smile.

'Mr Ardèvol is very absent-minded.' He made a politely conspiratorial expression and continued: 'We spoke about it just last night. I only have to examine the instrument for five minutes.'

'Look. Maybe it'd be better if you came back some other time when they're here ...'

'Forgive me, but I've come from Cremona, Lombardy, Italy,

just for this, do you understand? Does that ring a bell? Call Mr Ardèvol and ask him for permission.'

'I wouldn't know how to locate him.'

'Darn ...'

'Besides, lately he keeps it inside a safe.'

'I understand that you know the combination.'

Silence. The nice young man hadn't made any brusque movements, but he already had both feet inside the flat. Caterina was betrayed by her silence. He unzipped his briefcase and pulled out a wad of five-thousand notes, to help her make up her mind.

'This always stimulates the memory, dear Caterina Fargues.'

'Seven two eight zero six five. How do you know my name?'

'I told you, I'm an appraiser.'

As if that were an incontestable argument, Caterina Fargues took a step back and let the nice young man in.

'Come with me,' he said to her. First the man gave her the wad of notes, which she gripped tightly in her hand.

In my study, the man put on some very thin gloves – appraiser's gloves, he said – and opened the safe with the seven two eight zero six five, extracted the violin. He heard Caterina saying if he thinks he can take the violin, he's got another thing coming, and he replied, without looking at her, I told you I'm an appraiser, woman. And she kept quiet just in case. He put the violin beneath my loupe lamp, he examined its label, he read Laurentius Storioni Cremonensis me fecit, and then he said mille settecento sessantaquattro, winked at Caterina, who, leaning beside the friendly appraiser, wanting to justify her salary by making it clear that, no matter how friendly he was, that man was not going to leave the house with the violin in his hands. And his grey eyes were now more metallic than expressive. The appraiser noticed the double line beneath Cremonensis and his heart gave such a leap that surely even that idiot realised it.

'Va bene, va bene ...' he said, as if he were a doctor who'd just listened to the patient's chest and was keeping his diagnosis to himself for the moment. He turned the instrument over, ran his eyes along the wood, the little scratches, the curves, the flaming, as he mechanically repeated va bene, va bene.

'Is it valuable?' Caterina tightened the hand that held the guilty wad, tightly folded.

The appraiser didn't reply; he was smelling the violin's varnish. Or its wood. Or its age. Or its beauty. Finally, he put the violin down delicately on the table and pulled a Polaroid camera out of his briefcase. Caterina moved aside because she didn't want any photographic evidence that revealed her indiscretion. Five photos, with that calm of his, shaking each photo so it would dry, a smile plastered on his face, one eye on that woman and his ear trying to make out any noise from the stairwell. Once he was finished, he picked up the instrument and put it back in the safe. He closed it. He didn't take off his gloves. Caterina felt relieved. The affable man looked around him. He went over to some bookcases. He noticed the shelf with the incunabula. He nodded his head, and for the first time in a long while he looked Caterina in the eye: 'Whenever you're ready.'

'Excuse me: how did you know that I knew it?' she said pointing to the safe.

'I didn't know.'

The man left my study silently and turned around suddenly, so suddenly that Caterina bumped into him. And he said to her:

'But now I know that you know that I know.'

He left silently with his gloves still on and he closed the door himself after bowing his head slightly towards Caterina, who, despite her confusion, found him awfully elegant. You know that I know that; no, what was it? Once she was left alone, she opened up her hand. A wad of five-thousand notes. No: the first one was five-thousand; the others were oh, what a son of a bitch, that affable appraiser and the horse he rode in on! She opened the door about to … About to what, idiot? To make a scene with a man she'd just let into the house? Like a thief the Lord will come. She could still hear the regular, confident, affable footsteps of the mysterious thief on the last few steps of the staircase, heading towards the street. Caterina closed the door, looked at the wad of notes and stood there for a while saying no, no, no, it can't be. And I don't know what she saw in those grey eyes, because you could barely see them under those eyebrows, so thick he looked like a sheepdog.

I received a letter from Oxford. I think it changed my life. It forced me to start writing again. In fact, it was the spark and the vitamins I needed to roll up my sleeves and get down to work on what would end up being a work as long as a day without bread, which brought me much joy and I'm pleased to have written: *Història del pensament europeu*. It is my way of saying to myself, you see, Adrià? You've done something that holds a candle to the *Griechische Geistesgeschichte* and, therefore, you can feel a bit closer to Nestle. Without that letter, I wouldn't have had the strength to get down to work on it. Adrià had read the missive, his curiosity piqued: an airmail letter. Instinctively, he looked at the sender: I. Berlin, Headington House, Oxford, England, UK.

'Sara!'

Where was Sara? Adrià, wandering perfunctorily through the Created World, yelled Sara, Sara, until he reached her studio and saw that she had the door closed. He opened it. Sara was making sketches of faces and houses, in that frantic way that sometimes came over her like a fit, and she would fill half a dozen sheets of paper with those irrational impulses, and then she would spend a few days looking at the results and deciding what should be tossed and what should be worked on further. She was wearing headphones.

'Sara!'

Sara turned and saw Adrià with wild eyes, pulled off the headphones and said what's wrong, what's going on? Adrià held up the letter so she could see it and for a few moments she thought no, not more bad news, no.

'What's wrong?' she said, frightened.

Sara saw how Adrià, pale, sat down on the drawing stool and extended the envelope to her. She took it and said who is it? Adrià gestured for her to turn it over. She did and read I.

Berlin, Headington House, Oxford, England, UK. She looked
at Adrià and asked him who is it?

'Isaiah Berlin.'

'Who is Isaiah Berlin?'

Adrià left and, a few seconds later, came back with four
or five books by Berlin and put them beside a sheet of paper
filled with sketching attempts.

'This man,' he said, pointing to the books.

'And what does he want?'

'I don't know. But why could he possibly be writing to
me?'

Then you took my hand, you forced me to sit down and, as
if you were the teacher calming the excitable child in the class,
you told me you know what you have to do to find out what it
says in a letter, right? Isn't that right, Adrià? You have to open
it up. And then, you have to read it …

'But it's from Isaiah Berlin!'

'It doesn't matter if it's from the tsar of the entire Russian
empire. You have to open it.'

You gave me a letter opener. It was hard to slice it neatly so
that it didn't pinch the paper inside or ruin the envelope.

'But what could he want?' I said, hysterical. You just pointed
to the envelope in response. But Adrià, once he had it open,
left it on Sara's table.

'Don't you want to read it?'

'I'm terrified.'

You picked up the envelope and I, like a boy, took it from
you and extracted the letter. A single page, hand written, that
said Oxford, April 1987, dear sir, your book moved me deeply,
etcetera, etcetera, etcetera, and that, even after so much time,
I still know by heart. Until the end that said please, don't
stop thinking and, every once in a while, writing down your
thoughts. Sincerely yours, Isaiah Berlin.

'Holy mother of …'

'That's good, right?'

'But what book is he talking about?'

'From what he says, I think it's *La voluntat estètica*,' said
Sara, taking the page to read it herself. You gave me back the

letter, smiled and said and now you will explain to me who this Isaiah Berlin is, in detail.

'But how did he get my book?'

'Here, save the letter, don't lose it,' you said. And from then on I've kept it among my most private treasures even though soon I won't even know where it is. And yes, that letter helped me to get down to writing for a few years that, apart from teaching the minimum amount of classes I could get away with, were filled with the history of European thought.

## 40

A single, patchily paved landing strip received the plane with
some jolts that made them think they would never make it
to the baggage carousel, if there even was one at the Kikwit
airport. To keep from losing face in front of that young woman
with a bored expression, he pretended to be reading while, in
his head, he was thinking if he remembered exactly where
the emergency exits were. It was the third plane he'd taken
since boarding in Brussels. In this one, he was the only white
person; he wasn't worried about sticking out too much. That
came with the job. The plane left them more than a hundred
metres from the small building. They had to walk the rest,
trying not to leave their shoes stuck to the boiling asphalt. He
collected his small travel bag, bought a taxi driver who, with
his four by four and his jerry cans of petrol, was anxious to
be bribed, and who, after three hours of following the Kwilu's
course, asked for more dollars because they were entering a
dangerous area. Kikongo, you know what I mean. He paid
without complaint because it was all in his expected budget
and plan, even the lies. Another long hour of jolts, as if it were
a landing strip, and as they advanced there were more trees,
taller, thicker trees. The car stopped in front of a half-rotted
sign.

'Bebenbeleke,' he said in a tone that left no room for a reply.

'Where the heck is the hospital?'

The taxi driver pointed with his nose towards the reddish
sun. Four planks in the shape of a house. It wasn't as hot as at
the airport.

'When should I come pick you up?' he said.

'I'll walk back.'

'You're crazy.'

'Yes.'

He grabbed his bag and walked towards the four poorly positioned planks without turning to say goodbye to the taxi driver, who spat on the ground, happier than ever because he could still go through Kikongo to visit his cousins and try to drum up some unlikely passenger to Kikwit, and he wouldn't need to work again for four or five days.

Without turning around, he waited for the sound of the taxi to completely vanish. He headed towards the only tree around, a strange tree that must have had one of those impossible names, and he picked up a bulky bag of military camouflage fabric, which seemed to be waiting for him, leaning against the trunk like someone having a nap. Then he turned the corner and found what could be the main door to Bebenbeleke. A long porch where three women sat in deckchairs of some sort, carefully observing the passing of the hours in silence. There was no actual door. And inside there was no reception area. A dimly lit corridor with a bulb that gave off a shaky light, from a generator. And a hen that ran outside as if realising she'd been caught red-handed. He went back to the porch and addressed the three women, in general.

'Doctor Müss?'

One of the women, the oldest, pointed inside with a nod of her head. The youngest corroborated it by saying, to the right, but he's with a patient now.

He went back inside and took the hallway to the right. Soon he found himself in a room where an old man wearing a white coat, which was impeccable even amid so much dust, was listening to the torso of a child who wasn't so sure about the whole examination and wanted to be rescued by his mother, who stood beside him.

He sat down on a bright green bench next to two other women, who were excited by something breaking the routine in Bebenbeleke that had them repeating, like a litany, the same words over and over for quite some time. He put down the larger bag beside his feet, making a metallic noise. It was getting dark. When Doctor Müss finished with the last patient, he looked up at him for the first time, as if his being there was the most normal thing in the world.

'Do you need a check-up as well?' he said in greeting.

'I just wanted to confess.'

The newcomer now realised that the doctor wasn't old: he was beyond old. From the way he moved it seemed he had an inexhaustible inner energy, and that was deceiving. His body was what it was, that of a man over eighty. The photo that he had been able to lay his hands on was of a man in his sixties, at most.

As if a European showing up at dusk to the Bebenbeleke hospital asking for confession was a common occurence, Doctor Müss washed his hands in a sink that, miraculously, had a tap with running water and he gestured for the newcomer to follow him. Just then, two men with dark glasses and cocky attitudes sat on the green bench they'd just shooed the excited women off of. The doctor led the visitor to a small room, perhaps his office.

'Will you be staying for dinner?'

'I don't know. I don't make long-term plans.'

'As you wish.'

'It took me a lot of work to find you, Doctor Budden. I lost your trail in a Trappist monastery and there was no way to find where you'd gone.'

'How did you do it, then?'

'By visiting the main archives of the order.'

'Ah, yes, their obsession with having everything documented and archived. Were they helpful?'

'They probably still don't know I visited their archives.'

'What did you find there?'

'Besides the false lead on the Baltic, there was a reference to Stuttgart, to Tübingen and to Bebenhausen. In that small town I was able to tie up some loose ends with the help of a very kindly old lady.'

'My cousin Herta Landau, right? She's always been a windbag. She must have been overjoyed to have someone to listen to her. Forgive me, go on.'

'Well, that's it. It took me years to fit the pieces together.'

'That's for the best: it's given me time to make amends for a fraction of the evil I've done.'

'My client would have liked me to have found you sooner.'

'Why don't you arrest me and take me to trial?'

'My client is old: he doesn't want any delays because he is going to die soon, according to what he says.'

'Right.'

'And he doesn't want to die without seeing you dead.'

'I understand. And how did you manage to find me?'

'Oh, a lot of purely technical work. My trade is very boring: long hours of poking around in different places until you finally put the pieces together. And like that, for days and days, until I understood that the Bebenhausen I was looking for wasn't exactly in Baden-Württemberg. At some points I even thought that it was some sort of a clue left for someone who might be wanting to follow your trail.'

He realised that the doctor was repressing a smile.

'Did you like Bebenhausen?'

'Very much.'

'It is my lost paradise.' Doctor Müss shook off a recollection with a wave of his hand and now he did smile: 'You took a long time,' he said.

'As I said … When I took on the assignment you were very well hidden.'

'To be able to work and make amends.' Curious, 'How do these assignments work?'

'It's very professional and very … cold.'

Doctor Müss got up and, from a small cabinet that seemed to be a refrigerator, he pulled out a bowl of something vague and possibly edible. He put it on the table, with two plates and two spoons.

'If you don't mind … At my age I have to eat like a sparrow … little and often. Otherwise, I might faint.'

'Do people trust such an old doctor?'

'They have no other options. I hope they don't close the hospital when I die. I am in negotiations with the village authorities in Beleke and Kikongo.'

'I'm very sorry, Doctor Budden.'

'Yes.' About the vague contents of the bowl: 'It's millet. It's better than nothing, believe me.'

He served himself and passed the bowl to the other man.
With his mouth full: 'What did you mean by that, that it's a
very cold, very professional job?'

'Well, things …'

'No, please, I'm interested.'

'Well, for example, I never meet my clients. And they never
meet me either, of course.'

'That's seems logical. But how do you organise it?'

'Well, there's a whole technique. Indirect contact is always
a possibility, but you must be very meticulous to ensure that
you are always connecting with the right person. And you
have to learn how to not leave a trail.'

'That seems logical as well. But today you came in Makub-
ulo Joseph's car. He's an incorrigible gossip and by now must
have told everyone that …'

'He's telling them what I want him to tell them. I am giving
up a false lead. You'll understand that I can't go into details …
And how did you know who my taxi driver was?'

'I founded the Bebenbeleke hospital forty years ago. I know
the name of every dog that barks and every hen that cackles.'

'So you came here straight from Mariawald.'

'Does that interest you?'

'It fascinates me. I've had a lot of time to think about you.
Have you always worked alone?'

'I don't work alone. Before day breaks there are already three
nurses seeing patients. I get up early as well, but not that early.'

'I'm very sorry to be keeping you from your work.'

'I don't think the interruption is very important, not today.'

'And do you do anything else?'

'No. I devote all my energy to helping the needy during
every hour of life I have left.'

'It sounds like a religious vow.'

'Well … I'm still somewhat of a monk.'

'Didn't you leave the monastery?'

'I left the Trappist order; I left the monastery, but I still feel
that I am a monk. A monk without a community.'

'And do you lead mass and all that stuff?'

'I'm not a priest. Non sum dignus.'

They used the silence to take a sizeable chunk out the plate of millet.

'It's good,' said the newcomer.

'To tell you the truth, I'm sick of it. I miss a lot of foods. Like Sauerkraut. I can't even remember what it tastes like, but I miss it.'

'Aw, if I'd known …'

'No, I miss them but I don't …' He swallowed a spoonful of millet. 'I don't deserve Sauerkraut.'

'Isn't that a bit of an exaggeration … I mean, I'm no one to …'

'I can assure you full well that you are not no one.'

He wiped his lips with the back of his hand and brushed his still immaculate white coat. He pushed aside the tray of food without asking the other man and they remained face to face, with the bare table between them.

'And the piano?'

'I gave it up. Non sum dignus. Even the memory of the music I used to adore makes me heave.'

'Isn't that a bit of an exaggeration?'

'Tell me your name.'

Silence. The newcomer thinks it over.

'Why?'

'Curiosity. I have no use for it.'

'I'd rather not.'

'Your call.'

They couldn't help it: they both smiled.

'I don't know the client. But he gave me a key word that will give you a clue, if you are curious. Don't you want to know who sent me?'

'No. Whoever it was who sent you, you are welcome.'

'My name is Elm.'

'Thank you, Elm, for trusting me. Don't take this the wrong way, but I have to ask you to change your profession.'

'I am doing my last few jobs. I'm retiring.'

'I'd be happier if this were your last job.'

'I can't promise you that, Doctor Budden. And I would like to ask you a personal question.'

'Go ahead. I just asked you one.'

'Why haven't you turned yourself in? I mean, when you left prison, if you felt you hadn't purged your crimes … well …'

'In prison or dead I wouldn't have been able to make amends for my evil.'

'When it is beyond repair, what do you hope to make amends for?'

'We are a community that lives on a rock that sails through space, as if we were always searching for God amid the fog.'

'I don't understand.'

'I'm not surprised. I mean that you can always repair with one person the evil you've done to another. But you have to repair it.'

'And you must not have wanted your name …'

'Yes. I didn't want that, it's true. My life, since I left prison, has consisted of hiding and repairing. Knowing that I will never repair all the evil I've done. I've been carrying it around inside me for years and never told anyone.'

'Ego te absolvo, etcetera. Right?'

'Don't laugh. I tried it once. But the problem is that my sin cannot be forgiven because it is too big. I devoted my life to atoning for it knowing that when you got here I would still be on the starting line.'

'From what I remember, if the penitence is enough …'

'Nonsense. What do you know!'

'I had a religious education.'

'What good did it do you?'

'Look who's talking.'

They both smiled again. Doctor Müss stuck a hand under his white coat and into his shirt. The other, quickly, leaned over the table and immobilised his arm, grabbing him by the wrist. The doctor, slowly, pulled out a dirty, folded rag. Seeing what it was, the newcomer released his wrist. The doctor put the cloth, which seemed to have been cut in half at one point, onto the table, and with vaguely ritualistic gestures, he unfolded it. It was a handspan and a half square and still had traces of the white and blue threads that made up the checks. The newcomer observed him with curiosity. He glanced at the doctor, who had closed his eyes. Was he praying? Was he remembering?

'How were you able to do what you did?'

Doctor Müss opened his eyes.

'You don't know what I did.'

'I've done my research. You were part of a team of doctors who trampled on the Hippocratic oath.'

'Despite your profession, you are educated.'

'Like you. I don't want to miss my chance to tell you that you disgust me.'

'I deserve the disdain of hitmen.' He closed his eyes and said, as if reciting: 'I sinned against man and against God. In the name of an idea.'

'Did you believe in it?'

'Yes. Confiteor.'

'And what about piety and compassion?'

'Have you killed children?' Doctor Müss looked him in the eye.

'I'm the one asking the questions.'

'Right. So you know how it feels.'

'Watching a child cry as you rip off the skin on his arm to study the effects of the infections ... means you have no compassion.'

'I wasn't a man, Father,' confessed Doctor Müss.

'How is it that, without being a man, you were able to regret?'

'I don't know, Father. Mea maxima culpa.'

'None of your colleagues have repented, Doctor Budden.'

'Because they know that the sin was too large to ask for forgiveness, Father.'

'Some have committed suicide and others have fled and hid like rats.'

'I am no one to judge them. I am like them, Father.'

'But you are the only one who wants to repair the evil.'

'Let's not jump to conclusions: I may not be the only one.'

'I've done my research. By the way, Aribert Voigt.'

'What?'

Despite his self-control, Doctor Müss was unable to avoid

a tremor through his entire body at just the mention of that name.

'We hunted him down.'

'He deserved it. And may God forgive me, Father, because I deserve it too.'

'We punished him.'

'I can't say anything more. It is too big. The guilt is too deep.'

'We hunted him down years ago. Aren't you pleased to hear it?'

'Non sum dignus.'

'He cried and begged for forgiveness. And he shat himself.'

'I won't cry for Voigt. But the details you give me don't make me happy either.'

The newcomer stared at the doctor for some time.

'I am Jewish,' he finally said. 'I work for hire, but I put my all into it. Do you understand me?'

'Perfectly, Father.'

'Deep down, do you know what I think?'

Konrad Budden opened his eyes, frightened, as if he feared finding himself before the old Carthusian who stared at a crack in the wood of the frozen confessional. In front of him, this Elm, seated, looking him up and down, with his face already furrowed with the weight of many confessions, wasn't looking at any crack: he was staring into his eyes. Müss held his gaze, 'Yes, I know what you are thinking, Father: that I have no right to paradise.'

The newcomer looked at him in silence, concealing his surprise. Konrad Budden continued, 'And you are right. The sin is so atrocious that the true hell is what I have chosen: assuming my guilt and continuing to live.'

'Don't think that I understand it.'

'I don't even try for that. I don't take refuge in the idea that we followed or in the coldness of our souls that allowed us to inflict that hell. And I don't seek forgiveness from anyone. Not even from God. I have only asked for the chance to repair that hell.'

He covered his face with his hands and said doleo, mea

culpa. Every day I live the same feeling with the same intensity.

Silence. Outside, a sweet stillness overcame the hospital. The newcomer thought he could hear, muffled, in the distance, the sound of a television. Doctor Müss said, in a softer voice, hiding his distress, 'Will it be a secret or will my identity be revealed once I'm dead?'

'My client wants it to remain a secret. And the customer is king.'

Silence. Yes, a television. It sounded strange in that place. The newcomer leaned back in his chair. 'Don't you want to know who sent me now?'

'I don't need to know. You were sent by them all.'

And he put his hands flat on the dirty rag with a delicate, somewhat solemn, gesture.

'What is that rag?' the other man asked. 'A napkin?'

'I have my secrets too.'

The doctor kept his hands on the rag and he said if you don't mind, I'm ready.

'If you would be so kind as to open your mouth ...'

Konrad Budden closed his eyes, piously, and said when you're ready, Father. And from the other side of the window he heard the scandalous cackling of a hen about to roost. And further away, laughter and applause from the television. Then Eugen Müss, Brother Arnold Müss, Doctor Konrad Budden opened his mouth to receive the viaticum. He heard the bag's zipper being opened briskly. He heard metallic sounds that transported him to hell and he assumed it as an extra penance. He didn't close his mouth. He couldn't hear the shot because the bullet had gone too quickly.

The visitor put the pistol in his belt and pulled a Kalashnikov out of his bag. Before leaving the room, he carefully folded that man's rag as if it were a rite for him as well, and he put it in his pocket. His victim was still sitting, neatly, in his chair, with his mouth destroyed and barely a trickle of blood. He hadn't even stained his white coat. Too old to have enough blood flow, he thought, as he took the safety off the automatic rifle and prepared to distort the scene. He calculated where the sound of the television came from. He knew that was where he needed to head. It was important that the doctor's death go unnoticed but in order for that to happen he had decided that there'd have to be talk – a lot of talk – about the rest of it. Just part of the job.

## 41

Everything I am explaining to you, esteemed friends and colleagues, was prior to the *Història del pensament europeu*. Anyone who wants more practical information on our man, can consult two sources in particular: the *Gran Enciclopèdia Catalana* and the *Encyclopaedia Britannica*. The latter, which is the one I had closer at hand, says, in its fifteenth edition:

Adrià Ardèvol i Bosch (Barcelona, 1946). Professor of aesthetic theory and the history of ideas, earned a doctorate in 1976 at Tübingen and is author of of *La revolució francesa* (1978), an argument against violence in the service of an ideal, in which he calls into question the historical legitimacy of figures such as Marat, Robespierre and Napoleon himself, and with skilful intellectual work, compares them to the bloodthirsty dictators of the twentieth century such as Stalin, Hitler, Franco and Pinochet. Deep down, at that moment, young Professor Ardèvol couldn't give a rat's arse about history: as he was writing the book, he was still indignant, as he had been for years, over the disappearance of his Sara ↑Voltes-Epstein (Paris, 1950–Barcelona, 1996) without any explanation and he was feeling that the world and life owed him one. And he was unable to explain it all to his good friend Bernat ↑Plensa i Punsoda (Barcelona, 1945), who, on the other hand, often cried on Ardèvol's shoulder over his misfortunes. The work caused ripples in French intellectual circles, which turned their back on him, until they forgot about it. Which was why *Marx?* (1980) went unnoticed and not even the few remaining Catalan Stalinists noticed its appearance in order to annihilate it. Following a visit to ↑Little Lola (La Barceloneta, 1910–1982), he picked up the trail of his beloved Sara (vid. supra) and peace returned to his life except for a few specific incidents with Laura ↑Baylina (Barcelona, 1959?), with whom

he hadn't been able to decently end a relationship that he ac-
knowledges was very unfair, mea culpa, confiteor. For many
years it's been said that he is milling over a *Història del mal*,
but since he's not entirely convinced of the project, it will be
slow to come to fruition, if he ever feels up to the task. Once
he regained his inner peace, he was able to dedicate his efforts
to the creation of what he considers his finest work, *La voluntat estètica* (1987), which received the enthusiastic support
of Isaiah ↑Berlin (cf. *Personal Impressions*, Hogarth Press,
1987 [1998, Pimlico]), and, after years of feverish dedication,
to the culmination of the impressive *Història del pensament
europeu* (1994), his most internationally known work and the
one that brings us today to the Assembly Hall of the Brechtbau, the Faculty of Philosophy and Letters of this university.
It is an honour for me to have the opportunity to present this
modest introduction to the event. And I struggled to not get
carried away by subjective, personal memories, since my relationship with Doctor Ardèvol dates back many years to the
hallways, classrooms and offices of this university, when I was
a new professor (I was once young too, dear students!) and
Ardèvol was a young man desperate with a heartache that led
him to spend a few months sleeping around until he got into
a very complicated relationship with a young woman named
Kornelia ↑Brendel (Offenbach, 1948) who put him through
some real tribulations because she, who wasn't as pretty as he
thought anyway, even though it must be noted that she looked
like she was good in bed, insisted on having new experiences
and that, for a passionate Mediterranean man like Doctor
Ardèvol, was hard to bear. Well: it would have been for a cold,
square Germanic man, too. Don't ever speak a word of this,
because he could take it very badly, but I myself was one of
Miss Brendel's new experiences. Let me explain; after a huge
basketball player and a Finn who played ice hockey, and after
a painter with fleas, Miss Brendel opted for another sort of
experience and she looked at me and wondered what it would
be like to bed a professor. In fact, I have to confess that I was
just a hunting trophy, and my head, with a mortarboard cap,
hangs over the fireplace of her castle beside the Finn's with its

bright red helmet. And that's quite enough of that, because we haven't come here today to talk about me but to talk about Doctor Ardèvol. I was saying that his relationship with Miss Brendel was torment, which he was able to overcome when he decided to take refuge in his studies. Which is why we should erect a monument to Kornelia Brendel beside the Neckar. Ardèvol finished his studies at Tübingen and read his doctoral thesis on Vico that, I'll remind you although there is no need, was praised highly by Professor Eugen Coşeriu (vid. Eugenio Coşeriu-Archiv, Eberhard Karls Universität) who, old but lucid and energetic, is nervously moving his foot in the front row although the expression on his face is a satisfied one. I'm told that Doctor Ardèvol's thesis is one of the most requested texts by students of the history of ideas at this university. And I'll stop here because all I'll do is keep singing his praises: I'll let the fatuous and conceited Doctor Schott have the floor. Kamenek, with a smile, slide the microphone towards Professor Schott, winked at Adrià and sat more comfortably in his chair. There were about a hundred people in the assembly hall. An interesting mix of professors and intrigued students. And Sara thought how handsome he looked, with his new suit jacket.

It was the world premiere of the suit jacket that she had made him buy as a condition of her accompanying him to Tübingen for the presentation of his *Història del pensament europeu*. And Adrià, seated at the table beside those illustrious presenters, looked towards her and I said to myself Sara, you are my life and this is a dream. Not the profound, scrupulous and sensitive presentation by Kamenek, with slight, discreet concessions to a more personal and subjective tone; not the enthusiastic speech by Professor Schott, who insisted that *Die Geschichte des europäischen Denkens* is a major reflection that must be disseminated to every European university and I beg you all to read promptly. I beg you? I order you all to read it! Professor Kamenek didn't refer to Isaiah Berlin and his *Personal Impressions* (vid. supra) in vain. I would have to add, if you'll allow me, Professor Kamenek, the explicit references that Berlin makes to Ardèvol both in conversation with

Jahanbegloo and in Ignatieff's canonical biography. No, none
of this is the miracle, Sara. Nor the Lesung that will surely last
a good long hour. That's not it, Sara. It's seeing you here, in
the chair where I sat so many times, with your dark ponytail
spilling down your back and you looking at me, holding back
a smile and thinking I'm handsome in my new suit jacket,
isn't that so, Professor Ardèvol?

'Excuse me, Professor Schott?'

'What do you think?'

What do I think. My God.

'Love, that moves the sun and the other stars.'

'What?' Puzzled, the professor looked at the audience and
turned his confused gaze on Adrià.

'I'm in love and I often lose the thread of things. Can you
repeat the question?'

The hundred or so members of the audience didn't know
whether to laugh or not. Nervous glances, the half-frozen
smiles of deer in the headlights; until Sara broke out in a generous laugh and they were able to follow suit.

Professor Schott repeated the question. Professor Ardèvol
answered it with precision, many people's eyes gleamed with
interest, and life is wonderful, I was thinking. And then I read
the third chapter, the most subjective, which I had devoted
to my discovery of the historical nature of knowledge before
reading a single line of Vico. And the shock I felt when I discovered his work on the suggestion of Professor Roth, who
unfortunately is no longer among us. And as I read I couldn't
help thinking that many years back Adrià had fled to Tübingen to lick his wounds over his sudden, inexplicable desertion
by Sara, who now was laughing with satisfaction before him;
that twenty years earlier he went through Tübingen sleeping with everyone he could, as had been pointed out in the
presentation, and wandered through the classrooms searching every girl for some feature that reminded him of Sara.
And now, in Room 037, he had her before him, more mature,
looking at him with an ironic smirk as he closed the book
and said a book like this requires many years of work and I
hope I don't feel inspired to write another for many, many,

many years, amen. And the audience rapped their knuckles on the table with polite enthusiasm. And afterwards, dinner with Professor Schott, Dean Vartten, a thrilled Kamenek, and two female professors who were fairly mute and timid. One of them, perhaps the shorter one, said in a wisp of a voice that she had been moved by the human portrait that Kamenek had given of Doctor Ardèvol, and Adrià celebrated Professor Kamenek's sensitivity while Kamenek lowered his eyes, a bit confused by the unexpected praise. After dinner, Adrià took Sara for a stroll through the park, which in the last light of day gave off a scent of cold spring bursting forth, and she kept saying this is all so lovely. Even though it's cold.

'They say it's going to snow tonight.'

'It's still lovely.'

'Whenever I was sad and thinking of you I would come walking here. And I would jump over the cemetery fence.'

'You can do that?'

'See? I just did.'

She didn't think twice and leapt over the fence as well. After walking some thirty metres they found the entrance gate, which was open, and Sara struggled to hold back a nervous laugh, as if she didn't want to laugh in the house of the dead. They reached the grave at the back and Sara read the name on it, curious.

'Who are they?' asked the commander with no stars.

'Germans from the resistance.'

The commander went over to get a better look at them. The man was middle-aged, and looked more like an office worker than a guerrilla fighter; and she looked like a peaceful housewife.

'How did you get here?'

'It's a long story. We want explosives.'

'Where the hell did you come from and who the hell do you think you are?'

'Himmler has to visit Ferlach.'

'Where is that?'

'In Klagenfurt. Here, on the other side of the border. We know the territory.'

'And?'

'We want to offer him a warm reception.'

'How?'

'By blowing him up.'

'You won't be able to get close enough.'

'We know how to do it.'

'You don't know how to do it.'

'Yes. Because we are willing to die to kill him.'

'Who did you say you were?'

'We didn't say. The Nazis dismantled our resistance group. They executed thirty of our comrades. And our leader committed suicide in prison. Those of us who are left want to give meaning to the death of so many heroes.'

'Who was your leader?'

'Herbert Baum.'

'You are the group that …'

'Yes.'

Nervous glances from the commander with no stars at his assistant with the blond moustache.

'When did you say Himmler was visiting?'

They studied the suicide plan in depth; yes, it was possible, quite possible. Therefore, they assigned them a generous ration of dynamite and the supervision of Danilo Janicek. Since they were very short of resources, they decided that after five days Janicek would rejoin the partisan group, whether or not the operation had been carried out. And Janicek was not to commit suicide along with them, under any circumstances.

'It's dangerous,' protested Danilo Janicek, who wasn't the least bit thrilled with the idea when they explained it to him.

'Yes. But if it comes off …'

'I'm not sure about this.'

'It's an order, Janicek. Take someone with you to cover your back.'

'The priest. I need strong shoulders and good marksmanship.'

And that was how Drago Gradnik ended up on the paths of Jelendol, emulating a krošnjar, loaded down with explosives and just as happy as if he were transporting spoons and wooden plates. The explosives reached their destination safely. A rail-thin man received them in a dark garage on Waidischerstrasse and assured them that Himmler's visit to Ferlach was confirmed for two days later.

No one was able to explain how the tragedy happened. Not even the activists in Herbert Baum's group can understand it still. But the day before their planned assassination, Danilo and the priest were preparing the explosives.

'It must have been unstable material.'

'No. It was used for military operations: it wasn't unstable.'

'I'm sure it must have been sweating. I don't know if you know but when dynamite sweats ...'

'I know: but the material was fine.'

'Well, then they bungled it.'

'It's hard to believe. But there's no other explanation.'

The fact is that at three in the morning, when they had already packed the charges into the rucksacks that the two members of the suicide commando planned to use to blow themselves up, with Himmler as their dance partner, Danilo, tired, anxious, said don't touch that, damn it, and the priest, weary and annoyed by the other man's tone, put down the rucksack they'd just loaded up, too hard. There was light and noise and the dark garage lit up for a fraction of a second before blowing up with the glass, bricks from the partition wall and bits of Danilo and Father Gradnik mixed into the rubble.

When the occupying military authorities tried to reconstruct the events, all they found were the remains of at least two people. And one of those people had honking big feet. And amid the scrap iron, intestines and blood splatters they found, around a wide neck, the ID tag of missing SS-Obersturmführer Franz Grübbe, who according to the only approved version, the version of SS-Hauptsturmführer Timotheus Schaaf, was the abject cause of that humiliating defeat of a Waffen-SS division that had heroically succumbed at the entrance to Kranjska Gora, since as soon as he heard the first shots, he ran towards the enemies with his hands in the air begging for mercy. An SS officer begging for mercy from a communist guerrilla commando! Now we understand it: the abject traitor reappeared, mixed up in the preparation of an abject attempt on the Reichsführer himself, because that was nothing less than a plan to kill Reichsführer Heinrich Himmler.

'And who is this Grübbe?'

'A traitor to the fatherland, to the Führer and the sacred vow he solemnly swore when he joined the Schutzstaffel. SS-Haupsturmführer Schaaf can give you more details.'

'May he be shamefully reviled.'

The telegram that Lothar Grübbe received was curt and to the point, informing him of the infamy committed by his abject son, who wanted to make an attempt on the life of his highest direct superior, the Reichsführer, but had been blown up into a thousand abject bits when handling the explosive. And it added that they had made twelve arrests of German traitors belonging to an already crushed group like that of the abject Jew Herbert Baum. The shame of the empire will fall on your abject son for a thousand years.

And Lothar Grübbe cried with a smile and that night he told Anna, you see, my love, our son had a change of mind. I wanted to spare you this, but it turns out that our Franz had got his head filled with all of Hitler's crap; and something made him realise that he was wrong. The infamy of the regime has befallen us, which is the greatest joy they can give a Grübbe.

To celebrate the bravery of little Franz, the hero of the family, the only one who up until now has responded with valour to the beast of the Reich, he asked Günter Raue to repay the favour; yes, after so many years. And Günter Raue weighed the pros and cons and said yes, Lothar, my friend, but with one condition. What's that? That, for the love of God, you be discreet. And I will tell you how much of a tip you should give the gravediggers. And Lothar Grübbe said all right, that seems fair. And five days later – as they said that the Western front was starting to be a problem and no one talked about the Byelorussian disaster, where mother Earth had swallowed up a group of whole armies – in the tranquil Tübingen cemetery, in the Grübbe-Landau family plot, in front of a sad man and his cousin Herta Landau, of the Landaus of Bebenhausen, the memory of a brave hero was buried inside an empty coffin. When better times come, we will honour him with flowers as white as his soul. I am proud of our son, dear Anna, who is now reunited with you. I won't be long in coming because I have nothing more to do here.

Darkness had fallen. They left, pensive, through the gate that was still open, she took his hand, they walked in silence to the street lamp that illuminated the park's path and when they reached there she said I think what Professor Schott said is true.

'He said a lot of things.'

'No, that your history of European thought is a truly important work.'

'I don't know. I would like it to be true, but I can't know that.'

'It is,' insisted Sara. And what's more, I love you.

'Well, I've been batting around some other ideas for a while now.'

'What kind of ideas?'

'I don't know. The history of evil.'

As they left the cemetery, Adrià said the problem is I haven't really got my bearings. I haven't been able to really reflect. I don't know, I come up with examples but not an idea that …'

'Just write, I'm by your side.'

I wrote with Sara by my side as she drew with me close by. Sara illustrating stories and drawing in charcoal and Adrià beside her, admiring her skill. Sara cooking kosher food and teaching him about the richness of Jewish cuisine and Adrià responding with the eternal potato omelette, boiled rice and grilled chicken. Every once in a while, Max would send a package with bottles from excellent years. And laughing just because. And going into her studio while she was absorbed, for over ten minutes, in the easel with a blank sheet of paper, thinking her things, her mysteries, her secrets, her tears that she won't allow me to wipe away.

'I love you too, Sara.'

And she turned and went from the blank paper to my pale
face (extremely pale according to the valiant Black Eagle) and
took three seconds to smile because it was hard for her to
abandon her things, her mysteries, her secrets, her mysterious tears. But we were happy. And now, leaving the cemetery,
in Tübingen, she said you just write, I'm by your side.

When it's cold, even in springtime, nocturnal footsteps
make a different noise, as if the cold had a sound. Adrià was
thinking that as they walked in silence to the hotel. The footsteps in the night of two happy people.

'Sie wünschen?'

'Adrià Ardèvol? Adrià? Is that you?'

'Ja. Yes. Bernat?'

'Hello. Can you talk?'

Adrià looked at Sara, who was taking off her anorak and
about to draw the curtains in their room in the little hotel
Am Schloss.

'What are we doing? What do you want?'

Sara had time to brush her teeth, put on her pyjamas and
get into bed. Adrià was saying aha, yes, sure, sure, yes. Until
he decided not to say anything and just to listen. When he
hadn't spoken for five minutes, he looked at Sara, who was
contemplating the ceiling and lulled by the silence.

'Listen, I ... Yes. Yes. Of course.'

Three more minutes. I think that you, my love, were thinking about the two of us. Every once in a while I would look at
you out of the corner of my eye and you were hiding a satisfied
smile. I think, my beloved, that you were proud of me, and I
felt like the happiest man in the world.

'Wait, what?'

'Haven't you been listening to me?'

'Of course.'

'Well, look: that's it. And I'm ...'

'Bernat: maybe you should think about separating. If it's
not working, it's not working.' Pause. Adrià heard his friend's
breathing on the other end of the line. 'No?'

'Man, it's just that ...'

'How's the novel going?'

'It's not. How can it, with all this crap?' Distant silence. 'Besides, I don't know how to write and on top of it all you want me to get separated.'

'I don't want you to get separated. I don't want anything. I just want to see you happy.'

Three and a half more minutes until Bernat said thanks for listening and decided to hang up. Adrià sat for a few seconds in front of the telephone. He got up and pulled the thin curtain open a tiny bit. Outside it was snowing silently. He felt sheltered, by Sara's side. I felt sheltered by your side, Sara: then it was impossible to imagine that now, as I write to you, I would be living exposed to the elements.

I returned from Tübingen puffed up like a balloon and vain as a peacock. I was looking down on humanity from so far up that I wondered, in admiration, how the rest of the world could live so far down there below. Until I went to have a coffee at the university bar.

'Hey there.'

Even prettier. She had sidled up to me without me even realising.

'Hey, how's it going?'

Yes, even prettier. That irritation she made an effort to show when I was around had softened in the last few months. Maybe out of boredom. Maybe because things were going well for her.

'Well. And you? It went really well in Germany, didn't it?'

'Yes.'

'But I like *La voluntat estètica* better. Much better.'

Small sip of coffee. I liked that declaration of principles.

'Me too, but don't spread that around.'

Silence. Now I took a small sip of black coffee; now she took a small sip of her white coffee.

'You are very good,' she said after a little while.

'Excuse me?'

'You heard me. You are very good.'

'Thank you. I ...'

'No. Don't ruin it. Devote yourself to thinking and writing a book occasionally. But don't touch people. Just avoid them, you know?'

She finished her white coffee in one last sip. I really wanted to ask her for explanations, but I understood that it would be foolish to start that conversation. And especially when I still hadn't told you anything about Laura. I hadn't said anything even though I could have, easily. And now she, instead of going for my jugular, was praising me. And it had been a month since, with the renovations, she had chosen the desk in front of mine, now that I finally had one to myself. I had to get used to a new kind of relationship with Laura. I even thought that this would save me from ever having to tell you about her.

'Thank you, Laura,' I said.

She tapped her knuckles twice on the table and left. I had to wait a little while to avoid running into her on the stairs. But I thought it was better that Laura was done pouting over me. And Omedes had said Laura Baylina, you know that little blonde, so cute you just want to eat her up? Well, she's a sensational teacher. She has all her students by the short hairs. And I thought, I'm glad. And I also thought that probably all the shitty things I did to her helped her to improve. To Omedes, I said I've heard that; every once in a while there has to be a good professor, doesn't there?

Adrià Ardèvol got up and walked around his spacious study several times. He was thinking about what Laura had said to him that morning. He stopped in front of the incunabula and said to himself that he didn't know why he studied and studied, to the exclusion of all else. To quench a strange thirst. To comprehend the world. To comprehend life. Who knows. And he didn't think any more about it because he heard rsrsrsrsrsrsrsrs. He waited a little while, thinking that Little Lola would open the door, and he sat back down in front of his Lewis and read a few lines of the reflection he makes on realism in literature.

'How.'

'What.'

'Caterina.'

'Rsrsrsrsrsrsrsrs.'

He lifted his head. Caterina must have left. He checked the time. Seven-thirty in the evening. He grudgingly abandoned Lewis.

He opened the door and found Bernat with a sports bag in his hand, and he said hello, can I come in?, and he entered before Adrià had a chance to say come in, of course, come in.

After a long hour Sara arrived, and from the hall said in a loud, happy voice two Grimm stories!, closed the door and entered the study loaded down with drawings as she said didn't you put the vegetables on?

'Hey, hello, Bernat,' she added. And she noticed his sports bag.

'Uh, you see …' said Adrià.

Sara understood everything and said to Bernat stay for dinner. She said it as if it were an order. And to Adrià: six drawings for each story. And she went out to unload the drawings and put the pot on the stove. Bernat looked timidly at Adrià.

'We'll set you up in the guest room,' said Sara to break the silence, all of them before the monastery of Santa Maria de Gerri, which, even though it was night-time, was drenched in the sun coming from Trespui. The two men looked up from their plates of vegetables, surprised.

'Well: I imagine you've come to stay for a few days, right?'

The truth is, Sara, that Bernat hadn't asked me yet. I knew that he wanted to stay, but I was resistant, I don't know why. Maybe because it annoyed me that he didn't have the balls to ask.

'If you don't mind.'

I always wished I were like you, Sara, direct. But I am someone incapable of taking any bull by the horns. And this was my best friend. And now that we had cleared up the most important thing, the dinner continued, more relaxed. And Bernat felt obliged to explain that he didn't want to separate, but every day we argue more and I feel bad for Llorenç, who …

'How old is he?'

'I don't know. Seventeen or eighteen.'

'He's big, isn't he?' I said.

'Big for what?' said Bernat defensively.

'For if you separate.'

'What concerns me,' said Sara, 'is that you don't know your son's age.'

'I said seventeen or eighteen.'

'Is he seventeen or is he eighteen?'

'Well ...'

'When is his birthday?'

Guilty silence. And you, when you feel you are in the right, no one can stop you, and you insisted, 'Let's see: what year was he born?'

After thinking it over for a while Bernat said 1977.

'Summer, autumn, winter, spring?'

'Summer.'

'He's seventeen. Voilà.'

You didn't say it, but you surely had a few choice words for a man who doesn't know his own son's age and who, poor Tecla, with such a distracted guy, who's always doing his own thing, as if we were all at his beck and call, you know?, and stuff like that. But you just shook your head and kept all your comments to yourself. We finished our dinner in peace. Sara turned in early and left us alone, which was her way of encouraging me to get him to talk.

'You should separate,' I told him.

'It's my fault. I don't know my own son's age.'

'Come on, seriously: separate and try to live a happy life.'

'I won't live a happy life. I'll be eaten up by guilt.'

'Guilty over what?'

'Everything. What are you reading?'

'Lewis.'

'Who?'

'Clive Staples Lewis. A wise man.'

'Ah.' Bernat paged through the book and left it on the table. He looked at Adrià and said the thing is I still love her.

'And does she love you?'

'I think so.'

'All right. But you are hurting each other and hurting Llorenç.'

'No. If I ... It doesn't matter.'

'That's why you're running away from home, right?'

Bernat sat at the table, covered his face with his hands and began to cry, in irrepressible sobs. He was like that for a good long while and I didn't know what to do, whether I should go over to him, whether I should hug him, whether I should tap him on his shoulder or tell him a joke. I didn't do anything. Or I did. I moved aside the C.S. Lewis book so it wouldn't get wet. Sometimes I hate myself.

Tecla answered the door and stood there for a good long while staring at me in silence. She had me come in and then closed the door.

'How is he?'

'Confused. Shattered. And you?'

'Confused. Shattered. Have you come to act as an intermediary?'

Actually, Adrià never really had much to talk about with Tecla. She was too different, her gaze was too unsettling. And she was very pretty. Sometimes it seemed that she was sorry for being so pretty. Now she wore her hair pulled back in an improvised ponytail, and he would have gladly French kissed her. She folded her arms modestly and looked me in the eyes, as if inviting me to finally say something already; to say that Bernat was shattered and that he was down on his knees begging to come home; that he understands how unbearable he is and he will try his best to ... and that yes, yes, I know he left with a slam of the door, that he's the one who left and not you, that ... But he is asking, begging on his knees to come back because he can't live without you and ...

'I'm here to pick up his violin.'

Tecla remained stock still for a few seconds and when she reacted she went down the hall, I think a bit offended. As she disappeared, I still had time to say and his scores ... The ones in a blue folder, the thick one ...

She came back with the violin and a thick folder that she put down on the dining room table, maybe a little too hard. From what I could tell she was very offended. I understood that it was inappropriate to make any sort of reflection and I just took the violin and the thick folder.

'I'm very sorry about all this,' I said in parting.

'So am I,' she said when she closed the door. The door

closed a little too hard, as well. Just then Llorenç was coming up the stairs two by two, with a sports bag on his back. I got into the lift before the boy could see who the person hiding in such a shameful way was. I know, I'm a coward.

The second day, in the afternoon, Bernat was studying and decent violin playing was again heard in that house. It had been quite some time. Adrià, in his study, looking up to hear better. Bernat, in the guest room, filling the inner courtyard with Enescu's sonatas. And that evening he asked me if he could use the Storioni and he made it cry for twenty or thirty delicious minutes. He interpreted some sonatas by Tonton Leclair, but now all by himself. For a few moments I thought that I had to give Vial to him. That he could really make use of it. But I stifled the desire in time.

I don't know if music helped him. After dinner we were all three talking for a good long while. Sara made an exceptional reference to her Uncle Haïm and from the uncle we moved on to the banality of evil, because I had recently devoured Arendt and there were things going through my head that I didn't know what to do with.

'Why does it bother you?' said Bernat.

'If evil can be gratuitous, we're screwed.'

'I don't understand you.'

'If I can commit evil just because and that's fine, humanity has no future.'

'You mean crime without a motive, just because.'

'A crime just because is the most inhumane thing you can imagine. I see a man waiting for the bus and I kill him. Horrible.'

'Does hatred justify crime?'

'No, but it explains it. Gratuitous crime, the more horrific, is inexplicable.'

'And a crime in the name of God?' intervened Sara.

'That's a gratuitous crime but with a subjective alibi.'

'And if it's in the name of freedom? Or of progress? Or of the future?'

'Killing in the name of God or in the name of the future

is the same thing. When the justification is ideological, empathy and compassion vanish. One kills coldly, without one's conscience being affected. Like the gratuitous crime of a psychopath.'

They were silent for a little while. Without looking each other in the eye, as if they were subdued by the conversation.

'There are things that I don't know how to explain,' said Adrià in a mournful voice. 'Cruelty. The justification of cruelty. Things that I don't know how to explain except through narration.'

'Why don't you try it?' you said, looking at me with those eyes of yours that still bore right through me.

'I don't know how to write. That's Bernat's thing.'

'Don't mess with me, I'm not up for it.'

The conversation waned and we went to sleep. I remember, my love, that that was the day I took the decision. I grabbed some blank pages and the fountain pen and I tried to remedy it by coming from a distance, thinking that, gradually, I would approach us, and I wrote the rocks shouldn't be too small, because then they would be harmless. But they shouldn't be too big either, because then they would curtail the torture of the guilty too much. Because we are talking about punishing the guilty, let us not ever forget. All those good men who lift their fingers, anxious to participate in a stoning, must know that the sin requires atonement through suffering. That's how it is. It has always been that way. Therefore, wounding the adulterous woman, taking out an eye, showing ourselves insensitive to her sobs, that pleases the Almighty, the One God, the Compassionate, the Merciful.

Alí Bahr hadn't volunteered: he was the accuser and, as such, had the privilege of throwing the first stone. Before him, the infamous Amani, buried in a hole, only her indecent face showing, which was now covered in tears and had been repeating for too long, don't kill me, Alí Bahr lied to you. And Alí Bahr, impatient, made uncomfortable by the guilty woman's words, stepped forward at the Qadi's signal and threw the first stone to see if that whore would finally ffucking shut up, blessed be the Most High. And the stone that had to silence the slut moved too slowly, like he when he went into Amani's house with the pretext of selling her a basket of dates, and Amani, seeing a man enter, covered her face with the kitchen cloth she had in her hands and said what are you doing here and who are you.

'I came to sell these dates to Azizzadeh Alfalati, the merchant.'

'He's not here; he won't be back until the evening.'

Which was what Alí Bahr was hoping someone would confirm for him. Besides, he had been able to see her face: more lovely, much more lovely than he had been told in the hostel in Murrabash. Blasphemous women tend to be the most beautiful. Alí Bahr put down the basket of dates on the floor.

'We haven't ordered them,' she said, suspicious. 'I don't have the authority to ...'

He advanced two steps towards the woman and, opening his arms, with a serious air, he just said I want to unmask your secret, little Amani. With his eyes sparkling, he curtly concluded: 'I come in the name of the Most High to confound blasphemy.'

'What do you mean?' frightened, lovely Amani.

He advanced even more towards the girl. 'I find myself forced to search for your secret.'

'My secret?'

'Your blasphemy.'

'I don't know what you are talking about. My father ... He ... He will demand an explanation.'

Alí Bahr could no longer conceal the sparkle in his eye. He brusquely said, 'Take off your clothes, blasphemous dog.'

Insidious Amani, instead of obeying, ran into the house and Alí Bahr was forced to follow her and grab her by the neck. And when she began to scream for help, he was forced to cover her mouth with one hand while, with the other, he tore at her clothes to reveal the provocation to sin.

'Look, blasphemer!'

And he ripped off the medallion she wore around her neck, cutting her and making her bleed.

The man looked at the medallion in his open palm. A human figure: a woman with a child in her arms and a lush, strange tree in the background. And on the other side, Christian letters. So it was true what the women said about lovely Amani: she worshipped false gods or, at the very least, was disobeying the law of not sculpting, drawing, painting, buying, wearing, having or concealing any human figure under any circumstance, blessed be the Most High.

He hid the medallion among the folds of his clothes because he knew he could get a nice sum for it from the merchants on their way to the Red Sea and Egypt, with his spirit tranquil because he wasn't the one who had sculpted or drawn, nor painted nor bought, worn, carried or hidden any object that featured the human figure.

As he was thinking that and had made the pendant vanish, he noticed that lovely Amani, with her clothes half-torn, was showing part of that lascivious body that was a sin in and of itself. He had already heard it from some men, that beneath those insinuating clothes there must be an exceptional body.

In the background was the sound of the mufti calling the people to the Zuhr prayer.

'If you scream, I'll have to kill you. Don't make me do that,' he warned.

He forced her to lean forward against a shelf that held jars of grain, finally naked, resplendent, sobbing. And the minx let Alí Bahr penetrate her and it was a pleasure beyond paradise except for her whimpering, and I was too trusting and I closed my eyes, carried away on waves of infinite pleasure, blessed be ... anyway, you get the picture.

'Then I felt that horrible stab and when I opened my eyes and stood up, honourable Qadi, I saw before me those crazy eyes and the hand that had stabbed me, still holding the skewer. I had to interrupt my praying of the Zuhr because of the pain.'

'And why do you think she was compelled to stab you when you were absorbed in prayer?'

'I believe she wanted to rob me of my basket of dates.'

'And what did you say this woman's name was?'

'Amani.'

'Bring her here,' he said to the twins.

The bell tower of the Concepció rang out twelve and then one. The traffic had lessened hours earlier and Adrià didn't want to get up, not even to make a pee pee or to prepare a chamomile tea. He wanted to know what the Qadi would say.

'First you must know,' said the Qadi patiently, 'that I am the one asking the questions. And then, you must remember that, if you lie to me, you will pay with your life.'

She answers: 'Honourable Qadi: a strange man entered my home.'

'With a basket of dates.'

'Yes.'

'That he wanted to sell to you.'

'Yes.'

'And why didn't you want to buy them?'

'My father doesn't allow me to.'

'Who is your father?'

'Azizzadeh Alfalati, the merchant. And besides, I have no money to buy anything.'

'Where is your father?'

'They forced him to kick me out of the house and to not cry for me.'

'Why?'

'Because I have been dishonoured.'

'And you say it like that, so calmly?'

'Honourable Qadi: I told you that I am not lying and I swear that on my life.'

'Why are you dishonoured?'

'I was raped.'

'By whom?'

'By the man who wanted to sell me the dates. His name is Alí Bahr.'

'And why did he do it?'

'Ask him. I do not know.'

'Did you make advances on him?'

'No. Never! I am a modest woman.'

Silence. The Qadi observed her closely. Finally, she lifted

her head and said I know: he wanted to steal a jewel I was wearing.

'What jewel?'

'A pendant.'

'Show it to me.'

'I cannot. He stole it from me. And then he raped me.'

The kind Qadi, once he had Alí Bahr before him for the second time, waited patiently until they taken the woman out of his presence. When the twins had closed the door, he said in a soft voice what's this about a stolen pendant, Alí Bahr?

'Pendant? Me?'

'You didn't steal any pendant from Amani?'

'She's a liar!' He lifted his arms: 'Search my clothes, sir.'

'So it is a lie.'

'A filthy lie. She has no jewels in her home, just a skewer to stab he who pauses in the conversation to pray the Zuhr, or perhaps the Asr, I no longer recall exactly which it was.'

'Where is the skewer?'

Alí Bahr pulled the skewer he carried hidden in his clothes and held it out with extended arms, as if making an offering to the Most High.

'She stabbed me with this, kind Qadi.'

The Qadi took the skewer, one of those used to impale bits of lamb meat, examined it and, gestured with his head to send Alí Bahr out of the room. He waited, meditating, as the twins brought the murderous Amani before him. He showed her the skewer. 'Is this yours?' he said.

'Yes! How do you have it?'

'You confess that it is yours?'

'Yes. I had to defend myself against the man who …'

The Qadi addressed the twins, who were holding up the room's far wall: 'Take away this carrion,' he said to them, without yelling, tired of having to put up with such malice in the world.

The merchant Azizzadeh Alfalati was warned not to shed a tear because crying for a stoned woman is a sin that offends the Most High. And he was not allowed to show any grief, blessed be the Merciful One. Nor did they let him say goodbye since, like the good man he was, he had disowned her when he found out that she had allowed herself to be raped. Azizzadeh locked himself in his house and no one was able to know whether he was crying or talking to his wife who had died many years earlier.

And finally the first stone, not too small nor too large, accompanied by a roar of rage that enflamed the pain he felt in his belly ever since the murderous stab, hit the left cheek of that whore Amani who was still shouting saying Alí Bahr raped me and robbed me. Father! My father! Lut, don't hurt me, you and I are … Help! Is there a single compassionate man here? But the stone thrown by her friend Lut landed on her temple and left her half dazed, there in the hole that prevented her from moving her hands and defending herself. And Lut was proud of having as good an aim as Drago Gradnik. The rocks began to rain down, not excessively big nor too tiny, and now they came from the hands of twelve volunteers, and Amani's face was painted red, like the carmine some whores put on their lips to attract men's attention and make them lose their good judgement. Alí Bahr hadn't thrown another stone because Amani had stopped shouting and now stared him down. She had penetrated him, skewered him, run through him with her gaze, like Gertrud, exactly like Gertrud, and the pain in his belly had flared up with intensity. Now, lovely Amani could no longer cry because a rock had smashed her eye. And a larger, more angular stone had hit her mouth and the girl was choking on her own broken teeth, and what hurt the most was that the twelve just men continued to throw stones and if someone missed, even though they were so close, he would stifle a curse and try to be more precise with the next one. And the names of the twelve just men were Ibrahim, Bàqir, Lut, Marwan, Tàhar, Uqba, Idris, Zuhayr, Hunayn, another Tàhar, another Bàqir and Màhir, blessed be the Most High, the Compassionate One, the Merciful One. Azizzadeh, from his house, heard the roars of the twelve volunteers and he knew that three of the boys were from the town and as children had played with his daughter until she began to bleed each month and he had to hide her away, blessed be the Merciful One. And when he heard a general howl he understood that his Amani, after that atrocious suffering, was dead. Then, he kicked out the stool and his whole body fell, held around the neck by a rope used for bundling forrage. His body danced with the convulsions of his choking and, before the howling had faded out, Azizzadeh was already dead, searching for his daughter to bring her before his distant wife. Ill-fated Azizzadeh Alfalati's lifeless body pissed on a basket of dates, in the corridor of the shop. And a few streets away, Amani, her neck broken by a rock that was too large, I warned you not to use such big ones! You see? She's dead now. Who was it? And the twelve volunteers pointed at Alí Bahr, who had done it because he could no longer bear the blind gaze of that whore who stared at him with the only eye she had left, as if that were her vengeance: the gift of a stare that he would be unable to shake, not awake nor in dreams. And I still wrote that Alí Bahr, the very next day, showed up at the merchants' caravan that was planning to head to Alexandria in Egypt to trade with Christian seamen, now that the city had fallen into British hands. Alí Bahr approached the one who looked most resolute and opened his palm before him, making sure there were no witnesses from the town nearby. The other man looked at the pendant, picked it up to have a closer look, Alí Bahr made a prudent gesture, the other man understood it and led him into a corner near a resting camel. Despite the laws, despite the holy words of the Koran, he was interested in the object. The merchant examined the pendant more closely and ran his fingers over the medallion as if he wanted to wipe it clean.

'It is gold,' said Alí Bahr. 'And the chain is, too.'

'I know. But it is stolen.'

'What are you saying! Do you wish to offend me?'

'Take it however you wish.'

He gave the pendant that belonged to lovely Amani back to Alí Bahr, who didn't want to take it, shaking his head, his arms out at his sides, surely because that gold had already begun to burn his insides. He had to accept the scandalously low price the merchant offered him. When Alí Bahr left, the merchant contemplated the medallion. Christian letters. In Alexandria he'd sell it easily. Satisfied, he ran his fingers over it, as if he wanted to wipe it clean. He thought for a while, moved away from the oil lamp he had lit and said, looking at young Brocia: 'I know this medallion from somewhere.'

'Well, it's ... the Madonna of Moena, I think.'

'Santa Maria dai Ciüf.' He turned the medallion over so the young man could see the other side: 'Of Pardàc, you see?'

'Really?'

'You can't read. Are you a Mureda?'

'Yes, sir,' lied young Brocia. 'I need money because I am going to Venice.'

'You Muredas are a restless bunch.' Still examining the medallion, he added, 'You want to be a sailor?'

'Yes. And go far away. To Africa.'

'They're after you, aren't they?'

The jeweller put the medallion down on the table and looked into his eyes.

'What did you do?' he asked.

'Nothing. How much will you give me for it?'

'You know that the sea moves more the further inland you get?'

'How much will you give me for the medallion, Godfather?'

'Hold onto it for when the bad times come, Son.'

Instinctively, young Brocia glanced quickly around the workshop of that nosy Jew. They were alone.

'I want money now, you understand me?'

'What happened to Jachiam Mureda?' asked the old goldsmith of La Plana, curiously.

'He is with his family, with Agno, Jenn, Max, Hermes, Josef, Theodor, Micurà, Ilse, Erica, Katharina, Matilde, Gretchen and little blind Bettina.'

'I'm glad. I mean it.'

'Me too. They are all together, underground, being eaten by worms, who when they can't find any more meat on them will gnaw on their souls.' He took the pendant from his fingers. 'Are you going to buy the ffucking medallion already or should I pull out my knife?'

Just then, the bells of the Concepció sounded three in the morning and Adrià thought tomorrow I won't be good for anything.

As if it were a grain of sand, the drama also began with a harmless, unimportant gesture. It was the comment that Adrià made the day after the stonings, at dinner, when he said, well, have you had a chance to think it over?

'Think what over?'

'No, whether … I mean, whether you're going back home or

'Or I should look for a pension. All right, fine.'

'Hey, don't get cross. I just want to know what … eh?'

'And what's your hurry?' you said, cutting me off, haughty, curt, totally taking Bernat's side.

'Nothing, nothing, I didn't say a thing.'

'Don't worry. I'll leave tomorrow.'

Bernat looked towards Sara and said I really appreciate your putting me up for these last few days.

'Bernat, I didn't want to …'

'Tomorrow, after rehearsal, I will come for my things.' With one hand he cut off my attempt at an excuse. 'You're right, it was getting to be time for me to move my arse.' He smiled at us. 'I was starting to go to seed.'

'And what will you do? Go back home?'

'I don't know. I'll decide tonight.'

While Bernat was thinking it over, Adrià felt that Sara's silence, as she put on her pyjamas and brushed her teeth, was too thick. I think that I'd only seen her that cross one other time. So I took refuge in Horace. Stretched out on the bed, I read Solvitur acris hiems grata vice veris et Favoni / trahuntque siccas machinae carinas …

'You really outdid yourself, you know?' said Sara, hurt, as she entered the room.

… ac neque iam stabulis gaudet pecus aut arator igni. Adrià looked up from the odes and said what?

'You really outdid yourself there with your friend.'

'Why?'

'If he's suuuuch a good friend …'

'Since he's suuuuch a good friend I always tell him the truth.'

'Like he does, when he tells you that he admires your wisdom and that he is proud to see how the European universities are asking for you and how your reputation is becoming established and …'

'I wish I could say something like that about Bernat. I can say it about his music, but he pays me no mind.'

And he went back to Horace and read ac neque iam stabulis gaudet pecus aut arator igni / nec prata canis albiant pruinis.

'Fine. Fantastic. Merveilleux.'

'Huh?' Adrià lifted his head again as he thought nec prata cani albicant pruinis. Sara looked at him furiously. She was going to say something, but chose instead to leave the room. She half-closed the door angrily, but without making noise. Even when you got mad, you did it discreetly. Except for that one day. Adrià looked at the half-open door, not entirely aware of what was happening. Because what came into his head, like a tumultuous torrent, offended by being put off for so long, was that dum gravis Cyclopum/Volcanus ardens visit officinas.

'Huh?' said Sara, opening the door but keeping her hand on the knob.

'No, sorry. I was thinking out loud.'

She half-closed the door again. She must have been standing on the other side. She didn't like to go around the house in a nightgown when other people were there. I didn't know that you were debating between being true to your word and going for my jugular. She opted to be true to her word and came back in, got into bed and said goodnight.

For whom do you tie back your blonde hair with such simple elegance? thought Adrià absurdly, looking puzzled at his Sara, lying with her back to him, cross about who knows what, with her black hair spilling over her shoulders. With such simple elegance. I didn't know what to think and I opted for closing the book of odes and turning off the light. I lay there for a long time with my eyes open.

The next day, when Sara and Adrià got up, at the usual hour, there was no trace of Bernat, nor his violin and scores, nor his clothes. Just a note on the kitchen table that said, thank you, dear friends. Really, thank you. In the guest room, the sheets he had used were folded on the bed. He was completely gone and I felt very badly.

'How.'

'What.'

'You really screwed up, dear hunting companion.'

'I didn't ask for your opinion.'

'But you really screwed up. Right, Carson?'

Adrià could only hear the unpleasant sound of the valiant sheriff's disdainful spit hitting the ground.

Strangely, Sara, when she realised that Bernat had fled, didn't reproach me at all. Life continued along its course. But it took me years to put the pieces together.

Adrià had spent the whole afternoon looking at the wall of his study, unable to write a line, unable to concentrate on any reading, staring at the wall, as if searching for the answer to his perplexity there. At mid-afternoon, when he hadn't even made good use of ten minutes, he decided to prepare some tea. From the kitchen he said would you like a cuppa?, and he heard a mmm that came from Sara's studio and he interpreted it as yes, thank you, what a good idea. When he went into the studio with the steaming cup, he contemplated the nape of her neck. She had gathered her hair in a ponytail, as she usually did when she was drawing. I love your plait, your ponytail, your hair, no matter what you do with it. Sara was drawing, on an oblong sheet, some houses that could have been a half-abandoned village. In the background, she was now sketching a farmhouse. Adrià took a sip of tea and stood there with his mouth open, watching how the abandoned farmhouse grew bit by bit. And with a cypress tree half-split, most likely by lightning. And without warning, Sara returned to the fore-ground with the street of houses, on the left side of the sheet, and made the voussoirs that marked a window which didn't yet exist. She drew it so quickly that Adrià had to wonder how that had happened, how had Sara been able to see the window there where there'd been only white paper. Now that it was fin-ished, it seemed to him that it had always been there; he even had the impression that when she'd bought the paper at Can Terricabres they had sold it to her with the window already drawn on to it; and he also thought that Sara's talent was a miracle. Without giving it the slightest importance, Sara went back to the farmhouse and darkened the open front door, and the house – which up until that point was a drawing – began to come to life, as if the darkness of the blurred charcoal had given her permission to imagine the life that had been inside. Adrià took another slurp of Sara's tea, awestruck.

'Where do you get that from?'

'From here,' she said, pointing to her forehead with a blackened finger and leaving a print there.

Now she started to age the path, restoring the wagon tracks that had gone from the farmhouse to the town over decades, and I envied Sara's creative ability. When I finished the tea I had brought for her, I returned to my initial bewilderment that had kept me from working all afternoon. When she had come back from the gynaecologist, Sara had left her bag open by the door and gone quickly into the toilet, and Adrià went through her bag because he was looking for some money so he wouldn't have to go by the bank and he found the report from Doctor Andreu for her general practitioner that I couldn't help but read, mea culpa, yes, because she hadn't showed it to me, and the report said that the womb of the patient Mrs Sara Voltes-Epstein, which had only carried one gestation to term, despite the sporadic metrorrhagias, was perfectly healthy. Therefore, she had decided to remove her IUD, which was the most likely cause of the metrorrhagias. And I secretly consulted the dictionary, like when I looked up what brothel and poof meant, and I remembered that 'metro-' was the prefixed form of the Greek word *mētra*, which means 'uterus', and that '-rrhagia' was the suffixed form of the Greek word *rhēgnymi*, which means 'to spurt'. Spurting uterus, which could be the name of one of Black Eagle's relatives, but no: it was the bleeding that had her so worried. He'd forgotten that Sara had to go to the doctor about that bleeding. Why hadn't she mentioned it? And then Adrià reread the part that said she had only carried one gestation to term and he understood why so much silence. Holy hell.

And now Adrià was before her, his mouth hanging open like an idiot, drinking her cuppa and admiring her ability to create profound worlds in just two dimensions, and her obsession with keeping everything secret.

A fig tree; it looked like a fig tree. To one side of the farmhouse a fig tree grew and, leaned against one wall, a cart wheel.

And Sara said are you going to stand there all day breathing down my neck?

'I like to watch you draw.'

'I'm shy and I hold back.'

'What did the doctor say? Didn't you have an appointment today?'

'Nothing, fine. I'm fine.'

'And the bleeding?'

'It's the IUD. She took it out, as a precaution.'

'So nothing to worry about.'

'Right.'

'Well, we'll have to think about what to use now.'

What is that about your womb only having carried one gestation to term? Eh, Sara? Eh?

Sara turned around and looked at him. She had a small charcoal mark on her forehead. Did I think out loud?, thought Adrià to himself. Sara looked at the cup and wrinkled her nose and said hey, you drank my tea!

'Oh, man, sorry!' said Adrià. And she laughed with that laugh of hers that always reminded me of the babbling of a brook. I pointed to a drawing: 'Where is that supposed to be?'

'It's how I imagine Tona from the way you describe it, back when you were a boy.'

'It's lovely … But it looks abandoned.'

'Because one day you grew up and abandoned it. You see?' She pointed to the road. 'This is where you tripped and grazed your knees.'

'I love you.'

'I love you more.'

Why didn't you tell me anything about that pregnancy you had, when a child is the most important thing in the world. Is your child alive? Did it die? What was it called? Was it really born? Was it a girl or a boy? What was it like? I know that you have every right to not tell me everything about your life, but you can't keep all the pain to yourself and I'd like to share in it.

'Rsrsrsrsrsrsrsrsrsr.'

'Coming,' said Adrià. About the drawing, 'When you finish it, I'd like to reserve half an hour of contemplation.'

When he opened the door for the messenger, he still had the empty cup in his hand.

At dinnertime they opened the bottle that looked like it was the most expensive one in the package Max had sent them. Six bottles of wine, all top-quality reds and all jotted down in the little book that Max himself had had published with his own tasting comments. The lavish book, filled with fine photographs, was some sort of 'Easy Guide to Wines' aimed at the rushed palate of the American gourmet.

'You have to taste it in a glass.'

'Pouring straight from the pitcher into my mouth is more fun.'

'Sara: if your brother suspected that you drink his wines like that …'

'Fine. But only for the tasting.' She picked up the glass. 'What does Max say about this one?'

Adrià, all serious, served two glasses, picked one up by the stem and was about to read the text with a solemn expression; vaguely, he thought about school, in the times that, because of some scheduling error, he had attended mass and seen the priest up on the altar, with patens and cups, and cruets, officiating mysteries muttered in Latin. And he began to pray and he said domina mea, aged Priorat is a complex, velvety wine. It has a dense aroma, with a clove aftertaste and toasted notes, due to the quality of the oak barrels in which it was aged.

He gestured to Sara and they both had a taste as they'd seen Max do when he taught them how to taste wines. That day they had almost ended up dancing the conga on the dining room table.

'Do you notice the clove?'

'No. I notice the traffic on València Street.'

'Try to block that out and focus,' ordered Adrià, clicking his tongue. 'I … I think I note some sort of coconut aftertaste.'

'Coconut?'

Why don't you tell me your secrets, Sara? What aftertaste does your life have, with the episodes I don't know? Truffle or blackberry? Or the aftertaste of a child I've never met? But having a child is something normal, something everyone wants. What do you have against life?

As if she had heard his thoughts, Sara said look, look, look, look what Max says: this Priorat is virile, complex, intense, potent and structured.

'My giddy aunt.'

'Sounds like he's talking about a stud.'

'Do you like it or not?'

'Yes. But it's too strong for me. I'll have to dilute it.'

'Poor you. Max will kill you.'

'He doesn't need to know about it.'

'I could tell on you.'

'Mouchard, salaud.'

'It's a joke.'

They drank, read the poetic prose that Max directed at the American buyers of Priorats, Costers del Segre, Montsants and I don't remember what other wines, and we got tipsy enough that the shrill explosion of a rushing motorcycle, instead of annoying us, made us burst into laughter. And you ended up pouring the diluted wine straight into your mouth with your little spouted pitcher, may Max forgive you, and I will never tell your brother. And I was unable to ask you what was all that about having had a child or having been pregnant. Had you lost it? Whose child was it? And then the damn phone rang, appearing in my life when it shouldn't. I wasn't strong enough to get rid of the telephone altogether but, given the results, my life without it would have been a bit more tolerable. Bloody hell, I was quite dizzy. No, no, I'm on my way. Hello.

'Adrià.'

'Max?'

'Yes.'

'Bloody hell. We are celebrating with your wines! I swear Sara isn't using the pitcher, all right? We started with a Priorat that was virile, potent, complex and I don't know what the hell else. It was so strong it could walk. Thanks for the gift, Max.'

'Adrià.'

'Fantastic.'

'Father's died.'

'And the book is wonderful. The photos and the text.'

Adrià swallowed hard, still a bit cloudy, and said what did you say? And Sara, you always attentive, said what's wrong?

'Father's died, did you hear, Adrià?'

'Holy hell.'

Sara got up and came over to the telephone. I said it's your father, Sara. And into the telephone: we're on our way, Max.

The two notices of the deaths of your parents, both over the phone and unexpectedly, even though Mr Voltes had been in poor health for a several years and his heart had been acting up, and we already knew that at his age one day we would get the unpleasant news. And Max seemed very affected because even though he'd been taking care of him – he had never moved out of his parents' house – he hadn't seen it coming and wasn't home when he died, and as soon as he arrived, the nurse told him Mr Voltes, your father. He felt vaguely guilty; and I took him aside and I said Max, you've been a model son, always by your parents' side. Don't beat yourself up because it would be as unfair to you as … how old was he? Eighty?

'Eighty-six.'

I didn't dare to use his advanced age as an argument to assuage Max's conscience. I merely repeated eighty-six a couple of times, without knowing what else to say, strolling through the grandiose parlour of the Voltes-Epstein house, beside Max who, even though he was more than a head taller than me, looked like a disconsolate child. Yes, yes: I was capable of preachiness. It's so easy to give others advice.

This time I was allowed to accompany the family to the synagogue and the cemetery. Max explained to me that his father had wanted to be buried according to the Jewish ritual and so they wrapped him in a white shroud and put his tallit over it, which the Chevra Kaddisha asked Max, as first-born son, to tear. And in the Jewish cemetery of Les Corts, he was buried in the earth, beside his Rachel, the mother that no one allowed me to love. Sara, what a shame that things went the way they did, I thought as, at the cemetery, the rabbi recited the maleh rachamim. And when silence fell, Max and Sara stepped forward and, holding hands, recited the kaddish for Pau Voltes and I began to cry, hiding from myself.

Sara lived through those days in profound grief and the questions that I wanted to ask you were no longer urgent because what was about to happen to us would erase it all.

The area around Headington House was tranquil and placid, just as Adrià had imagined it. Before Sara rang the bell, she looked at him, smiled and Adrià knew he was the most loved being on earth and he had to hold himself back to keep from covering her in kisses just as a maid opened the door. Behind her rose the splendid figure of Aline de Gunzbourg. Sara and her distant aunt embraced in silence, as if they were old friends who hadn't seen each other for donkey's years; or as if they were two colleagues who respected each other deeply but still maintained a certain rivalry; or like two polite ladies, one much younger than the other, who had to treat each other with extreme courtesy for some professional reasons; or like a niece and aunt who had never met before; or like two people who knew that they had only narrowly escaped the long hand of the Abwehr, the Gestapo and the SS because life's calendar had kept them from being in the wrong place at the wrong time. Because evil strives to corrupt all plans of happiness, no matter how humble, and struggles to exert as much destruction as possible in its immediate surroundings. Spermatozoa, ova, frenetic dances, premature deaths, voyages, escapes, knowledge, hope, doubts, breakups, reconciliation, moves and many other difficulties that could have kept that encounter from happening had been defeated by the warm embrace between two strangers, two grown women, one forty-six and the other over seventy, both silent, both smiling, at the front door of Headington House, before me. Life is so strange.

'Come in.'

She extended her hand to me without losing her smile. We shook hands in silence. Two framed scores by Bach greeted the visitors. I made an effort to remain calm and was thus able to offer a polite smile to Aline de Gunzbourg.

We spent two unforgettable hours in Isaiah Berlin's study, on the upper floor of Headington House, surrounded by books, with the clock on the mantelpiece making the time pass too quickly. Berlin was very downcast, as if he were certain his time was drawing near. He listened to Aline, repressing a smile, and said I haven't got much rope left. You are the ones who must keep on. And then, in a softer voice, he said I don't fear death; I just get angry with it. Death makes me mad but it doesn't scare me. Where you are, death isn't; where death is, you aren't. Therefore, fearing it is a waste a time. And he talked about it so much that I am sure he was scared of it, perhaps as much as I am. And then he added Wittgenstein said that death isn't an event in life. And Adrià thought to ask him what surprised him about life.

'Surprises me?' He pondered the question. As if arriving slowly from a distance, the tick tock of the clock took over the room and our thoughts. 'Surprises me ...' he repeated. And he made up his mind, 'Well, yes: the simple fact that I've been able to live with such serenity and pleasure through such horrors, in the worst century that humanity has ever known. Because it has been the worst, by a long shot. And not only for the Jews.'

He looked at me shyly, as if hesitating, searching for the appropriate expression and in the end added I've been happy, but survivor's guilt and remorse have always gnawed at me.

'What?' said Aline and Sara at the same time.

Then I realised that he had mumbled those last few words in Russian. And I translated them without moving, without taking my eyes off of him, because Berlin hadn't yet finished speaking. And now, in English, he took up the thread of his thoughts and said what did I do, why did nothing happen to me? He shook his head: 'Unfortunately most Jews of this century live with this weight burdening us.'

'I believe Jews of other centuries did as well,' said Sara.

Berlin looked at her with his mouth open and nodded in silence. And then, as if it were a way of banishing sad thoughts, he spoke about Professor Adrià Ardèvol's publications. It seems he had read *Història del pensament europeu* with interest; he liked it, but he still considered *La voluntat estètica* the real gem.

'I still can't believe it found its way into your hands.'

'Oh! It was through a friend of yours. Right, Aline? Those two awkward figures, one six feet tall and the other not even five, who just stood there ...' Smiling, he reminisced staring straight ahead, at the wall. 'Strange pair.'

'Isaiah ...'

'They were convinced I would be interested in it and so they brought it to me.'

'Isaiah, wouldn't you like a tea?'

'Yes, tell me ...'

'Would you like tea as well?' Now Tante Aline asked all of us.

'What two friends of mine?' asked Adrià, surprised.

'A Gunzbourg. Aline has so many relatives ... sometimes I mix them up.'

'Gunzbourg ...' said Adrià, not grasping it.

'One moment ...'

Berlin got up with some effort and went into one corner. I caught a glance between Aline Berlin and Sara, and I still found it all very strange. Berlin returned with a copy of my book. I puffed up with pride to see that there were five or six little slips of papers sticking out of its pages. He opened it, pulled one out and read Bernat Plensa of Barcelona.

'Ah, of course, yes,' said Adrià, not knowing what he was saying.

I don't remember much more of the conversation because I went blank. And just then the maid came in with a huge tray filled with all the tools and elements necessary to enjoy a proper tea as God and the Queen dictate. They spoke of many more things that I can only scarcely and indistinctly remember. What a pleasure, what luxury, that long conversation with Isaiah Berlin and Tante Aline ...

'What do I know!?' said Sara the three times Adrià wondered, on the trip home, if she knew what Bernat had to do with all that. And on the fourth she said why don't you invite him over for one of these new teas we bought?

'Mmm ... Superb. British tea always tastes different. Don't you find?'

'I knew you'd like it. But don't change the subject.'

'Me?'

'Yes. When did you go visit Isaiah Berlin?'

'Who?'

'Isaiah Berlin.'

'Who's that?'

'*The Power of Ideas. Liberty. Russian Thinkers.*'

'What are you talking about?' To Sara: 'What's wrong with Adrià?' And both of them, lifting their cups, repeated: 'Superb tea.' And he scratched his noggin.

'*The Hedgehog and the Fox,*' said Adrià, making a concession to a wider audience.

'Bloody hell, you're off your rocker.' And to Sara: 'Has he been like this long?'

'Isaiah Berlin told me that you had made him read *La voluntat estètica.*'

'What are you talking about?'

'Bernat, what's going on?'

Adrià looked at Sara, who was very busy serving more tea even though no one had asked for any.

'Sara, what's going on?'

'Huh?'

'Someone is hiding something from me here ...' Suddenly he remembered: 'You and a very short bloke. 'A strange pair,' was how Berlin defined you. Who was the other man?'

'Well, Berlin is off his rocker. I've never been to Oxford.'

Silence. There was no clock on any mantelpiece going tick tock. But the soft breeze that emanated from the Urgell on the wall could be felt, the sun still illuminating the bell tower of Santa Maria de Gerri in the dining room of the house. And the murmur of the water on the river that came down from Burgal. Suddenly, Adrià pointed to Bernat and, calmly, imitating Sheriff Carson: 'You gave yourself away, kid.'

'Me?'

'You don't even know who Berlin is, you've never even heard of him, but somehow you know he lives in Oxford.'

Bernat looked towards Sara, who avoided his gaze. Adrià observed them both and said tu quoque, Sara?

'She quoque,' admitted Bernat. With his head lowered he said I think I forgot to mention one little detail.

'Go ahead. I'm listening.'

'It all started …' Bernat looked at Sara, 'five or six years ago?'

'Seven and a half.'

'Yes. With ages … I'm not … Seven and a half years ago.'

As soon as she came into the bar, he put a copy of the German edition of *La voluntat estètica* in front of her. She looked at the book, she looked at Bernat, she looked back at the book and she made a sign of not knowing what was going on as she sat down.

'Would the lady like anything?' The smile of a somewhat obsequious bald waiter who had emerged from the darkness.

'Two waters,' said Bernat, impatiently. And the waiter left without hiding his displeasure and muttering you can dress up a pig, as my father used to say. Bernat continued, ignoring him:

'I have an idea. I wanted to check with you about it, but you have to swear you won't say a word to Adrià.'

Negotiations: how can I swear over something when I don't know what it is. He can't know. All right, but first tell me what this is about so I can swear whatever you need me to. It's madness. More reason not to swear, unless it's some madness that's really worth it. It's madness that's really worth it. For goodness sake, Bernat. I need you in on this, Saga.

'My name is not Saga.' Peevish: 'My name is Sagga.'

'Oh, sorry.'

After that push and pull, they reached the conclusion that Sagga's swearing would be provisional, with the option of rescinding it if the idea was too too too crazy that there was just no way.

'You told me that your family knew Isaiah Berlin. Is that still true?'

'Well, yeah … His wife is … I think she's a distant relative of some Epstein cousins.'

'Is there any way of ... You putting me in touch with him?'

'What do you want to do?'

'Bring him this book: so he can read it.'

'Listen, people don't just ...'

'I'm sure he's going to like it.'

'You're insane. How do you expect him to read something by a stranger who ...'

'I already told you it was madness,' he interrupted. 'But I want to try.'

Sara thought it over. I can imagine you rubbing your forehead, the way you do when you think things over, my love. And I see you sitting at the table of some bar, looking at Bernat the Mad, not quite able to believe what he's telling you. I see you telling him wait, and flipping through your address book, and finding Tante Chantal's phone number, and calling from the bar telephone, which took tokens; Bernat had asked the waiter for dozens of tokens that started dropping when she said allô, ma chère tante, ça marche bien? ( ... ) Oui. ( ... ) Oui. ( .... ) Aoui. ( ....... ) Aaooui. ( ......... ... . ), and Bernat, undaunted, putting more tokens into the phone and asking the waiter for even more, with a peremptory gesture, it's an emergency, and leaving a hundred-peseta note on the table as a guarantee, and Sara still saying Oui. ( .................. ) Oui. ( ...................... ) Aoui. ( ......... .................. ), until the waiter said that's it, did he think this was the phone company, he didn't have any more tokens and then, Sara quickly asked her auntie about the Berlins and started jotting things down in her address book and saying oui, oui, ouiii! ..., and in the end, when she was thanking her, ma chère tante, for her help, and the telephone made a click and cut off for lack of tokens and she was left with that uncomfortable sensation that she hadn't had a chance to say goodbye to her chère tante Chantal.

'What did she say?'

'That she will try to talk to Aline.'

'Who is Aline?'

'Berlin's wife.' Sara checked the pages with undecipherable handwriting: 'Aline Elisabeth Yvonne de Gunzbourg.'

'Brilliant! We've got it!'

'Wait, we've got the contact. But that's just …'

Bernat snatched her address book from her, 'What did you say her name was?'

She took it back and consulted it: 'Aline Elisabeth Yvonne de Gunzbourg.'

'Gunzbourg?'

'Yes, what? It's a family that's very … Half Russian and half French. Barons and things like that. These ones are rich.'

'Holy Mother of God.'

'Shhh, don't swear.'

Bernat gave her a kiss; well: or two or three or four, because I think Bernat has always been a bit enamoured of you. I say that now, now that you are over your desire to contradict me; just so you know, I think that every man fell a little bit in love with you. I fell completely and utterly.

'But Adrià should know about this!'

'No. I already told you it's pure madness.'

'It's pure madness, but he should know.'

'No.'

'Why not?'

'It's my gift to him. I think it's more of a gift if he never finds out about it.'

'If he never finds out, he'll never be able to thank you for it.'

And that must have been when the waiter, from one corner of the table, concealed a smile when he saw the man saying in a slightly louder voice this conversation is over, Mrs Voltes-Epstein. This is how I want it. Will you swear?

After a few seconds of silent tension, the man got down on one knee before the lady, in an imploring pose. Then, the elegant woman lowered her eyes and said, 'I swear it to you, Bernat.'

The waiter ran a hand over his bald skull and concluded that lovers were always making fools of themselves. If they could see themselves through my eyes … Now, the woman is beautiful, lovely as a summer's day, that's a fact. I'd make a fool of myself over her too.

It turned out that yes, Franz-Paul Decker's model French horn, Romain Gunzbourg, timid, blond and short, a secret pianist, was a member of the Gunzbourg family and knew Aline Elisabeth Yvonne de Gunzbourg, of course. Romain was from the poor branch of the family, and if you'd like, I can call Tante Aline right now.

'Bloody hell ... Tante Aline!'

'Yes. She married some important philosopher or something like that. But they've been living in England forever. What's it for?'

And Bernat gave him a kiss on each cheek, even though he wasn't enamoured of Romain. Everything was coming up roses. They had to wait for the spring, for the Easter week gigs, and before that Romain had long conversations with Tante Aline to get her on their side. And when they were in London, which was the end of the orchestra's mini-tour, they hopped on a train that left them in Oxford at mid-morning. Headington House seemed deserted when they rang the doorbell, which made a noble sound. They looked at each other, somewhat expectant, and no one came to open the door. And it was the time they'd agreed on. No. Yes, tiny footsteps. And finally the door opened. An elegant woman looked at them, puzzled.

'Tante Aline,' said Romain Gunzbourg.

'Romain?'

'Yes.'

'You've grown so much!' she lied. 'You were like this ...' She pointed to her waist. Then she had them come in, pleased with her role as a co-conspirator.

'He will see you; but I can't guarantee that he'll read it.'

'Thank you, madam. Truly,' said Bernat.

She had them go into some sort of small hallway. On the walls were framed scores by Bach. Bernat pointed with his chin to one of the reproductions. Romain went over to it. In a whisper: 'I told you I was from the poor branch.' About the framed score: 'I'm sure it's an original.'

A door opened and Tante Aline had them come into a large room, filled with books from top to bottom, ten times more

books than in Adrià's house. And a table filled with folders
stuffed with papers. And some piles of books with numerous
slips of long paper as bookmarks. And before the desk, sitting
in an armchair was Isaiah Berlin, with a book in his hand,
who looked curiously at that strange pair who had entered his
sanctuary.

'How did it go?' asked Sara, when he came back.

Berlin seemed tired. He spoke little and when Bernat gave
him the copy of *Der ästhetische Wille*, the man took it, turned
it over and then opened it at the index. For a long minute no
one said a peep. Tante Aline winked at her nephew. When
Berlin finished examining the book he closed it and left it in
his hands.

'And why do you think I should read it?'

'Well, I … If you don't want to …'

'Don't cringe, man! Why do you want me to read it?'

'Because it is very good. It's excellent, Mr Berlin. Adrià
Ardèvol is a profound and intelligent man. But he lives too far
from the centre of the world.'

Isaiah Berlin put the book on a small table and said every
day I read and every day I realise that I have everything left to
read. And every once in a while I reread, even though I only
reread that which deserves the privilege of rereading.

'And what earns it that privilege?' Now Bernat sounded
like Adrià.

'Its ability to fascinate the reader; to make him admire it
for its intelligence or its beauty. Even though with rereading,
by its very nature, we always enter into contradiction.'

'What do you mean, Isaiah?' interrupted Tante Aline.

'A book that doesn't deserve to be reread doesn't deserve to
be read either.' He looked at the guests. 'Have you asked them
if they would like some tea?' He looked at the book and he
immediately forgot his pragmatic suggestion. He continued:
'But before reading it we don't know that it's not worthy of a
rereading. Life is cruel like that.'

They spoke about everything for a little while, both of the
visitors sitting on the edge of the sofa. They didn't have any
tea because Romain had given his auntie a signal that it was

best to take advantage of the little time they had. And they spoke of the orchestra's tour.

'French horn? Why do you play the French horn?'

'I fell in love with the sound,' replied Romain Gunzbourg.

And then the strange pair told them that the next evening they would perform at the Royal Festival Hall. And the Berlins promised they would listen to them on the radio.

In the programme there was *Leonora* (number three), Robert Gerhard's second symphony and Bruckner's fourth with Gunzbourg on the French horn and dozens more musicians. It went well. Gerhard's widow attended, was moved, and received the bouquet of flowers meant for Decker. And the next day they returned home after five concerts in Europe that had left them worn out and with divided opinions about whether it was good to do microtours during the season or ruin the summer gigs with a more properly set-up tour or forget about tours altogether, with what they pay us we do enough just going to all the rehearsals, don't you think?

In the hotel, Bernat found an urgent message and thought what's happened to Llorenç, and that was the first time he worried about his son, perhaps because he was still thinking about the unwrapped book he had given him.

It was an urgent telephone message from Mr Isaiah Berlin that said, in the evening receptionist's handwriting, that he should come urgently to Headington House, if possible the next day, that it was very important.

'Tecla.'

'How did it go?'

'Well. Poldi Feichtegger came. Adorable: eighty-something years old. The bouquet of flowers was bigger than she was.'

'You are coming home tomorrow, right?'

'Well. I, it's that … I have to stay one more day, because …'

'Because of what?'

Bernat, loyal to his special way of complicating his life, didn't want to tell Tecla that Isaiah Berlin had asked him to come back to talk about my book, which he had found very, very interesting, which he had read in a matter of hours but was starting to reread because it had a series of perceptions

that he considered brilliant and profound, and that he wanted
to meet me. It would have been easy to tell her that. But Bernat
wouldn't be Bernat if he wasn't making his life more complicated. He didn't trust Tecla's ability to keep a secret, which I
have to admit he was right about. But he chose silence and
replied because an urgent job came up.

'What job?'

'This thing. It's … it's complicated.'

'Drinking French wine with a French horn?'

'No, Tecla. I have to go to Oxford to … There's a book that
… anyway I'll be home the day after tomorrow.'

'And they're going to change your ticket?'

'Ay, that's right.'

'Well: I think it'd be best, if you plan on flying back. If you
plan on coming back at all.'

And she hung up. Bollocks, thought Bernat; I screwed up
again. But the next morning he changed his plane ticket, took
the train to Oxford and Berlin told him what he had to tell
him and he gave him a note for me that read dear sir, your
book moved me deeply. Particularly the reflection on the
why behind beauty. And how this why can be asked in every
period of humanity. And also how it is impossible to separate
it from the inexplicable presence of evil. I just recommended
it effusively to some of my colleagues. When will it be published in English? Please, don't stop thinking and, every once
in a while, writing down your thoughts. Sincerely yours,
Isaiah Berlin. And I am so grateful to Bernat, for the consequences of his persuading Berlin to read my book, which were
essential for me, but even more so for the tenacity with which
he has always tried to help me. And I reward his efforts by
talking to him sincerely about his writings and causing him
severe bouts of depression. Friend, life is so hard.

'And swear to me one more time that you will never
mention it to Adrià.' He looked at her with fervent eyes. 'You
understand me, Sara?'

'I swear.' And after a pause: 'Bernat.'

'Hmmm?'

'Thank you. From me and from Adrià.'

'No need for that. I always owe Adrià things.'

'What do you owe him?'

'I don't know. Things. He's my friend. He's a kid who ... Even though he's so wise, he still wants to be my friend and put up with my crises. After all these years.'

## 45

Vissarion Grigoryevich Belinsky was to blame for the fact that when I turned fifty I started to brush up my neglected Russian. To distance myself from fruitless approaches to the nature of evil, I immersed myself in the suicidal attempt to bring Berlin, Vico and Llull together in one book and I was starting to see, to my surprise, that it was possible. As usually happened in moments of unexpected discoveries, I had to distance myself in order to reassure myself that the intuition wasn't a mirage and so I spent a few days paging through completely different things, including Belinsky. It was Belinksy, the scholar and enthusiastic propagandist of Pushkin, who gave me a pressing desire to read in Russian. Belinsky talking about Alexander Sergeyevich Pushkin and not Pushkin's work directly. I understood what the interest in others' literature meant, that which pushes you to create literature without realising it. I was passionate about Belinsky's passion, so much so that what I knew of Pushkin didn't impress me until I reread him after reading Belinsky. Before my eyes, Ruslan, Ludmila, Farlaf, Ratmir, Rodgay and also Chernomor and the Boss came to life, recited out loud thanks to what Belinsky had inspired in me. Sometimes I think about the power of art and about the study of art and I get frightened. Sometimes I don't understand why humanity is always fighting when there are so many other things to do. Sometimes I think that we are more wicked than we are poets and, therefore, that we are hopeless. The problem is that no one is without sin. Very, very few people, to be more precise. Very, very few. And then Sara came in and Adrià, whose gaze was on the inextricable whole: verses of jealousy, love and Russian language, could tell without looking at her that Sara's eyes were gleaming. He lifted his gaze.

'How did it go?'

She put down the folders with the portrait samples on the sofa.

'We are going to do the exhibition,' she said.

'Bravo!'

Adrià got up, glanced with a bit of nostalgia at Ludmila's doom and hugged Sara.

'Thirty portraits.'

'How many do you have?'

'Twenty-eight.'

'All charcoal?'

'Yes, yes: that will be the leitmotif: seeing the soul in charcoal or something like that. They have to find a really lovely phrase.'

'Make them show it to you first: to make sure they don't come up with something ridiculous.'

'Seeing the soul in charcoal isn't ridiculous.'

'No, of course not! But gallery owners aren't poets. And the ones at Artipèlag …' Pointing to the folders resting on the sofa: 'I'm so pleased. You deserve it.'

'I need to make two more portraits.'

I already knew that you wanted to make one of me. I wasn't thrilled with the idea, but I did like your enthusiasm. At my age I was starting to learn that more than things, what was important was the excitement we projected into them. That is what makes us people. And Sara was in an exceptional moment: every day she was more respected for her drawings. I had only twice asked why she didn't try her hand at painting, and she, with that gentle but definitive stance, both times told me no, Adrià, what makes me happy is drawing with pencil and charcoal. My life is in black and white, perhaps in memory of my family, who lived in black and white. Or perhaps …

'Perhaps there's no need for you to explain.'

'You're right.'

At dinnertime I said that I knew whom the other portrait should be of and she said who? and I answered a self-portrait. She stopped with her fork in the air, thinking it over;

I surprised you, Sara. You hadn't thought of that. You never think of yourself.

'I'm embarrassed,' you said, after a few long seconds of silence. And you put the bite of croquette into your mouth.

'Well, get over it. You're a big girl.'

'It's not arrogant?'

'No, quite the opposite; it is a display of humility: you bare the souls of twenty-nine people and you subject yourself to the same interrogation as the others. It would seem that you're restoring the order of things.'

Now I caught you again with your fork in the air. You put it down and you said you know, you might be right. And thanks to that, today as I write to you I have your extraordinary self-portrait on the wall in front of me, beside the incunabula, presiding over my world. It is the most valuable object in this study. Your self-portrait that was to be the last drawing in the exhibition you prepared so meticulously, whose opening you were unable to attend.

For me, Sara's work is some sort of window into inner silence. An invitation to introspection. Sara, I love you. And I remember you suggesting an order for the thirty artworks, and secretly making the first sketches for your self-portrait. And those at the Artipèlag Gallery outdid themselves: *Sara Voltes-Epstein. Charcoal drawings. A window into the soul.* It was a gorgeous catalogue that made one want to be sure to see the exhibition, or buy up every drawing. Your mature work that took you two years to complete. Without rushing, naturally, calmly, the way you've always done things.

The self-portrait is the work that took her the longest, locked up in her studio without witnesses, because she was embarrassed to be seen observing herself in the mirror, looking at herself on paper and working the details, the sweet crease at the corners of her lips, the small defeats that huddle inside the wrinkles. And the little lines at your eyes that are so much a part of you, Sara. And all those tiny signs that I don't know how to reproduce but which make a face, as if it were a violin, become a landscape that reflects the long winter voyage in full detail, with total immodesty, my God. As if it were the cruel tachograph that records the lorry driver's life, your face draws our tears, your tears without me, which I don't entirely know about and the tears for the misfortunes that befell your family and your people. And some joys that were beginning to show in the brightness of your eyes and illuminate the splendid face that I have before me now as I write you this long letter that was only meant to be a few pages. I love you. I discovered you, I lost you and I found you again. And above all we had the privilege to begin to grow old together. Until the moment that misfortune entered our house.

During those days she was unable to do any illustrations and the assignments began to pile up in a way that had never happened to her before. All her thoughts were focused on the charcoal portraits.

It was one month before the opening at the Artipèlag and I, before returning to Vico, Llull and Berlin, had gone from Pushkin and Belinsky to Hobbes, with his sinister vision of human nature, always prone to evil. And between one thing and another I ended up in his translation of the *Iliad*, which I read in a delicious mid-nineteenth-century edition. And yes, the misfortune.

Thomas Hobbes was trying to convince me that I had to choose between liberty and order because, otherwise, the wolf would come, the wolf that I had seen so many times in human nature when studying history and knowledge. I heard the sound of a key in the lock, the door closing silently and it wasn't the wolf Hobbes warned of, but Sara's mute footsteps, which entered the study. She stood there for a few seconds, still and soundless. I looked up and immediately realised that we had a problem. Sara sat on the sofa behind which I had spied on so many secrets with Carson and Black Eagle. She had trouble getting the words out. It was all too clear that she was searching for the right way to say it and Adrià took off his reading glasses and helped her along, saying, hey, Sara, what's wrong?

Sara got up, went to the instrument cabinet and pulled out

Vial. She put it on the reading table with a bit too much emphasis, almost covering up poor Hobbes who was in no way
to blame.

'Where did you get it from?'

'Father bought it.' Suspicious pause. 'I already showed you
the buyer's certificate. Why?'

'It's Vial, the only Storioni with a proper name.'

Sara kept silent, prepared to listen. And Guillaume-François Vial took a step out of the darkness, so the person inside
the carriage could see him. The coachman stopped the horses
right in front of him. He opened the door and Monsieur Vial
got into the coach.

'Good evening,' said La Guitte.

'You can give it to me, Monsieur La Guitte. My uncle has
agreed to the price.'

La Guitte laughed to himself, proud of his nose. So many
days roasting in Cremona's sun had been worth it. To make
sure: 'We are talking about five thousand florins.'

'We are talking about five thousand florins,' Monsieur Vial
reassured him.

'Tomorrow you will have the famous Lorenzo Storioni's
violin in your hands.'

'Don't try to deceive me: Storioni isn't famous.'

'In Italy, in Naples and Florence … they speak of no one
else.'

'And in Cremona?'

'The Bergonzis and the others aren't happy at all about the
appearance of that new workshop.'

'You already explained all that to me …' Sara, standing,
impatient, like a strict teacher expecting an awkward child's
excuses.

But Adrià, tuning her out, said 'mon cher tonton! …' he
declared as he burst into the room early the next morning.
Jean-Marie Leclair didn't even deign to look up; he was
watching the flames in the fireplace. 'Mon cher tonton,' repeated Vial, with less enthusiasm.

Leclair half turned. Without looking him in the eyes he
asked him if he had the violin with him. Leclair was soon

running his fingers over the instrument. From a painting on the wall emerged a servant with a beak-like nose with a violin bow in his hand, and Leclair spent some time searching out all of that Storioni's possible sounds with fragments of three of his sonatas.

'It's very good,' he said when he had finished. 'How much did it cost you?'

'How.'

'Ten thousand florins, plus a five-hundred coin reward that you'll give me for finding this jewel.'

'Hey, how!'

With an authoritative wave, Leclair sent out the servants. He put a hand on his nephew's shoulder and smiled. And I heard Sheriff Carson's curt spit hitting the ground, but I paid him no heed.

'You are a bastard. I don't know who you take after, you son of a rotten bitch. Your poor mother, which I doubt, or your pathetic father. Thief, conman.'

'Why? I just ...' Fencing with their eyes. 'Fine: I can forget about the reward.'

'You think that I would trust you, after so many years of you being such a thorn in my side?'

'So why did you entrust me to ...'

'As a test, you stupid son of a sickly, mangy bitch. This time you won't escape prison.' After a few seconds, for emphasis: 'You don't know how I've been waiting for this moment.'

'How, Adrià, you're drifting! Look her in the face!'

'You've always wanted my ruin, Tonton Jean. You envy me.'

'Christ, child. Listen to Black Eagle! She already knows all that. You've already told her.'

Leclair looked at him in surprise and pointed to him: 'No flea-ridden cowboy should even address me.'

'Hey, hey ... I didn't say anything to you. And I deserve to be treated with respect.'

'Piss off, both of you, you and your friend with the feathers on his head who looks like a turkey.'

'How.'

'How what?' Leclair, absolutely irritated.

'Instead of making friends, you'd be wise to continue the argument with your nephew before the sun sets over the western hill.'

Leclair looked at Guillaume Vial, somewhat disconcerted. He had to make an effort to concentrate and then pointed at him: 'What do you think I could envy about you, you wretched, crappy fleabag?'

Vial, red as a tomato, was too enraged to be able to respond.

'It's better if we don't go into details,' he said just to say something.

Leclair looked at him with contempt.

'Why not go into details? Physique? Height? People skills? Friendliness? Talent? Moral stature?'

'This conversation is over, Tonton Jean.'

'It will end when I say so. Intelligence? Culture? Wealth? Health?'

Leclair grabbed the violin and improvised a pizzicato. He examined it with respect.

'Adrià.'

'What?'

Sara sat down in front of me. I faintly heard Sheriff Carson saying watch out, kid, this is serious; and then don't tell me we didn't warn you. You looked me in the eyes: 'I said I already know that. You explained it to me a long time ago!'

'Yes, yes, it's just that Leclair said the violin is very good, but I don't give a damn, you understand me? I only want to be able to send you to prison.'

'You are a bad uncle.'

'And you are a bastard who I've finally been able to unmask.'

'The brave warrior has lost his marbles after so many battles.' A curt gob of spit corroborated the valiant Arapaho chief's statement.

Leclair pulled on the little bell's rope and the servant with the beak-like nose entered through the door to the back of the room.

'Call the commissioner. He can come whenever he's ready.' To his nephew: 'Have a seat, we'll wait for Monsieur Béjart.'

They didn't have a chance to sit down. Instead Guillaume-François Vial walked in front of the fireplace, grabbed the poker and bashed in his beloved tonton's head. Jean-Marie Leclair, known as l'Aîne, was unable to say another word. He collapsed without even a groan, the poker stuck in his head. Splattered blood stained the violin's wooden case. Vial, breathing heavily, wiped his clean hands on his uncle's coat and said you don't know how much I was looking forward to this moment, Tonton Jean. He looked around him, grabbed the violin, put it into the blood-spattered case and left the room through the balcony that led to the terrace. As he ran away, in the light of day, it occurred to him that he should make a not very friendly visit to La Guitte the bigmouth. And Father bought it long before I was born from someone named Saverio Falegnami, the legal owner of the instrument.

Silence. Unfortunately, I had nothing more to say. Well, I had no interest in saying anything further. Sara stood up.

'Your father bought it in nineteen forty-five.'

'How do you know?'

'And he bought it from a fugitive.'

'From someone named Falegnami.'

'Who was a fugitive. And his name was surely not Falegnami.'

'That I don't know.' I think you could see a mile off that I was lying.

'I *do* know.' With her hands on her hips, leaning towards me: 'He was a Bavarian Nazi who had to flee and thanks to your father's money he was able to disappear.'

A lie, or a half-truth, or a few lies cobbled together for the coherence that transforms them into something believable, can hold up for a while. Even for a long while. But they can never last an entire lifetime because there is an unwritten law that speaks of the hour of truth of all things.

'How do you know all that?' trying to seem surprised and not defeated.

Silence. She, like a statue, icy, authoritarian, imposing. Since she was silent, I kept talking, a bit desperately: 'A Nazi? Well, it's better that we have it than some Nazi, right?'

'This Nazi had confiscated it from a Belgian or Dutch family that had the poor taste to show up in Auschwitz-Birkenau.'

'How do you know?'

How did you know, Sara … How did you know that, which I only knew because my father had left it written in Aramaic on a piece of paper that surely only I had read.

'You have to give it back.'

'To who?'

'To its owners.'

'I am its owner. We are.'

'Don't involve me in this. You have to return it to its real owners.'

'I don't know who they are. Dutch, you say?'

'Or Belgian.'

'That's not much to go on. Should I just go to Amsterdam and stand in the middle of the street with the violin in my hand saying, is this yours, dames en heren?'

'Don't play the cynic.'

He didn't know how to answer. What could he say when he always feared that day would come? Without knowing the details, but that what he was going through would someday happen: I, seated, with my glasses in one hand, my Storioni on the table and Sara with her hands on her hips and saying well, research it. There are detectives in the world. Or we can go to a centre for the recovery of stolen assets. Surely there are a dozen Jewish organisations that could help us.

'At the first step you take, the house would fill with people trying to take advantage.'

'Or maybe the owners would show up.'

'We are talking about fifty years ago, you realise that?'

'The owners of the instrument have direct or indirect descendants.'

'Who probably couldn't care less about the violin.'

'Have you asked them that?'

Little by little, the tone of your voice grew harsher and I was feeling attacked and offended because the harshness in your voice was accusing me of something I hadn't felt guilty of until then: the horrible crime of being my father's son. And, what's more, your voice was changing, the timbre sharpening, as it always did when you talked about your family or when you talked about the Shoah, or when Uncle Haïm came up.

'I'm not lifting a finger until I know that what you are saying is true. Where did you get all this from?'

Tito Carbonell had been sitting at the steering wheel of his car on the corner for half an hour. He saw his uncle come out, with his diminishing hair, his briefcase in one hand, heading up València Street towards the university. Tito stopped drumming his fingers on the wheel. The voice from the back seat said Ardèvol's balder every day. Tito didn't think he needed to add any comment; he just checked his watch. The voice from the back seat was going to say I don't think it'll be long, relax, when a policeman put his hand to his cap in greeting, leaned over to talk to the driver and said gentleman, you can't be here.

'We're waiting for someone who … Here she is,' he improvised.

Tito got out of the car and the policeman was distracted by a Coca-Cola lorry trying to unload, invading Llúria Street by a good half metre. Tito got back inside the car and when he saw that Caterina was coming through the doorway, he said in a cheery voice that is the famous Caterina Fargues. The voice from the back seat didn't respond. They waited four more minutes until Sara stepped out on the street and looked both ways. She glanced at the opposite corner and, with quick, decisive steps, went towards the car.

'Get in, they won't let us stay here,' said Tito, pointing to the back door of the car with his head. She hesitated for a few seconds and got in the car, in the back, as if it were a taxi.

'Good day,' said the voice.

Sara saw an older man, very thin, hidden behind a dark mackintosh, who looked at her with interest. With a flat palm, he patted the empty part of the seat between them, to invite her to sit beside him.

'So you are the famous Sara Voltes-Epstein.'

Sara sat down just as Tito started the car. When they passed the policeman, he thanked him with a nod and entered the traffic that was heading up Llúria.

'Where are we going?' she said with a slightly scared voice.

'Relax: somewhere where we can speak comfortably.'

The place where they could speak comfortably was a luxurious bar on the Diagonal. They had reserved a table in an isolated corner. They sat down and for a few seconds they all three looked at each other in silence.

'This is Mr Berenguer,' said Tito, pointing to the thin older man. He nodded his head slightly in greeting. And then Tito explained that he personally, some time ago, had checked that in her house they had a Storioni violin named Vial –

'And would you mind telling me how you checked that?'

– that was very valuable and that, unfortunately, had been stolen more than fifty years ago from its legitimate owners –

'The owner is Mr Adrià Ardèvol.'

– and it turns out that its legitimate owner has been looking for it for ten years and it seems we've finally found it –

'And why am I supposed to believe you?'

– and we already know that the instrument was acquired by its legitimate owner on the fifteenth of February of nineteen thirty-eight in the city of Antwerp. Then it was appraised at far below its true value. Then it was stolen. Confiscated. The legitimate owner has moved heaven and earth to find it and, when he finally did, he took a few years to reflect and now it seems that he's decided to reclaim it.

'Well, then let him reclaim it legally. And prove this strange tale.'

'There are legal problems. It's a very long story.'

'I've got time.'

'I don't want to bore you.'

'Aha. And how did the violin come into my husband's hands?'

'Mr Adrià Ardèvol is not your husband. But if you'd like, I can explain how it came into Mr Adrià Ardèvol's hands.'

'My husband has an ownership certificate for the instrument.'

'Have you seen it?'

'Yes.'

'Well, it's a fake.'

'And why should I believe that?'

'Who was the owner according to that certificate?'

'How do you expect me to remember that? He showed it to me a long time ago.'

'None of this makes any sense,' said Adrià without looking at Sara. He stroked the violin instinctively, but pulled away his hand as though he'd received a shock.

I was too young, but Father had me enter the study as if to tell me a secret, even though there was no one else at home. And he told me have a good look at this violin. Vial was resting on the table. He brought over the loupe and had me look through it. I stuck my hand in my pocket and Sheriff Carson said pay attention, boy, this must be important. I pulled my hand away as if I'd been burned and I contemplated the violin through the magnifying glass. The violin, the scratches, the fine lines. And the ribs, with little varnish left on them ...

'Everything you see is its history.'

I remembered that at other times he had explained similar things about the violin. That was why I wasn't at all surprised to hear: how, this rings a bell. And so I responded to Father, yes, its history. And what do you mean by that?

'That its history has travelled through many homes and touched many people whom we will never meet. Imagine, from millesettecentosessantaquattro to today, that's ... !

'Mmmm ... Vediamo ... Centonovantatrè anni.'

'That's right. I see that you've understood me.'

'No, Father.'

It had been eight months since I'd begun to learn

'Uno.'

'Uno.'

'Due.'

'Due.'

'Tre.'

'Tre.'

'Quattro.'

'Quattro.'

'Cinque.'

'Cinque.'

'Sei.'

'Sei.'

'Sette.'

'Sette.'

'Otto.'

'Octo.'

'Otttto!'

'Otttto!'

'Bravissimo!'

because you can learn Italian easily, in just four classes, trust me.

'But Fèlix … The boy is already studying French, German, English …'

'Signor Simone is a great teacher. In a year my son will be able to read Petrarch and that's that.'

And he pointed to me, so there was no doubt: 'You've been warned: tomorrow you start Italian.'

Now, before the violin, hearing me say centonovantatrè anni, Father couldn't repress a proud expression that, I confess, made me feel utterly satisfied and self-important. Pointing with one hand to the instrument and putting the other on my shoulder, he said now it is mine. It has been many places, but now it's mine. And it will be yours. And it will be your children's. My grandchildren. And it will belong to our great grandchildren because it will never leave our family. Swear that to me.

I wonder how I can swear in the name of those who have yet to be born. But I know that I also swore in my own name. And every time I pick up Vial I remember that vow. And a few months later they killed my father, and it was my fault. I came to the conclusion that it was also the violin's fault.

'Mr Berenguer,' said Adrià giving her an accusatory look, 'is a former employee of the shop. He fought with Father and with Mother. And with me. He is a con man, did you know that?'

'I am quite sure that he is an undesirable who wants to hurt you. But he knows exactly how your father bought the violin: he was there.'

'And this Albert Carbonell is a half-relative who goes by the name of Tito and now runs the shop. Doesn't that seem like a plot?'

'If what they say is true, I don't care about the plot. Here you have the owner's address. All you have to do is get in touch with him and then you and I won't have to wonder any more.'

'It's a trap! Any owner those two give us is an accomplice. What they want is to get their hands on the violin, can't you see?'

'No.'

'How can you be so blind?'

I think that comment hurt you; but I was convinced that there was nothing innocent behind Mr Berenguer's movements.

She handed him a folded piece of paper. Adrià took it but didn't unfold it. He held it for quite some time before putting it down on the table.

'Matthias Alpaerts,' she said.

'Huh?'

'The name you didn't read.'

'It's not true. The owner's name is Netje de Boeck,' I said angrily.

Thus, as if I were a five-year-old boy, you unmasked me. I looked at the piece of paper that read Matthias Alpaerts and I put it down on the table again.

'This is all ridiculous,' said Adrià after a long silence.

'You are in a position to right a wrong and you refuse to do it.'

Sara left the study and I never heard her laugh again.

## 46

Silence reigned in the house for three or four days. It is horrible when two people who live together stay silent because they don't want to say or they don't dare to say things that could hurt. Sara focused on her exhibition and I wasn't good for anything. I'm convinced that if your self-portrait has a slightly sad gaze, it's because there was that silence in the house as you were making it. But I couldn't give in. So Adrià Ardèvol made up his mind and went to the Law Faculty to consult Doctor Grau i Bordas about the problem a friend of mine had with a valuable object acquired by his family many years ago that presumably had been pillaged during the war, and Doctor Grau i Bordas stroked his chin and listened to what was happening to my friend and then he began to digress about generalisations regarding international law and Nazi pillaging and after five minutes Adrià Ardèvol understood that the man didn't have a clue.

In the university's department of musicology, Doctor Casals gave him a lot of information about the various families of luthiers in Cremona and recommended an authority on historic violins. And you can trust him, Ardèvol. And the question that he wanted to ask him from the moment they'd opened the case: 'Can I try it?'

'You play the violin too?'

In the hallway of Musicology, four students stopped to hear the enigmatic, sweet music that emerged from one of the offices. Until Doctor Casals put the violin in its case and said it is extraordinary; like a Gesù, truly.

He left the violin in his departmental office, in one corner. And he saw two students who wanted to improve their grades. And another student who wanted to know why did you only just pass me when I came to every class. You? Well, to a lot of classes. Ah, yes? To some, yeah. When the young lady left, Laura came in and sat at the desk in front of his. She was simply lovely and he said hello, without looking her in the eyes. She made a distracted wave and opened up a folder filled with notes or exams to correct or one of those things that make her sigh. They were alone for quite a while, each with their own work. Twice, no, three times, they both looked up at the same time and their gazes played timidly for a few moments. Until the fourth time, when she said how are you. Was it the first time she took the initiative? I don't remember. But I know that she accompanied the question with a slight smile. That was an obvious declaration of armistice.

'Well, all right.'

'That's all?'

'That's all.'

'But you're a celebrity.'

'Now you're having a laugh.'

'No: I envy you. Like half of the department.'

'Now you're really having a laugh. And how are you?'

'Well, all right.'

They were quiet and smiled, each with their own thoughts.

'Are you writing?'

'Yes.'

'Do you mind telling me what you're working on?'

'I am rewriting three conferences.'

She, with a smile, invited me to continue, and I, obedient, said Llull, Vico and Berlin.

'Wow.'

'Yes. But you know what? I am rewriting everything so it will be a new book, you know? Not three conferences, but ...'

Adrià made a vague gesture, as if he were in the middle of the problem: 'There has to be something that ties them all together.'

'And have you found it?'

'Maybe. The historical narrative. But I don't know.'

Laura rearranged the papers, which is what she always did when she was thinking.

'Is that the famous violin?' she said pointing with a pencil to the corner.

'Famous?'

'Famous.'

'Well, yes.'

'Gosh: don't leave it there.'

'Don't worry: I'll take it to class with me.'

'Don't tell me that you are planning on playing it in front of …' she said, tickled.

'No, no.'

Or yes. Why not? He decided suddenly. Like when he asked Laura to come with him to Rome to play his lawyer. Laura inspired him to rash decisions.

Adrià Ardèvol, in the History of Aesthetic Ideas class, second quarter, at the University of Barcelona, had the nerve to start the class with the partita number one played on his Storioni. Surely none of the thirty-five students noticed the five unjustifiable errors nor the moment when he got lost and even had to improvise the Tempo di Borea. And when he finished he carefully stored the violin in its case, placed it on the desk and said what relationship do you think there is between artistic manifestation and thought. And no one dared to say anything because gosh, I don't know.

'Now imagine that we are in the year seventeen twenty.'

'Why?' said a boy with a beard sitting at the back, isolated from the rest, perhaps to avoid contamination.

'The year when Bach composed what I just played so badly.'

'And our thinking has to change?'

'At the very least you and I would be wearing wigs.'

'But that doesn't change our thinking.'

'It doesn't? Men and women in wigs, stockings and high heels.'

'It's just that the aesthetic idea of the eighteenth century is different from ours today.'

'Just the aesthetic? In the eighteenth century, if you weren't wearing a wig, makeup, stockings and heels, they wouldn't let you into the salons. Today, a man wearing makeup, a wig, stockings and heels would be locked up in prison without any questions being asked.'

'We have to take morality into account?'

It was the timid voice of a lanky girl from the front row. Adrià, who was between desks, turned around.

'That's what I like to hear,' he said. And the girl turned red, which wasn't my intention. 'Aesthetics, as hard as we try to separate it, is never alone.'

'No?'

'No. It has a great capacity to drag other forms of thought with it.'

'I don't understand.'

Anyway, it was a class that worked very well to establish the bases of what I had to explain for the next few weeks. And, for a few moments, I even forgot that at home we were living in silence, Sara and I. And Adrià was very sorry not to find Laura in the office when he went there to pick up his things because he would have liked to explain to her how well her idea had worked.

As soon as I opened the case inside the workshop of Pau Ullastres, the luthier told me it's an authentic Cremona. Just by its scent and its outward mien. Even so, Pau Ullastres didn't know Vial's specific history; he had heard some vague talk about it, but he thought a Storioni could be worth a serious pile of dough and you should have brought it in to be appraised earlier. For insurance purposes, you know? It took me a few seconds to understand, because I had been captivated by the still atmosphere of his workshop. A warm, reddish light the colour of violin wood, made that unexpected silence, right in the heart of Gràcia, more solid. The window overlooked an interior courtyard at the back of which was a wood drying shed with its door open. There the wood aged unhurriedly while the world, now round, spun like a compulsive spinning top.

I looked at the luthier, frightened: I didn't know what he had said to me. He smiled and repeated it.

'I never thought to have it appraised,' I responded. 'It was like another piece of furniture in the house, just always there. And we've never wanted to sell it.'

'What a lucky family.'

I didn't tell him I disagreed because it wasn't any of Pau Ullastres's business and there was no way I could have read these lines that weren't yet written. The luthier asked for permission before playing it. He played better than Doctor Casals. It almost sounded as if Bernat were playing.

'It's marvellous,' he said. 'Like a Gesù: it's on the same level.'

'Are all the Storionis as good as this one?'

'Not all of them; but this one is.' He smelled it with his eyes closed. 'You've kept it locked up?'

'Not for some time now. There was a period where …'

'Violins are alive. The wood of a violin is like wine. It needs to age slowly over time and it enjoys the pressure of the strings; it likes to be played, it likes to live at a comfortable temperature, to be able to breathe, not be banged, always be clean … Only lock it up when you go on a trip.'

'I would like to get in touch with the former owners.'

'Do you have an ownership title?'

'Yes.'

I showed him Father's contract of sale from Signor Saverio Falegnami.

'The certificate of authenticity?'

'Yes.'

I showed him the certificate cooked up by Grandfather Adrià and the luthier Carlos Carmona in a period when for a few grand you could have even counterfeit banknotes authenticated. Pau Ullastres looked at it curiously. He gave it back to me without comment. He thought it over: 'Do you want to get it appraised now?'

'No. In fact, what I want is to be sure of who its previous owners were. I want to meet with them.'

Ullastres looked at the ownership certificate: 'Saverio Falegnami, it says here.'

'The ones prior to that man.'

'You mind telling me why you want to get in touch with them?'

'I don't even know myself. For me it's as if this violin had always belonged to my family. I've never worried about its genealogy. But now …'

'You are concerned about its authenticity?'

'Yes,' I lied.

'If it helps you at all, I would swear on all that is holy that this is an instrument from Lorenzo Storioni's finest period. And not because of the certificate, but because of what I can see, hear and feel.'

'I've been told it is the first violin he ever made.'

'The best Storionis were the first twenty. They say it's because of the wood he used.'

'The wood?'

'Yes. It was exceptional.'

'Why?'

But the luthier was stroking my violin and didn't answer. All those caresses were making me feel jealous. Then Ullastres looked at me: 'What exactly do you want to do? Why exactly have you come?'

It is hard to make enquiries without being entirely truthful with those who could help you.

'I would like to make a family tree of its owners since the beginning.'

'That's a good idea ... But it'll cost you an arm and a leg.'

I didn't know how to tell him that what I wanted was to work out if Mr Berenguer and Tito had made up the name Alpaerts. And to know whether the name that Father had given me, Netje de Boeck, was the correct one. Or maybe find out that neither of those names were authentic and that the violin had always been mine. Because I was seeing that yes, that if there had been a legal owner prior to the Nazi, that it was in my best interests for me to get in touch with them, whoever they were, to get down on my knees and beg them to let me have it until my death; just thinking about Vial leaving my home forever gave me chills. And I had made up my mind to do whatever it took to keep that from happening.

'Did you hear me, Mr Ardèvol? An arm and a leg.'

If I'd had any doubt, Vial was authentic. Perhaps I went to see Ullastres just for that: to be hear it for myself; to make sure that I had fought with Sara over a valuable violin; not over some pieces of wood in the shape of an instrument. No, deep down I don't know why I went there to see him. But I believe it was since my visit to Ullastres's workshop that I began to muse on that fine wood and on Jachiam Mureda.

For lunch they gave him a bland semolina soup. He thought he should let them know that he didn't like semolina soup like the one they gave to whatshername … ffucking semolina soup. But things weren't that simple because he didn't know if it was his vision or what, but he was having more and more trouble reading and retaining things. Fucking ceiling. Retaining things. Retaining.

'Aren't you hungry, my prince?'

'No. I want to read.'

'They should give you alphabet soup.'

'Yes.'

'Come on, eat a little.'

'Little Lola.'

'Wilson.'

'Wilson.'

'What, Adrià?'

'Why am I so befuddled?'

'What you need to do is eat and rest. You've worked enough.'

He gave him five spoonfuls of the semolina soup and was satisfied that Adrià had had enough lunch.

'Now you can read.' He looked at the floor, 'Oh, we've made a real mess with the soup,' he said. 'And if you want to take a nap, let me know and I'll put you into bed.'

Adrià, obedient, only read for a little while. He slowly read how Cornudella explained his reading of Carner. He read with his mouth open. But soon he was overcome by I don't know what's wrong with me, Little Lola, and he grew tired because Carner and Horace blurred together on the table. He took off his glasses and ran his palm over his fatigued eyes. He didn't know if he should sleep in the chair or the bed or … I don't think they've explained it well enough to me, he thought. Maybe it was the window?

'Adrià.'

Bernat had come into cinquantaquattro and was looking at his friend.

'Where should I sleep?'
'Are you tired?'
'I don't know.'
'Who am I?'
'Little Lola.'
Bernat kissed him on the forehead and examined the room.
Adrià was sitting in a comfortable chair beside the window.
'Jònatan?'
'Huh?'
'Are you Jònatan?'
'I'm Bernat.'
'No: Wilson!'
'Wilson is that lively bloke, the one from Ecuador?'
'I don't know. I think ...' He looked at Bernat, perplexed: 'I'm
all mixed up now,' he confessed finally.

Outside it was an overcast, cold, windy day; but even if it'd
been a sunny, gorgeous day it wouldn't have mattered because
the glass separated the two worlds too efficiently. Bernat went
towards the bedside table and opened the drawer: he placed
Black Eagle and Sheriff Carson inside it, so they could continue
their useless but loyal watch, lying on the dirty rag where some
dark and light checks and a large scar in the middle could still
be made out; a rag that had been the source of much speculation by the doctors because during the first few days Mr Ardèvol
wouldn't let go of it, clutching it with both hands. A disgusting,
dirty rag, yes, Doctor. How strange, no? What is this rag, eh,
sweetie?

Adrià scratched with his fingernail at a small stain on the
chair's arm. Bernat turned when he heard the slight sound and
said are you all right?

'There's no way to get rid of it.' He scratched harder. 'You
see?'

Bernat came closer, put on his eyeglasses and examined the
spot as if it were very interesting. Since he didn't know what to
do or what to say, he folded his glasses and said, don't worry, it
won't spread. After fifteen minutes of silence, no one had interrupted them because life is made up of the sum of solitudes that
lead us to

'Very well: look at me. Adrià, look at me, for God's sake.'

Adrià stopped scratching and looked at him, a bit frightened; he gave him an apologetic smile, as if he'd been caught with his hand in the cookie jar.

'I just finished typing up your papers. I liked them very much. Very much. And the flipside of the pages, I plan on having them published. Your friend Kamenek says I should.'

He looked him in the eyes. Adrià, disorientated, kept scratching at the itchy stain on the arm of the chair.

'You aren't Wilson.'

'Adrià. I'm talking to you about what you wrote.'

'Forgive me.'

'I don't have anything to forgive you for.'

'Is that good or bad?'

'I really like what you wrote. I don't know if it's very good, but I really, really like it. You've no right, you son of a bitch.'

Adrià looked at his interlocutor, scratched at the stain, opened his mouth and closed it again. He lifted up his arms, perplexed: 'Now what do I do?'

'Listen to me. All my life. Sorry: all my ffucking life trying to write something decent, something that would affect and move the reader, and you, a total novice, the first day you put pen to paper you rub salt into the most sensitive wounds of the soul. At least, of my soul. You've no right, damn it.'

Adrià Ardèvol didn't know whether to scratch at the stain or look at his interlocutor. He chose to look at the wall, worried: 'I think you're making some mistake. I haven't done anything.'

'You have no right.'

Two large tears began to roll down Adrià's face. He couldn't look at the other man. He wrung his hands.

'What can I do?' he implored.

Bernat, absorbed, didn't respond. Then Adrià looked at him and begged, 'Listen, sir.'

'Don't call me sir. I'm Bernat and I'm your friend.'

'Bernat, listen.'

'No: you listen. Because now I know what you think of me. I'm not complaining; you've revealed me and I deserve it; but I still have secrets you'll never be able to even suspect.'

'I'm very sorry.'

They grew quiet. And then Wilson came in and said everything OK, sweetie? And he lifted up Adrià's chin to examine his face, as if he were a boy. He wiped away his tears with a tissue and gave him a little pill and a half-full glass that Adrià drank up eagerly, with an eagerness that Bernat had never seen in him before. Wilson said is everything OK, looking at Bernat, who made an expression that said fantastic, man, and Wilson glanced at the semolina all over the floor. With a paper napkin he picked up some of it, displeased, and left the room with the empty glass, whistling some strange music in six by eight time.

'I'm so envious that …'

Ten minutes passed in silence.

'Tomorrow I'll bring the papers to Bauçà. All right? All the ones written in green ink. I've sent the ones in black ink to Johannes Kamenek and a colleague of yours at the university named Parera. Both sides. All right? Your memoir and your reflection. All right, Adrià?'

'I have an itch here,' said Adrià pointing to the wall. He looked at his friend. 'How can I have an itch on the wall?'

'I'll keep you posted.'

'My nose itches too. And I'm very tired. I can't read because the ideas get mixed up in my head. I already don't remember what you said.'

'I admire you,' said Bernat, looking him in the eyes.

'I won't do it again. I promise.'

Bernat didn't even laugh. He stared at him in silence. He took him by the hand that was still sporadically battling the rebellious stain and he kissed it like you would a father or an uncle. He looked into his eyes. Adrià held his gaze for a few seconds.

'You know who I am,' Bernat declared, almost. 'Right?'

Adrià stared at him. He nodded as he traced a faint smile.

'Who am I?' A hint of frightened hope in Bernat.

'Yes, of course … Mr … whatshisname. Right?'

Bernat got up, serious.

'No?' said Adrià, worried. He looked at the other man, who

*was standing. 'But I know it. What's his name. That guy. I can't quite come up with the name. I don't know yours, but there is that other one, yeah. One named … right now I can't remember, but I know it. I take very good care of myself. Very. My name is … now I don't remember my name, but yes, it's him.'*

*And after a heartrending pause: 'Isn't that right, sir?'*

*Something vibrated in Bernat's pocket. He pulled out his mobile phone. An SMS: 'Where are you hiding?' He leaned over and kissed the sick man's forehead.*

'Goodbye, Adrià.'

'Take care. Come back whenever you'd like …'

'My name is Bernat.'

'Bernat.'

'Yes, Bernat. And forgive me.'

*Bernat went out into the hallway and headed off; he wiped away a runaway tear. He looked furtively from side to side and made a phone call.*

'Where in God's name are you?' *Xènia's voice, a bit upset.*

'Hey, no, sorry.'

'Where are you?'

'Nowhere. Work.'

'I thought you didn't have rehearsal.'

'No; it's just that some things came up.'

'Come on, come over, I want to screw.'

'It'll take me about an hour.'

'Are you still at the tax office?'

'Yes. I have to go now, all right? Bye.'

*He hung up before Xènia could ask for more explanations. A cleaning lady passed by him with a cart filled with supplies and gave him a severe look because he had a mobile in his hands. She reminded him of Trullols. A lot. The woman grumbled as she headed down the corridor.*

Doctor Valls *brought his hands together, in a prayer pose, and shook his head: 'Today's medicine can't do anything more for him.'*

'But he's wise! He's intelligent. Gifted!' *He had a feeling of déjà vu, as if he were Quico Ardèvol from Tona. 'He knows something like ten or fifteen languages!'*

'All that is in the past. And we've talked about it many times. If they cut off an athlete's leg, he can't break any more records. Do you understand that? Well, this is similar.'

'He wrote five emblematic studies in the field of cultural history.'

'We know … But the illness doesn't give a fig about that. That's just how it is, Mr Plensa.'

'There's no possible improvement?'

'No.'

Doctor Valls checked his watch, not obviously, but making sure Bernat noticed. Still, he was slow to react.

'Does anyone else come, to see him?'

'The truth is that …'

'He has some cousins in Tona.'

'They come sometimes. It's hard.'

'There's no one else who …'

'Some colleagues from the university. A few others, but … he spends a lot of time alone.'

'Poor thing.'

'From what we know, that doesn't worry him much.'

'He can live on the memories.'

'Not really. He doesn't remember anything. He lives in the moment. And he forgets it very quickly.'

'You mean that now he doesn't remember that I came to see him?'

'Not only doesn't he remember that you came to see him, but I don't think he really has any idea who you are.'

'He doesn't seem to be clear on it. If we took him to his house, maybe that would spark something for him.'

'Mr Plensa: this disease consists of the formation of intra-neuronal fibres …'

The doctor is quiet and thinks briefly.

'How can I say this to you? …' He thought for a few more seconds and added, 'It's the conversion of the neurons into coarse, knot-shaped fibres …' He looked from side to side as if asking for help. 'To give you an idea, it's as if the brain were *being invaded by cement, irreversibly. If you took Mr Ardèvol home he wouldn't recognise it or remember anything. Your friend's brain is permanently destroyed.'*

*'So,' insisted Bernat, 'he doesn't even know who I am.'*

*'He's polite about it because he's a polite person. He is start-ing not to know who anyone is, and I think he doesn't even know who he is.'*

*'He still reads.'*

*'Not for long. He'll soon forget. He reads and he can't re-member the paragraph he's read; and he has to reread it, do you understand? And he's made no progress. Except for tiring himself out.'*

*'So then he's not suffering since he doesn't remember anything?'*

*'I can't tell you that for sure. Apparently, he's not. And soon, the deterioration will spread to his other vital functions.'*

*Bernat stood up with his eyes weepy; an era was ending forever. Forever. And he was dying a little bit with his friend's slow death.*

Trullols *went into cinquantaquattro with the cleaning cart. She pushed Adrià's wheelchair into one corner so he wasn't in the way.*

*'Hello, sweetie.' Examining the floor of the room: 'Where's the disaster?'*

*'Hello, Wilson.'*

*'What a mess you've made!'*

*The woman started scrubbing the area laid waste by the semolina and said looks like we're going to have to teach you not to be such a piglet, and Adrià looked at her, scared. With her cleaning cloth, Trullols approaches the chair where Adrià is observing her, about to pout over her scolding. Then she undoes the top button on his shirt and looks at his thin chain with the medallion, the way Daniela had forty years earlier.*

*'It's pretty.'*

*'Yes. It's mine.'*

*'No: it's mine.'*

*'Ah.' A bit disorientated, with no comeback at the ready.*

'You'll give it back to me, won't you?'

Adrià Ardèvol looked at the woman, unsure as to what to do. She glanced at the door and then, gently, picked up the chain and lifted it over Adrià's head. She gazed at it for a quick second and then stuck it into the pocket of her smock.

'Thanks, kid,' she said.

'You're welcome.'

## 47

He opened the door himself. Older, just as thin, with the same penetrating gaze. Adrià got an intense whiff of the air inside, and wasn't sure if he liked it or not. For a few seconds, Mr Berenguer stood with the door open, as if he were having trouble placing the visitor. He wiped a few drops of sweat from his brow with a carefully folded white handkerchief. Finally he said, 'Goodness gracious. Ardèvol.'

'May I come in?' asked Ardèvol.

A few seconds of hesitation. In the end, he let him in. Inside it was hotter than outside. By the entrance was a relatively large, neat, polished room with a splendid Pedrell coat-rack from eighteen seventy that must have cost a fortune, with an umbrella stand, mirror and a lot of mouldings. And a definitive Chippendale console table with a bouquet of dried flowers on it. He led him into a room where a Utrillo and a Rusiñol hung on the same stretch of wall. The sofa, by Torrijos Hermanos, was a unique piece, surely the only one that had survived the historic workshop fire. And on another stretch of wall was a double manuscript page, very carefully framed. He didn't dare go over to see what it was. There, from a distance, it looked like a text from the sixteenth or early seventeenth century. Adrià couldn't say why, but it seemed that all of that impeccable, undisputable order lacked a woman's touch. Everything was too emphatic, too professional to live in. He couldn't help looking around the entire room, with a lovely Chippendale confident sofa in one corner. Mr Berenguer let him look, surely with a hint of pride. They sat down. The fan, which uselessly tried to lessen the mugginess, seemed like an anachronism in poor taste.

'Goodness gracious,' repeated Mr Berenguer.

Adrià looked into his eyes. Now he understood what the

intense scent mixed with the heat was: it was the smell of the
shop, the same smell of every time he had visited there, under
the watchful eye of Father, Cecília or Mr Berenguer himself.
A home with the scent and atmosphere of a business. At seventy-five, Mr Berenguer obviously hadn't retired.

'What is all this about the violin?' I said, too abruptly.

'These things happen.' And he looked at me, not trying to
conceal his satisfaction.

What things happen? spat out Sheriff Carson.

'What things happen?'

'Well, the owner has shown up.'

'He's right in front of you: me.'

'No. He is a gentleman from Antwerp who is quite elderly.
The Nazis took the violin from him when he got to Auschwitz.
He had acquired it in nineteen thirty-eight. If you want more
details, you'll have to ask the gentleman.'

'And how can he prove that?'

Mr Berenguer smiled and said nothing.

'You must be getting a good commission.'

Mr Berenguer ran his handkerchief over his forehead, still
smiling and saying nothing.

'My father acquired it legally.'

'Your father stole it in exchange for a fistful of dollars.'

'And how do you know that?'

'Because I was there. Your father was a bandit who took
advantage of whomever he could: first the Jews fleeing any
which way they could and then the Nazis, fleeing in an
orderly, organised fashion. And always, anyone who was skint
and needed money desperately.'

'That surely is part of the business. And surely you took
part in it.'

'Your father was a man without scruples. He made an ownership title that was inside the violin disappear.'

'You know what? I don't believe you and I don't trust you. I
know what you are capable of. I would like to know where you
got that Torrijos and the Pedrell in the entryway.'

'Everything is in order, don't worry. I have the ownership papers for each and every one of my things. I'm not a

blabbermouth like your father. In the end he chose the end he met with.'

'What?' Silence. Mr Berenguer looked at me with a poorly concealed cunning smile. Surely to gain a bit of time to think, Carson had me say did I understand you correctly, Mr Berenguer?

Signor Falegnami had pulled out a feminine little parlour gun and aimed it at him nervously. Fèlix Ardèvol didn't even flinch. He pretending to be stifling a smile and shook his head as if he were very displeased, 'You are alone. How will you get rid of my corpse?'

'It will be a pleasure to face that challenge.'

'You'll still be left with an even bigger one: if I don't walk out of here on my own two feet, the people waiting for me on the street already have their instructions.' He pointed to the gun, sternly. 'And now I'll take it for two thousand. Don't you know that you are one of the Allies' ten most wanted?' He improvised that part in the tone of someone scolding an unruly child.

Doctor Voigt watched as Ardèvol pulled out a wad of notes and put them on the table. He lowered the gun, with his eyes wide, incredulous: 'That's not even fifteen hundred!'

'Don't make me lose my patience, Sturmbannführer Voigt.'

That was Fèlix Ardèvol's doctorate in buying and selling. A half an hour later he was out on the street with the violin, striding quickly with his heart beating fast and the satisfaction of a job well done. No one was waiting for him downstairs to do what they had to do if he didn't emerge, and he was proud of his shrewdness. But he had underestimated Falegnami's little notebook. And he hadn't even noticed his hate-filled gaze. And that afternoon, without telling anyone, without entrusting himself to God, or the devil, or Mr Berenguer, or Father Morlin, Fèlix Ardèvol turned in that Doctor Aribert Voigt, officer of the Waffen-SS, who was hiding at the Ufficio della Giustizia e della Pace disguised as a harmless, fat, bald consierge with a lost stare and a puffy nose. Fèlix was unaware of his medical activities. Just as there had been no way to tie Doctor Budden to Auschwitz-Birkenau, there was no way to tie Doctor Voigt to the camp either. Someone must have burned the specific papers and all the inquisitorial gazes were focused on the vanished Doctor Mengele and those around him while the enterprising investigators assigned to other Lager had time to destroy compromising evidence. And if we add to that the general confusion, the numerous lists of the accused, the incompetence of Sergeant-Major O'Rourke, who opened the file and who, it must be said, was overwhelmed by the task, all of it colluded to obscure the true personality and activities of Doctor Voigt, who was sentenced to five years of prison as an officer of the Waffen-SS, and about whom there was no record of participation in any act of war or annihilation in the cruel style of most of the SS units.

A few years later, on the street of the Sun, which was filled with people wearing jellabah coming out of the majestic Umayyad Mosque and commenting on some of the reflections of that Friday's sura, or perhaps only mentioning, shocked, the rise in the prices of shoes, tea or vegetables. But there were also many people who didn't look as if they'd ever set foot in a mosque and were smoking their hookahs on the narrow rows of outdoor tables at the Concord Café or the Café of the Scissors, trying not to think about whether there would be another coup d'état that year.

Two minutes from there, lost in the labyrinth of backstreets, sitting on a rock of the Deer Fountain, two silent men looked at the ground, lost in thought, as if they were keeping an eye on the sun as it headed west, along Bab al-Jabiyah, towards the Mediterranean. More than one distracted observer must have thought that those individuals were fervent men waiting for the sun to set and the shadows to begin their reign, for the magical moment when it was impossible to distinguish a white thread from a black thread and Mawlid began and the name of the Prophet was forever remembered and venerated. And the moment came when the human eye couldn't distinguish a white thread from a black thread and, despite the soldiers paying little attention, the entire city of Damascus entered into Mawlid. The two men didn't move from the rock until they heard some rather hesitant footsteps. A Western person, from the gait, the excessive noise, the panting. They looked at each other in silence and stood up. From the corner of the street of the mosques came a fat man, with a big nose, who was wiping his brow with a handkerchief, as if that Mawlid was a hot night. He went straight over to the two men.

'I am Doctor Zimmermann,' said the Western man.

The two men, without saying a word, began to walk swiftly through the backstreets around the bazaar and the fat man had quite a time keeping them in his sight around each corner or when they mingled among the increasingly fewer people circulating on those backstreets. Until they went through a half-open door to a shop stuffed with copper utensils, and he went in after them. They went along the only aisle left by the piles of utensils, a narrow path that led to the back of the shop, where there was a curtain that opened onto a courtyard lit by a dozen candles where a short bald man in a jellabah was pacing, visibly impatient. When they arrived, he extended his hand to the Westerner, ignoring the two guides, and said I was worried. The two guides disappeared as silently as they had come.

'I had problems at the customs control in the airport.'

'Everything taken care of?'

The man removed his hat, as if he wanted to show off his baldness, and he used it to fan himself. He made a gesture that said, yes, everything taken care of.

'Father Morlin,' he said.

'Here I am always David Duhamel. Always.'

'Monsieur Duhamel. What were you able to find out?'

'Many things. But I want to dot the i's.'

Father Félix Morlin, standing, dotted the i's in the light of the twelve candles, and spoke in a murmur that the other man listened to attentively, as if it were a confession without a confessional. He told him that Fèlix Ardèvol had betrayed his confidence by taking advantage of Mr Zimmermann's situation, robbing him, practically, of that valuable violin. And violating the sacred rule of hospitality, he had also turned Mr Zimmermann in, revealing his hidey hole to the Allies.

'Because of his unjust actions, I have enjoyed five years of forced labour for having served my country in times of war.'

'A war against the expansion of communism.'

'Against the expansion of communism, yes.'

'And now what do you want to do?'

'Find him.'

'Enough blood,' declaimed Father Morlin. 'You do know that, even though Ardèvol is unpredictable and has harmed you, he is still my friend.'

'I just want to get my violin back.'

'Enough blood, I said. Or I personally will make you pay.'

'I haven't the slightest interest in harming a hair on his head. Gentleman's promise.'

As if those words were a definitive assurance of good conduct, Father Morlin nodded and pulled a folded piece of paper out of his trousers pocket and passed it to Herr Zimmermann. He opened it up, drew near one of the candles, read it quickly, folded it again and made it disappear into his pocket.

'At least the trip wasn't in vain.' He pulled out a handkerchief and ran it over his face as he said ffucking heat, I don't know how people can live in these countries.

'How have you earned a living, since you were released?'

'As a psychiatrist, of course.'

'Ah.'

'And what do you do, in Damascus?'

'Internal things for the order. At the end of the month I will go back to my monastery, Santa Sabina.'

He didn't say that he was trying to revive the noble espionage institution that Monsignor Benigni had founded many years earlier and had had to shut down because of the blindness of the Vatican authorities, who didn't realise that the only real danger was communism spreading throughout Europe. Nor did he say that the next day it would be forty-seven years since he had joined the Dominican order with the firm, holy intention of serving the church, offering up his life if necessary. Forty-seven years already, since he had asked to be admitted to the order's monastery in Liège. Félix Morlin had been born during the winter of 1320 in the same city of Girona where he was raised in an atmosphere of fervour and piety in a family who gathered each day to pray after finishing their work. And no one was surprised by the young man's decision to become a member of the fledgling Dominican order. He studied medicine at the University of Vienna and, at twenty-one years of age, joined the Austrian National Socialist Party with the name Alí Bahr. He was preparing to begin the studies that would make him a good Qadi or a good mufti, since he had already modelled himself on the gifts of wisdom, deliberation and justice of his teachers and shortly afterward he joined the SS as member number 367,744. After serving on the battlefield of Buchenwald under the orders of Doctor Eisel, on 8 October, 1941, he was named chief medic on the dangerous battle front of Auschwitz-Birkenau, where he worked selflessly for the good of humanity. Misunderstood, Doctor Voigt had to flee disguised with various names such as Zimmermann and Falegnami and he was willing to wait, among the chosen, for the moment to regain the Earth when it became flat again, when the sharia had spread all over the world and only the faithful would have the right to live there in the name of the Most Merciful. Then the end of the world would be a mysterious fog and we will be able to go back to managing this mystery and all the mysteries that derive from it. So be it.

Doctor Aribert Voigt instinctively patted his pockets. Father Morlin told him that it would be better if he took a train to Aleppo. And from there another train to Turkey. The Taurus Express.

'Why?'

'To avoid ports and airports. And if the train line is down, which can happen, rent a car with a chauffeur: dollars make miracles.'

'I already know how to get around.'

'I doubt that. You arrived in an aeroplane.'

'But it was totally secure.'

'It's never totally secure. They held you there for a little while.'

'You don't think I was followed.'

'My men made sure you weren't. And you've never seen me in your life.'

'Obviously I would never put you in any danger, Monsieur Duhamel. I am infinitely grateful to you.'

Up until then he hadn't unbuttoned his trousers, as if it hadn't occurred to him. On some sort of fabric belt he wore various small hidden objects. He pulled out a tiny black bag and gave it to Morlin, who loosened the string that closed it. Three large tears of a thousand faces were reflected, multiplied, in the light of the twelve candles. Morlin made the bag disappear among the mysteries of his jellabah while Doctor Voigt buttoned his trousers.

'Good night, Mr Zimmermann. The first train for the north departs at six in the morning.'

'Ffucking heat,' said Mr Berenguer in response as he stood up and aimed the fan more directly onto himself.

Adrià, in a hushed voice – since he remembered how Mr Berenguer threatened Father when he was spying on them from behind the sofa – said, Mr Berenguer, I am the legitimate owner of the violin. And if they want to take this to court, they can, but I warn you that if they continue along this path, I will spill the beans and you'll be left exposed.

'As you wish. You have the same character as your mother.'

No one had ever told me that before. And I didn't believe it when he did. Mostly I felt hatred for that man because he was the one who had caused Sara to fight with me. And he could say whatever balderdash he wanted to.

I stood up because I had to look tough if I wanted my words to be credible. By the time I'd stood up, I was already regretting everything I'd said and the way I was handling things. But Mr Berenguer's amused expression made me decide to continue, albeit fearfully.

'It'd be best if you don't mention my mother. I understand she made you toe the line.'

I started to head back towards the door, thinking that I was a bit of an idiot: what had I got out of that visit? I hadn't cleared up anything. I had merely made a unilateral declaration of war that I wasn't at all sure I wanted to follow through on. But Mr Berenguer, walking behind me, lent me a hand: 'Your mother was a horrid cunt who wanted to make my life miserable. The day she died I opened up a bottle of Veuve Clicquot champagne.' I felt Mr Berenguer's breath on the nape of my neck as we walked towards the door. 'I drink a sip each day. It's gone flat, but it forces me to think about ffucking Mrs Ardèvol, the horrid cunt.' He sighed. 'When I drink the last drop, then I can die.'

They reached the entrance and Mr Berenguer overtook him. He mimed drinking: 'Every day, glug, down the hatch. To celebrate that the witch is dead and I'm still alive. As you can imagine, Ardèvol, your wife isn't going to change her mind. Jews are so sensitive about some things ...'

He opened the door.

'I could reason with your father and he gave me freedom of movement for the good of the business. Your mother was a nag. Like all women: but with particular malice ... And I – glug! – one sip down the hatch each and every day.'

Adrià went out onto the landing of the stairwell and turned to say some worthy phrase like you'll pay dearly for these insults or something like that. But instead of Mr Berenguer's sly smile, he found the dark varnish of the door that Mr Berenguer was slamming in his face.

That evening, alone at home, I tried the sonatas and the partitas. I didn't need the score despite the years; but I would have liked to have other fingers. And Adrià, as he played the second sonata, began to cry because he was sad about everything. Just then Sara came in off the street. When she saw that it was me and not Bernat, she left again without even saying hello.

## 48

My sister died fifteen days after my conversation with Mr
Berenguer. I didn't know she was ill, just like had happened
with my mother. Her husband told me that neither she nor
anyone else had known either. She had just turned seventy-
one and, even though I hadn't seen her in a long time, lying
in the coffin she looked to me like an elegant woman. Adrià
didn't know what he felt: grief, distance, something strange.
He didn't know which feeling he was experiencing. He was
more worried about Sara's anger than about how he felt about
Daniela Amato de Carbonell, as the funeral card read.

I didn't say Sara, my sister died. When Tito Carbonell
called me to tell me that his mother had died, I was so focused
on him possibly mentioning the violin that at first I didn't
understand what he was saying, and it was as simple as she
is at the Les Corts funeral home, if you want to go, and we're
burying her tomorrow, and I hung up and I didn't say Sara,
my sister died because I think you would have said you have a
sister? Or you wouldn't have said anything, because in those
days you and I weren't on speaking terms.

In the funeral home, there were quite a few people. At the
Montjuïc cemetery we were about twenty. Daniela Amato's
niche has a wonderful view of the sea. Not that it will do her
any good, I heard someone say behind me, while the workers
sealed up the niche. Cecília hadn't shown up or she hadn't
been told or she was already dead. Mr Berenguer pretended
he hadn't seen me the entire time. And Tito Carbonell stood
beside him as if he wanted to mark his territory. The only
person who seemed perplexed and sad over her death was
Albert Carbonell, who was debuting as a widower without
having had time to get used to the idea of so much unexpected solitude. Adrià had only seen him a couple of times in

his life, but he felt some grief over the desolation of that man who had aged considerably. As we went down the long paths of the cemetery, Albert Carbonell approached me, took me by the arm and said thank you for coming.

'It's the least I could do. I'm so sad.'

'Thank you. You might be the only one. The others are crunching numbers.'

We grew silent; the sound of the group's footsteps on the dirt path, broken by whispers, by the occasional curse against Barcelona's mugginess, by the odd cough that couldn't be stifled, lasted until we reached where we had left our cars. And meanwhile, almost into my ear, as if he wanted to take advantage of the proximity, Albert Carbonell said watch it with that nosy parker Berenguer.

'Did he work with Daniela in the shop?'

'For two months. And Daniela threw him out on his ear. Since then they've hated each other and never missed the chance to show it.'

He paused, as if he were having trouble speaking and walking at the same time. I vaguely recalled that he was asthmatic. Or maybe I made that part up. Anyway, he continued, saying Berenguer is a crafty devil; he's sick.

'In what sense?'

'There's only one possible sense. He's not right in the head. And he hates all women. He can't accept that a woman is more intelligent than him. Or that she makes the decisions instead of him. That pains him and eats him up inside. Be careful that he doesn't hurt you.'

'Do you mean that he could?'

'You never know with Berenguer.'

We said goodbye in front of Tito's car. We shook hands and he said take care of yourself; Daniela spoke affectionately of you. It's a shame you didn't spend more time together.

'As a boy I was in love with her for one whole day.'

I said it as he was getting into the car and I don't know if he heard me. He waved vaguely from inside. I never saw him again. I don't know if he's still alive.

It wasn't until I was right in the middle of the dense traffic around the statue of Columbus covered in tourists taking photos of themselves, on my way home and wondering whether I should speak to you about it or not, that I realised that Albert Carbonell was the first person who didn't call Mr Berenguer Mr Berenguer.

When I opened the door, Sara could have asked me where are you coming from, and I, from burying my sister; and she, you have a sister? And I, yes, a half-sister. And she, well, you could have told me; and I, you never asked, we barely ever saw each other, you know. Why didn't you tell me now, that she'd died? Because I would have had to tell you about your friend Tito Carbonell, who wants to steal the violin from me, and we would've had another argument. But when I opened the door to the house, you didn't ask me where are you coming from and I didn't respond from burying my sister and you couldn't respond you have a sister? And then I realised that your suitcase was in the entryway. Adrià looked at it, surprised.

'I'm going to Cadaqués,' replied Sara.

'I'll come.'

'No.'

She left without any explanation. It happened so fast that I wasn't aware of the importance it would have for us both. When Sara was gone, Adrià, still disorientated, with his heart heavy and restless, opened Sara's wardrobe and suddenly felt relieved: her clothes were still there. I thought that you must have just taken a few outfits.

## 49

Since he didn't know what to do, Adrià didn't do anything. He had been abandoned by Sara again; but now he knew why. And it was only a momentary escape. Momentary? To keep from thinking about it too much, he threw himself into his work, but he had trouble concentrating on what would be the definitive version of *Llull, Vico, Berlin, tres organitzadors de les idees*, a book with a dense title. He felt personally compelled to write it in order to distance himself from his *Història del pensament europeu*, which was weighing on him perhaps because he had dedicated many years to it, perhaps because he had much hope placed in it, perhaps because people he admired had made mention of it ... The unity, one of the unities of the book, was created by the historical narrative. And he rewrote the three essays entirely. He had been working on that for months. I had begun, my beloved, the day when I saw on television the horrifying images of the building in Oklahoma City gutted by a bomb placed by Timothy McVeigh. I didn't say anything to you about it because it's better to do these things and then later, if necessary, talk about them. I got to work on it because I've always believed that those who kill in the name of something have no right to sully history. One hundred and sixty-eight deaths, caused by Timothy McVeigh. And much more grief and suffering not reflected in the statistics. In the name of what intransigence, Timothy? And, I don't know how, I imagined another intransigent, of another sort of intransigence, asking him the question, why, Timothy, why such destruction when God is Love?

'The American government can shove it up their ass.'

'Timothy, son: what religion do you practise?' interjected Vico.

'Sticking it to the people who are screwing up the country.'

'There is no such religion,' Ramon Llull, patient. 'There are three known religions, Timothy: namely, Judaism, which is a terrible error with apologies to Mr Berlin; Islam, which is the mistaken belief system of the infidel enemies of the church, and Christianity, which is the only just and true religion, because it is the religion of the Good God, who is Love.'

'I don't understand you, old man. I kill the government.'

'And the forty children you killed are the government?' Berlin, wiping his glasses with a handkerchief.

'Collateral damage.'

'Now I don't understand.'

'1:1'

'What?'

'One to one.'

'The colonel who doesn't stop the massacre of women and children,' states Vico, 'must go to jail.'

'But not if he kills men?' Berlin, mockingly, to his colleague, putting on his glasses.

'Why don't you three just all shove it up your ass, huh?'

'This boy has a strange verbal obsession with the posterior,' observed Llull, very perplexed.

'All those who live by the sword, die by the sword, Timothy,' Vico reminded him just in case. And he was going to say which verse of Matthew it was, but he couldn't remember because it had all been too long ago.

'Would you doddering old fogies mind fucking leaving me alone?'

'They are going to kill you tomorrow, Tim,' Llull pointed out.

'168:1.'

And he began to fade out.

'What did he say? Did you understand anything?'

'Yes. One hundred and sixty-eight, colon, one.'

'It sounds cabbalistic.'

'No. This kid has never heard of the cabbala.'

'One hundred and sixty-eight to one.'

*Llull, Vico, Berlin* was a feverish book, written quickly, but it left me exhausted because each day, when I got up and when

I went to sleep, I opened Sara's wardrobe and her clothes were still there. Writing under such circumstances is very difficult. And one day I finished writing it, which doesn't mean that it was finished. And Adrià was overcome with a desire to throw all the pages off the balcony. But he just said Sara, ubi es? And then, after a few minutes in silence, instead of going out on the balcony, he made a pile of all the pages, put them on one corner of the table, said I'm going out, Little Lola, without realising that Caterina wasn't there, and he headed to the university, as if it were the ideal place to distract himself.

'What are you doing?'

Laura turned around. From the way she was walking, it looked as if she were taking measurements of the cloister.

'Thinking. And you?'

'Trying to distract myself.'

'How's the book?'

'I just finished it.'

'Wow,' she said, pleased.

She took both of his hands in hers, but immediately pulled them away as if she'd been burned.

'But I'm not at all convinced. It's impossible to bring together three such strong personalities.'

'Have you finished it or not?'

'Well, yes. But now I have to read it all the way through and I'll come up against many obstacles.'

'So it's not finished.'

'No. It's written. Now I just have to finish it. And I don't know if it's publishable, honestly.'

'Don't give in, coward.'

Laura smiled at him with that gaze that disconcerted him. Especially when she called him a coward because she was right.

Ten days later, in mid-July, it was Todó, with his deliberateness, who said hey, Ardèvol, are you going ahead with the book in the end or what. They were both looking out from the first floor of the sunny, half-empty cloister.

I have trouble writing because Sara is not around.

'I don't know.'

'Shit: if *you* don't know …'

She's not around: we aren't speaking because of a damn violin.

'I'm having trouble bringing together personalities that are so … so …'

'Such strong personalities, yes: that's the official version that everyone knows,' interrupted Todó.

Why don't you all just leave me alone, for fuck's sake?

'Official version? And how do people know, that I'm writing …'

'You're the star, mate.'

Bloody hell.

They were in silence for a long while. Ardèvol's lengthy conversations were filled with silences, according to reliable sources.

'Llull, Vico, Berlin,' recited Todó, his voice arriving from a distance.

'Yes.'

'Shit. Vico and Llull, all right: but Berlin?'

No, no, please, leave me alone, you annoying fuck.

'The desire to organise the world through scholarship: that is what unites them.'

'Hey, that could be interesting.'

That's why I wrote it, you bloody idiot, you're making me swear and everything.

'But I think it's still going to take me some time. I don't know if I'll be able to finish it: you can consider that the official version.'

Todó leaned on the stone railing.

'Do you know what?' he said after a long pause. 'I really hope you work it out.' He looked at him out of the corner of his eye. 'It'd do me good to read something like that.'

He patted him on the arm in a show of support and went towards his office, in the corner of the cloister. Below, a couple walked through the cloister holding hands, uninterested in the rest of the word, and Adrià envied them. He knew that when Todó had told him that it would do him good to read something like that, it wasn't to butter him up and even less because it would do his spirit good to read a book where the unlinkable was linked and he struggled to show that the great thinkers were doing the same thing as Tolstoy but with ideas. Todó's spirit was featherweight and if he was yearning for a book that didn't yet exist it was because he had been obsessed for years now with undermining Doctor Bassas's position in their department and in the university, and the best way to do that was by creating new idols, in whatever discipline. If not for you, I would have even felt flattered to be used in other people's power struggles. The violin belongs to my family, Sara. I can't do that, because of my father. He died over this violin and now you want me to just give it away to some stranger who claims it's his? And if you can't understand that it's because when it comes to Jewish matters, you don't listen to reason. And you let yourself be hoodwinked by gangsters like Tito and Mr Berenguer. Eloi, Eloi, lema sabachthani.

In the deserted office, it suddenly came to him. Or, to put it better, he came to a decision all of a sudden. It must have been the euphoria of the half-finished book. He dialed a number and waited patiently as he thought please let her be there, let her be there, let her be there because otherwise … He looked at his watch: almost one. They must be having lunch.

'Hello.'

'Max, it's Adrià.'

'Hey.'

'Can you put her on?'

Slight hesitation.

'Let's see. One sec.'

That meant she was there! She hadn't run off to Paris, to the huitième arrondissement, and she hadn't gone to Israel. My Sara was still in Cadaqués. My Sara hadn't wanted to flee too far … On the other side of the line, still silence. I couldn't even hear footsteps or any murmur of conversation. I don't know how many eternal seconds passed. When a voice came on it was Max again: 'Listen, she says that … I'm really sorry … She says to ask you if you've returned the violin.'

'No: I want to talk to her.'

'It's that … Then she says … she says she doesn't want to talk to you.'

Adrià gripped the phone very tightly. Suddenly, his throat was dry. He couldn't find the words. As if Max had guessed that, he said I'm really sorry, Adrià. Really.

'Thank you, Max.'

And he hung up as the office door opened. Laura looked surprised to find him there. In silence, she went over to her desk and shuffled through the drawers for a few minutes. Adrià had barely changed position, looking into the void, hearing Sara's brother's delicate words as if they were a death sentence. After a little while he sighed loudly and looked over at Laura.

'Are you all right?' she asked as she gathered some very thick folders, the kind she was always carrying around everywhere.

'Of course. I'll buy you lunch.'

I don't know why I said that. It wasn't out of any sort of revenge. I think it was because I wanted to show Laura and the whole world that nothing was wrong, that everything was under control.

Seated before Laura's blue eyes and perfect skin, Adrià left half of his pasta on his plate. They had barely spoken. Laura filled his water glass and he made an appreciative gesture.

'So, how's everything going?' said Adrià, putting on a friendly face as if they had lifted the conversation ban.

'Well. I'm going to the Algarve for fifteen days.'

'How nice. Todò is a bit loony, yeah?'

'Why?'

They reached, after a few minutes, the conclusion that yes, a bit loony; and that it was best if you didn't tell him anything about my book that doesn't yet exist because there is nothing more unpleasant than writing knowing that everyone is on the edge of their seats wondering whether you will be able to tie together Vico and Llull and all that.

'I talk too much, I know.'

And to prove it, she explained that she had met some really nice people and they were meeting up in the Algarve because they were bicycling all over the Iberian peninsula and

'Are you a biker, too?'

'I'm too old. I'm going to lie on a beach chair. To disconnect from the dramas in the department.'

'And flirt a bit.'

She didn't answer. She glanced at him to convey that I was going too far, because women have an ability to understand things that I've always envied.

What do I know, Sara? But this is how it went. In Laura's flat, which was tiny but always spick and span, there was a controlled disorder that was particularly concentrated in the bedroom. A disorder that wasn't chaotic in the least, the disorder of someone about to go on a trip. Clothing in piles, shoes lined up, a couple of tourist guides and a camera. Like a cat and a dog, they carefully watched each other's moves.

'Is it one of the electronic ones?' said Adrià, picking up the camera suspiciously.

'Uh-huh. Digital.'

'You're always into the latest thing.'

Laura took off her shoes, standing, and put on some sort of flip-flops that were very flattering.

'And you must use a Leica.'

'I don't have a camera. I never have.'

'And your memories?'

'Here.' Adrià pointed to his head. 'They never break down. And they're always here when I need them.'

I said it without irony because I can't predict anyone's future.

'I can take two hundred photos, with this.' She took the camera from him with a gesture that strove to conceal her impatience and put it down on the night table, beside the telephone.

'Bravo,' he said, uninterested.

'And then I can put them into my computer. I look at them more there than in an album.'

'Bravissimo. But for that you need a computer.'

Laura stood before him, defiant.

'What?' she said, her hands on her hips. 'Now you want a lecture on the quality of digital photos?'

Adrià looked into those oh so blue eyes and embraced her.
They held each other for a long time and I cried a little bit.
Luckily, she didn't notice.

'Why are you crying?'

'I'm not crying.'

'Liar. Why are you crying?'

By mid afternoon they had turned the bedroom's disorder
into chaos. And they spent close to an hour lying down,
looking at the ceiling. Laura studied Adrià's medallion.

'Why do you always wear it?'

'Just because.'

'But you don't believe in …'

'It's a reminder.'

'A reminder of what?'

'I don't know.'

Then the telephone rang. It rang on the bedside table next
to Laura's side of the bed. They looked at each other, as if
wanting to ask, in some sort of guilty silence, whether they
were expecting any call. Laura didn't move, with her head on
Adrià's chest, and they both heard how the telephone, monotonously, insisted, insisted, insisted. Adrià stared at Laura's
hair, expecting her to reach for it. Nothing. The telephone
kept ringing.

# VI

## STABAT MATER

We are granted all that we fear.

Hélène Cixous

## 50

Two years later, the telephone rang suddenly and gave Adrià a start, just like every time he heard it. He stared at the device for a long time. The house was dark except for the reading light on in his study. The house was silent, the house without you, except for the insistent ringing of the telephone. He put a bookmark in Carr, closed it and stared at the shrieking telephone for a few more minutes, as if that solved everything. He let it ring for a good long while and finally, when whoever was calling had already made their stubborness clear, Adrià Ardèvol rubbed his face with his palms, picked up and said hello.

His gaze was sad and damp. He was nearing eighty and gave off a worn, infinitely beaten air. He stood on the landing of the staircase breathing anxiously, gripping a small travel bag as if his contact with it was what was keeping him alive. When he heard Adrià walking up the stairs slowly, he turned. For a few seconds, they both stared at each other.

'Mijnheer Adrian Ardefol?'

Adrià opened the door to his home and invited him in while the man, in something approximating English, confirmed that he was the one who'd called that morning. I was convinced that a sad story was entering my house together with the stranger, but I no longer had any choice. I closed the door to keep the secrets from scampering out onto the landing and into the stairwell; standing, I offered to speak in Dutch and then I saw that the stranger's damp eyes brightened a tad as he made an appreciative gesture to Adrià, who had to brush up on his rusty Dutch straightaway to ask the stranger what he wanted.

'It's a long story. That's why I asked if you had some time.'

He led him into the study. He noticed that the man hadn't tried to hide his admiration, which was like someone who suddenly happens upon an unexpected room filled with surprises when visiting the Louvre. Right in the middle of the study, the newcomer spun around timidly, taking in the shelves filled with books, the paintings, the incunabula, the instrument cabinet, the two desks, your self-portrait, the Carr on top of the table, which I still hadn't been able to finish, and the manuscript beneath the loupe, my latest acquisition: sixty-three handwritten pages of *The Dead* with curious comments in the margin that were probably by Joyce himself. Once he had seen it all, he looked at Adrià in silence.

Adrià had him sit on the other side of the desk, one in front of the other, and for a few seconds I wondered what specific grief could have produced the rictus of pain that had dried onto the stranger's face. He unzipped his bag with some difficulty and pulled out something covered carefully in paper. He unwrapped it meticulously and Adrià saw a dirty piece of cloth, dark with filth, on which a few dark and light checks could still be made out. The stranger moved aside the paper and placed the rag on the desk and, with gestures that seemed liturgical, he unfolded it carefully, as if it contained a valuable treasure. He seemed like a priest laying out an altar cloth. Once he had spread it out, I was somewhat disappointed to see that there was nothing inside. A stitched line separated it into two equal parts, like a border. I couldn't perceive the memories. Then the stranger took off his glasses and wiped his right eye with a tissue. Noting Adrià's respectful silence and without looking him in the eye, he said that he wasn't crying, that for the last few months he'd been suffering a very uncomfortable allergy that caused etcetera, etcetera, and he smiled as if in apology. He looked around him and tossed the tissue into the bin. Then, with a vaguely liturgical gesture, he pointed to the filthy old rag with both hands extended in front of him. As if it were an invitation to the question.

'What is that?' he asked.

The stranger put both palms onto the cloth for a few seconds, as if he were mentally reciting a deep prayer, and he said, in a transformed voice, now imagine you are having lunch at home, with your wife, your mother-in-law and your three little daughters; your mother-in-law has a bit of a chest cold, and suddenly …

The stranger lifted his head and now his eyes were definitely filled with tears, not allergies and etceteras. But he didn't make any motion to wipe away the tears of pain, he looked intently straight ahead, and he repeated imagine you are having lunch at home, with your wife, your sick mother-in-law and your three little daughters, with the new tablecloth set out, the blue-and-white chequered one, because today is the eldest girl's birthday – little Amelietje – and suddenly someone breaks down the door without even knocking first and comes in armed to the teeth, followed by five more soldiers, storming in, and they all keep shouting schnell, schnell and raus, raus, and they take you out of your house forever in the middle of lunch, for the rest of your life, with no chance of looking back, the party tablecloth, the new one, the one my Berta had bought two years earlier, without the chance to grab anything, with just the clothes on your back. What does raus mean, Daddy, says Amelietje, and I couldn't keep her from getting smacked on the nape of her neck by an impatient rifle who insisted raus, raus because everyone can understand German because it is the language and whoever says they don't understand it is lying and will get what's coming to them. Raus!

Two minutes later they were going down the street, my mother-in-law coughing, with a violin case in her arms because her daughter had left it in the hall after returning home from rehearsal; the girls with their eyes wide, my Berta, pale, squeezing little Juliet in her arms. Down the street, almost running because it seemed the soldiers were in a big hurry, and the mute gazes of the neighbours from the windows, and I grabbed the little hand of Amelia, who turned seven today and was crying because the blow to her neck hurt and because the German soldiers were scary, and poor Trude, just five years old, begged me to pick her up and I put her on my shoulders, and Amelia had to run to keep up with us and until we reached Glass Square, where the lorry was, I didn't realise that I was still gripping a blue-and-white chequered napkin.

There were more humane ones, they told me later. The ones who said you can take twenty-five kilos of luggage and you have half an hour to gather it, schnell, eh? And then you think about everything there is in a house. What would you grab, to take with you? To take where? A chair? A book? The shoebox with family photos? China? Light bulbs? The mattress? Mama, what does schnell mean. And how much are twenty-five kilos? You end up grabbing that useless key ring that hangs forgotten in the hall and that, if you survive and don't have to trade it for a crumb of mouldy bread, will become the sacred symbol of that normal, happy life you had before the disaster. Mama, why did you bring that? Shut up, my mother-in-law responded.

Leaving the house forever, accompanied by the rhythm of the soldiers' boots, leaving that life with my wife pale with panic, the girls terrified, my mother-in-law about to faint and I unable to do anything about it. Who turned us in? We live in a Christian neighbourhood. Why? How did they know? How did they sniff out the Jews? On the lorry, to keep from seeing the girls' desperation, I thought who, how and why. When they made us get into the lorry, which was filled with frightened people, Berta the Brave with the little one and I with Trude stayed to one side. My mother-in-law and her cough, a bit further down, and Berta started to shout where is Amelia, Amelietje, my daughter, where are you, stay close to us, Amelia, and a little hand made its way over and grabbed my trouser leg and then poor Amelietje, scared, even more scared after finding herself alone for a few moments, looked up at me, asking for help, she too wanted to climb into my arms, but she didn't ask because Truu was littler and that gaze that I've never been able to forget for the rest of my life, never, the help that your daughter begs you for and you don't know how to give, and you will go to hell for not having helped your little daughter in her moment of need. All you can think to do is give her the blue-and-white chequered napkin and she clung to it with both hands and looked at me gratefully, as if I'd given her a precious treasure, the talisman that would keep her from getting lost wherever she went.

The talisman didn't work because after that rough journey in a lorry and two, three or four days in a smelly, stifling sealed goods train, they snatched Truu out of my hands despite my desperation, and when they slammed my head so hard I was left stunned, little Amelia had disappeared from my side, I think pursued by dogs that wouldn't stop barking. Little Juliet in Berta's arms, I don't know where they were, because we hadn't even been able to exchange a last glance, Berta and I, not even to communicate the mute desperation our hard-earned happiness had become. And Berta's mother, still coughing, clinging to the violin, and Trude, where is Truu, I've let them take her from my hands. I never saw them again. They had made us get out of the train only a few moments before and I had lost my women forever. Rsrsrsrsrsrsrs. And even though they pushed me and shrieked orders in my ear as I twisted my neck, desperate, towards where they might be, I had time to see two soldiers, with cigarettes in their mouths, grabbing suckling babes like my Juliet from the arms of their mothers and smashing them against the wood of the train carriage to make the women obey for once and ffucking all. That was when I decided to stop speaking to the God of Abraham and the God of Jesus.

'Rsrsrsrsrsrs. Rsrsrsrsrsrsrsrs.'

'Excuse me …' Adrià had to say.

The man looked at me, confused, absent. Perhaps he wasn't even conscious of being with me, as if he'd repeated that story thousands of times in attempts to mitigate his pain.

'Someone's at the door …' said Adrià, looking at his watch as he stood up. 'It's a friend who …'

And he left the study before the other man could react.

'Come on, come on, come on, this is heavy …' said Bernat, entering the flat and breaking the atmosphere, with a bulky package in his arms. 'Where should I put it?'

He was already in the study and surprised to see a stranger there.

'Oh, pardon me.'

'On the table,' said Adrià, coming in behind him.

Bernat rested the package on the table and smiled timidly at the stranger.

'Hello,' he said to him.

The old man tilted his head in greeting, but said nothing.

'Let's see if you can help me,' said Bernat as he tried to extract the computer from the box. Adrià pulled down on the box and the contraption emerged, in Bernat's hands.

'Right now I'm …'

'I can see that. Should I come back later?'

Since we were speaking in Catalan, I could be more explicit and I told him that it was an unexpected visit and I had the feeling it would be a while. Let's get together tomorrow, if that works for you.

'Sure, no problem.' Referring discreetly to the strange visitor. 'Is there any problem?'

'No, no.'

'Very well then. See you tomorrow.' About the computer: 'And until then, don't mess with it.'

'I wouldn't dream of it.'

'Here's the keyboard and the mouse. I'll take the big box. And tomorrow I'll bring you the printer.'

'Thanks, eh.'

'Thank Llorenç; I'm only the intermediary.'

He looked at the stranger and said farewell. The other man tilted his head again. Bernat left saying you don't need to walk me to the door, go ahead, go ahead.

He left the study and they heard the door to the hall slam shut. I sat down again beside my guest. I made a gesture to excuse the brief interruption and said sorry. I indicated with my hand for him to continue, as if Bernat hadn't come in and brought me Llorenç's old computer, to see if I'd finally give up my unhealthy habit of writing with a fountain pen. The donation included a commitment of a short speed course of x sessions, in which the value of x depended on the patience of both the student and the teacher. But it was true that I had finally agreed to find out for myself what was the big deal about computers, which everyone found so wonderful and I had no need for.

Seeing my signal, the little old man continued, apparently not very affected by the interruption, as if he knew the text by heart, and said for many years I asked myself the question, the questions, which are many and muddle together into one. Why did I survive? Why, when I was a useless man who allowed, without putting up any resistance, the soldiers to take my three daughters, my wife and my mother-in-law with a chest cold. Not even a sign of resistance. Why did I have to survive; why, if my life up until then had been absolutely useless, doing the accounting for Hauser en Broers, living a boring life, and the only worthwhile thing I'd done was conceive three daughters, one with jet-black hair, the other a brunette like the finest woods of the forest and the little one honey blonde. Why? Why, and with the added anguish of not being sure, because I never saw them dead, not knowing for sure if they really are all dead, my three little girls and my wife and my coughing mother-in-law. Two years of searching when the war ended led me to accept the words of a judge who determined that, based on the indications and signs – he called them evidence – I could be sure they were all dead, most likely they had all been killed the very day they arrived in Auschwitz-Birkenau, because in those months, according to the confiscated Lager documents, all the women, children and old people were taken to the gas chambers and only the men who could work were saved. Why did I survive? When they took me away from my girls and Berta, I thought I was the one being taken to die because, in my innocence, I thought I was the danger to them and not the women. Yet, for them, it was the women and children that were dangerous, especially the girls, because it was through them that the accursed Jewish race could spread and through them that, in the future, the great revenge could come. They were coherent with that thought and that is why I am still alive, ridiculously alive now that Auschwitz has become a museum where only I sense the stench of death. Perhaps I survived until today and am able to tell you all this because I was a coward on Amelietje's birthday. Or because that rainy Saturday, in the barracks, I stole a crumb of clearly mouldy bread from old Moshes who came from Vilnius. Or because I crept away when the Blockführer decided to teach us a lesson and let loose with the butt of his rifle, and the blow that was meant to wound me killed a little boy whose name I'll never know but who was from a Ukrainian village near Upper Hungary and who had hair black as coal, blacker than my Amelia's, poor little thing. Or perhaps it was because … What do I know? … Forgive me, brothers, forgive me, my daughters, Juliet, Truu and Amelia, and you, Berta, and you, Mama, forgive me for having survived.

He stopped his account of the facts, but he kept his gaze fixed forward, looking nowhere because such pain could not be expressed while looking into anyone's eyes. He swallowed hard, but I, tied to my chair, didn't even think that the stranger, with all his talking, might need a glass of water. As if he didn't, he continued his tale, saying and so I went through life with my head bowed, crying over my cowardice and looking for some way to make amends for my evilness until I thought of hiding myself there where the memory could never reach me. I sought out a refuge: I probably made a mistake, but I needed shelter and I tried to get closer to the God I distrusted because he hadn't moved a muscle to save innocents. I don't know if you can understand it, but absolute desperation makes you do strange things: I decided to enter a Carthusian monastery, where they counselled me that what I was doing wasn't a good idea. I have never been religious; I was baptised as a Christian although religion in my house was never more than a social custom and my parents passed down their disinterest in religion to me. I married my beloved Berta, my brave wife who was Jewish but not from a religious family, and who didn't hesitate to marry a goy for love. She made me Jewish in my heart. After the Carthusians refused me I lied and at the next two places I tried I didn't mention the reasons for my grief; I didn't even show it. In one place and the other I learned what I had to say and what I had to keep quiet, so that when I knocked on the door of Saint Benedict's Abbey in Achel I already knew that no one would put up obstacles to my belated vocation and I begged, if obedience didn't demand otherwise, that they let me live there and fulfil the humblest tasks in the monastery. That was when I began speaking again, a bit, with God and I learned to get the cows to listen to me. And then I realised that the telephone had been ringing for some time, but I didn't have the heart to answer it. At least that was the first time in two years that it had rung without giving me a start. The stranger named Matthias, who was no longer such a stranger, and who had been called Brother Robert, looked at the telephone and at Adrià, waiting for some reaction. Since his host showed no interest in answering it, he continued speaking.

'And that's it,' he said, to help himself get started again. But maybe he had already said everything, because he started to fold up the dirty cloth, as if gathering up his stand after a very hard day at the street market. He did it carefully, using all five of his senses. He left the folded cloth in front of him. He repeated en dat is alles, as if no further explanations were necessary. Then Adrià broke his long silence and asked why have you come to explain this to me. And then he added, what does this have to do with me?

Neither of the two men realised that the telephone, at some point, had got fed up with ringing in vain. Now the only noise that reached them was the very muffled sounds of the traffic on València Street. They were both silent, as if exceedingly interested in the traffic noise of Barcelona's Eixample district. Until I looked the old man in the eye, and he, without returning my gaze, said and with all that, I confess that I don't know where God is.

'Well, I ...'

'For many years, in the monastery, he was part of my life.'

'Was that experience useful to you?'

'I don't believe so. But they wanted to show me that pain is not the work of God, but a consequence of human freedom.'

Now he did look at me and continued, raising his voice slightly, as if it were a mass meeting, and he said what about earthquakes? And floods? And why doesn't God doesn't stop people from committing evil? Huh?

He put his palms on the folded cloth: 'I talked a lot with cows, when I was a peasant monk. I always came to the maddening conclusion that God is guilty. Because it can't be that evil only resides in the desire for evil. That's too easy. He even gives us permission to kill the evil: dead dogs don't bite, says God. And it's not true. Without the dog, the bite continues to gnaw on us from inside, forever and ever.'

He looked from side to side without focusing on the books that had amazed him when he'd first entered the study. He picked up the thread: 'I came to the conclusion that if all-powerful God allows evil, God is an invention in poor taste. And I broke inside.'

'I understand. I don't believe in God either. The guilty always have a first and last name. They are named Franco, Hitler, Torquemada, Amalric, Idi Amin, Pol Pot, Adrià Ardèvol or whatever. But they have first and last names.'

'Not always. The tool of evil has a first and last name, but evil, the essence of evil … I still haven't resolved that.'

'Don't tell me that you believe in the devil.'

He looked at me in silence for a few seconds, as if weighing my words, which made me feel proud. But no: his head was somewhere else. He obviously didn't want to philosophise: 'Truu, the brunette, Amelia, the one with jet-black hair, Juliet, the littlest, blonde as the sun. And my coughing mother-in-law. And my strength, my wife, who was named Berta and who I have to believe has been dead for the last fifty-four years and ten months. I can't stop feeling guilty about still being alive. Every day I wake up thinking that I am failing them, day in, day out … and now I'm eighty-five and I still haven't known how to die, I keep living the same pain with the same intensity of the first day. Which is why – since despite everything I have never believed in forgiveness – I tried to get vengeance …'

'Excuse me?'

'… and I discovered that vengeance can never be complete. You can only take it out on the idiot who let himself get caught. You are always left with the disappointment of those who got away with it.'

'I understand.'

'You don't understand,' he interrupted, abruptly. 'Because vengeance causes even more pain and brings no satisfaction. And I wonder: if I can't forgive, why doesn't vengeance make me happy? Huh?'

He grew quiet and I respected his silence. Had I ever taken vengeance on anyone? Surely I had, in the thousand evil things of daily life surely I had. I looked into his eyes and I insisted, 'Where do I show up in this story?'

I said it with some confusion, I don't know if I was expecting to have some sort of starring role in that life of pain or if I wanted to get to the part I was already fearing.

'You are entering the stage right now,' he responded, half hiding a smile.

'What do you want?'

'I came to get back Berta's violin.'

The telephone started to ring, as if it were feverishly applauding the interpreters of a memorable recital.

Bernat plugged in the computer and turned it on. As he waited for the screen to come to life, I explained what had happened the day before. As he listened, his jaw dropped in amazement.

'What?' he said, absolutely beside himself.

'You heard me right,' I replied.

'You're … you're … you're crazy, man!'

He connected the mouse and the keyboard. He banged angrily on the table and started to walk around the room. He went over to the instrument cabinet and opened it with a bit too much force, as if he wanted to check what I'd just told him. He slammed it shut.

'Careful you don't break the glass,' I warned him.

'Fuck the glass. Fuck you, bloody hell, why didn't you tell me?'

'Because you would have talked me out of it.'

'Obviously! But how could you …'

'It was as simple as the man standing up, going over to the cabinet, opening it and pulling out the Storioni.' He stroked it and Adrià watched him with curiosity and a bit of suspicion.

The man burst into tears, hugging the violin; Adrià let him do it. The man pulled a bow from the cabinet, tightened it, looked at me to ask for my permission and began to play. 'It didn't sound very good. Actually, it sounded awful.'

'I'm not a violinist. She was. I was only a hobbyist.'

'And Berta?'

'She was a great woman.'

'Yes, but ...'

'She was first violinist of the Antwerp Philharmonic.'

He began playing a Jewish melody that I had heard once but couldn't place where. But since he played so terribly, he ended up singing it. I got goose bumps.

'And now I've got fucking goose bumps, because you gave away that violin, for fuck's sake!'

'Justice was done.'

'He was an imposter, you blockhead! Can't you see? Bloody hell, my God. Our Vial is gone forever. After so many years of ... What would your father say? Huh?'

'Don't be ridiculous. You've never wanted to use it.'

'But I was dying to, for fuck's sake! Don't you know how to interpret a no?' Don't you know that when you told me use it, take it on tour, Bernat smiled timidly and left the instrument in the cabinet as he shook his head and said I can't, I can't, it's too big a responsibility? Huh?

'That means no.'

'It doesn't mean no, bloody hell. It means I'm dying to!' Bernat, with his eyes wanting to pounce on me: 'Is that so hard to understand?'

Adrià was silent for a few moments, as if he was having trouble digesting so much life philosophy.

'Look, laddie: you're a bastard,' continued Bernat. 'And you let yourself be swindled by some bloke who came to you with a sob story.'

He pointed to the computer: 'And I came here to help you.'

'Maybe we should do it some other day. Today we're ... a little ...'

'Fuck, you're an idiot, giving the violin to the first cry-baby who knocks on your door! I can't fucking believe it.'

When he had finished singing the melody, the old man put the violin and bow into the cabinet and sat back down as he timidly said at my age you can only play the violin for yourself. Nothing works any more, your fingers fail you, and your arm isn't strong enough to hold up the instrument correctly.

'I understand.'

'Being old is obscene. Ageing is obscene.'

'I understand.'

'You don't understand. I would have liked to die before my wife and daughters and yet I'm becoming a decrepit old man, as if I had the slightest interest in clinging to life.'

'You're in good shape.'

'Poppycock. My body is falling apart. And I should have died more than fifty years ago.'

'So what the fuck did that stupid old man want with a violin if what he wanted was to die? Can't you see that it's contradictory?'

'It was my decision, Bernat. And it's done.'

'Bastard. Tell me where that hapless cretin is and I'll convince him that ...'

'It's over. I don't have the Storioni any more. Inside, I feel that ... I contributed towards justice being done. I feel good. Two years too late.'

'I feel terrible. Now I see: the hapless cretin is you.'

He sat down, he stood up again. He couldn't believe it. He faced Adrià, challenging him: 'Why do you say two years too late?'

The old man sat down. His hands were trembling a bit. He rested them on the dirty cloth that was still on top of the table, well folded.

'Have you thought about suicide?' My tone came out like a doctor asking a patient if he likes chamomile tea.

'Do you know how Berta was able to buy it?' he responded.

'No.'

'I don't need it, Matthias, my love. I can spend my life with ...'

'Yes, of course. You can use your same old violin forever.

But I'm telling you it's worth making the effort. My family can lend me half of the price.'

'I don't want to be indebted to your family.'

'They're your family too, Berta! Why can't you accept that? ...'

That was when my mother-in-law intervened; that was before she got the chest cold. The time between one war and the other, when life came back with a vengeance and musicians could devote themselves to playing music and not rotting in the trenches; that was when Berta Alpaerts spent countless hours trying out a Storioni that was beyond her reach, with a beautiful, confident, deep sound. Jules Arcan was asking for a price that wasn't the least bit reasonable. That was the day that Trude, our second daughter, turned six months old. We didn't have Juliet yet. It was dinnertime and, for the first time since we'd been living together, my mother-in-law wasn't at home. When we returned from work no one had made anything for supper. While Berta and I threw something together, my mother-in-law arrived, loaded down, and placed a magnificent dark case on the table. There was a thick silence. I remember that Berta looked at me for a response I was unable to give her.

'Open it, my girl,' said my mother-in-law.

Since Berta didn't dare, her mother encouraged her: 'I've just come from Jules Arcan's workshop.'

Then Berta leapt towards the case and opened it. We all looked inside and Vial winked at us. My mother-in-law had decided that since she was well taken care of at our house, her savings could be spent on her daughter. Poor Berta was struck dumb for a couple of hours, unable to play anything, unable to pick up the instrument, as if she weren't worthy, until Amelietje, our eldest who was still very little, the one with jet-black hair, said come on, Mama, I want to hear how it sounds. Oh, how she made it sound, my Berta ... How lovely ... My mother-in-law had spent all of her savings. Every last penny. Plus some other secret that she never would tell us. I think she sold a flat she had in Schoten.

The man was silent, his gaze lost beyond the book-covered

wall. Then, as if in conclusion to his story, he told me it took me many years to find you, to find Berta's violin, Mr Ardefol.

'That's no argument, Adrià, bloody hell. He could be telling you any old story he'd made up, can't you see that?'

'How did you find me?' said Adrià, his curiosity piqued.

'Patience and help ... the detectives assured me that your father left many trails behind him. He made a lot of noise as he moved.'

'That was many years ago.'

'I've spent many years crying. Until now I wasn't prepared to do certain things, including getting back Berta's violin. I waited a couple of years to come and see you.'

'A couple of years ago some opportunists spoke to me about you.'

'Those weren't my instructions. I only wanted to locate the violin.'

'They wanted to be intermediaries in its sale,' insisted Adrià.

'God save me from intermediaries: I've had bad experiences with people like that.' He stared into Adrià's eyes. 'I never would have thought to talk about buying it.'

Adrià observed him, stock-still. The old man came over to him as if he wanted to erase any possible intermediaries between them: 'I didn't come here to buy it: I came here for restitution.'

'They hoodwinked you, Adrià. You've been swindled by a conman. A clever chap like you ...'

Since Adrià didn't reply, the man continued speaking: 'When I located it, first I wanted to meet you. At this point in life, I'm in no rush about anything.'

'Why did you want to do it this way?'

'To find out if I had to hold you accountable for your role.'

'I should tell you that I feel guilty about everything.'

'That's why I studied you before coming to see you.'

'What do you mean?'

'I read *La voluntat estètica* and the other one, the fat one. *Història del ... del ...*'

He snapped his fingers to help along his senior memory.

'... *del pensament europeu*,' said Adrià with very well concealed pride.

'Exactly. And a collection of articles that I don't remember
the title of now. But don't make me talk about them because
...'

He touched his forehead to make it clear that his brain
wasn't as sharp as it used to be.

'But why?'

'I don't really know. I suppose because I ended up respecting you. And because from what the investigators told me,
you didn't have anything to do with ...'

I didn't want to contradict him. I didn't have anything to
do with ... , but I had a lot to do with Father. Possibly it wasn't
aesthetic to talk about that now. So I kept quiet. I only repeated why did you want to study me, Mr Alpaerts.

'All I have is time. And in trying to make amends for evil,
I've made many mistakes: the first, believing that if I hid the
horror would disappear; and the worst, causing other horrors
because of lack of foresight.'

We talked for hours on end and I didn't even think to offer
him a glass of water. I understood that such profound pain
came out of confusing, chaotic stories that made it even more
profound and bloody.

Matthias Alpaerts had entered my home after lunch,
around two or two-thirty in the afternoon. We didn't leave
the study until nine in the evening except for a couple of interruptions to go to the toilet. Now it had been hours since
the windows had begun to allow in darkness from the street
and the moving reflection of car headlights going down it.
Then we looked at each other and I realised that I was about
to faint.

Given the hour, the negotiation was quick: green beans,
potatoes and onions, boiled. And an omelette. As I prepared
it, he asked if he could use the toilet again and I apologised
for being such an inattentive host. Matthias Alpaerts excused
it with a wave and urgently slipped into the bathroom. As the
pressure cooker released its warning, I went back to the study
and put the violin on the table. I looked at it carefully. I took

a dozen photos of it with your historic camera that was right where you had left it; until the roll of film ended. Face, back, side, scroll and pegbox, neck and a few details of the fillets. Half way through the operation, Matthias Alpaerts came back from the toilet and watched me in silence.

'Are you feeling all right?' I said without looking at him, as I tried to photograph the Laurentius Storioni me fecit through the f-hole.

'At my age I have to be alert; nothing special.'

I put the violin back in the cabinet and looked Matthias Alpaerts in the eye.

'How do I know that you are telling me the truth? How do I know that you are Matthias Alpaerts?'

The old man pulled out an identification card with his photo on it and passed it to me.

'I'm me, as you can see.' He took back the card. 'I'm afraid I can't give you any proof that I'm telling the truth.'

'I hope you understand that I need to make sure,' said Adrià, thinking more about Sara and how happy you would be if I were brave enough to give the violin back.

'I don't know what more I can show you ...' said Alpaerts, slightly alarmed, as he hid the card in his wallet. 'My name is Matthias Alpaerts and I am the sole – unfortunately – owner of this violin.'

'I don't believe you.'

'I don't know what more I can tell you. As you can imagine, when I went back to the house I didn't find the certificate of ... Nor did I find our family photos. They had destroyed everything: they had devastated all my memories.'

'Allow me to distrust you,' I said without wanting to.

'You have every right,' he said. 'But I will do what it takes to get back that instrument: it is what ties me to my history and the history of my women.'

'I understand you, really. But ...'

He looked at me as if he emerging from the well of his memories, his entire face dripping with pain.

'Having to explain all that to you forced me to return to hell. I hope it wasn't in vain.'

'I understand you. But I have a document, and your name doesn't appear as the instrument's owner.'

'No?' Surprised, confused, so much so that I felt a bit bad for him.

They were both silent for a while. The smell of the vegetables boiling in the pressure cooker began to reach them from the kitchen.

'Ah! Of course!' he said suddenly. 'It must be my wife's name, of course: what was I thinking.'

'And what is your wife's name?'

'Her name was,' he corrected me, cruel with himself: 'Her name was Berta Alpaerts.'

'No, sir. That isn't the name I have either.'

We were quiet. I even regretted having started that sort of desperate haggling. But Adrià kept silent. Then Matthias Alpaerts gave a little shriek and said, of course, it was my mother-in-law who bought it!

'What was your mother-in-law's name?'

He thought for a few seconds, as if he was having trouble remembering such a simple thing. He looked at me with gleaming eyes and said Netje de Boeck.

Netje de Boeck. Netje de Boeck … The name my father had written down and I'd never forgotten, only because it weighed on my conscience. And it turns out that this Netje de Boeck was a mother-in-law with a chest cold.

'They've conned you!'

'Bernat, shut up. That sealed it for me.'

'Fucking idiot.'

Netje de Boeck, repeated the stranger. I only know that the violin went to Birkenau as if it were another member of the family: in the train that took us there I realised that my coughing mother-in-law held it tightly in her arms, as if it were a granddaughter. It was so cold our thoughts froze. With difficulty, I made it over to the corner where she sat beside another elderly woman. I felt Amelia's little hands clinging to my trousers and following me on that arduous route through the train carriage filled with sad people.

'Mama, why did you take it?'

'I don't want it to get stolen. It belongs to Berta.' Netje de Boeck was a woman of strong character.

'Mama, but if …'

Then she looked at me with those black eyes and said Matthias, don't you see that these are times of tragedy? They didn't even give me time to gather my jewels; but they won't steal this violin from me. Who knows if …

And she looked straight ahead again. Who knows if they'll give us food any time soon, the mother-in-law must have wanted to say. I didn't dare to grab the violin out of her hands and throw it to the rotten train floor and tell her to take care of Amelia, because the girl was still clinging to my trouser leg and didn't want to let me go. I had Truu on my shoulders, and I never saw Juliet and Berta again, because they were in another carriage. How could I lie to you, Mr Ardefol? In another carriage, towards the uncertainty of certain death. Because we knew we were heading to our deaths.

'Papa, it hurts me a lot here.'

Amelietje touched the nape of her neck. Best I could, I put Trude down and examined Amelia's neck. A considerable lump with a cut in the middle of it, which was starting to get infected. All I could do was apply a useless, loving kiss. The poor thing, she didn't complain again after that. I picked up the littler one again. After a while, Truu took my face in both hands so I would look into her eyes and said I'm hungry, Papa, when are we going to get there. Then I said to little Amelietje since you are the oldest, you have to help me, and she said yes, Papa. I put Truu down, with difficulty, and asked her sister for the napkin and, with a knife a taciturn, bearded man lent me, carefully cut the napkin into two equal parts. I gave one to each of my daughters, and poor Trude stopped saying that she was hungry and Amelietje and Truu stood together, leaning against my legs, silently gripping their pieces of the miraculous napkin.

The cruellest part was knowing that we were leading our little daughters by the hand to their deaths: I was an accomplice in the murder of my daughters, who clung to my neck and legs as the freezing air in the train carriage became unbreathable and no one looked each other in the eye because we were all haunted by the same thoughts. Only Amelietje and little Truitje had a chequered napkin just for them. And Matthias Alpaerts went over to the table and placed his palm on the dirty cloth that was carefully folded. This is all I have left of Amelia's birthday, my eldest girl, who they killed when she'd just turned seven. And Truu was five, and Julietje, two, and Berta thirty-two, and Netje, my mother-in-law with a chest cold, was over sixty …

He picked up the rag and looked at it fervidly and recited I still don't know by what miracle I was able to recover both halves. He placed the napkin on the table, again with the devotion of a priest folding and unfolding an altar cloth.

'Mr Alpaerts,' I said, raising my voice slightly.

The old man looked at me, surprised by the interruption. For a few moments it seemed he didn't know where he was.

'We should eat something.'

We ate in the kitchen, as if it were a casual visit. Despite his grief, Alpaerts ate hungrily. He curiously examined the oil cruet; I showed him how to use it and he bathed his vegetables in olive oil. Seeing how well it went over, I pulled out your spouted wine pitcher, which I hadn't used in so long, since your death: I had put it away out of fear it would get broken. I don't think I ever mentioned that. I put a bit of wine inside, demonstrated how to use it and, for the first and last time, Matthias Alpaerts laughed heartily. He drank from the pitcher's long spout, stained himself, still smiling, and said, out of the blue, bedankt, heer Ardefol. Perhaps he was thanking me for the laugh that had come out of him; I didn't want to ask.

I will never know for sure whether Matthias Alpaerts lived through all the things he explained to me. Deep down I know it; but I will never be entirely certain. In any case, I surrendered to a story that had defeated me, thinking of you and what you would have wanted me to do.

'You squandered your inheritance, my friend. If I can still call you a friend.'

'The violin was mine, why are you so worked up about it?'

Because I always thought that, if you died before I did, you would leave me the violin.

'Because it's not at all clear that this man's story is true. And even if we're not going to be friends any more, I'll show you how to use the computer later.'

'He told me if you look through the sound hole, mijnheer Ardefol, you'll see that it says Laurentius Storioni Cremonensis me fecit 1764 and next to that there are two marks, like little stars. And beneath Cremonensis, there is an irregular line, thicker in some parts, that goes from the m to the last n. If I remember correctly, because it's been more than fifty years.'

Adrià picked up the violin and looked at it. He had never noticed, but it was true. He looked at Matthias, opened his mouth, closed it again and placed the violin on the table.

'Yes, that's true,' ratified Bernat. But I knew that too and the violin wasn't mine, unfortunately.

Adrià placed the violin on the table again. Now it was time to make a decision. Deep down I know that it wasn't that hard for me to do. But we still spent a couple of hours together before saying farewell. I gave him the original case, the one with the dark stain that was impossible to get off.

'You are a complete fool.'

'The atrocious pain made Matthias Alpaerts continue living as if he were the same age as when he lost everything. That pain is what defeated me.'

'You were defeated by his history. No: his story.'

'Perhaps. So?'

The man caressed the top of the violin delicately with his fingertips. His hand began to tremble. He hid it, embarrassed, and turned towards me: 'Pain becomes concentrated and more intense when a defenceless being suffers it. And the certainty that it could have been avoided by a heroic act torments you throughout your life and throughout your death. Why didn't I cry out; why didn't I strangle the soldier who hit little Amelia with his rifle butt; why didn't I kill the SS who were saying you to the right, you to the left, you, you hear me?'

'Where are my daughters!'

'What?'

'Where are my daughters. They've snatched them from my hands!'

Matthias stood – his arms open, his eyes wide – before the soldier that had called over the officer.

'What are you telling me for. Come on. Get moving!'

'No! Amelia, with jet-black hair, and Truu, the one with brown hair the colour of forest wood, they were with me.'

'I said get moving. Go to the right and stop pestering me.'

'My daughters! And Juliet, the one with the golden ringlets! A clever little girl. She was in the other train carriage, do you hear me!?'

The soldier, bored by his insistence, rammed his rifle butt into his forehead. As he fell, half dazed, he saw one of the napkin halves on the ground, and he grabbed it and clung to it as if it were one of his daughters.

'You see?' he leaned towards Adrià, moving aside the few hairs he had left: there was something strange on his head, some sort of distant scar from that pain that was still so near.

'Get in the queue or I'll smash your skull,' said the deliberate voice of Doctor Budden, the officer, putting his hand on the closed holster. It was later than usual and he was a bit anxious; especially after his conversation with Doctor Voigt, who was demanding results in one thing or another, make it up, for goodness sake, it's not that hard. But I want a report with the results. And Matthias Alpaerts was unable to see that monster's eyes because his visor covered most of his face. He got into the right queue obediently, which didn't take him – though he couldn't know that – to the gas chambers, but rather to the disinfection blocks to become free labour ad maiorem Reich gloriam. And Budden – like the pied piper of Hamelin – was able to make his selection of boys and girls. Voigt, a few metres further on, was able to blow off the head of Netje de Boeck, Matthias's mother-in-law with a chest cold. And he kept telling Adrià that in the face of that officer's threat I lowered my head and ever since then I think that my daughters died because I didn't rebel, and so did Berta and

my mother-in-law with a chest cold. I hadn't seen Berta and
Juliet since we'd got on the train. Poor Berta: we weren't able
to look at each other one last time. Look at each other, just
look at each other, my God; just look at each other, even from
a distance. Look at each other … My beloved women, I abandoned you. And I wasn't able to avenge the fear that those
ogres made Truu, Amelia and Juliet go through. Forgive me,
if this cowardice is worthy of forgiveness.

'Don't torture yourself.'

'I was thirty-one years old. I could fight.'

'They would have cracked your skull and your family
would have died anyway. Now they live on in your memory.'

'Nonsense. This is torment. That ridiculous protest was the
only act of rebellion that I allowed myself.'

'I understand you saying that: you must not be able to get
it out of your head; that is what I believed about Alpaerts:
his pain. Which will lead him to his death today or tomorrow or the day after. That was what pained him, that and
having moved to one side when he should have taken a blow
that ended up killing a child. Or not giving a bread crumb to
someone: his great sins ate away at his soul.'

'Like Primo Levi?'

It was that first time in the whole afternoon that Bernat
wasn't insulting me. I looked at him with my mouth open in
surprise and he finished his thought: I mean how he committed suicide when he was already old. He could have done it
before then, the moment he emerged from the horror. Or Paul
Celan, who waited for years and years.

'They committed suicide not because they'd lived through
the horror, but because they had written about it.'

'Now I don't follow you.'

'They had already written it down; now they could die.
That's how I see it. But they also realised that writing is reliving, and spending years reliving the hell is unbearable: they
died for having written about the horror they had already lived
through. And in the end, so much pain and panic reduced to
a thousand pages or to two thousand verses; making so much
pain fit into a stack of paper almost seemed like sarcasm.'

'Or on a disk like this,' said Bernat, pulling one out of a case. 'An entire life of horrors here inside.'

By then I had already realised that, when he'd departed, Matthias Alpaerts had left the filthy cloth on the table in the study. Or he had abandoned it. Or he had given it to me. I had realised but I hadn't dared to touch it. An entire life of horror inside the filthy rag as if it were a computer disk. Or as if it were a book of poems written after Auschwitz.

'Yes. Listen … about that, Bernat.'

'Yeah.'

'I'm not up for computers right now.'

'Typical. You get discouraged just seeing the screen.'

Bernat sat down, dejected, and rubbed his face with his hands, a gesture that I considered mine and mine alone. Then the telephone started ringing and a shiver went through Adrià.

## 51

'Horace said it: Tu ne quaesieris (scire nefas) quem mihi, quem tibi / finem di dederint, Leuconoe, nec Babylonios / temptaris numeros.'

Silence. Some looked out of the window. Others kept their gaze down.

'And what does that mean, Prof?' the daring girl with the huge plait.

'Haven't you studied Latin?' Adrià, surprised.

'Man …'

'And you?' to the boy looking out the window.

'Me, weelll …'

Silence. Alarmed, Adrià Ardèvol addresses the entire class: 'Has anyone studied Latin? Is there a single student of aesthetics and its history who has ever taken a Latin class?'

After a laborious push and pull, it turned out that only one girl had: the one with the green ribbon in her hair. Adrià took a few deep breaths to calm himself down.

'But, Prof, what does that mean, what Horace said?'

'It's talking about what's said in Acts, in Peter's second epistle and in Revelations.'

An even thicker silence. Until someone with more criteria said and what does it say in Acts and all that?

'In Acts and all that it says that the Lord will come like a thief in the night.'

'What lord?'

'Has anyone here ever read the Bible, even once?'

Since he couldn't tolerate another ominous silence, he said you know what? Let's just drop it. Or no: on Friday bring me a phrase taken from a literary work that speaks on this topos.

'What's a topos, Prof?'

'And between now and Friday you all have to read a poem. And go to the theatre. I will expect a full account.'

Then, before the disorientated faces of his students, he woke up, with wide eyes. And when he remembered that it wasn't a dream but rather a memory of his last class, he felt like crying. Just then he realised that he had awoken from his nightmare because the telephone was ringing. Always the damn telephone.

A computer was turned on, atop the table in the study. He never would have thought it possible. The light from the screen made Llorenç and Adrià's faces look pale, as they both observed it attentively.

'Do you see?'

Llorenç moved the mouse and the cursor shifted on the screen.

'Now you do it.'

And Adrià, sticking out the tip of his tongue, made the cursor move.

'Are you left-handed?'

'Yes.'

'Wait. I'll get on your other side.'

'Hey, wait, I don't have enough pad. It's really small.'

Llorenç kept his laughter to himself, but Adrià still perceived it.

'Don't mock me: it's true; it's too small.'

Once he had overcome that obstacle with some practice motions, Adrià Ardèvol was initiated into the mysteries of the creation of a text document, which was, more or less, an infinite, extraordinary, magical spool. And the telephone started ringing, but it went into one of Adrià's ears and right out the other.

'No, I can already see that …'

'That what?'

'That it must be very practical; but ugh, what a drag.'

'And next you need to learn how to write an email.'

'Oh, no. No, no … I have work to do.'

'It's super easy. And email is basic.'

'I already know how to write letters and I have a letter box downstairs. I also have a telephone.'

'My dad told me that you don't want a mobile.' Incredulous silence: 'Is that true?'

The telephone grew tired of its useless shouting and was silent.

'I don't need one. I have a lovely telephone here at home.'

'But you don't even answer it when it rings!'

'No,' Adrià cut him off. 'You are wasting your time. Show me how to write with this thing and … How old are you?'

'Twenty.' Pointing to the dialogue box: 'Here it tells you how to save the text so you don't lose what you've written.'

'Now you're scaring me … You see? You can't lose paper.'

'Yeah, you can lose paper. And it can burn.'

'Do you know I remember when you were two days old, in the hospital?'

'Yeah, really?'

'Your father was wild with joy. He was unbearable.'

'He still is.'

'Well, I meant …'

'You see?' Llorenç pointed to the screen. 'That's how you save the document.'

'I didn't see how you did it.'

'Like this, see?'

'You're going too fast.'

'Look: grab the mouse.'

Adrià grabbed it fearfully, as if the little beast could bite him.

'Get a good hold of it. Like this. Put the little arrow there where it says document.'

'Why do you say he's unbearable?'

'Who?'

'Your father.'

'Pfff … It's just that …' Stopping his hand on the mouse. 'No, no, to the left.'

'It doesn't want to go there.'

'Drag it along the mouse pad.'

'Damn, this is harder than it looks.'

'This is nothing. A few minutes of practice. Now click.'

'What do you mean click?'

'Make a click on the mouse. Like this.'

'Whoa! How did I do that? Oh, it disappeared!'

'All right … let's try again.'

'Why is your father unbearable?' Pause, moving the cursor with serious difficulties. 'Do you hear me, Llorenç?'

'Look, just things.'

'He makes you study violin against your will.'

'No, it's not that …'

'No?'

'Well, that's part of it.'

'You don't like the violin.'

'I do like it.'

'What year are you in?'

'In the old plan it would be seventh.'

'Wow.'

'According to my Dad, I should be doing virtuosity.'

'Everyone has their own pace.'

'According to my Dad, I don't put enough interest into it.'

'And is he right?'

'Pfff … No. He'd like me to … Should we get back to the lesson?'

'What would Bernat like?'

'Me to be a Perlman.'

'And who are you?'

'Llorenç Plensa. And I don't think my Dad gets that.'

'And your mother?'

'She does.'

'Your father is a very good man.'

'I know. You two are very good friends.'

'Despite that, he's a good man.'

'Well, yeah. But he's a pain.'

'What are you studying? Just violin?'

'Oh, no! … I'm enrolled in architecture.'

'That's good, right?'

'No.'

'So why are you studying it?'

'I didn't say I'm studying architecture. I said I'm enrolled in it.'

'And why aren't you studying it?'

'I'd like to be a teacher.'

'That's great, right?'

'Oh, really? Tell that to my father.'

'He doesn't like the idea?'

'It's not enough for his son. He wants me to be the best violinist in the world, the best architect or the best whatever in the world. And that's exhausting.'

Silence. Adrià was pressing hard on the mouse, which couldn't complain. When he realised, he let it go. He had to breathe deeply to calm himself down: 'And why don't you tell him that you want to be a teacher?'

'I already told him.'

'And?'

'A teacher? A teacher, you? My son, a teacher?'

'What's wrong? What do you have against teachers?'

'Nothing: what do you think? But why can't you be an engineer or an I don't know what, eh?'

'I want to teach reading and writing. And multiplying. It's nice.'

'I agree.' Tecla, shooting her husband a defiant look.

'I don't.' Bernat, serious, wiping his lips with a napkin. He places the napkin down on the table and, looking at the empty plate, says the life of a teacher is exhausting and filled with hardship. And they don't make much. Shaking his head: 'It's not a good idea.'

'But I like it.'

'I don't.'

'Hey, it's the boy who has to study it. Not you. You understand?'

'Fine, fine … do what you want. You always do anyway …'

'What do you mean, we always do anyway?' Tecla, cross. 'Huh?'

'No, that … nothing.'

'No, no, go ahead … Tell me, what is it that we always do and you don't want us to?'

And then Llorenç stood up with his plate in his hand, brought it to the kitchen and went to his room and closed the door while Tecla and Bernat continued sharpening their axes because you said that I always do what I want and that's not true! Not at all! Ever!

'But you ended up enrolling in Architecture,' remarked Adrià.

'Why don't we talk about something else?'

'You're right. Come on, what more can I do with this computer?'

'You want to try writing a text?'

'No. I think that, for today, I've …'

'Write a sentence and we'll save it as if it were a valuable document.'

'All right. Do you know what I think? You'd make a good teacher.'

'Tell that to my father.'

Adrià wrote Llorenç Plensa is teaching me how to work all this. Who will lose their patience first, him or me? Or perhaps the Mac?

'Oof, that's already a novel! Now you'll see how we save it, so you can reopen it when you want.'

Adrià, guided by his patient Virgil, did all the steps to save a document for the first time in his life, then closed the folders, put everything away and turned off the computer. Meanwhile Llorenç said I think I'm going to move out.

'Well … That's something that …'

'Don't mention it to my father, eh?'

'No, no. But first you have to find a place.'

'I'll share a flat.'

'That must be a pain. And what will you do with the violin if you live with other people?'

'Why?'

'Because it could bother them.'

'Well, then I won't bring it with me.'

'Hey, unless you're living with a girl.'

'I don't have a girlfriend.'

'I mention that because …'

Llorenç stands up, a bit peeved. Adrià tries to undo what he's done: 'Sorry ... It's none of my business, whether you have a girlfriend or not.'

'I told you I don't have a girlfriend, all right?'

'I heard you.'

'I have a boyfriend.'

A few seconds of awkwardness. Adrià was a bit too slow to react.

'Great. Does your father know?'

'Of course! That's part of the problem. And if you tell my father that we talked about all this ... He'll kill me and he'll kill you.'

'Don't worry. And you, you should do your own thing, trust me.'

Once Llorenç had wrapped up his first basic computer class – with a student who was hard to work with and particularly inept – and was heading down the stairs, Adrià thought how easy it was to give advice to other people's children. And I was overwhelmed by a desire to have had a child with you, whom I could talk to about his life the way I had for a few minutes with Llorenç. How is it possible that Bernat and I spoke so little that I knew nothing about Llorenç?

They were in the dining room and the telephone wouldn't stop ringing, and Adrià didn't clutch his head in a fed-up gesture because Bernat was there explaining his idea. So he wouldn't hear the telephone, he opened up the door to the balcony and a gust of traffic and noise entered, mixed with the shrieks of some children and the cooing of the dirty pigeons that puffed up on the balcony above. He went out onto the balcony and Bernat followed him. Inside, almost in penumbra, Santa Maria de Gerri received the western light from Trespui.

'There's no need for you to organise this! You've had a stable position as a professional musician for a dozen years now.'

'I'm fifty-three years old. That's no accomplishment.'

'You play in the OBC.'

'What?'

'You play in the OBC!' he raised his voice.

'So what?'

'And you are in a quartet with the Comas, for goodness sake!'

'As second violin.'

'You're always comparing yourself to others.'

'What?'

'You're always ...'

'Why don't we go inside?'

Adrià went into the dining room and Bernat followed suit. The telephone was still ringing. They closed the door to the balcony and the street sounds became an easily ignorable backdrop.

'What were you saying?' said Bernat, a bit on edge because of the constantly ringing telephone.

Adrià thought now you'll tell him to rethink his relationship with Llorenç. He's suffering and you're all suffering, right?

'No, that you're always comparing yourself to other people.'

'I don't think so. And if I do, so what?'

Your son is sad. You are using the same parenting style my father did with me and it's hell.

'I have the feeling that you want to keep from getting splashed with even the slightest drop of happiness.'

'What's your point?'

'For example, if you organise this conference, you are setting yourself up for failure. And you'll put yourself in an awful mood. And put everyone around you in an awful mood. There's no need for you to do it.'

'That's for me to decide.'

'As you wish.'

'And why did you say it was a bad idea?'

'You run the risk of no one attending.'

'What a bastard.' He looked at the traffic through the windowpane. 'Listen, why don't you answer the phone?'

'Because right now I'm with you,' lied Adrià.

He looked towards Santa Maria de Gerri without seeing it. He sat in an armchair and glanced at his friend. Now I will talk to him about Llorenç, he swore to himself.

'Will you come, if I set it up?' Bernat, back to his own thing.

'Yes.'

'And Tecla. And Llorenç, that's already three in the audience.'

'Yes: me, Tecla and Llorenç, three. And the scholar, four. And you, five. Bingo.'

'Don't be such a dickhead.'

'How are you and Tecla?'

'It's no bed of roses, but we're sticking it out.'

'I'm glad. What's Llorenç up to?'

'Fine, fine.' He thinks it over before continuing: 'Tecla and I are in some sort of unstable stability.'

'And what does that mean?'

'Well, for months she's been insinuating the possibility of us separating.'

'Shit …'

'And Llorenç finds a thousand reasons not to be around much.'

'I'm so sorry. How are things going for Llorenç?'

'I'm walking on eggshells to keep from screwing things up, and Tecla tries her best to be patient despite her insinuations of throwing in the towel. That is an unstable stability.'

'How are things going for Llorenç?'

'Fine.'

Silence. The ringing of the phone, apparently, makes only Bernat uncomfortable.

Now I will tell him how, lately, since I've been seeing Llorenç, he's seemed a bit sad. And Bernat: that's just how he is. And I, no: it's your fault, Bernat, you plan his life without asking him what he thinks about it. And Bernat would curtly say mind your business. And I, I have to say something: it pains me to watch. And Bernat, marking each syllable: it-is-none-of-your-busi-ness. Understood? And I, all right, but he's sad: he wants to be a teacher. Why don't you let your son be what he wants to be? And Bernat would stand up, furious, as if I'd given away our Storioni again and he'd leave muttering curses and we'd never speak another word to each other.

'What are you thinking?' asked Bernat, interested.

'That … That you have to prepare it really well. Make sure there'll be about twenty people. And choose a location with the capacity for twenty-five. Then it will be well attended.'

'Very clever.'

They were quiet. I have the courage to tell him that I don't like what he writes, but I don't know how to talk to him about Llorenç. The telephone's ringing invaded the silence again. Adrià stood up, picked up the receiver and put it down again. Bernat didn't dare to comment. Adrià sat back down and took up the conversation as if nothing had happened.

'You can't expect a big crowd. In Barcelona there are eighty to a hundred cultural events every day, at least. Besides, people know you as a musician, not as a writer.'

'Not as a musician, no: I am just another one of the violins scraping away on stage. As a writer I am the sole author of five books of short stories.'

'That haven't sold even a thousand copies between them.'

'*Plasma* alone sold a thousand.'

'You know what I mean.'

'You sound like my editor: always encouraging.'

'Who is going to present it?'

'Carlota Garriga.'

'That's good.'

'Good? Great. She alone draws a crowd.'

When Bernat left, Adrià hadn't said a single word to him about Llorenç. And he remained firm in his idea of creating the suicidal session devoted to his literary oeuvre: Bernat Plensa, a narrative trajectory, the invitations would read. Then the telephone, as if it had been lying in wait, began to ring again and, as always, Adrià was startled.

Adrià decided to switch one of his History of Aesthetic Ideas classes for something else and so he had them meet at a different place and time, like when they'd gone down into the lobby of the metro at Plaça Universitat. Or when they'd done, I don't know, those fun things that daft Ardèvol comes up with. They say that one day he held a class in the garden on Diputació Street, and people were passing by and he just carried on.

'Does anyone have a problem making it at that time?'

Three hands went up.

'So I expect everyone else will be there, and punctual.'

'And what are we going to do there?'

'Listen. And take part, if you feel like it.'

'But listen to what?'

'Finding that out there is part of the content of the class.'

'How late will it go?' the blond boy in the middle, the one with the two loyal admirers who were now looking at him, thrilled by his opportune question.

'Is it going to be on the exam?' asked the boy with the Quaker beard who always sat by the window and away from everyone else.

'Do we have to take notes?' the girl with the huge plait.

After answering all their questions, the class ended as always, with his ordering them to read poetry and go to the theatre.

When he got home he found a telegram from Johannes Kamenek inviting him to give a conference at the university tomorrow. Stop. Tomorrow Stop? Kamenek had lost his mind.

'Johannes.'

'Oh, finally!'

'What's wrong?'

'It's a favour.' Kamenek's voice was slightly panicked.

'And what's the rush?'

'Your phone must be off the hook. Or broken.'

'Well, no. It's just that … If you call in the morning, there is someone who …'

'Are you all right?'

'Well. I was before your telegram. You are asking me to come and give a conference tomorrow. Is that a mistake?'

'No, no. You have to put out a fire. Ulrike Hörstrup can't make it. Please.'

'Wow: what's it on?'

'Whatever you want. There's a guaranteed audience because they're participants in the seminars. Which are going very well. And at the last minute …'

'What happened to Hörstrup?'

'She's got a fever of thirty-nine. She couldn't even make the trip. You'll have plane tickets at your house before this evening.'

'And it has to be tomorrow?'

'At two in the afternoon. Say yes.'

I said no, that I still didn't even know what I wanted to talk about yet, for god's sake, Johannes, don't do this to me, and he said talk about whatever you want but, please, come, and then I had to say yes. They mysteriously delivered the tickets to my house and the next day I flew to Stuttgart and then to my beloved Tübingen. Up in the plane I thought about what I'd like to talk about and I sketched an outline. In Stuttgart I was met by a Pakistani taxi driver with strict instructions and he dropped me off in front of the university after speeding dizzily for several kilometres.

'I don't know how to repay the favour,' said Johannes, receiving me at the entrance to the faculty.

'It's a favour: you don't need to repay it. I'm going to talk about Coşeriu.'

'No. They've already talked about him today.'

'Bollocks.'

'I should have … Shoot, I'm so sorry. You can … I don't know …'

Johannes, despite his hesitation, grabbed me by the arm and made me walk towards the auditorium.

'I'll improvise. Give me a few minutes to

'We don't have a few minutes,' said Kamenek, still leading me by the arm.

'Whoa. Do I have time to have a piss?'

'No.'

'And they say that we Mediterraneans are all improvisation and the Germans always methodically prepare …'

'You are right: but Ulrike was already a substitution.'

'Oh: so I'm third-string. And why didn't you adjourn?'

'Impossible. It's never been done. Never. And we have people from abroad who …'

We stopped in front of the door to the assembly hall. He embraced me, embarrassed, he said thank you, my friend,

and he led me into the hall, where thirty per cent of the couple
of hundred people attending the seminars on linguistics and
thought looked surprised at Ulrike Hörstrup's strange appearance: bald and with a growing pot belly, and not very
feminine in the slightest. As Adrià organised in his head the
ideas he didn't have, Johannes Kamenek reminded the audience about Professor Hörstrup's health problems and how
lucky they all were to be able to hear Professor Adrià Ardèvol
who will speak on … who will speak right now.

And he sat at my side, I suppose in some sort of gesture of
solidarity. I felt how he physically deflated and decompressed,
poor Johannes. And in order to be able to order my ideas I
began to recite, slowly and in Catalan, that poem by Foix that
begins by saying: 'És per la Ment que se m'obre Natura / A l'ull
golós; per ella em sé immortal / Puix que l'ordén, i ençà i enllà
del mal, / El temps és u i pel meu ordre dura'. And I translated
it literally: It is through the Mind that Nature opens up to me
/ To my greedy eye; through it I know I am immortal / Since
order, and on both sides of evil, / Time is one and through my
order endures. And from Foix and the importance of thought
and the present, I began to explain what beauty means and
why humanity has been pursuing it for centuries. Professor Ardèvol posed many questions and didn't know how or
didn't want to answer them. And, inevitably, evil showed up.
And the sea, the dark sea. He spoke of the love of knowledge,
without worrying about making everything fit into the seminars on linguistics and thought. He spoke little of linguistics
and much about I am thinking about the nature of life but
death intervenes. And then, like a flash of lightning, Sara's
funeral came to him, with Kamenek silent and perplexed.
And after a long time he said that is why Foix ends the sonnet
by saying: '… i en els segles em moc / Lent, com el roc davant
la mar obscura' and fifty minutes had passed. '… and I move
through the centuries / Slowly, like the rock before the dark
sea.' And he left quickly to take a long piss, longer than a rainy
day.

Before the dinner with the organising committee to thank
him, Adrià wanted to do two things in Tübingen, since he

didn't have to fly back until the next day. Alone, please. Really, Johannes. I want to do them alone.

Bebenhausen. It had been fully restored. They still gave guided tours, but no one asked the guide what secularised meant. And he thought distantly of, Bernat and his books. More than twenty years had passed and nothing had changed: not Bebenhausen and not Bernat. And when it began to get dark, he went into the Tübingen cemetery and strolled, as he had done so many times, alone, with Bernat, with Sara ... He heard the sound of his footsteps, a hard, curt sound on the compressed earth paving. Without meaning to, his stroll led him to the empty tomb of Franz Grübbe, at the end. In front of it, Lothar Grübbe and his niece Herta Landau, from Beben-hausen, the one who was kind enough to take a photo of him and Bernat, were still placing some white roses there, white as the soul of their heroic son and nephew. Hearing his footsteps, Herta Landau turned and concealed her fear at seeing him.

'Lothar ...' she said in a choked voice, completely terrified.

Lothar Grübbe turned. The SS officer had stopped in front of him and for the moment was mutely waiting for them to explain themselves.

'I'm cleaning all these graves,' Lothar Grübbe finally said.

'Identification,' said the SS-Obersturmführer Adrian Hartbold-Bosch, planted before the old man and the younger woman. Herta, very frightened, couldn't manage to open her purse. Lothar was so panicked that he began to act as if he were covered in a veil of indifference, as if he were already finally dead by your side, Anna, and beside brave Franz.

'Oh ...' he exclaimed. 'I've left it at home.'

'I've left it at home, Obersturmführer!' scolded SS-Obersturmführer Hartbold-Bosch.'

'I've left it at home, Obersturmführer!' shouted Lothar, looking into the officer's eyes, imperceptibly martial. The lieutenant pointed to the grave.

'What are you doing here, at the grave of a traitor. Eh?'

'He is my son, Obersturmführer,' said Lothar. And pointing to Herta, rigid and horrified: 'I don't even know this young woman.'

'Come with me.'

The interrogation was led by Obersturmführer Adrian Hartbold-Bosch himself. To ensure that, despite his age, Lothar had no contact with abject Herbert Baum's group. But he's an old man! (Friar Miquel). Old men and babies are equally dangerous to the safety of the Reich. At your orders (Friar Miquel). Make him vomit all the information. Using any means at my disposal? Using any means at your disposal. Torture the soles of his feet, to start with. How long? The length of three well prayed hailmaries. And then continue with the rack for the length of a credoinunumdeum. Yes, Your Excellency.

It took Herta Landau, who was miraculously not arrested, a desperate half hour to establish phone contact with Berlin, where she was given advice on how to speak with Auschwitz and, miraculously, after a long hour, was able to hear Konrad's voice: 'Heil Hitler. Hallo.' Impatient. 'Ja, bitte?'

'Konrad, this is Herta.'

'Who?'

'Herta Landau, your cousin. That is if you still have family.'

'What's going on?'

'They've arrested Lothar.'

'Who is this Lothar?' Peeved.

'Lothar Grübbe, your uncle. Who do you think.'

'Ah! Abject Franz's father?'

'Franz's father, yes.'

'And what do you want?'

'Intercede, have compassion on him. They could torture him and they'll end up killing him.'

'Who arrested him?'

'The SS.'

'But why?'

'For putting flowers on Franz's grave. Do something.'

'Girl … Here I really …'

'For the love of God!'

'I'm very busy right now. You want to expose us all?'

'He's your uncle!'

'He must have done something.'

'Don't say that, Konrad!'

'Look, Herta: someone's got to pay the piper.'

'Holländisch?' Berta heard Konrad saying. And then, into the telephone: 'I don't know about you, but I'm working. I have too much work to waste time on such nonsense. Heil Hitler!'

And she heard Konrad Budden – that bastard – hang up the phone, condemning Lothar. Then she cried inconsolably.

Lothar Grübbe, sixty-two years of age, was not a dangerous individual. But his death could serve as an example: the father of an abject traitor putting flowers on a grave as if it were a monument to the domestic resistance? A grave that …

Obersturmführer Hartbold-Bosch remained with his mouth open, thinking. Of course! To the twins who were holding up the wall: 'Have the traitor's grave dug up!'

The tomb of the cowardly abject traitor Franz Grübbe was empty. Lothar the Elder had mocked the authorities by secretly putting flowers somewhere where there was nothing. An empty grave is more dangerous than one with a bag of bones inside: the emptiness makes it universal and converts it into a monument.

'What do we do with the prisoner, Your Excellency?'

Adrian Hartbold-Bosch took a deep breath. With his eyes closed he said in a low, trembling voice, hang him from a butcher's hook, the punishment for traitors to the Reich.

'You mean … isn't that too cruel? He's an old man.'

'Friar Miquel …' said the Obersturmführer's threatening voice. Realising the silence, he looked at his subordinates, who had their heads bowed. Then he added, shouting, vomiting: 'Take away this carrion!'

Lothar Grübbe, horrified by the death that awaited him, was taken to the punishment cell. They no longer punished a traitor every day, they had to set up the mechanism to hang the hook, which they'd first had to carefully sharpen. As they were hoisting him up with a rope, he was sweating and choking on panicked vomit. He had time to say relax, Anna, it's all right. He died of fear half a second before being skewered with the rage necessary to impale traitors.

'Who is this Anna?' wondered aloud one of the twins.

'Doesn't matter now,' said the other.

## 52

The Sagarra Room at the Athenaeum, at seven forty-five on that dark, cloudy Tuesday had the fifty-something available chairs filled with young people who seemed to be spellbound listening to the extremely saccharine background music. An older man, who seemed disorientated, hesitated endlessly before choosing a seat at the back, as if he were afraid that, when it was over, they would ask him what the lesson was. Two elderly women – clearly disappointed because they hadn't seen any sign of cheese and biscuits afterwards – shared confidences in the front row, propelled by their fluttering fans. On a side table were the five books that comprised the complete work of Bernat Plensa, displayed. Tecla was there, in the front row, which Adrià was surprised to see. Tecla was looking back, as if monitoring who came in. Adrià approached her and gave her a kiss, and she smiled at him for the first time since the last argument in which he'd intervened, in vain, to make peace. It had been a long time since they'd seen each other.

'Good, right?' said Adrià, lifting his eyebrows to refer to the room.

'I wasn't expecting this. And, young people, even.'

'Uh huh.'

'How's it going with Llorenç?'

'Great. I already know how to make word documents and save them on a disk.' Adrià thought for a few moments: 'But I'm still unable to write anything directly onto the computer. I'm a paper man.'

'All in good time.'

'Or not.'

Then the telephone rang and no one paid any attention to it. Adrià raised his head and his eyebrows. No one paid it any heed, as if it weren't even ringing.

Bernat's five published books were also on the speakers' table, placed so that people could see the covers. The extremely saccharine background music stopped, but the telephone, not as loud, kept ringing and Bernat appeared, accompanied by Carlota Garriga. Adrià was surprised to see him without the violin in his hands and he smiled at the idea. Author and speaker sat down. Bernat winked at me and smiled with satisfaction at the room. Carlota Garriga began by saying that she had always admired the literature of Bernat Plensa, and he winked at me again and for a few moments I imagined that he had set up that whole fandango just for me. So I decided to listen carefully to what Doctor Garriga was saying.

Quotidian worlds, with mostly unhappy characters, who can't make up their minds to love or leave, all served up with considerable stylistic skill, and that is part of another feature that I will touch on later.

After half an hour, when Garriga had already touched on every subject, even the subject of influences, Adrià raised his hand and asked if he could query the author as to why the characters in his first four books all had so many physical and psychological resemblances, and he immediately regretted the question. Bernat, after a few seconds of reflection, stated yes, yes, the gentleman is right. It is on purpose. A way to affirm that these characters are the precursors to the ones who will appear in the novel I am writing now.

'You're writing a novel?' I asked, surprised.

'Yes. It's still a long way off, but yes.'

A hand in the back: it was the girl with the huge plait who asked if he could explain his process for inventing the stories, and Bernat snorted in satisfaction and said oof, the question. I don't know if I can answer it. But he spent five minutes talking about how he invented the stories. And then the boy with the Quaker beard was inspired to ask about his literary role models. Then I looked back at the audience with satisfaction, and I was shocked to see Laura entering the room just then. It had been a few months since I'd last seen her because she had returned to somewhere in Sweden. I didn't even know she was back. She looked pretty, yes. But no. What was she doing there? And later, the blond boy with the two admirers got up and said that he or Mrs ...

'Doctor Garriga,' said Bernat.

'Yeah, that,' corroborated the young man with the two admirers. 'Well, she said in passing that you were a musician and I didn't understand why you write if you are musician. I mean, can you do a lot of different arts at the same time? Like, maybe you also paint in secret or make sculpture.'

The admirers laughed at the cleverness of the subject of their admiration and Bernat responded that all art springs from the deep dissatisfaction of man's soul. And then his eyes met Tecla's and I noticed an oh so slight hesitation, and Bernat quickly added what I mean is that art is born from dissatisfaction; no one makes art with their belly full, they just take a nap. And some of the spectators smiled.

When the event was finished, Adrià went to greet Bernat and he said you see?, full house, and Adrià said yeah, congratulations. Tecla gave Adrià a kiss: she seemed more calm, as if a weight had been lifted from her shoulders, and before Garriga joined them she said I wasn't expecting so many people to come, will you look at that? And Adrià didn't dare to ask why didn't my friend Llorenç come? And Garriga joined the group and wanted to meet Doctor Ardèvol and Bernat suggested why don't we all have dinner together?

'Oh, I can't. I'm so sorry. Really. Go celebrate, you've earned it.'

When they left, the room was already empty. In the hall, Laura pretended she was looking at the information on upcoming events and turned as soon as she heard Adrià's footsteps: 'Hello.'

'Hello.'

'Let's have dinner. My treat,' she said, serious.

'I can't.'

'Come on ...'

'I can't, really. I have to go to the doctor.'

Laura was left with her mouth hanging open, as if her words had got stuck in her throat. She looked at her watch, but didn't say anything. Somewhat offended, she said all

right, fine, sure, no problem. And with a forced smile: are you
all right?

'No. And you?'

'Me neither. I might stay in Uppsala.'

'Wow. If that's the best thing for you …'

'I don't know.'

'Can we talk some other time?' said Adrià, lifting his wrist
that held his watch as an excuse.

'Go ahead, go to your appointment.'

Adrià gave her a chaste kiss on the cheek and left quickly,
without looking back. He could still make out Bernat's relaxed
laughter and I felt very good, truly, because Bernat deserved it
all. Outside, it was starting to rain and, with his glasses splattered with drops, he searched for an impossible taxi.

'Sorry.' He wiped his soaked shoes on the mat in the hall.

'Don't worry about it.' He had him come to the left, straight
towards the examining room. 'I thought you'd forgotten
about me.'

On the right side of the flat you could hear the murmur of
dishes and silverware, of everyday life. Doctor Dalmau had
him enter and closed the door without locking it. He went for
the white coat he had hanging, but changed his mind. They
both sat down, one on each side of the desk. They looked at
each other in silence. Behind the doctor there was a Modigliani reproduction filled with yellows. Outside, a smattering of
spring rain.

'Come on, what's wrong?'

Adrià raised a hand to get attention.

'Do you hear it?'

'What?'

'The telephone.'

'Yes. They'll answer it soon. I bet it's for my daughter and
she'll have the line tied up for a couple of hours.'

'Ah.'

Indeed, the telephone at the other end of the flat stopped
ringing and a female voice was heard saying hello? Yeah, it's
me; who'd you expect?

'What else?' asked Doctor Dalmau.

'Just that: the telephone. I'm always hearing the telephone ring.'

'Let's see if you can explain yourself a little better.'

'I keep hearing the telephone ringing, a ringing that blames me and eats away at me inside and I can't get it out of my head.'

'How long has this been going on?'

'Two long years. Almost three. Since the fourteenth of July, nineteen ninety-six.'

'Quatorze juillet.'

'Oui. The phone has been ringing since the fourteenth of July, nineteen ninety-six. It rang on Laura's bedside table, in a disorganised room with half-packed suitcases. They looked at each other, as if wanting to ask, in some sort of guilty silence, whether they were expecting any call. Laura didn't move, with her head on Adrià's chest, and they both heard how the telephone, monotonously, insisted, insisted, insisted. Adrià stared at Laura's hair, expecting her to reach for it. Nothing. The telephone kept ringing. And, finally, like a miracle, silence was re-established. Adrià relaxed; then he realised that while it was ringing, he had stiffened up. He ran his fingers through Laura's hair. He stopped abruptly because the telephone started ringing again.

'Damn, they don't give up, do they,' she said, curling up more towards Adrià.

It rang for another good long while.

'Answer it,' he said.

'I'm not here. I'm with you.'

'Answer it.'

Laura sat up grudgingly, picked up the receiver and said yes with a very subdued voice. A few seconds of silence. She turned and passed the receiver to him, hiding her shock very well.

'It's for you.'

Impossible, thought Adrià. But he took the receiver. He realised, with admiration, that the telephone was cordless. It must have been the first time he'd used a cordless phone. And he was surprised to be thinking that and to be remembering it now in front of Doctor Dalmau almost three full years later.

'Hello.'

'Adrià?'

'Yes.'

'It's Bernat.'

'How did you find me?'

'It's a long story. Listen ...'

I understood that Bernat's hesitation was a bad portent.

'What ...'

'Sara.'

Everything ended here, my beloved. Everything.

53

The all too brief days by your side, washing you, covering you up, airing you out, asking for your forgiveness. The days I devoted to lessening the pain I caused you. Those days of torment, particularly your torment and – forgive me, I mean no offence, but – also my torment, changed me. Before I had interests. Now I've been left without motivation and I spend the day thinking by your side, as you seem to sleep placidly. What were you doing, at the house? Had you come back to embrace me or to scold me? Were you looking for me or just wanting to get some more clothes to take to the huitième arrondissement? I called you, you must remember that, and Max told me that you didn't want to speak with me. Yes, yes, forgive me: Laura, yes; it's all so pitiful. You didn't have to come back: you never should have gone because we should never have fought over a crappy violin. I swear I'll give it back to its owner when I find out who that is. And I will do it in your name, my beloved. Do you hear me? Somewhere I have the piece of paper you gave me with his name.

'Go home and get some rest, Mr Ardèvol,' the nurse with the plastic-framed glasses, the one named Dora.

'The doctor told me I should talk to her.'

'You've been talking to her all day long. Poor Sara's head must be throbbing.'

She examined the serum, regulated its flow and observed the monitor in silence. Without looking him in the eye: 'What do you talk to her about?'

'Everything.'

'You've spent two days explaining thousands of stories.'

'Haven't you ever been sorry about the silences you had with the person you love?'

Dora glanced around and, holding his gaze, said do us both

a favour: go home, get some rest and come back tomorrow.'

'You haven't answered me.'

'I have no answer.'

Adrià Ardèvol looked at Sara: 'And what if she wakes up when I'm not here?'

'We'll call you, don't worry. She's not going anywhere.'

He didn't dare to say and what if she dies?, because that was unthinkable, now that the exhibition of Sara Voltes-Epstein's drawings would open in September.

And at home I kept talking to you, remembering the things I used to explain to you. And a few years later I am writing you, hurriedly, so that you won't completely die when I am no longer here. Everything is a lie, you already know that. But everything is a great, deep truth that no one can ever deny. This is you and I. This is me with you, light of my life.

'Max came today,' said Adrià. And Sara didn't respond, as if she didn't care.

'Hey, Adrià.'

He, absorbed in staring at her, turned towards the door. Max Voltes-Epstein, with an absurd bouquet of roses in his hand.

'Hello, Max.' About the roses: 'You didn't have to ...'

'She loves flowers.'

Thirteen years living with you without knowing that you loved flowers. I'm ashamed of myself. Thirteen years without realising that every week you changed the flowers in the vase in the hall. Carnations, gardenias, irises, roses, all different kinds. Now, suddenly, the image had exploded over me, like an accusation.

'Leave them here, yes, thank you.' I pointed vaguely outside: 'I'll ask for a vase.'

'I can stay this afternoon. I've arranged things so that ... If you want you can go rest ...'

'I couldn't.'

'You look ... you look really bad. You should lie down for a few hours.'

Both men contemplated Sara for a good long while, each living his own history. Max thought why didn't I go with her?, she wouldn't have been alone. And I, how could I know, what did I know? And Adrià again thinking obstinately that if I hadn't been in bed with Laura, I would have been at home retouching Llull, Vico and Berlin and I would have heard rsrsrsrsrsrsrsrsrs, I would have opened the door, you would have put down your travel bag and when you had the ffucking stroke, the bloody embolism, I would have picked you up off the floor, I would have taken you to bed and I would have called Dalmau, the Red Cross, the emergency room, Medicus Mundi, and they would have saved you, that was my fault, that when it happened I wasn't with you and the neighbours say that you went out onto the landing of the staircase, because your bag was already inside, and when they went to pick you up you must have fallen three or four steps, and Doctor Real told me that the first thing they did was save your life and now they'll see if you have any dislocation or any broken ribs, poor thing, but at least they saved your life because one day you will wake up and you'll say I'd love a cup of coffee, like the first time you came back. After spending the first night with you at the hospital, with Laura's scent still on me, when I went home I saw that your bag was in the hall and I checked that you had returned with everything you'd taken with you and from then on I like to think that you were coming back to stay. And I swear I heard your voice saying I'd love a cup of coffee. They tell me that when you wake up you won't remember anything. Not even the fall you took on the stairs. The Mundós that live downstairs heard you and they gave the alarm, and I was fucking Laura and hearing a telephone I didn't want to answer. And a thousand years later Adrià woke up.

'Did she tell you she was coming to the house?'

A few seconds of silence. Was it hesitation or was it that he didn't remember?

'I don't know. She didn't tell me anything. Suddenly she grabbed the bag and left.'

'What was she doing, before?'

'She'd been drawing. And strolling in the garden, looking at the sea, looking at the sea, looking at the sea ...'

Max didn't usually do that, repeat himself. He was shaken up.

'Looking at the sea.'

'Yes.'

'It's just that I wanted to know if she had decided to come back or ...'

'What does that matter now?'

'It matters a lot. To me. Because I think she was, coming home.'

Mea culpa.

Adrià spent a silent afternoon with a perplexed Max, who still didn't quite understand what had happened. And the next day I went back to your side with your favourite flowers.

'What's that?' asked Dora, wrinkling her nose, as soon as I arrived.

'Yellow gardenias.' Adrià hesitated. 'They're the ones she likes best.'

'A lot of people come through here.'

'They are the best flowers I can bring her. The ones that have kept her company while she worked over many years.'

Dora looked at the small painting carefully.

'Who is it by?' she said.

'Abraham Mignon. Seventeenth century.'

'It's valuable, isn't it?'

'Yes, very. That's why I brought it for her.'

'It's in danger here. Take it home.'

Instead of listening to her, Professor Roig put the bouquet of yellow gardenias into the vase and poured the bottle of water into it.

'I told you I'll take care of it.'

'Your wife has to stay in the hospital. At least for a few months.'

'I'll come every day. I'll spend the day here.'

'You have to live. You can't spend every day here.'

I couldn't spend the whole day there, but I spent many hours and I understood how a silent gaze can hurt you more than a sharpened knife; what horror, Gertrud's gaze. I fed her and she looked me in the eyes and swallowed, obediently, her soup. And she looked into my eyes and accused me without words.

The worst is the uncertainty; what's horrible is not knowing if. She looks at you and you can't decipher her gaze. Is she accusing me? Does she want to talk about her vast grief and cannot? Does she want to explain that she hates me? Or perhaps she wants to tell me that she loves me and that I should save her? Poor Gertrud is in a well and I can't rescue her.

Every day Alexandre Roig went to see her and spent long periods of time there, looking at her, letting himself be wounded by her gaze, wiping the sweat off her forehead, without daring to say anything to her, to avoid making the situation worse. And she, after an eternity, was starting to hear the shouts of Tiberium in Tiberim, Tiberium in Tiberim, which was the last thing she had read before the darkness. And she was starting to see a face, two or three faces that said things to her, that put a spoon in her mouth, that wiped away her sweat, and she wondered what is going on, where am I, why don't you say anything to me?, and then she saw herself far, far away, at night, and at first she didn't understand a thing, or she didn't want to understand it and, filled with confusion, she again took shelter in Suetoni and said morte eius ita laetatus est populus, ut ad primum nuntium discur-rentes pars: 'Tiberium in Tiberim!' clamitarent. They shouted it, but all of Suetonius crowded together in her head and it seems no one could hear her. Perhaps because she was speak-ing Latin and … No. Yes. And then it took her centuries to remember who the face was that she constantly had in front of her, telling her I don't know what that I couldn't make out. And one day she understood what it was that she was remem-bering about that night and she began to tie the loose ends together and she was horrified from the top of her head to the tips of her toes. And, as best she could, she started shriek-ing in fear. And Alexandre Roig didn't know what was worse, tolerating the intolerable silence or facing the consequences of his actions once and for all. He didn't know if he was doing the right thing, but one day: 'Doctor, why doesn't she speak?'

'She does speak.'

'Pardon me, but my wife hasn't spoken since she came out of the coma.'

'Your wife speaks, Mr Roig. She has been for a few days now; didn't they tell you? We can't understand a thing because she speaks in some weird language and we don't ... But she speaks. Boy does she ever.'

'In Latin?'

'Latin? No. I don't think so. Well, I, languages aren't my ...'

Gertrud was speaking and reserved her silence just for him. That scared him more than the knife-like gaze.

'Why don't you say anything to me, Gertrud?' he said, before giving her that bloody semolina soup; it seemed they had no other menu options at this hospital.

But the woman just looked at him with the same intensity as ever.

'Do you hear me? Can you hear me now?'

He repeated it in Estonian and, in honour of his grandfather, in Italian. Gertrud remained silent and opened her mouth to receive the semolina soup each day, as if she hadn't the slightest interest in conversation.

'What are you telling the others?'

More soup. Alexandre Roig had the feeling that Gertrud was holding back an ironic smile and his hands started to sweat. He fed her the soup in silence, trying to keep his eyes from meeting his wife's. When he'd finished, he moved very close to her, almost able to smell her thoughts, but he didn't kiss her. Right into her ear he said what are you telling them, Gertrud, that you can't tell me? And he repeated it in Estonian.

She had come out of the coma two weeks earlier; it had been two weeks since they'd told him Professor Roig, as we feared, your wife has been left quadriplegic from the traumas suffered. There isn't anything we can do for her now, but who knows, in a few years we can imagine hope for alleviating and even curing this type of injury, and I was speechless because many things that were too big were happening to me and I didn't realise the true dimensions of my misfortune. My entire life was in a stir. And now the anguish over finding out what Gertrud was saying.

'No, no, no. It's normal for the patient to have a slight regression: it's normal for them to speak whatever language they spoke as children. Swedish?'

'Yes.'

'I'm terribly sorry, but here, among the staff ...'

'Don't worry.'

'What's strange is that she doesn't speak to you.'

Fucking bitch. Poor thing.

Only two weeks passed before Professor Alexandre Roig finally managed to bring his wife home. He left the technical aspects to Dora, a vast expert in palliative treatments who'd been recommended by the hospital, and he devoted himself to feeding Gertrud her soup, and avoiding her eyes and thinking what do you know and what do you think about what I know and I don't know if you know and no one better hear you.

'What's strange is that she doesn't speak to you,' repeated Dora.

More than strange, it was worrisome.

'And she gets more chatty with each passing day, Mr Roig, as soon as I get close to her she starts saying things in Norwegian, isn't it, as if ... You should hide so you can see it.'

And he did, with the complicity of that matron with the nurse's wimple who had taken Gertrud as something personal and every day she said to her today you are prettier than ever, Gertrud, and when Gertrud spoke she clasped her unfeeling hand and she told her what are you saying, I can't understand you, sweetie, can't you see I don't understand Icelandic, much as I'd like to. And Professor Alexandre Roig, who should have been locked up in his study at that time of the day, waited in the next room for as long as it took Gertrud to start speaking again, and in the mid-afternoon, that drowsy time after lunch, when the complicit nurse approached her to carry out the ritual changing of position, Gertrud said exactly what I was fearing and I began to tremble like a birch leaf.

Heaven forbid, it wasn't something he sought out although

in the blackest depths of his soul it was a desire that nestled unconfessed. It was his drowsiness, after two long hours on the dark highway, Gertrud napping intermittently in the passenger seat and I driving and thinking desperately of how to tell Gertrud that I wanted to leave, that I was very sorry, very, but that I had made up my mind, and that was that, that life sometimes has these things and that I didn't care what the family or my co-workers might say, or the neighbours, because everyone has the right to a second chance and now I have that. I am so deeply in love, Gertrud.

And then the unexpected bend and the decision that he made without making it, since everything was dark so it seemed simpler, and he opened the door and he took off his seat belt and he leapt onto the asphalt and the car continued, without anyone to step on the brake, and the last thing he heard from Gertrud was a scream that said what's going on, what's going on, Saaaaaandreee ... and something else that he couldn't catch and the void swallowed up the car, Gertrud and her frightened shriek, and since then, nothing more, the knife-sharp gaze and that was it. And I at home, alone, when Dora had kicked me out of the hospital, thinking about you, thinking what had I done wrong and searching desperately for the slip of paper where you had written the name of the owner of the violin and dreaming of travelling to Ghent or to Brussels with Vial in its blood-stained case, arriving at a well-to-do home, ringing a doorbell that first made a noble clonk and then an elegant clank, and a maid with a starched cap opening the door and asking me what I had come for.

'I've come to return the violin.'

'Ah, yes, come in. It's about time, eh?'

The starched maid closed the door and disappeared. And her muffled voice said sir, they've come to return Vial. And, immediately, a patriarchal man with white hair came out, dressed in a burgundy and black plaid robe, tightly gripping a baseball bat, and he said are you the bastard Ardefol?

'Well, yeah.'

'And you've brought Vial?'

'Here.'

'Fèlix Ardefol, right?' he said lifting the bat over his shoulders.

'No. Fèlix was my father. I'm the bastard Adrià Ardefol.'

'And what took you so long to bring it back to me?' The bat, still threatening my skull.

'It's a very long story, sir, and right now … I'm tired and my beloved is in hospital, sleeping.'

The man with white hair and patriarchal bearing tossed the bat to the floor, where the maid picked it up, and he snatched the case from me. He opened it right there, on the floor, lifted the protective chamois cloths and pulled out the Storioni. Magnificent. Just then I regretted what I was doing because the man with the white hair and patriarchal bearing wasn't worthy of that violin. I woke up covered in sweat and went back to the hospital to be by your side and I told you I'm doing what I can but I haven't found the paper. No, don't ask me to get it from Mr Berenguer because I don't trust him and he would sully everything. Where were we?

Alexandre Roig put the spoon in front of her mouth. For a few seconds, Gertrud didn't open it; she just stared into his eyes. Come on, open up your little mouth, I said to her, so I wouldn't have to tolerate that gaze. Finally, thank God, she opened up and I was able to get her to swallow the warm broth with a bit of pasta and thought that surely the best thing to do was pretend that I hadn't heard what she'd said to Dora when she thought I wasn't home and I said Gertrud, I love you, why won't you speak to me, what's wrong, they tell me you speak when I'm not here, why, it's as if you had something against me. And Gertrud, in response, opened her mouth. Professor Roig gave her a couple more spoonfuls and looked into her eyes: 'Gertrud. Tell me what's wrong. Tell me what you're thinking.'

After a few days, Alexandre Roig was already able to recognise that he wasn't feeling sorry for that woman, he was afraid of her. I'm sorry that I don't feel bad for you, but that's how life is. I am in love, Gertrud, and I have the right to remake my life and I don't want you to stand in the way, not by being pitiful nor with threats. You were a vibrant woman, always wanting to impose your criteria, and now you are limited to opening your mouth for soup. And staying quiet. And speaking Estonian. And how will you read your Martials and your Livys? Doctor Dalmau – that imbecile – says that this regression is common. Until one day when Alexandre Roig, anxious, decided not to lower his guard; this isn't regression: it's cunning. She does it to make me suffer … She just wants to make me suffer! If she wants to hurt me, I won't allow it. But she doesn't want me to know what she's up to. I don't know how to neutralise her scheme. I don't know how. I had found the perfect way, but she didn't go along with it. The perfect way, but very risky, because I don't know how I was able to get out of the car.

'Weren't you wearing your seatbelt?'

'Yes. I guess so. I don't know.'

'It's not broken or forced.'

'Maybe. I don't know: I was … The car hit such a bad bump that the door opened and I flew out.'

'To save yourself?'

'No, no. The bump sent me flying out. Once I was on the ground I saw the car sinking and I couldn't see it any more and she was screaming Saaaaandreeeee.'

'The drop was three metres.'

'For me it was as if it had been swallowed up by the land-scape. And I suppose I fainted.'

'She called you Sandre?'

'Yes. Why?'

'Why do you only suppose you fainted?'

'No … I'm confused. How is she?'

'In a bad way.'

'Will she pull through?'

Then the inspector said what he had been so fearing; he said I don't know if you are a believer or not, but there's been a miracle here; the Lord has listened to your prayers.

'I'm not a believer.'

'Your wife is not going to die. Although …'

'My God.'

'Yes.'

'Tell me exactly what you want, Mr Ardèvol.'

I had to spend a little while ordering unorderable ideas. The stillness of Pau Ullastres's workshop helped to calm me down. And finally I said this violin was stolen during World War II. By a Nazi. I think it was seized in Auschwitz itself.

'Whoa.'

'Yes. And through circumstances that are irrelevant to the case, it has been in my family for years.'

'And you want to return it,' prompted the luthier.

'No! Or yes, I don't know. But I wanted to know whom it was seized from. Who was its previous owner. And then, well, we'll see.'

'If the previous owner ended up in Auschwitz ...'

'I know. But he must have some relative, right?'

Pau Ullastres picked up the violin and began to play fragments of a Bach partita, I can't remember which. The third? And I felt dirty because it had been too long since I'd been by your side and when I finally was I took your hand and I said I am taking steps to return it, Sara, but so far I haven't had much luck. I want to return it to its real owner, not some opportunist. And the luthier strongly recommended, Mr Ardèvol, that you are very careful and don't do anything hasty. There are a lot of vultures hovering around stories like this one. Do you understand me, Sara?

'Gertrud.'

The woman looked at the ceiling; she didn't even bother to shift her gaze. Alexandre waited for Dora to close the door to the flat and leave them alone before he spoke: 'It was my fault,' he said in a soft tone. 'Forgive me ... I guess I fell asleep ... It was my fault.'

She looked at him as if coming from a far distance. She opened her mouth as if she were about to say something. After a few endless seconds, though, she just swallowed hard and shifted her gaze.

'I didn't do it on purpose, Gertrud. It was an accident ...'

She looked at him and now he was the one who swallowed hard: this woman knows everything. A gaze had never cut me to the quick like that. My God. She's capable of saying something crazy to the first person who shows up because now she knows that I know that she knows. I am afraid I have no choice. I don't want you to be an obstacle to this happiness I deserve.

My husband wants to kill me. No one understands me here. Warn my brother; Osvald Sikemäe; he is a teacher in Kunda; tell him to save me. Please, I am afraid.

'No ...'

'Yes.'

'Say it again,' asked Dora.

Àgata glanced quickly at the notebook. She looked at the waiter who was heading off and repeated my husband wants to kill me. No one understands me here. Warn my brother; Osvald Sikemäe; he is a teacher in Kunda; tell him to save me. Please, I am afraid. And she added I am alone in the world, I am alone in the world. Someone who understands me, whom I can understand.

'But what did you tell her? This is the first time, since I've been taking care of her, that she's had a conversation. Up until now, she just talked to the walls, poor woman. What did you tell her?'

'Ma'am ... that must be the nerves over ...'

'My husband knows that I know that he wants to kill me. I am very afraid. I want to go back to the hospital. Here alone with him ... everything frightens me ... Don't you believe me?'

'Of course I believe you. But ...'

'You don't believe me. He will kill me.'

'Why would he want to kill you?'

'I don't know. We were fine until now. I don't know. The accident ...' Àgata turned a page in the notebook and continued deciphering her bad, hasty handwriting ... I think the accident ... How come he didn't ... She lifted her head, devastated: 'Poor woman, she went on, saying incoherent things.'

'Do you believe her?' Dora, sweating, distressed.

'What do I know!?'

They looked at the third woman, the silent one. As if they
had asked her the question, she spoke for the first time.

'I believe her. Where is Kunda?'

'On the northern coast. On the Gulf of Finland.'

'And how is it that you know Estonian and you know …'
Dora, impressed.

'Look …'

Which meant that I met Aadu Müür, yes, that oh so handsome young man, six foot two, kind smile … you can imagine.
I met him eight years ago and I fell head over heels in love; I
fell in love with Aadu Müür the watchmaker, and I went to
live in Tallinn by his side and I would have gone to the ends of
the earth, there where the contours of the mountains end and
the horrific precipice begins, which leads you straight to hell,
if you slip, for having thought, at any point, that the Earth was
round. I would have gone there if Aadu had asked me to. And
in Tallinn I worked in a hair salon and then I sold ice creams
in a place where at night they allowed alcohol and the time
came when I spoke Estonian so well that they didn't know if
my accent was because I was from Saaremaa Island or what,
and when I told them I was Catalan, they couldn't believe it.
Because they say that the Estonians are cold like ice, but it's
a lie because with vodka in their bodies they turn warm and
talkative. And Aadu disappeared one awful day and I've never
heard from him again; well, yes, but it hurts me to remember it and I came back because I had nothing to do there, in
the middle of the ice, without Aadu the watchmaker, selling
ice creams to Estonians who were about to get drunk. I still
hadn't recovered from the shock and Helena called me and
said let's see if we get lucky, you know Estonian, right? And I,
yes, why? And she, well, I have a friend who's a nurse, Dora,
and she has a problem that … She's frightened and … it could
be something really serious … And I'm still willing to sign up
for anything that could help me forget about all six foot two
of Aadu and that hesitant sweet soul that one fine day stopped
being hesitant and sweet, and I said sure, I speak Estonian:
where do we go, what needs to be done?

'No, no … I mean … How do you know it so well? Because

it took me forever to figure out that she was speaking Estonian. It didn't sound like anything I'd ever heard before, you
know? Until she said something, can't remember what and I,
after saying Norwegian, Swedish, Danish, Finnish, Icelandic,
I said Estonian and it seemed that her eyes gleamed a bit differently. That was my only clue, yeah. And I hit the nail on
the head.'

'The funny thing is that we don't know if her husband is a
serial killer or if she's lost her marbles. If we are in danger or
not, you know what I mean?'

'I don't think I've ever,' – Helena's second contribution to
the conversation – 'seen a woman so afraid. From now on
we'd better be on our guard.'

'We have to ask her more things.'

'Do you want me to talk to her again?'

'Yes.'

'And what if the husband shows up … Hmm?'

Alexandre Roig, after having paid his beloved a brief
but passionate visit, had come to a final decision. I'm sorry,
Gertrud, but I have no choice: you are forcing me to it. Now
it's my turn to live. He climbed the metro stairs mechanically
and said to himself tonight's the night.

Meanwhile, Gertrud was saying more and more things in
Estonian and Àgata, dressed as a nurse – she who fainted at
the first sight of blood – with her heart in her throat, translated
them for Dora, and she said I was watching him in the dark,
I was watching his profile. Yes, because he had been strange,
very strange, for several days and I don't know what's happening with him, and he went like this, tightening his jaw and
poor Gertrud wanted to lift an arm to show what like this was,
but she was realising she could only move her thoughts and
then she said it seemed like he was showing me his soul, that
he was loathing me just for existing. And he said that's it, to
hell with everything; yes, yes; that's it, to hell with everything.

'He said it in Estonian?'

'What?'

'Did he say it in Estonian?'

'What do I know? … That was when I saw him struggling

with his seat belt and the car started flying and I said Saaaandreeee son of a biiiiiitcccch … And nothing more; nothing more … Until I woke up and he was there before me and he said it wasn't my fault, Gertrud, it was an accident.'

'Your husband doesn't speak Estonian.'

'No. But he understands it. Or yes, he does speak it.'

'And couldn't you speak in Catalan?'

'What am I speaking now?'

Then they heard the sound of a key in the lock and the three women's blood froze in their veins.

'Put the thermometer in her mouth. No, rub her legs!'

'How?'

'Rubbing, for god's sake. He shouldn't be here.'

'Oh, is there a guest?' he said, hiding his surprise.

'Good evening, Mr Roig.'

He looked at the two of them. The three of them. A quick, suspicious glance. He opened his mouth. He saw how the strange nurse was rubbing Gertrud's right foot as if she were playing with modelling clay.

'Uh … She came to help me.'

'How is she?' referring to Gertrud.

'The same. No change.' Referring to Àgata: 'She is a colleague who …'

Professor Roig came all the way into the room, looked at Gertrud, gave her a kiss on the forehead, pinched her cheek and said I'll be right back, dear, I forgot to buy noodles. And he went out, without giving the other women any explanation. When they were alone again, the two of them looked at each other. The three of them.

Sara, last night I found your slip of paper with the name. Matthias Alpaerts, it says. And he lives in Antwerp. But do you know what? I don't trust your source, not in the least. It is a source corrupted by Mr Berenguer and Tito's resentment. Mr Berenguer is a thief who only wants revenge on my father, my mother and me. And he's used you for his ends. Let me think it over. I have to know … I'm not sure; I promise you, I'm doing what I can, Sara.

I know you want to kill me, Sandre, even though you call me dear and you buy me noodles. I know what you did because I dreamt it. They told me that I was in a coma for five days. For me, those five days were a crystal-clear, slow-motion vision of the accident: I was looking at you in the dark because you'd been very strange for several days, a bit elusive, nervous, always lost in thought. The first thing that a woman thinks when her husband is like that is that there's another woman he's thinking of; the ghost of the other woman. Yes, that's the first thing you think; but I didn't know what to say. I couldn't imagine you cheating on me. And the first day I said out loud help, I think my husband wants to kill me; help, I think he wants to kill me because he made a strange face in the car and he took off his seat belt and he said that's it, and I Saandreeee, son of a biiiiiiitcccccccccch, and after a slow dream that repeated everything until, it seems, five days had passed. I no longer know what I'm saying. Yes, that's the first time I dared to say out loud that I think you want to kill me, no one paid me any mind, as if they didn't believe me. But then they looked at me, and this Dora told me what are you saying, I can't understand you; when it was clear as day that I was saying I think my husband wants to kill me, now shamelessly, and panicking over another fear: that no one believed me or paid me any mind. It is like being buried alive. It's terrible, Sandre, this. I look into your eyes and you don't hold my gaze: what must you be planning? Why don't you tell me what you say to the others that you won't tell me? What do you want? For me to tell you to your face that I think you wanted to kill me, that I think you want to kill me? That I tell you, holding your gaze, that I believe you want to kill me, because I am in the way of your life and it's easier to just get rid of me like snuffing out a candle than to have to explain? At this point, Sandre … I don't think I need any explanations; but don't blow out my flame: I don't want to die. I am stock-still and buried in this shell and all I have left is a weak flame. Don't take that from me. Go, divorce me, but don't snuff out my flame.

Àgata left the house when the scents of the first suppers were timidly rising in the stairwell. Her legs were still shaking. Out on the streets he was greeted by the stench of a bus. She went straight towards the metro. She had looked a killer in the eyes and it was quite an experience. That is if Mr Roig was a killer. He was. And when she was about to go down the stairs, the killer himself, with his eyes like daggers, came up beside her and said miss, please. She stopped, terrified. He gave her a shy smile, ran a hand through his hair and said, 'What do you think, about my wife's state?'

'Not good.' What else could she say?

'Is it true that there is no hope of recovery?'

'Unfortunately … Well, I …'

'But the process of myoma is solvable, from what they've told me.'

'Yes, of course.'

'So you also believe that it has a solution.'

'Yes, sir. But I …'

'If you're a nurse, I'm the pope in Rome.'

'Pardon me?'

'What were you doing at my house?'

'Look, I'm in a hurry right now.'

What does one do in such cases? What does the killer who realises that someone is sticking their nose in his business do? What does the victim who isn't entirely sure if the killer is a killer do? They both hesitated for a few seconds like real dummies. Then it occurred to Àgata to say farewell and she took off down the stairs, and Professor Roig, planted there in the middle of the stairwell, didn't really know what to do. Àgata went down to the platform. Just then a train arrived. Once she was inside it, she turned towards the door and looked: no, that madman hadn't followed her. She didn't breathe easily until the carriage doors closed.

At night, in the dark, so he wouldn't have to bear her gaze. At night, as she pretended to be sleeping, Gertrud made out the shadow of cowardly Sandre and smelled the sofa cushion, which, when her life was alive, she would put behind her head to watch TV comfortably. And she even still had time to think Sandre chose the cushion, like Tiberius did to murder Augustus. It won't take much because I'm already half dead, but you should know that you're even more of a coward than you are a bastard. You haven't even been able to look me in the eye and say goodbye. And Gertrud couldn't think anything more because the spasm of the smothering was more intense than life itself and in an instant it transformed into death.

Dora put a hand on his back and said Mr Ardèvol, go rest. That's an order.

Adrià woke up and turned, surprised. The light in the room was tenuous and Mignon's gardenias gave off a magic brilliance. And Sara slept and slept and slept. Dora and a stranger kicked him out of the hospital. And Dora put a pill to help him sleep into his hand, and, mechanically, he got the metro at the Clínic stop while Professor Alexandre Roig, at the entrance to the Verdaguer metro stop, met up with a girl who could have been his daughter, who was surely a student, and the best detective of them all, Elm Gonzaga, hired by the three brave women, followed them ever so discreetly after having captured their kiss with a camera like Laura's, digital or whatever they're called, and all three waited on the platform until the train arrived and the happy couple entered the carriage along with the detective, and at Sagrada Família Friar Nicolau Eimeric and Aribert Voigt got on, chatting excitedly about the big ideas that were going through their heads, and seated in one corner, Doctor Müss or Budden was reading Kempis and looking out the window into the darkness of the tunnel, and at the other end of the carriage, dressed in the Benedictine habit, Brother Julià of Sant Pere del Burgal was dozing off. Standing beside him, Jachiam Mureda of Pardàc was looking, with wide eyes, at the new world around him, and surely he was thinking of all the Muredas and of poor Bettina, his little blind sister. And next to him was a frightened Lorenzo Storioni who didn't understand what was going on and clung to the pole in the centre of the carriage to keep from falling. The train stopped at the Hospital de Sant Pau station, a few passengers got out and Guillaume-François Vial got on, decked out in his moth-eaten wig and chatting with Drago Gradnik, who was more corpulent than I ever could have imagined and had to duck his head to get into the carriage, and whose smile reminded me of Uncle Haïm's serious expression, even though in the portrait Sara made of him he wasn't smiling. And the train started up again. Then I realised that Matthias, Berta the Strong, Truu, the one with hair brown as wood from the forest, Amelietje with her jet-black hair, Juliet, the littlest, blonde like the sun, and brave Netje de Boeck, the mother-in-law with a chest cold, were talking, near the end of the carriage, with Bernat. With Bernat? Yes. And with me, who was also in the train carriage. And they were telling us about the last train trip they'd taken together, in a sealed carriage, and Amelietje was showing her the nape of her neck, wounded by the rifle blow, you see, you see?, to Rudolf Höss, who was seated alone, looking at the platform, and wasn't very interested in looking at her bump. And the girl's lips already had the dark colour of death, but her parents didn't seem to mind much. They were all young and fresh except for Matthias, who was old, with weepy eyes and slow reflexes. It seemed they were looking at him suspiciously, as if they had difficulty accepting or forgiving their father's old age. Especially Berta the Strong's gaze, which was sometimes reminiscent of Gertrud's, or no, a bit different. And we reached Camp de l'Arpa, where Fèlix Morlin got on, chatting animatedly with Father: it had been so many years since I'd seen my father that I could barely make out his face, but I know that it was him. Behind him was Sheriff Carson accompanied by his loyal friend Black Eagle, both very silent, making an effort not to look at me. I saw that Carson was about to spit on the floor of the train carriage, but valiant Black Eagle stopped him with a brusque gesture. The train was stopped, I don't know why, with the doors of every carriage open. Mr Berenguer and Tito still had time to enter leisurely, by the arm I think. Lothar Grübbe hesitated just as he was stepping inside the carriage, and Mother and Little Lola, who came up behind, helped him finally make up his mind. And as the doors started to close, Alí Bahr ran in, forcing them open slightly, all alone without infamous Amani. The doors closed completely, the train started off and when we'd already been in the tunnel towards La Sagrera for thirty seconds, Alí Bahr planted himself in the middle of the carriage and started shouting like a wild man, take away, Merciful Lord, all this carrion! He opened his jellabah, shrieked Allahu Akbar! and pulled on a cord that emerged from his clothes and everything became luminously white and none of us could see the immense ball of

Someone was shaking him. He opened his eyes. It was Caterina, leaning over him.

'Adrià! Can you hear me?'

It took him a few seconds to situate himself because his sleepiness came from very far away. She insisted: 'Can you hear me, Adrià?'

'Yes, what's wrong?'

Instead of telling him that they'd just called from the hospital or that he had a call from the hospital or even that he had an urgent call, or perhaps even better, instead of saying the phone is for you and going off to iron, which was an unbeatable excuse, Caterina, always anxious to be in the front row, repeated Adrià, can you hear me, and I, yes, what's wrong, and she, Saga woke up.

Then I did wake up completely and instead of thinking she's awake, she's awake, I thought and I wasn't there, and I wasn't there. Adrià got out of bed without realising that he was in the nude, and Caterina, with a quick glance, criticised his excessive belly but saved her comment for another occasion.

'Where?' I said, disorientated.

'On the telephone.'

Adrià picked up the receiver in his study: it was Doctor Real herself, who said she's opened her eyes and begun to speak.

'In what language?'

'Pardon?'

'Can you understand her?' and without waiting for a reply: 'I'll be right there.'

'We need to speak before you see her.'

'Fine. I'll be right there.'

If not for Caterina, who stood square in front of the door to the stairwell, I would have gone to the hospital in the buff, because I hadn't even realised the incidental circumstances, totally overcome by happiness as I was. Adrià showered, crying, dressed crying and laughing, and went to the hospital laughing, and Caterina locked the apartment when she had finished with the laundry and said this man cries when he should cry and laughs when he should cry.

The skinny doctor with a slightly wrinkled face had him come into some sort of an office.

'Hey, I just want to say hello to her.'

'One moment, Mr Ardèvol.'

She had him sit down. She sat down in her spot and looked at him in silence.

'What's wrong?' Adrià grew frightened. 'She's all right, yeah?'

Then the doctor said what he had been so fearing; she said I don't know if you are a believer or not, but there's been a miracle here; the Lord has listened to your prayers.

'I'm not a believer,' I said. 'And I don't pray,' I lied.

'Your wife is not going to die. Although, the injuries …'

'My God.'

'Yes.'

'On one hand we have to wait and see how the stroke has affected her.'

'Yeah.'

'The problem is that there are other problems.'

'What problems?'

'We've been noticing, in the last few days, some flaccid paralysis, do you understand me?'

'No.'

'Yes. And the neurologist ordered a CAT scan and we found a fracture of the sixth cervical vertebra.'

'What does that all mean?'

Doctor Real leaned imperceptibly and changed the inflection of her voice: 'That Sara has a serious spinal cord injury.'

'Does that mean that she's paralytic?'

'Yes.' After a brief silence, in a lower voice: 'Quadriplegic.'

With the prefix 'quadri-', which means 'four', and the suffix '-plegic', from the word *plēgē*, which means 'blow' and also 'affliction', they had described Sara's state. My Sara is afflicted by four blows. What would we do without Greek? We would be unable to take in or understand the great tragedies of humankind.

I couldn't turn my back on God because I didn't believe in God. I couldn't punch Doctor Real in the face because it wasn't her fault. I could only cry out to the heavens saying I wasn't there and I could have saved her; if I had been there, she wouldn't have gone out into the stairwell, she would have fallen on the floor and just got a cut on her head and that's it. And I was fucking Laura.

They let him see Sara. She was quite sedated and could barely open her eyes. He thought she was smiling at him. He told her that he loved her very, very, very much, and she half-opened her mouth but said nothing. Four or five days passed. Mignon's gardenias were his loyal companions as they slowly woke her up. Until one Friday, the psychologist and the neurologist, with Doctor Real, refused to let me in with them and they spent a long hour in Sara's room, with Dora keeping watch like Cerberus the hellhound. And I cried in some sort of waiting room and when they came out they didn't let me go in to give her a kiss until not a trace of my tears remained on my face. And as soon as she saw me she didn't say I'd love a cup of coffee, she said I want to die, Adrià. And I felt like a stupid idiot, with that bouquet of white roses in my hand and a smile frozen on my face.

'My Sara,' I ended up saying.

She looked at me, serious, without saying anything.

'Forgive me.'

Nothing. I think she swallowed some saliva with difficulty. But she didn't say anything. Like Gertrud.

'I'll give back the violin. I have the name.'

'I can't move.'

'Well, listen. That's now. We'll have to see if ...'

'They've already told me. Never again.'

'What do they know?'

Despite everything, she gave a hint of a resigned smile when she heard my response.

'I won't ever be able to draw again.'

'But can't you move one finger?'

'Yes, this one. And that's it.'

'That's a good sign, isn't it?'

She didn't dignify my question with an answer. To dispel the uncomfortable silence, Adrià continued, in a falsely cheerful tone: 'First we have to talk to all the doctors. Isn't that right, Doctor?'

Adrià turned towards Doctor Real who had just come into the room, he still with the bouquet of flowers in his hand, as if he wanted to offer them to the newcomer.

'Yes, of course,' said the doctor.

And she took the bouquet, as if it were for her. Sara closed her eyes as if she were infinitely weary.

## 54

Bernat and Tecla were the first to visit her. Flummoxed, they didn't know what to say. Sara wasn't up for smiling or joking. She said thank you for coming and didn't open her mouth again. I kept saying as soon as we can we'll go back home and we'll set it up so she'll be real comfortable; but she looked up at the ceiling, flat on her back, and didn't even bother to smile. And Bernat, exaggerating his excitement, said you know what, Sara?, I was in Paris with the quartet and I played in the same Pleyel chamber hall, the medium-sized one, where Adrià played a million years ago.

'Oh, really?' Adrià, surprised.

'Yeah.'

'And how'd you know I played there?'

'You told me.'

Should we have told him that that was where you and I met? Because of Master Castells and your auntie, whose name escapes me now? Or should we keep it to ourselves?

'You could say that that was where we met, Sara and I.'

'Oh, really? That's lovely,' pointing to Mignon's gardenias.

Tecla, meanwhile, approached Sara and put a hand on her cheek. For a long while she caressed her, in silence, as Bernat and I tried to pretend that everything was going swimmingly. Stupid, stupid Adrià hadn't even realised; if he wanted her to, if he wanted Sara to, if he wanted her to feel him, he had to touch her face and not her dead hands. They aren't dead. Well, then sleeping.

Later, when they were alone, Adrià put a hand on her cheek and she rebuffed him with a very brusque gesture, filled with silence.

'You're angry with me.'

'I have bigger problems than being angry with you.'

'Sorry.'

They were silent. Our life was beginning to have broken glass all over the floor and we could get hurt.

At night, at home, with the balconies open because of the heat, Adrià wandered like a ghost, not knowing what he had to do and indignant with himself because, after so much grief, deep down he had the feeling that he was the victim. It was very hard for me to get that there was only one victim: you. So, two or three days later, I sat by your side, I took your hand, I noticed its lack of sensitivity, I delicately put it back where it was, I placed my fingertips on your cheek and I said Sara, I am working on returning the violin to its owners. She didn't respond to my half-truth, but she didn't rebuff my fingers. After five infinite minutes of silence, and from deep inside, she said thank you in a thin voice and I felt the tears about to stream from my eyes, but I stifled them in time because I knew that, in that hospital room, I had no right to cry.

'*Or in a state that I consider, freely, to be not worth living in.* That's exactly what it says there.'

'That's very easy to say.'

'No: that's how it is. It was very hard for me to write, but it is my living will. And I am completely lucid and can stand by it.'

'You aren't lucid. You are demoralised.'

'You're mistaking the smoke for the fire.'

'What?'

'I'm lucid.'

'You are alive. You can continue living. I will always be by your side.'

'I don't want you by my side. I want you brave and doing what I am begging you to do.'

'I can't.'

'You're a coward.'

'Yes.'

We heard some voices saying cinquantaquattro. Here it is. The door opened and I smiled at the people who entered the room and interrupted our conversation. Some friends from Cadaqués. They knew about the roses, too.

'Look how lovely they are, Sara,' said the woman.

'Very lovely.'

Sara smiled pallidly and was very polite. She told them that she was fine, don't worry. And the friends from Cadaqués were able to leave half an hour later a bit reassured because they had come in not knowing what to say, poor thing.

Over many days, many visits interrupted our conversation, which was always the same one. And when it had been fifteen or twenty days since Sara had awoken, one night, when I was about to go home, Sara asked me to put the painting by Mignon before her. For a few minutes, she ran her eyes over it, gluttonously, without blinking. And, suddenly, she burst into tears. It must have been those tears that made me brave.

## 55

The exhibition opened without you. The gallerists couldn't postpone it because their calendar was booked for the next two years and Sara Voltes-Epstein would never able to visit it, so just go ahead and you'll tell me all about it, really. You can just videotape it all anyway, right?

A few days before, Sara gathered Max and I together beside her bed and said I want to add two drawings.

'Which ones?'

'Two landscapes.'

'But ...' Max, perplexed. 'It's a show of portraits.'

'Two landscapes,' she insisted, 'that are portraits of a soul.'

'Which ones are they?' I asked.

'My landscape of Tona and the apse of Sant Pere del Burgal.'

Your composure left me dumbstruck. Because you continued giving orders: they are both in the black folder that's still in Cadaqués. The drawing of Tona is called *In Arcadia Hadriani* and the other, *Sant Pere del Burgal: A Dream.*'

'Whose soul are they the portrait of?' Max needed everything to be explained to him.

'The person who needs to know already does.'

'Anima Hadriani,' I said, about to cry or to jump with joy, I still don't know which.

'But the people at the gallery ...'

'Just two more drawings, shit, Max! And if there is no budget for it, they can leave them unframed.'

'No, no: I mean about the portrait concept ...'

'Max, look at me.'

You blew a lock of hair out of your eyes, I pushed it aside with my hand and you said thank you. And to Max: the exhibition will be the way I say it'll be. You owe that to me. Thirty portraits and two landscapes dedicated to the man I love.

'No, no, I wasn't …'

'Wait. One is a free interpretation of Adrià's lost paradise. And the other is a monastery in ruins that, I don't know why, but that Adrià has always had in his head, even though he only saw it for the first time recently. And that's how you'll do it. You will do it for me. Even though I won't be able to see the exhibition.'

'We'll take you there.'

'I shudder at the thought of making a scene with ambulances and stretchers … No. Make a video for me.'

So, it was an opening without the artist. Max officiated as the strong man and said my sister isn't here but it's as if she were. This evening we will show her the photos and the video we're making, and Sara, sitting up with some good cushions, saw all the portraits and the two landscapes together for the first time and, in a repetition of the opening in cinquantaquattro with Max, Dora, Bernat, Doctor Dalmau, me and I don't know who else, when the camera landed on Uncle Haïm, Sara said stop there for a moment. And she spent a few seconds looking at the frozen image and thinking who knows what and then they showed the rest. She didn't ask to stop the tape at my portrait, head bowed, reading. The camera travelled to her self-portrait, with that enigmatic gaze, and she didn't want to look closer at that one either. She listened attentively to Max saying a few words to the crowd, she saw that many people had come, and as they showed the images again, she said thank you, Max, very lovely words. And she mentioned that she had seen Murtra, Josée and Chantal Cases, the Rieras from Andorra, everybody, and wow, that's Llorenç, he's grown so much.

'And Tecla, you see?' I said.

'And Bernat. How nice.'

'Ooh, who's that handsome one?' exclaimed Dora.

'A friend of mine,' said Max. 'Giorgio.'

Silence. To break it, Max himself said: 'Every piece sold. Did you hear me?'

'Who's that one? Stop, stop!' Sara almost miraculously sat up: 'It's Viladecans! It looks like he wants to eat Uncle Haïm up with his eyes! …'

'Yeah, yes, it's true, he was there. He spent a million hours staring at each portrait.'

'Whoa …'

Seeing her eyes gleam, I thought she's getting her lust for life back and I thought a new life is possible, changing priorities, changing style, changing all the values of everything. No? She grew serious, as if she had heard my thoughts. After a few seconds: 'The self-portrait isn't for sale.'

'What?' Max, scared.

'It's not for sale.'

'Well, that was the first one to sell.'

'Who bought it?'

'I don't know. I'll ask.'

'I told you that …' She grew silent, slightly confused.

You hadn't told us anything. But the world was starting to mix up the things you say, the things you think, the things you hope for and the things that could have been if not for.

'Can I call from here?' Max, desolate.

'There's a telephone at reception.'

'You don't have to call,' Adrià interrupted, as if he'd been caught red-handed.

I felt Max, Sara, Doctor Dalmau and Bernat looking at me. That happens to me sometimes. As if I had entered life without an invitation and they'd all just realised I was a fraud, with reproachful, stabbing stares.

'Why?' someone said.

'Because I bought it.'

Silence. Sara pulled a face: 'Silly,' she said.

Adrià looked at her, his eyes wide.

'I wanted to give it to you,' I improvised.

'I wanted to give it to you, too.' She let out a new timid giggle, one I had never heard before she'd fallen ill.

The opening at the hospital ended with a toast, everyone with a sad plastic cup filled with water. And Sara never said I really would have liked to be there. But you looked at me and you smiled. I'm sure that you had reconciled with me thanks to that half-truth about the violin. I wasn't honest enough to refute it.

When she had drank the ritual sip with my help, she moved her head from one side to the other and said, out of the blue, I'm going to cut my hair real short, it's bothering me at the back of my neck.

Laura had come back from the Algarve very tanned. We saw each other in the office, between the turmoil and the pressing September exams; she asked me about Sara, I said yeah, what can you do and she didn't insist. Even though we spent hours together in the office, we didn't say anything more to each other and we pretended not to see each other. Some days later, I had lunch with Max because I had come up with the idea of making a book with the title of the exhibition, with all of the portraits, eight and a half by twelve and a half, what do you think? That's a brilliant idea, Adrià: and with the two land-scapes. Sure, with the two landscapes. An expensive book, done well, not some rush job. Sure, done well. We fought over who would pay for it and we ended up agreeing to split it and I got to work with the help of the gallerists at Artipèlag and Bauçà. And I was excited at the idea that we might be able to start another life, you at home, well attended, if you still wanted to live with me, something I wasn't sure about, if you agreed and gave up on those strange thoughts. I spoke with all the doctors: Dalmau warned me that, from the informa-tion he had, Sara still wasn't well and that I shouldn't rush to get her home, that Doctor Real was right. And that it was much better for everyone's mental health if we didn't make too many plans yet. That we weren't out of the woods yet and that it was best to take it one day at a time, trust me. And Laura cornered me one day in a hallway by the classrooms and said I'm going back to Uppsala. They've offered me a job at the Centre for Language Studies and ...

'That's great.'

'It depends. I'm leaving. If you want a lawyer, I'll be in Uppsala.'

'Laura, I don't want anything.'

'You've never known what you want.'

'Fine. But now I know that I won't go to Uppsala to see you.'

'You already said that.'

'You can't wait around hoping others will …'

'Hey.'

'What.'

'It's my life, not yours. I'll write the instruction manual.'

She got on tiptoe and gave me a kiss on the cheek, and I don't remember us ever speaking again. I know that she lives in Uppsala. I know that she's published six or seven quite good articles. I miss her but I hope she's found someone more whole than me. And meanwhile, Max and I decided that the book of portraits would be a surprise, basically to keep her from talking us out of it. We wanted to shock her a little with our excitement, and have it be contagious. So we asked Joan Pere Viladecans to write a short prologue and he did, gladly. In just a few lines he said so many things about Sara's art that I was overcome with a pressing, feverish attack of jealousy thinking how is it possible that there are so many aspects and so many details to Sara's drawings that I don't know how to see. As many as the aspects of your life that I was also unable to grasp.

Gradually, paying attention to you in the hospital, I discovered a woman capable of directing the world without moving a finger, just speaking, organising, suggesting, demanding, begging, and looking at me with those eyes that still today go right through me and wound me with love and other things I can't pinpoint. I was wracked by my bad conscience. I had a name: Alpaerts. I didn't know for sure if he was the true owner of the violin. I knew that wasn't the name my father had put in that quasi-final testament, written in Aramaic. I didn't tell you, Sara, but I wasn't doing anything to solve that. Confiteor.

That pale, slow afternoon, with no visitors, as was beginning to be the norm because people have their work and their lives, you said stay a little longer.

'If Dora lets me.'

'She'll let you. I already took care of it. I have to tell you something.'

I had sensed that you and Dora had understood each other

right off, from the first moment, without the need for much discussion.

'Sara, I don't think it's …'

'Hey. Look at me.'

I looked at her, sadly. Her hair was still long and she was just lovely. And you said take my hand. Like that. Higher up, so I can see. Like that.

'What do you have to tell me?' I was afraid the topic would come up again.

'That I had a daughter.'

'That what?'

'In Paris. Her name is Claudine and she died at two months old. Fifty-nine days of life. I must not have been a good enough mother, because I wasn't able to detect her illness. Claudine, eyes dark as coal, defenceless, she cried a lot. And one day I don't know what came over her. She died in my arms on the way to the hospital.'

'Sara …'

'The most profound pain a person can experience: the death of a child. That was why I never wanted to have another. It seemed unfair to Claudine.'

'Why didn't you tell me?'

'It was my fault and I had no right to transfer that much pain to you. Now I will find her again.'

'Sara.'

'What.'

'It wasn't your fault. And you don't have to die.'

'I want to die, you know that already.'

'I won't let you die.'

'That's just what I said to Claudine in the taxi. I don't want you to die, don't die, don't die, don't die, don't die, Claudine, do you hear me, itty-bitty one?'

For the first time since you'd been in hospital, you cried. For your daughter, not for yourself, strong woman. You were quiet for a while, letting the tears stream down. I wiped them away gently with a handkerchief, in silence and with respect. You made an effort and continued: 'But death is stronger than us and my itty-bitty Claudine died.' She was silent, exhausted by the effort. Two more tears and she continued: 'That's why I know that I will meet up with her again. I called her my itty-bitty Claudine.'

'Why do you say you'll meet up with her again?'

'Because I know I will.'

'Sara ... you don't believe in anything.' Sometimes I don't know when to keep my mouth shut.

'You're right. But I know that mothers meet up with their dead daughters again. Otherwise, life would be impossible to bear.'

I kept my mouth shut because, as was almost always true, you were right. Adrià kept his mouth shut because he also knew that it was impossible. And he couldn't explain to her that evil is capable of everything and more, and that was before he even knew the story of Matthias Alpaerts's life, about Berta the Strong, his mother-in-law with a chest cold, Amelietje with the jet-black locks, Truu with hair the colour of fine wood, and Juliet, the littlest with her golden tresses.

When Sara returned to her house in the huitième arrondissement, she searched the flat for Bitxo, thinking where could he be, where could he be, where could he be, where could he be hiding?

The cat was under the bed, as if he had sensed that things had gone terribly wrong. Sara made him emerge with chicanery, lying and saying come here, pretty boy, come here and when Bitxo trusted his owner's tone and came out from under the bed, she grabbed him, ready to throw him out of the window into the interior courtyard because I don't ever want another living thing in this house. Never again anything that can die on me. But the cat's disconcerted meow saved him and made her snap out of it. She took him to the local animal sanctuary knowing that she was being unfair to the poor creature. Sara Voltes-Epstein spent some months grieving, drawing black abstractions and spending her work hours, mute, illustrating stories that mothers would read to their laughing, living daughters, and thinking that her little itty-bitty Claudine would never see those drawings and trying to keep the pain from eating away at her insides. And after

exactly one year she was visited by an encyclopaedia salesman. Do you understand that I couldn't go back with you
right away? Do you understand that I didn't want to live with
anyone who could die on me? Do you understand that I was
insane?

She was silent. We were silent. I placed her hand on her
chest and I stroked her cheek: she let me do it. I said I love
you and I wanted to think that she was calmer. I never dared
to ask you who Claudine's father was and if he lived with you
when the girl died. With the explanation of just a few strokes
of your life, as if you were drawing in charcoal, underlining
one shadow but leaving out another stroke, you were asserting your right to keep your secrets to yourself, in Bluebeard's
locked room. And Dora let me stay until a scandalously inad-
missible hour.

## 56

The day you went back to that conversation and again you asked me to help you die, that you couldn't do it alone, I was horrified because I had wanted to think that you'd put it behind you. Then Adrià said how can you want to die when we are about to give you a surprise? What? Your book. My book, my book? Yes, with all the portraits; Max and I made it.

Sara smiled and was pensive for a little while. And she said thank you, but what I want is the end. I don't like dying, but I don't want to be a burden and I can't accept this life I have to live, always looking at the same stretch of the fucking ceiling. I think it was the first and only curse word I ever heard you say. Or maybe it was the second.

But. Yes, I understand the but. I don't know how. I do, Dora explained it to me, but I need someone. Don't ask me that. And you don't mind if someone else does it? No; I mean, don't ask that of anyone. I'm the one in charge here; this is my life, not yours; I write the instruction manual.

I was flabbergasted. As if, between Laura and Sara, there was some ... I'm sorry to admit that I began to cry like a baby by Sara's bed, who, by the way, was gorgeous with her short hair. I had never seen you with short hair before, Sara. Since she couldn't run her hand over my head to console me, she just looked up at the fucking ceiling and waited for it to pass. I think Dora came in just then with her pills but, seeing the scene, she discreetly left again.

'Adrià.'

'Yes ...'

'Do you love me more than anyone?'

'Yes, Sara. You know I love you.'

'Then do what I say.' And after a pause: 'Adrià.'

'Yes.'

'Do you love me more than anyone?'

'Yes, Sara. You know I love you.'

'Then do what I'm asking.' And almost immediately: 'My beloved Adrià.'

'Yes.'

'Do you love me?'

And Adrià was sad that she was asking him that again because I would give my life for you and every time you ask me that all I can think is that …

'Do you love me or not?'

'You know everything and you know that I love you.'

'Then help me die.'

Leaving the hospital gave me a pang of bad conscience. Walking through Universal Creation, looking halfheartedly at the spines of books without really seeing them. Just as at other times strolling through Romance Language Prose made me recall pleasurable readings; or entering Poetry meant, inevitably, pulling out a book and furtively reading a couple of poems at random or with every intention, as if Universal Creation were Paradise, and the poems, apples that had never been forbidden. Just as entering Essays made me identify with those who had one day tried to put order into their reflections, now I wandered looking at spines without seeing the titles on them, dejected, my eyes filled only with Sara's pain. It was impossible to work. I would sit before a pile of manuscript papers, trying to reread where I had left off, but then you arose saying kill me if you love me, or you stock-still for years, patient, level-headed, and me having to leave your room every five minutes to scream with rage. I asked Dora if you'd saved the hair when you had it cut …

'No.'

'Damn! …'

'She told us to throw it away.'

'Shit, but …'

'Yes, it's a shame. I thought the same thing.'

'Did you really do as she said?'

'It's impossible not to do what your wife says.'

And the nights were one long insomnia. To the point that I had to do strange things to get to sleep, like going over texts in Hebrew, which was the language I had most neglected because I had few opportunities to work with it. And I searched for texts from the fifteenth and sixteenth centuries and contemporary texts and I was reminded of the venerable Assumpta Brotons with her pince-nez and a half smile that I at first took for kindly and later found out was a smirk. And the patience she had. And the patience I had to have.

'Echad.'

'Eshad.'

'Echad.'

'Ehad.'

'Very good. Do you understand it?'

'Yes.'

'Schtayim.'

'Shtaim.'

'Very good. Do you understand it?'

'Yes.'

'Schalosh.'

'Shalosh.'

'Very good. Do you understand it?'

'Yes.'

'Arba.'

'Arba.'

'Khamesh.'

'Kamesh.'

'Yes, that's it, very good!'

The letters danced before my eyes because nothing mattered to me, because all my desire remained by your side. I went to bed in the wee hours and at six in the morning I was still lying there with my eyes open. I barely slept a few minutes and was up before Little Lola arrived, shaved and showered and ready to return to the hospital if I didn't have class, to witness some miracle for the love of God.

Until one night I felt so ashamed of myself that I decided to try to really put myself in Sara's shoes in an attempt to understand her fully. And the next day Adrià contrived to bump

into Dora alone, who wasn't as scared as I was, but very reticent because it wasn't a case of some irreversible disease that
would sooner or later be life-threatening; she could spend
years in that state; she … and I had to hear myself pleading
in favour of Sara's arguments, which could be summed up in
one "do it because you love me". Alone again. Alone before
your request, your entreaty. But I didn't feel capable of it. And
one night I said to Sara that yes, that I would do it, and she
smiled at me and she said if I could move I would get up and
French kiss you right now. And I'd said it knowing I was lying,
because I had no intention of carrying it out. In the end, Sara,
I always lied to you; about that and about trying to return the
violin, which according to my version was full steam ahead
and I was about to get in touch with … The edifice of lies
I constructed just to buy time was pathetic. Buy time from
whom? Buy time from fear, thinking that each passing day
was a victory, things like that. I spoke about it with Dalmau,
who advised me not to involve Doctor Real.

'You say it like it's a crime.'

'It is a crime. According to our current legislation.'

'So why are you helping me?'

'Because one thing is the law and another is the cases that
the law doesn't dare to legislate.'

'In other words, you agree with me.'

'What do you want? A signed declaration?'

'No. Sorry. I … Anyway.'

He grabbed me, he had me sit down and, even though we
were in his office and there was no one else home, he lowered
his voice and, with the yellow Modigliani as a mute, shocked
witness, gave me a speed course on assisted suicide for love.
And I knew that I would never make use of that knowledge.
I spent a couple of weeks relatively calm until one day Sara
looked me in the eyes and said when, Adrià? I opened my
mouth. I looked up at the fucking ceiling and I looked at her
without knowing what to say. I said I talked to … I'm … eh?

The next day you died all on your own. I will always believe
that you died on your own because you understood that I was
a coward and you so wanted to die and I wasn't brave enough

to accompany you on the final stretch and make it easier on you. Doctor Real's version was that you had another haemorrhage like the one that had caused the accident, despite the treatment they were giving you. And even though you were in hospital, there was nothing that could be done. You left with your exhibition of portraits still up. And Max, who came with Giorgio, crying, said what a shame, she didn't know we were making the book for her; we should have told her.

That was how it all went, Sara. Since I was unable to help you, you had to go on your own, in a rush, secretly, without looking back, without being able to say goodbye. Do you understand my disquiet?

## 57

'Adrià?' Just hearing him say that I could tell that Max was upset.

'Yes, what?'

'I got the fax.'

'Is it all right?'

'No. It's not.'

'It's just that, the fax ... I must have hit the wrong key ...'

'Adrià.'

'Yes.'

'I received the fax perfectly. You pushed the right button and I got it.'

'Very good. So then there's no problem, yeah?'

'No problem? Do you know what you sent me?' His tone was like Trullols when she told me to do arpeggios in G major and I started them in D major.

'Of course, Sara's bio.'

'Yes. What note did you start with?' insisted Trullols.

'Hey, what's wrong with you?'

'To put where?' now it was Max.

'At the end of the book of portraits. Are you pleased?'

'No. Now I'll read you what you sent me.'

It wasn't a question: it was a warning. And I immediately heard him saying Sara Voltes-Epstein was born in Paris in nineteen fifty and when she was very young she met a stupid boy who fell in love with her and while he never intended any harm, he was never really able to make her happy.

'Listen, I ...'

'Shall I continue?'

'No need for that.'

But Max read the whole thing to me. He was very cross and when he finished there was a terribly strange silence. I swallowed hard and said Max, I sent you that?

More silence. I looked at the papers on top of the desk. There were the Aesthetics exams to correct. Surely Little Lola had moved things around. And more papers and … Wait. I grabbed a paper, the one I had faxed, written with the Olivetti. I looked it over quickly.

'Damn.' Silence. 'Are you sure I sent you that?'

'Yes.'

'Forgive me.'

Max's voice sounded calmer: 'If you don't mind, I'll write the bio myself. I already have her exhibition history.'

'Thanks.'

'No, and sorry about my … nerves … It's just that the printers want the text right away if we want it to be finished before the exhibition closes.'

'If you want I'll try to …'

'No, no: I'll take care of it.'

'Thank you, Max. Give my regards to Giorgio.'

'I will. By the way: why do you write fucking with two f's?'

I hung up. That was the first warning, but I didn't know it yet. I went through the papers on the desk again. There was only that text. I reread it, concerned. On the paper I had written Sara Voltes-Epstein was born in Paris in nineteen fifty and when she was very young she met a stupid boy who fell in love with her and while he never intended any harm, he was never really able to make her happy. After some painful back and forth, after some coming and going, she agreed to live with the aforementioned stupid boy over what were long (too short) years of shared life that became the most important of my life. The most essential. Sara Voltes-Epstein died in Barcelona in the autumn of ninety-six. Proof that life is a ffucking bitch, she didn't make it to fifty years old. Sara Voltes-Epstein devoted herself to drawing life for other people's children. She only very occasionally and reluctantly exhibited her pencil and charcoal drawings, as if she only cared about the essential: the relationship with the paper via the stroke of a pencil or a stick of charcoal. She was very good, drawing. She was very good. She was.

Life went on, sadder, but alive. The appearance of the book of portraits by Sara Voltes-Epstein filled me with a profound and inexhaustible melancholy. The biographical note that Max had come up with was brief but impeccable, like everything Max does. Afterwards, things sped up: Laura didn't come back from Uppsala, just as she had threatened to do, and I locked myself up to write about evil because I had many things going through my head. But Adrià Ardèvol, no matter how desperately he wrote and how many pages he filled, knew that he wasn't making progress; that it was impossible to make progress because all he heard was the ringing of the telephone: a sustained and very unpleasant D.

'Rsrsrsrsrsrsrsrsrs.' It was the door.

'Do you mind?'

Adrià opened the door the rest of the way. That time, Bernat had gone straight to the point; he was carrying his violin and a bulky bag with half his life in it.

'Did you have another argument?'

Bernat went inside without responding to the obvious. He spent the first five days in silence, while I battled with a sterile text and against the telephone's insistence.

With that good faith, Bernat, starting on the sixth day, spent a few dinners trying to convince me to finally take the computer into my life, having me go over what Llorenç had taught me, which I had forgotten because I never put it to use.

'No, I understand the concept. But to use it … I'd have to use it and I just don't have the time.'

'You're hopeless.'

'How can I start with that when I still haven't even got used to the typewriter?'

'But you use it.'

'Because I don't have a secretary to type things up for me.'

'You don't know how much time you'd save.'

'I am a child of the codex, not of volume and scroll.'

'I don't understand you now.'

'I'm a child of the codex and not of volume.'

'Still don't understand you. I just want to save you time, with the computer.'

Bernat wasn't able to convince me and I wasn't able to talk to him about Llorenç and how he had to avoid being a father like mine. Until one day I saw him packing a suitcase; it had only been a couple of weeks since he'd sought refuge at my house. He was going back home because, according to what he told me before leaving, he couldn't live like this, which I didn't exactly understand. He left my flat half-reconciled with Tecla, and I was alone again at home. Alone forever.

I hadn't been able to get the idea out of my head until one fine day I called Max and I asked him if he would be there because I needed to see him. And I went to Cadaqués ready for everything.

The Voltes-Epstein house is large and spacious, not particularly lovely but designed to maximise the gorgeous view of the coves and the Homeric blue of the Mediterranean. It is a paradise I was entering for the first time. I was very pleased when Max hugged me as soon as I set foot in the house. I understood that as the official way of becoming part of the family, even though it was too late. The best room in the house, since Mr Voltes's death, had been turned into Max's study: an impressive library, they say the largest in Europe on wine: sunny slopes, vineyards, vines, tendrils, diseases, grapes, monographs on Cabernet, Tempranillo, Chardonnay, Riesling, Shiraz and company; history, geographic distribution, historic crises, epidemics, phylloxera, the start of varieties, the vineyard and the ideal latitude and altitude. Fog and the vineyard. The wine that comes from the cold. The raisin. Wines of the mountain and highest mountains. Green vineyards beside the sea. Cellars, caves, barrels, oak from Virginia and from Portugal, sulphites, years of ageing, humidity, darkness, cork oaks, caps, cork-making families, companies that export wine, grapes, cork, barrel wood, biographies of famous oenologists, of families of winemakers, books of photographs of the different colours of the vineyards. Types of soils. Denominations of origin; the various controlled and qualified and protected regions, with publications on legislation, lists, maps, borders and histories. The great years throughout history. Winegrowing lands, regions, districts. Interviews with oenologists and entrepreneurs. The world of wine packaging. Champagne. Cava. Sparkling wine. Gastronomy and wine. White wine, red wine, rosé, young wine, mature wine. Sweet, mellow wines. And a section devoted to sweet and dry liqueurs. Monasteries and liqueurs, chartreuse, cognacs and armagnacs, brandies, whiskies from around the world, bourbons, calvados, grappa, aguardientes, orujo, anisette, vodka; distillation as a concept. The universe of rum. Temperatures. Wine thermometers. The sommeliers who had made history ... When he entered that room, Adrià made the same face of surprise and admiration that Matthias Alpaerts had when going into his study in Barcelona.

'Impressive,' he summed up. 'You're a wine scholar and your sister would mix it with soda and pour it straight into her mouth from a pitcher.'

'It takes all kinds. But only up to a point: the pitcher isn't necessarily bad. But the soda, that's a real sin.

'Stay for dinner,' he added. 'Giorgio is an excellent cook.'

We sat down, surrounded by the world of wine and the unspoken question: what do you want, what do you want to talk about, why?, that Max was trying not to formulate. We were also surrounded by a silence mixed with sea air that conjoined one not to do anything, to let the day pass placidly and not allow anyone or any conversation to complicate our lives. It was hard to get to the point of why he'd come.

'What do you want, Adrià?'

It wasn't easy to say. Because what Adrià wanted to know was what the hell had they told Sara, eh, to make her run away from one day to the next without saying anything and without even ...

There was a silence only sliced, and then just partially, by the faint salty breeze.

'Sara didn't tell you all that?'

'No.'

'Did you ask her about it?'

'Don't ask me again, Adrià. It's best that ...'

'Well, if she said that, then I ...'

'Max, look into my eyes. She is dead. Sara is dead! And I want to know what the hell happened.'

'Perhaps you no longer need to.'

'Yes, I do. And your parents and my parents are dead too. But I have a right to know what I'm guilty of.'

Max got up, went over to the window, as if he suddenly had to check some detail of the seascape that it framed like a painting. He stood there for a while, taking in the details. Or thinking, perhaps.

'So you don't know a thing,' he concluded without turning towards me.

'I don't know what I'm supposed to know or not.'

His reticence had made me nervous. I struggled to calm myself down. And I wanted to be more precise: 'The only thing that Sara told me, when I went to see her in Paris, was that I had written her a letter saying that she was a stinking Jewess who could shove her shitty, snotty family, where the sun don't shine, that they had a big broomstick firmly up their arses.'

'Wow. I didn't know that part.'

'That was more or less what she said. But I didn't write that!'

Max made a vague gesture and left the study. After a little while he came back with a chilled bottle of white wine and two glasses.

'Let's see what you think of this.'

Adrià had to contain his anxiousness and taste that Saint-Émilion and try to distinguish the flavours that Max explained to him; they slowly emptied the first glass like that, with little sips, discussing aromas and not what their mothers had told Sara.

'Max.'

'I know.'

He served himself half a glass and drank it not like an oenologist, but like a drinker. And when he was done he clicked his tongue, said help yourself and began to say that Fèlix Ardèvol was surprised by his customer's appearance and I'll tell you, beloved, because from what Max told me you only knew the tip of the iceberg. You have a right to the details: it is my penance. So, I have to say that Fèlix Ardèvol was surprised by his customer's appearance, a man so weedy that when he wore his hat he looked like an open umbrella in the middle of the romantic garden at the Athenaeum.

'Mr Lorenzo?'

'Yes,' said Fèlix Ardèvol. 'You must be Abelard.'

The other sat in silence. He took off his hat and placed it delicately on the table. A blackbird passed shrieking between the two men and headed to the lushest patch of vegetation. The weedy man said, in a deep voice and in very artificial Spanish, that my client will send you a packet today right here. Half an hour after I've left.

'Fine. I have time.'

'When are you leaving?'

'Tomorrow morning.'

The next day, Fèlix Ardèvol took a plane, as he did so often. Once he was in Lyon, he rented a Stromberg, as he did so often, and in a few hours he was in Geneva. The same weedy man with the voice of a Lower Bulgarian was waiting for him at the Hôtel du Lac, and had him go up to a room. Ardèvol delivered the packet and the man, after delicately placing his hat on the chair, parsimoniously unwrapped it and opened the security seal. He slowly counted five wads of banknotes. It took him a good ten minutes. On a piece of paper, he took notes and made calculations, and he wrote the results meticulously into a small notebook. He even checked the bills' serial numbers.

'Such trust, it's really appalling,' muttered Ardèvol, impatient. The weedy man didn't deign to respond until he had finished what he was doing.

'What did you say?' he asked as he placed the banknotes into a small briefcase, hid the little notebook, tore up the paper with the notes, gathered the pieces and put them in his pocket.

'That such trust is really appalling.'

'As you wish.' He stood up, extended a packet he had pulled out of the briefcase and slid it over to Ardèvol.

'That is for you.'

'Now I have to start counting?'

The man gave a corpse-like smile, rescued the umbrella from the chair, put it on as a hat, and said if you want to rest, your room is paid up until tomorrrow. And he left without turning around or saying goodbye. Fèlix Ardèvol carefully counted the notes and felt satisfied with life.

He repeated the operation with slight variants. And soon he did it with new intermediaries and with increasingly fatter packets. And larger profits. What's more, he took advantage of the trips to scrutinise corners and sniff library shelves, archives and warehouses. And one day, the weedy man who went by the name of Abelard, had a voice like thunder and spoke an artificial Spanish, as if he liked to hear himself speak, made a mistake. He left the torn up pieces of the paper where he'd jotted down his sums on the table of the room in the Hôtel du Lac instead of putting them in his pocket. And that night, after patiently constructing the puzzle on the glass top, Fèlix Ardèvol could read the words on the other side. The two words: Anselmo Taboada. And some indecipherable scribblings. Anselmo Taboada. Anselmo Taboada.

Fèlix Ardèvol took two months to put a face to that name. And one rainy Tuesday he showed up at military government headquarters and waited patiently to be seen. After a very long delay, after seeing soldiers of every rank pass before him, after hearing snippets of strange conversations, they had him enter an office twice the size of his, but without a single book. Behind a desk was the slightly curious face of Lieutenant Colonel Anselmo Taboada Izquierdo. Viva Franco. Long may he live. Viva. Without further ado, they struck up an educational and profitable conversation.

'According to my calculations, Colonel, this is the amount that I have got into Switzerland for you,' said Fèlix, sliding a paper along the desk with one hand, as he had seen the man who went by the name of Abelard do with his envelope of money.

'I don't know what you are talking about.'

'I am Lorenzo.'

'You've got the wrong person.' He stood up, anxious.

'I don't have the wrong person.' Ardèvol, seated, tranquil: 'Actually, I came by headquarters because it was on my way: I'm going to see my good friend, the Civil Governor of Barcelona. A good friend of mine and also of the Captain-General here in the office next door.'

'You are a friend of Don Wenceslao?'

'A very close friend.'

As the lieutenant colonel sat back down, hesitating, Ardèvol placed one of the Civil Governor's personal business cards on the desk and said call him and he'll get you up to speed.

'There's no need for that. You can explain it to me.'

There wasn't much explanation necessary, my beloved, because Father was very skilled at luring people into his spider web: 'Oh!' sycophantic leer from Fèlix Ardèvol as he cursed him in his head. The Civil Governor picked up the terracotta broken into three pieces.

'Is this valuable?' he said.

'It's worth a fortune, Your Excellency.'

Fèlix Ardèvol made an effort not to show his irritation in front of that clumsy oaf. Wenceslao González Oliveros placed the three pieces on the desk and in his florid Spanish said, with the surprising voice of an emasculated bullfighter, I'll have it put together with good glue, like we've done with Spain after it was shattered and besmirched by rebels.

'You can't do that!' It slipped out too passionately. 'I'll restore it myself and in two days' time you'll have your gift back here in your office.'

Wenceslao González Oliveros put a hand on his shoulder and trumpeted dear Ardèvol, this pagan idol is a symbol of Spain wounded by communism, Catalanism, Judaism and Freemasonry that obliges us to make a necessary war against evil.

Ardèvol made a gesture of profound reflection that pleased the civil governor, who boldly picked up the smallest piece, an arm broken off the figure, and showed it to his disciple, explaining that there were also two Catalonias: one that is false, treacherous, cynically optimistic ...

'I've come to ask for a specific favour.'

' ... imbued with materialism and, therefore, sceptical of religious and ethical realms, and fundamentally stateless.'

'In exchange for the services I will provide you. Something that is simple for you: permission to have freedom of movement.'

'Another Catalonia is emerging, friendly and admirable, healthy, vital, confident, exquisitely sensitive, like this figure here.'

'It is a Punic terracotta piece, very dear, bought with my savings from a Jewish doctor who needed money urgently.'

'The Jewish race is perfidious, the Bible teaches us.'

'No, Your Excellency: the Catholic Church tells us that. The Bible was written by Jews.'

'You have a good point, Ardèvol. I see that you are a man of culture, such as I am. But that doesn't mean the Jews are any less perfidious.'

'No, of course not, Your Excellency.'

'And don't contradict me again,' he said with one finger lifted, just in case.

'No, Your Excellency.' Pointing to the three pieces of terracotta: 'Punic statuette, very valuable, very dear, unique, ancient: Carthaginians and Romans.'

'Yes. A Catalonia powered by intelligence, rich in illustrious, noble origins ...'

'And I can assure you that I'll make it good as new. This right here is more than two thousand years old. It is incredibly dear.'

' ... fertile with initiatives, distinguished for its chivalry and a participant with emotion, action and intuition ...'

'I only ask for an unrestricted passport, Your Excellency.'

' ... in the final fate of Spain, the mother that shelters us all. A Catalonia that knows how to use its charming dialect with moderation, prudence and private decorum, only in the home so as not to offend anyone.'

'To enter and exit the great country that is Spain, without obstacles; even though Europe is at war; precisely because Europe is at war, I can do business buying and selling.'

'Like a vulture in search of carrion?'

'Yes, Your Excellency: and I will show my immense gratitude, in the form of objects and pieces even more valuable
than this Punic terracotta statuette, for this document in my
name.'

'A spiritual, dynamic, entrepreneurial Catalonia that the
rest of Spain has so much to learn from.'

'I am merely a merchant. But I can spread joy. Yes, exactly,
without any geographical restrictions, as if I were a diplomat.
No, I'm not afraid of the dangers: I always know which doors
to knock on.'

'From the very prow, we could say, of the great ship that
spies the new horizons.'

'Thank you, Your Excellency.'

'With Franco, our beloved Caudillo, these horizons, once
blackened and vile, are now, in this radiant dawn, within our
reach.'

'Long live Franco, Your Excellency.'

'I prefer cash to statuettes, Ardèvol.'

'Deal. Long live Spain.' And to Lieutenant Colonel Anselmo
Taboada Izquierdo, a few weeks later, in his office without a
single book: 'Would you like me to call His Excellency the
Civil Governor?'

Hesitation from Lieutenant Colonel Anselmo Taboada.
Then Fèlix Ardèvol reminded him and I am also very close
friends with the Captain-General. Does the name Lorenzo
mean anything to you now?

Brief: a second at most, was all it took for the lieutenant
colonel to smile widely and say did you say Lorenzo? Sit
down, man, sit down!

'I'm already sitting down.'

Just fifteen minutes of conversation. Having lost his smile
after some negotiation, Lieutenant Colonel Anselmo Taboada
Izquierdo had to give in and Fèlix Ardèvol doubled his alloca-
tion for the next three operations plus a fixed bonus at the end
of the year of

'Granted,' said Anselmo Taboada hastily. 'Granted.'

'Long live Franco.'

'Long may he live.'

'And I will be silent as the grave, Lieutenant Colonel.'

'That would be the best thing. For your health, I mean.'

He never saw the weedy man with the umbrella for a hat who went by the name Abelard again; he was surely jailed for professional incompetence. Ardèvol, on the other hand, managed to get his new friend's colleagues, a commander and a captain, also in administration, as well as a judge and three businessmen, to entrust him with their savings so he could take them to a safe place with a better return. It seems he did that over four or five years, when Europe was at war and when it was over as well, Max told me. And he earned himself a good gang of enemies among those Francoist military men and politicians who had room for financial manoeuvring. Perhaps it was an attempt to balance the scales and avoid repercussions that led him to denounce four or five professors at the university.

Quite a panorama, my beloved: he took money from everyone and spent it buying objects for the shop or manuscripts for himself ... It seems he had a sixth sense for sniffing out those anxious to sell out or those with so many secrets and so many worries that he could pressure them without fear of consequences. Max told me that it was well known in your family because one of your uncles, an Epstein from Milan, was a victim of his. And he was so affected by Father's scams that he committed suicide. My father did all that, Sara. My father who was my father, Sara. And my mother, it seems, was clueless. It was very hard for Max to explain all of that to me, but he did it just like that, like ripping off a plaster, to get it off his chest. And now I too have vomited it out because it was a secret you only knew a part of. And Max ended up saying because of that, your father's death ...

'What, Max?'

'In our house they said that when someone went to mess with him for whatever reason, Franco's police looked the other way.'

They were silent for a long while, taking little sips of wine, looking into the void, thinking it would have been better not to have started this conversation.

'But I …' said Adrià after a long time.

'Yes, all right. You, nothing. The thing is he brought ruin to one of my parents' cousins, and his family. Ruin and death.'

'I don't know what to say.'

'You don't have to say anything.'

'Now I understand your mother better. But I loved Sara.'

'Capuleti i Montecchi, Adrià.'

'And I can't do anything to repair the evil done by my father?'

'What you can do is finish your wine. What do you want to repair?'

'You don't hold it against me.'

'My sister's love for you made that easy for me.'

'But she ran away to Paris.'

'She was a girl. Our parents forced her to go to Paris: at twenty years old you can't … They brainwashed her. It's that simple.'

Silence fell, and the sea, the splashing of the waves, the shrieks of the seagulls, the saltiness of the air entered the room. After a thousand years: 'And now when we argued, she ran away again. Here to Cadaqués.'

'And she spent her days crying.'

'You never told me that.'

'She made me promise not to.'

Adrià finished his glass of wine and thought that at lunch they would serve even more. He heard a little bell that vaguely reminded him of a nineteenth-century mail boat and Max got up, well-trained.

'We'll eat out on the terrace. Giorgio doesn't like it if we make him wait once the meal is ready.'

'Max.' He stopped, the tray of glasses in his hand. 'Did Sara ever talk about me when she was here?'

'She made me promise I wouldn't tell you about anything we discussed.'

'All right.'

Max headed towards the terrace. But before leaving the study he turned and told me my sister loved you madly. He lowered his voice so Giorgio wouldn't hear him. That's why she couldn't accept that you wouldn't return a stolen violin. That was what she couldn't understand. Should we go?

My God, my beloved.

'Adrià?'

'Yes?'

'Where are you?'

Adrià Ardèvol looked at Doctor Dalmau and blinked. He focused on the Modigliani filled with yellows that had been in front of him such a long time, the whole time.

'Pardon?' he said, a tad disorientated, searching for where he really was.

'Do you have lapses?'

'Me?'

'For quite some time you were … out of it.'

'I was thinking,' he said as an excuse.

Doctor Dalmau looked at him seriously and Adrià smiled and said yes, I've always had lapses. Everyone says I'm an absent-minded professor.' Pointing at him with an accusing finger: 'You say it too.'

Doctor Dalmau smiled slightly and Adrià continued: 'I'm not much of a professor, but I'm more and more absent-minded by the day.'

We talked about Dalmau's children, his favourite subject, subdivided into the little one, Sergi, who was no problem, but Alícia … And I had the feeling that I'd been in my friend's office for months on end. When I was already leaving, I pulled a copy of *Llull, Vico i Berlin* out of my briefcase and signed it for him. For Joan Dalmau, who has been looking out for me ever since he passed Anatomy II. With profound gratitude.

'For Joan Dalmau, who has been looking out for me every since he passed Anatomy II. With profound gratitude. Barcelona, Spring 1998.' He looked at him, pleased. 'Thanks, mate. You know I'll really treasure it.'

I already knew that Dalmau didn't read my books. He had them impeccably ordered on a high shelf in his office bookcase. To the left of the Modigliani. But I didn't give them to him for him to read.

'Thanks, Adrià,' he said, brandishing the book. And we stood up.

'There's no rush,' he added, 'but I would like to give you a thorough check-up.'

'Oh, really? Well, if I'd known that, I wouldn't have brought you the book.'

The two friends parted with a laugh. As hard as it is to believe, Dalmau's teenage daughter was still on the phone, saying of course he's a total ratbag, I've told you that a million times, girl!

Out on the street I was greeted by Vallcarca's damp night. Few cars passed and those that did splattered the puddles in that thoughtless way of theirs. If I couldn't explain my horror to my friends, I was beyond hope. You had been dead for some time when you came to talk to me and I still haven't been able to accept it. I live clinging to rotted driftwood from a shipwreck; I cannot row towards any destination. I am at the mercy of any gust of wind thinking of you, thinking why couldn't it have gone some other way, thinking of the thousand missed opportunities to love you more tenderly.

It was that Tuesday night in Vallcarca, without an umbrella and with a hard rain falling, that I understood that I am entirely an exaggeration. Or worse: I am entirely an error, beginning with having been born into the wrong family. And I know that I can't delegate the weight of thought and the responsibility for my actions to gods or friends. But thanks to Max, besides knowing more details about my father, I know something that keeps me afloat: that you loved me madly. Mea culpa, Sara. Confiteor.

# VII

## ... USQUE AD CALCEM

Let us try, if we can, to enter into death
with open eyes ...*

Marguerite Yourcenar

---

* Marguerite Yourcenar, *Memoirs of* Hadrian, trans. Grace Frick, Farrar,
Straus & Giroux, 1963.

# VII

## USQUE AD CALCEM

## 58

There are starting to be too many skeletons in this house, Adrià thought his father had grumbled. And he strolled through the Creation of the Universe without seeing the books' spines. And at work, classes had lost their vitality because all his desire was limited to sitting before Sara's self-portrait, in the study, contemplating your mystery, my beloved. Or, also in silence, before the Urgell in the dining room, as if wanting to witness the impossible flight of the sun on the Trespui side. And very occasionally he looked half-heartedly at the pile of papers and some days he picked them up, sighed and wrote a few lines or reread, sceptically, the work he'd done the day or the week before and found it painfully insignificant. The thing is he didn't know what to do about it. Because even his hunger had abandoned him.

'Adrià, listen.'

'Yes.'

'You haven't eaten anything in two days.'

'Don't worry: I'm not hungry.'

'Well, of course I worry.'

Caterina had just come into the study, taken Adrià by one arm and started to pull on him.

'What are you doing?' Adrià raising his voice, disconcerted.

'I don't care if you start bellowing. You're coming to the kitchen with me, right now.'

'Hey! Leave me be, woman!' indignant, Adrià Ardèvol.

'No. Sorry, but no.' More indignant than him, and shouting louder: 'Have you looked at yourself in the mirror?'

'There's no need.'

'Come on, one foot in front of the other.' Brusque, authoritative voice.

He was Haïm Epstein, and Little Lola was the Hauptsturmführer taking him to barracks number twenty-six against the orders of Sturmbannführer Barber because someone had invented a terribly fun rabbit hunting game. Hauptsturmführer Katharine forced him into the kitchen and, instead of half a dozen frightened Hungarian women, he found rice soup and noodles and a steak with a tomato cut in two. Hauptsturmführer Katharine made him sit at the little table and Haïm Ardèvol was hungry for the first time in many days and he started eating, head bowed, as if he feared the Hauptsturmführer's recrimination.

'Delicious,' about the soup.

'Would you like more?'

'Yes. Thank you.'

During dinner, Katharine, with the visor of her cap hiding her gaze, standing, with the staff threateningly tapping the leg of her shiny boot, watched to make sure the prisoner didn't escape from the kitchen. She even got him to have a yogurt for dessert. When he finished the prisoner said thank you, Little Lola, then got up and left the kitchen.

'Caterina.'

'Caterina. Shouldn't you be home by now?'

'Yes. But I don't want to show up tomorrow and find you stiff as a board in the corner.'

'Oh, please. What an imagination.'

'No, sir. Stiff as a board: deader than the Dead Sea.'

Adrià went back to the study because he thought that his problem was some pages he had written that he didn't entirely believe in. Too many things for him to deal with on his own. And the days kept passing. The months, too, slow, endless. Until one day he heard a curt spitting onto the floor and he said what do you want, Carson?

'Maybe this is enough already, don't you think?'

'There's never enough when you feel …'

'How do you feel?'

'What do I know?'

'How.'

'Yes, go on.'

'If you'll allow me …'

'Go ahead, come on, Black Eagle.'

'The wind on the open plain will do your sickly spirit good.'

'Yes. I thought about taking a trip, but I don't know where to go or what to do.'

'It would be enough to just accept the invitations to Oxford, Rennes, Tübingen and I don't know where else.'

'Konstanz.'

'That was it.'

'You're right.'

'The hunt will be fruitful if the noble warrior offers up his valiant chest to the new challenges of war and the hunt.'

'I understand already, thank you. Thank you both.'

I listened to my advisers and I took some air along the plains of Europe in search of noble exploits. The anxiety over his writing returned shyly, hesitantly, perhaps thanks to the travel and the encouragement he got from those who asked when are you going to publish another book, Ardèvol?

And in the end, a pile of pages written on one side, that he wasn't at all convinced about. I've lost all steam. I don't know where evil is and I don't know how to explain my agnostic perplexity. I lack the tools of the philosopher to continue the journey. I insist on searching for the place where evil resides and I know that it is not inside a person. Inside many people? Is evil the fruit of a perverse human will? Or not: does it come from the Devil, who inoculates those he wishes to with it, as poor weepy-eyed Matthias Alpaerts seemed to think? Evil is that the Devil doesn't exist. And God, where is He? Abraham's severe God, Jesus's inexplicable God, cruel and loving Allah ... Ask the victims of any perverse act. If God exists, his coldness in the face of evil's consequences would be shocking. What do the theologians say? As poetic as they make it, in the end, deep down, they come up against its limits: absolute evil, relative evil, physical evil, moral evil, the evil of guilt, the evil of pain ... My God. It would be laughable, if evil wasn't accompanied by pain. And natural catastrophes, are they evil as well? Are they another evil? And the pain that they provoke, is that another pain?

'How.'

'What.'

'You've lost me.'

'Me too, Black Eagle,' murmured Adrià, before the pile of manuscript pages in his neat but illegible handwriting. He got up and walked around the study, to loosen up his ideas. Do you know what was wrong with me, Sara? Instead of reasoning, I was shouting. Instead of thinking, I cried or laughed, and that's not the way to do scholarship. And then I thought seven, two, eight, zero, six, five.

I opened my father's safe, which I hadn't visited in years. Seven, two, eight, zero, six, five. I was curious because I couldn't remember what I had stored there. I found a couple of thick envelopes with various documents belonging to my parents that were almost certainly of no use to anyone: receipts from a thousand years ago, hastily written notes that had lost their urgency after fifty years. And some stock certificates and things like that, which I put to one side so the accountant could have a look at them and tell me what to do with them. And a sole, sad, blue folder, the manuscript in Aramaic that Father had written too many years ago. That message with delayed effects. If Father could now know that I had got rid of Vial, he would surely scream and give me a hard smack to the nape of the neck. In the same folder there was another, also solitary, amulet: the letter that Isaiah Berlin had sent me thanks to Bernat's manoeuvrings. Thank you, Bernat, my friend, who will be reading these pages before the others – if all goes according to plan – and you'll be able to cut out this final expansiveness.

And there was still something in one corner. A Kodak envelope. I opened it with curious fingers: inside were photos that I had taken of my Storioni the day I gave it back to Matthias Alpaerts. I didn't even remember that, after I'd had the photos developed, I'd hidden them all in the safe. I was only thinking, and I still think it today, of the uncertainty over having done the stupidest thing in the world by allowing myself to be taken in by a story that was too dramatic to be fake. I went through the photos one by one: they were those kind that have the month and year they were taken stamped right on them. I went through them: its face, its back, its ribs, its lovely scroll, the f-holes; and the one that I took by getting right up to the f-hole: you could barely make out the Laurentius Storioni cremonensis me fecit inside. Oof. I looked at the next photo and my mouth dropped open: it was a photo you had taken of yourself in the mirror on your wardrobe. Like a kind of self-portrait, perhaps prior to drawing yourself. It was dated two years earlier than the others. Had you forgotten about it? Or maybe you'd started the roll and left it inside the camera, waiting to finish the reel before taking it to be developed? There were another couple of photos taken by you. Adrià's vision blurred and he had to make an effort to calm himself down. It was him, working, with his head leaning towards the desk, writing. A photo taken in secret when we were no longer speaking to each other. You were irritated and angry with me, but you took my picture secretly. Now I realise what I hadn't thought enough about: the fight hurt you more than it hurt me, because you started it. And what if the stroke was caused by having to suffer such pressure?

The third photo was a drawing on the easel in your studio. A drawing I've never seen and that Sara never mentioned to me. A drawing saved in a photo because you had probably torn it into a thousand pieces. Poor thing. I struggled to hold back my tears and I thought that the next day, if I could find the negatives, I would have an enlargement made. I looked at it under the table's magnifying glass. They were six studies, in search of a face. Six drawings, increasingly more complete, in three-quarter views, of a baby's face. I couldn't say if they were drawings made with the baby in front of her or if they were an exercise in remembering Claudine's face, what she could recall of it. Or if she'd had the cold bloodedness to draw her dead daughter. All this time that photograph had been in the safe beside the others. The photograph of your pain. Because once you had lived through the drama, you were still able to draw it; perhaps you didn't know that it is impossible to resist. Look at Celan. Look at Primo Levi. Drawing, like writing, is reliving. And as if wanting to corroborate it with applause, the bloody telephone rang and I began to tremble, as if I were worse off than I already was. I forced myself, on the orders of Dalmau in fact, to undertake the gruelling task of lifting the receiver: 'Hello.'

'Hey, Adrià. It's Max.'

'Hi.'

'How are you?'

'Fine.' Five seconds. 'And you?'

'Fine. Listen: do you want to come to a wine tasting in the Priorat?'

'Wow ...'

'I've decided to write a book ... One with a lot of photos, eh, not like yours.'

'On what?'

'On the tasting process ...'

'It must be difficult to put such fragile sensations into words.'

'Poets do it.'

Now I will ask him what he knew about Claudine and Sara's grief.

'Max Voltes-Epstein, the poet of wine.'

'Are you up for it?'

'Listen. I wanted to ask you a question that ...' He ran a hand over his bald skull and was in time to stop himself. 'Sure, why not: when is it?'

'This weekend: at the Quim Soler Centre.'

'Will you pick me up?'

'Deal.'

Max hung up. I had no right to rummage around in the life of a good man like Max. And maybe he didn't know anything about it. Because Sara's secrets could have been secrets from everyone. What a shame: I would have been able to help you bear your pain. That seems a tad pretentious. Or bear a part of it. I would have liked to be your refuge and I wasn't able to and I didn't know enough about it. At best, I sheltered you from a few scattered showers but not a single storm.

I had asked Dalmau how fast the process is, how much of a rush we're in, how urgent is it, you understand?, and he pressed his lips together to help him think.

'Every case is different.'

'Obviously, I'm interested in my case.'

'They'll have to do some tests. What we have now are signs.'

'Is it really irreversible?'

'With today's medicine, yes.'

'Bugger.'

'Yeah.'

They were silent. Doctor Dalmau looked at his friend, seated on the other side of his office desk, refusing to bury his head between his shoulders, thinking urgently, refusing to focus his eyes on the yellows of the Modigliani.

'I'm still working. I read well.'

'You yourself have admitted that you have inexplicable lapses. That you go blank. That ...'

'Yes, yes, yes ... But that happens to everyone at my age.'

'Sixty-two, today, isn't that old. You've had a lot of warning signs. You haven't even noticed many of them.'

'Let's say that this is the third warning.' Silence. 'Can you give me a date?'

'I don't know. There isn't a date; it is a process that advances at its own pace, which is different in each individual. We will monitor you. But you have to ...' He stopped.

'I have to what?'

'To make arrangements.'

'What do you mean?'

'Put your affairs ... in order.'

'You mean a will?'

'Um ... I don't know how ... You don't have anyone, do you?'

'Well, I do have friends.'

'You don't have anyone, Adrià. You have to leave everything in order.'

'That's brutal, man.'

'Yes. And you'll have to hire someone, so you spend the minimum amount of time alone.'

'I'll cross that bridge when I come to it.'

'All right. But come every fifteen days.'

'Deal,' I said, imitating Max.

That was when I made the decision I had begun to ponder on that rainy night in Vallcarca. I took the three hundred pages where I had worn my fingers to the bone struggling to discuss evil, which I already knew was ineffable and mysterious like beliefs, and on the back side, like some sort of palimpsest, I started the letter that seems to be drawing to a close as I reach the hic et nunc. Despite Llorenç's efforts, I didn't use the computer, which lies, obedient, on one corner of my desk. These pages are the day-to-day record of something written chaotically, in many tears mixed with a little ink.

All these months I have been writing frenetically, in front of your self-portrait and the two landscapes you gave me: your subjective vision of my Arcadia and the small lobed apse of Sant Pere del Burgal. I have observed them obsessively and I know their every detail, every line and every shadow. And every one of the stories they've evoked in me. I have written steadily in front of this altar made up of your drawings, as if in a race between memory and oblivion, which will be my first death. I wrote without thinking, pouring onto the paper everything I could put into words, and trusting that, afterwards, someone with the soul of a palaeontologist, Bernat if he accepts the task, can decipher it in order to be able to give it to I don't even know whom. Perhaps this is my testament. Very disorganised, but a testament.

I began with these words: 'It wasn't until last night, walking along the wet streets of Vallcarca, that I finally comprehended that being born into my family had been an unforgivable mistake.' And, now that it's written, I understand that I had to begin at the beginning. In the beginning there was always the word. Which is why I've now returned to the beginning and reread: 'Up until last night, walking along the wet streets of Vallcarca, I didn't comprehend that being born into that family had been an unforgivable mistake.' I lived through that long ago; and much time has slipped away since I wrote it. Now is different. Now is the following day.

*After much paperwork with notaries and lawyers, and three
or four consultations with the cousins in Tona, who didn't
know how to thank him for everything he was doing for Adrià,
Bernat went to see this Laura Baylina in Uppsala.*

'What a shame, poor Adrià.'

'Yes.'

'Forgive me, but I feel like I'm about to start crying.'

'Go ahead.'

'No. What is it Adrià sent you here for?'

*As he blew on his scalding hot tea, Bernat explained the
details of the will that concerned her.*

An Urgell? The one in the dining room?

'Oh, you know it?'

'Yes. I was over at his house a few times.'

*How many things you hid from us, Adrià. I had never really
met her before today. How many things we friends hide from
each other, thought Bernat.*

*Laura Baylina was pretty, blonde, short, nice, and she said
she wanted to think over whether she would accept it or not.
Bernat told her that it was a gift, there were no strings.*

'Taxes. I don't know if I'll be able to pay the taxes for accepting that painting. Or whatever you call this bequeathing thing.
Here in Sweden I'd have to ask for a loan, inherit, pay the taxes
and sell the painting to liquidate the loan.'

*He left Baylina thinking over her decision, with the tea still
steaming, and Bernat Plensa returned to Barcelona in time to
ask for permission from management to miss two orchestra
rehearsals for serious family matters, fearlessly enduring the
manager's disapproving looks and took the second plane in the
last two months, this time to Brussels.*

*It was a nursing home for the elderly, in Antwerp. At recep-
tion, he smiled at a fat woman who was handling the telephone
and a computer at the same time and waited for her to finish
the call she was on. When the woman hung up, he exaggerated*

*his smile, said English or French, the receptionist answered
English and he asked for Mr Matthias Alpaerts. The woman
looked at him, intrigued. It was actually more like she was observing him. Or that's how he felt: intently observed.*

*'Who did you say you were looking for?'*

*'Mr Matthias Alpaerts.'*

*The woman thought it over for a few moments. Then she
checked the computer. She looked at it for some time. She
answered the phone twice to transfer calls and continued consulting the computer. Until she said of course, Alpaerts! She hit
another key, looked at the screen and looked at Bernat: 'Mr
Alpaerts died in 1997.'*

*'Oh... I ...'*

*He was about to leave, but he got a crazy idea: 'Could I have
a look at his file?'*

*'You aren't family, are you?'*

*'No, madam.'*

*'Can you tell me what brings you? ...'*

*'I wanted to buy a violin from him.'*

*'Now I recognise you!' she exclaimed, as if it had been both-
ering her.*

*'Me?'*

*'Second violin in the Antigone quartet.'*

*For a few seconds, Bernat Plensa dreamed of glory. He
smiled, flattered.*

*'What a good memory you have,' he said finally.*

*'I'm very good with faces,' she responded. 'Besides, such a tall
man ...' Timidly: 'But I don't remember your name.'*

*'Bernat Plensa.'*

*'Bernat Plensa ...' She held out her hand to shake his.
'Liliana Moor. I heard you in Ghent two months ago. Mendelssohn, Schubert, Shostakovich.'*

*'Wow ... I ...'*

*'I like to be in the front row, right by the musicians.'*

*'Are you a musician?'*

*'No. I'm just a music lover. Why do you want information
about Mr Alpaerts?'*

*'Because of the violin ...' He hesitated for a few seconds. 'I*

*just wanted to see a photo of his face.'* He smiled. *'Please ...
Liliana.'*

*Miss Moor thought it over for a few moments and in honour
of the Antigone quartet she turned the computer screen so that
Bernat could see it. Instead of a thin man with weepy eyes,
bushy white hair and protruding ears – that electric presence
he had seen for thirty silent seconds in Adrià's study when he
went to drop off the computer – on the flat screen before him
he had a sad man, but who was bald and fat, with round eyes
the colour of jet like one of his daughters, he couldn't remember
which. Fucking sneaky bastards.*

*The receptionist turned the screen back to its original po-
sition and Bernat began to sweat anxiously. Just in case, he
repeated I wanted him to sell me his violin, you know?*

*'Mr Alpaerts never had any violin.'*

*'How many years was he here?'*

*'Five or six.'* She looked at the screen and corrected herself:
*'Seven.'*

*'Are you sure that the man in the photo was Matthias
Alpaerts?'*

*'Completely. I've been working here for twenty years.'* Satisfied: *'I remember all the faces. The names, that's another
story.'*

*'Did he have any relative who ...'*

*'Mr Alpaerts was alone.'*

*'No, but did he have any distant relative who ...'*

*'Alone. They had killed his family in the war. They were Jews.
Only he survived.'*

*'Not a single relative?'*

*'He was always telling his dramatic story, poor man. I think
in the end he went mad. Always telling it, over and over, compelled by ...'*

*'By guilt.'*

*'Yes. Always. To everyone. His story had become his reason
for living. Living only to explain how he had two daughters ...'*

*'Three.'*

*'Three? Well, three daughters named so-and-so, so-and-so
and so-and-so and who ...'*

'Amelietje with the jet-black hair, Truu with the tresses the colour of fine wood and Juliet, the littlest, blonde like the sun.'

'Did you know him?' Her eyes wide with surprise.

'In a way. Are there many people who know that story?'

'In this home, yes. The ones who are still alive, of course. We're talking about a few years ago now.'

'Of course.'

'Bob did a very good imitation of him.'

'Who's that?'

'He was Alpaerts's roommate.'

'Is he alive?'

'Very alive. He keeps us on our toes.' She lowered her voice, totally taken by that second violin of the Antigone Quartet, tall as a Maypole. 'He organises secret domino matches between the residents.'

'Could I ...'

'Yes. I'm going against all the rules ...'

'In the name of music.'

'Exactly! In the name of music.'

In the waiting room there were five magazines in Dutch and one in French. And a cheap reproduction of a Vermeer; a woman beside a window who looked, shocked, towards Bernat, as if he were about to enter the room inside the painting.

The man arrived five minutes later. Thin, with weepy eyes and bushy white hair. From his expression, he hadn't recognised Bernat.

'English or French?' smiled Bernat.

'English.'

'Good morning.'

Bernat had before him the man from that afternoon, the man who had convinced Adrià ... I told you, Adrià, he thought. They saw you a mile away. Instead of going right over and throttling him, he smiled and said have you ever heard of a Storioni violin named Vial?

The man, who hadn't sat down, headed towards the door. Bernat kept him from leaving the little room, standing between him and the door, covering the exit with his whole body.

'You stole the violin from him.'

'Do you mind telling me who you are?'

'Police.'

He pulled out his ID card as a member of the Barcelona Symphony Orchestra and National Orchestra of Catalonia and added: 'Interpol.'

'My God,' said the man. And he sat down, defeated. And he explained that he didn't do it for the money.

'How much did they give you for it?'

'Fifty thousand francs.'

'Hell's bells.'

'I didn't do it for the money. And they were Belgian francs.'

'Then why did you do it?'

'Matthias Alpaerts drove me batty, every day during the five years we shared a room he would tell me about his bloody little daughters and his mother-in-law with a chest cold. Every day he would tell me, looking out the window, not even seeing me. Every single day. And he got sick. And then those men showed up.'

'Who were they?'

'I don't know. From Barcelona. One was thin and the other was young. And they told me we've heard you do a very good impression of him.

'I'm an actor. Retired, but an actor. And I play the accordion and the sax. And the piano a little.'

'Let's see how your impression is.'

They took him to a restaurant, they let him eat and try a white wine and a red. And he looked at them, puzzled, and asked them why don't you just talk to Alpaerts?

'He's on his last legs. He won't live long.'

'What a relief it'll be to not hear him talk about his coughing mother-in-law.'

'Don't you feel sorry for the poor man?'

'Matthias has been saying he wants to die for sixty years. How can I feel sorry for him when he finally gets his wish?'

'Come on, Bob: show us what you can do.'

And Bob Mortelmans started to say because imagine you are having lunch at home, with your Berta, your sick mother-in-law *and the three lights of your life, Amelietje, the eldest, who was turning seven that day; Truu, the middle daughter, with hair the colour of mahogany, and Juliet, the littlest one, blonde like the sun. And out of nowhere, they bust down the front door and all these soldiers burst in shouting raus, raus and Amelietje, who said what does raus mean, Papa?, and I couldn't stop them and I didn't do a single thing to protect them.*

'*Perfect. That's enough.*'

'*Hey, hey, hey! I can do more than ...*'

'*I said that's perfect. Do you want to make some serious dough?*'

'*And since I said yes, they put me on a plane and in Barcelona we rehearsed a couple of times, with variations; but it was always the true story of Matthias the pain in the arse.*'

'*And your friend, meanwhile, was lying in bed, dying.*'

'*He wasn't my friend. He was a broken record. When I got back to Antwerp he was already dead.*' *And, rehearsing insouciance with the tall policeman:* '*As if he'd missed me, you know?*'

*Bernat was quiet. And Bob Mortelmans made a run for the door. Bernat, without getting up from his chair or moving a muscle, said try to run away and I'll break your spine. Understood?*

'*Yup. Perfectly.*'

'*You're scum. You stole the violin from him.*'

'*But he didn't even know that anyone had it ...*'

'*You're scum. Selling out for a hundred thousand francs.*'

'*I didn't do it for the money. And they were fifty thousand. And Belgian.*'

'*And you also robbed poor Adrià Ardèvol.*'

'*Who's that?*'

'*The man in Barcelona you hoodwinked.*'

'*I swear I didn't do it for the money.*'

*Bernat looked at him, curious. He made a gesture with his head, as if inviting him to continue speaking. But the other man was silent.*

'*Why did you do it then?*'

'*It was ... it was an opportunity ... It was ... the role of a lifetime. That's why I said yes.*'

'You were also well paid.'

'That's true. But because I embellished it. And, besides, I had to improvise because that bloke struck up a conversation and so, after the monologue, I had to improvise the whole conversation.'

'And?'

'And I nailed it.' Proud: 'I was able to completely inhabit the character.'

Bernat thought now I'll throttle him. And he looked around, to see if there were any witnesses. Meanwhile, Bob Mortelmans returned to his favourite role, fired up by the policeman's admiring silence. Performing, overdoing it slightly: 'Perhaps I survived until today and am able to tell you all this because I was a coward on Amelietje's birthday. Or because that rainy Saturday, in the barracks, I stole a crumb of clearly mouldy bread from old Moshes who came from Vilnius. Or because I crept away when the Blockführer decided to teach us a lesson and let loose with the butt of his rifle, and the blow that was meant to wound me killed a little boy whose …'

'That's enough!'

Bernat got up and Bob Mortelmans thought he was about to thrash him. He shrank down in his chair, cowering, thoroughly prepared to answer more questions, to answer each and every one that Interpol agent wanted to ask him.

*Bernat said open your mouth and Adrià opened it as if he were Llorenç at a year old; he gave him a spoonful and said, yum, semolina soup, eh? Adrià stared at Bernat and said nothing.*

*'What are you thinking?'*

*'Me?'*

*'You.'*

*'I don't know.'*

*'Who am I?'*

*'That guy.'*

*'Here, have another spoonful. Come on, open your mouth, it's the last one. That's it, very good.'*

*He uncovered the second course and said oh, how nice, boiled chicken. Do you like that?*

*Adrià placed his gaze on the wall, indifferent.*

*'I love you, Adrià. And I'll spare you the story of the violin.'*

*He looked at him with Gertrud's gaze, or with the gaze that Adrià saw Sara giving him when she looked at him with Gertrud's gaze. Or with the gaze that Bernat thought Sara gave Adrià when she looked at him with Gertrud's gaze.*

*'I love you,' repeated Bernat. And he picked up a quite sad piece of pale chicken thigh and said ooh how nice, how nice. Come on, open up your mouth, Llorenç.*

*When they'd finished the supper, Jònatan came to take the tray and said do you want to lie down?*

*'I can take care of that, if that's all right.'*

*'Fine: if you need help, just whistle.'*

*Once they were alone, Adrià scratched his head and sighed. He looked at the wall with an empty stare. Bernat shuffled through his briefcase and pulled out a book.*

*'The Problem of Evil,' he read from the cover. 'Adrià Ardèvol.'*

*Adrià looked into his eyes and then at the book. He yawned.*

*'Do you know what this is?'*

*'Me?'*

*'Yes. You wrote it. You asked me not to publish it, but in the*

*university they assured me that it was well worth it. Do you remember it?'*

Silence. Adrià, *uncomfortable. Bernat took his hand and felt his friend calming down. Then he explained to him that the edition had been done by Professor Parera.*

*'I think she did a very good job. And she was advised by Johannes Kamenek, who, from what I've seen, is a real workhorse. And loves you very much.'*

*He stroked his hand and Adrià smiled. They remained like that for some time, in silence, as if they were sweethearts. Adrià's eyes landed on the book's cover, apathetically, and he yawned.*

*'I gave each of your cousins in Tona a copy. They were very excited. Before New Year's they'll come visit.'*

*'Very good. Who are they?'*

*'Xevi, Rosa and one more whose name escapes me.'*

*'Ah.'*

*'Do you remember them?'*

*As he did every time Bernat asked him that question, Adrià clicked his tongue as if he were peeved or perhaps offended.*

*'I don't know,' he admitted, uncomfortable.*

*'Who am I?' said Bernat for the third time that evening.*

*'You.'*

*'And what's my name?'*

*'You. That guy. Wilson. I'm tired.'*

*'Well, come on, to bed, it's quite late. I'll leave your book on the bedside table.'*

*'Fine.'*

*Bernat grabbed the chair to push it over to the bed. Adrià half-turned, somewhat frightened. Timidly: 'Now I don't know ... if I'm supposed to sleep in the chair or in the bed. Or in the window.'*

*'In the bed, come on. You'll be more comfortable.'*

*'No, no, no: I think it's the window.'*

*'Whatever you say, dear friend,' said Bernat, pushing the chair over to the bed. And then he added: 'Forgive me, forgive me, forgive me.'*

He was awoken by the intense cold entering through all

the cracks in the window. It was still dark. He struck the flint until he managed to light the candle's wick. He put on his habit and his travel cape on top of that and he went out into the narrow corridor. A hesitant light emerged from one of the cells, on the side overlooking the Santa Bàrbara knoll. With a shiver of cold and grief he headed towards the church. The taper that had illuminated the coffin where Friar Josep de Sant Bartomeu was resting had burned down. He put his candle in its place. The birds, feeling dawn near, began to chirp despite the cold. He fervidly prayed an Our Father, thinking of the salvation of the good father prior's soul. The twinkling light of his candle provoked a strange effect on the paintings in the apse. Saint Peter, Saint Paul and ... and ... and the other apostles, and the Madonna and the severe Pantocrater seemed to be moving along the wall, in an un-hurried, silent dance.

Chaffinches, greenfinches, goldfinches, blackbirds and sparrows were singing the arrival of the new day as the monks had sung the praises of the Lord over centuries. Chaffinches, greenfinches, goldfinches, blackbirds and sparrows seemed joyous at the news of the death of the prior of Sant Pere del Burgal. Or perhaps they were singing the joy of knowing he was in paradise, because he had been a good man. Or perhaps God's little birdies couldn't care less and were singing because that was all they knew how to do. Where am I? Five months living in the fog and only once in a while does a little light come on, reminding me that you exist.

'Friar Adrià,' he heard behind him. He lifted his head. Brother Julià approached him, his candle flickering.

'We will have to bury him immediately after Matins,' he said.

'Yes, of course. Have the men arrived from Escaló?'

'Not yet.'

He got up and stood beside the other monk, looking at the altar. Where am I. He tucked his chilblained hands into the wide sleeves of his habit. They weren't chaffinches, green-finches, goldfinches, blackbirds nor sparrows, just two sad monks because that was the last day of monastic life at their monastery after so many centuries of continued existence. It had been several months since they'd sung; they just recited their prayers and left the singing to the birds and their oblivious joy. Closing his eyes, Friar Adrià murmured the words that, over centuries, had served to break the vast silence of the night: 'Domine, labia mea aperies.'

'Et proclamabo laudem tuam,' responded Friar Julià in the same murmuring tone.

That Christmas night, the first one without Missa in Nocte, the two lay friars could only pray Matins. Deus, in adiutorium meum intende. It was the saddest chanting of Matins in all the centuries of monastic life at Sant Pere del Burgal. Domine, ad adiuvandum me festina.

The conversation with Tito Carbonell was unexpectedly relaxed. As they ordered, Tito admitted he was a coward, that it had been more than a year since he'd gone to the nursing home to visit Zio Adriano.

'Give it a try.'

'It's too depressing. I don't have your mettle.' Picking up the menu and signalling the waiter: 'By the way, I appreciate the time and effort you devote to him.'

'I consider it my obligation as his friend.'

Tito Carbonell skilfully navigated the menu, ordered and ate his first course with few comments. And there was a somewhat uncomfortable silence when the plate was empty. Until Tito decided to break it: 'And what, exactly, did you want?'

'To talk about Vial.'

'Vial? Zio Adriano's violin?'

'Yes. I went to Antwerp a few months ago, to visit Mr Bob Mortelmans.'

Tito received those words with a spirited laugh: 'I thought you'd never bring it up!' he said. 'What could you possibly want to know from me?'

They waited for the waiter to place the second course in front of them; then, since Bernat remained in silence, Tito, looking him in the eyes, said: 'Yes, yes, it was my idea; brilliant, yes. Since I know Zio Adriano, I knew that everything would be easier with Mr Mortelmans's help.' He pointed at him with his knife. 'And I was right!'

Bernat ate in silence, looking at him without saying a word. Tito Carbonell continued: 'Yes, yes, Mr Berenguer sold the Storioni to the highest bidder; yes, we made a bundle; do you like that codfish?; isn't it the best you've ever had?; yes, it's a shame to have such a fine violin locked up in a safe. Do you know who bought it from us?'

'Who?' He heard the question coming too much from his stomach, like a shriek.

'Joshua Mack.' Tito waited for some reaction from Bernat, who was making titanic efforts to control himself. 'You see? It ended up going to a Jew.' Laughing: 'Justice, right?'

Bernat counted to ten to keep from doing anything rash. To take the sting out of his rage he said you disgust me. Tito Carbonell didn't even bat an eyelash.

'And I don't care what Mack does with it. I confess that I did it all for the money.'

'But I am going to report you to the police now,' said Bernat, staring him in the eye, brimming with rage. 'And don't think I can be bought.'

Tito Carbonell chewed, attentive to his meal; he wiped his lips with a napkin, took a tiny sip of wine and smiled.

'Me, buy you? You?' He smacked his lips, irked. 'I wouldn't give you a red tuppence for your silence.'

'And I wouldn't accept it. I am doing this for the memory of my dear friend.'

'I wouldn't make too many speeches, if I were you, Mr Plensa.'

'Does it bother you that I have principles?'

'No, please. It's very sweet. But you should know that I know what I need to know.'

Bernat looked him in the eye. Tito Carbonell smiled again and said I've moved some pieces as well.

'Now you've lost me.'

'Your editor has been working on your new book for about a month now.'

'I'm afraid that's none of your business.'

'Oh, but it is! I'm in it and everything! With another name and as a supporting character, but I'm in it.'

'How do you know that? ...'

Tito Carbonell moved his face right up to Bernat's, and said is it a novel or an autobiography? Because if Zio Adriano wrote it, it's an autobiography; if you wrote it, it's a novel. I understand that the changes you made were very slight ... It's a shame you changed the names ... That'll make it hard to know who is who. The only name you kept was Adrià's. It's strange. But since you had the cheek to appropriate the entire text, we *have to conclude that it's a novel. He clicked his tongue, as if he were worried. 'And then it turns out that we are all pure fiction. Even me!' He patted his body, shaking his head, 'What can I say? It's frustrating ...'*

*He put the napkin down on the table, suddenly serious: 'So don't talk to me about principles.'*

*Bernat Plensa was left with a bite of suddenly dry cod in his mouth. He heard Tito say I kept half the profits of the sale of the violin. But you kept the whole book. Zio Adriano's whole life.*

*Tito Carbonell pushed back his chair, carefully observing Bernat. He continued: 'I know that the book you supposedly wrote is going to come out in a couple of months. Now you decide whether we set up a press conference or we just let it go.'*

*He opened his arms, inviting him to make up his mind. Since Bernat didn't move, he went on: 'Would you like dessert?' He snapped his fingers at the waiter. 'They do a fabulous flan here.'*

When Bernat went into cinquantaquattro Wilson had just finished putting some brand-new tennis shoes on Adrià, who was sitting in the wheelchair.

'Look how handsome he is,' said the nurse.

'Gorgeous. Thank you, Wilson. Hello, Adrià.'

Adrià didn't recognise his name. It seemed that he was smiling. The room was the same as ever, although it had been a long time since he'd been there.

'I brought you this,' he said.

He gave him a fat book. Adrià took it in his hands, somewhat fearful. He looked at Bernat, not really knowing what to do with it.

'I wrote it,' he said to him. 'It's hot off the presses.'

'Oh, how nice,' said Adrià.

'You can keep it. And forgive me, forgive me, forgive me.'

Adrià, seeing the stranger with his head bowed and almost crying, began to cry.

'Is it my fault?'

'No, not at all. I'm crying because … Just because.'

'Sorry.' He looked at him, concerned. 'Come on, don't cry, sir.'

Bernat pulled a CD case out of his pocket, took out the CD and put it in Adrià's player. He took him by the hands and said listen to this, Adrià: it's your violin. Prokofiev. His second concerto. Soon the lament that Joshua Mack extracted from Adrià's Storioni could be heard. They were like that for twenty-six minutes. Holding hands, listening to the concert and the applause on the live recording.

'This CD is for you. Tell Wilson it's yours.'

'Wilson!'

'Not now, that's OK. I'll tell him myself.'

'Booooy!' insisted Adrià.

As if he were waiting for the moment, as if he were spying on them, Wilson stuck his nose into the room: 'What is it? Are you all right?'

'It's just that … I brought him this CD and this book, too. All right?'

'I'm sleepy.'

'But I just got you dressed, my prince!'

'I need to make a poo poo.'

'Oh, you're such a pill.' To Bernat: 'Do you mind? It'll be five minutes.'

Bernat went out into the hallway with the book. He headed towards the terrace and flipped through the pages. A shadow came up beside him: 'Nice, eh?' Doctor Valls pointed to the book: 'It's yours, right?'

'It just …'

'Oy!' the doctor interrupted. 'I have no time to read.' And as if it were a threat: 'But I promise that I will read it one day.' Joking: 'I don't know much about literature, but I will review it mercilessly.'

There's no fear of that, thought Bernat as he watched the doctor head off. And his mobile buzzed. He went into a corner of the terrace because you weren't allowed to use your mobile inside.

'Hello.'

'Where are you?'

'At the hospital.'

'Do you want me to come there?'

'No, no, no,' he said, a little too hastily. 'I'll be at your house at two.'

'You really don't want me to come?'

'No, no, no … there's no need, really.'

'Bernat.'

'What?'

'I'm proud of you.'

'Me … Why?'

'I just finished the book. From what little I know, you've captured your dear friend perfectly…'

'Weeelll … thanks, really.' Recomposing himself: 'I'll be at your house at two.'

'I won't put on the rice until you get here.'

'All right, Xènia: I have to go now.'

*'Give him a kiss from me.'*

*As he hung up, musing on the impossible figure of the Klein bottle, Wilson pushed Adrià out onto the terrace in his wheelchair. Adrià put up one hand for a visor, as if the sun was blinding.*

*'Hello,' said Bernat. To Wilson: 'I'll take him to the corner with the wisteria.'*

*Wilson shrugged his shoulders and Bernat dragged Adrià towards the corner with the wisteria. From there you could see a good stretch of the city of Barcelona and the sea in the background. Klein. He sat down and opened the book to its final pages. And he read:* I lived through that long ago; and much time has slipped away since I wrote it. Now is different. Now is the following day.

And why have I explained all that? Because if Friar Miquel hadn't had a pang of bad conscience at the cruelties of the holy inquisitor, he wouldn't have fled and he wouldn't have become Friar Julià, the one with the maple seeds in his pocket, and Guillaume-François Vial wouldn't have sold his Storioni to the Arcan family at an exorbitant price.

'A Storioni.'

'I don't know that name.'

'Don't tell me you've never heard of Laurent Storioni!'

'No.'

'Purveyor to the courts of Bavaria and Weimar,' he improvised.

'Never heard of him. Don't you have anything by Ceruti or Pressenda?'

'For the love of God!' Exaggeratedly scandalised, Monsieur Vial. 'Pressenda learned his trade from Storioni!'

'And Stainer?'

'Right now I don't have anything.' He pointed to the violin that rested on the table. 'Try it. For as many hours as you'd like, Heer Arcan.'

Nicolas Arcan took off his wig and picked up the violin with a displeased or perhaps disdainful expression, but dying to give it a try. His extremely agile fingers, using his customary bow and strange playing position, began to make it speak an extraordinary sound almost from the very first note. Guillaume-François Vial had to go through the humiliation of seeing a Flemish violinist play by heart one of disgusting Tonton Leclair's sonatas; but he didn't show his feelings because the sale was at stake. After an hour, his bald pate and forehead sweaty, Nicolas Arcan gave the violin back to Guillaume-François Vial, who assumed that he had him convinced.

'No. I don't like it,' said the violinist.

'Fifteen thousand florins.'

'I don't want to buy it.'

Monsieur Vial got up and took the instrument. He put it away carefully in its case, which still bore a dark stain of unknown origin.

'I have a customer a half hour from Antwerp. Will you forgive me if I leave without greeting your wife?'

'Ten thousand.'

'Fifteen thousand.'

'Thirteen.'

'Fourteen thousand.'

'Deal, Monsieur Vial.' And with the price already set, Heer Arcan admitted in a soft voice: 'Exceptional acoustics.'

Vial left the case on the table and opened it up again. He saw Heer Arcan's gluttonous eyes. He whispered to himself: 'If I know one thing it's that this instrument will bring much joy.'

Nicolas Arcan grew old beside the violin and passed it down to his daughter, a spinet player, and she to her nephew Nestor, the composer of the famous estampes, and Nestor to his son, and his son to a nephew, and like that until, after many decades, Jules Arcan made a series of mistakes on the stock market and had to squander his inheritance. And the coughing mother-in-law lived in Antwerp, as did Arcan. Wonderful sound, proportions, touch, shape … A true Cremona. And if Father had had scruples, if Voigt had been an honourable man and hadn't shown an interest in the violin; if … I wouldn't be talking about all this. If I hadn't had the Storioni, I wouldn't have made friends with Bernat. I wouldn't have met you at

a concert in Paris. I would be someone else and I wouldn't
be talking to you now. I know: I explained everything out
of order, but it's just that my head is a bit unfurnished these
days. I only just reached here, with little chance of going back
over what I've written. I don't have the heart to look back; on
one hand, because I cried as I wrote some of these things; and
on the other, because I can tell that with each passing day a
chair or a cornucopia disappears from inside my head. And I
am slowly becoming a character from a Hopper, looking out
a window or out at life, with an empty gaze and my tongue
thick from so much tobacco and whisky.

*Bernat looked at Adrià, who seemed entertained by a wis-
teria leaf that fell close to his head. After a second's hesitation,
he dared to say: 'Does any of what I'm reading ring a bell with
you?'*

*Adrià, after a few moments of uncertainty, replied guiltily:
'Should it ring a bell, sir?'*

*'Please, don't call me sir: I'm Bernat.'*

*'Bernat.'*

*But the wisteria leaf was more interesting. And Bernat con-
tinued reading where he'd left off, which was when Adrià was
saying* I want to tell you something that has been obsessing
me, my beloved: after spending my life trying to ponder the
cultural history of humanity and trying to play an instrument that resisted being played, I mean that we are, all of us,
we and our penchants, ffucking random. And the facts that
weave together actions and events, the people we meet, those
we happen upon or never meet at all, are also just random. It
is all chance: or perhaps it's not chance, but it's just already
drawn. I don't know which affirmation to stick with because
both are true. And if I don't believe in God, I can't believe in
a previous drawing, whether it is called destiny or something
else.

My beloved: it is late, night-time. I am writing before your
self-portrait, which retains your essence because you were
able to capture it. And before the two landscapes of my life. A
neighbour, Carreres on the third, I imagine, remember that
tall blond?, is closing the door to the lift, too noisily for this

time of night. Goodbye, Carreres. All these months I've been writing on the other side of the manuscript where I tried, unsuccessfully, to reflect on evil. Wasting the time I devoted to it. Paper scribbled on both sides. On one, my failed reflection; on the other, the narration of my facts and my fears. I could have told you a thousand things about my life, things that are inaccurate but true. And I could talk to you and I could conjecture or invent things about my parents' lives, my parents whom I hated, judged, undervalued and, now, miss a little.

This narration is for you, because you are alive somewhere, even if it is just in my story. It's not for me, who won't make it to tomorrow. I feel like Anicius Manlius Torquatus Severinus Boethius, who was born in Rome around four hundred seventy-five, and received many honours for his life devoted to the study of the philosophy of the classics; I earned my doctorate in nineteen seventy-six at the University of Tübingen and then I taught at the University of Barcelona, a fifteen-minute walk from my home. I have published several works, the fruit of my reflections out loud in class. I was appointed to political posts, which brought me fame and then disgrace, and imprisoned at the Ager Calventianus in Pavia before it was called Pavia; I await the judges' verdict, which I already know will be my death sentence. Which is why I stop time by writing *De consolatione philosophiae* while I wait for the end to come, writing these memories to you, which can be called by no other name than their own. My death will be slow, not like Boethius's. My murderous emperor is not named Theodoric, but rather Alzheimer the Great.

Through my fault, through my fault, through my most grievous fault, they taught me at school, I who am not even baptised, I don't think. And they spiced it up with an incredible story about original sin. I am guilty of everything; if need be, of all the earthquakes, fires and floods in history. I don't know where God is. Not mine, not yours, not the God of the Epsteins. The sensation of loneliness is excruciating, my beloved, my dearest beloved.

There is no redemption for the sinner. At most, forgiveness from the victim. But often one can't live with the forgiveness either. Müss decided on reparation, without waiting for forgiveness from anyone, not even God. I feel guilty of many things and I've tried to go on living. Confiteor. I write with much difficulty, wearily, bewildered because I've started to have worrisome lapses. From what the doctor tells me, when these pages are printed, my beloved, I will already be a vegetable unable to ask for anyone's help – not out of love but out of compassion – to give up on living.

*Bernat looked at his friend, who returned his gaze in silence. For a few moments, he was afraid because it looked like Gertrud's gaze. Despite everything, he kept reading* I wrote all of this in a desperate attempt to hold onto you. I descended to the infernos of memory and the gods allowed me to rescue you with one, impossible condition. Now I understand Lot's wife, who also turned at the wrong moment. I swear that I turned to make sure you wouldn't trip on the staircase's uneven step. The implacable gods of Hades took you back to the inferno of death. I didn't know how to resuscitate you, beloved Eurydice.

'*Eurydice.*'

'*What.*'

'*No, nothing, sorry.*'

*Bernat was silent for a few minutes. Cold sweat. Fear.*

'*Do you understand me?*'

'*Huh?*'

'*Do you know what this is, that I'm reading?*'

'*No.*'

'*Really?*'

'*Boooy!*'

'*One moment,*' *said Bernat, making up his mind.* '*I'll be right back.*' *Without the slightest irony:* '*Don't move. And don't call for Wilson, I'll be back in a second.*'

'*Wilson!*'

*With his heart about to leap out of his chest, Bernat burst into the doctor's office and blurted out* Doctor Valls, *he corrected my pronunciation.*

*The doctor looked up from the document he was reading. It took him a few seconds to process the information, as if his patients' slowness was contagious:* '*A reflex.*' *He looked at his*

*papers and then at Bernat. 'Mr Ardèvol cannot remember any-*
*thing. Not at this point. Just a coincidence. Unfortunately for*
*all of us.'*

*'But he said Eurydice when I said Eurydice.'*

*'Random chance. I assure you it's just a coincidence.'*

*Bernat returned to his friend's side, in the corner with the*
*wisteria, and he said forgive me, Adrià: I'm very anxious*
*because ...*

*Adrià looked at him somewhat askance.*

*'Is that good or bad?' he replied, slightly scared.*

*Bernat thought my poor friend, all his life spent reasoning*
*and reflecting and now he can only formulate one question*
*about morality. Is that good or bad? As if life could be summed*
*up as doing evil or not doing it. Maybe he's right. I don't know.*

*They remained in silence for a while longer until Bernat,*
*in a loud, clear voice, continued his reading with* now I've
finally reached the end. It has been several months of intense
writing, of reviewing my life; I was able to reach the end, but
I no longer have the strength to order it as the canons dictate.
The doctor explained that my light will gradually fade out,
at a speed they can't predict because every case is different.
We have decided, that as long as I'm still me, that what's her
name, uh ... that she will work full-time because they say I
need someone to keep an eye on me. And soon we'll have to
hire two more people to complete the cycle ... You see how
I'm spending the money from the sale of the shop? I decided
that while I still have a shred of consciousness I don't want to
be separated from my books. When I've lost that, I'm afraid I
won't care about anything any more. Since you aren't here to
take care of me; since Little Lola left hastily many years ago
now ... I had to make the preparations myself. In the nursing
home in Collserola, close to my beloved Barcelona, they will
take care of my body when I've passed over to another world,
which may or may not be one of shadows. They assure me that
I won't miss my reading. It's ironic that I spent my entire life
trying to be aware of the steps I took; my entire life lugging
around my many guilts, and the guilts of humanity, and in the
end I will leave without knowing that I'm leaving. Farewell,

Adrià. I'll say it now, just in case. I look around me, the study where I've spent so many hours. 'But one moment still, let us gaze together on these familiar shores, on these objects which doubtless we shall not see again ... Let us try, if we can, to enter into death with open eyes ...' says Emperor Adrià before dying. Small soul. Supple, gentle, wandering soul, Sara, my body's companion: you went first to the pale, frozen, naked places. Bugger. I pick up the telephone and stop writing. I dial my friend's mobile number: it's been months since I've spoken with him, locked up here, writing to you.

'Hey! It's Adrià. How are you? Oh, were you already sleeping? No: what time is it? What? Four in the mor ...? Ohh, sorry! ... Yikes ... listen, I want to ask you for a favour and explain a couple of things to you. Yes. Yes. No, you can come over tomorrow: well, today. Yeah, it's best if you come here. Any time that's good for you, of course. I'm not going anywhere. Yeah, yeah. Thank you.'

I just explained the hic et nunc of what I'm living through. I had to write that last part in the present, which is very distressing. I am almost at the end of my text. Outside, the rosy fingers of dawn paint the still-dark sky. My hands are stiff with cold. I move the pages I've written, the inkwell and the writing implements and I look out the window. What cold, what loneliness. The brothers from Gerri will climb the path that I'll glimpse when dawn wins the battle. I look at the Sacred Chest and I think that there's nothing sadder than having to give up a monastery that has never stopped singing God's praises. I can't stop feeling guilty over this disaster, my beloved. Yes, I know. We all end up dying ... But you, thanks to the generosity of my friend, who has been patient enough to be my friend all these years, you will continue living in these lines every time someone reads these pages. And one day, they tell me, my body will also decompose. Forgive me, but, like Orpheus, I was unable to go beyond. Resurrection is only for the gods. Confiteor, my beloved. L'shanah haba'ah b'Yerushalayim. Now is the following day.

This long letter that I've written you has reached its end. Je n'ai fait celle-ci plus longue que parce que je n'ai pas eu le loisir de la faire plus courte. After so many intense days, I have reached my rest. The autumn enters. End of the inventory. Now it is the following day forever. I turned on the television and saw the weatherman's sleepy face assuring me that in the next few hours there will be a sudden drop in temperature and sporadic showers. It made me think of Szymborska, who said that even though it's mostly sunny, those who continue living are advised to have an umbrella. I, of course, won't need one.

*In the room beside cinquantaquattro, some weak children's voices sing a carol followed by kindly applause and a woman's voice: 'Happy Christmas, Papa.' Silence. 'Children, say happy Christmas to Granddad.'*

*And then the running started. Someone, perhaps Jònatan, emerged from cinquantaquattro frightened: 'Wilson!'*

*'Yes.'*

*'Where is Mr Ardèvol?'*

*'Where do you think? In cinquantaquattro.'*

*'What I'm saying is that he's not in there.'*

*'For the love of God! Where else could he be?'*

*Wilson opened the door to the room, tense inside and saying sweetie, my prince. And there was no sweetie and no prince. Not in the bed, not in the chair, not by the wall that itches me. Wilson, Jònatan, Olga, Ramos, Maite, Doctor Valls, Doctor Roure, after fifteen minutes Doctor Dalmau, and Bernat Plensa and all the staff who weren't on duty, looking on terraces, in the toilets of every room and in the staff toilets, in offices, in every room, in every wardrobe of every room, God, God, God, how can this be when the poor man can barely walk? Ónde estás? They even called Caterina Fargues to see if she had any idea. And then they widened the search to include the area around the home when the case had already been put in the hands of the police and they were already searching Collserola Park, behind a tree, beside a fountain, lost in the thick forest among the wild boars or, God forbid, at the bottom of one of the lakes, God help us. And Bernat thought teño medo dunha cousa que vive e que non se ve. Teño medo á desgracia traidora que ven, e que nunca se sabe ónde ven. Adrià, ónde estás. Because Bernat was the only one who could know the truth.*

That day, after burying the father prior, they had definitively abandoned the monastery and left it alone, for the woodland mice who, despite the monks, had already ruled there for centuries – owners without Benedictine habits – of the sacred spot. Like the bats who made their home in the small counter-apse of Saint Michael, above the counts' tombs. But in a question of a few days the mountain's wild animals would also begin to rule there and there was nothing they could do about it.

'Friar Adrià.'

'Yes.'

'You don't look well.'

He looked around him. They were alone in the church. The front door was open. Not long before, when the sun had already set, the men from Escaló had buried the prior. He looked at his open palms, in a gesture he quickly deemed too theatrical. He glanced at Friar Julià and said, in a soft voice, what am I doing here?

'The same thing I am. Preparing to close up Burgal.'

'No, no … I live … I don't live here.'

'I don't understand you.'

'What? How?'

'Sit down, Brother Adrià. Unfortunately, we are in no hurry.' He took him by the arm and forced him to sit on a bench. 'Sit,' he repeated, even though the other man was already sitting.

Outside, the rosy fingers of dawn painted the still-dark sky and the birds carried on with their racket. Even a rooster from Escaló joined in on the fun, from a distance.

'*Adrià, my prince! How could you manage to hide so well?*' In a whisper: '*What if he's been kidnapped?*'

'*Don't say such things.*'

'What do we have to do now?'

Friar Julià looked, puzzled, at the other monk. He remained in worried silence. Adrià insisted, saying eh?

'Well … prepare the Sacred Chest, close up the monastery, put away the key and pray for God to forgive us.' After an eternity: 'And wait for the brothers from Santa Maria de Gerri to arrive.' He observed him, perplexed: 'Why do you ask?'

'Flee.'

'What did you say?'

'That you must flee.'

'Me?'

'You. They are coming to kill you.'

'Brother Adrià …'

'Where am I?'

'I'll bring you a bit of water.'

Friar Julià disappeared through the door to the small cloister. Outside, birds and death; inside, death and the snuffed
out candle. Friar Adrià gathered in devout prayer almost until
the light took possession of the Earth, which was once again
flat, with mysterious limits he could never reach.

'*Go through each and every one of his friends. And when I
say each and every one, I mean each and every one!*'

'*Yes, sir.*'

'*And don't give up on the search operation. Widen the circle
to include the entire mountain. And Tibidabo. And the amusement park too.*'

'*This patient has reduced mobility.*'

'*Doesn't matter: search the entire mountain.*'

'*Yes, sir.*'

Then he shook his head as if awakening from a deep sleep,
got up and went to a cell to collect the Sacred Chest and the key
he'd used to close the door to the monastery during Vespers
for thirty years. Thirty years as the doorkeeper brother of
Burgal. He went through each of the empty cells, the refectory
and the kitchen. He also went into the church and the tiny
chapterhouse. And he felt that he was the sole person guilty
of the extinction of the monastery of Sant Pere del Burgal.
With his free hand he beat on his chest and said confiteor,
Dominus. Confiteor: mea culpa. The first Christmas without
Missa in Nocte and without the praying of Matins.

He collected the little box of pine cones and fir and maple
seeds, the desperate gift of a disgraced woman striving to be
forgiven for the lack of divine hope implicit in her abominable act of suicide. He contemplated the little box for a few
moments, remembering the poor woman, the disgraced Wall-
eyed Woman of Salt; murmured a brief prayer for her soul in

case salvation was possible for the desperate, and placed the little box in the deep pocket of his habit. He picked up the Sacred Chest and the key and went out into the narrow corridor. He was unable to resist the impulse to take a last stroll through the monastery, all alone. His footsteps echoed in the corridor beside the cells, the chapterhouse, the cloister … He finished his walk with a glance into the tiny refectory. One of the benches was touching the wall, chipping away at the dirty plaster. Out of habit, he moved the bench. A rebellious tear fell from his eye. He wiped it away and left the grounds. He closed the door to the monastery, inserted the key and made two turns that resonated in his soul. He put the key in the Sacred Chest and sat down to wait for the newcomers who were climbing wearily, despite having spent the night in Soler. My God, what am I doing here when …

*Bernat thought it's impossible, but I can't think of any other explanation. Forgive me, Adrià. It's my fault, I know, but I can't give up the book. Confiteor. Mea culpa.*

Before the shadows had shifted much, Friar Adrià got up, dusted off his habit and walked a few steps down the path, clinging to the Sacred Chest. Three monks were coming up. He turned, with tears in his heart, to say farewell to the monastery and he began his descent to save his brothers the final stretch of the steep slope. Many memories died with that gesture. Where am I? Farewell, landscapes. Farewell, ravines and farewell, glorious babbling waters. Farewell, cloistered brothers and centuries of chanting and prayers.

'Brothers, may peace be with you on this day of the birth of Our Lord.'

'May the Lord's peace be with you as well.'

Three strangers. The tallest one pulled back his hood, revealing a noble forehead.

'Who is the dead man?'

'Josep de Sant Bartomeu. The father prior.'

'Praise be the Lord. So you are Adrià Ardèvol.'

'Well, I …' He lowered his head: 'Yes.'

'You are dead.'

'I've been dead for some time.'

'No: now you will be dead.'

The dagger glimmered in the faint light before sinking into his soul. The flame of his candle went out and he neither saw nor lived anything more. Nothing more. He wasn't even able to say where am I because he was no longer anywhere.

Matadepera, 2003–2011

I deemed this novel definitively unfinished
on 27 January, 2011, the anniversary of
the liberation of Auschwitz.
During the years in which the novel grew in my life,
I asked many people for help and opinions.
There are so many of you,
and I've been pestering you for so many years,
that I'm terrified I'll leave out someone's name.
So I would instead like to once again count
on your generosity as I make a generic
acknowledgement in which, I hope, each and every one
of you will see yourselves included and reflected.
I am deeply grateful to you all.

# Dramatis Personae

Adrià Ardèvol i Bosch
Sara Voltes-Epstein
Bernat Plensa i Punsoda
Black Eagle
    Valiant Arapaho Chief
Sheriff Carson
    Of Rockland
Fèlix Ardèvol i Guiteres
    Adrià Ardèvol's father
Carme Bosch
    Adrià Ardèvol's mother
Adrià Bosch
    Adrià Ardèvol's grandfather
Vicenta Palau
    Adrià Ardèvol's grandmother
Little Lola (Dolors Carrió i Solegibert)
    Carme Bosch's trusted maid
Big Lola
    Little Lola's mother
Caterina
Angeleta
    Seamstress to the Ardèvol i Bosch family
Cecília
    Fèlix Ardèvol's employee
Mr Berenguer
    Fèlix Ardèvol's employee
Signor Falegnami / Mr Zimmermann
    Concierge at the Ufficio della Giustizia e della Pace
Doctor Prunés and Mrs Prunés
    Visitors

Tecla
  Bernat Plensa's wife
Llorenç Plensa
  Bernat Plensa's son
Xènia
  Journalist friend of Bernat Plensa
Mrs Trullols
  Violin teacher to Adrià Ardèvol and Bernat Plensa
Master Joan Manlleu
  Adrià Ardèvol's violin teacher
Herr Casals, Herr Oliveres, Herr Romeu, Mr Prats, Signor
Simone, Doctor Gombreny
  Adrià Ardèvol's language instructors
Father Anglada, Father Bartrina, Mr Badia, Brother Climent
  Adrià Ardèvol's teachers at the Jesuit School on Casp
Street
Esteban, Xevi, Quico, Rull, Pedro, Massana, Riera, Torres,
Escaiola, Pujol, Borrell
  Adrià Ardèvol's classmates at the Jesuit School on Casp
Street
Mr Castells and Antònia Marí
  Piano accompanists
Uncle Cinto, from Tona
  Fèlix Ardèvol's brother
Aunt Leo
  Cinto Ardèvol's wife
Rosa, Xevi and Quico
  Adrià Ardèvol's cousins
Eugen Coşeriu
  Linguist, professor at the University of Tübingen
Johannes Kamenek
  Professor at the University of Tübingen
Doctor Schott
  Professor at the University of Tübingen
Kornelia Brendel
  Adrià Ardèvol's classmate at Tübingen
Sagrera
  Lawyer

Calaf
  Notary
Morral
  Bookseller at the Sant Antoni Market
Caterina Fargues
  Little Lola's replacement
Gensana
  Adrià Ardèvol's classmate at the university
Laura Baylina
  Professor at the University of Barcelona and Adrià
Ardèvol's girlfriend
Eulàlia Parera, Todó, Dr. Bassas, Dr. Casals, Omedes
  Professors at the University of Barcelona
Heribert Bauçà
  Editor
Mireia Gràcia
  Presenter of one of Bernat Plensa's books
Saverio Somethingorother
  Luthier in Rome
Daniela Amato
  Carolina Amato's daughter
Albert Carbonell
  Daniela Amato's husband
Tito Carbonell Amato
  Daniela Amato and Albert Carbonell's son
Jascha Heifetz
  World famous violinist
Master Eduard Toldrà
  Musical composer and director of the Barcelona
Symphony Orchestra
Rachel Epstein
  Sara Voltes-Epstein's mother
Pau Voltes
  Sara and Max Voltes-Epstein's father
Max Voltes-Epstein
  Sara Voltes-Epstein's brother
Giorgio
  Max Voltes-Epstein's friend

Franz-Paul Decker
    Director of the Barcelona Symphony Orchestra and
National Orchestra of Catalonia (OBC)
Romain Gunzbourg
    French horn in the OBC
Isaiah Berlin
    Philosopher and historian of ideas
Aline de Gunzbourg
    Isaiah Berlin's wife
Pau Ullastres
    Luthier in Barcelona
Doctor Dalmau
    Doctor and Adrià Ardèvol's friend
Doctor Valls
Doctor Real
Jònatan, Wilson and Dora
    Nurses
Plàcida
    Adrià Ardèvol's maid
Eduard Badia
    Director of the Artipèlag Gallery
Bob Mortelmans
    Matthias Alpaerts's roommate in the nursing home
Gertrud
    Accident victim
Alexandre Roig
    Gertrud's husband
Helena and Àgata
    Dora's friends
Osvald Sikemäe
    Gertrud's brother
Aadu Müür
    Àgata's ex-boyfriend
Eugen Müss
    Doctor at Bebenbeleke
Turu Mbulaka
    Tribal chief

Elm Gonzaga
  Detective

## VIC AND ROME 1914–1918
Josep Torras i Bages
  Bishop of Vic
Félix Morlin, from Lieja
  Fèlix Ardèvol's classmate
Drago Gradnik, from Ljubljana
  Fèlix Ardèvol's classmate
Faluba, Pierre Blanc, Levinski and Daniele D'Angelo, S. J.
  Fèlix Ardèvol's professors at the Pontificia Università
Gregoriana
Carolina Amato
Saverio Amato
  Carolina Amato's father
Sandro
  Carolina Amato's uncle
Muñoz
  Bishop of Vic
Father Ayats
  Episcopal secretary

## BARCELONA, '40s AND '50s
Commissioner Plasencia
Inspector Ocaña
Ramis
  The best detective in the world
Felipe Acedo Colunga
  Civil Governor
Abelardo
  Client of Fèlix Ardèvol
Anselmo Taboada
  Lieutenant Coronel
Wenceslao González Oliveros
  Civil Governor

## GIRONA, SANTA MARIA DE GERRI, SANT PERE DEL BURGAL (14th AND 15th CENTURIES)
Nicolau Eimeric
  Inquisitor General
Miquel de Susqueda
  Secretary to the Inquisitor
Ramon de Nolla
  Assassin for the Inquisitor
Julià de Sau
  Monk at Sant Pere del Burgal
Josep de Sant Bartomeu
  Father Prior of Sant Pere del Burgal
Wall-eyed Man of Salt
Wall-eyed Woman of Salt
  Wife of the Wall-eyed Man of Salt
Friar Maur and Friar Mateu
  Monks at the monastery of Santa Maria de Gerri
Josep Xarom, from Girona
  Jewish doctor
Dolça Xarom
  Josep Xarom's daughter
Emanuel Meir, from Varna
  Dolça Xarom's descendant
The twins

## PARDÀC, CREMONA, PARIS (17th AND 18th CENTURIES)
Jachiam Mureda
  Tonewood tracker
Mureda
  The father of the Mureda family
Agno, Jenn, Max, Hermes, Josef, Theodor and Micurà. Ilse, Erica, Katharina, Matilde, Gretchen and Bettina
  Jachiam Mureda's siblings
Bulchanij Brocia
  The fattest man in Moena
The Brocias of Moena
  Enemies of the Muredas of Pardàc

Brother Gabriel
  Monk at the abbey of La Grassa
Blond of Cazilhac
  Jachiam Mureda's assistant
Antonio Stradivari
  Luthier
Omobono Stradivari
  Son of Antonio Stradivari
Zosimo Bergonzi
  Luthier, disciple of Antonio Stradivari
Lorenzo Storioni
  Luthier, disciple of Zosimo Bergonzi
Maria Bergonzi
  Zosimo Bergonzi's daughter
Monsieur La Guitte
  Instrument dealer
Jean-Marie Leclair, l'Aîné
  Violinist and composer
Guillaume-François Vial
    Jean-Marie Leclair's nephew
Jewish goldsmith

**AL-HISW**
Amani Alfalati
Azizzadeh Alfalati
  Amani's father
Azizzadeh's wife
Alí Bahr
  Merchant
Honourable Qadi
The twins

**DURING THE THIRD REICH AND WORLD WAR II**
Rudolph Höss
    SS-Obersturmbannführer (lieutenant colonel),
commander of Auschwitz
Hedwig Höss
  Rudolph Höss's wife

Aribert Voigt
SS-Sturmbannführer (commander), doctor
Konrad Budden
SS-Obersturmführer (lieutenant), doctor
Brother Robert
Novitiate at the abbey of Saint Benedict of Achel
Bruno Lübke
SS soldier
Mathäus
Rottenführer (section leader)
Uncle Haïm Epstein
Rachel Epstein's uncle
Gavriloff
Deportee
Heinrich Himmler
Reichsführer
Elisaveta Meireva
Unit 615428
Hansch
Gefreiter (corporal)
Barabbas
Oberscharführer (sergeant)
Matthias Alpaerts, from Antwerp
Berta Alpaerts
Matthias Alpaerts's wife
Netje de Boeck
Matthias Alpaerts's mother-in-law with a chest cold
Amelia, Trude and Julia Alpaerts
Matthias Alpaerts's daughters
Franz Grübbe, from Tübingen
SS-Obersturmführer (lieutenant) of the SS Division Reich
Lothar Grübbe
Franz Grübbe's father
Anna Grübbe
Lothar Grübbe's wife
Herta Landau, of Bebenhausen
Konrad Budden and Franz Grübbe's cousin

Vlado Vladić
 Serbian partisan
Danilo Janicek
 Partisan
Timotheus Schaaf
 Hauptsturmführer (captain) of the SS Division Reich
The twins

the midst of this discussion when the prosecutor, Mr. Bosch, entered the room and then asked Bob to excuse himself.

"Mandela," he said, after Bob had left, "I did not want to come to court today. For the first time in my career, I despise what I am doing. It hurts me that I should be asking the court to send you to prison." He then reached out and shook my hand, and expressed the hope that everything would turn out well for me. I thanked him for his sentiments, and assured him that I would never forget what he had said.

The authorities were on alert that day. The crowd inside the courtroom seemed even larger than on the first day of the case. All one hundred fifty "non-European" seats were filled. Winnie was present, in Xhosa dress, as well as a number of my relatives from the Transkei. Hundreds of demonstrators stood a block from the courthouse, and there seemed to be as many policemen as spectators.

When I walked in the courtroom, I raised my right fist and called out *"Amandla!"* which was met by a mighty *"Ngawethu!"* The magistrate pounded his gavel and cried for order. When the court was quiet, he summed up the charges, after which I had my opportunity to speak. My plea in mitigation lasted over an hour. It was not a judicial appeal at all but a political testament. I wanted to explain to the court how and why I had become the man I was, why I had done what I had done, and why, if given the chance, I would do it again.

Many years ago, when I was a boy brought up in my village in the Transkei, I listened to the elders of the tribe telling stories about the good old days before the arrival of the white man. Then our people lived peacefully, under the democratic rule of their kings and their *amapakati* [literally "insiders," but meaning those closest in rank to the king], and moved freely and confidently up and down the country without let or hindrance. The country was our own, in name and right. We occupied the land, the forests, the rivers; we extracted the mineral wealth beneath the soil and all the riches of this beautiful country. We set up and operated our own government, we controlled our own arms and we organized our trade and commerce. The elders would tell tales of the wars fought by our ancestors in defense of the Fatherland, as well as the acts of valor by generals and soldiers during these epic days. . . .

The structure and organization of early African societies in this country fascinated me very much and greatly influenced the evolution of my political outlook. The land, then the main means of production, belonged to the whole tribe and there was no individual ownership whatsoever. There were no classes, no rich or poor and no exploitation of man by man. All men were free and equal and this was the foundation of government. Recognition of this general principle found expression in the constitution of the council, variously called "Imbizo" or "Pitso" or "Kgotla," which governs the affairs of the tribe. The council was so completely democratic that all members of the tribe could participate in its deliberations. Chief and subject, warrior and medicine man, all took part and endeavored to influence its decisions. It was so weighty and influential a body that no step of any importance could ever be taken by the tribe without reference to it.

There was much in such a society that was primitive and insecure and it certainly could never measure up to the demands of the present epoch. But in such a society are contained the seeds of revolutionary democracy in which none will be held in slavery or servitude, and in which poverty, want and insecurity shall be no more. This is the history which, even today, inspires me and my colleagues in our political struggle.

I told the court how I had joined the African National Congress and how its policy of democracy and nonracialism reflected my own deepest convictions. I explained how as a lawyer I was often forced to choose between compliance with the law and accommodating my conscience.

I would say that the whole life of any thinking African in this country drives him continuously to a conflict between his conscience on the one hand and the law on the other. This is not a conflict peculiar to this country. The conflict arises for men of conscience, for men who think and who feel deeply in every country. Recently in Britain, a peer of the realm, Earl [Bertrand] Russell, probably the most respected philosopher of the Western world, was sentenced and convicted for precisely the type of activities for which I stand before you today — for following his conscience in defiance of the law, as a protest against the nuclear weapons policy being pursued by his own government. He could do no other than to oppose the law and to suffer the consequences for it. Nor can I. Nor can many Africans in this country. The law as it is applied, the law as it has been developed over a long period of history, and especially the law as it is written and designed by the Nationalist government is a law which, in our views, is immoral, unjust, and intolerable. Our consciences dictate that we must protest against it, that we must oppose it and that

we must attempt to alter it. . . . Men, I think, are not capable of doing
nothing, of saying nothing, of not reacting to injustice, of not protesting
against oppression, of not striving for the good society and the good life
in the ways they see it.

I recounted in detail the numerous times the government had
used the law to hamper my life, career, and political work, through
bannings, restrictions, and trials.

I was made, by the law, a criminal, not because of what I had done, but
because of what I stood for, because of what I thought, because of my
conscience. Can it be any wonder to anybody that such conditions make
a man an outlaw of society? Can it be wondered that such a man, having
been outlawed by the government, should be prepared to lead the life
of an outlaw, as I have led for some months, according to the evidence
before this court?

It has not been easy for me during the past period to separate myself
from my wife and children, to say good-bye to the good old days when,
at the end of a strenuous day at an office I could look forward to joining
my family at the dinnertable, and instead to take up the life of a man
hunted continuously by the police, living separated from those who are
closest to me, in my own country, facing continually the hazards of
detection and of arrest. This has been a life infinitely more difficult than
serving a prison sentence. No man in his right senses would voluntarily
choose such a life in preference to the one of normal, family, social life
which exists in every civilized community.

But there comes a time, as it came in my life, when a man is denied
the right to live a normal life, when he can only live the life of an outlaw
because the government has so decreed to use the law to impose a state
of outlawry upon him. I was driven to this situation, and I do not regret
having taken the decisions that I did take. Other people will be driven
in the same way in this country, by this very same force of police persecution and of administrative action by the government, to follow my
course, of that I am certain.

I enumerated the many times that we had brought our grievances
before the government and the equal number of times that we were
ignored or shunted aside. I described our stay-away of 1961 as a last
resort after the government showed no signs of taking any steps to
either talk with us or meet our demands. It was the government
that provoked violence by employing violence to meet our nonviolent demands. I explained that because of the government's actions
we had taken a more militant stance. I said that I had been privileged

throughout my political life to fight alongside colleagues whose abilities and contributions were far greater than my own. Many others had paid the price of their beliefs before me, and many more would do so after me.

Before sentencing, I informed the court that whatever sentence the state imposed, it would do nothing to change my devotion to the struggle.

I do not believe, Your Worship, that this court, in inflicting penalties on me for the crimes for which I am convicted should be moved by the belief that penalties will deter men from the course that they believe is right. History shows that penalties do not deter men when their conscience is aroused, nor will they deter my people or the colleagues with whom I have worked before.

I am prepared to pay the penalty even though I know how bitter and desperate is the situation of an African in the prisons of this country. I have been in these prisons and I know how gross is the discrimination, even behind the prison wall, against Africans. . . . Nevertheless these considerations do not sway me from the path that I have taken nor will they sway others like me. For to men, freedom in their own land is the pinnacle of their ambitions, from which nothing can turn men of conviction aside. More powerful than my fear of the dreadful conditions to which I might be subjected in prison is my hatred for the dreadful conditions to which my people are subjected outside prison throughout this country. . . .

Whatever sentence Your Worship sees fit to impose upon me for the crime for which I have been convicted before this court, may it rest assured that when my sentence has been completed I will still be moved, as men are always moved, by their conscience; I will still be moved by my dislike of the race discrimination against my people when I come out from serving my sentence, to take up again, as best I can, the struggle for the removal of those injustices until they are finally abolished once and for all. . . .

I have done my duty to my people and to South Africa. I have no doubt that posterity will pronounce that I was innocent and that the criminals that should have been brought before this court are the members of the government.

When I had finished, the magistrate ordered a ten-minute recess to consider the sentence. I turned and looked out at the crowd before exiting the courtroom. I had no illusions about the sentence I would receive. Exactly ten minutes later, in a courtroom heavy with tension, the magistrate pronounced sentence: three years for inciting people to strike and two years for leaving the country without a passport; five years in all, with no possibility of parole. It was a stern sentence and there was wailing among the spectators. As the court rose, I turned to the gallery and again made a clenched fist, shouting *"Amandla!"* three times. Then, on its own, the crowd began to sing our beautiful anthem, *"Nkosi Sikelel' iAfrika."* People sang and danced and the women ululated as I was led away. The uproar among the gallery made me forget for a moment that I would be going to prison to serve what was then the stiffest sentence yet imposed in South Africa for a political offense.

Downstairs, I was permitted a brief good-bye to Winnie, and on this occasion she was not at all grim: she was in high spirits and shed no tears. She seemed confident, as much a comrade as a wife. She was determined to brace me. As I was driven away in the police van I could still hear the people outside singing *"Nkosi Sikelel' iAfrika."*

# 52

PRISON NOT ONLY robs you of your freedom, it attempts to take away your identity. Everyone wears the same uniform, eats the same food, follows the same schedule. It is by definition a purely authoritarian state that tolerates no independence or individuality. As a freedom fighter and as a man, one must fight against the prison's attempt to rob one of these qualities.

From the courthouse, I was taken directly to Pretoria Local, the gloomy red-brick monstrosity that I knew so well. But I was now a convicted prisoner, not an awaiting-trial prisoner, and was treated without even that little deference that is afforded to the latter. I was stripped of my clothes and Colonel Jacobs was finally able to confiscate my kaross. I was issued the standard prison uniform for Africans: a pair of short trousers, a rough khaki shirt, a canvas jacket, socks, sandals, and a cloth cap. Only Africans are given short trousers, for only African men are deemed "boys" by the authorities.

I informed the authorities that I would under no circumstances wear shorts and told them I was prepared to go to court to protest. Later, when I was brought dinner, stiff cold porridge with a half teaspoonful of sugar, I refused to eat it. Colonel Jacobs pondered this and came up with a solution: I could wear long trousers and have my own food, if I agreed to be put in isolation. "We were going to put you with the other politicals," he said, "but now you will be alone, man. I hope you enjoy it." I assured him that solitary confinement would be fine as long as I could wear and eat what I chose.

For the next few weeks, I was completely and utterly isolated. I did not see the face or hear the voice of another prisoner. I was locked up for twenty-three hours a day, with thirty minutes of exercise in the morning and again in the afternoon. I had never been in isolation before, and every hour seemed like a year. There was no natural light in my cell; a single bulb burned overhead twenty-four hours a day. I did not have a wristwatch and I often thought it was the middle of the night when it was only late afternoon. I had nothing to read, nothing to write on or with, no one to talk to. The mind begins to turn in on itself, and one desperately wants something outside of oneself on which to fix one's attention. I have known men who took half-a-dozen lashes in preference to being locked up alone. After a time in solitary, I relished the company even of the insects in my cell, and found myself on the verge of initiating conversations with a cockroach.

I had one middle-aged African warder whom I occasionally was able to see, and one day I tried to bribe him with an apple to get him to talk to me. *"Baba,"* I said, which means Father, and is a term of respect, "can I give you an apple?" He turned away, and met all my subsequent overtures with silence. Finally, he said, "Man, you wanted long trousers and better food, and now you have them and you are still not happy." He was right. Nothing is more dehumanizing than the absence of human companionship. After a few weeks, I was ready to swallow my pride and tell Colonel Jacobs that I would trade my long trousers for some company.

During those weeks I had plenty of time to ponder my fate. The place of a freedom fighter is beside his people, not behind bars. The knowledge and contacts I had recently made in Africa were going to be locked away rather than used in the struggle. I cursed the fact that my expertise would not be put to use in creating a freedom army.

I soon began to protest vigorously against my circumstances and demanded to be put with the other political prisoners at Pretoria Local. Among them was Robert Sobukwe. My request was ultimately granted, accompanied by a stern warning from Colonel Jacobs that serious consequences would result if I returned to my impudent ways. I don't think I ever looked forward to eating cold mealie pap so much in my life.

Apart from my desire for company, I was keen to talk with Sobukwe and the others, most of whom were PAC, because I thought that in prison we might forge a unity that we could not on the outside. Prison conditions have a way of tempering polemics, and making individuals see more what unites them than what divides them.

When I was taken to the courtyard with the others, we greeted each other warmly. Besides Sobukwe, there was also John Gaetsewe, a leading member of the South African Congress of Trade Unions; Aaron Molete, an ANC member who worked for *New Age;* and Stephen Tefu, a prominent Communist, trade unionist, and PAC member. Robert asked me to give them an account of my African tour, which I did gladly. I was candid about how both the PAC and the ANC were perceived in the rest of Africa. At the end of my narrative I said there were issues that I wanted us to examine. But after initially allowing Sobukwe and me a certain proximity, the authorities took pains to keep us apart. We lived in single cells along a corridor and he and I were given cells at opposite ends.

Occasionally, we did have a chance to talk as we sat next to each other on the ground of the prison courtyard sewing and patching up shabby old mailbags. I have always respected Sobukwe, and found him a balanced and reasonable man. But we differed markedly about the principal subject at hand: prison conditions. Sobukwe believed that to fight poor conditions would be to acknowledge the state's right to have him in prison in the first place. I responded that it was always unacceptable to live in degrading conditions and that political prisoners throughout history had considered it part of their duty to fight to improve prison conditions. Sobukwe responded that prison conditions would not change until the country changed. I completely agreed with this, but I did not see why that ought to prevent us from fighting in the only realm in which we now could fight. We never resolved this issue, but we did make some progress when we submitted a joint letter to the commanding officer setting out our complaints about prison conditions.

Sobukwe never broke in prison. But in Pretoria he was a bit sensitive and testy, and I attribute this to Stephen Tefu. Tefu had become a kind of goad to Sobukwe, teasing, taunting, and challenging him. Even at the best of times, Tefu was a difficult fellow: dyspeptic, argumentative, overbearing. He was also articulate, knowledgeable, and an expert in Russian history. Above all, he was a fighter, but he would fight everyone, even his friends. Tefu and Sobukwe quarreled every day.

I was keen to discuss policy issues with Sobukwe, and one of the matters I took up with him was the PAC slogan "Freedom in 1963." It was already 1963 and freedom was nowhere to be seen. "My brother," I said to Sobukwe, "there is nothing so dangerous as a leader making a demand that he knows cannot be achieved. It creates false hopes among the people."

I said this in a most respectful manner, but Tefu jumped in and started to berate Sobukwe. "Bob," he said, "you have met your match with Mandela. You know he is right." Tefu continued in this vein, annoying Sobukwe to the point where he would tell Tefu, "Leave me alone." But Tefu would not stop. "Bob, the people are waiting for you. They are going to kill you because you have deceived them. You are just an amateur, Bob. You are not a real politician."

Tefu did his best to alienate me as well. Every morning, when we were visited by the warders, he would complain to them about something — the food, the conditions, the heat or the cold. One day, an officer said to Tefu: "Look, man, why do you complain every morning?"

"I complain because it is my duty to complain," Steve said.

"But, look at Mandela," the officer said, "he does not complain every day."

"Ah," said Tefu with disgust, "Mandela is a little boy who is afraid of the white man. I don't even know who he is. One morning, I woke up and found every newspaper saying, 'Mandela, Mandela, Mandela,' and I said to myself, 'Who is this Mandela?' I will tell you who Mandela is. He is a chap built up by you people for some reason that I don't understand. That is who Mandela is!"

\*          \*          \*

We were joined for two weeks by Walter, who had been on trial in Johannesburg for incitement to strike while I had been in Pretoria. He was sentenced to six years. We had a number of opportunities to talk in jail and we discussed Walter's application for bail while his appeal was pending, a move I wholeheartedly supported. After two weeks he was released on bail, and he was instructed by the movement to go underground, from where he was to continue to lead the struggle, which he ably did.

Not long after Walter left, I was walking to the prison hospital with Sobukwe when I spotted Nana Sita in the courtyard about twenty-five yards away. Sita, the distinguished Indian campaigner who had led our defiance at Boksburg in 1952, had just been convicted by a Pretoria magistrate for refusing to vacate his house — the house he had lived in for more than forty years — which was in a precinct that had been proclaimed "white" in terms of the Group Areas Act. He was hunched over, and the fact that he was barefoot despite an acute arthritic condition made me uncomfortable in my own sandals. I wanted to go over to greet him, but we were marching under the eyes of a half-dozen warders.

Suddenly and without warning, I suffered a blackout. I crumpled to the concrete and sustained a deep gash above my left eye, which required three stitches. I had been diagnosed back in the Fort with high blood pressure and had been given certain pills. The cause of the blackout was evidently an overdose of these pills; I was taken off them, and put on a low-salt diet, which solved the problem.

That afternoon was my first scheduled visit from Winnie since I had been sentenced. Stitches or no stitches, I was not going to miss it. She was extremely concerned when she saw me but I assured her I was fine and explained what happened. Even so, rumors circulated that my health had broken down.

# 53

IN OCTOBER 1962, during my trial, the ANC held its first annual conference since 1959. Because the organization was illegal, the conference took place in Lobatse, just over the border in Bechuanaland. The conference was a milestone, for it explicitly linked the ANC and MK. Although the National Executive Committee stated, "Our emphasis still remains mass political action," Umkhonto was referred to as the "military wing of our struggle." This was done in part to try to quell the more irresponsible acts of terrorism then being committed by Poqo. Poqo, Xhosa for "independent" or "standing alone," was loosely linked to the PAC, and their acts of terrorism targeted both African collaborators and whites. The ANC wanted the people to see its new militancy, but also to see that it was controlled and responsible.

The government had decided to accelerate the program of "separate development" to show the world that apartheid allowed races their individual "freedom." The prototype would be the Transkei. In January 1962, Verwoerd had announced that South Africa intended to grant the Transkei "self-government." In 1963, the Transkei became a "self-governing" homeland. In November 1963, an election was held for the Transkei legislative assembly. But by a margin of more than three to one, Transkei voters elected members opposed to the homeland policy.

The bantustan system was nevertheless instituted; the voters had opposed it, but participated in it simply by voting. Though I abhorred the bantustan system, I felt the ANC should use both the system and those within it as a platform for our policies, particularly as so many of our leaders were now voiceless through imprisonment, banning, or exile.

Terrorism against the Bantu Authorities increased. As acts of sabotage mounted, so did the government's vigilance. John Vorster, the new minister of justice, who had himself been detained during World War II for opposing the government's support of the Allies, was a man unsentimental in the extreme. For him, the iron fist was the best and only answer to subversion.

On May 1, 1963, the government enacted legislation designed "to break the back" of Umkhonto, as Vorster put it. The General Law Amendment Act, better known as the Ninety-Day Detention Law, waived the right of habeas corpus and empowered any police officer to detain any person without a warrant on grounds of suspicion of a political crime. Those arrested could be detained without trial, charge, access to a lawyer, or protection against self-incrimination for up to ninety days. The ninety-day detention could be extended, as Vorster ominously explained, until "this side of eternity." The law helped transform the country into a police state; no dictator could covet more power than the Ninety-Day Detention Law gave to the authorities. As a result, the police became more savage: prisoners were routinely beaten and we soon heard reports of electric shock, suffocation, and other forms of torture. In Parliament, Helen Suzman, the representative of the liberal Progressive Party, cast the lone vote against the act.

Increased penalties were ordered for membership in illegal organizations; sentences from five years to the death penalty were instituted for "furthering the aims" of communism or of other banned organizations. Political prisoners were redetained as I found out in May 1963, when Sobukwe's three-year sentence was up; instead of releasing him, the government simply redetained him without charging him, and then sent him to Robben Island.

Vorster also championed the Sabotage Act of June 1962, which allowed for house arrests and more stringent bannings not subject to challenge in the court, restricting the liberties of citizens to those in the most extreme fascist dictatorships. Sabotage itself now carried a minimum penalty of five years without parole and a maximum of death. Because the wording of the act was so broad, even activities such as trespassing or illegal possession of weapons could constitute sabotage. Another act of Parliament prohibited the reproduction of any statement made by a banned person. Nothing I said or had ever said could be reported in the newspapers. *New Age* was banned at the end of 1962, and possession of a banned publication became a criminal offense, punishable by up to two years in prison. Provision was also made for house arrest, the most well-known use of which was imposed on the white political activist Helen Joseph.

# 54

ONE NIGHT, toward the end of May, a warder came to my cell and ordered me to pack my things. I asked him why, but he did not answer. In less than ten minutes, I was escorted down to the reception office where I found three other political prisoners: Tefu, John Gaetsewe, and Aaron Molete. Colonel Aucamp curtly informed us that we were being transferred. Where? Tefu asked. Someplace very beautiful, Aucamp said. Where? said Tefu. *"Die Eiland,"* said Aucamp. The island. There was only one. Robben Island.

The four of us were shackled together and put in a windowless van that contained only a sanitary bucket. We drove all night to Cape Town, and arrived at the city's docks in the late afternoon. It is not an easy or pleasant task for men shackled together to use a sanitary bucket in a moving van.

The docks at Cape Town were swarming with armed police and nervous plainclothes officials. We had to stand, still chained, in the hold of the old wooden ferry, which was difficult as the ship rocked in the swells off the coast. A small porthole above was the only source of light and air. The porthole served another purpose as well: the warders enjoyed urinating on us from above. It was still light when we were led on deck and we saw the island for the first time. Green and beautiful, it looked at first more like a resort than a prison.

*Esiquithini.* At the island. That is how the Xhosa people describe the narrow, windswept outcrop of rock that lies eight miles off the coast of Cape Town. Everyone knows which island you are referring to. I first heard about the island as a child. Robben Island was well known among the Xhosas after Makanna (also known as Nxele), the six foot six inch commander of the Xhosa army in the Fourth Xhosa War, was banished there by the British after leading ten thousand warriors against Grahamstown in 1819. He tried to escape from Robben Island by boat, but drowned before reaching shore. The memory of that loss is woven into the language of my people who speak of a "forlorn hope" by the phrase *"Ukuza kuka Nxele."*

Makanna was not the first African hero confined on the island. In 1658, Autshumao, known to European historians as Harry the Strandloper, was banished by Jan Van Riebeeck during a war between the Khoi Khoi and the Dutch. I took solace in the memory of Autshumao, for he is reputed to be the first and only man to ever escape from Robben Island, and he did so by rowing to the mainland in a small boat.

The island takes its name from the Dutch word for seal, hundreds of which once cavorted in the icy Benguela currents that wash the shores. Later the island was turned into a leper colony, a lunatic asylum, and a naval base. The government had only recently turned the island back into a prison.

*          *          *

We were met by a group of burly white warders shouting: *"Dis die Eiland! Hier gaan julle vrek!"* (This is the island. Here you will die.) Ahead of us was a compound flanked by a number of guardhouses. Armed guards lined the path to the compound. It was extremely tense. A tall, red-faced warder yelled at us: *"Hier is ek jou baas!"* (Here I am your boss!) He was one of the notorious Kleynhans brothers, known for their brutality to prisoners. The warders always spoke in Afrikaans. If you replied in English they would say, *"Ek verstaan nie daardie kafferboetie se taal nie."* (I don't understand that kaffir-lover's language.)

As we walked toward the prison, the guards shouted "Two-two! Two-two!" — meaning we should walk in pairs, two in front, two behind. I linked up with Tefu. The guards started screaming, *"Haas! . . . Haas!"* The word *haas* means "move" in Afrikaans, but it is customarily reserved for cattle.

The warders were demanding that we jog, and I turned to Tefu and under my breath said that we must set an example; if we gave in now we would be at their mercy. Tefu nodded his head in agreement. We had to show them that we were not everyday criminals but political prisoners being punished for our beliefs.

I motioned to Tefu that we two should walk in front, and we took the lead. Once in front, we actually decreased the pace, walking slowly and deliberately. The guards were incredulous. "Listen," Kleynhans said, "this is not Johannesburg, this is not Pretoria, this is Robben Island, and we will tolerate no insubordination here. *Haas! Haas!"* But we continued at our stately pace. Kleynhans ordered us to halt, and stood in front of us: "Look, man, we will kill you, we are not fooling around, your wives and children and mothers and fathers will never know what happened to you. This is the last warning. *Haas! Haas!"*

To this I said: "You have your duty and we have ours." I was determined that we would not give in, and we did not, for we were already at the cells. We were ushered into a rectangular stone building and taken to a large open room. The floor was covered with water a few inches deep. The guards yelled: *"Trek uit! Trek uit!"* (Undress! Undress!) As we removed each item of clothing, the guards would grab it, search it quickly, and then throw it in the water. Jacket off, searched, thrown in the water. Then the guards commanded us to get dressed, by which they meant for us to put on our soaking clothes.

Two officers entered the room. The less senior of the two was a captain whose name was Gericke. From the start, we could see that he was intent on manhandling us. The captain pointed to Aaron Molete, the youngest of the four of us and a very mild and gentle person, and said, "Why is your hair so long?" Aaron said nothing. The captain shouted, "I'm talking to you! Why is your hair so long? It is against regulations. Your hair should have been cut. Why is it long . . ." and then he paused and turned to look at me, and said, ". . . like this boy's!" pointing at me. I began to speak: "Now, look here, the length of our hair is determined by the regulations . . ."

Before I could finish, he shouted in disbelief: "Never talk to me that way, boy!" and began to advance. I was frightened; it is not a pleasant sensation to know that someone is about to hit you and you are unable to defend yourself.

When he was just a few feet from me, I said, as firmly as I could, "If you so much as lay a hand on me, I will take you to the highest court in the land and when I finish with you, you will be as poor as a church mouse." The moment I began speaking, he paused, and by the end of my speech, he was staring at me with astonishment. I was a bit surprised myself. I had been afraid, and spoke not from courage, but out of a kind of bravado. At such times, one must put up a bold front despite what one feels inside.

"Where's your ticket?" he asked, and I handed it to him. I could see he was nervous. "What's your name?" he said. I nodded my head toward the ticket, and said, "It is written there." He said, "How long are you in for?" I said again, gesturing toward the ticket, "It is written there." He looked down and said, "Five years! You are in for five years and you are so arrogant! Do you know what it means to serve five years?" I said, "That is my business. I am ready to serve five years but I am not prepared to be bullied. You must act within the law."

No one had informed him who we were, or that we were political prisoners, or that I was a lawyer. I had not noticed it myself, but the other officer, a tall, quiet man, had vanished during our confrontation; I later discovered that he was Colonel Steyn, the commanding officer of Robben Island. The captain then left, much quieter than he had entered.

We were then by ourselves and Steve, his nerves jangling, could not stop speaking. "We have provoked the Boere," he said. "Now we are in for a rough time." He was in the midst of speaking when a stocky fellow named Lieutenant Pretorius walked in. To our surprise, Pretorius spoke to us in Xhosa, which he seemed to know quite well. "We have looked at your records and they are not so bad. All except this one," he said, nodding toward Steve. "Your record is filthy."

Steve exploded. "Who are you to talk to me like that? You say I have a filthy record. You have read my files, eh. Well, you will find that all those convictions were for cases I was fighting for the rights of my people. I am not a criminal; you are the criminal." The lieutenant then warned Steve that he would charge him if he ever addressed him in that way again. Before leaving, the lieutenant said he was placing us in a single large cell with windows that faced outside and then added, rather ominously, "But I don't want you to talk to anyone through those windows, especially you, Mandela."

We were then taken to our cell, one of the best I had ever seen. The windows were large and within easy reach. From one set of windows we could see other prisoners and warders as they walked past. It was spacious, certainly large enough for the four of us, and had its own toilets and showers.

It had been an exhausting day and a short while later, after a supper of cold porridge, the others went to sleep. I was lying on my blanket on the floor, when I heard a tapping at the window. I looked up and saw a white man, beckoning me to come to the glass. I remembered the lieutenant's admonition and stayed put.

Then I heard the fellow whisper: "Nelson, come here." The fact that he knew my name intrigued me and I decided to take a chance. I went over to the window and looked at him. He must have realized that I thought he was white, because the first thing he whispered was, "I'm a Coloured warder from Bloemfontein." He then gave me news of my wife. There had been a report in the Johannesburg newspapers that my wife had come to see me at Pretoria Local, but that they had not informed her that I had been taken to Robben Island. I thanked him for the information.

"Do you smoke?" he said. I told him that I did not and he seemed disappointed. I then got the idea: "Yes, but my comrades do." He brightened at this and said he would return in a few minutes with tobacco and sandwiches. Everyone was now awake. Tefu and John Gaetsewe smoked, and I split the pouch of tobacco between them, and we all divided the sandwiches.

For the next few weeks the Coloured warder came almost every night with tobacco and sandwiches. And each night I would divide up the tobacco evenly between Tefu and Gaetsewe. The warder was taking great risks, and he warned me that he was only prepared to deal directly with me, or the arrangement was off.

When we arrived on the island we had no idea how many other prisoners were there. Within a few days we learned there were about a thousand men, all Africans, all recent arrivals. Most of these men were common-law prisoners, but I knew there would be some political prisoners among them. I wanted to contact them, but we were completely isolated. For the first few days we were kept locked in our cell and not even permitted outside. We demanded to be taken to work like the other prisoners, and this was soon granted, but we were taken out alone, supervised by Kleynhans. Our first job was covering up some newly laid pipe and we were on a small hill and could see some of the island, which was wild and lovely.

We worked hard that first day, but on each succeeding day Kleynhans pushed us harder. He did this crudely, as one would urge on a horse or cow. *"Nee, man. Kom aan! Gaan aan!"* (No, man. Come on. Go on.) At one point, Steve, who was older than the rest of us, put down his shovel and was immediately threatened by Kleynhans. But Steve, in Afrikaans, responded: "You ignoramus who cannot even speak your own language properly — you cannot tell me what to do. I will work at my own rate, that is what I am prepared to do, and that is all I can do." Then, with great dignity, he picked up his shovel and resumed work. Steve had been a teacher of Afrikaans, and he not only spoke perfect Afrikaans but its antecedent, High Dutch. Steve would speak to the warders in a condescending and grandiloquent style that they probably did not understand. But they knew better than to engage him in a verbal battle.

There were two Kleynhans brothers on the island, both reputed to have viciously assaulted prisoners. We were looked after by the older brother, who must have been warned to restrain himself, for he never touched us. The younger one was under no such constraints. One day, we were walking back from work along a road and passed a workspan of several hundred prisoners carting sand in wheelbarrows. They were nonpolitical prisoners and both of our groups were ordered to halt while the two brothers had a chat; the younger brother ordered one of his men to polish his boots while he talked. I recognized some of the men in the other workspan as those who had been sentenced to death in the Sekhukhuneland peasant revolt of 1958, and I turned around to get a better look at them. The younger brother rudely ordered me to look the other way. I do not know how I would have reacted had I not been standing in full view of the other prisoners, but my pride was now at stake. I refused to turn around. The younger Kleynhans advanced with the obvious intent of assaulting me, but when he was a few steps away, his brother ran over, grabbed him, whispered a few words, and the incident passed.

One day we were visited by the head of prison, who was responsible for running all of Robben Island and had come to hear our complaints. Theron was a sour fellow who did not like to deal with prisoners face to face. I did not want to alienate him but I was not going to cringe. "We are grateful that you have come to see us," I said, speaking for the group, "because we have a number of problems which I am certain you will be able to sort out." I enumerated the problems and when I finished, he said, "I will see what I can do."

Perhaps he thought he had given in too easily because as he was walking out he turned to Tefu, who had a large belly, and said, *"Jou groot pens sal in die plek verdwyn,"* Afrikaans for "That great stomach of yours is going to disappear here in prison." *Pens* means stomach, but is used to refer to the stomach of animals like sheep or cattle. The word for the stomach of a human being is *maag*.

Steve did not take kindly to the prison head's jab, and he was incapable of letting an insult go unanswered. "You know, Captain," he said, "there is nothing you can do to me that can truly affect me for I am a member of the most revolutionary political organization in the world, the Communist Party, which has a distinguished record of service to oppressed people around the globe. You and your poor National Party will be on the ash-heap of history while we are ruling the world. I am better known internationally than your witless state president. Who are you? A small functionary not even worth paying attention to. By the time I leave prison I won't even know your name." Theron turned on his heel and left.

The nightly visits of our Coloured warder went a long way to mitigate the harshness of the island. But even with this luxury, Steve was still dissatisfied. Tefu was a heavy smoker; he would sometimes puff away the entire night, leaving himself no tobacco for the next day. Gaetsewe, however, conserved his tobacco, and never ran out. One evening, in a particularly irritable mood, Tefu confronted me. "Nelson," he said, "you are shortchanging me. You are giving Gaetsewe more tobacco than me."

This was not true, but I thought I would play a game with him. "Very well then," I said. "Every night when I get the tobacco I will first divide it into two portions and then I will let you choose which one you want." That night, and each night afterward, I separated the tobacco into equal piles and said to Steve, "Choose."

Tefu would be in an agony of indecision. He would look at both piles, his head swinging back and forth between the two. Finally, in frustration, he would grab one of the piles and go off and begin to smoke. Though this process seemed to me eminently fair — and also humorous — Tefu was still unhappy. He began to hover about when the warder came to the window in order to make sure that I was not hoarding the tobacco. This made the warder uncomfortable. "Look," he said to me, "I only deal with you. It is a question of security." I said I understood, and told Tefu that he could not be around when I was dealing with the warder.

The next night, however, when the warder came to the window, Tefu strode up to the bars and said to him, "From now on I want my own tobacco. Just give it to me directly." The warder panicked. "Mandela," he said, "you have broken our agreement. No more. I won't be bringing you these things." I shooed Tefu away and remonstrated with the warder. I said, "Look, man, this is an old chap," meaning Tefu. "And he's not very normal," I said pointing to my head. "Make an exception." So he softened and gave me the supplies, but warned if it happened again, that would be the end.

That night, I thought it necessary to punish Tefu. I said, "Now, look, you have jeopardized our supplies. You are not going to have any tobacco or sandwiches tonight. You have almost lost us these privileges. So we're cutting you off until you improve." Tefu was silent.

We stayed in one corner of the cell that night, eating our sandwiches and reading the paper the warder also brought for us. Tefu sat by himself in the opposite corner. Eventually we drifted off to sleep. At about midnight, I felt an arm on my shoulder, jostling me awake. "Nelson . . . Nelson." It was Tefu.

"Nelson," he said, speaking softly, "you have hit me in a weak spot. You have deprived me of my tobacco. I am an old man. I have suffered for my commitment to my people. You are the leader here in jail, and you are punishing me like this. It is not fair, Nelson."

He had hit *me* in a weak spot. I felt as though I had abused my power. He had indeed suffered, far more than I had. I had not eaten half my sandwich, and I immediately gave it to him. I roused Gaet-sewe — I had given him all the tobacco — and asked him if he would share it with Tefu. Tefu was always difficult, but from that point on he behaved much better.

Once we started working, I got some sense of what life was like for other prisoners on the island. The authorities also moved some young political prisoners from the PAC into the cells opposite ours. At night, we were able to talk with them through the barred door. Among these young men, I discovered, was Nqabeni Menye, a nephew of mine from Mqhekezweni whom I had last seen when he was a baby in 1941.

We conversed about the Transkei and caught up on family history. One night, while his friends were gathered around him, he said, "Uncle, what organization do you belong to?" The ANC, I said, of course. My response caused consternation among those young men and suddenly their faces disappeared from the window. After some time, my nephew reappeared and asked me whether or not I had ever been a member of the PAC. I replied that I had not. He then said he had understood that I joined the PAC during my Africa tour. I told him that I had not, that I had always been a member of the ANC, and that I always would be. This again caused dismay among them and they vanished.

I later learned that PAC propaganda claimed that I had joined the organization when I was traveling elsewhere on the continent. Although I was not pleased to hear this, it did not surprise me. In politics, one can never underestimate how little people know about a situation. A short while later my nephew was back and asked me if I had met and talked with Sobukwe at Pretoria Local. I said that I had and that we had very good discussions. This pleased them and they said good night, and that was the last I saw of them.

A few hours later that same evening a captain came to our cell and commanded the four of us to pack our belongings. Within minutes my comrades were taken away, leaving me in the cell by myself. In prison, one counts oneself lucky to be able to wave good-bye to one's comrades. One can be in extraordinarily intimate circumstances with someone for months, and then never see the person again. It is dehumanizing, for it forces one to adapt by becoming more self-contained and insulated.

Now that I was alone, I was also somewhat anxious. There is sometimes safety in numbers; when you are alone, there are no witnesses. I realized I had not been served any food, and banged on the door: "Warder, I have not received my supper."

"You must call me *baas*," he yelled. I went hungry that night.

Very early the next morning I was taken back to Pretoria. The Department of Prisons released a statement to the press that I had been removed from the island for my own safety because PAC prisoners were planning to assault me. This was patently false; they had brought me back to Pretoria for their own motives, which soon became clear.

I was kept in solitary confinement at Pretoria Local. But prisoners are resourceful and I was soon receiving secret notes and other communications from some of the ANC people there. I had a communication from Henry Fazzie, one of the MK cadres who had undergone military training in Ethiopia and been arrested while attempting to return to South Africa. They were among the first ANC members to be tried under the Sabotage Act.

Through the prison grapevine, I attempted to help them with their defense and suggested they contact Harold Wolpe. I later heard that Wolpe was in police detention. This was my first intimation that something had gone seriously wrong. One day, as I was being led away from the courtyard after exercise, I saw Andrew Mlangeni. I had last seen him in September of 1961 when he was leaving the country for military training. Wolpe, Mlangeni — who else was under arrest?

Early in 1961, Winnie had been banned for two years. I heard from another prisoner that Winnie had recently been charged with violating her bans, which could lead to imprisonment or house arrest. Winnie was headstrong; a banning order was just the type of thing that would make her angry. I had no doubt that she violated her orders, and I would never counsel her not to do so, but it concerned me greatly that she might spend time in prison.

One morning in July 1963, as I was walking along the passage to my cell, I saw Thomas Mashifane, who had been the foreman at Liliesleaf Farm. I greeted him warmly, though I realized that the authorities had undoubtedly led him to my passage to see if I recognized or acknowledged him. I could not help but do otherwise. His presence there could mean only one thing: the authorities had discovered Rivonia.

A day or two later I was summoned to the prison office where I found Walter; Govan Mbeki; Ahmed Kathrada; Andrew Mlangeni; Bob Hepple; Raymond Mhlaba, a member of the MK High Command who had recently returned from training in China; Elias Motsoaledi, also a member of MK; Dennis Goldberg, an engineer and a member of the Congress of Democrats; Rusty Bernstein, an architect and also a member of the COD; and Jimmy Kantor, an attorney who was Harold Wolpe's brother-in-law. We were all charged with sabotage, and scheduled to appear in court the next day. I had served just nine months of my five-year sentence.

In bits and pieces, I learned what had happened. On the afternoon of July 11, a dry cleaner's van entered the long driveway of the farm. No one at Liliesleaf had ordered a delivery. The vehicle was stopped by a young African guard, but he was overwhelmed when dozens of armed policemen and several police dogs sprang from the vehicle. They surrounded the property and a handful of officers entered the main building and the principal outbuilding. In the latter they found a dozen men around a table discussing a document. Walter jumped out a window but was cut off by a snarling police dog. The arrests also included Arthur Goldreich, who had driven into the farm as the police raid was in progress.

The police searched the entire farm and confiscated hundreds of documents and papers, though they found no weapons. One of the most important documents remained right on the table: Operation Mayibuye, a plan for guerrilla warfare in South Africa. In one fell swoop, the police had captured the entire High Command of Umkhonto we Sizwe. Everyone was detained under the new Ninety-Day Detention Law.

Joe Slovo and Bram Fischer were fortunately not there at the time of the raid. But Joe and Bram often went to the farm two or three times a day. In hindsight, it is extraordinary that Liliesleaf was not discovered sooner. The regime had become stricter and more sophisticated. Wiretaps had become common, as was twenty-four-hour surveillance. The raid was a coup for the state.

On our first day in court we were not given the opportunity to instruct counsel. We were brought before a magistrate and charged with sabotage. A few days later we were allowed to meet with Bram, Vernon Berrangé, Joel Joffe, George Bizos, and Arthur Chaskalson, all of whom were acting for us. I was still being kept separately as I was a convicted prisoner, and these sessions were my first opportunity to talk with my colleagues.

Bram was very somber. In his quiet voice, he told us that we were facing an extremely serious trial and that the state had formally advised him they would ask for the supreme penalty permitted by law, the death sentence. Given the climate of the times, Bram said, this result was a very real possibility. From that moment on we lived in the shadow of the gallows. The mere possibility of a death sentence changes everything. From the start, we considered it the most likely outcome of the trial. Far lesser crimes than ours had recently been punished by life sentences.

Prison officials never let you forget that you might hang. That night, a warder rapped on my cell door at bedtime. "Mandela, you don't have to worry about sleep," he said. "You are going to sleep for a long, long time." I waited a moment and said, "All of us, you included, are going to sleep for a long, long time." It was small consolation.

# 55

ON OCTOBER 9, 1963, we were picked up in a heavily fortified police van. It had a steel divider running along the center, segregating the white prisoners from the Africans. We were driven to the Palace of Justice in Pretoria, where the Supreme Court sits, for the opening of *The State versus the National High Command and others,* what later became known as *The State versus Nelson Mandela and others,* and is still better known as the Rivonia Trial. Near the court stands a statue of Paul Kruger, the president of the Republic of the Transvaal who fought against British imperialism in the nineteenth century. Underneath this Afrikaner hero is a quotation from one of his speeches. The inscription reads, "In confidence we lay our cause before the whole world. Whether we win or whether we die, freedom will rise in Africa like the sun from the morning clouds."

Our van was in the center of a convoy of police trucks. At the front of this motorcade were limousines carrying high police officials. The Palace of Justice was teeming with armed policemen. To avoid the enormous crowd of our supporters, who had grouped in front of the building, we were driven into the rear of the building and taken in through great iron gates. All around the building police officers with machine guns stood at attention. As we descended from the van, we could hear the great crowd singing and chanting. Once inside, we were held in cells below the courtroom before the opening of what was depicted in the newspapers at home and around the world as the most significant political trial in the history of South Africa.

As we emerged from the cells, each of the accused was accompanied by two armed warders. When we entered the ornate, high-ceilinged courtroom, we each turned to the crowd and made a clenched-fist ANC salute. In the visitors' gallery our supporters shouted *"Amandla! Ngawethu!"* and *"Mayibuye Afrika!"* This was inspiring, but dangerous: the police took the names and addresses of all the spectators in the galleries, and photographed them as they left the court. The courtroom was filled with domestic and international journalists, and dozens of representatives of foreign governments.

After we filed in, a group of police officers formed a tight cordon between us and the spectators. I was disgusted to have to appear in court wearing my prison clothes of khaki shorts and flimsy sandals. As a convicted prisoner, I did not have the choice of wearing proper clothes. Many people later commented on how poorly I looked, and not just because of my wardrobe. I had been in and out of solitary confinement for months and I had lost more than twenty-five pounds. I took pains to smile at the gallery when I walked into the courtroom, and seeing our supporters was the best medicine I could have had.

Security was particularly tight as only a few weeks before Arthur Goldreich, Harold Wolpe, Mosie Moola, and Abdulhay Jassat had bribed a young guard and escaped from jail. Arthur and Harold made their way to Swaziland disguised as priests, then flew to Tanganyika. Their escape came at a time of hysteria about the underground and was greeted with blaring newspaper headlines. It was an embarrassment to the government and a boost to our morale.

Our judge in the Rivonia Trial was Mr. Quartus de Wet, judge-president of the Transvaal, who sat in his flowing red robes beneath a wooden canopy. De Wet was one of the last judges appointed by the United Party before the Nationalists came to power and was not considered a government lackey. He was a poker-faced judge who did not suffer fools gladly. The prosecutor was Dr. Percy Yutar, deputy attorney general of the Transvaal, whose ambition was to become attorney general of South Africa. He was a small, bald, dapper fellow, whose voice squeaked when he became angry or emotional. He had a flair for the dramatic and for high-flown if imprecise language.

Yutar rose and addressed the court: "My Lord, I call the case of the state against the National High Command and others." I was accused number one. Yutar handed in the indictment and authorized that we be charged immediately and tried summarily. This was the first time we were given a copy of the indictment. The prosecution had kept it from us, though they gave it to the *Rand Daily Mail,* which had splashed it all over that day's edition of the paper. The indictment charged eleven of us with complicity in over two hundred acts of sabotage aimed at facilitating violent revolution and an armed invasion of the country. The state contended that we were actors in a conspiracy to overthrow the government.

We were charged with sabotage and conspiracy rather than high treason because the law does not require a long preparatory examination (which is highly useful to the defense) for sabotage and conspiracy as it does for treason. Yet the supreme penalty — death by hanging — is the same. With high treason, the state must prove its case beyond a reasonable doubt and needs two witnesses to testify to each charge. Under the Sabotage Law, the onus was on the defense to prove the accused innocent.

Bram Fischer stood up and asked the court for a remand on the grounds that the defense had not had time to prepare its case. He noted that a number of the accused had been held in solitary confinement for unconscionable lengths of time. The state had been preparing for three months, but we had only received the indictment that day. Justice de Wet gave us a three-week adjournment until October 29.

I was disturbed to discover that first day that Winnie was unable to attend. Because of her banning and her restriction to Johannesburg, she needed police permission to come to court. She had applied and been refused. I also learned that our house had been raided and the police had detained a young relative of Winnie's. Winnie was not the only wife being harassed. Albertina Sisulu and Caroline Motsoaledi were detained under the Ninety-Day Detention Act, and Walter's young son Max was also arrested. This was one of the state's most barbarous techniques of applying pressure: imprisoning the wives and children of freedom fighters. Many men in prison were able to handle anything the authorities did to them, but the thought of the state doing the same thing to their families was almost impossible to bear.

Winnie subsequently appealed to the minister of justice, who granted her permission to attend the trial on the condition that she did not wear traditional dress. Ironically, the same government that was telling us to embrace our culture in the homelands forbade Winnie from wearing a Xhosa gown into court.

During the next three weeks, we were permitted to spend our days together preparing our case. I was now among my fellow accused, and the company of my colleagues was a tonic. As awaiting-trial prisoners we were entitled to two half-hour visits a week, and one meal a day could be sent in from the outside. I soon gained back my lost weight with Mrs. Pillay's delicious dinners.

While we were preparing our defense, the government was trying the case in the newspapers. Normally, a case that is sub judice cannot be commented upon in public or in the press. But since the men arrested at Rivonia were Ninety-Day detainees, and therefore not technically charged with a crime, this judicial principle went by the wayside. We were publicly branded as violent revolutionaries by everyone from the minister of justice on down. Newspapers regularly featured headlines like "REVOLUTION ON MILITARY BASIS."

On October 29, we again entered the Palace of Justice; again the crowds were large and excited; again the security was extremely tight; again the court was filled with dignitaries from many foreign embassies. After three weeks with my comrades I felt rejuvenated, and I was far more comfortable in court this time in a suit. Our attorneys had objected to our having to come to court in prison garb and we had won the right to wear our own clothes. We again raised clenched fists to the gallery, and were warned that if we did it again, we would be forced to come to court in our prison khakis. To prevent such outbursts, the authorities reversed the normal order of the prisoners preceding the judge into the courtroom. After that first day, the judge entered first so that court would already be in session when we entered.

We went on the attack immediately — Bram Fischer criticized the state's indictment as shoddy, poorly drawn, and containing absurdities such as the allegation that I had participated in certain acts of sabotage on dates when I was in Pretoria Local. Yutar was flummoxed. Judge de Wet looked to him to reply to Bram's argument, and instead of offering particulars he began to give what the judge derided as "a political speech." De Wet was impatient with Yutar's fumbling and told him so. "The whole basis of your argument as I understand it, Mr. Yutar, is that you are satisfied that the accused are guilty." De Wet then quashed the indictment and gaveled the session to a close.

For that moment we were technically free, and there was pandemonium in the court. But we were rearrested even before Judge de Wet left his seat. Lieutenant Swanepoel clapped each of us on the shoulder and said, "I am arresting you on a charge of sabotage," and we were herded back to our cells. Even so, this was a blow to the government, for they now had to go back to the drawing board in the case they were calling the trial to end all trials.

The state redrew their indictment and we were back in court in early December. We all sensed that in the interim Justice de Wet had grown more hostile to us. We suspected his previous independence had brought down the wrath of the government and pressure had been applied. The new charges were read: we were alleged to have recruited persons for sabotage and guerrilla warfare for the purpose of starting a violent revolution; we had allegedly conspired to aid foreign military units to invade the republic in order to support a Communist revolution; and we had solicited and received funds from foreign countries for this purpose. The orders for munitions on the part of the accused, said Yutar melodramatically, were enough to blow up Johannesburg.

The registrar then requested our pleas. We had agreed not to plead in the traditional manner but to use the moment to show our disdain for the proceedings.

"Accused number one, Nelson Mandela, do you plead guilty or not guilty?"

I rose and said, "My Lord, it is not I, but the government that should be in the dock. I plead not guilty."

"Accused number two, Walter Sisulu, do you plead guilty or not guilty?"

Sisulu: "The government is responsible for what has happened in this country. I plead not guilty."

Justice de Wet said he was not interested in hearing political speeches, that we should merely plead not guilty or guilty. But his direction was ignored. Each of the accused suggested that it was the government that was criminal before pleading not guilty.

To enhance the drama of the proceedings, the state had made arrangements for a live broadcast of Yutar's speech on the South African Broadcasting System. Microphones had been placed on the prosecution table as well as in front of the judge. But just as Yutar was clearing his throat, Bram Fischer rose and made an application to the court for the removal of the microphones on the grounds that the broadcasts would unfairly prejudice the case and were not in keeping with the dignity of the court. Despite Yutar's shrill plea for their retention, Justice de Wet ordered them removed.

In his address, Yutar argued that from the time the ANC had been driven underground, the organization had embarked on a policy of violence designed to lead from sabotage through guerrilla warfare to an armed invasion of the country. He asserted that we planned to deploy thousands of trained guerrilla units throughout the country, and these units were to spearhead an uprising that would be followed by an armed invasion by military units of a foreign power. "In the midst of the resulting chaos, turmoil, and disorder," Yutar proclaimed, "it was planned by the accused to set up a Provisional Revolutionary Government to take over the administration and control of the country." The engine of this grand plan was Umkhonto we Sizwe, under the political direction of the ANC and the Communist Party, and the headquarters of Umkhonto was Rivonia.

In his orotund prose, Yutar described how we recruited members for MK, how we planned our national uprising for 1963 (here he was confusing us with the PAC), how we erected a powerful radio transmitter at Rivonia, and how we were collectively responsible for two hundred twenty-two acts of sabotage. He said Elias Motsoaledi and Andrew Mlangeni were in charge of recruiting members and that Dennis Goldberg ran a special school for recruits in the Cape. He detailed the production of various bombs, as well as the solicitation of money abroad.

Over the next three months, the state produced one hundred seventy-three witnesses and entered into the record thousands of documents and photographs, including standard works on Marxism, histories of guerrilla warfare, maps, blueprints, and a passport made out to one David Motsamayi. The first witness was a police photographer who had taken pictures of Rivonia, and the next witnesses were domestic workers for the Goldreich family, who had been held in detention all this time even though they had no connection to the politics of the household. These servants identified most of us by pointing to us in the dock, but old Mr. Jelliman, in a brave attempt to help me, pretended that he did not see me when he was asked to point to accused number one. Look again, the prosecutor said, go over all the faces carefully. "I do not think he is here," Jelliman said quietly.

We wondered what evidence the state had to prove my guilt. I had been out of the country and in prison while much of the planning at Rivonia had taken place. When I saw Walter in Pretoria Local just after my sentencing, I urged him to make sure that all my books and notes were removed from the farm. But during the first week of the trial, when Rusty Bernstein applied for bail, Percy Yutar dramatically produced the sketch of the Fort and the accompanying note about escape that I had made while detained there. Yutar exclaimed that this was evidence that all of the accused meant to escape. It was a sign that nothing of mine had been removed from Rivonia. Later, I was told that my colleagues at Rivonia had decided to preserve my escape note because they thought it would be historic in the future. But in the present, it cost Rusty Bernstein his bail.

The state's star witness was Bruno Mtolo, or "Mr. X" as he was known in court. In introducing "Mr. X," Yutar informed the court that the interrogation would take three days and then, in theatrical tones, he added that the witness was "in mortal danger." Yutar asked that the evidence be given in camera, but that the press be included provided that they not identify the witness.

Mtolo was a tall, well-built man with an excellent memory. A Zulu from Durban, he had become the leader of the Natal region of MK. He was an experienced saboteur, and had been to Rivonia. I had met him only once, when I addressed his group of MK cadres in Natal after my return from the continent. His evidence concerning me in particular made me realize that the state would certainly be able to convict me.

He began by saying that he was an MK saboteur who had blown up a municipal office, a power pylon, and an electricity line. With impressive precision, he explained the operation of bombs, land mines, and grenades, and how MK worked from underground. Mtolo said that while he had never lost faith in the ideals of the ANC, he did lose faith in the organization when he realized that it and MK were instruments of the Communist Party.

His testimony was given with simplicity and what seemed like candor, but Mtolo had gone out of his way to embellish his evidence. This was undoubtedly done on police instructions. He told the court that during my remarks to the Natal Regional Command I had stated that all MK cadres ought to be good Communists but not to disclose their views publicly. In fact, I never said anything of the sort, but his testimony was meant to link me and MK to the Communist Party. His memory appeared so precise the ordinary person would assume that it was accurate in all instances. But this was not so.

I was bewildered by Mtolo's betrayal. I never ruled out the possibility of even senior ANC men breaking down under police torture. But by all accounts, Mtolo was never touched. On the stand, he went out of his way to implicate people who were not even mentioned in the case. It is possible, I know, to have a change of heart, but to betray so many others, many of whom were quite innocent, seemed to me inexcusable.

During cross-examination we learned that Mtolo had been a petty criminal before joining MK and had been imprisoned three previous times for theft. But despite these revelations, he was an extremely damaging witness, for the judge found him reliable and believable, and his testimony incriminated nearly all of us.

The keystone of the state's case was the six-page Plan of Action confiscated in the Rivonia raid. The leaders of the High Command had had this very document before them on the table when the police stormed the farm. Operation Mayibuye sketches out in general form the plan for the possible commencement of guerrilla operations, and how it might spark a mass armed uprising against the government. It envisions an initial landing of small guerrilla forces in four different areas of South Africa and the attacking of preselected targets. The document set a goal of seven thousand MK recruits in the country who would meet the initial outside force of one hundred twenty trained guerrillas.

The prosecution's case rested in large part on their contention that Operation Mayibuye had been approved by the ANC executive and had become the operating plan of MK. We insisted that Operation Mayibuye had not yet been formally adopted and was still under discussion at the time of the arrests. As far as I was concerned, Operation Mayibuye was a draft document that was not only not approved, but was entirely unrealistic in its goals and plans. I did not believe that guerrilla warfare was a viable option at that stage.

The plan had been drafted in my absence so I had very little knowledge of it. Even among the Rivonia Trialists there was disagreement as to whether the plan had been adopted as ANC policy. Govan, who had drafted the document with Joe Slovo, insisted that it had been agreed upon and felt that it was wrong for us to argue in court that it was still under discussion. But all the other accused contended that the document, while drawn up by the High Command, had not been approved by the ANC executive or even seen by Chief Luthuli.

Although a capital trial can be quite grim, our spirits were generally high. There was a good deal of gallows humor among us. Dennis Goldberg, the youngest of the accused, had an irrepressible sense of humor and often had us laughing when we should not have been. When one of the prosecution witnesses described how Raymond Mhlaba had worn a clerical collar as a disguise, Dennis took to calling him Reverend Mhlaba.

In our consulting room downstairs, we often communicated through notes, which we would then burn and throw in the wastebasket. One of the Special Branch officers who looked after us was Lieutenant Swanepoel, a burly, red-faced fellow who was convinced we were always putting one over on him. One day, while Swanepoel was observing us from the door, Govan Mbeki began to write a note in a conspicuously secretive manner. With similar drama he handed me the note. I read it, nodded my head sagely, and passed it to Kathy, who ostentatiously took out his matches as if to burn the note when Swanepoel swooped into the room, grabbed the paper out of Kathy's hands, and said something about the dangers of lighting matches indoors. He then left the room to read his prize; a few seconds later, he stormed back saying, "I will get all of you for this!" Govan had written in capital letters: "ISN'T SWANEPOEL A FINE-LOOKING CHAP?"

We were locked up in prison and on trial for our lives, but outside new life was blossoming. Jimmy Kantor's wife was to give birth any day. Jimmy was an attorney who had been roped into the trial by the state for no other reason than that he was Harold Wolpe's brother-in-law.

One morning, when we were sitting in the dock, a note was passed down to me from the other end.

> Barbara and I have discussed godfathers at length and we have come to
> the conclusion that, whether the baby is a girl or boy, we would consider
> it an honour if you would agree to accept this office as an adjunct to the
> more disreputable positions you have held in the past.

By return mail I sent Jimmy back a note.

I would be more than delighted, and the honour is mine, not the baby's. Now they dare not hang me.

# 56

THE STATE CASE continued through the Christmas season of 1963, ending on February 29, 1964. We had a little over a month to examine the evidence and prepare our defense. We were not all equally affected by the evidence. There was no evidence against James Kantor; he was not even a member of our organization and should not have been on trial at all. For Rusty Bernstein, Raymond Mhlaba, and Ahmed Kathrada, the evidence of involvement in conspiracy was slight and we decided they should not incriminate themselves. In Rusty's case, the evidence was negligible; he had merely been found at Rivonia with the others. The remaining six of us would make admissions of guilt on certain charges.

Bram was deeply pessimistic. He avowed that even if we proved that guerrilla war had not been approved and our policy of sabotage was designed not to sacrifice human life, the state could still impose the death sentence. The defense team was divided on whether or not we should testify. Some asserted that it would hurt our case if we testified. George Bizos, though, suggested that unless we gave evidence and convinced the judge that we had not decided on guerrilla warfare, he would certainly impose the supreme penalty.

Right from the start we had made it clear that we intended to use the trial not as a test of the law but as a platform for our beliefs. We would not deny, for example, that we had been responsible for acts of sabotage. We would not deny that a group of us had turned away from nonviolence. We were not concerned with getting off or lessening our punishment, but with having the trial strengthen the cause for which we were all struggling — at whatever cost to ourselves. We would not defend ourselves in a legal sense so much as in a moral sense. We saw the trial as a continuation of the struggle by other means. We would readily admit what was known by the state to be true but refuse to give away any information we thought might implicate others.

We would dispute the state's central contention that we had embarked on guerrilla warfare. We would admit that we had made contingency plans to undertake guerrilla warfare in the event sabotage failed. But we would claim it had not yet failed, for it had not been sufficiently attempted. We would deny the claims of murder and damage to innocent bystanders that the state alleged; either these claims were outright lies, or the incidents were the work of someone else. We had never contemplated the intervention of foreign military forces. In order to make these claims, we believed we would have to explain Operation Mayibuye to the court.

In my own case, the court had sufficient evidence for a conviction. Documents in my handwriting showed that I had left the country illegally, had arranged for military training for our men, and had been behind the formation of Umkhonto we Sizwe. There was also a document in my handwriting called "How to be a good Communist," which the state suggested was proof that I was a card-carrying Communist. In fact the document's title was taken from the work of a Chinese theoretician named Liu Shao Chi, and was written by me to prove a point to Moses Kotane. We had been engaged in a running debate about the appeal of communism to ordinary South Africans. I had long argued that Communist literature was, for the most part, dull, esoteric, and Western-centered, but ought to be simple, clear, and relevant to the African masses. Moses insisted it could not be done. To prove my point, I had taken Liu's essay and rewritten it for an African audience.

I would be the first witness and therefore set the tone for the defense. In South African courts, evidence from the witness box can be given only in the form of an answer to a question. I did not want to be limited to that format. We decided that instead of giving testimony, I would read a statement from the dock, while the others would testify and go through cross-examination.

Because a witness making a statement from the dock does not submit to cross-examination or questions from the bench, the statement does not have the same legal weight as ordinary testimony. Those who choose to make such a statement usually do so to avoid cross-examination. Our attorneys warned me that it would put me in a more precarious legal situation; anything I said in my statement regarding my own innocence would be discounted by the judge. But that was not our highest priority. We believed it was important to open the defense with a statement of our politics and ideals, which would establish the context for all that followed. I wanted very much to cross swords with Percy Yutar, but it was more important that I use the platform to highlight our grievances.

All of this was agreed upon in consultation, mainly through notes because the consultation room was bugged. We even used the state's eavesdropping to our advantage by supplying them with disinformation. We gave every indication that I was going to testify so that they would spend their time planning their cross-examination. In a staged conversation, I told our attorney Joel Joffe that I would need the Treason Trial record to prepare my testimony. We smiled at the notion of Yutar poring over the hundred or so volumes of Treason Trial transcripts.

I spent about a fortnight drafting my address, working mainly in my cell in the evenings. When I was finished, I read it first to my comrades and fellow accused. They approved of it, suggesting a few changes, and then I asked Bram Fischer to look it over. Bram became concerned after reading it and had a respected advocate named Hal Hanson read it. Hanson told Bram, "If Mandela reads this in court they will take him straight out in back of the courthouse and string him up." That confirmed Bram's anxieties and he came to me the next day and urged me to modify the speech. I felt we were likely to hang no matter what we said, so we might as well say what we truly believed. The atmosphere at the time was extremely grim, with newspapers routinely speculating that we would receive the death sentence. Bram begged me not to read the final paragraph, but I was adamant.

On Monday, the twentieth of April, under the tightest of security, we were taken to the Palace of Justice, this time to begin our defense. Winnie was there with my mother, and I nodded to them as we entered the court, which was again full.

Bram announced that certain parts of the state's evidence would be conceded by the accused, and there was a buzz in the court. But he went on to say that the defense would deny a number of the state's assertions, including the contention that Umkhonto we Sizwe was the military wing of the ANC. He said that the leaders of MK and the ANC "endeavored to keep these two organizations entirely separate. They did not always succeed in this," he said, "but . . . every effort was made to achieve that object." He emphatically denied that the ANC took orders from the Communist Party. He said the defense would challenge the allegation that Goldberg, Kathrada, Bernstein, and Mhlaba were members of Umkhonto. He stated that the defense would show that Umkhonto had not in fact adopted Operation Mayibuye, and that MK had not embarked on preparations for guerrilla warfare.

"That will be denied?" asked Justice de Wet incredulously.

"That will be denied," replied Bram. "The evidence will show that while preparations for guerrilla warfare were being made, no plan was ever adopted. It was hoped throughout that such a step could be avoided."

Then, in his soft voice, Bram said, "The defense case, My Lord, will commence with a statement from the dock by accused number one, who personally took part in the establishment of Umkhonto, and who will be able to inform the court of the beginnings of that organization."

At this, Yutar popped up from the table and cried, "My Lord! My Lord!" He was distressed that I would not be testifying for he had undoubtedly prepared for my cross-examination. "My Lord," he said rather despondently, "a statement from the dock does not carry the same weight as evidence under oath."

"I think, Dr. Yutar," Justice de Wet responded dryly, "that counsel for the defense have sufficient experience to advise their clients without your assistance." Yutar sat down.

"Neither we nor our clients are unaware of the provisions of the criminal code," replied Bram. "I call on Nelson Mandela."

I rose and faced the courtroom and read slowly.

I am the first accused.

I hold a Bachelor's degree in Arts, and practiced as an attorney in Johannesburg for a number of years in partnership with Mr. Oliver Tambo. I am a convicted prisoner, serving five years for leaving the country without a permit and for inciting people to go on strike at the end of May 1961.

I admit immediately that I was one of the persons who helped to form Umkhonto we Sizwe and that I played a prominent role in its affairs until I was arrested in August 1962.

At the outset, I want to say that the suggestion made by the state in its opening that the struggle in South Africa is under the influence of foreigners or Communists is wholly incorrect. I have done whatever I did, both as an individual and as a leader of my people, because of my experience in South Africa, and my own proudly felt African background, and not because of what any outsider might have said.

In my youth in the Transkei, I listened to the elders of my tribe telling stories of the old days. Amongst the tales they related to me were those of wars fought by our ancestors in defense of the fatherland. The names of Dingane and Bambatha, Hintsa and Makanna, Squngthi and Dalasile, Moshoeshoe and Sekhukhuni, were praised as the pride and glory of the entire African nation. I hoped then that life might offer me the opportunity to serve my people and make my own humble contribution to their freedom struggle. This is what has motivated me in all that I have done in relation to the charges made against me in this case.

Having said this, I must deal immediately and at some length with the question of violence. Some of the things so far told the court are true and some are untrue. I do not, however, deny that I planned sabotage. I did not plan it in a spirit of recklessness nor because I have any love of violence. I planned it as a result of a calm and sober assessment of the political situation that had arisen after many years of tyranny, exploitation, and oppression of my people by whites.

I wanted to impress upon the court that we had not acted irresponsibly or without thought to the ramifications of taking up violent action. I laid particular emphasis on our resolve to cause no harm to human life.

We of the ANC have always stood for a nonracial democracy, and we shrank from any action which might drive the races further apart than they already were. But the hard facts were that fifty years of nonviolence had brought the African people nothing but more repressive legislation, and fewer and fewer rights. It may not be easy for this court to understand, but it is a fact that for a long time the people had been talking of violence — of the day when they would fight the white man and win back their country, and we, the leaders of the ANC, had nevertheless always prevailed upon them to avoid violence and to use peaceful methods. While some of us discussed this in May and June of 1961, it could not be denied that our policy to achieve a nonracial state by nonviolence had achieved nothing, and that our followers were beginning to lose confidence in this policy and were developing disturbing ideas of terrorism. . . .

Umkhonto was formed in November 1961. When we took this decision, and subsequently formulated our plans, the ANC heritage of nonviolence and racial harmony was very much with us. We felt that the country was drifting towards a civil war in which blacks and whites would fight each other. We viewed the situation with alarm. Civil war would mean the destruction of what the ANC stood for; with civil war racial peace would be more difficult than ever to achieve. We already have examples in South African history of the results of war. It has taken more than fifty years for the scars of the South African [Anglo-Boer] War to disappear. How much longer would it take to eradicate the scars of interracial civil war, which could not be fought without a great loss of life on both sides?

Sabotage, I said, offered the best hope for future race relations. The reaction of the white rulers to our first efforts was swift and brutal: sabotage was declared to be a crime punishable by death. We did not want civil war, I said, but we needed to be prepared for it.

> Experience convinced us that rebellion would offer the government limitless opportunities for the indiscriminate slaughter of our people. But it was precisely because the soil of South Africa is already drenched with the blood of innocent Africans that we felt it our duty to make preparations as a long-term undertaking to use force in order to defend ourselves against force. If war were inevitable, we wanted the fight to be conducted on terms most favorable to our people. The fight which held out prospects best for us and the least risk of life to both sides was guerrilla warfare. We decided, therefore, in our preparations for the future, to make provision for the possibility of guerrilla warfare.
>
> All whites undergo compulsory military training, but no such training was given to Africans. It was in our view essential to build up a nucleus of trained men who would be able to provide the leadership which would be required if guerrilla warfare started. We had to prepare for such a situation before it became too late to make proper preparations.

I explained that at this stage in our discussions I left the country to attend the PAFMECSA conference and undergo military training. I said that I underwent training because if there was to be a guerrilla war, I wanted to be able to stand and fight beside my own people. Even so, I believed that the possibilities of sabotage were far from exhausted and should be pursued with vigor.

I told the court of the dividing line between the ANC and MK, and how we made good-faith attempts to keep the two separate. This was our policy, but in practice, it was not so simple. Because of bannings and imprisonment, people often had to work in both organizations. Though this might have sometimes blurred the distinction, it did not abolish it. I disputed the allegations of the state that the aims and objects of the ANC and the Communist Party were one and the same.

> The ideological creed of the ANC is, and always has been, the creed of African Nationalism. It is not the concept of African Nationalism expressed in the cry, "Drive the white man into the sea." The African Nationalism for which the ANC stands is the concept of freedom and fulfillment for the African people in their own land. The most important political document ever adopted by the ANC is the Freedom Charter. It is by no means a blueprint for a socialist state. . . . The ANC has never at any period of its history advocated a revolutionary change in the economic structure of the country, nor has it, to the best of my recollection, ever condemned capitalist society. . . .
>
> The ANC, unlike the Communist Party, admitted Africans only as members. Its chief goal was, and is, for the African people to win unity and full political rights. The Communist Party's main aim, on the other hand, was to remove the capitalists and to replace them with a working-class government. The Communist Party sought to emphasize class distinctions whilst the ANC seeks to harmonize them.
>
> It is true that there has often been close cooperation between the ANC and the Communist Party. But cooperation is merely proof of a common goal — in this case the removal of white supremacy — and is not proof of a complete community of interests. The history of the world is full of similar examples. Perhaps the most striking illustration is to be found in the cooperation between Great Britain, the United States of America and the Soviet Union in the fight against Hitler. Nobody but Hitler would have dared to suggest that such cooperation turned Churchill or Roosevelt into Communists or Communist tools, or that Britain and America were working to bring about a Communist world. . . .
>
> It is perhaps difficult for white South Africans, with an ingrained prejudice against communism, to understand why experienced African politicians so readily accepted Communists as their friends. But to us the reason is obvious. Theoretical differences amongst those fighting against oppression is a luxury we cannot afford at this stage. What is more, for many decades Communists were the only political group in South Africa who were prepared to treat Africans as human beings and their equals; who were prepared to eat with us; talk with us, live with and work with us. Because of this, there are many Africans who, today, tend to equate freedom with communism.

I told the court that I was not a Communist and had always regarded myself as an African patriot. I did not deny that I was attracted by the idea of a classless society, or that I had been influenced by Marxist thought. This was true of many leaders of the newly independent states of Africa, who accepted the need for some form of socialism to enable their people to catch up with the advanced countries of the West.

> From my reading of Marxist literature and from conversations with Marxists, I have gained the impression that Communists regard the parliamentary system of the West as undemocratic and reactionary. But, on the contrary, I am an admirer of such a system.
>
> The Magna Carta, the Petition of Rights and the Bill of Rights, are documents which are held in veneration by democrats throughout the world. I have great respect for British political institutions, and for the country's system of justice. I regard the British Parliament as the most democratic institution in the world, and the independence and impartiality of its judiciary never fail to arouse my admiration. The American Congress, the country's doctrine of separation of powers, as well as the independence of its judiciary, arouse in me similar sentiments.

I detailed the terrible disparities between black and white life in South Africa. In education, health, income, every aspect of life, blacks were barely at a subsistence level while whites had the highest standards in the world — and aimed to keep it that way. Whites, I said, often claim that Africans in South Africa were better off than Africans in the rest of the continent. Our complaint, I said, was not that we were poor by comparison with the people in the rest of Africa, but that we were poor by comparison with the whites in our country, and that we were prevented by legislation from righting that imbalance.

> The lack of human dignity experienced by Africans is the direct result of the policy of white supremacy. White supremacy implies black inferiority. Legislation designed to preserve white supremacy entrenches this notion. Menial tasks in South Africa are invariably performed by Africans. When anything has to be carried or cleaned the white man looks around for an African to do it for him, whether the African is employed by him or not. . . .
>
> Poverty and the breakdown of family life have secondary effects. Children wander about the streets of the townships because they have

no schools to go to, or no money to enable them to go to school, or no parents at home to see that they go to school, because both parents (if there be two) have to work to keep the family alive. This leads to a breakdown in moral standards, to an alarming rise in illegitimacy and to growing violence which erupts, not only politically, but everywhere. . . .

Africans want a just share in the whole of South Africa; they want security and a stake in society. Above all, we want equal political rights, because without them our disabilities will be permanent. I know this sounds revolutionary to the whites in this country, because the majority of voters will be Africans. This makes the white man fear democracy. . . .

This then is what the ANC is fighting for. Their struggle is a truly national one. It is a struggle of the African people, inspired by their own suffering and their own experience. It is a struggle for the right to live.

I had been reading my speech, and at this point I placed my papers on the defense table, and turned to face the judge. The courtroom became extremely quiet. I did not take my eyes off Justice de Wet as I spoke from memory the final words.

During my lifetime I have dedicated myself to this struggle of the African people. I have fought against white domination, and I have fought against black domination. I have cherished the ideal of a democratic and free society in which all persons live together in harmony and with equal opportunities. It is an ideal which I hope to live for and to achieve. But if needs be, it is an ideal for which I am prepared to die.

The silence in the courtroom was now complete. At the end of the address, I simply sat down. I did not turn and face the gallery, though I felt all their eyes on me. The silence seemed to stretch for many minutes. But in fact it lasted probably no more than thirty seconds, and then from the gallery I heard what sounded like a great sigh, a deep, collective "ummmm," followed by the cries of women.

I had read for over four hours. It was a little after four in the afternoon, the time court normally adjourned. But Justice de Wet, as soon as there was order in the courtroom, asked for the next witness. He was determined to lessen the impact of my statement. He did not want it to be the last and only testimony of the day. But nothing he did could weaken its effect. When I finished my address and sat down, it was the last time that Justice de Wet ever looked me in the eye.

The speech received wide publicity in both the local and foreign press, and was printed, virtually word for word, in the *Rand Daily Mail*. This despite the fact that all my words were banned. The speech both indicated our line of defense and disarmed the prosecution, which had prepared its entire case based on the expectation that I would be giving evidence denying responsibility for sabotage. It was now plain that we would not attempt to use legal niceties to avoid accepting responsibility for actions we had taken with pride and premeditation.

Accused number two, Walter Sisulu, was next. Walter had to bear the brunt of the cross-examination that Yutar had prepared for me. Walter withstood a barrage of hostile questions and rose above Yutar's petty machinations to explain our policy in clear and simple terms. He asserted that Operation Mayibuye and the policy of guerrilla warfare had not been adopted as ANC policy. In fact, Walter told the court that he had personally opposed its adoption on the grounds that it was premature.

Govan followed Walter in the witness box and proudly related to the court his longtime membership in the Communist Party. The prosecutor asked Govan why, if he admitted many of the actions in the four counts against him, he did not simply plead guilty to the four counts? "First," Govan said, "I felt I should come and explain under oath some of the reasons that led me to join these organizations. There was a sense of moral duty attached to it. Secondly, for the simple reason that to plead guilty would to my mind indicate a sense of moral guilt. I do not accept there is moral guilt attached to my answers."

Like Govan, Ahmed Kathrada and Rusty Bernstein testified to their membership of the Communist Party as well as the ANC. Although Rusty was captured at Rivonia during the raid, the only evidence of a direct nature that the state had against him was that he had assisted in the erection of a radio aerial at the farm. Kathy, in his sharp-witted testimony, denied committing acts of sabotage or inciting others to do so, but he said he supported such acts if they advanced the struggle.

We had all been surprised when accused number eight, James Kantor, had been arrested and grouped with us. Apart from being the brother-in-law and legal partner of Harold Wolpe, who performed a number of transactions for us through his office, he had no involvement whatsoever with the ANC or MK. There was virtually no evidence against him, and I assumed the only reason the state kept up the charade of prosecuting him in prison was to intimidate progressive lawyers.

On the day that Justice de Wet was to rule on Jimmy's case, we were waiting in the cells underneath the court and I said to Jimmy, "Let us exchange ties for good luck." But when he saw the wide, old-fashioned tie I gave him compared to the lovely, silk tie he gave me, he probably thought I was merely trying to improve my wardrobe. Jimmy was something of a clotheshorse, but he wore the tie to court and when Justice de Wet dismissed the charges against him, he lifted the tie up to me as a kind of salute and farewell.

Raymond Mhlaba was one of the leading ANC and MK figures in the eastern Cape, but because the state did not have much evidence against him, he denied he was a member of MK and that he knew anything about sabotage. We all decided that neither Elias Motsoaledi, accused number nine, nor Andrew Mlangeni, accused number ten, should testify. They were low-level members of MK, and could not add much to what had already been said. Elias Motsoaledi, despite having been beaten and tortured in prison, never broke down. Andrew Mlangeni, the last accused, made an unsworn statement admitting that he carried messages and instructions for MK and had disguised himself as a priest to facilitate this work. He, too, informed the court that he had been assaulted while in prison, and subjected to electric shock treatment. Andrew was the last witness. The defense rested. All that remained were the final arguments and then judgment.

On the twentieth of May, Yutar handed out a dozen blue leather-bound volumes of his final speech to the press and one to the defense. Despite its handsome packaging, Yutar's address was a garbled summary of the prosecution's case and did not explain the indictment or assess the evidence. It was filled with ad hominem insults. "The deceit of the accused is amazing," he said at one point. "Although they represented scarcely 1% of the Bantu population they took it upon themselves to tell the world that the Africans in South Africa are suppressed, oppressed and depressed." Even Judge de Wet seemed mystified by Yutar's speech, and at one point interrupted him to say, "Mr. Yutar, you do concede that you failed to prove guerrilla warfare was ever decided upon, do you not?"

Yutar was stunned. He had assumed precisely the opposite. We were surprised as well, for the judge's question gave us hope. Yutar haltingly told the court that preparations for guerrilla warfare were indeed made.

"Yes, I know that," de Wet replied impatiently, "the defense concedes that. But they say that prior to their arrest they took no decision to engage in guerrilla warfare. I take it that you have no evidence contradicting that and that you accept it?"

"As Your Worship wishes," Yutar said in a strangled voice.

Yutar finished by saying that the case was not only one of high treason "par excellence," but of murder and attempted murder — neither of which was mentioned in the indictment. In a fit of bluster, he proclaimed, "I make bold to say that every particular allegation in the indictment has been proved." He knew, even as he uttered those words, that they were patently false.

Defense counsel Arthur Chaskalson rose first to deal with some of the legal questions raised by the prosecution. He rejected Yutar's statement that the trial had anything to do with murder, and reminded the court that MK's express policy was that there should be no loss of life. When Arthur began to explain that other organizations committed acts of sabotage for which the accused were blamed, de Wet interrupted to say he already accepted that as a fact. This was another unexpected victory.

Bram Fischer spoke next and was prepared to tackle the state's two most serious contentions: that we had undertaken guerrilla warfare and that the ANC and MK were the same. Though de Wet had said he believed that guerrilla warfare had not yet begun, we were taking no chances. But as Bram launched into his first point, de Wet interjected somewhat testily, "I thought I made my attitude clear. I accept that no decision or date was fixed upon for guerrilla warfare."

When Bram began his second point, de Wet again interrupted him to say that he also conceded the fact that the two organizations were separate. Bram, who was usually prepared for anything, was hardly prepared for de Wet's response. He then sat down; the judge had accepted his arguments even before he made them. We were jubilant — that is, if men facing the death sentence can be said to be jubilant. Court was adjourned for three weeks while de Wet considered the verdict.

# 57

THE WORLD had been paying attention to the Rivonia Trial. Night-long vigils were held for us at St. Paul's Cathedral in London. The students of London University elected me president of their Students' Union, in absentia. A group of experts at the U.N. urged a national convention for South Africa that would lead to a truly representative parliament, and recommended an amnesty for all opponents of apartheid. Two days before Judge de Wet was due to give his decision, the U.N. Security Council (with four abstentions, including Great Britain and the United States) urged the South African government to end the trial and grant amnesty to the defendants.

In the days before we were due to reconvene, I wrote papers for a set of London University examinations for my LL.B. It might seem odd that I was taking law exams a few days before the verdict. It certainly seemed bizarre to my guards, who said I would not need a law degree where I was going. But I had continued my studies through the trial and I wanted to take the examinations. I was single-minded about it, and I later realized that it was a way to keep myself from thinking negatively. I knew I would not be practicing law again very soon, but I did not want to consider the alternative. I passed the exams.

On Thursday, June 11, we reassembled in the Palace of Justice for the verdict. We knew that for at least six of us, there could be no verdict but guilty. The question was the sentence.

De Wet wasted no time in getting down to business. He spoke in low, rapid tones. "I have recorded the reasons for the conclusions I have come to. I do not propose to read them out.

"Accused number one is found guilty on all four counts. Accused number two is found guilty on all four counts. Accused number three is found guilty on all four counts. . . ."

De Wet pronounced each of the main accused guilty on all counts.

Kathy was found guilty on only one of four counts, and Rusty Bernstein was found not guilty and discharged.

"I do not propose to deal with the question of sentence today," de Wet said. "The state and the defense will be given opportunities to make any submission they want tomorrow morning at ten o'clock." Court was then adjourned.

We had hoped that Kathy and Mhlaba might escape conviction, but it was another sign, if one was necessary, that the state was taking a harsh line. If he could convict Mhlaba on all four counts with little evidence, could the death sentence be far behind for those of us against whom the evidence was overwhelming?

That night, after a discussion among ourselves, Walter, Govan, and I informed counsel that whatever sentences we received, even the death sentence, we would not appeal. Our decision stunned our lawyers. Walter, Govan, and I believed an appeal would undermine the moral stance we had taken. We had from the first maintained that what we had done, we had done proudly, and for moral reasons. We were not now going to suggest otherwise in an appeal. If a death sentence was passed, we did not want to hamper the mass campaign that would surely spring up. In light of the bold and defiant line we had taken all along, an appeal would seem anticlimactic and even disillusioning. Our message was that no sacrifice was too great in the struggle for freedom.

Counsel were unhappy about our decision, and wanted to talk about an appeal. But Walter, Govan, and I wanted to discuss the mechanics of the sentencing procedure the next day. If we were sentenced to death, what would then happen? We were told that after de Wet pronounced the death sentence, he would ask me, as the first accused, "Have you any reason to advance why the sentence of death should not be passed?" I told Bram, Joel, and Vernon that in that case I would have quite a lot to say. I would tell de Wet that I was prepared to die secure in the knowledge that my death would be an inspiration to the cause for which I was giving my life. My death — our deaths — would not be in vain; if anything we might serve the cause greater in death as martyrs than we ever could in life. Counsel said that such a speech would not be very helpful for an appeal, and I reaffirmed that we would not be appealing.

Even if — especially if — we did not receive the death penalty, there were practical reasons not to appeal. For one thing, we might lose. An appellate court might decide that de Wet had been too lenient and that we deserved the death penalty. An appeal would forestall international pressure to release us.

For the state, a death sentence would be the most practical verdict. We had heard that John Vorster, the minister of justice, had told friends that Prime Minister Smuts's greatest blunder during the Second World War was not hanging him for his treason. The Nationalists, he said, would not make the same mistake.

I was prepared for the death penalty. To be truly prepared for something, one must actually expect it. One cannot be prepared for something while secretly believing it will not happen. We were all prepared, not because we were brave but because we were realistic. I thought of the line from Shakespeare: "Be absolute for death; for either death or life shall be the sweeter."

# 58

ON FRIDAY, JUNE 12, 1964, we entered court for the last time. Nearly a year had passed since the fateful arrests at Rivonia. Security was extraordinarily high. Our convoy raced through the streets with sirens wailing. All the roads leading to the courthouse had been blocked off to normal traffic. The police checked the identification of anyone attempting to go near the Palace of Justice. They had even set up checkpoints at the local bus and railway stations. Despite the intimidation, as many as two thousand people assembled in front of the courthouse holding banners and signs such as "WE STAND BY OUR LEADERS." Inside, the spectators' gallery was full, and it was standing room only for the local and foreign press.

I waved hello to Winnie and my mother. It was heartening to see them there; my mother had journeyed all the way from the Transkei. It must be a very odd sensation to come to a courtroom to see whether or not your son will be sentenced to death. Though I suspect my mother did not understand all that was going on, her support never wavered. Winnie was equally stalwart, and her strength gave me strength.

The registrar called out the case: "The State against Mandela and others." Before the sentence was to be passed, there were two pleas in mitigation. One was delivered by Harold Hanson and the other by the author Alan Paton, who was also national president of the Liberal Party. Hanson spoke eloquently, saying that a nation's grievances cannot be suppressed, that people will always find a way to give voice to those grievances. "It was not their aims which had been criminal," said Hanson, "only the means to which they had resorted." Hanson said the judge would do well to recall that his own people, the Afrikaners, had struggled violently for their freedom.

Though Paton did not himself support violence, he said the accused had had only two alternatives: "to bow their heads and submit, or to resist by force." The defendants should receive clemency, he said, otherwise the future of South Africa would be bleak.

But de Wet did not seem to be listening to either man. He neither looked up nor took any notes while they spoke. He seemed absorbed in his own thoughts. He had obviously already decided; he was merely waiting for the moment to reveal his decision.

He nodded for us to rise. I tried to catch his eye, but he was not even looking in our direction. His eyes were focused on the middle distance. His face was very pale, and he was breathing heavily. We looked at each other and seemed to know: it would be death, otherwise why was this normally calm man so nervous? And then he began to speak.

> I have heard a great deal during the course of this case about the grievances of the non-European population. The accused have told me and their counsel have told me that the accused who were all leaders of the non-European population were motivated entirely by a desire to ameliorate these grievances. I am by no means convinced that the motives of the accused were as altruistic as they wish the court to believe. People who organize a revolution usually take over the government and personal ambition cannot be excluded as a motive.

He paused for a moment as if to catch his breath. De Wet's voice, which was muted before, was now barely audible.

> The function of this court as is the function of the court in any other country is to enforce law and order and to enforce the laws of the state within which it functions. The crime of which the accused have been

convicted, that is the main crime, the crime of conspiracy, is in essence one of high treason. The state has decided not to charge the crime in this form. Bearing this in mind and giving the matter very serious consideration I have decided not to impose the supreme penalty which in a case like this would usually be the proper penalty for the crime, but consistent with my duty that is the only leniency which I can show. The sentence in the case of all the accused will be one of life imprisonment.

We looked at each other and smiled. There had been a great collective gasp in the courtroom when de Wet announced that he was not sentencing us to death. But there was consternation among some spectators because they had been unable to hear de Wet's sentence. Dennis Goldberg's wife called to him, "Dennis, what is it!?"

"Life!" he yelled back, grinning. "Life! To live!"

I turned and smiled broadly to the gallery, searching out Winnie's face and that of my mother, but it was extremely confused in the court, with people shouting, police pushing the crowd this way and that. I could not see them. I flashed the thumbs-up ANC salute as many of the spectators were dashing outside to tell the crowd the verdict. Our police guardians began to hustle us out of the dock and toward the door leading underground, and although I looked again for Winnie's face, I was not able to see her before I ducked through the door leading to the cells below.

We were kept handcuffed in the cells underneath the courthouse. The police were extremely nervous about the crowd outside. They kept us underground for more than half an hour, hoping people would disperse. We were taken through the back of the building and entered the black van. We could hear the motorcycle escort revving up beside us. To avoid the crowd, the van took a different course, but even so, we could hear the crowd shouting *"Amandla!"* and the slow beautiful rhythms of *"Nkosi Sikelel' iAfrika."* We made clenched fists through the bars of the window, hoping the crowd could see us, not knowing if they could.

All of us were now convicted prisoners. We were separated from Dennis Goldberg because he was white and he was taken to a different facility. The rest of us were locked up in cells in Pretoria Local away from all the other prisoners. Instead of shouts and songs, we now heard only the clanging of doors and gates.

*          *          *

That night, as I lay on my mat on the floor of my cell, I ran over the reasons for de Wet's decision. The demonstrations throughout South Africa and the international pressure undoubtedly weighed on his mind. International trade unions had protested the trial. Dockworkers' unions around the world threatened not to handle South African goods. The Russian prime minister, Leonid Brezhnev, wrote to Dr. Verwoerd asking for leniency. Members of the United States Congress protested. Fifty members of the British Parliament had staged a march in London. Alex Douglas-Home, the British foreign secretary, was rumored to be working behind the scenes to help our cause. Adlai Stevenson, the U.S. representative at the U.N., wrote a letter saying that his government would do everything it could to prevent a death sentence. I thought that once de Wet had accepted that we had not yet initiated guerrilla warfare and that the ANC and MK were separate entities, it would have been difficult to impose the death penalty; it would have seemed excessive.

Verwoerd told Parliament that the judgment had not been influenced by the telegrams of protest and representations that had come in from around the world. He boasted that he had tossed into the wastebasket all the telegrams from socialist nations.

Towards the end of the proceedings, Judge de Wet had remarked in passing to Bram Fischer that the defense had generated a great deal of worldwide propaganda in the case. This was perhaps his own way of acknowledging the pressure. He knew that if we were executed, the great majority of the people would regard him as our killer.

Yet he was under even greater pressure from his own people. He was a white Afrikaner, a creature of the South African system and mind-set. He had no inclination to go against the belief system that had formed him. He had succumbed to these pressures by sentencing us to life and resisted them by not giving us death.

I was surprised and displeased by the sentences de Wet imposed on Kathrada, Motsoaledi, and Mlangeni. I had expected him to discharge Kathy, and to give Elias and Andrew lighter sentences. The latter two were comparatively junior members of MK, and the combined offenses of the three of them could hardly be compared with those of the rest of us. But by not appealing, we undoubtedly cost Kathy, Andrew, and Elias: an appeals court might have cut down their sentences.

Every evening, in Pretoria Local, before lights were out, the jail would echo to African prisoners singing freedom songs. We too would sing in this great swelling chorus. But, each evening, seconds before the lights were dimmed, as if in obedience to some silent command, the hum of voices would stop and the entire jail would become silent. Then, from a dozen places throughout the prison, men would yell *"Amandla!"* This would be met by hundreds of voices replying *"Ngawethu!"* Often, we would start this call-and-response ourselves, but that night, other nameless prisoners took the initiative, and the voices from around the prison seemed uncommonly strong as though steeling us for what lay ahead.

*Part Eight*

# ROBBEN ISLAND: THE DARK YEARS

# 59

AT MIDNIGHT, I was awake and staring at the ceiling — images from the trial were still rattling around in my head — when I heard steps coming down the hallway. I was locked in my own cell, away from the others. There was a knock at my door and I could see Colonel Aucamp's face at the bars. "Mandela," he said in a husky whisper, "are you awake?"

I told him I was. "You are a lucky man," he said. "We are taking you to a place where you will have your freedom. You will be able to move around; you'll see the ocean and the sky, not just gray walls."

He intended no sarcasm, but I well knew that the place he was referring to would not afford me the freedom I longed for. He then remarked rather cryptically, "As long as you don't make trouble, you'll get everything you want."

Aucamp then woke the others, all of whom were in a single cell, ordering them to pack their things. Fifteen minutes later we were making our way through the iron labyrinth of Pretoria Local, with its endless series of clanging metal doors echoing in our ears.

Once outside, the seven of us — Walter, Raymond, Govan, Kathy, Andrew, Elias, and myself — were handcuffed and piled into the back of a police van. It was well after midnight, but none of us was tired, and the atmosphere was not at all somber. We sat on the dusty floor, singing and chanting, reliving the final moments of the trial. The warders provided us with sandwiches and cold drinks and Lieutenant Van Wyck was perched in the back with us. He was a pleasant fellow, and during a lull in the singing, he offered his unsolicited opinion on our future. "Well," he said, "you chaps won't be in prison long. The demand for your release is too strong. In a year or two, you will get out and you will return as national heroes. Crowds will cheer you, everyone will want to be your friend, women will want you. Ag, you fellows have it made." We listened without comment, but I confess his speech cheered me considerably. Unfortunately, his prediction turned out to be off by nearly three decades.

\*　　　\*　　　\*

We were departing quietly, secretly, under a heavy police escort, in the middle of the night, and in less than half an hour we found ourselves at a small military airport outside the city. We were hustled onto a Dakota, a large military transport plane that had seen better days. There was no heat, and we shivered in the belly of the plane. Some of the others had never flown before and they seemed more anxious about our voyage than our destination; bumping up and down in a plane at fifteen thousand feet seemed far more perilous than being locked in a cell behind high walls.

After about an hour in the air, dawn lightened the terrain below. The plane had portholes, and as soon as we could see in the half-light, my comrades pressed their faces to the glass. We flew south-east, over the dry, flat plains of the Orange Free State and the green and mountainous Cape peninsula. I, too, craned to see out the portholes, examining the scenery not as a tourist but as a strategist, looking for areas where a guerrilla army might hide itself.

There had been a running argument since the formation of MK as to whether the countryside of South Africa could support a guer-rilla army. Most of the High Command thought that it could not. When we flew over a wooded, mountainous area called Matroosberg in the Cape, I yelled to my colleagues that here was terrain where we could fight. The men became excited and craned to get a better look, and indeed, the heavily forested area appeared as though it could shelter a nascent guerrilla force.

Minutes later we approached the outskirts of Cape Town. Soon, we could see the little matchbox houses of the Cape Flats, the gleam-ing towers of downtown, and the horizontal top of Table Mountain. Then, out in Table Bay, in the dark blue waters of the Atlantic, we could make out the misty outline of Robben Island.

We landed on an airstrip on one end of the island. It was a grim, overcast day, and when I stepped out of the plane, the cold winter wind whipped through our thin prison uniforms. We were met by guards with automatic weapons; the atmosphere was tense but quiet, unlike the boisterous reception I had received on my arrival on the island two years before.

We were driven to the old jail, an isolated stone building, where we were ordered to strip while standing outside. One of the ritual indignities of prison life is that when you are transferred from one

486

prison to another, the first thing that happens is that you change from the garb of the old prison to that of the new. When we were undressed, we were thrown the plain khaki uniforms of Robben Island.

Apartheid's regulations extended even to clothing. All of us, except Kathy, received short trousers, an insubstantial jersey, and a canvas jacket. Kathy, the one Indian among us, was given long trousers. Normally Africans would receive sandals made from car tires, but in this instance we were given shoes. Kathy, alone, received socks. Short trousers for Africans were meant to remind us that we were "boys." I put on the short trousers that day, but I vowed that I would not put up with them for long.

The warders pointed with their guns where they wanted us to go, and barked their orders in simple one-word commands: "Move!" "Silence!" "Halt!" They did not threaten us in the swaggering way that I recalled from my previous stay, and betrayed no emotion.

The old jail was only temporary quarters for us. The authorities were in the process of finishing an entirely separate maximum-security structure for political prisoners. While there, we were not permitted to go outside or have any contact with other prisoners.

The fourth morning we were handcuffed and taken in a covered truck to a prison within a prison. This new structure was a one-story rectangular stone fortress with a flat cement courtyard in the center, about one hundred feet by thirty feet. It had cells on three of the four sides. The fourth side was a twenty-foot-high wall with a catwalk patrolled by guards with German shepherds.

The three lines of cells were known as sections A, B, and C, and we were put in Section B, on the easternmost side of the quadrangle. We were each given individual cells on either side of a long corridor, with half the cells facing the courtyard. There were about thirty cells in all. The total number of prisoners in the single cells was usually about twenty-four. Each cell had one window, about a foot square, covered with iron bars. The cell had two doors: a metal gate or grille with iron bars on the inside and a thick wooden door outside of that. During the day, only the grille was locked; at night, the wooden door was locked as well.

The cells had been constructed hurriedly, and the walls were perpetually damp. When I raised this with the commanding officer, he told me our bodies would absorb the moisture. We were each issued three blankets so flimsy and worn they were practically transparent. Our bedding consisted of a single sisal, or straw, mat. Later we were given a felt mat, and one placed the felt mat on top of the sisal one to provide some softness. At that time of year, the cells were so cold and the blankets provided so little warmth that we always slept fully dressed.

I was assigned a cell at the head of the corridor. It overlooked the courtyard and had a small eye-level window. I could walk the length of my cell in three paces. When I lay down, I could feel the wall with my feet and my head grazed the concrete at the other side. The width was about six feet, and the walls were at least two feet thick. Each cell had a white card posted outside of it with our name and our prison service number. Mine read, "N Mandela 466/64," which meant I was the 466th prisoner admitted to the island in 1964. I was forty-six years old, a political prisoner with a life sentence, and that small cramped space was to be my home for I knew not how long.

We were immediately joined by a number of prisoners who had been held in the general section of the prison, a squat brick building not far from Section B. The general prison, known as sections F and G, contained about a thousand mostly common-law prisoners. As many as a quarter of them were political prisoners, and a handful of those men were put with us in Section B. We were isolated from the general prisoners for two reasons: we were considered risky from a security perspective, but even more dangerous from a political standpoint. The authorities were concerned we might "infect" the other prisoners with our political views.

Among the men put with us was George Peake, one of the founders of the South African Coloured People's Organization, a Treason Trialist, and most recently a member of the Cape Town City Council. He had been sentenced for planting explosives outside a Cape Town prison. Dennis Brutus, another Coloured political activist, was a poet and writer from Port Elizabeth imprisoned for violating his bans. We were also joined by Billy Nair, a longtime member of the Natal Indian Congress, sentenced for sabotage as a member of Umkhonto we Sizwe.

Within a few days we had more company, including Neville Alexander, a prominent Coloured intellectual and member of the Non-European Unity Movement, who had formed a tiny radical offshoot called the Yu Chi Chan Club in Cape Town, which studied guerrilla warfare. Neville had a B.A. from the University of Cape Town and a doctorate in German literature from Tubingen University in Germany. Along with Neville, there was Fikile Bam, a law student of the University of Cape Town and another member of the Yu Chi Chan Club; and Zephania Mothopeng, a member of the PAC National Executive. Zeph had been a teacher in Orlando, and was a staunch opponent of Bantu Education, and one of the most level-headed of the PAC's leaders. Three aged peasants from the Transkei, sentenced for plotting to assassinate K. D. Matanzima, now the chief minister of the "self-governing" Transkei, were also imprisoned with us.

This became our core group of about twenty prisoners. Some I knew, some I had heard of, while others I did not know at all. Normally, in prison, one of the few festive times is seeing old friends and new faces, but the atmosphere in those first few weeks was so oppressive we were not even able to greet each other. We had as many guards as prisoners, and they enforced every regulation with threats and intimidation.

That first week we began the work that would occupy us for the next few months. Each morning, a load of stones about the size of volleyballs was dumped by the entrance to the courtyard. Using wheelbarrows, we moved the stones to the center of the yard. We were given either four-pound hammers or fourteen-pound hammers for the larger stones. Our job was to crush the stones into gravel. We were divided into four rows, about a yard-and-a-half apart, and sat cross-legged on the ground. We were each given a thick rubber ring, made from tires, in which to place the stones. The ring was meant to catch flying chips of stone, but hardly ever did so. We wore makeshift wire masks to protect our eyes.

Warders walked among us to enforce the silence. During those first few weeks, warders from other sections and even other prisons came to stare at us as if we were a collection of rare caged animals. The work was tedious and difficult; it was not strenuous enough to keep us warm but it was demanding enough to make all our muscles ache.

June and July were the bleakest months on Robben Island. Winter was in the air, and the rains were just beginning. It never seemed to go above forty degrees Fahrenheit. Even in the sun, I shivered in my light khaki shirt. It was then that I first understood the cliché of feeling the cold in one's bones. At noon we would break for lunch. That first week all we were given was soup, which stank horribly. In the afternoon, we were permitted to exercise for half an hour under strict supervision. We walked briskly around the courtyard in single file.

On one of our first days pounding rocks, a warder commanded Kathy to take a wheelbarrow filled with gravel to the truck parked by the entrance. Kathy was a slender fellow unused to hard physical labor. He could not budge the wheelbarrow. The warders yelled: *"Laat daardie kruiwa loop!"* (Let that wheelbarrow move!) As Kathy managed to nudge it forward, the wheelbarrow looked as if it would tip over, and the warders began to laugh. Kathy, I could see, was determined not to give them cause for mirth. I knew how to maneuver the wheelbarrows, and I jumped up to help him. Before being ordered to sit down, I managed to tell Kathy to wheel it slowly, that it was a matter of balance not strength. He nodded and then carefully moved the wheelbarrow across the courtyard. The warders stopped smiling.

The next morning, the authorities placed an enormous bucket in the courtyard and announced that it had to be half full by the end of the week. We worked hard and succeeded. The following week, the warder in charge announced that we must now fill the bucket three-quarters of the way. We worked with great diligence and succeeded. The next week we were ordered to fill the bucket to the top. We knew we could not tolerate this much longer, but said nothing. We even managed to fill the bucket all the way, but the warders had provoked us. In stolen whispers we resolved on a policy: no quotas. The next week we initiated our first go-slow strike on the island: we would work at less than half the speed we had before to protest the excessive and unfair demands. The guards immediately saw this and threatened us, but we would not increase our pace, and we continued this go-slow strategy for as long as we worked in the courtyard.

*        *        *

Robben Island had changed since I had been there for a fortnight's stay in 1962. In 1962, there were few prisoners; the place seemed more like an experiment than a fully-fledged prison. Two years later, Robben Island was without question the harshest, most iron-fisted outpost in the South African penal system. It was a hardship station not only for the prisoners but for the prison staff. Gone were the Coloured warders who had supplied cigarettes and sympathy. The warders were white and overwhelmingly Afrikaans-speaking, and they demanded a master-servant relationship. They ordered us to call them *"baas,"* which we refused. The racial divide on Robben Island was absolute: there were no black warders, and no white prisoners.

Moving from one prison to another always requires a period of adjustment. But journeying to Robben Island was like going to another country. Its isolation made it not simply another prison, but a world of its own, far removed from the one we had come from. The high spirits with which we left Pretoria had been snuffed out by its stern atmosphere; we were face to face with the realization that our life would be unredeemably grim. In Pretoria, we felt connected to our supporters and our families; on the island, we felt cut off, and indeed we were. We had the consolation of being with each other, but that was the only consolation. My dismay was quickly replaced by a sense that a new and different fight had begun.

From the first day, I had protested about being forced to wear short trousers. I demanded to see the head of the prison and made a list of complaints. The warders ignored my protests, but by the end of the second week, I found a pair of old khaki trousers unceremoniously dumped on the floor of my cell. No pin-striped three-piece suit has ever pleased me as much. But before putting them on I checked to see if my comrades had been issued trousers as well.

They had not, and I told the warder to take them back. I insisted that all African prisoners must have long trousers. The warder grumbled, "Mandela, you say you want long pants and then you don't want them when we give them to you." The warder balked at touching trousers worn by a black man, and finally the commanding officer himself came to my cell to pick them up. "Very well, Mandela," he said, "you are going to have the same clothing as everyone else." I replied that if he was willing to give me long trousers, why couldn't everyone else have them? He did not have an answer.

# 60

AT THE END of our first two weeks on the island, we were informed that our lawyers, Bram Fischer and Joel Joffe, were going to be visiting the following day. When they arrived, we were escorted to the visiting area to meet them. The purpose of their visit was twofold: to see how we had settled in, and to verify that we still did not want to appeal our sentences. It had only been a few weeks since I had seen them, but it felt like an eternity. They seemed like visitors from another world.

We sat in an empty room, a major just outside supervising the consultation. I felt like hugging them, but I was restrained by the presence of the major. I told them that all of us were well, and explained that we were still opposed to an appeal for all the reasons we had previously enunciated, including the fact that we did not want our appeal to interfere with the cases of other ANC defendants. Bram and Joel seemed resigned to this, though I knew Bram believed we should mount an appeal.

When we were winding up our conversation, I briefly asked Bram about Molly, his wife. No sooner had I pronounced Molly's name than Bram stood up, turned away, and abruptly walked out of the room. A few minutes later, he returned, once again composed, and resumed the conversation, but without answering my question.

Our meeting ended shortly afterward, and when we were walking back to our cells with the major, he said to me, "Mandela, were you struck by the behavior of Bram Fischer?" I said that I had been. He told me that Molly had died in a car accident the previous week. Bram, he said, had been driving and had swerved to avoid an animal in the road, and the car had plunged into a river. Molly had drowned.

We were devastated by the news. Molly was a wonderful woman, generous and unselfish, utterly without prejudice. She had supported Bram in more ways than it was possible to know. She had been wife, colleague, and comrade. Bram had already experienced disaster in his life: his son had died of cystic fibrosis in adolescence.

The act of turning away when I asked about Molly was typical of Bram's character. He was a stoic, a man who never burdened his friends with his own pain and troubles. As an Afrikaner whose conscience forced him to reject his own heritage and be ostracized by his own people, he showed a level of courage and sacrifice that was in a class by itself. I fought only against injustice, not my own people.

I informed the major that I intended to write Bram a condolence letter, and he responded that I could do so. The rules governing letter-writing were then extremely strict. We were only permitted to write to our immediate families, and just one letter of five hundred words every six months. I was therefore surprised and pleased when the major did not oppose my writing Bram. But he didn't live up to his agreement. I wrote the letter and handed it over to the major, but it was never posted.

Within a few months, our life settled into a pattern. Prison life is about routine: each day like the one before; each week like the one before it, so that the months and years blend into each other. Anything that departs from this pattern upsets the authorities, for routine is the sign of a well-run prison.

Routine is also comforting for the prisoner, which is why it can be a trap. Routine can be a pleasant mistress whom it is hard to resist, for routine makes the time go faster. Watches and timepieces of any kind were barred on Robben Island, so we never knew precisely what time it was. We were dependent on bells and warders' whistles and shouts. With each week resembling the one before, one must make an effort to recall what day and month it is. One of the first things I did was to make a calendar on the wall of my cell. Losing a sense of time is an easy way to lose one's grip and even one's sanity.

Time slows down in prison; the days seem endless. The cliché of time passing slowly usually has to do with idleness and inactivity. But this was not the case on Robben Island. We were busy almost all the time, with work, study, resolving disputes. Yet, time nevertheless moved glacially. This is partially because things that took a few hours or days outside would take months or years in prison. A request for a new toothbrush might take six months or a year to be filled. Ahmed Kathrada once said that in prison the minutes can seem like years, but the years go by like minutes. An afternoon pounding rocks in the courtyard might seem like forever, but suddenly it is the end of the year, and you do not know where all the months went.

The challenge for every prisoner, particularly every political prisoner, is how to survive prison intact, how to emerge from prison undiminished, how to conserve and even replenish one's beliefs. The first task in accomplishing that is learning exactly what one must do to survive. To that end, one must know the enemy's purpose before adopting a strategy to undermine it. Prison is designed to break one's spirit and destroy one's resolve. To do this, the authorities attempt to exploit every weakness, demolish every initiative, negate all signs of individuality — all with the idea of stamping out that spark that makes each of us human and each of us who we are.

Our survival depended on understanding what the authorities were attempting to do to us, and sharing that understanding with each other. It would be very hard if not impossible for one man alone to resist. I do not know that I could have done it had I been alone. But the authorities' greatest mistake was keeping us together, for together our determination was reinforced. We supported each other and gained strength from each other. Whatever we knew, whatever we learned, we shared, and by sharing we multiplied whatever courage we had individually. That is not to say that we were all alike in our responses to the hardships we suffered. Men have different capacities and react differently to stress. But the stronger ones raised up the weaker ones, and both became stronger in the process. Ultimately, we had to create our own lives in prison. In a way that even the authorities acknowledged, order in prison was preserved not by the warders but by ourselves.

As a leader, one must sometimes take actions that are unpopular, or whose results will not be known for years to come. There are victories whose glory lies only in the fact that they are known to those who win them. This is particularly true of prison, where one must find consolation in being true to one's ideals, even if no one else knows of it.

I was now on the sidelines, but I also knew that I would not give up the fight. I was in a different and smaller arena, an arena for whom the only audience was ourselves and our oppressors. We regarded the struggle in prison as a microcosm of the struggle as a whole. We would fight inside as we had fought outside. The racism and repression were the same; I would simply have to fight on different terms.

Prison and the authorities conspire to rob each man of his dignity. In and of itself, that assured that I would survive, for any man or institution that tries to rob me of my dignity will lose because I will not part with it at any price or under any pressure. I never seriously considered the possibility that I would not emerge from prison one day. I never thought that a life sentence truly meant life and that I would die behind bars. Perhaps I was denying this prospect because it was too unpleasant to contemplate. But I always knew that some-day I would once again feel the grass under my feet and walk in the sunshine as a free man.

I am fundamentally an optimist. Whether that comes from nature or nurture, I cannot say. Part of being optimistic is keeping one's head pointed toward the sun, one's feet moving forward. There were many dark moments when my faith in humanity was sorely tested, but I would not and could not give myself up to despair. That way lay defeat and death.

# 61

WE WERE AWAKENED at 5:30 each morning by the night warder, who clanged a brass bell at the head of our corridor and yelled, *"Word wakker! Staan op!"* (Wake up! Get up!) I have always been an early riser and this hour was not a burden to me. Although we were roused at 5:30, we were not let out of our cells until 6:45, by which time we were meant to have cleaned our cells and rolled up our mats and blankets. We had no running water in our cells and instead of toilets had iron sanitary buckets known as "ballies." The ballies had a diameter of ten inches and a concave porcelain lid on the top that could contain water. The water in this lid was meant to be used for shaving and to clean our hands and faces.

At 6:45, when we were let out of our cells, the first thing we did was to empty our ballies. The ballies had to be thoroughly cleansed in the sinks at the end of the hallway or they created a stench. The only pleasant thing about cleaning one's ballie was that this was the one moment in those early days when we could have a whispered word with our colleagues. The warders did not like to linger when we cleaned them, so it was a chance to talk softly.

During those first few months, breakfast was delivered to us in our cells by prisoners from the general section. Breakfast consisted of mealie pap porridge, cereal made from maize or corn, which the general prisoners would slop in a bowl and then spin through the bars of our cells. It was a clever trick and required a deft hand so as not to spill any of the porridge.

After a few months, breakfast was delivered to us in the courtyard in old metal oil drums. We would help ourselves to pap using simple metal bowls. We each received a mug of what was described as coffee, but which was in fact ground-up maize, baked until it was black, and then brewed with hot water. Later, when we were able to go into the courtyard to serve ourselves, I would go out into the courtyard and jog around the perimeter until breakfast arrived.

Like everything else in prison, diet is discriminatory.

In general, Coloureds and Indians received a slightly better diet than Africans, but it was not much of a distinction. The authorities liked to say that we received a balanced diet; it was indeed balanced — between the unpalatable and the inedible. Food was the source of many of our protests, but in those early days, the warders would say, "Ag, you kaffirs are eating better in prison than you ever ate at home!"

In the midst of breakfast, the guards would yell, *"Val in! Val in!"* (Fall in! Fall in!), and we would stand outside our cells for inspection. Each prisoner was required to have the three buttons of his khaki jacket properly buttoned. We were required to doff our hats as the warder walked by. If our buttons were undone, our hats unremoved, or our cells untidy, we were charged with a violation of the prison code and punished with either solitary confinement or the loss of meals.

After inspection we would work in the courtyard hammering stones until noon. There were no breaks; if we slowed down, the warders would yell at us to speed up. At noon, the bell would clang for lunch and another metal drum of food would be wheeled into the courtyard. For Africans, lunch consisted of boiled mealies, that is, coarse kernels of corn. The Indian and Coloured prisoners received samp, or mealie rice, which consisted of ground mealies in a souplike mixture. The samp was sometimes served with vegetables whereas our mealies were served straight.

For lunch we often received *phuzamandla,* which means "drink of strength," a powder made from mealies and a bit of yeast. It is meant to be stirred into water or milk and when it is thick, it can be tasty, but the prison authorities gave us so little of the powder that it barely colored the water. I would usually try to save my powder for several days until I had enough to make a proper drink, but if the authorities discovered that you were hoarding food, the powder was confiscated and you were punished.

After lunch we worked until four, when the guards blew shrill whistles and we once again lined up to be counted and inspected. We were then permitted half an hour to clean up. The bathroom at the end of our corridor had two seawater showers, a saltwater tap, and three large galvanized metal buckets, which were used as bathtubs. There was no hot water. We would stand or squat in these buckets, soaping ourselves with the brackish water, rinsing off the dust from the day. To wash yourself with cold water when it is cold outside is not pleasant, but we made the best of it. We would sometimes sing while washing, which made the water seem less icy. In those early days, this was one of the only times that we could converse.

Precisely at 4:30, there would be a loud knock on the wooden door at the end of our corridor, which meant that supper had been delivered. Common-law prisoners were used to dish out the food to us and we would return to our cells to eat it. We again received mealie pap porridge, sometimes with the odd carrot or piece of cabbage or beetroot thrown in — but one usually had to search for it. If we did get a vegetable, we would usually have the same one for weeks on end, until the carrots or cabbage were old and moldy and we were thoroughly sick of them. Every other day, we received a small piece of meat with our porridge. The meat was usually mostly gristle.

For supper, Coloured and Indian prisoners received a quarter loaf of bread (known as a *katkop,* that is, a cat's head, after the shape of the bread) and a slab of margarine. Africans, it was presumed, did not care for bread as it was a "European" type of food.

Typically, we received even less than the meager amounts

stipulated in the regulations. This was because the kitchen was rife with smuggling. The cooks — all of whom were common-law prisoners — kept the best food for themselves or their friends. Often they would lay aside the tastiest morsels for the warders in exchange for favors or preferential treatment.

At 8 P.M., the night warder would lock himself in the corridor with us, passing the key through a small hole in the door to another warder outside. The warder would then walk up and down the corridor, ordering us to go to sleep. No cry of "lights out" was ever given on Robben Island because the single mesh-covered bulb in our cell burned day and night. Later, those studying for higher degrees were permitted to read until ten or eleven.

The acoustics along the corridor were quite good, and we would try to chat a bit to each other before going to sleep. But if we could hear a whisper quite clearly, so could the warder, who would yell, *"Stilte in die gang!"* (Quiet in the passage!) The warder would walk up and down a few times to make sure we were not reading or writing. After a few months, we would sprinkle a handful of sand along the corridor so that we could hear the warder's footsteps and have time to stop talking or hide any contraband. Only when we were quiet did he take a seat in the small office at the end of the passage where he dozed until morning.

# 62

ONE MORNING, several days after my meeting with Bram and Joel, we were taken to the head office. The head office was only about a quarter of a mile away and was a simple stone structure that resembled our own section. Once there, we were lined up to have our fingerprints taken, which was routine prison service business. But while waiting, I noticed a warder with a camera. After our fingerprints had been taken, the chief warder ordered us to line up for photographs. I motioned to my colleagues not to move, and I addressed the warder: "I would like you to produce the document from the commissioner of prisons authorizing our pictures to be taken." Photographs of prisoners required such authorization.

It was always valuable to be familiar with regulations, because the warders themselves were often ignorant of them and could be intimidated by one's superior knowledge. The warder was taken aback by my request and was unable to offer any explanation or produce anything in writing from the commissioner of prisons. He threatened to charge us if we did not consent to have our photographs taken, but I said that if there was no authorization, there would be no pictures, and that is where the matter remained.

As a rule, we objected to having our pictures taken in prison on the grounds that it is generally demeaning to be seen as a prisoner. But there was one photograph I did consent to, the only one I ever agreed to while on Robben Island.

One morning, a few weeks later, the chief warder, instead of handing us hammers for our work in the courtyard, gave us each needles and thread and a pile of worn prison jerseys. We were instructed to repair the garments, but we discovered that most of these jerseys were frayed beyond repair. This struck us as a curious task, and we wondered what had provoked the change. Later that morning, at about eleven o'clock, the front gate swung open, revealing the commanding officer with two men in suits. The commanding officer announced that the two visitors were a reporter and photographer from the *Daily Telegraph* in London. He related this as if visiting members of the international press were a regular diversion for us.

Although these men were our first official visitors, we regarded them skeptically. Firstly, they were brought in under the auspices of the government, and second, we were aware that the *Telegraph* was a conservative newspaper unlikely to be sympathetic to our cause. We well knew that there was great concern in the outside world about our situation and that it was in the government's interest to show that we were not being mistreated.

The two journalists walked slowly around the courtyard, surveying us. We kept our heads down concentrating on our work. After they had made one circuit, one of the guards plucked me by the shoulder and said, "Mandela, come, you will talk now." In those early days, I often spoke on behalf of my fellow prisoners. The prison service regulations were explicit that each prisoner was permitted to speak only for himself. This was done to negate the power of organization and to neutralize our collective strength. We objected to this rule, but made little headway. We were not even permitted to use the word *we* when we made complaints. But during the first few years, when the authorities needed one prisoner to speak on behalf of others, that individual would be me.

I talked to the reporter, whose name was Mr. Newman, for about twenty minutes, and was candid about both prison and the Rivonia Trial. He was an agreeable fellow, and at the end of our talk, he said he would like the photographer to take my picture. I was reluctant, but in this case relented because I knew the photograph would only be published overseas, and might serve to help our cause if the article was even the least bit friendly. I told him I would agree provided Mr. Sisulu could join me. The image shows the two of us talking in the courtyard about some matter that I can no longer remember. I never saw the article or heard anything about it. The reporters were barely out of sight when the warders removed the jerseys and gave us back our hammers.

The men from the *Telegraph* were the first of a small stream of visitors during those early months. While the Rivonia Trial still resonated in people's minds, the government was eager to show the international community that we were being treated properly. There were stories in the press about the inhuman conditions on the island, about how we were being assaulted and tortured. These allegations embarrassed the government, and to combat them they brought in a string of outsiders meant to rebut these critical stories.

We were briefly visited by a British lawyer who had argued for Namibian independence before the World Court, after which we were informed that a Mr. Hynning, a representative of the American Bar Association, would be coming to see us. Americans were then a novelty in South Africa, and I was curious to meet a representative of so august a legal organization.

On the day of Mr. Hynning's visit we were called into the courtyard. The American arrived in the company of General Steyn, the commissioner of prisons, who rarely made appearances on the island. General Steyn was that unusual thing in the prison service, a polished and sophisticated man. His suits were always of a fine quality and a fashionable cut. He was courtly, and referred to us as "gentlemen," even doffing his hat to us, something no one else in the prison service ever did. Yet General Steyn oppressed us by omission rather than commission. He basically turned a blind eye to what was happening on the island. His habitual absence emboldened the more brutal prison officials and gave them carte blanche to do whatever they wanted. In his most gracious manner, the general introduced our guest and said, "Gentlemen, please select your spokesman." A number of the prisoners called out my name.

General Steyn nodded in my direction, and I stood up. In contrast to General Steyn, Mr. Hynning was a heavyset, unkempt man. I thanked him for visiting us and said we were honored by his presence. I then summarized our complaints, beginning with the central and most important one, that we were political prisoners, not criminals, and that we should be treated as such. I enumerated our grievances about the food, our living conditions, and the work detail. But as I was speaking, Mr. Hynning kept interrupting me. When I made a point about the long hours doing mindless work, he declared that as prisoners we had to work and were probably lazy to boot.

When I started to detail the problems with our cells, he interjected that the conditions in backward American prisons were far worse than Robben Island, which was a paradise by comparison. He added that we had been justly convicted and were lucky not to have received the death penalty, which we probably deserved.

Mr. Hynning perspired a great deal and there were those among us who thought he was not altogether sober. He spoke in what I assumed was a southern American accent, and had a curious habit of spitting when he talked, something none of us had ever seen before.

Finally, I had heard enough, and I interrupted him, "No, sir, you misunderstand the points that I am making." Hynning took offense that I was now contradicting him, while General Steyn watched and listened without comment. Under the circumstances, it was difficult to keep tempers down. The men were angered by Mr. Hynning's remarks and annoyed that he had been permitted to see us at all. Normally, a visit of any kind lifted our spirits but the visit of Mr. Hynning was demoralizing. Perhaps that is what the authorities wanted. To meet someone with so impressive an affiliation and so little understanding was depressing. Hynning finally just turned and walked away without so much as a good-bye. We were not sorry to see him go.

We discussed Mr. Hynning for years afterward and many of the men imitated the way he spoke to comic effect. We never heard about him again, and he certainly did not win any friends on Robben Island for the American Bar Association.

# 63

IN JAIL, all prisoners are classified by the authorities as one of four categories: A, B, C, or D. A is the highest classification and confers the most privileges; D is the lowest and confers the least. All political prisoners, or what the authorities called "security prisoners," were automatically classified as D on admission. The privileges affected by these classifications included visits and letters, studies, and the opportunity to buy groceries and incidentals — all of which are the lifeblood of any prisoner. It normally took years for a political prisoner to raise his status from D to C.

We disdained the classification system. It was corrupt and demeaning, another way of repressing prisoners in general and political prisoners in particular. We demanded that all political prisoners be in one category. Although we criticized it, we could not ignore it: the classification system was an inflexible feature of prison life. If you protested that, as a D Group prisoner, you could receive only one letter every six months, the authorities would say, Improve your behavior, become a C Group prisoner, and you will be able to receive two letters every six months. If you complained that you did not receive enough food, the authorities would remind you that if you were in A Group, you would be able to receive money orders from the outside and purchase extra food at the prison canteen. Even a freedom fighter benefits from the ability to buy groceries and books.

The classifications generally ran parallel to the length of one's sentence. If you were sentenced to eight years, you would generally be classified as D for the first two years, C for the next two, B for the following two, and A for the last two. But the prison authorities wielded the classification system as a weapon against political prisoners, threatening to lower our hard-won classifications in order to control our behavior.

Though I had been in prison for nearly two years before I was taken to Robben Island, I was still in D Group when I arrived. While I desired the privileges that came with higher classifications,

I refused to compromise my conduct. The fastest way to raise one's classification was to be docile and not complain. "Ag, Mandela, you are a troublemaker," the warders would say. "You will be in D Group for the rest of your life."

Every six months, prisoners were called before the prison board to have their classifications evaluated. The board was meant to assess our behavior in terms of prison regulations, but we found that it preferred to act as a political tribunal rather than a mere evaluator of behavior. During my first meeting with the board, the officials asked me questions about the ANC and my beliefs. Although this had nothing to do with the classification system, I was vain enough to answer and think that I might convert them to my beliefs. It was one of the few times we were treated as human beings, and I for one responded. Later I realized that this was simply a technique on the part of the authorities to glean information from us, and I had fallen for it. Shortly afterward, we agreed among ourselves not to discuss politics with the prison board.

As a D Group prisoner, I was entitled to have only one visitor, and to write and receive only one letter, every six months. I found this one of the most inhumane restrictions of the prison system. Communication with one's family is a human right; it should not be restricted by the artificial gradations of a prison system. But it was one of the facts of prison life.

Visits and letters were restricted to "first degree" relatives. This was a restriction we not only found irksome but racist. The African sense of immediate family is far different from that of the European or Westerner. Our family structures are larger and more inclusive; anyone who claims descent from a common ancestor is deemed part of the same family.

In prison, the only thing worse than bad news about one's family is no news at all. It is always harder to cope with the disasters and tragedies one imagines than with the reality, however grim or disagreeable. A letter with ill tidings was always preferable to no letter at all.

But even this miserable restriction was abused by the authorities. The anticipation of mail was overwhelming. Mail call took place once a month, and sometimes six months would go by without a letter. To be allowed one letter in six months and then not to receive it is a great blow. One wonders: What has happened to my wife and children, to my mother and my sisters? When I did not receive a letter I felt as dry and barren as the Great Karroo desert. Often the authorities would withhold mail out of spite. I can remember warders saying, "Mandela, we have received a letter for you, but we cannot give it to you." No explanation of why, or whom the letter was from. It required all my self-discipline not to explode at such times. Afterward, I would protest through the proper channels, and sometimes get it.

When letters did arrive, they were cherished. A letter was like the summer rain that could make even the desert bloom. When I was handed a letter by the authorities, I would not rush forward and grab it as I felt like doing, but take it in a leisurely manner. Though I yearned to tear it open and read it on the spot, I would not give the authorities the satisfaction of seeing my eagerness, and I would return slowly to my cell as though I had many things to occupy me before opening a letter from my family.

During the first few months, I received one letter from Winnie, but it was so heavily censored that not much more than the salutation was left. The island's censors would black out the offending passages in ink, but they later changed this when they realized we could wash away the ink and see what was underneath. They began to use razors to slice out whole paragraphs. Since most letters were written on both sides of a single piece of paper, the material on the other side would also be excised. They seemed to relish delivering letters in tatters. The censorship delayed the delivery of mail because warders, some of whom were not proficient in English, might take as long as a month to censor a letter. The letters we wrote were censored as well; they were often as cut up as the letters we received.

At the end of August, after I had been on the island less than three months, I was informed by the authorities that I would have a visitor the following day. They would not tell me who it was. Walter was informed that he, too, would have a visitor, and I suspected, I hoped, I wished — I believed — that it would be a visit from Winnie and Albertina.

From the moment Winnie learned we had been brought to the island, she had been trying to arrange a visit. As a banned person,

Winnie had to receive a special dispensation from the minister of justice, for she was technically not permitted to communicate with me.

Even with the help of the authorities, visiting Robben Island was not an easy proposition. Visits were a maximum of thirty minutes long, and political prisoners were not permitted contact visits, in which the visitor and prisoner were in the same room.

Visits did not seem to be planned in advance by the authorities. One day, they would contact your wife and say, "You have permission to visit your husband tomorrow." This was enormously inconvenient, and often had the effect of making visits impossible. If a family member was able to plan a visit in advance, the authorities would sometimes deliberately delay issuing a permit until after the plane had departed. Since most of the men's families lived far from the Cape and had very little money, visits by family members were often far beyond their means. Some men who came from poor families did not see their wives for many years at a time, if at all. I knew of men who spent a decade or more on Robben Island without a single visit.

The visiting room for noncontact visits was cramped and windowless. On the prisoner's side, there was a row of five cubicles with small square pieces of glass that looked out on identical cubicles on the other side. One sat in a chair and looked through the thick, smudged glass that had a few small holes drilled into it to permit conversation. One had to talk very loudly to be heard. Later the authorities installed microphones and speakers in front of the glass, a marginal improvement.

Walter and I were called to the visitors' office in the late morning and took seats at the far end of the room. I waited with some anxiety, and suddenly, filling out the glass on the other side of the window was Winnie's lovely face. Winnie always dressed up for prison visits, and tried to wear something new and elegant. It was tremendously frustrating not to be able to touch my wife, to speak tenderly to her, to have a private moment together. We had to conduct our relationship at a distance under the eyes of people we despised.

I could see immediately that Winnie was under tremendous strain. Seeing me in such circumstances must have been trying. Just getting to the island itself was difficult, and added to that were the harsh rituals of the prison, the undoubted indignities of the warders, and the impersonality of the contact.

Winnie, I later discovered, had recently received a second banning order and had been terminated from her job at the Child Welfare Office as a result. Her office was searched by the police shortly before she was fired. The authorities were convinced that Winnie was in secret communication with me. Winnie loved her job as a social worker. It was the hands-on end of the struggle: placing babies with adoptive parents, finding work for the unemployed and medical help for the uninsured. The banning and harassment of my wife greatly troubled me: I could not look after her and the children, and the state was making it difficult for her to look after herself. My powerlessness gnawed at me.

Our conversation was awkward at first, and was not made easier by the presence of two warders standing directly behind her and three behind me. Their role was not only to monitor but to intimidate. Regulations dictated that conversation had to be in either English or Afrikaans — African languages were forbidden — and could involve family matters only. Any line of talk that departed from the family and verged on the political might mean the abrupt termination of the visit. If one mentioned a name unfamiliar to the warders, they would interrupt the conversation, and ask who the person was and the nature of the relationship. This happened often, as the warders were generally unfamiliar with the variety and nature of African names. It was frustrating to spend precious minutes of one's visit explaining to a warder the different branches of one's family tree. But their ignorance also worked in our favor: it allowed us to invent code names for people we wanted to talk about and pretend that we were referring to family members.

That first visit was important, for I knew that Winnie was anxious about my health: she had heard stories that we were being physically abused. I quickly informed her that I was fine and she could see that I was fit, though a bit thinner than before. She, too, was thinner, something I always attributed to stress. After a visit in which Winnie's face looked drawn or tense, I would urge her to put on a bit of weight. She was always dieting, and I was always telling her not to. I inquired one by one about all the children, about my mother and sisters, and Winnie's own family.

Suddenly, I heard the warder behind me say, "Time up! Time up!" I turned and looked at him with incredulity. It was impossible that half an hour had passed. But, in fact, he was right; visits always seemed to go by in the blink of an eye. For all the years that I was in prison, I never failed to be surprised when the warder called, "Time up!" Winnie and I were both hustled from our chairs and we waved a quick farewell. I always felt like lingering after Winnie left, just to retain the sense of her presence, but I would not let the warders see such emotion. As I walked back to the cell, I reviewed in my head what we had talked about. Over the next days, weeks, and months, I would return to that one visit again and again. I knew I would not be able to see my wife again for at least six months. As it turned out, Winnie was not able to visit me for another two years.

# 64

ONE MORNING in early January, as we lined up to be counted before beginning work in the courtyard, we were instead marched outside and ordered into a covered truck. It was the first time that we had left our compound. No announcement was made as to our destination, but I had an idea of where we were headed. A few minutes later we emerged from the truck in a place that I had first seen when I was on the island in 1962: the lime quarry.

The lime quarry looked like an enormous white crater cut into a rocky hillside. The cliffs and the base of the hillside were blindingly white. At the top of the quarry were grass and palm trees, and at the base was a clearing with a few old metal sheds.

We were met by the commanding officer, Colonel Wessels, a rather colorless fellow who cared only about strict adherence to prison regulations. We stood at attention as he told us that the work we would be doing would last six months and afterward we would be given light tasks for the duration of our terms. His timing was considerably off. We remained at the quarry for the next thirteen years.

After the C.O.'s speech, we were handed picks and shovels and given rudimentary instructions as to the mining of lime. Mining lime is not a simple task. That first day, we were clumsy with our new tools and extracted little. The lime itself, which is the soft, calcified residue of seashells and coral, is buried in layers of rock, and one had to break through to it with a pick, and then extract the seam of lime with a shovel. This was far more strenuous than the work in the courtyard, and after our first few days on the quarry we fell asleep immediately after our supper at 4:30 in the afternoon. We woke the next morning aching and still tired.

The authorities never explained why we had been taken from the courtyard to the quarry. They may simply have needed extra lime for the island's roads. But when we later discussed the transfer, we assumed it was another way of enforcing discipline, of showing us that we were not different from the general prisoners — who worked in the island's stone quarry — and that we had to pay for our crimes just as they did. It was an attempt to crush our spirits.

But those first few weeks at the quarry had the opposite effect on us. Despite blistered and bleeding hands, we were invigorated. I much preferred being outside in nature, being able to see grass and trees, to observe birds flitting overhead, to feel the wind blowing in from the sea. It felt good to use all of one's muscles, with the sun at one's back, and there was simple gratification in building up mounds of stone and lime.

Within a few days, we were walking to the quarry, rather than going by truck, and this too was a tonic. During our twenty-minute march to the quarry, we got a better sense of the island, and could see the dense brush and tall trees that covered our home, and smell the eucalyptus blossoms, spot the occasional springbok or kudu grazing in the distance. Although some of the men regarded the march as drudgery, I never did.

Although our work at the quarry was meant to show us that we were no different from the other prisoners, the authorities still treated us like the lepers who once populated the island. Sometimes we would see a group of common-law prisoners working by the side of the road, and their warders would order them into the bushes so they would not see us as we marched past. It was as if the mere sight of us might somehow affect their discipline. Sometimes out of the corner of an eye we could see a prisoner raise his fist in the ANC salute.

Near the quarry, the dirt road diverged, and to the right the general prisoners trooped off to the rock quarry. This crossroads was later to become an important site of communications with them. Where the road branched, we could see in the brush the small white cottage where Robert Sobukwe lived. The house had been built for a black warder years before, and now Sobukwe lived in it by himself. It was a tiny plot, unkempt and overgrown, and one would not even know that anyone lived there, except for the guard who stood in front.

Sobukwe's sentence had ended in 1963, but under what became known as the Sobukwe clause of the General Law Amendment Act of 1963, the minister of justice could hold political prisoners indefinitely without charge. That is precisely what they did with Bob. For six years, Sobukwe lived a kind of half-life on the island; he was a free man who was denied his liberty. Sometimes we were able to get a glimpse of him in his garden, but that was all.

After arriving in the morning, we would fetch our picks, shovels, hammers, and wheelbarrows from a zinc shed at the top of the quarry. Then we would array ourselves along the quarry face, usually in groups of three or four. Warders with automatic weapons stood on raised platforms watching us. Unarmed warders walked among us, urging us to work harder. *"Gaan aan! Gaan aan!"* (Go on! Go on!), they would shout, as if we were oxen.

By eleven, when the sun was high in the sky, we would begin to flag. By that time, I would already be drenched in sweat. The warders would then drive us even harder. *"Nee, man! Kom aan! Kom aan!"* (No, man! Come on! Come on!), they would shout. Just before noon, when we would break for lunch, we would pile the lime into wheelbarrows and cart it over to the truck, which would take it away.

At midday, a whistle would blow, and we would make our way to the bottom of the hill. We sat on makeshift seats under a simple zinc shed shielding us from the sun. The warders ate at a larger shed with tables and benches. Drums of boiled mealies were delivered to us. Hundreds of seagulls, screaming and swooping, circled above us as we ate, and a well-aimed dropping could sometimes spoil a man's lunch.

We worked until four, when we again carted the lime to the waiting truck. By the end of the day, our faces and bodies were caked with white dust. We looked like pale ghosts except where rivulets of sweat had washed away the lime. When we returned to our cells, we would scrub ourselves in the cold water, which never seemed to completely rinse away the dust.

Worse than the heat at the quarry was the light. Our backs were protected from the sun by our shirts, but the sun's rays would be reflected into our eyes by the lime itself. The glare hurt our eyes and, along with the dust, made it difficult to see. Our eyes teared and our faces became fixed in a permanent squint. It would take a long time after each day's work for our eyes to adjust to the diminished light.

After our first few days at the quarry, we made an official request for sunglasses. The authorities refused. This was not unexpected, for we were then not even permitted reading glasses. I had previously pointed out to the commanding officer that it did not make sense to permit us to read books but not permit us glasses to read them with.

During the following weeks and months, we requested sunglasses again and again. But it was to take us almost three years before we were allowed to have them, and that was only after a sympathetic physician agreed that the glasses were necessary to preserve our eyesight. Even then, we had to purchase the glasses ourselves.

For us, such struggles — for sunglasses, long trousers, study privileges, equalized food — were corollaries to the struggle we waged outside prison. The campaign to improve conditions in prison was part of the apartheid struggle. It was, in that sense, all the same; we fought injustice wherever we found it, no matter how large, or how small, and we fought injustice to preserve our own humanity.

Shortly after we started working at the quarry, we were joined in Section B by a number of other prominent political prisoners. Several were MK men who had been arrested in July of 1964 and convicted of more than fifty acts of sabotage in what became known as the "little Rivonia Trial." These included Mac Maharaj, a member of the SACP and one of the sharpest minds in the struggle; Laloo Chiba, also a member of the MK High Command, and a stalwart colleague who proved a great asset in prison; and Wilton Mkwayi, the Treason Trialist who had been mistakenly let go during a mo-

ment of confusion when the State of Emergency was declared in
1960. He had left South Africa secretly, received military training,
and become commander-in-chief of MK after the Rivonia Trial. We
were also joined by Eddie Daniels, a Coloured member of the Liberal
Party, who had been convicted for sabotage operations undertaken
by the African Resistance Movement, a small sabotage group composed of members of the Liberal Party. Eddie was to become one
of my greatest friends in prison.

To counterbalance the effect of these new political allies, the
authorities also put a handful of common-law prisoners in our section. These men were hardened criminals, convicted of murder, rape,
and armed robbery. They were members of the island's notorious
criminal gangs, either the Big Fives or the Twenty-Eights, which
terrorized other prisoners. They were brawny and surly, and their
faces bore the scars of the knife fights that were common among
gang members. Their role was to act as agents provocateurs, and
they would attempt to push us around, take our food, and inhibit
any political discussions we tried to have. One of these fellows was
known as Bogart, after the American tough-guy movie actor. He
had a cell opposite Walter's and Walter used to complain that he
would demand Walter's breakfast from him each morning, and that
he was too scared to refuse.

The gang members worked in their own clique apart from us at
the quarry. One day, they began singing what sounded like a work
song. In fact, it was a famous work song with their own adapted
lyrics: *"Benifunani eRivonia?,"* which means "What did you want at
Rivonia?" The next line was something like "Did you think that
you would become the government?" They sang exuberantly and
with a mocking tone. They had obviously been encouraged by the
warders, who were hoping that the song would provoke us.

Although the more hotheaded among us wanted to confront
them, instead, we decided to fight fire with fire. We had far more
and better singers among us than they had, and we huddled together
and planned our response. Within a few minutes, we were all singing
the song *"Stimela,"* a rousing anthem about a train making its way
down from Southern Rhodesia. *"Stimela"* is not a political song,
but in the context, it became one, for the implication was that the
train contained guerrillas coming down to fight the South African
army.

For a number of weeks our two groups sang as we worked, adding songs and changing lyrics. Our repertoire increased, and we were soon singing overt political songs, such as *"Amajoni,"* a song about guerrilla soldiers, the title of which was a corruption of the English slang word for soldier, Johnny; and *"Tshotsholoza,"* a song that compares the struggle to the motion of an oncoming train. (If you say the title over and over, it mimics the sound of the train.) We sang a song about the Freedom Charter, and another about the Transkei, whose lyrics said, "There are two roads, one road is the Matanzima road, and one road is the Mandela road, which one will you take?"

The singing made the work lighter. A few of the fellows had extraordinary voices, and I often felt like putting my pick down and simply listening. The gang members were no competition for us; they soon became quiet while we continued singing. But one of the warders was fluent in Xhosa and understood the content of our songs, and we were soon ordered to stop singing. (Whistling was also banned.) From that day on we worked in silence.

I saw the gang members not as rivals but as raw material to be converted. There was a nonpolitical prisoner among us, nicknamed Joe My Baby, who later joined the ANC and proved invaluable in helping us smuggle material in and out of prison.

One day we heard that Bogart had been savagely beaten by a warder at the quarry. I did not see the assault, but I saw the results. His face cut and badly bruised, Bogart approached me in our corridor and asked for help. I immediately agreed to take up his case.

We were always looking for ways to stand up to the authorities, and the report of a beating was the kind of incident we could raise with the head office. Shortly before this, we had learned that a certain PAC man named Ganya had been beaten by a warder. In my role as an attorney, I wrote a letter to the commissioner of prisons protesting on behalf of Ganya. I was brought to the Head Office, where I was confronted by prison officials. In the same breath they denied that the beating had occurred and wanted to know how I had heard about it. I insisted that the warder who had beaten Ganya be removed from the island. They refused, saying there was no evidence against him. But shortly afterward the warder in question was transferred off the island.

I had been emboldened by this case, so when Bogart asked for help I immediately demanded to see the commanding officer. The next day I was summoned to the head office, where the commander blandly informed me that the case had been investigated and dismissed. "That's a violation of regulations," I said. "The case must be tried."

"No," he said, "we have attempted to interview the so-called complainant and he denies that he was ever assaulted."

"That's impossible," I said. "I spoke to him only yesterday." The commander gestured to a lieutenant and said, "Then see for yourself." The lieutenant led Bogart into the room. His face was covered with bandages. The commander asked him whether or not he had been beaten. "No, *baas*," he said quietly, without meeting my gaze, "I was never assaulted." He was then dismissed.

"Well, Mandela," the commander said. "The case is closed." The commander had succeeded in humiliating me. He had obviously bribed Bogart with extra food and tobacco to drop his charges. From that point on, I demanded a signed and written statement from a prisoner before I agreed to take up his case.

# 65

ONE DAY in the summer of 1965, we discovered some fat glistening on our porridge at breakfast and chunks of fresh meat with our pap at supper. The next day some of the men received new shirts. The guards at the quarry and the warders in our section seemed a bit more deferential. All of us were suspicious; in prison, no improvement happens without a reason. A day later we were notified that the International Red Cross would be arriving the following day.

This was a crucial occasion, more important than any of our previous visitors. The Red Cross was responsible and independent, an international organization to whom the Western powers and the United Nations paid attention. The prison authorities respected the Red Cross — and by respected, I mean feared, for the authorities respected only what they were afraid of. The prison service distrusted all organizations that could affect world opinion, and regarded them not as legitimate investigators to be dealt with honestly but as meddling interlopers to be hoodwinked if possible. Avoiding international condemnation was the authorities' principal goal.

In those early years, the International Red Cross was the only organization that both listened to our complaints and responded to them. This was vital, because the authorities ignored us. Regulations required that the authorities provide some official procedure for acknowledging our complaints. They did so, but only in the most perfunctory manner. Every Saturday morning, the chief warder would come into our section and call out, *"Klagtes en Versoeke! Klagtes en Versoeke!"* (Complaints and Requests! Complaints and Requests!) Those of us with *klagtes* and *versoeke* — which was nearly everyone — lined up to see the chief warder. One by one, we would make formal complaints about food, or clothing, or visits. To each, the chief warder would nod his head and simply say, *"Ja, ja,"* and then, "Next!" He did not even write down what we said. If we tried to speak for our organizations, the warders would yell, "No ANC or PAC here! *Verstaan?"* (Understand?)

Shortly before the Red Cross's visit we had submitted a formal list of complaints to the commissioner of prisons. At the time we were only permitted paper and pencil to write letters. We had secretly consulted with each other at the quarry and in the lavatory, and put together a list. We submitted it to our chief warder, who did not want to take it and accused us of violating regulations by making such a list. One of our complaints to the Red Cross would be that the authorities did not listen to our complaints.

On the day of their visit, I was called to the head office to meet with the Red Cross representative. That year, and for the following few years, the representative was a Mr. Senn, a former director of prisons in his native Sweden who had emigrated to Rhodesia. Senn was a quiet, rather nervous man in his mid-fifties who did not seem at all comfortable in his surroundings.

The meeting was not monitored, a critical difference from nearly all of our other visitors. He asked to hear all of our complaints and grievances, and listened very carefully, taking extensive notes. He was very courteous and thanked me for all that I told him. Even so, that first visit was rather tense. Neither of us yet knew what to expect from the other.

I complained quite vociferously about our clothing, affirming that we did not want to wear short trousers and needed proper clothing including socks and underwear, which we were not then given. I recounted our grievances regarding food, visits, letters, studies, exercise, hard labor, and the behavior of warders. I made certain requests I knew the authorities would never satisfy, such as our desire to be transferred to prisons nearer our homes.

After our session, Senn met with the commissioner of prisons and his staff while I waited. I assumed that he relayed our complaints to the authorities, indicating the ones he thought were reasonable. Not long after Senn's visit our clothing did improve and we were given long trousers. But Senn was not a progressive fellow by any means; his years in Rhodesia seemed to have acclimatized him to racism. Before I had returned to my cell, I reminded him of our complaint that African prisoners did not receive bread. Mr. Senn appeared flustered, and glanced over at the colonel, who was head of the prison. "Bread is very bad for your teeth, you know, Mandela," Mr. Senn said. "Mealies are much better for you. They make your teeth strong."

In later years, the International Red Cross sent more liberal men who wholeheartedly fought for improvements. The organization also played a critical role in an area that was less obvious but no less important to us. They often provided money to wives and relatives who would not otherwise have been able to visit us on the island.

After we had been sent to Robben Island, there was concern among our supporters that we would not be permitted to study. Within a few months of our arrival, the authorities announced that those who wanted to study could apply for permission. Most of the men did so and even though they were D Group prisoners, permission was granted. The state, after the Rivonia Trial, was feeling confident and thought giving us study privileges would be harmless. Later, they came to regret it. Postgraduate study was not permitted, but they made an exception in my case because I had established a precedent when I was in Pretoria.

Very few of the men in our section had B.A.'s and many registered for university-level courses. Quite a few did not have high school degrees and elected courses to qualify for that degree. Some of the men were already well educated, like Govan Mbeki and Neville Alexander, but others had not gone past Standard V or VI. Within months, virtually all of us were studying for one degree or another.

At night, our cell block seemed more like a study hall than a prison.

But the privilege of studying came with a host of conditions. Certain subjects, such as politics and military history, were prohibited. For years, we were not permitted to receive funds except from our families, so that poor prisoners rarely had money for books or tuition. This made the opportunity to study a function of how much money one had. Nor were we permitted to lend books to other prisoners, which would have enabled our poorer colleagues to study.

There was always controversy about whether or not we should accept study privileges. Some members of the Unity Movement at first felt that we were accepting a handout from the government, which compromised our integrity. They argued that studying should not be a conditional privilege but an unfettered right. While I agreed, I could not accept that we should therefore disavow studying. As freedom fighters and political prisoners, we had an obligation to improve and strengthen ourselves, and study was one of the few opportunities to do so.

Prisoners were permitted to enroll at either the University of South Africa (UNISA) or Rapid Results College, which was for those studying for their high school qualification. In my own case, studying under the auspices of the University of London was a mixed blessing. On the one hand I was assigned the sorts of stimulating books that would not have been on a South African reading list; on the other, the authorities inevitably regarded many of them as unsuitable and thus banned them.

Receiving books at all was often a challenge. You might make an application to a South African library for a book on contract law. They would process your request and then send you the book by post. But because of the vagaries of the mail system, the remoteness of the island, and the often deliberate slowness of the censors, the book would reach you after the date that it needed to be returned. If the date had passed, the warders would typically send the book back without even showing it to you. Given the nature of the system, you might receive a late fine without ever having received the book.

In addition to books, we were permitted to order publications necessary to our studies. The authorities were extremely strict about this, and the only kind of publication that would pass muster might be a quarterly on actuarial science for a prisoner studying accounting. But one day, Mac Maharaj told a comrade who was studying economics to request *The Economist*. We laughed and said we might as well ask for *Time* magazine, because *The Economist* was also a news-weekly. But Mac simply smiled and said the authorities wouldn't know that; they judged a book by its title. Within a month, we were receiving *The Economist* and reading the news we hungered for. But the authorities soon discovered their mistake and ended the subscription.

Once most of the men began to study, we complained that we did not even have the minimum facilities necessary for studying, such as desks and chairs. I made this complaint to the International Red Cross. Finally, the authorities built in each cell a kind of stand-up desk, a simple wooden board that jutted out from the wall at about chest-level.

This was not precisely what we had envisaged. After a tedious day at the quarry, one did not much feel like working at a stand-up desk. A number of us complained about the desks, and Kathy was the most vociferous. He informed the commanding officer that not only was it an imposition to have stand-up desks, but that they sloped so steeply that the books fell off. The commanding officer made a surprise visit to Kathy's cell, asked for a book, and plunked it on his desk. It did not move. He asked Kathy for another and placed it on top of the first one; again, nothing happened. Finally, after placing four books on the desk, he turned to a sheepish Kathy and said, "Ag, there's nothing wrong with these desks," and walked out. But about six months later, the authorities relented and we were given three-legged wooden stools and the stand-up desks were lowered.

One complaint I voiced to the International Red Cross concerned the arbitrary way we were charged by the warders. To be "charged" meant that a warder claimed that a prisoner had violated a specific regulation, which could be punished by isolation or by loss of meals and privileges. Warders generally did not treat this lightly, for when a prisoner was charged he was allowed a judicial hearing and, depending on the seriousness of the offense, a magistrate was brought in from Cape Town. At the time, the authorities were refusing to permit hearings. When I complained to the International Red Cross about this, I had yet to experience the problem myself. But that situation was soon remedied.

On weekends, during our first year on the island, we were kept inside our cells all day except for a half hour of exercise. One Saturday, after returning from exercise in the courtyard, I noticed that a warder had left a newspaper on the bench at the end of the corridor. He had become rather friendly to us, and I assumed that he had not left the newspaper there by accident.

Newspapers were more valuable to political prisoners than gold or diamonds, more hungered for than food or tobacco; they were the most precious contraband on Robben Island. News was the intellectual raw material of the struggle. We were not allowed any news at all, and we craved it. Walter, even more than myself, seemed bereft without news. The authorities attempted to impose a complete blackout; they did not want us to learn anything that might raise our morale or reassure us that people on the outside were still thinking about us.

We regarded it as our duty to keep ourselves current on the politics of the country, and we fought long and hard for the right to have newspapers. Over the years, we devised many ways of obtaining them, but back then we were not so adept. One of the advantages of going to the quarry was that warders' sandwiches were wrapped in newspaper and they would often discard these newsprint wrappers in the trash, where we secretly retrieved them. We would distract the warders' attention, pluck the papers out of the garbage, and slide them into our shirts.

One of the most reliable ways to acquire papers was through bribery, and this was the only area where I tolerated what were often unethical means of obtaining information. The warders always seemed to be short of money, and their poverty was our opportunity.

When we did get hold of a paper, it was far too risky to pass around. Possession of a newspaper was a serious charge. Instead, one person would read the paper, usually Kathy or, later, Mac Maharaj. Kathy was in charge of communications, and he had thought of ingenious ways for us to pass information. Kathy would go through the paper and make cuttings of relevant stories, which were then secretly distributed to the rest of us. Each of us would write out a summary of the story we were given; these summaries were then passed among us, and later smuggled to the general section. When the authorities were particularly vigilant, Kathy or Mac would write out his summary of the news and then destroy the paper, usually by tearing it into small pieces and placing it in his ballie, which the warders never inspected.

When I noticed the newspaper lying on the bench, I quickly left my cell, walked to the end of the corridor, looked in both directions, and then plucked the newspaper off the bench and slipped it into my shirt. Normally, I would have hidden the newspaper somewhere in my cell and taken it out only after bedtime. But like a child who eats his sweet before his main course, I was so eager for news that I opened the paper in my cell immediately.

I don't know how long I was reading; I was so engrossed in the paper that I did not hear any footsteps. Suddenly, an officer and two other warders appeared and I did not even have time to slide the paper under my bed. I was caught black-and-white-handed, so to speak. "Mandela," the officer said, "we are charging you for possession of contraband, and you will pay for this." The two warders then began a thorough search of my cell to see if they could turn up anything else.

Within a day or two a magistrate was brought in from Cape Town and I was taken to the room at headquarters that was used as the island's court. In this instance, the authorities were willing to call in an outside magistrate because they knew they had an open-and-shut case. I offered no defense, and was sentenced to three days in isolation and deprivation of meals.

I do not think that I was set up by the warder who left the newspaper on the bench, though some assumed I had been. At the hearing, the authorities grilled me as to how I got the newspaper, and I refused to answer. If I had been railroaded, the authorities would have known how I'd gotten it.

The isolation cells were in our same complex, but in another wing. Although just across the courtyard, they felt enormously distant. In isolation, one was deprived of company, exercise, and even food: one received only rice water three times a day for three days. (Rice water is simply water in which rice has been boiled.) By comparison, our normal ration of pap seemed like a feast.

The first day in isolation was always the most painful. One grows accustomed to eating regularly and the body is not used to being deprived. I found that by the second day I had more or less adjusted to the absence of food, and the third passed without much craving at all. Such deprivation was not uncommon among Africans in everyday life. I myself had gone without food for days at a time in my early years in Johannesburg.

As I have already mentioned, I found solitary confinement the most forbidding aspect of prison life. There is no end and no beginning; there is only one's own mind, which can begin to play tricks. Was that a dream or did it really happen? One begins to question everything. Did I make the right decision, was my sacrifice worth it? In solitary, there is no distraction from these haunting questions.

But the human body has an enormous capacity for adjusting to trying circumstances. I have found that one can bear the unbearable if one can keep one's spirits strong even when one's body is being tested. Strong convictions are the secret of surviving deprivation; your spirit can be full even when your stomach is empty.

In those early years, isolation became a habit. We were routinely charged for the smallest infractions and sentenced to isolation. A man might lose his meals for a sidelong glance or be sentenced for failing to stand when a warder entered the room. Some PAC prisoners, who often flouted the rules simply for the sake of doing so, spent a great deal of time in isolation. The authorities believed that isolation was the cure for our defiance and rebelliousness.

The second time I was charged and spent time in isolation occurred shortly after the first. As I have mentioned, we were having great difficulty making our complaints heard. The remoteness of the prison made the authorities feel they could ignore us with impunity. They believed that if they turned a deaf ear to us, we would give up in frustration and the people on the outside would forget about us.

One day we were working at the lime quarry when the commanding officer came to observe us, accompanied by a gentleman whom we at first did not recognize. One of my colleagues whispered to me that it was Brigadier Aucamp from the Head Office, our commanding officer's commanding officer. (He is not to be confused with the Aucamp of Pretoria Local, who looked after us during the Rivonia Trial.) The two men stood at a distance, watching us.

Aucamp was a short, heavyset fellow in a suit rather than a military uniform. He normally came to the island on biannual inspections. On those occasions, we were ordered to stand at attention at the grille of our cells and hold up our prison cards as he walked by.

I decided that Aucamp's unexpected appearance was a singular opportunity to present our grievances to the man who had the power to remedy them. I put down my pick and began to walk over to them. The warders immediately became alarmed and moved toward me. I knew that I was violating regulations, but I hoped the warders would be so surprised by the novelty of my action that they would do nothing to stop me. That proved to be the case.

When I reached the two men, the commanding officer said bluntly, "Mandela, go back to your place. No one called you." I disregarded him and addressed Aucamp, saying I had taken this extraordinary action because our complaints were being ignored. The C.O. interrupted me: "Mandela, I order you back to your place." I turned to him and said in a measured tone, "I am here already, I will not go back." I was hoping that Aucamp would agree to hear me out, but he studied me coldly and then turned to the warders and said calmly, "Charge him."

I continued to speak as the guards led me away. "Take him back to the cells," the C.O. said. I was charged and, once again, I had no defense. The punishment this time was four days in isolation. There was a lesson in what I had done, a lesson I already knew but had disobeyed out of desperation. No one, least of all prison officials, ever likes to have his authority publicly challenged. In order to respond to me, Aucamp would have had to humiliate his subordinate. Prison officials responded much better to private overtures. The best way to effect change on Robben Island was to attempt to influence officials privately rather than publicly. I was sometimes condemned for appearing to be too accommodating to prison officials, but I was willing to accept the criticism in exchange for the improvement.

# 66

THE MOST IMPORTANT PERSON in any prisoner's life is not the minister of justice, not the commissioner of prisons, not even the head of prison, but the warder in one's section. If you are cold and want an extra blanket, you might petition the minister of justice, but you will get no response. If you go to the commissioner of prisons, he will say, "Sorry, it is against regulations." The head of prison will say, "If I give you an extra blanket, I must give one to everyone." But if you approach the warder in your corridor, and you are on good terms with him, he will simply go to the stockroom and fetch a blanket.

I always tried to be decent to the warders in my section; hostility was self-defeating. There was no point in having a permanent enemy among the warders. It was ANC policy to try to educate all people, even our enemies: we believed that all men, even prison service warders, were capable of change, and we did our utmost to try to sway them.

In general we treated the warders as they treated us. If a man was considerate, we were considerate in return. Not all of our warders were ogres. We noticed right from the start that there were some among them who believed in fairness. Yet, being friendly with warders was not an easy proposition, for they generally found the idea of being courteous to a black man abhorrent. Because it was useful to have warders who were well disposed toward us, I often asked certain men to make overtures to selected warders. No one liked to take on such a job.

We had one warder at the quarry who seemed particularly hostile to us. This was troublesome, for at the quarry we would hold discussions among ourselves, and a warder who did not permit us to talk was a great hindrance. I asked a certain comrade to befriend this fellow so that he would not interrupt our talks. The warder was quite crude, but he soon began to relax a bit around this one prisoner. One day, the warder asked this comrade for his jacket so that he could lay it on the grass and sit on it. Even though I knew it went against the comrade's grain, I nodded to him to do it.

A few days later, we were having our lunch under the shed when this warder wandered over. The warder had an extra sandwich, and he threw it on the grass near us and said, "Here." That was his way of showing friendship.

This presented us with a dilemma. On the one hand, he was treating us as animals to whom he could toss a bit of slop, and I felt it would undermine our dignity to take the sandwich. On the other hand, we were hungry, and to reject the gesture altogether would humiliate the warder we were trying to befriend. I could see that the comrade who had befriended the warder wanted the sandwich, and I nodded for him to take it.

The strategy worked, for this warder became less wary around us. He even began to ask questions about the ANC. By definition, if a man worked for the prison service he was probably brainwashed by the government's propaganda. He would have believed that we were terrorists and Communists who wanted to drive the white man into the sea. But as we quietly explained to him our nonracialism, our desire for equal rights, and our plans for the redistribution of wealth, he scratched his head and said, "It makes more bloody sense than the Nats."

Having sympathetic warders facilitated one of our most vital tasks on Robben Island: communication. We regarded it as our duty to stay in touch with our men in F and G, which was where the general prisoners were kept. As politicians, we were just as intent on fortifying our organization in prison as we had been outside. Communication was essential if we were to coordinate our protests and complaints. Because of the greater numbers of prisoners coming and going in the general section, the men in F and G tended to have more recent information about not only what was happening in the movement, but about our friends and families.

Communication between sections was a serious violation of regulations. We found many effective ways around the ban. The men who delivered our drums of food were from the general section, and in the early months we managed to have whispered conversations with them in which we conveyed brief messages. We formed a clandestine communications committee, composed of Kathy, Mac Maharaj, Laloo Chiba, and several others, and their job was to organize all such practices.

One of the first techniques was engineered by Kathy and Mac, who had noticed that on our walks to the quarry, the warders often tossed away empty matchboxes. They began secretly collecting them, and Mac had the idea of constructing a false bottom to the box and placing in it a tiny written message. Laloo Chiba, who once trained as a tailor, wrote out minuscule coded messages that would be placed in the converted matchbox. Joe Gqabi, another MK soldier who was with us, would carry the matchboxes on our walks to the quarry and drop them at a strategic crossing where we knew the general prisoners would pass. Through whispered conversations at food deliveries, we explained the plan. Designated prisoners from F and G would pick up the matchboxes on their walks, and we retrieved messages in the same fashion. It was far from perfect, and we could easily be foiled by something as simple as the rain. We soon evolved more efficient methods.

We looked for moments when the warders were inattentive. One such time was during and after meals. We helped ourselves to our food, and we worked out a scheme whereby comrades from the general section who worked in the kitchen began placing letters and notes wrapped in plastic at the bottom of the food drums. We sent return communication in a similar way, wrapping notes in the same plastic and placing them at the bottom of the mounds of dirty dishes that were routed back to the kitchen. We would do our best to create a mess, scattering food all over the plates. The warders even complained about the disarray, but never bothered to investigate.

Our toilets and showers were adjacent to the isolation section. Prisoners from the general section were often sentenced to isolation there and would use the same set of toilets we did, though at different times. Mac devised a method of wrapping notes in plastic and then taping them inside the rim of the toilet bowl. We encouraged our political comrades in the general section to be charged and placed in isolation so that they could retrieve these notes and send replies. The warders never bothered to search there.

In order not to have our notes read or understood by the authorities if they were found, we devised ways of writing that could not easily be seen or deciphered. One way was to write messages with milk. The milk would dry almost immediately, and the paper would look blank. But the disinfectant we were given to clean our cells, when sprayed on the dried milk, made the writing reappear. Unfortunately, we did not regularly receive milk. After one of us was diagnosed with an ulcer, we used his.

Another technique was to write in tiny, coded script on toilet paper. The paper was so small and easily hidden that this became a popular way of smuggling out messages. When the authorities discovered a number of these communications, they took the extraordinary measure of rationing toilet paper. Govan was then ailing and not going to the quarry, and he was given the task of counting out eight squares of toilet paper for each prisoner per day.

But even with all these ingenious methods, one of the best ways was also the easiest: getting sent to the prison hospital. The island had one hospital, and it was difficult to segregate us from the general prisoners while we were there. Sometimes prisoners from the different sections even shared the same wards, and men from Section B and prisoners from F and G mingled and exchanged information about political organizations, strikes, go-slows, whatever the current prison issues were.

Communication with the outside world was accomplished in two ways: through prisoners whose sentences were completed and who were leaving the island, and through contact with visitors. Prisoners who were leaving would smuggle out letters in their clothes or baggage. With outside visitors, the situation was even more dangerous, because the risks were also borne by the visitor. When lawyers visited us, warders were not permitted in the room and we would sometimes pass a letter to the lawyer to be taken out. Lawyers were not searched. In these meetings, we could also communicate by writing as we had during the Rivonia Trial. Because the room was bugged, we might say, "Please tell . . ." and then pause and write "O.T.," meaning Oliver Tambo, on a piece of paper, "that we approve of his plan to cut down the size of the . . ." and then write, "National Executive."

Through a plastic-wrapped note hidden in our food drums, we learned in July of 1966 that the men in the general section had embarked on a hunger strike to protest poor conditions. The note was imprecise, and we did not know exactly when the strike had started or exactly what it was about. But we would support any strike of prisoners for whatever reason they were striking. Word was passed among us, and we resolved to initiate a sympathetic strike beginning with our next meal. A hunger strike consists of one thing: not eating.

Because of the time lag in communications, the general prisoners probably did not learn of our participation for a day or so. But we knew that the news would hearten them. The authorities would be telling them that we were not participating in the strike, that we were gorging ourselves on gourmet meals. This was standard operating procedure; in a crisis, the authorities inevitably started a disinformation campaign to play one section against the other. In this case, while the ANC unanimously supported the strike, some PAC men in the general section did not.

During the first day of our strike, we were served our normal rations and refused to take them. On the second day, we noticed that our portions were larger and a few more vegetables accompanied our pap. On the third day, juicy pieces of meat were served with supper. By the fourth day, the porridge was glistening with fat, and great hunks of meat and colorful vegetables were steaming on top. The food was positively mouthwatering. The warders smiled when we passed up the food. The temptation was great, but we resisted, even though we were being driven especially hard at the quarry. We heard that in the main section, prisoners were collapsing and being taken away in wheelbarrows.

I was called to the Head Office for an interview with Colonel Wessels. Such sessions were delicate, as my fellow prisoners knew that the authorities would attempt to influence me to call off the strike. Wessels was a direct man and demanded to know why we were on a hunger strike. I explained that as political prisoners we saw protest to alter prison conditions as an extension of the anti-apartheid struggle. "But you don't even know why they are striking in F and G," he said. I said that did not matter, that the men in F and G were our brothers and that our struggle was indivisible. He snorted, and dismissed me.

The following day we learned of an extraordinary course of events: the warders had gone on their own food boycott, refusing to go to their own cafeteria. They were not striking in support of us, but had decided that if we could do such a thing, why couldn't they? They were demanding better food and improved living conditions. The combination of the two strikes was too much for the authorities. They settled with the warders and then, a day or two later, we learned the authorities had gone to the general section and asked for three representatives to negotiate changes. The general prisoners declared victory and called off the hunger strike. We followed suit a day later.

*        *        *

That was the first and most successful of the hunger strikes on the island. As a form of protest, they did not have a high success rate and the rationale behind them always struck me as quixotic. In order for a hunger strike to succeed, the outside world must learn of it. Otherwise, prisoners will simply starve themselves to death and no one will know. Smuggled-out information that we were on a hunger strike would elicit newspaper stories, which in turn would generate pressure from advocacy groups. The problem, particularly in the early years, was that it was next to impossible to alert people on the outside that we were waging a hunger strike inside.

For me, hunger strikes were altogether too passive. We who were already suffering were threatening our health, even courting death. I have always favored a more active, militant style of protest such as work strikes, go-slow strikes, or refusing to clean up; actions that punished the authorities, not ourselves. They wanted gravel and we produced no gravel. They wanted the prison yard clean and it was untidy. This kind of behavior distressed and exasperated them, whereas I think they secretly enjoyed watching us go hungry.

But when it came to a decision, I was often outvoted. My colleagues even jokingly accused me of not wanting to miss a meal. The proponents of hunger strikes argued that it was a traditionally accepted form of protest that had been waged all over the world by such prominent leaders as Mahatma Gandhi. Once the decision was taken, however, I would support it as wholeheartedly as any of its advocates. In fact, during the strikes I was often in the position of remonstrating with some of my more wayward colleagues who did not want to abide by our agreement. "Madiba, I want my food," I remember one man saying. "I don't see why I should go without. I have served the struggle for many years."

Comrades would sometimes eat on the sly. We knew this for a simple reason: by the second day of a hunger strike, no one needs to use the toilet. Yet one morning you might see a fellow going to the toilet. We had our own internal intelligence service because we knew that certain men were weak in this regard.

# 67

IN THE MIDST of the July 1966 hunger strike I had my second visit from my wife. It was almost exactly two years after the first visit, and it nearly did not happen at all. Winnie had been under constant harassment since her first visit in 1964. Her sisters and brother were persecuted by the police, and the authorities attempted to forbid anyone in her family from living with her. Some of this I learned at the time, much of it I found out later. Some of the nastiest items were known to me because when I would return from the quarry, I often would find neatly cut clippings about Winnie that had been anonymously placed on my bed by the warders.

In small and spiteful ways, the authorities did their best to make Winnie's journeys as unpleasant as possible. For the previous two years, her visits had been stymied by local magistrates and by the repeated bannings that prevented her from traveling. I had recently heard through counsel that Winnie had been informed by the police that she could visit me only if she carried a pass. Winnie, who had been protesting the government's policy regarding women's passes since the 1950s, rightly refused to carry the hated document. The authorities were clearly attempting to humiliate her and me. But I thought it was more important that we see each other than to resist the petty machinations of the authorities, and Winnie consented to carry a pass. I missed her enormously and needed the reassurance of seeing her, and we also had vital family matters to discuss.

The regulations governing each of Winnie's visits were long and complicated. She was barred from taking a train or car and had to fly, making the trip much more expensive. She was required to take the shortest route from the airport to Caledon Square, the Cape Town police station, where she was required to sign various documents. She had to report to the same station on the way back and sign more documents.

I had also learned from a newspaper clipping that a Special Branch officer broke into our Orlando house while Winnie was dressing and she reacted angrily, pushing the officer out of the bedroom. The lieutenant laid a charge of assault against her, and I asked my friend and colleague George Bizos to defend her, which he ably did. We had seen stories about this in the newspapers, and some of the men even joked with me about Winnie's bellicosity. "You are not the only boxer in the family, Madiba," they said.

This second visit was for only half an hour, and we had much to discuss. Winnie was a bit agitated from the rough treatment in Cape Town and the fact that, as always, she had to ride in the hold of the ferry where the fumes from the engine made her ill. She had taken pains to dress up for me, but she looked thin and drawn.

We reviewed the education of the children, the health of my mother, which was not very good, and our finances. A critical issue was the education of Zeni and Zindzi. Winnie had placed the girls in a school designated as Indian, and the authorities were harassing the principal on the grounds that it was a violation of the law for the school to accept African pupils. We made the difficult decision to send Zeni and Zindzi to boarding school in Swaziland. This was hard on Winnie, who found her greatest sustenance in the two girls. I was consoled by the fact that their education would probably be superior there, but I worried about Winnie. She would be lonely and prey for people who sought to undermine her under the guise of being her friends. If anything, Winnie was too trusting of people's motives.

To get around the restrictions on discussing nonfamily matters, we used names whose meaning was clear to us, but not to the warders. If I wanted to know how Winnie was really doing, I might say, "Have you heard about Ngutyana recently; is she all right?" Ngutyana is one of Winnie's clan names, but the authorities were unaware of that. Then Winnie could talk about how and what Ngutyana was doing. If the warder asked who Ngutyana was, we would say she was a cousin. If I wanted to know about how the external mission of the ANC was faring, I would ask, "How is the church?" Winnie would discuss "the church" in appropriate terms, and I might then ask, "How are the priests? Are there any new sermons?" We improvised and managed to exchange a great deal of information that way.

As always, when the warder yelled, "Time up!," I thought only a few minutes had passed. I wanted to kiss the glass good-bye, but restrained myself. I always preferred for Winnie to leave first so she would not have to see me led away by the warders, and I watched as she whispered a good-bye, hiding her pain from the warders.

After the visit, I replayed all the details in my mind, what Winnie wore, what she said, what I said. I then wrote her a letter going over some of what we had discussed, and reminding her of how much I cared for her, how unshakable our bond was, how courageous she was. I saw my letters to her both as love letters and as the only way I could give her the emotional support she needed.

Soon after the visit, I learned that Winnie had been charged for failing to report to the police on her arrival in Cape Town as well as refusing to furnish the police with her address when she left. Having already given her address at the ferry, she was asked again when she returned, and refused, saying she had done so earlier.

Winnie was arrested and released on bail. She was tried and sentenced to a year's imprisonment, which was suspended except for four days. Winnie was subsequently dismissed from her second job as a social worker because of the incident, and lost her main source of income.

The state did its utmost to harass me in ways they thought I would be powerless to resist. Toward the end of 1966, the Transvaal Law Society, at the instigation of the minister of justice, made a motion to strike me off the roll of practicing attorneys as a result of my conviction in the Rivonia Trial. Apparently they were not discouraged by the earlier unsuccessful attempt to remove my name from the roll because of my conviction in the Defiance Campaign.

I found out about the Law Society's action only after it had been initiated. The Transvaal Law Society was an extremely conservative organization, and they were seeking to punish me at a time when they assumed I would be unable to defend myself. It is not easy for a prisoner on Robben Island to defend himself in court, but that is precisely what I intended to do.

I informed the authorities that I planned to contest the action and would prepare my own defense. I told prison officials that in order to prepare adequately, I would need to be exempt from going to the quarry and would also require a proper table, chair, and reading light to work on my brief. I said I needed access to a law library and demanded to be taken to Pretoria.

My strategy was to overwhelm the prison authorities and the

courts with legitimate requests, which I knew they would have a difficult time satisfying. The authorities always found it distressing when I wanted to defend myself in court because the accompanying publicity would show that I was still fighting for the same values I always had.

Their first response was, "Mandela, why don't you retain a lawyer to defend you? He will be able to handle the case properly. Why put yourself out?" I went ahead and applied to the registrar of the Supreme Court for the records, documents, and books that I would need. I also requested a list of the state's witnesses and summaries of their prospective testimony.

I received a letter stating that before the court would grant my requests they would need to know the nature of my defense. This was extraordinary. To ask the nature of a lawyer's defense before the trial? No defendant can be compelled to reveal his defense before he is actually in court. I wrote back to tell them that the nature of my defense would become clear to them when I filed my papers — and not until then.

This was the beginning of a flurry of correspondence between me and the registrar as well as the state attorney, who was representing the Law Society. I would not back down on any of my requests. The authorities were equally intransigent: I could not be taken off quarry detail, I could not have a table and chair, and under no circumstances would I be able to go to Pretoria to use the law library.

I continued to bedevil the Law Society and registrar with demands, which they continued to deflect. Finally, several months and many letters later, without any fanfare and with just a cursory notification to me, they dropped the entire matter. The case was becoming more than they had bargained for. They had reckoned I would not have the initiative or wherewithal to defend myself; they were mistaken.

I was able to read in detail about the official reactions to my opposition to the Law Society's actions because we were receiving a daily newspaper just as if it were delivered to our door. In effect, it was.

The warder who supervised us at night was a quiet, elderly Jehovah's Witness whom Mac Maharaj had befriended. One night, he wandered over to Mac's cell and told him that he wanted to enter a newspaper contest that required an essay. Would Mac, he wondered, be willing to assist him in writing it? The old warder hinted that if Mac helped him, there would be a reward. Mac agreed, and duly wrote the essay. A fortnight later, the old man came to Mac very excited. He was now a finalist in the competition; would Mac write him another essay? The warder promised Mac a cooked chicken in return. Mac told the old warder that he would think about it.

The next day, Mac came to Walter and me and explained the situation. While Walter encouraged Mac to accept the food, I appreciated his reluctance to do so, because it would appear that he was getting special treatment. That night, he told the warder he would write the essay in exchange for a pack of cigarettes. The old warder agreed, and the following evening presented Mac with a newly bought pack of cigarettes.

The next day, Mac told us that he now had the leverage he wanted over the old warder. How? we asked. "Because I have his fingerprints on the cigarette pack," Mac said, "and I can blackmail him." Walter exclaimed that that was immoral. I did not criticize Mac, but asked what he would blackmail him for. Mac raised his eyebrow: "Newspapers," he said. Walter and I looked at each other. I think Walter was the only man on Robben Island who relished newspapers as much as I did. Mac had already discussed his plan with the communications committee, and although we both had reservations about Mac's technique, we did not stop him.

That night Mac told the warder that he had his fingerprints on the pack of cigarettes and that if the old man did not cooperate, he would expose him to the commanding officer. Terrified of being fired and losing his pension, the warder agreed to do whatever Mac wanted. For the next six months, until the warder was transferred, the old man would smuggle that day's newspaper to Mac. Mac would then summarize the news and reduce it to a single small piece of paper, which would circulate among us. The unfortunate warder did not win the contest, either.

It would be hard to say what we did more of at the quarry: mine lime or talk. By 1966, the warders had adopted a laissez-faire attitude: we could talk as much as we wanted as long as we worked. We would cluster in small groups, four or five men in a rough circle, and talk all day long, about every subject under the sun. We were in a perpetual conversation with each other on topics both solemn and trifling.

There is no prospect about prison which pleases — with the possible exception of one. One has time to think. In the vortex of the struggle, when one is constantly reacting to changing circumstances, one rarely has the chance to carefully consider all the ramifications of one's decisions or policies. Prison provided the time — much more than enough time — to reflect on what one had done and not done.

We were constantly engaged in political debates. Some were dispatched in a day, others were disputed for years. I have always enjoyed the cut-and-thrust of debating, and was a ready participant. One of our earliest and longest debates concerned the relationship between the ANC and the Communist Party. Some of the men, especially those MK soldiers who had been trained in socialist countries, believed that the ANC and the party were one and the same. Even some very senior ANC colleagues, such as Govan Mbeki and Harry Gwala, subscribed to this theory.

The party did not exist as a separate entity on Robben Island. In prison, there was no point in making the distinction between the ANC and the party that existed on the outside. My own views on the subject had not altered in many years. The ANC was a mass liberation movement that welcomed all those with the same objectives.

Over time, the debate concerning the ANC and the party grew progressively acrimonious. A number of us proposed one way to resolve it: we would write to the ANC in exile in Lusaka. We prepared a secret twenty-two-page document on the subject with a covering letter from myself to be sent to Lusaka. It was a risky maneuver to prepare and smuggle out such a document. In the end, Lusaka confirmed the separation of the ANC and the party and the argument eventually withered away.

Another recurrent political discussion was whether or not the ANC leadership should come exclusively from the working class. Some argued that because the ANC was a mass organization made up mainly of ordinary workers, the leadership should come from those same ranks. My argument was that it was as undemocratic to specify that the leaders had to be from the working class as to declare that they should be bourgeois intellectuals. If the movement had insisted on such a rule, most of its leaders, men such as Chief Luthuli, Moses Kotane, Dr. Dadoo, would have been ineligible. Revolutionaries are drawn from every class.

Not all debates were political. One issue that provoked much discussion was circumcision. Some among us maintained that circumcision as practiced by the Xhosa and other tribes was not only an unnecessary mutilation of the body, but a reversion to the type of tribalism that the ANC was seeking to overthrow. It was not an unreasonable argument, but the prevailing view, with which I agreed, was that circumcision was a cultural ritual that had not only a salutary health benefit but an important psychological effect. It was a rite that strengthened group identification and inculcated positive values.

The debate continued for years, and a number of men voted in favor of circumcision in a very direct way. A prisoner working in the hospital who had formerly practiced as an *ingcibi* set up a secret circumcision school, and a number of the younger prisoners from our section were circumcised there. Afterward, we would organize a small party of tea and biscuits for the men, and they would spend a day or two walking around in blankets, as was the custom.

One subject we hearkened back to again and again was the question of whether there were tigers in Africa. Some argued that although it was popularly assumed that tigers lived in Africa, this was a myth and they were native to Asia and the Indian subcontinent. Africa had leopards in abundance, but no tigers. The other side argued that tigers were native to Africa and some still lived there. Some claimed to have seen with their own eyes this most powerful and beautiful of cats in the jungles of Africa.

I maintained that while there were no tigers to be found in contemporary Africa, there was a Xhosa word for tiger, a word different from the one for leopard, and that if the word existed in our language, the creature must have once existed in Africa. Otherwise, why would there be a name for it? This argument went round and round, and I remember Mac retorting that hundreds of years ago there was a Hindi word for a craft that flew in the air, long before the airplane was invented, but that did not mean that airplanes existed in ancient India.

# 68

"ZITHULELE," the Quiet One, was what we called the tolerant, soft-spoken warder in charge of us at the quarry. He routinely stood a great distance from us while we worked and did not appear to care what we did as long as we were orderly. He never berated us when he found us leaning on our spades and talking.

We responded in kind. One day, in 1966, he came to us and said, "Gentlemen, the rains have washed away the lines on the roads, we need twenty kilos of lime today. Can you help?" Although we were working very little at the time, he had approached us as human beings, and we agreed to assist him.

That spring, we had felt a certain thawing on the part of the authorities, a relaxation of the iron-fisted discipline that had prevailed on the island. The tension between prisoners and warders had lessened somewhat.

But this lull proved to be short-lived and came to an abrupt end one morning in September. We had just put down our picks and shovels on the quarry face and were walking to the shed for lunch. As one of the general prisoners wheeled a drum of food toward us, he whispered, "Verwoerd is dead." That was all. The news quickly passed among us. We looked at each other in disbelief and glanced over at the warders, who seemed unaware that anything momentous had occurred.

We did not know how the prime minister had died. Later, we heard about the obscure white parliamentary messenger who stabbed Verwoerd to death, and we wondered at his motives. Although Verwoerd thought Africans were beneath animals, his death did not yield us any pleasure. Political assassination is not something I or the ANC has ever supported. It is a primitive way of contending with an opponent.

Verwoerd had proved to be both the chief theorist and master builder of grand apartheid. He had championed the creation of the bantustans and Bantu Education. Shortly before his death he had led the Nationalists in the general election of 1966, in which the party of apartheid had increased its majority, winning 126 seats to the 39 achieved by the United Party, and the single seat won by the Progressive Party.

As often happened on the island, we had learned significant political news before our own guards. But by the following day, it was obvious the warders knew, for they took out their anger on us. The tension that had taken months to abate was suddenly at full force. The authorities began a crackdown against political prisoners as though we had held the knife that stabbed Verwoerd.

The authorities always imagined that we were secretly linked with all kinds of powerful forces on the outside. The spate of successful guerrilla attacks against the South African police forces in Namibia by the South-West African People's Organization (SWAPO) — an ally of the ANC — had also unnerved them. I suppose we should have been flattered that the government thought our nascent military ability was sophisticated enough to successfully eliminate their head of state. But their suspicions merely reflected the insecurities of narrow, shortsighted men who blamed their problems not on their own misguided policies but on an opponent by the name of the ANC.

The punishment against us was never enunciated as an official policy, but it was a renewal of the harsh atmosphere that prevailed upon our arrival on the island. The Quiet One was replaced with a man who was a vicious martinet. His name was Van Rensburg and he had been flown to the island on twenty-four hours' notice after the assassination. His reputation preceded him, for his name was a byword among prisoners for brutality.

Van Rensburg was a big, clumsy, brutish fellow who did not speak but shouted. During his first day on the job we noticed he had a small swastika tattooed on his wrist. But he did not need this offensive symbol to prove his cruelty. His job was to make our lives as wretched as possible, and he pursued that goal with great enthusiasm.

Each day over the next few months, Van Rensburg would charge one of us for insubordination or malingering. Each morning, he and the other warders would discuss who would be charged that afternoon. It was a policy of selective intimidation, and the decision on who would be charged was taken regardless of how hard that prisoner had worked that day. When we were trudging back to our cells, Van Rensburg would read from a list, "Mandela [or Sisulu or Kathrada], I want to see you immediately in front of the head of prison."

The island's administrative court began working overtime. In response, we formed our own legal committee made up of myself, Fikile Bam, and Mac Maharaj. Mac had studied law and was adept at putting the authorities on the defensive. Fiks, who was working toward a law degree, was a bright, resourceful fellow who had become the head of the prisoners' committee in our section. The job of our legal committee was to advise our comrades on how to conduct themselves in the island's administrative court.

Van Rensburg was not a clever fellow, and while he would lord it over us at the quarry, we could outwit him in court. Our strategy was not to argue with him in the field, but to contest the charges in court where we would have a chance to make our case before slightly more enlightened officers. In administrative court, the charge would be read by the presiding magistrate. "Malingering at the quarry," he might say, at which Van Rensburg would look smug. After the charge had been read in full, I always advised my colleagues to do one thing and one thing only: ask the court for "further particulars." This was one's right as a defendant, and though the request became a regular occurrence, Van Rensburg would almost always be stumped. Court would then have to be adjourned while Van Rensburg went out to gather "further particulars."

Van Rensburg was vindictive in large ways and small. When our lunch arrived at the quarry and we would sit down to eat — we now had a simple wooden table — Van Rensburg would inevitably choose that moment to urinate next to our food. I suppose we should have been grateful that he did not urinate directly on our food, but we lodged a protest against the practice anyway.

One of the few ways prisoners can take revenge on warders is through humor, and Van Rensburg became the butt of many of our jokes. Among ourselves we called him "Suitcase." Warders' lunch boxes were known as "suitcases" and normally a warder would designate a prisoner, usually his favorite, to carry his "suitcase," and then reward him with half a sandwich. But we always refused to carry Van Rensburg's "suitcase," hence the nickname. It was humiliating for a warder to carry his own lunch pail.

One day, Wilton Mkwayi inadvertently referred to "Suitcase" within Van Rensburg's hearing. "Who is Suitcase?" Van Rensburg bellowed. Wilton paused for a moment and then blurted out, "It's you!"

"Why do you call me Suitcase?" Van Rensburg asked. Wilton paused. "Come, man," Van Rensburg said. "Because you carry your own 'suitcase,' " Wilton replied tentatively. "The general prisoners carry the 'suitcases' of their warders, but we won't carry yours — so we call you Suitcase."

Van Rensburg considered this for a moment, and instead of getting angry, announced, "My name is not Suitcase, it's Dik Nek." There was silence for a moment, and then all of us burst into laughter. In Afrikaans, Dik Nek literally means "Thick Neck"; it suggests someone who is stubborn and unyielding. Suitcase, I suspect, was too thick to know that he had been insulted.

One day at the quarry, we resumed our discussion of whether or not the tiger was native to Africa. We were not able to talk as freely during Van Rensburg's tenure as we had been before, but we were able to talk nonetheless while we worked.

The principal advocate of those who argued that the tiger was not native to Africa was Andrew Masondo, an ANC leader from the Cape who had also been a lecturer at Fort Hare. Masondo could be a volatile fellow, and he was vehement in his assertions that no tigers had ever been found in Africa. The argument was going back and forth and the men had put down their picks and shovels in the heat of the argument. This attracted the attention of the warders, and they shouted at us to get back to work. But we were so absorbed in the argument that we ignored the warders. A few of the lower-ranking warders ordered us to go back to work, but we paid them no attention. Finally, Suitcase marched over and bellowed at us in English, a language in which he was not expert: "You talk too much, but you work too few!"

The men now did not pick up their tools because they were bent over in laughter. Suitcase's grammatical mistake struck everyone as extremely comical. But Suitcase was not at all amused. He immediately sent for Major Kellerman, the commanding officer.

Kellerman arrived on the scene a few minutes later to find us in much the same state as we had been before. Kellerman was relatively new to the island, and was determined to set the right tone. One of the warders then reported to Kellerman that Andrew Masondo and I had not been working, and we were to be charged with malingering and insubordination. Under Kellerman's authority, we were then handcuffed and taken to isolation.

From that point on, Suitcase seemed to hold a special grudge against me. One day, while he was supervising us at the quarry, I was working next to Fikile Bam. We were off by ourselves, on the far side of the quarry. We worked diligently, but since we were both studying law at the time, we were discussing what we had read the night before. At the end of the day, Van Rensburg stood in front of us and said, "Fikile Bam and Nelson Mandela, I want to see you in front of the head of prison."

We were brought before the lieutenant, who was the head of prison, and Van Rensburg announced, "These men did not work the whole day. I'm charging them for defying orders." The lieutenant asked if we had anything to say. "Lieutenant," I responded, "we dispute the charge. We have been working and, in fact, we have evidence that we have been working, and it is essential to our defense." The lieutenant scoffed at this. "All you men work in the same area," he said. "How is it possible to have evidence?" I explained that Fiks and I had been working apart from the others and that we could show exactly how much work we had done. Suitcase naively confirmed that we had been off by ourselves, and the lieutenant agreed to have a look. We drove back to the quarry.

Once there, Fiks and I walked to the area where we had been working. I pointed to the considerable pile of rocks and lime that we had built up and said, "There, that is what we have done today." Suitcase had never even bothered to examine our work and was rattled by the quantity of it. "No," he said to the lieutenant, "that is the result of a week's work." The lieutenant was skeptical. "All right, then," he said to Suitcase, "show me the small pile that Mandela and Bam put together today." Suitcase had no reply, and the lieutenant did something I have rarely seen a superior officer do: he chastised his subordinate in the presence of prisoners. "You are telling lies," he said, and dismissed the charges on the spot.

One morning in early 1967, during Suitcase's tenure, we were preparing to walk to the quarry when Suitcase informed us that an order had come down from Major Kellerman forbidding us to talk. Not only was conversation banned on our walks; henceforth, there would be no conversation permitted at the quarry. "From now on, silence!" he yelled.

This command was greeted by profound dismay and outrage. Talking and discussing issues were the only things that made the work at the quarry tolerable. Of course, we could not discuss it on the way to the quarry because we were ordered not to talk, but during our lunch break the ANC leadership and the heads of the other political groups managed secretly to hash out a plan.

While we were surreptitiously hatching our plan, Major Kellerman himself appeared and walked into our lunch shed. This was highly unusual; we had never had such a high-ranking visitor in our lowly shed. With a cough of embarrassment, he announced that his order had been a mistake and that we could resume talking at the quarry, just as long as we did it quietly. He then told us to carry on and spun on his heel and was gone. We were glad the order was rescinded, but suspicious as to why.

For the remainder of the day, we were not forced to work very hard. Suitcase did his best to be friendly, and said that as a gesture of goodwill he had decided to withdraw all pending charges against us.

That afternoon, I discovered that my cell had been moved from number 4, near the entrance of the passageway, to number 18, at the back. All of my belongings had been dumped into the new cell. As always, there was no explanation.

We guessed that we were to have a visitor and I had been moved because the authorities did not want me to be the first among the prisoners to talk to whoever was coming. If each prisoner in turn voiced his complaints, the authorities could yell "Time up!" before a visitor reached cell 18. We resolved that in the interest of unity, each individual along the passageway would inform any visitor that while everyone had individual complaints, the prisoner in number 18 would speak for all.

The following morning, after breakfast, we were informed by Suitcase that we would not be going to the quarry. Then Major Kellerman appeared to say that Mrs. Helen Suzman, the lone member of the liberal Progressive Party in Parliament and the only voice of true opposition to the Nationalists in Parliament, would be arriving shortly. In less than fifteen minutes, Mrs. Suzman — all five feet two inches of her — came through the door of our passageway, accompanied by General Steyn, the commissioner of prisons. As she was introduced to each prisoner, she asked him whether or not he had any complaints. Each man replied the same way: "I have many complaints, but our spokesman is Mr. Nelson Mandela at the end of the corridor." To General Steyn's dismay, Mrs. Suzman was soon at my cell. She firmly shook my hand and cordially introduced herself.

Unlike judges and magistrates, who were automatically permitted access to prisons, members of Parliament had to request permission to visit a prison. Mrs. Suzman was one of the few, if not the only, members of Parliament who took an interest in the plight of political prisoners. Many stories were circulating about Robben Island, and Mrs. Suzman had come to investigate for herself.

As this was Mrs. Suzman's first visit to Robben Island, I attempted to put her at ease. But she was remarkably confident and utterly unfazed by her surroundings, and proposed that we get down to business right away. General Steyn and the commanding officer stood by her, but I did not mince words. I told her of our desire to have the food improved and equalized and to have better clothing; the need for facilities for studying; our right to information such as newspapers; and many more things. I told her of the harshness of the warders, and mentioned Van Rensburg in particular. I pointed out that he had a swastika tattooed on his forearm. Helen reacted like a lawyer. "Well, Mr. Mandela," she said, "we must not take that too far because we don't know when it was made. Perhaps, for example, his parents had it tattooed on him?" I assured her that was not the case.

Normally, I would not complain about an individual warder. One learns in prison that it is better to fight for general principles than to battle each individual case. However callous a warder may be, he is usually just carrying out prison policy. But Van Rensburg was in a class by himself, and we believed that if he were gone, it would make a disproportionate difference for all of us.

Mrs. Suzman listened attentively, jotting down what I said in a small notebook, and promised to take these matters up with the minister of justice. She then made an inspection of our cells, and talked a bit with some of the other men. It was an odd and wonderful sight to see this courageous woman peering into our cells and strolling around our courtyard. She was the first and only woman ever to grace our cells.

Van Rensburg was exceedingly nervous during Mrs. Suzman's visit. According to Kathy, while Mrs. Suzman and I were talking, Van Rensburg apologized for all his past actions. But his contrition did not last long, for the next day he informed us he was reinstating all the charges against us. We later learned that Mrs. Suzman had taken up our case in Parliament, and within a few weeks of her visit, Suitcase was transferred off the island.

# 69

I NEVER IMAGINED the struggle would be either short or easy. The first few years on the island were difficult times both for the organization outside and those of us in prison. After Rivonia, much of the movement's underground machinery had been destroyed. Our structures had been discovered and uprooted; those who were not captured were scrambling to stay one step ahead of the enemy. Virtually every one of the ANC's senior leaders was either in jail or in exile.

In the years after Rivonia, the ANC's External Mission, formerly responsible for fund-raising, diplomacy, and establishing a military training program, took up the reins of the organization as a whole. The External Mission not only had to create an organization in exile, but had the even more formidable task of trying to revitalize the underground ANC inside South Africa.

The state had grown stronger. The police had become more powerful, their methods more ruthless, their techniques more sophisticated. The South African Defense Force was expanding. The economy was stable, the white electorate untroubled. The South African government had powerful allies in Great Britain and the United States who were content to maintain the status quo.

But elsewhere the struggle against imperialism was on the march. In the middle to late 1960s, armed struggles were being fought throughout southern Africa. In Namibia (then South-West Africa), SWAPO was making its first incursions in the Caprivi Strip; in Mozambique and Angola, the guerrilla movement was growing and spreading. In Zimbabwe (then Rhodesia), the battle against white minority rule was advancing. Ian Smith's white government was bolstered by the South African Defense Force, and the ANC regarded the battle in Zimbabwe as an extension of our struggle at home. In 1967, we learned that the ANC had forged an alliance with the Zimbabwe African People's Union (ZAPU), which had been formed by Joshua Nkomo.

That year, a group of MK soldiers who had been training in Tanzania and Zambia crossed the Zambezi River into Rhodesia with the intention of making their way home. This first group of MK soldiers was christened the Luthuli Detachment and they were the spearhead of the armed struggle. In August, as the Luthuli Detachment, accompanied by ZAPU troops, moved southward, they were spotted by the Rhodesian army. Over the next few weeks, fierce battles were fought and both sides sustained casualties. Finally, our troops were overpowered by the superior numbers of the Rhodesian forces. Some were captured, and others retreated into Bechuanaland — which had become independent Botswana. By the beginning of 1968, another larger ANC detachment had entered Rhodesia and fought not only the Rhodesian army but South African policemen who had been posted to Rhodesia.

We heard of this months later by rumor, but did not learn the full story until some of the men who had fought there were imprisoned with us. Though our forces were not victorious, we quietly celebrated the fact that our MK cadres had engaged the enemy in combat on their own terms. It was a milestone in the struggle. "Justice" Panza, one of the commanders of the Luthuli Detachment, was later imprisoned with us. He briefed us on the detachment's military training, political education, and valor in the field. As a former commander-in-chief of MK, I was terribly proud of our soldiers.

*         *         *

Before receiving the news of MK's battles abroad, we also learned of Chief Luthuli's death at home in July 1967. The circumstances were curious: he had been hit by a train in an area near his farm where he often walked. I was granted permission to write a letter to his widow. Luthuli's death left a great vacuum in the organization; the chief was a Nobel Prize winner, a distinguished, internationally known figure, a man who commanded respect from both black and white. For these reasons, he was irreplaceable. Yet in Oliver Tambo, who was acting president-general of the ANC, the organization found a man who could fill the chief's shoes. Like Luthuli, he was articulate yet not showy, confident but humble. He too epitomized Chief Luthuli's precept: "Let your courage rise with danger."

We organized a small memorial service for the chief in Section B and permitted everyone who wanted to speak to do so. It was a quiet, respectful service, with only one sour note. When Neville Alexander of the Unity Movement rose to speak, it was apparent that he had come not to praise the chief but to bury him. Without even perfunctory regrets at the man's passing, he accused Luthuli of being a patsy of the white man, mainly on the grounds that the chief had accepted the Nobel Peace Prize.

Apart from its wrong-headedness, Neville's speech was entirely contrary to the climate of cooperation between organizations we were trying to create on the island. From the moment I arrived on the island, I had made it my mission to seek some accommodation with our rivals in the struggle. I saw Robben Island as an opportunity to patch up the long and often bitter differences between the PAC and the ANC. If we could unite the two organizations on the island, that could set a precedent for uniting them in the liberation struggle as a whole.

Yet from the beginning, relations with the PAC had been more competitive than cooperative. Some of the PAC men had already been on the island, and saw our arrival as an encroachment on their territory. We heard from some of our men that the most senior PAC prisoners had expressed regret that we had not been hanged.

In 1962, when I had first been on the island, the PAC had greatly outnumbered the ANC. In 1967, the numbers were reversed. Yet this seemed to harden the PAC in their positions. They were unashamedly anti-Communist and anti-Indian. In the early years, I had talks with Zeph Mothopeng, who had been on the PAC's National Executive Committee. Zeph argued that the PAC was more militant than the ANC, and that in prison, the ANC should follow the PAC's lead. The PAC maintained that negotiations with the authorities were a betrayal, but that did not stop them from taking advantage of the benefits that resulted from negotiations. In 1967, I held talks with Selby Ngendane on the question of unity. Outside of prison, Ngendane had been violently opposed to the Freedom Charter, but in prison, particularly when sent to our section, Selby mellowed. We eventually wrote separate letters to our respective organizations in the general section advocating the idea of unity. The ANC also worked well with Clarence Makwetu, who later became president of the PAC. Makwetu, who had once been a member of the ANC Youth League, was in our section and was a balanced, sensible man. We had many fruitful discussions about the unity of our two organizations, but after Makwetu was released and was succeeded in the PAC leadership on Robben Island by John Pokela, the talks foundered.

The PAC's insecurity occasionally had comical results. At one point, an order came from Pretoria that I was to be isolated from all other prisoners at the quarry. I would work separately, eat separately, and have my own guard. We noticed that this new ruling caused some agitation among the PAC. Several days later, the PAC decided that their leader, Zeph Mothopeng, would also be isolated, and on their own they had him work and eat separately from everyone else for as long as I did.

The PAC often refused to participate in meetings that had no overt party affiliation. When we called meetings to discuss our grievances and later had news sessions to discuss what we had learned from the paper, the PAC boycotted these gatherings. I found this greatly annoying. The PAC, we learned, were ignorant of changes in their own organization on the outside. At the time, the PAC members on the island refused to believe our claims that the exiled PAC had opened its doors to whites and Indians as members. That was heresy. Yet we had read in the paper that the white activist Patrick Duncan had become a member of the PAC executive. The PAC members derided this at the time as ANC propaganda.

*      *      *

The ANC formed its own internal organization on the island. Known as the High Command, or more officially, the High Organ, it consisted of the most senior ANC leaders on Robben Island, the men who had been members of the National Executive Committee: Walter Sisulu, Govan Mbeki, Raymond Mhlaba, and myself. I served as the head of the High Organ.

From its inception, we decided the High Organ would not try to influence external ANC policy. We had no reliable way of evaluating the situation in the country, and concluded it would neither be fair nor wise for us to offer guidance on matters about which we were uninformed. Instead, we made decisions about such matters as prisoners' complaints, strikes, mail, food — all of the day-to-day concerns of prison life. We would, when possible, convene a general members' meeting, which we regarded as vital to the health of our organization. But as these meetings were extremely dangerous and thus infrequent, the High Organ would often take decisions that were then communicated to all the other members. The High Organ also operated a cell system, with each cell consisting of three members.

In the first few years on the island, the High Organ also acted as a representative committee for all the political prisoners in our section. In 1967, we organized a petition demanding better treatment that was signed by virtually everyone, including members of the PAC, the Unity Movement, and the Liberal Party, represented by Eddie Daniels. This arrangement was acceptable to all until Neville Alexander complained that the High Organ was neither democratic nor truly representative, and that some other body ought to be created.

Neville's original suggestion eventually turned into a prisoners' committee composed of people from all political parties. There was fear among the other organizations that the ANC would attempt to dominate it, and the committee's rules were crafted so that its powers were purely consultative and its decisions not binding. Even so, it was still difficult to agree on a common approach to problems. We suggested that Fikile Bam, a member of the Yu Chi Chan Club, preside over meetings. Later, the committee leadership would rotate. Eventually the committee became known as Ulundi, and acted as a disciplinary committee for all political prisoners.

The High Organ was the source of some controversy because of its ethnic composition: all four permanent members were from Xhosa backgrounds. This was a matter of coincidence rather than design; the senior ANC leadership on the island, the only four to have served on the National Executive Committee, happened to be Xhosa. It would not have been proper to take a less senior comrade and put him on the High Organ simply because he was not a Xhosa. But the fact that the High Organ was Xhosa-dominated disturbed me because it seemed to reinforce the mistaken perception that we were a Xhosa organization.

I have always found this criticism to be vexing and based on both ignorance of ANC history and maliciousness. I would refute it by noting that the presidents of the ANC have been Zulus, Basotho, Pedis, and Tswanas, and the executive has always been a mixture of tribal groups. I recall once working in our courtyard on a sunny afternoon, while some men from the general section were working on the roof above me. They shouted at me, "*Mdala!* [Old man!], why do you only talk to Xhosas?" The accusation stung me. I looked up and said, "How can you accuse me of discrimination? We are one people." They seemed satisfied by that, but their perception stuck in my mind. From then on, whenever I knew I would be walking in front of men from the general section, I would try to converse with Kathy or Eddie Daniels, or someone who was not a Xhosa.

We subsequently decided that there should be a fifth, rotating member of the High Organ. This member was usually not a Xhosa; Kathy, for example, was the fifth member of the High Organ for more than five years. Laloo Chiba also served for a time, and in the end, the criticism died a slow and unremarkable death.

I did not by any means dominate the High Organ, and in fact, a number of proposals that I felt strongly about were rejected. This is as it should be, but I sometimes found it frustrating. There were two issues regarding the authorities about which I could never persuade my colleagues. Prison regulations stated that prisoners must stand in the presence of a senior officer. I advocated that we should remain seated, as it was demeaning to have to recognize the enemy when he did not recognize us as political prisoners. My comrades believed this was a trivial matter and the negative consequences of resistance would outweigh any benefits.

The second issue was rejected by the High Organ on similar

grounds. The warders called us by either our surnames or our Christian names. Each, I felt, was degrading, and I thought we should insist on the honorific "Mister." I pressed for this for many years, without success. Later, it even became a source of humor as my colleagues would occasionally call me "Mr." Mandela.

# 70

TIME MAY SEEM to stand still for those of us in prison, but it did not halt for those outside. I was reminded of this when I was visited by my mother in the spring of 1968. I had not seen her since the end of the Rivonia Trial. Change is gradual and incremental, and when one lives in the midst of one's family, one rarely notices differences in them. But when one doesn't see one's family for many years at a time, the transformation can be striking. My mother suddenly seemed very old.

She had journeyed all the way from the Transkei, accompanied by my son Makgatho, my daughter Makaziwe, and my sister Mabel. Because I had four visitors and they had come a great distance, the authorities extended the visiting time from a half an hour to forty-five minutes.

I had not seen my son and daughter since before the trial and they had become adults in the interim, growing up without me. I looked at them with amazement and pride. But though they had grown up, I am afraid I still treated them more or less as the children they had been when I went to prison. They may have changed, but I hadn't.

My mother had lost a great deal of weight, which concerned me. Her face appeared haggard. Only my sister Mabel seemed unchanged. While it was a great pleasure to see all of them and to discuss family issues, I was uneasy about my mother's health.

I spoke with Makgatho and Maki about my desire for them both to pursue further schooling and asked Mabel about relatives in the Transkei. The time passed far too quickly. As with most visits, the greatest pleasure often lies in the recollection of it, but this time, I could not stop worrying about my mother. I feared that it would be the last time I would ever see her.

Several weeks later, after returning from the quarry, I was told to go to the Head Office to collect a telegram. It was from Makgatho, informing me that my mother had died of a heart attack. I immediately made a request to the commanding officer to be permitted to attend her funeral in the Transkei, which he turned down. "Mandela," he said, "while I know you are a man of your word and would not try to escape, I cannot trust your own people, and we fear that they would try to kidnap you." It added to my grief that I was not able to bury my mother, which was my responsibility as her eldest child and only son.

Over the next few months I thought about her a great deal. Her life had been far from easy. I had been able to support her when I was practicing as an attorney, but once I went to prison, I was unable to help her. I had never been as attentive as I should have been.

A mother's death causes a man to look back on and evaluate his own life. Her difficulties, her poverty, made me question once again whether I had taken the right path. That was always the conundrum: Had I made the right choice in putting the people's welfare even before that of my own family? For a long time, my mother had not understood my commitment to the struggle. My family had not asked for or even wanted to be involved in the struggle, but my involvement penalized them.

But I came back to the same answer. In South Africa, it is hard for a man to ignore the needs of the people, even at the expense of his own family. I had made my choice, and in the end, she had supported it. But that did not lessen the sadness I felt at not being able to make her life more comfortable, or the pain of not being able to lay her to rest.

In the early hours of the morning of May 12, 1969, the security police awakened Winnie at our home in Orlando and detained her without charge under the 1967 Terrorism Act, which gave the government unprecedented powers of arrest and detention without trial. The raid, I later learned, was part of a nationwide crackdown in which dozens of others were detained, including Winnie's sister. The police dragged Winnie away while Zeni and Zindzi clung to her skirts. She was placed in solitary confinement in Pretoria, where she was denied bail and visitors; over the next weeks and months, she was relentlessly and brutally interrogated.

446 LONG WALK TO FREEDOM

When Winnie was finally charged — six months later — I managed to send instructions that she be represented by Joel Carlson, a longtime anti-apartheid lawyer. Winnie and twenty-two others were charged under the Suppression of Communism Act for attempting to revive the ANC. Later, George Bizos and Arthur Chaskalson, both members of the Rivonia team, joined the defense. In October, seventeen months after her arrest, the state withdrew its case without explanation, and Winnie was released. Within two weeks, she was again banned, and placed under house arrest. She immediately applied for permission to visit me and was rebuffed.

There was nothing I found so agonizing in prison as the thought that Winnie was in prison too. I put a brave face on the situation, but inwardly I was deeply disturbed and worried. Nothing tested my inner equilibrium as much as the time that Winnie was in solitary confinement. Although I often urged others not to worry about what they could not control, I was unable to take my own advice. I had many sleepless nights. What were the authorities doing to my wife? How would she bear up? Who was looking after our daughters? Who would pay the bills? It is a form of mental torture to be constantly plagued by such questions and not have the means to answer them.

Brigadier Aucamp allowed me to send letters to Winnie, and relayed one or two from her. Normally, prisoners awaiting trial are not permitted mail, but Aucamp permitted it as a favor to me. I was grateful, but knew the authorities had not granted permission out of altruism: they were reading our letters, hoping to glean some information that would assist their case against Winnie.

During this time I experienced another grievous loss. One cold morning in July of 1969, three months after I learned of Winnie's incarceration, I was called to the main office on Robben Island and handed a telegram. It was from my youngest son, Makgatho, and it was only a sentence long. He informed me that his older brother, my first and oldest son, Madiba Thembekile, whom we called Thembi, had been killed in a motorcar accident in the Transkei. Thembi was then twenty-five years old, and the father of two small children.

What can one say about such a tragedy? I was already overwrought about my wife, I was still grieving for my mother, and then to hear such news ... I do not have words to express the sorrow, or the loss I felt. It left a hole in my heart that can never be filled.

I returned to my cell and lay on my bed. I do not know how long I stayed there, but I did not emerge for dinner. Some of the men looked in, but I said nothing. Finally, Walter came to me and knelt beside my bed, and I handed him the telegram. He said nothing, but only held my hand. I do not know how long he remained with me. There is nothing that one man can say to another at such a time.

I asked permission of the authorities to attend my son's funeral. As a father, it was my responsibility to make sure that my son's spirit would rest peacefully. I told them they could send a security cordon with me, and that I would give my word that I would return. Permission was denied. All I was permitted to do was write a letter to Thembi's mother, Evelyn, in which I did my best to comfort her and tell her that I shared her suffering.

I thought back to one afternoon when Thembi was a boy and he came to visit me at a safe house in Cyrildene that I used for secret ANC work. Between my underground political work and legal cases, I had not been able to see him for some time. I surprised him at the house and found him wearing an old jacket of mine that came to his knees. He must have taken some comfort and pride in wearing his father's clothing, just as I once did with my own father's. When I had to say good-bye again, he stood up tall, as if he were already grown, and said, "I will look after the family while you are gone."

*Part Nine*

---

# ROBBEN ISLAND: BEGINNING TO HOPE

# 71

THE GRAPH of improvement in prison was never steady. Progress was halting, and typically accompanied by setbacks. An advancement might take years to win, and then be rescinded in a day. We would push the rock up the hill, only to have it tumble down again. But conditions did improve. We had won a host of small battles that added up to a change in the atmosphere of the island. While we did not run the island, the authorities could not run it without us, and in the aftermath of Van Rensburg's departure, our life became more tolerable.

Within our first three years on the island we were all given long trousers. By 1969, we received our own individual prison uniforms, instead of being issued a different set each week. These uniforms actually fit us and we were allowed to wash them ourselves. We were permitted out in the courtyard at all hours during the weekend. Although our food was not yet equalized, African prisoners would occasionally receive bread in the morning. We were allowed to pool our food anyway, so that the differences did not matter. We had been given board games and cards, which we often played on Saturdays and Sundays. At the quarry, our talk was rarely interrupted. If the commanding officer was coming, the warders on duty would blow a whistle to warn us to pick up our tools. We had neutralized the worst warders and befriended the more reasonable ones, though the authorities realized this and rotated warders every few months.

We were able to meet among ourselves virtually whenever we wanted. Meetings of the High Organ, general members' meetings, and meetings of Ulundi were generally not broken up unless they were too conspicuous. The inmates seemed to be running the prison, not the authorities.

Stern and God-fearing, the Afrikaner takes his religion seriously. The one inflexible event on our weekly schedule was Sunday morning religious services. This was an observance the authorities considered mandatory. It was as if they believed their own mortal souls would be in peril if they did not give us the benefit of worship on Sunday.

Every Sunday morning, a minister from a different denomination would preach to us. One Sunday it would be an Anglican priest, the next a Dutch Reform predikant, the next a Methodist minister. The clerics were recruited by the prison service, whose one edict was that they must preach exclusively on religious matters. Warders were present at all services and if the minister strayed from religion, he was not invited back.

During the first two years on the island, we were not even permitted to leave our cells for Sunday services. The minister would preach from the head of our corridor. By our third year, services were held in the courtyard, which we preferred. In those years, this was the only time we were permitted in the courtyard on Sunday, except for our half hour of exercise. Few of our men were religious, but no one minded long sermons; we enjoyed being outside.

Once services were held outside, we were given the option of attending. Some men only attended services in their own denomination. Though I am a Methodist, I would attend each different religious service.

One of our first ministers was an Anglican priest by the name of Father Hughes, a gruff, burly Welshman who had served as a chaplain in the submarine corps during the Second World War. When he first arrived, he was perturbed by having to preach in the corridor, which he found inimical to the contemplation of God. On his first visit, instead of preaching to us, he recited passages of Winston Churchill's wartime radio addresses in his beautiful baritone: "We shall fight on the beaches, we shall fight on the landing grounds, we shall fight in the fields and in the streets, we shall fight in the hills; we shall never surrender."

Father Hughes soon preached to us in the courtyard and we found his sermons splendid. He made a point of discreetly inserting bits and pieces of news into his sermons, something we appreciated. He might say, for example, that like the pharaoh of ancient Egypt, the prime minister of South Africa was raising an army.

We always sang hymns at the end of services, and I think Father Hughes visited us so frequently just to hear us sing. He brought along a portable organ, and he would play for us. He praised our singing, saying that it was the only singing that matched the choirs in his native Wales.

The Methodist minister was a Reverend Jones, a nervous and gloomy fellow who had been based in the Congo during its revolution. His experience there seemed to be the source of his melancholy. Over and over, he preached the importance of reconciliation — implying that it was we who needed to reconcile ourselves to the whites.

One Sunday, during the reverend's one-sided message, I noticed Eddie Daniels shifting uneasily. Finally, Eddie could take it no longer. "You're preaching reconciliation to the wrong people," Eddie called out. "We've been seeking reconciliation for the last seventy-five years." This was enough for Reverend Jones and we never saw him again.

Reverend Jones was not the only minister Eddie scared away. We were visited by a Coloured minister known as Brother September. One Sunday, a prisoner named Hennie Ferris, who was an eloquent speaker, volunteered to lead a prayer. Brother September was pleased to recognize such devotion. Hennie began speaking in lofty language, and at one point, asked the congregation to close its eyes and pray. Everyone, including Brother September, obliged. Eddie then tiptoed to the front, opened Brother September's briefcase, and removed the *Sunday Times* of that day. No one suspected anything at the time, but Brother September never brought newspapers again.

Reverend Andre Scheffler was a minister of the Dutch Reformed Mission Church in Africa, a sister church of the Dutch Reformed Church, the faith of nearly all the Afrikaner people. The Mission Church catered only to Africans. Reverend Scheffler was a crusty, conservative fellow who usually preached to the general prisoners. One Sunday, he wandered over to our section and we asked him why he didn't preach to us. "You men think you are freedom fighters," he said contemptuously. "You must have been drunk on liquor or high on *dagga* [marijuana] when you were arrested. Freedom fighters, my foot!" But we challenged him to come to preach to us, and eventually, in the late 1960s, he responded.

Reverend Scheffler was unorthodox in one respect: he took a scientific approach to religion. I found this very appealing. Many people use science to debunk religion, but Reverend Scheffler enlisted science to bolster his beliefs. I recall one sermon in which he talked about the three Wise Men from the East who followed a star until it led them to Bethlehem. "This is not just a superstition or a myth," he said, and then cited evidence from astronomers that at that time in history there was a comet that followed the path outlined in the Bible.

As Reverend Scheffler became familiar with us, he became more sympathetic. He had a dry sense of humor and liked to poke fun at us. "You know," he would say, "the white man has a more difficult task than the black man in this country. Whenever there is a problem, we have to find a solution. But whenever you blacks have a problem, you have an excuse. You can simply say, '*Ingabilungu.*' " We burst into laughter not only because his pronunciation was unintentionally comical, but also because we were amused by the idea. "*Ngabelungu*" is a Xhosa expression that means, "It is the whites." He was saying that we could always blame all of our troubles on the white man. His message was that we must also look within ourselves and become responsible for our actions — sentiments with which I wholeheartedly agreed.

What Sundays were to the rest of the week, Christmas was to the rest of the year. It was the one day when the authorities showed any goodwill toward men. We did not have to go to the quarry on Christmas Day, and we were permitted to purchase a small quantity of sweets. We did not have a traditional Christmas meal, but we were given an extra mug of coffee for supper.

The authorities permitted us to organize a concert, hold competitions, and put on a play. The concert was the centerpiece. Our choirmaster was Selby Ngendane of the PAC. Selby had been a member of the ANC Youth League before switching allegiance to the Pan Africanist Congress. He was a natural entertainer with a lovely voice and a fine ear.

Selby chose the songs, arranged the harmonies, selected the soloists, and conducted the performance. The concert took place on Christmas morning in the courtyard. We would mix in traditional English Christmas songs with African ones, and include a few protest songs — the authorities did not seem to mind or perhaps know the difference. The warders were our audience, and they enjoyed our singing as much as we did.

Before coming to prison, Ngendane was perceived as something of a political lightweight. But in prison, Selby showed his mettle. In prison, one likes to be around men who have a sunny disposition, and Selby had one.

Prison was a kind of crucible that tested a man's character. Some men, under the pressure of incarceration, showed true mettle, while others revealed themselves as less than what they had appeared to be.

In addition to the concerts, we held a chess and draughts (or checkers) tournament, and also played Scrabble and bridge. Every year, I competed in the draughts competition, and some years, I won the grand prize, which was usually a candy bar. My style of play was slow and deliberate; my strategy conservative. I carefully considered the ramifications of every option and took a long time between moves. I resist such analogies, but it is my preferred mode of operating not only in draughts but in politics.

Most of my opponents played more swiftly, and often lost patience with my manner of play. One of my most frequent opponents was Don Davis. A member of the Non-European Unity Movement, Don had grown up in the diamond-mining area of Kimberley and was a rugged, fearless fellow who was also highly strung. Don was an excellent draughts player, but his style contrasted with mine. When Don played, perspiration would flow down his face. He became tense and agitated as he played, and made his moves rapidly as though points were awarded for speed. Several times Don and I found ourselves in the finals of the annual tournament.

Don called me Qhipu because of a habit I had when playing draughts. I would ponder each possibility, and then when I was about to move, I would call out, *"Qhipu!"* — which means "I strike!" — and then move the piece. Don found this frustrating and he called me Qhipu more in irritation than in amity.

Don and I played in many tournaments, and even if he won, he would come back within a few minutes, challenging me to another match. Don always wanted to play draughts, and did not seem satisfied until I responded. Soon I was spending so much time playing with Don that my other pursuits languished. When I once failed to pass an exam in my studies, a few colleagues asked me why, and I responded, to much laughter, "Don Davis!"

Our amateur drama society made its yearly offering at Christmas. My thespian career, which had lain dormant since I played John Wilkes Booth while at Fort Hare, had a modest revival on Robben Island. Our productions were what might now be called minimalist: no stage, no scenery, no costumes. All we had were the words of the play.

I only performed in a few dramas, but I had one memorable role: that of Creon, the king of Thebes, in Sophocles' *Antigone*. I had read some of the classic Greek plays in prison, and found them enormously elevating. What I took out of them was that character was measured by facing up to difficult situations and that a hero was a man who would not break even under the most trying circumstances.

When *Antigone* was chosen as the play, I volunteered my services, and was asked to play Creon, an elderly king fighting a civil war over the throne of his beloved city-state. At the outset of the play, Creon is sincere and patriotic, and there is wisdom in his early speeches when he suggests that experience is the foundation of leadership and that obligations to the people take precedence over loyalty to an individual.

> Of course you cannot know a man completely,
> his character, his principles, sense of judgment,
> not till he's shown his colors, ruling the people,
> making laws. Experience, there's the test.

But Creon deals with his enemies mercilessly. He has decreed that the body of Polynices, Antigone's brother, who had rebelled against the city, does not deserve a proper burial. Antigone rebels, on the grounds that there is a higher law than that of the state. Creon will not listen to Antigone, nor does he listen to anyone but his own inner demons. His inflexibility and blindness ill become a leader, for a leader must temper justice with mercy. It was Antigone who symbolized our struggle; she was, in her own way, a freedom fighter, for she defied the law on the grounds that it was unjust.

# 72

SOME OF THE WARDERS began to engage us in conversation. I never initiated conversations with warders, but if they addressed a question to me, I tried to answer. It is easier to educate a man when he wants to learn. Usually, these questions were posed with a kind of exasperation: "All right, Mandela, what is it you really want?" Or, "Look, you have a roof over your head and enough food, why are you causing so much trouble?" I would then calmly explain our policies to the warders. I wanted to demystify the ANC for them, to peel away their prejudices.

In 1969 a young warder arrived who seemed particularly eager to get to know me. I had heard rumors that our people on the outside were organizing an escape for me, and had infiltrated a warder onto the island who would assist me. Gradually, this fellow communicated to me that he was planning my escape.

In bits and pieces he explained the plan: one night, he would drug the warders on duty at the lighthouse to allow for the landing of a boat on the beach. He would furnish me with a key to get out of our section so that I could meet the boat. On the boat I was to be equipped with underwater diving gear, which I would use to swim into the harbor at Cape Town. From Cape Town, I would be taken to a local airport and flown out of the country.

I listened to the plan in its entirety and did not communicate to him how far-fetched and unreliable it sounded. I consulted with Walter, and we agreed that this fellow was not to be trusted. I never told him that I would not do it, but I never took any of the actions required to implement the plan. He must have gotten the message, for he was soon transferred off the island.

As it turned out, my mistrust was justified, for we later learned that the warder was an agent of the Bureau of State Security (BOSS), South Africa's secret intelligence agency. The plot was that I was to be successfully taken off the island, but killed in a dramatic shootout with security forces at the airport as I tried to leave the country. The entire plan had been dreamed up by BOSS, even the rumors that reached me about the ANC's planning an escape. It was not the last time they would try to eliminate me.

The term of a commanding officer was usually no more than three years, and we had been through several by 1970. That year, Robben Island's commanding officer was Colonel Van Aarde, a rather amiable, harmless fellow who allowed us free rein. But at the end of the year, the authorities concluded that they wanted a different atmosphere on the island, and Colonel Piet Badenhorst was named the new C.O. of Robben Island.

This was an ominous development. Badenhorst was reputed to be one of the most brutal and authoritarian officers in the entire prison service. His appointment indicated one thing: the government believed that discipline on the island was too lax, and that a strong hand was needed to keep us in line. Badenhorst would supposedly make us yearn for the days of Suitcase.

Whenever a new commanding officer was appointed, I requested a meeting with him. I did this in order to impress upon him the seriousness of our cause and also to evaluate his character. I requested a meeting with Colonel Badenhorst and was turned down. He was the first commanding officer to spurn such a meeting.

We felt the effects of his regime before we ever saw him. A number of the newer regulations regarding study and free time were immediately rescinded. It was obvious that he intended to roll back every privilege we had won over the years. Our old warders were transferred off the island and replaced by Badenhorst's handpicked guards. They were younger, coarser men who enforced every niggling regulation, whose job was to harass and demoralize us. Within days of Badenhorst's appointment, our cells were raided and searched; books and papers were confiscated; meals were suspended without warning; and men were jostled on the way to the quarry.

Badenhorst attempted to turn back the clock to the way the island was in the early 1960s. The answer to every question was always no. Prisoners who requested to see their lawyers were given solitary confinement instead. Complaints were completely ignored. Visits were canceled without explanation. The food deteriorated. Censorship increased.

About a week after Badenhorst arrived, we were working at the quarry one morning when, without introduction or fanfare, Badenhorst and his driver pulled up in the commander's car. He got out and surveyed us from a distance. We paused to look at our new commander. Badenhorst returned my glance and called out, "Mandela, *Jy moet jou vinger uit jou gat trek*" (You must pull your finger out of your arse). I did not care for this expression at all, and without thinking, I started advancing toward Badenhorst. He was still a distance away, and before I got close he had returned to his car and driven away.

From his car, Badenhorst radioed a command to his staff, and within minutes a truck had arrived to transport us back to Section B. We were commanded to be silent in the truck, and when we arrived at the courtyard, we were ordered to stand at attention. Badenhorst appeared in front of us, pacing back and forth. He seemed incapable of uttering a sentence without including an oath or swearword. "*Jou ma se moer,*" was his favorite expression. "Your mother is a *moer*" — *moer* being a vulgar term for an intimate part of a woman's anatomy.

In his guttural voice, he told us he was disgusted to have observed our laziness at the quarry. As a result, he said, he was arbitrarily dropping all of our classifications by one notch. Though we despised the classification system, most of the men had by that time risen to at least C level, where they were permitted to study. D level prisoners were not allowed to study. The authorities rued the fact that they had allowed us study privileges, and Badenhorst was determined to rectify that mistake.

Later, after my anger abated, I realized that Badenhorst's crude remark to me at the quarry was a calculated one. He had been brought to Robben Island to restore order, and he had singled out the individual he assumed was the source of the disorder. Like a teacher who takes over a rowdy class, he sought to discipline the student he regarded as the principal troublemaker.

# 73

IN LATE MAY of 1971, a number of men from SWAPO (the South-West African People's Organization), an ally of the ANC fighting for independence in Namibia, were brought to the isolation section. They were led by Andimba Toivo ja Toivo, a founder of

SWAPO and a formidable freedom fighter. We learned that they had embarked on a hunger strike to protest their isolation, and we immediately decided to join in. This angered Badenhorst and the authorities who regarded this as unacceptable insubordination.

Late on the night of May 28, we were awakened by shouts and fierce knocking on our cell doors. "Get up! Get up!" the warders yelled. We were ordered to strip and then line up against the wall of the courtyard. The warders were obviously drunk and were yelling and taunting us. They were led by a sadistic fellow named Fourie, whom we privately called Gangster.

It was a bitterly cold night, and for the next hour, while we stood at attention naked and shivering, our cells were searched one by one. Warders kept up their abuse for the entire time. Toward the end of the hour, Govan experienced severe chest pains and collapsed. This seemed to scare Fourie, and he ordered us to return to our cells.

The warders searched high and low, and found nothing. But the search seemed only an excuse for Fourie's sadistic impulses. Only later did we learn that Fourie was reputed to have molested prisoners in the general section. The following day we discovered that the warders had brutally beaten some general prisoners before they came to us, and afterward, assaulted Toivo ja Toivo, who hit back and knocked down the warder who was beating him. Toivo was severely punished for this.

We filed a formal complaint about our treatment, but it was ignored. The incident stands out in my memory, but it was by no means unique; incidents like it were the rule rather than the exception during Badenhorst's command.

We were determined not to let conditions deteriorate entirely under Badenhorst. We smuggled messages to our people on the outside to agitate for his dismissal. At the same time, we resolved to create a delegation among ourselves to see Badenhorst. We discussed this for months and gradually decided on its composition; Walter and I represented the ANC, and each of the other parties had two representatives as well.

Badenhorst agreed to meet us, and at our parley we threatened work stoppages, go-slows, hunger strikes — every weapon at our disposal — unless he reformed his ways and restored many of the privileges that he had rescinded. He merely said he would take what we said under consideration. We regarded this confrontation as a victory, for he was wary of us and knew that we had alerted people on the outside of our complaints. These efforts soon produced a response.

A few weeks later, we knew an important visit must be imminent because when it rained that day at the quarry we were allowed to take shelter instead of continuing to work. The following day we were informed that a troika of judges were coming to the island. The authorities asked us to nominate a spokesman to express our grievances, and I was chosen.

As I was preparing for my meeting with the judges, I was informed by a reliable source that a prisoner in the general section had recently been severely beaten by a guard. The three judges were Justices Jan Steyn, M. E. Theron, and Michael Corbett of the Cape provincial division of the Supreme Court. They were escorted by the commissioner of prisons, General Steyn, and accompanied by Colonel Badenhorst. I met them that day outside, where we were working.

General Steyn introduced me to the judges and explained that I had been selected to represent the other prisoners. The judges then indicated that as a matter of course they would talk with me privately. I replied that I had nothing to hide and that in fact I welcomed the presence of General Steyn and the colonel. I could see that they were taken aback by my statement, and I added that it would be only proper for them to have the opportunity to reply to my charges. The judges reluctantly acquiesced.

I began by recounting the recent assault in the general section. I told them the details that had been reported to me, the viciousness of the beating, and the cover-up of the crime. I had barely begun to speak when I noticed Badenhorst shifting uncomfortably. When I had finished describing the incident, Badenhorst interjected in a gruff, aggressive manner: "Did you actually witness this assault?" I replied calmly that I had not but that I trusted the people who had told me of it. He snorted and wagged his finger in my face. "Be careful, Mandela," he said. "If you talk about things you haven't seen, you will get yourself in trouble. You know what I mean."

I ignored Badenhorst's remarks and turned to the judges and said, "Gentlemen, you can see for yourselves the type of man we are dealing with as commanding officer. If he can threaten me here, in your presence, you can imagine what he does when you are not here." Judge Corbett then turned to the others and said, "The prisoner is quite right."

I spent the remainder of the meeting enumerating complaints about our diet, work, and studying. Inwardly Badenhorst must have been fuming, but outwardly he seemed chastened. At the end of the session, the judges thanked me, and I bade them good-bye.

I have no idea what the judges said or did after the meeting, but over the next few months, Badenhorst seemed to have his hands tied. The harshness abated, and within three months of the judges' visit, we received word that Badenhorst was to be transferred.

A few days before Badenhorst's departure, I was called to the main office. General Steyn was visiting the island and wanted to know if we had any complaints. Badenhorst was there as I went through a list of demands. When I had finished, Badenhorst spoke to me directly. He told me that he would be leaving the island, and added, "I just want to wish you people good luck." I do not know if I looked dumbfounded, but I was amazed. He spoke these words like a human being, and showed a side of himself we had never seen before. I thanked him for his good wishes, and wished him luck in his endeavors.

I thought about this moment for a long time afterward. Badenhorst had perhaps been the most callous and barbaric commanding officer we had had on Robben Island. But that day in the office, he had revealed that there was another side to his nature, a side that had been obscured but that still existed. It was a useful reminder that all men, even the most seemingly cold-blooded, have a core of decency, and that if their heart is touched, they are capable of changing. Ultimately, Badenhorst was not evil; his inhumanity had been foisted upon him by an inhuman system. He behaved like a brute because he was rewarded for brutish behavior.

# 74

IT WAS ANNOUNCED that Colonel Willemse would succeed Colonel Badenhorst as commanding officer. I requested a meeting with the colonel after his appointment and visited with him shortly after his arrival. While he was obviously not a progressive man, he was courteous and reasonable, in marked contrast to his predecessor. Badenhorst's tenure, we hoped, would simply be a dip on the graph of the steady improvement of our conditions.

The aggressive young warders departed with Badenhorst as well, and we quickly resumed our customary behavior at the quarry and in our section. Willemse may have been a reasonable man, but when he saw that we spent more time at the quarry talking than working, he was shocked.

He had been on the island for only a few weeks when I was summoned to his office for a meeting. "Mandela," he said frankly, "you must help me." I asked him how. "Your men are not working. They don't listen to orders. They only do what they want to do. This is a prison. There must be some discipline. It is not only good for us but good for you. We must have some order or they will bring back someone like the previous head of prison."

What the colonel said made sense. I listened and told him that his request was a legitimate one, but before I could respond to him, I would need to meet with all my men. At that time, a meeting of all prisoners in the single cells was something that was expressly forbidden. By asking him to permit such a meeting, I was asking him for a significant extension of the rules. He knew this as well as I did, and he wanted some time to consider it.

Within days, I received a communication from Willemse saying he would allow it. All of us met one afternoon in the courtyard, without guards watching over us. I told the men what Willemse said, and noted that by compromising a bit now, we would be making our conditions better in the long run. We decided that we would at least appear to be working, but what work we did would be at a pace that suited us. From then on, that is what we did, and we heard no more complaints from the commanding officer.

During the early part of Willemse's tenure, in 1971–2, there was a steady influx of captured MK soldiers. These men had seen combat, and were well informed about the state of the exile movement. While I was never happy to see ANC men imprisoned, I was keen to debrief them after they arrived. I was extremely eager to know about Oliver, about the training camps, about MK's successes and failures.

The men were extremely militant, and they did not take to prison life easily. One of the first of these men was Jimmy April, an MK officer who had trained under Joe Slovo and had fought against the enemy in Rhodesia. MK had been slowly infiltrating men back into the country with forged identity documents. Jimmy had been one of them and he was arrested in South Africa.

Jimmy regaled us with war stories, but I also took him aside and asked him about MK's problems. As I was founder of MK and its first commander-in-chief, Jimmy and the others were more candid with me than they were with the others. He told me stories of discontent in the camps, and of abuses by MK officers. I asked him to keep the matter to himself, and I managed to smuggle a letter out to Oliver suggesting that some reforms must be made in the camps.

One day, I was at the Head Office meeting with Colonel Willemse when I saw Jimmy outside the office of another official. He turned to me and said in some agitation, "They are refusing to give me my letter."

"On what ground?" I replied.

"They claim it contains matter which I am not allowed to see," he said. I entered the office to discuss the matter, but before I could even open my mouth, Jimmy had barged in and loudly said to the official, "Give me my letter!" Jimmy began to push me aside to get to the officer's desk and take the letter himself. At this point, the official took the letter and moved behind me as if for protection from Jimmy. It might have been a comical scene in a film, but at the time it was nerve-racking. I turned to Jimmy and said quietly but sternly, "Please don't do this. Calm down. I'll sort out this matter and see to it that you get your letter. Now, please leave."

My speech had the intended effect, and Jimmy left the office. I then turned to the officer, who was extremely rattled. It was, for me, an odd position. I was not opposing the authorities but mediating between my own people and the men I had so long fought against. The militancy of those who were coming to the island put me in this position more and more frequently. While we were encouraged by their radicalism, these men sometimes made our day-to-day life more burdensome.

Within a week, the officer handed me Jimmy's letter.

# 75

ONE MORNING, instead of walking to the quarry, we were ordered into the back of a truck. It rumbled off in a new direction, and fifteen minutes later we were ordered to jump out. There in front of us, glinting in the morning light, we saw the ocean, the rocky shore, and in the distance, winking in the sunshine, the glass towers of Cape Town. Although it was surely an illusion, the city, with Table Mountain looming behind it, looked agonizingly close, as if one could almost reach out and grasp it.

The senior officer explained to us that we had been brought to the shore to collect seaweed. We were instructed to pick up the large pieces that had washed up on the beach, and wade out to collect seaweed attached to rocks or coral. The seaweed itself was long and slimy and brownish-green in color. Sometimes the pieces were six to eight feet in length and thirty pounds in weight. After fishing out the seaweed from the shallows, we lined it up in rows on the beach. When it was dry, we loaded it into the back of the truck. We were told it was then shipped to Japan, where it was used as a fertilizer.

The work did not seem too taxing to us that day, but in the coming weeks and months, we found it could be quite strenuous. But that hardly mattered because we had the pleasures and distractions of such a panoramic tableau: we watched fishing ships trawling, stately oil tankers moving slowly across the horizon; we saw gulls spearing fish from the sea and seals cavorting on the waves; we laughed at the colony of penguins, which resembled a brigade of clumsy, flat-footed soldiers; and we marveled at the daily drama of the weather over Table Mountain, with its shifting canopy of clouds and sun.

In the summer, the water felt wonderful, but in winter, the icy Benguela currents made wading out into the waves a torture. The rocks on and around the shore were jagged, and we often cut and scraped our legs as we worked. But we preferred the sea to the quarry, although we never spent more than a few days there at a time.

\*          \*          \*

The ocean proved to be a treasure chest. I found beautiful pieces of coral and elaborate shells, which I sometimes brought back to my cell. Once someone discovered a bottle of wine stuck in the sand that was still corked. I am told it tasted like vinegar. Jeff Masemola of the PAC was an extremely talented artist and sculptor, and the authorities allowed him to harvest pieces of driftwood, which he carved into fantastic figures, some of which the warders offered to buy. He constructed a bookcase for me, which I used for many years. The authorities told visitors that they had provided me with it.

The atmosphere at the shore was more relaxed than at the quarry. We also relished the seaside because we ate extremely well there. Each morning when we went to the shore, we would take a large drum of fresh water. Later, we would bring along a second drum, which we would use to make a kind of Robben Island seafood stew. For our stew we would pick up clams and mussels. We also caught crayfish, which hid themselves in the crevices of rocks. Capturing a crayfish was tricky; one had to grab it firmly between its head and tail or it would wiggle free.

Abalone, or what we call *perlemoen,* was my favorite dish. Abalones are mollusks that cling tenaciously to rocks, and one has to pry them loose. They are stubborn creatures, difficult to open, and if they are the slightest bit overcooked, they are too tough to eat.

We would take our catch and pile it into the second drum. Wilton Mkwayi was the chef among us and he would concoct the stew. When it was ready, the warders would join us and we would all sit down on the beach and have a kind of picnic lunch. In 1973, in a smuggled newspaper, we read about the wedding of Princess Anne and Mark Phillips, and the story detailed the bridal luncheon of rare and delicate dishes. The menu included mussels, crayfish, and abalone, which made us laugh; we were dining on such delicacies every day.

One afternoon, we were sitting on the beach eating our stew when Lieutenant Terblanche, who was then head of prison, made a surprise visit. We quickly pretended to be working, but we had not fooled him. He soon discovered the second drum containing a mussel stew bubbling over the fire. The lieutenant opened the pot and looked inside. He then speared a mussel, ate it, and pronounced it *"Smaaklik,"* Afrikaans for "tasty."

# 76

IN THE STRUGGLE, Robben Island was known as the University. This is not only because of what we learned from books, or because prisoners studied English, Afrikaans, art, geography, and mathematics, or because so many of our men, such as Billy Nair, Ahmed Kathrada, Mike Dingake, and Eddie Daniels, earned multiple degrees. Robben Island was known as the University because of what we learned from each other. We became our own faculty, with our own professors, our own curriculum, our own courses. We made a distinction between academic studies, which were official, and political studies, which were not.

Our university grew up partly out of necessity. As young men came to the island, we realized that they knew very little about the history of the ANC. Walter, perhaps the greatest living historian of the ANC, began to tell them about the genesis of the organization and its early days. His teaching was wise and full of understanding. Gradually, this informal history grew into a course of study, constructed by the High Organ, which became known as Syllabus A, involving two years of lectures on the ANC and the liberation struggle. Syllabus A included a course taught by Kathy, "A History of the Indian Struggle." Another comrade added a history of the Coloured people. Mac, who had studied in the German Democratic Republic, taught a course in Marxism.

Teaching conditions were not ideal. Study groups would work together on the quarry and station themselves in a circle around the leader of the seminar. The style of teaching was Socratic in nature; ideas and theories were elucidated through the leaders asking and answering questions.

It was Walter's course that was at the heart of all the education on the island. Many of the young ANC members who came to the island had no idea that the organization had even been in existence in the 1920s and 1930s. Walter guided them from the founding of the ANC in 1912 through to the present day. For many of these young men, it was the only political education they had ever received.

As these courses became known in the general section, we began to get queries from our men on the other side. This started what became a kind of correspondence course with the prisoners in the general section. The teachers would smuggle lectures over to them and they would respond with questions and comments.

This was beneficial for us as well as for them. These men had little formal education, but a great knowledge of the hardships of the world. Their concerns tended to be practical rather than philosophical. If one of the lectures stated that a tenet of socialism is "From each according to his ability and to each according to his need," we might receive a question back that said, "Yes, but what does that mean in practice? If I have land and no money, and my friend has money but no land, which of us has a greater need?" Such questions were immensely valuable and forced one to think hard about one's views.

For a number of years, I taught a course in political economy. In it, I attempted to trace the evolution of economic man from the earliest times up to the present, sketching out the path from ancient communal societies to feudalism to capitalism and socialism. I am by no means a scholar and not much of a teacher, and I would generally prefer to answer questions than to lecture. My approach was not ideological, but it was biased in favor of socialism, which I saw as the most advanced stage of economic life then evolved by man.

In addition to my informal studies, my legal work continued. I sometimes considered hanging a shingle outside my cell, because I was spending many hours a week preparing judicial appeals for other prisoners, though this was forbidden under prison service regulations. Prisoners from all different political stripes sought my help.

South African law does not guarantee a defendant the right to legal representation, and thousands upon thousands of indigent men and women went to prison every year for lack of such representation. Few Africans could afford a lawyer, and most had no choice but to accept whatever verdict the court handed down. Many men in the general section had been sentenced without benefit of counsel, and a number of them sought me out to make an appeal. For most of these men, it was the first time they had ever dealt with an attorney.

I would receive a smuggled note from a prisoner in F or G asking for help. I would then request the particulars of the case, the charge, the evidence, and the testimony. Because of the clandestine nature of these exchanges, information would come slowly in bits and pieces. A consultation that would last no more than half an hour in my old Mandela and Tambo office might take a year or more on the island.

I advised my "clients" to write a letter to the registrar of the Supreme Court asking for a record of their case. I told the prisoner to inform the registrar that he had limited funds and would like the record at no charge. Sometimes the registrars were kind enough to supply that material gratis.

Once I had the record of the case, I could put together an appeal, usually based on some judicial irregularity such as bias, incorrect procedure, or insufficient evidence. I drafted a letter to the judge or magistrate in my own handwriting, and then sent it to the other side. Because it was a violation of regulations for me to prepare a man's case, I would instruct the prisoner to copy the document in his own hand. If he could not write, and many prisoners could not, I told him to find someone who could.

I enjoyed keeping my legal skills sharp, and in a few cases verdicts were overturned and sentences reduced. These were gratifying victories; prison is contrived to make one feel powerless, and this was one of the few ways to move the system. Often I never met the men I worked for, and sometimes, out of the blue, a man who was serving us pap for lunch would whisper a thank-you to me for the work I had done on his behalf.

# 77

THE OPPRESSION of my wife did not let up. In 1972, security policemen kicked down the door of 8115 Orlando West. Bricks were hurled through the window. Gunshots were fired at the front door. In 1974, Winnie was charged with violating her banning orders, which restricted her from having any visitors apart from her children and her doctor. She was then working at a lawyer's office, and a friend brought Zeni and Zindzi to see her during her lunch hour. For this, Winnie was charged and then sentenced to six months' imprisonment. She was put in Kroonstad Prison, in the Orange Free State, but her experience there was not as horrendous as her previous stay in Pretoria. Winnie wrote to me that she felt liberated in prison this time, and it served to reaffirm her commitment to the struggle. The authorities permitted Zindzi and Zeni to visit her on Sundays.

When Winnie was released in 1975, we managed, through letters and communications with our lawyers, to work out a plan for me to see Zindzi. Prison regulations stated that no child between the ages of two and sixteen may visit a prisoner. When I went to Robben Island, all my children were in this legal limbo of age restrictions. The reasoning behind the rule is not pernicious: the lawmakers presumed that a prison visit would negatively affect the sensitive psyches of children. But the effect on prisoners was perhaps equally damaging. It is a source of deep sorrow not to be able to see one's children.

In 1975, Zindzi turned fifteen. The plan was for her mother to alter Zindzi's birth documents to show that the girl was turning sixteen, not fifteen, and therefore able to see me. Birth records are not kept in a very uniform or organized way for Africans, and Winnie found that it was not hard to modify her documents to show that Zindzi was born a year earlier. She applied for a permit, and it was approved.

A few weeks before Zindzi's scheduled visit in December, I had a previously arranged visit with Winnie's mother. When I was seated across from her in the visiting area, I said to her, "Well, Ma, I'm very excited because I'm going to see Zindzi." My mother-in-law, who was a former teacher, regarded me with some surprise and then said in a rather peevish way, "No, Zindzi cannot come and see you because she is not yet sixteen."

I realized immediately that no one had told her about our gambit. There was a warder behind each of us, and I decided I would simply gloss over what she had said, and mumbled, "Ah, well, Ma, it is nothing."

But my mother-in-law is a stubborn woman and she did not let it pass. "Well, Mkonyanisi" — an affectionate term for son-in-law in Xhosa, which is what she always called me — "you have made a serious error because Zindzi is only fifteen."

I widened my eyes in a gesture of alarm and she must have gotten the message because she did not mention Zindzi again.

I had not seen Zindzi since she was three years old. She was a daughter who knew her father from old photographs rather than memory. I put on a fresh shirt that morning, and took more trouble than usual with my appearance: it is my own vanity, but I did not want to look like an old man for my youngest daughter.

I had not seen Winnie for over a year, and I was gratified to find that she looked well. But I was delighted to behold what a beautiful woman my youngest daughter had become and how closely she resembled her equally beautiful mother.

Zindzi was shy and hesitant at first. I am sure it was not easy for her finally to see a father she had never really known, a father who could love her only from a distance, who seemed to belong not to her but to the people. Somewhere deep inside her she must have harbored resentment and anger for a father who was absent during her childhood and adolescence. I could see right away that she was a strong and fiery young woman like her own mother had been when she was Zindzi's age.

I knew she would be feeling uncomfortable, and I did my best to lighten the atmosphere. When she arrived I said to her, "Have you met my guard of honor?," gesturing to the warders who followed me everywhere. I asked her questions about her life, her schooling, and her friends, and then tried to take her back to the old days that she barely remembered. I told her how I often recalled Sunday mornings at home when I dandled her on my knee while Mum was in the kitchen making a roast. I recollected small incidents and adventures in Orlando when she was a baby, and how she had rarely cried even when she was small. Through the glass, I could see her holding back her tears as I talked.

The one tragic note of the visit was when I learned from Winnie that Bram Fischer had died of cancer shortly after being let out of prison. Bram's death affected me deeply. Although the government left no fingerprints on Bram's body, it was the state's relentless harassment of him that brought on the final illness that took him too soon. They hounded him even after death — the state confiscated his ashes after his cremation.

Bram was a purist, and after the Rivonia Trial, he decided he could best serve the struggle by going underground and living the life of an outlaw. It burdened him that the men whom he was representing in court were going to prison while he lived freely. During the trial, I advised Bram not to take this route, stressing that he served the struggle best in the courtroom, where people could see this Afrikaner son of a judge president fighting for the rights of the powerless. But he could not let others suffer while he remained free. Like the general who fights side by side with his troops at the front, Bram did not want to ask others to make a sacrifice that he was unwilling to make himself.

Bram went underground while out on bail and was captured in 1965, and sentenced to life imprisonment for conspiracy to commit sabotage. I had tried to write him in prison, but regulations forbade prisoners from corresponding with each other. After he had been diagnosed with cancer, a newspaper campaign calling for his release on humanitarian grounds had influenced the government. It was just a few weeks after the authorities released him, still under house arrest, to his brother's house in Bloemfontein that he died.

In many ways, Bram Fischer, the grandson of the prime minister of the Orange River Colony, had made the greatest sacrifice of all. No matter what I suffered in my pursuit of freedom, I always took strength from the fact that I was fighting with and for my own people. Bram was a free man who fought against his own people to ensure the freedom of others.

A month after this visit I received word from Winnie that her most recent request for a visit had been turned down by the authorities on the absurd grounds that I did not wish to see her. I immediately made an appointment with Lieutenant Prins, who was then head of prison, to lodge a protest.

Prins was not what one would call a sophisticated man. When I went in to see him I explained the situation evenly and without animosity. But I said the situation as it stood was unacceptable and my wife must be permitted to visit.

Prins did not appear to be listening, and when I had finished he said, "Ag, Mandela, your wife is only seeking publicity." I told him that I resented his remark, and before I had even finished, he uttered

something so offensive and uncomplimentary about my wife that I
immediately lost my temper.

I rose from my chair and started to move around the desk toward
the lieutenant. Prins began to retreat, but I soon checked myself.
Instead of assaulting him with my fists, as I felt like doing, I pum-
meled him with words. I am not a man who approves of oaths or
curses, but that day I violated my own principle. I finished by telling
him that he was a contemptible man without honor, and that if he
ever repeated those same words I would not hold myself back as I
had that day.

When I had finished, I turned and stormed out of his office. As
I was leaving, I saw Kathy and Eddie Daniels outside but I did not
even greet them as I walked back to my cell. Even though I had
silenced Prins, he had caused me to violate my self-control and I
consider that a defeat at the hands of my opponent.

After breakfast the following morning, two warders entered my cell
and said I was wanted at the Head Office. When I reached the office,
I was surrounded by a half-dozen armed warders. Off to one side
was Lieutenant Prins and in the center of this circle was a warrant
officer who was the prison prosecutor. The atmosphere was tense.

"Well, Mandela," the prosecutor said, "I hear you had yourself
a nice time yesterday, but today will not be so pleasant. I am charging
you for having insulted and threatened the head of prison. It is a
grave charge." He then handed me the summons.

"Do you have anything to say?" he asked.

"No," I replied. "You can speak with my attorney." I then asked
to be taken back to my cell. Prins did not say a word.

I knew immediately what I would do: prepare a countersuit charging
everyone from the lieutenant all the way up to the minister of justice
with misconduct. I would indict the prison system as a whole as a
racist institution that sought to perpetuate white supremacy. I would
make the case a cause célèbre, and make them regret they had ever
charged me in the first place.

I asked George Bizos to represent me, and a meeting was soon
arranged. Before George's visit I informed the authorities that I
would be giving him written instructions. They asked me why and

I replied frankly that I assumed the consultation room was bugged. The authorities then refused permission for me to give a written statement; I must make an oral one. I told them that they had no right to withhold permission, and the fact that they did only confirmed my suspicions.

The truth was that the authorities were afraid George would leak a written statement to the press. This was indeed part of our strategy. They were also concerned that I was using George as a conduit to communicate with Oliver in Lusaka, and assumed that the written statement would contain sensitive information. I had previously used George for such purposes, but the document in question did not contain such material.

A date was set for the island's disciplinary court, and a magistrate from Cape Town was assigned. A day before the hearing, I was told that my attorney would be arriving the following day and I would be free to give him my written statement. I met George at the head office in the morning and we briefly consulted before court was called into session. But the hearing had no sooner started than the prosecutor announced that the prison was withdrawing its case. The judge gaveled the session to a close and abruptly left the room. George and I looked at each other in surprise, and congratulated one another on an apparent victory. I was putting away my papers when another warrant officer came over and, pointing to my written statement, said, "Hand me that file."

I refused, saying it was a confidential matter between myself and my attorney. I called over the prosecutor and said: "Inform this man that these documents are protected by attorney-client privilege, and that I do not have to turn them over." The prosecutor replied that they were, but that the case was over, court was no longer in session, and the only authority in the room was that of the warrant officer. The officer plucked the document off the table. There was nothing I could do to stop him. I believe the authorities dropped the case simply to get hold of that document — which, as they discovered, contained nothing they did not already know.

As unlikely a prospect as it may have seemed, I nevertheless thought about escape the entire time I was on the island. Mac Maharaj and Eddie Daniels, both brave and resourceful men, were always hatching plans and discussing possibilities. Most were far too dangerous, but that did not stop us from considering them.

We had made certain advances. Jeff Masemola, our master crafts-man, had managed to make a passkey that unlocked most of the doors in and around our section. One day, a warder had left his key on the desk in the office at the end of our corridor. Jeff took a piece of soap and made an imprint of the key. Using that outline, he took a piece of metal and filed it into the shape of the key. This key gave us access to some of the storerooms behind our cells as well as to the isolation section. But we never used it to leave our section. It was the sea, after all, that was the uncrossable moat around Robben Island.

In 1974, Mac had an idea how to cross that barrier. He had recently been taken to the dentist in Cape Town and discovered that the dentist himself was related by marriage to a well-known political prisoner. The dentist was sympathetic; he had refused to treat Mac unless Mac's leg irons were first removed. Mac had also noticed that the window in the dentist's second-floor waiting room was just a short drop to a small side-street where we might make a run for it.

When Mac returned, he met with a few of us and urged us to make appointments at the dentist. We did so, and learned that a day had been arranged for Mac, Wilton Mkwayi, me, and one other prisoner to go to Cape Town. The three of us were willing to make the attempt, but when Mac contacted the fourth man, he refused. We had doubts about this man's loyalty, and it concerned me that he knew what we were planning.

The three of us were taken by boat to Cape Town and then to the dentist's office under heavy guard. All three of us had trained as soldiers and we probably had the best chance of actually executing an escape. Mac was also carrying a knife, and was prepared to use it. At the dentist's office, the guards first cleared away all the other patients. We demanded to have our leg irons removed, and with the support of the dentist, our guards took them off.

Mac led us over to the window and pointed out the street that was our escape route. But something about the street bothered Mac as soon as he saw it: we were in the center of Cape Town in the middle of the day, and yet the street was empty. When he had been here before, the street had been filled with traffic. "It's a setup," Mac whispered. I, too, had the sense that something was not right, and I agreed with Mac. Wilton, whose adrenaline was flowing, said Mac was talking nonsense. "Madiba, you're losing your nerve," he said. But I agreed with Mac, and the three of us simply ended up having our teeth examined. The dentist was curious as to why I had come, because my teeth were fine.

While Mac considered the most practical escape plans, Eddie Daniels hatched the most imaginative ones. During the early years, airplanes were not permitted to fly over the island. But by the mid-1970s, we noticed that not only were planes flying over our heads, but helicopters on their way to and from the tankers that sailed off the coast. Eddie came to me with a plan that would involve the organization using a helicopter, painted with the South African military colors, to pick me up on the island and then deposit me on the roof of a friendly foreign embassy in Cape Town where I would seek asylum. It was not an ill-conceived plan, and I told Eddie he should smuggle out the suggestion to Oliver in Lusaka. Eddie did manage to get his idea to Lusaka, but we never received a response.

# 78

BIRTHDAY CELEBRATIONS were bare-bones affairs on Robben Island. In lieu of cake and gifts, we would pool our food and present an extra slice of bread or cup of coffee to the birthday honoree. Fikile Bam and I were born on the same date, July 18, and I would save a few sweets that I had purchased at Christmas for the two of us to share on our mutual anniversary. My fiftieth birthday had passed without much notice in 1968, but in 1975, when I turned fifty-seven, Walter and Kathy approached me with a long-term plan that would make my sixtieth birthday more memorable.

One of the issues that always concerned us was how to keep the idea of the struggle before the people. During the previous decade, the government had silenced most of the radical press, and there remained a prohibition on publishing the words or pictures of any banned or imprisoned individuals. An editor could go to jail and his newspaper be shuttered for publishing so much as a snapshot of me or my colleagues.

One day, Kathy, Walter, and myself were talking in the courtyard when they suggested that I ought to write my memoirs. Kathy noted that the perfect time for such a book to be published would be on my sixtieth birthday. Walter said that such a story, if told truly and fairly, would serve to remind people of what we had fought and were still fighting for. He added that it could become a source of inspiration for young freedom fighters. The idea appealed to me, and during a subsequent discussion, I agreed to go ahead.

When I decide to do something, I like to start immediately, and I threw myself into this new project. I adopted a rather unorthodox work schedule: I would write most of the night and sleep during the day. During the first week or two, I would take a nap after dinner, awake at ten o'clock, and then write until it was time for breakfast. After working at the quarry, I would then sleep until dinner, and the process would begin again. After a few weeks of this, I notified the authorities that I was not feeling well and would not be going to the quarry. They did not seem to care, and from then on I was able to sleep most of the day.

We created an assembly line to process the manuscript. Each day I passed what I wrote to Kathy, who reviewed the manuscript, and then read it to Walter. Kathy then wrote their comments in the margins. Walter and Kathy have never hesitated to criticize me, and I took their suggestions to heart, often incorporating their changes. This marked-up manuscript was then given to Laloo Chiba, who spent the next night transferring my writing to his own almost microscopic shorthand, reducing ten pages of foolscap to a single small piece of paper. It would be Mac's job to smuggle the manuscript to the outside world.

The warders grew suspicious. They went to Mac and said, "What is Mandela up to? Why is he sitting up late at night?" But Mac merely shrugged his shoulders and said he had no idea. I wrote rapidly, completing a draft in four months. I did not hesitate over choosing a word or phrase. I covered the period from my birth through the Rivonia Trial, and ended with some notes about Robben Island.

I relived my experiences as I wrote about them. Those nights, as

I wrote in silence, I could once again experience the sights and sounds of my youth in Qunu and Mqhekezweni; the excitement and fear of coming to Johannesburg; the tempests of the Youth League; the endless delays of the Treason Trial; the drama of Rivonia. It was like a waking dream and I attempted to transfer it to paper as simply and truthfully as I could.

Mac ingeniously hid the transcribed version of the manuscript inside the binding of a number of notebooks he used for his studies. In this way, he was able to safeguard the entire text from the authorities and smuggle it out when he was released in 1976. The arrangement was that Mac would secretly communicate when the manuscript was safely out of the country; only then would we destroy the original. In the meantime, we still had to dispose of a five-hundred-page manuscript. We did the only thing we could do: we buried it in the garden in the courtyard. Surveillance in the courtyard had become careless and sporadic. The warders usually sat in an office at the northern end talking among themselves. From that office, they could not see the southern end next to the isolation area where there was a small garden. I had casually inspected this area on my early morning walks, and it was there that I decided to bury the manuscript.

In order not to have to dig a great hole, we decided to bury the manuscript in three separate places. We divided it into two smaller segments and one larger one, wrapped each in plastic, and placed them inside empty cocoa containers. The work would have to be done quickly, and I asked Jeff Masemola to fashion some digging tools. Within a few days I was equipped with several sharp iron stakes.

One morning, after breakfast, Kathy, Walter, Eddie Daniels, and I drifted over to the garden at the southern end of the courtyard where we appeared to be having a political discussion. We were each hiding portions of the manuscript in our shirts. At a signal from me, we dropped down and began digging. I dug in the center, near a manhole cover that led to a drainpipe. When I reached the pipe, I carved out a space beneath it, and it was there that I placed the largest of the three containers. The others dug two shallower holes for their portions.

We finished just in time to line up for our march to the quarry. As I walked that morning, I felt a sense of relief that the manuscript was safely hidden. I then thought no more about it.

A few weeks later, just after our wake-up call, I heard a sound in the courtyard that made me uneasy: it was the thud of picks and shovels on the ground. When we were allowed out of our cells for wash-up, I walked to the front of the corridor and managed to peer out the door and around the corner. There, at the south end of the courtyard, was a work crew from the general section. To my alarm, they were digging in the area where the manuscript was buried.

The authorities had decided to build a wall in front of the isolation section because they had discovered that the prisoners in isolation were able to communicate with us in the courtyard. The work crew was digging a shallow trench for the concrete foundation of the wall.

While washing up I managed to inform Walter and Kathy about the digging outside. Kathy thought that the main part of the manuscript, which was buried under the pipe, would probably be safe, but that the other two were vulnerable. When the drums of breakfast porridge were wheeled into the courtyard, the warders commanding the work crew ordered the men out of the yard. This was done to prevent any fraternization with the political prisoners.

With our bowls of porridge in hand, I led Walter and Kathy over to the south end of the courtyard as though I wanted to confer with them privately. The beginnings of the trench were already perilously close to the two smaller containers. At the same time, we were joined by Eddie Daniels, who immediately recognized the problem.

There was only one thing to do: as inconspicuously as possible, the four of us began digging in the area where the two smaller pieces of manuscript would be. We managed to unearth the two containers rather quickly, and covered the area again with soil. To rescue the chunk of manuscript under the pipe would require more time, but we were confident that they would not find the manuscript because they would not dislodge the pipe in order to build the wall.

We hid the manuscript in our shirts as we walked back to our cells. Eddie was not going to the quarry that day, and we gave the containers to him, instructing him to destroy them as soon as possible. At great personal risk, Eddie agreed to do so. I breathed easier knowing that we had salvaged the two containers, and tried not to dwell on the remaining piece of manuscript as I worked that day.

When we returned from the quarry that afternoon, instead of washing up, which I normally did, I strolled over to the far end of the courtyard. I attempted to appear as casual as possible, but I was alarmed by what I saw. The prisoners had dug a trench that ran parallel to the wall of the isolation section and had actually removed the pipe altogether. They could not help but have uncovered the manuscript.

I must have flinched or reacted in some way that was noticeable. Unknown to me, I was being watched by a number of warders, who later said that my reaction confirmed that I knew a manuscript had been there. I returned to the corridor to wash up and told Walter and Kathy that I suspected the manuscript had been discovered. Eddie had meanwhile successfully disposed of the other two pieces.

Early the next morning, I was summoned to the office to see the commanding officer. Next to him stood a high prison official who had just arrived from Pretoria. Without any greeting whatsoever, the commanding officer announced: "Mandela, we have found your manuscript."

I did not reply. The commanding officer then reached behind his desk and produced a sheaf of papers.

"This is your handwriting, is it not?" he demanded. Again, I remained silent.

"Mandela," the commander said in some exasperation. "We know this is your work."

"Well," I replied, "you must produce some proof of that." They scoffed at this, and said they knew the notations in the margin were made by Walter Sisulu and Ahmed Kathrada. Again, I said that they must furnish evidence if they were going to impose any penalties.

"We do not need evidence," the commander said. "We have the evidence."

Although he did not impose a penalty that day, a short while later, Walter, Kathy, and I were called before General Rue, the deputy commissioner of prisons, who told us that we had abused our study privileges in order to illegally write the manuscript. For that offense, our study privileges were being suspended indefinitely. As it turned out, we lost study privileges for four years.

After Mac was released in December, he sent the notebooks overseas to England. He spent the next six months under house arrest in South Africa before slipping out of the country and going first to Lusaka to see Oliver, and then to London. He stayed there for six months; with a typist he reconstructed the manuscript and put together a typescript. He then returned to Lusaka and presented Oliver with a copy.

From there, the trail grows cold. I heard nothing from Lusaka about the manuscript and still do not know precisely what Oliver did with it. Although it was not published while I was in prison, it forms the spine of this memoir.

# 79

IN 1976, I RECEIVED an extraordinary visit: Jimmy Kruger, the minister of prisons, a prominent member of the prime minister's cabinet, came to see me. Kruger was not only influential about prisons policy but he was critical to the government's handling of the liberation struggle.

I had an inkling as to why he had come. The government was then engaged in a massive effort to make a success of its separate development policy, and "quasi-independent" homelands. The showpiece of separate development was the Transkei, led by my nephew and one-time benefactor, K. D. Matanzima, who had successfully repressed almost all legitimate opposition to his rule. I recalled that the commanding officer had recently said to me in a bantering way, "Mandela, you ought to retire to the Transkei and take a good long rest."

As it turned out, that was precisely what Jimmy Kruger was

proposing as well. He was a stout, blunt man, not nearly as polished as I would have expected from a cabinet minister. I approached the meeting as another opportunity to present our grievances, and at first he seemed content to listen. I began by reminding him of the letter we had sent him in 1969, which had gone unanswered. He merely shrugged. I then detailed the poor conditions on the island, reiterating once more that we were political prisoners, not criminals, and expected to be treated as such. But Kruger scoffed at this, saying, "Nah, you are all violent Communists!"

I then began to tell him a bit about the history of our organization and why we had turned to violence. It was clear that he knew almost nothing about the ANC, and what he did know was gleaned from the propaganda of the right-wing press. When I told him the organization was far older than the National Party, he was dumbfounded. I said that if he considered us Communists he should reread the Freedom Charter. He looked at me blankly. He had never heard of the Freedom Charter. I found it extraordinary that a cabinet minister should be so uninformed. Yet I should not have been surprised; Nationalist politicians routinely condemned what they didn't understand.

I raised the question of our release and reminded him of the case of the 1914 Afrikaner rebels, who had resorted to violence though they were represented in Parliament, could hold meetings, and could even vote. Even though General de Wet and General Kemp had led a force of twelve thousand and occupied towns and caused many deaths, they were both released soon after their convictions for high treason. I mentioned the case of Robey Leibbrandt, who set up an underground organization during the Second World War to oppose South Africa's support for the Allies; he was sentenced to life imprisonment but soon pardoned. Kruger seemed as ignorant of these episodes in the history of his own people as he was of the Freedom Charter. It is difficult to negotiate with those who do not share the same frame of reference.

Kruger waved all of this aside. "That is ancient history," he said. He came armed with a specific offer. Despite his reputation for brusqueness, he made his proposal in a deferential manner. He stated the matter simply: if I recognized the legitimacy of the Transkei government and was willing to move there, my sentence would be dramatically reduced.

With Walter and Winnie in 1990. *(Gideon Mendel/Magnum)*

Cyril Ramaphosa and Joe Slovo in Johannesburg, during preparatory talks for a new constitution. *(Associated Press)*

*Left:*
At the Chris Hani memorial at Orlando Stadium, Soweto, with Tokyo Sexwale (right) and Charles Ngekule (left). *(Magnum)*

*Below:*
In 1993, I revisited Robben Island. *(Copyright Island Pictures Corporation)*

*Opposite, above:*
The cell in which I lived for eighteen of my twenty-seven years in prison. *(Copyright Island Pictures Corporation)*

*Opposite, below:*
The waters of Table Bay separate Robben Island from Cape Town. In the distance is Table Mountain. *(Copyright Island Pictures Corporation)*

With Archbishop
Tutu. *(Peter
Magubane)*

With F. W. de Klerk.
*(Peter Magubane)*

Casting my vote in
South Africa's first
general election.
*(Peter Magubane)*

Singing the national
anthem at my
inauguration with
Thabo Mbeki and
my daughter Zinani.
*(Ian Berry/Magnum)*

A warm embrace with Bishop Tutu after the ceremony. *(Ian Berry/Magnum)*

With my children Zindzi, Zinani, Makaziwe, and Makgatho. *(Peter Magubane)*

*Left:*
With my great-granddaughter in September 1994. *(Peter Magubane)*

My family. *(Peter Magubane)*

With my grandson
Bambata. *(Peter Magubane)*

I listened respectfully until he had finished. First, I said, I wholly rejected the bantustan policy, and would do nothing to support it, and second, I was from Johannesburg, and it was to Johannesburg that I would return. Kruger remonstrated with me, but to no avail. A month later he returned with the same proposal, and again I turned him down. It was an offer only a turncoat could accept.

# 80

AS DILIGENT AS WE WERE in gathering news and information, our knowledge of current events was always sketchy. Happenings in the outside world were muffled by the fact that we heard of them first through rumor; only later might they be confirmed by a newspaper account or an outside visitor.

In June of 1976, we began to hear vague reports of a great uprising in the country. The whispers were fanciful and improbable: the youth of Soweto had overthrown the military and the soldiers had dropped their guns and fled. It was only when the first young prisoners who had been involved in the June 16 uprising began to arrive on Robben Island in August that we learned what truly happened.

On June 16, 1976, fifteen thousand schoolchildren gathered in Soweto to protest the government's ruling that half of all classes in secondary schools must be taught in Afrikaans. Students did not want to learn and teachers did not want to teach in the language of the oppressor. Pleadings and petitions by parents and teachers had fallen on deaf ears. A detachment of police confronted this army of earnest schoolchildren and without warning opened fire, killing thirteen-year-old Hector Pieterson and many others. The children fought with sticks and stones, and mass chaos ensued, with hundreds of children wounded, and two white men stoned to death.

The events of that day reverberated in every town and township of South Africa. The uprising triggered riots and violence across the country. Mass funerals for the victims of state violence became national rallying points. Suddenly the young people of South Africa were fired with the spirit of protest and rebellion. Students boycotted schools all across the country. ANC organizers joined with students to actively support the protest. Bantu Education had come back to haunt its creators, for these angry and audacious young people were its progeny.

In September, the isolation section was filled with young men who had been arrested in the aftermath of the uprising. Through whispered conversations in an adjacent hallway we learned firsthand what had taken place. My comrades and I were enormously cheered; the spirit of mass protest that had seemed dormant through the 1960s was erupting in the 1970s. Many of these young people had left the country to join our own military movement, and then smuggled themselves back home. Thousands of them were trained in our camps in Tanzania, Angola, and Mozambique. There is nothing so encouraging in prison as learning that the people outside are supporting the cause for which you are inside.

These young men were a different breed of prisoner than we had ever seen before. They were brave, hostile, and aggressive; they would not take orders, and shouted *"Amandla!"* at every opportunity. Their instinct was to confront rather than cooperate. The authorities did not know how to handle them, and they turned the island upside down. During the Rivonia Trial, I remarked to a security policeman that if the government did not reform itself, the freedom fighters who would take our place would someday make the authorities yearn for us. That day had indeed come on Robben Island.

In these young men we saw the angry revolutionary spirit of the times. I had had some warning. At a visit with Winnie a few months before, she had managed to tell me through our coded conversation that there was a rising class of discontented youth who were militant and Africanist in orientation. She said they were changing the nature of the struggle and that I should be aware of them.

The new prisoners were appalled by what they considered the barbaric conditions of the island, and said they could not understand how we could live in such a way. We told them that they should have seen the island in 1964. But they were almost as skeptical of us as they were of the authorities. They chose to ignore our calls for discipline and thought our advice feeble and unassertive.

It was obvious that they regarded us, the Rivonia Trialists, as moderates. After so many years of being branded a radical revolutionary, to be perceived as a moderate was a novel and not altogether pleasant feeling. I knew that I could react in one of two ways: I could scold them for their impertinence or I could listen to what they were saying. I chose the latter.

When some of these men, such as Strini Moodley of the South African Students' Organization and Saths Cooper of the Black People's Convention, came into our section, I had them give us papers on their movement and philosophy. I wanted to know what had brought them to the struggle, what motivated them, what their ideas were for the future.

Shortly after their arrival on the island, the commanding officer came to me and asked me as a favor to address the young men. He wanted me to tell them to restrain themselves, to recognize the fact that they were in prison and to accept the discipline of prison life. I told him that I was not prepared to do that. Under the circumstances, they would have regarded me as a collaborator of the oppressor.

These fellows refused to conform to even basic prison regulations. One day I was at the Head Office conferring with the commanding officer. As I was walking out with the major, we came upon a young prisoner being interviewed by a prison official. The young man, who was no more than eighteen years old, was wearing his prison cap in the presence of senior officers, a violation of regulations. Nor did he stand up when the major entered the room, another violation.

The major looked at him and said, "Please, take off your cap." The prisoner ignored him. Then in an irritated tone, the major said, "Take off your cap." The prisoner turned and looked at the major, and said, "What for?"

I could hardly believe what I had just heard. It was a revolutionary question: What for? The major also seemed taken aback, but managed a reply. "It is against regulations," he said. The young prisoner responded, "Why do you have this regulation? What is the purpose of it?" This questioning on the part of the prisoner was too much for the major, and he stomped out of the room, saying, "Mandela, you talk to him." But I would not intervene on his behalf, and simply bowed in the direction of the prisoner to let him know that I was on his side.

*          *          *

This was our first exposure to the Black Consciousness Movement. With the banning of the ANC, PAC, and Communist Party, the Black Consciousness Movement helped fill a vacuum among young people. Black Consciousness was less a movement than a philosophy and grew out of the idea that blacks must first liberate themselves from the sense of psychological inferiority bred by three centuries of white rule. Only then could the people rise up in confidence and truly liberate themselves from repression. While the Black Consciousness Movement advocated a nonracial society, they excluded whites from playing a role in achieving that society.

These concepts were not unfamiliar to me: they closely mirrored ideas I myself held at the time of the founding of the ANC Youth League a quarter-century before. We, too, were Africanists; we, too, stressed ethnic pride and racial self-confidence; we, too, rejected white assistance in the struggle. In many ways, Black Consciousness represented the same response to the same problem that had never gone away.

But just as we had outgrown our Youth League outlook, I was confident that these young men would transcend some of the strictures of Black Consciousness. While I was encouraged by their militancy, I thought that their philosophy, in its concentration on blackness, was exclusionary, and represented an intermediate view that was not fully mature. I saw my role as an elder statesman who might help them move on to the more inclusive ideas of the Congress Movement. I knew also that these young men would eventually become frustrated because Black Consciousness offered no program of action, no outlet for their protest.

Although we viewed the ranks of the BCM as a fertile ground for the ANC, we did not attempt to recruit these men. We knew that this would alienate both them and the other parties on the island. Our policy was to be friendly, to take an interest, to compliment them on their achievements, but not to proselytize. If they came to us and asked questions — "What is the ANC policy on the bantustans?" "What does the Freedom Charter say about nationalization?" — we would answer them — and a great many of them did come to us with questions.

I myself contacted some of these men through smuggled notes. I spoke with some who were from the Transkei and asked questions about my old home. Some of the men who arrived were already well known in the struggle. I had heard reports of the bravery of Patrick "Terror" Lekota, a leader of the South African Students' Organization, and sent him a note of welcome to Robben Island.

Terror's nickname comes from his prowess on the soccer field, but he was just as formidable in a debate. He disagreed with some of his colleagues on the issue of racial exclusiveness and inched closer to the ideas of the ANC. Once on the island, Terror decided that he wanted to join us, but we discouraged him — not because we did not want him but because we thought such a maneuver would create tensions in the general section.

But Terror would not take no for an answer and publicly switched his allegiance to the ANC. One day, not long afterward, he was assaulted with a garden fork by disgruntled BC members. After he was treated, the authorities charged the attackers and planned to put them on trial. But in the interest of harmony, we advised Terror not to lodge a complaint. He agreed, and refused to testify against those who had hurt him. The case was dropped. Such a trial, I felt, would only play into the hands of the authorities. I wanted these young men to see that the ANC was a great tent that could accommodate many different views and affiliations.

After that incident, the floodgates seemed to open and dozens of BC men decided to join the ANC, including some of those who had planned the attack on Terror. Terror rose to the top of the ANC hierarchy in the general section, and was soon teaching ANC policies to other prisoners. The courage and vision of men like Lekota confirmed to us that our views remained potent, and still represented the best hope for unifying the liberation struggle as a whole.

Political feuding continued in F and G. We learned of a clash among the ANC, the PAC, and the BCM in the general section. A number of ANC people had been beaten. A large number of ANC members were charged by the authorities, and a trial was set for the island's administrative court. The ANC men brought in an outside lawyer to handle the case. Although I had not witnessed the fight, I was asked to be a character witness. This was a troubling prospect. While I was more than willing to give testimonials for my comrades, I did not want to take any action that would heighten the bitterness between the ANC, the PAC, and the BCM.

I regarded my role in prison not just as the leader of the ANC, but as a promoter of unity, an honest broker, a peacemaker, and I was reluctant to take a side in this dispute, even if it was the side of my own organization. If I testified on behalf of the ANC, I would jeopardize my chances of bringing about reconciliation among the different groups. If I preached unity, I must act like a unifier, even at the risk of perhaps alienating some of my own colleagues.

I decided not to testify. This disappointed some of my colleagues, but I thought the issue was serious enough to risk their displeasure. It was more important to show the young Black Consciousness men that the struggle was indivisible and that we all had the same enemy.

# 81

IN THEIR ANXIOUSNESS to deal with these young lions, the authorities more or less let us fend for ourselves. We were in the second year of a go-slow strike at the quarry, demanding a complete end to all manual labor. Our requirement was for the right to do something useful with our days, like studying or learning a trade. We no longer even went through the motions of working at the quarry; we simply talked among ourselves. In early 1977, the authorities announced the end of manual labor. Instead, we could spend our days in our section. They arranged some type of work for us to do in the courtyard, but it was merely a fig leaf to hide their capitulation.

This victory was the combined result of our own unceasing protests and simple logistics. The authorities normally preferred to have a ratio of one warder for every three prisoners. Even before the arrival of the post-Soweto prisoners, there was a shortage of warders, and the rebellious young men required even greater supervision. They were so bold that each man seemed to require his own warder. If we remained in our section, we required less supervision.

The end of manual labor was liberating. I could now spend the day reading, writing letters, discussing issues with my comrades, or formulating legal briefs. The free time allowed me to pursue what became two of my favorite hobbies on Robben Island: gardening and tennis.

To survive in prison, one must develop ways to take satisfaction in one's daily life. One can feel fulfilled by washing one's clothes so that they are particularly clean, by sweeping a hallway so that it is empty of dust, by organizing one's cell to conserve as much space as possible. The same pride one takes in more consequential tasks outside of prison one can find in doing small things inside prison.

Almost from the beginning of my sentence on Robben Island, I asked the authorities for permission to start a garden in the courtyard. For years, they refused without offering a reason. But eventually they relented, and we were able to cut out a small garden on a narrow patch of earth against the far wall.

The soil in the courtyard was dry and rocky. The courtyard had been constructed over a landfill, and in order to start my garden, I had to excavate a great many rocks to allow the plants room to grow. At the time, some of my comrades jested that I was a miner at heart, for I spent my days at the quarry and my free time digging in the courtyard.

The authorities supplied me with seeds. I initially planted tomatoes, chilies, and onions — hardy plants that did not require rich earth or constant care. The early harvests were poor, but they soon improved. The authorities did not regret giving permission, for once the garden began to flourish, I often provided the warders with some of my best tomatoes and onions.

While I have always enjoyed gardening, it was not until I was behind bars that I was able to tend my own garden. My first experience in the garden was at Fort Hare where, as part of the university's manual labor requirement, I worked in one of my professors' gardens and enjoyed the contact with the soil as an antidote to my intellectual labors. Once I was in Johannesburg studying and then working, I had neither the time nor the space to cultivate a garden.

I began to order books on gardening and horticulture. I studied different gardening techniques and types of fertilizer. I did not have many of the materials that the books discussed, but I learned through trial and error. For a time, I attempted to grow peanuts, and used different soils and fertilizers, but finally I gave up. It was one of my only failures.

A garden was one of the few things in prison that one could control. To plant a seed, watch it grow, to tend it and then harvest it, offered a simple but enduring satisfaction. The sense of being the custodian of this small patch of earth offered a small taste of freedom.

In some ways, I saw the garden as a metaphor for certain aspects of my life. A leader must also tend his garden; he, too, plants seeds, and then watches, cultivates, and harvests the result. Like the gardener, a leader must take responsibility for what he cultivates; he must mind his work, try to repel enemies, preserve what can be preserved, and eliminate what cannot succeed.

I wrote Winnie two letters about a particularly beautiful tomato plant, how I coaxed it from a tender seedling to a robust plant that produced deep red fruit. But, then, either through some mistake or lack of care, the plant began to wither and decline, and nothing I did would bring it back to health. When it finally died, I removed the roots from the soil, washed them, and buried them in a corner of the garden.

I narrated this small story at great length. I do not know what she read into that letter, but when I wrote it I had a mixture of feelings: I did not want our relationship to go the way of that plant, and yet I felt that I had been unable to nourish many of the most important relationships in my life. Sometimes there is nothing one can do to save something that must die.

One unanticipated result of ending manual labor was that I began to gain weight. Though we were doing barely enough labor at the quarry to work up a sweat, the walk there and back was enough to keep me trim.

I have always believed that exercise is not only a key to physical health but to peace of mind. Many times in the old days I unleashed my anger and frustration on a punching bag rather than taking it out on a comrade or even a policeman. Exercise dissipates tension, and tension is the enemy of serenity. I found that I worked better and thought more clearly when I was in good physical condition, and so training became one of the inflexible disciplines of my life. In prison, having an outlet for one's frustrations was absolutely essential.

Even on the island, I attempted to follow my old boxing routine of doing roadwork and muscle-building from Monday through

Thursday and then resting for the next three days. On Monday through Thursday, I would do stationary running in my cell in the morning for up to forty-five minutes. I would also perform one hundred fingertip push-ups, two hundred sit-ups, fifty deep knee-bends, and various other calisthenics.

In my letters to my children, I regularly urged them to exercise, to play some fast-moving sport like basketball, soccer, or tennis to take their mind off whatever might be bothering them. While I was not always successful with my children, I did manage to influence some of my more sedentary colleagues. Exercise was unusual for African men of my age and generation. After a while, even Walter began to take a few turns around the courtyard in the morning. I know that some of my younger comrades looked at me and said to themselves, "If that old man can do it, why can't I?" They too began to exercise.

From the very first meetings I had with outside visitors and the International Red Cross, I stressed the importance of having the time and facilities for proper exercise. Only in the mid-1970s, under the auspices of the International Red Cross, did we begin to receive things like volleyball equipment and a Ping-Pong table.

At roughly the same time we finished working at the quarry, one of the warders had the idea of converting our courtyard into a tennis court. Its dimensions were perfect. Prisoners from the general section painted the cement surface green and then fashioned the traditional configuration of white lines. A few days later a net was put up and suddenly we had our own Wimbledon in our front yard.

I had played a bit of tennis when I was at Fort Hare, but I was by no means an expert. My forehand was relatively strong, my backhand regrettably weak. But I pursued the sport for exercise, not style; it was the best and only replacement for the walks to and from the quarry. I was one of the first in our section to play regularly. I was a back-court player, only rushing the net when I had a clean slam.

Once manual labor ended, I had much more time for reading, but the books I had been using were now out-of-bounds. When my studies were canceled, I was still in the midst of pursuing my LL.B. at the University of London. I had started studying for the LL.B.

during the Rivonia Trial and the suspension of study privileges for four years would undoubtedly assure me of the university record for the most number of years pursuing that degree.

But the suspension of study privileges had an unintended benefit, and that was that I began to read books that I would not otherwise have read. Instead of poring over tomes about contract law, I was now absorbed by novels.

I did not have an unlimited library to choose from on Robben Island. We had access to many unremembered mysteries and detective novels and all the works of Daphne du Maurier, but little more. Political books were off-limits. Any book about socialism or communism was definitely out. A request for a book with the word *red* in the title, even if it was *Little Red Riding Hood,* would be rejected by the censors. *War of the Worlds* by H. G. Wells, though it is a work of science fiction, would be turned down because the word *war* appeared in its title.

From the first, I tried to read books about South Africa or by South African writers. I read all the unbanned novels of Nadine Gordimer and learned a great deal about the white liberal sensibility. I read many American novels, and recall especially John Steinbeck's *The Grapes of Wrath,* in which I found many similarities between the plight of the migrant workers in that novel and our own laborers and farmworkers.

One book that I returned to many times was Tolstoy's great work, *War and Peace.* (Although the word *war* was in the title, this book was permitted.) I was particularly taken with the portrait of General Kutuzov, whom everyone at the Russian court underestimated. Kutuzov defeated Napoleon precisely because he was not swayed by the ephemeral and superficial values of the court, and made his decisions on a visceral understanding of his men and his people. It reminded me once again that to truly lead one's people one must also truly know them.

# 82

IN THE WAKE of the Soweto student uprising, I learned that Winnie, along with my old friend and physician, Dr. Nthato Motlana, had become involved with the Black Parents Association, an organization of concerned local professionals and church leaders who acted as a guiding hand and intermediary for the students. The authorities seemed to be as wary of the parents association as of the young rebels. In August, less than two months after the student revolt, Winnie was detained under the Internal Security Act and imprisoned without charge in the Fort in Johannesburg, where she was held for five months. During that time, I was able to write to her and my daughters, who were at boarding school in Swaziland, expressing support and solidarity. I was greatly distressed by her imprisonment, though she was apparently not mistreated this time and emerged from jail in December even firmer in her commitment to the struggle.

Though banned, Winnie picked up where she left off, and the authorities were dismayed about her popularity with the young radicals of Soweto. They were determined to lessen her influence and did it with a brazen and shameless act: they sent her into internal exile. On the night of May 16, 1977, police cars and a truck pulled up outside of the house in Orlando West and began loading furniture and clothing into the back of the truck. This time Winnie was not being arrested, or detained, or interrogated; she was being banished to a remote township in the Free State called Brandfort. I discovered the details from Kathy, who had been given the information from a visiting Hindu priest.

Brandfort is about two hundred fifty miles southwest of Johannesburg, just north of Bloemfontein, in the Free State. After a long and rough ride, Winnie, Zindzi, and all their possessions were dumped in front of a three-room tin-roofed shack in Brandfort's bleak African township, a desperately poor and backward place where the people were under the thumb of the local white farmers. Winnie was regarded with wariness and trepidation. The local language was Sesotho, which Winnie did not speak.

Her new circumstances saddened and angered me. At least when she was home in Soweto, I could picture her cooking in the kitchen or reading in the lounge, I could imagine her waking up in the house I knew so well. That was a source of comfort to me. In Soweto, even if she was banned, there were friends and family nearby. In Brandfort she and Zindzi would be alone.

I had passed through this township once on my way to Bloemfontein, and took no notice of it. There was nothing memorable in its all too typical poverty and desolateness. I did not know at the time how familiar the address — house number 802, Brandfort — would one day become to me. Once again, I felt as though Winnie and I were in prison at the same time.

Life in Brandfort was hard, as I learned from Winnie's letters. They had no heat, no toilet, no running water. The township had no shops and the stores in town were hostile to African customers. The whites for the most part were Afrikaans-speaking and deeply conservative.

Winnie and Zindzi were under constant police surveillance and intermittent harassment. Within a few months Zindzi — who was not banned — was upset by the security police's intimidation. In September, with the help of Winnie's lawyers, I brought an urgent application for an interdict against the local Brandfort security police to restrain them from harassing my daughter. Affidavits filed before the judge described policemen bursting into the house and threatening Zindzi. The judge ruled that Zindzi could receive visitors in peace.

Winnie is a resilient person, and within a relatively short time, she had won over the people of the township, including some sympathetic whites in the vicinity. She supplied food to the people in the township with the help of Operation Hunger, started a crèche or nursery school for the township's children, and raised funds to create a medical clinic in a place where few people had ever seen a doctor.

In 1978, Zeni, my second-youngest daughter and my first child with Winnie, married Prince Thumbumuzi, a son of King Sobhuza of Swaziland. They had met while Zeni was away at school. Being in prison, I was not able to fulfill the father's traditional duties. In our culture, the father of the bride must interview the prospective groom and assess his prospects. He must also determine *lobola,* the bride-price, which is paid by the groom to the bride's family. On the wedding day itself, the father gives away his daughter. Although I had no doubts about the young man, I asked my friend and legal adviser George Bizos to be a stand-in for me. I instructed George to interview the prince about how he intended to look after my daughter.

George met with the prince in his office and then arranged to consult with me on Robben Island. Because Zeni was under twenty-one years of age, it was necessary for me to give my legal consent for her to marry. I met George in the consulting room and he was surprised to find a warder in the consulting room with us. I explained that this was according to regulations because this was considered a family visit not a legal one. I jestingly reassured George by saying that I had no secrets from my guards.

George reported how much the two children loved one another and the bright prospects of my future son-in-law. His father, King Sobhuza, was an enlightened traditional leader and also a member of the ANC. As George relayed to me some of the requirements made by the young man's family, he was at pains to point out that the boy was a Swazi prince. I told George to tell the young man that he was getting a Thembu princess.

There was a tremendous advantage in Zeni's becoming a member of the Swazi royal family: she was immediately granted diplomatic privileges and could visit me virtually at will. That winter, after she and Thumbumuzi were married, they came to see me, along with their newborn baby daughter. Because of the prince's status, we were allowed to meet one another in the consulting room, not the normal visiting area where one is separated from one's family by thick walls and glass. I waited for them with some nervousness.

It was a truly wondrous moment when they came into the room. I stood up, and when Zeni saw me, she practically tossed her tiny daughter to her husband and ran across the room to embrace me. I had not held my now-grown daughter virtually since she was about her own daughter's age. It was a dizzying experience, as though time had sped forward in a science fiction novel, to suddenly hug one's fully grown child. I then embraced my new son and he handed me my tiny granddaughter whom I did not let go of for the entire visit. To hold a newborn baby, so vulnerable and soft in my rough hands, hands that for too long had held only picks and shovels, was a profound joy. I don't think a man was ever happier to hold a baby than I was that day.

The visit had a more official purpose and that was for me to choose a name for the child. It is a custom for the grandfather to select a name, and the one I had chosen was Zaziwe — which means

"Hope." The name had special meaning for me, for during all my years in prison hope never left me — and now it never would. I was convinced that this child would be a part of a new generation of South Africans for whom apartheid would be a distant memory — that was my dream.

# 83

I DO NOT KNOW whether it was the upheaval inside the prison after the Soweto uprising or the upheaval in my family's life outside of prison, but in the year or two following 1976 I was in a dreamy, nostalgic state of mind. In prison, one has time to review the past, and memory becomes both friend and foe. My memory transported me into moments of both great joy and sadness. My dream life became very rich, and I seemed to pass entire nights reliving the high and low times of the old days.

I had one recurring nightmare. In the dream, I had just been released from prison — only it was not Robben Island, but a jail in Johannesburg. I walked outside the gates into the city and found no one there to meet me. In fact, there was no one there at all, no people, no cars, no taxis. I would then set out on foot toward Soweto. I walked for many hours before arriving in Orlando West, and then turned the corner toward 8115. Finally, I would see my home, but it turned out to be empty, a ghost house, with all the doors and windows open, but no one at all there.

But not all my dreams of release were so dark. In 1976 I wrote to Winnie of a happier vision.

> The night of 24 February, I dreamt arriving at 8115 finding the house full of youth dancing away to a mixture of jive and infiba. I caught all of them by surprise as I walked in unexpectedly. Some greeted me warmly, whilst others simply melted away shyly. I found the bedroom equally full with members of the family and close friends. You were relaxing in bed, with Kgatho [my son Makgatho], looking young and sleeping against the opposite wall.
>
> Perhaps in that dream I was recalling the two weeks in December 1956 when he was six and when I left Makhulu [Evelyn's mother] alone in the house. He was living with his mother in O.E. [Orlando East]

then, but a few days before I came back he joined Makhulu and slept in my bed. He was missing me very much and using the bed must have relieved the feeling of longing a bit.

While I took joy from dwelling on happy moments, I rued the pain I had often caused my family through my absence. Here is another letter from 1976.

As I woke up on the morning of 25 February I was missing you and the children a great deal as always. These days I spend quite some time thinking of you both as Dadewethu [Sister], Mum, pal and mentor. What you perhaps don't know is how I often think and actually picture in my mind all that makes you up physically and spiritually — the loving remarks which came daily and the blind eye you've always turned against those numerous irritations that would have frustrated another woman. . . . I even remember a day when you were bulging with Zindzi, struggling to cut your nails. I now recall those incidents with a sense of shame. I could have done it for you. Whether or not I was conscious of it, my attitude was: I've done my duty, a second brat is on the way, the difficulties you are now facing as a result of your physical condition are all yours. My only consolation is the knowledge that I then led a life where I'd hardly enough time even to think. Only I wonder what it'll be like when I return. . . .

   Your beautiful photo still stands about two feet above my left shoulder as I write this note. I dust it carefully every morning, for to do so gives me the pleasant feeling that I'm caressing you as in the old days. I even touch your nose with mine to recapture the electric current that used to flush through my blood whenever I did so. Nolitha stands on the table directly opposite me. How can my spirits ever be down when I enjoy the fond attentions of such wonderful ladies.

Nolitha was the one person who was not a member of the family whose photo I kept. I revealed the secret of her identity to my daughter Zindzi in another letter from 1976.

By the way, has Mum ever told you about Nolitha, the other lady in my cell from the Andaman Islands? She keeps you, Zeni, Ndindi and Nandi, Mandla [these last three are grandchildren], Maki and Mum company. It's one matter over which Mum's comments are surprisingly economic. She regards the pygmy beauty as some sort of rival and hardly suspects that I took her picture out of the *National Geographic*.

I thought continually of the day when I would walk free. Over and over, I fantasized about what I would like to do. This was one of the pleasantest ways to pass the time. I put my daydreams on paper, again in 1976.

> I wish I could drive you on a long, long journey just as I did on 12/6/58, with the one difference that this time I'd prefer us to be alone. I've been away from you for so long that the very first thing I would like to do on my return would be to take you away from that suffocating atmosphere, drive you along carefully, so that you could have the opportunity of breathing fresh and clean air, seeing the beauty spots of South Africa, its green grass and trees, colourful wild flowers, sparkling streams, animals grazing in the veld and be able to talk to the simple people we meet along the road. Our first stop would be to the place where Ma Radebe and CK [Winnie's mother and father] sleep. I hope they lie next to each other. Then I would be able to pay my respects to those who have made it possible for me to be as happy and free as I am now. Perhaps the stories I've so much wanted to tell you all these years would begin there. The atmosphere should probably sharpen your ears and restrain me to concentrate on those aspects which are tasty, edifying and constructive. Thereafter, we would adjourn and resume next to Mphakanyiswa and Nosekeni [my parents] where the environment would be similar. I believe we would then be fresh and solid as we drive back to 8115.

When the authorities began to allow us to receive photographs of immediate family members in the early 1970s, Winnie sent me an album. Whenever I received a photograph of Winnie, the children, or the grandchildren, I would carefully paste it in. I cherished this album; it was the one way that I could see those I loved whenever I wanted.

But in prison no privilege comes without some accompanying impediment. Though I was permitted to receive pictures and to keep the album, warders would often search my cell and confiscate pictures of Winnie. Eventually, however, the practice of seizing pictures ceased, and I built up my album so that it was thick with pictures of my entire family.

I do not remember who first asked to borrow my photo album, but it was undoubtedly someone in my section. I happily loaned it, and someone else asked, and then someone else. Soon it became so widely known that I possessed a photo album that I was receiving requests from men in F and G.

The men of F and G rarely received visitors or even letters, and it would have been ungenerous to deny them this window on the world. But before long I found that my precious photo album was in tatters, and that many of my irreplaceable photographs had been removed. These men were desperate to have something personal in their cells and could not help themselves. Each time this happened, I resolved to build up my album once more.

Sometimes men would just ask me for a photograph rather than the album. I recall one day a young BC fellow from the general section who was bringing us food took me aside and said, "Madiba, I would like a photograph." I said fine, I would send him one. "When?" he said rather brusquely. I replied that I would try to send it that weekend. This seemed to satisfy him, and he began to walk away, but suddenly he turned round and said, "Look, don't send me a photograph of the old lady. Send me one of the young girls, Zindzi or Zeni — remember, not the old lady!"

# 84

IN 1978, after we had spent almost fifteen years agitating for the right to receive news, the authorities offered us a compromise. Instead of permitting us to receive newspapers or listen to radio, they started their own radio news service, which consisted of a daily canned summary of the news read over the prison's intercom system.

The broadcasts were far from objective or comprehensive. Several of the island's censors would compile a brief news digest from other daily radio bulletins. The broadcasts consisted of good news for the government and bad news for all its opponents.

The first broadcast opened with a report about the death of Robert Sobukwe. Other early reports concerned the victories of Ian Smith's troops in Rhodesia and detentions of government opponents in South Africa. Despite the slanted nature of the news, we were glad to have it, and prided ourselves on reading between the lines and making educated guesses based on the obvious omissions.

That year, we learned via the intercom that P. W. Botha had succeeded John Vorster as prime minister. What the warders did not tell us was that Vorster resigned as a result of press revelations about the Department of Information's misuse of government funds.

I knew little about Botha apart from the fact that he had been an aggressive defense minister and had supported a military strike into Angola in 1975. We had no sense that he would be a reformer in any way.

I had recently read an authorized biography of Vorster (this was one of the books the prison library did have) and found that he was a man willing to pay for his beliefs; he went to prison for his support of Germany during the Second World War. We were not sorry to see Vorster go. He had escalated the battle against freedom to new heights of repression.

But even without our expurgated radio broadcast, we had learned what the authorities did not want us to know. We learned of the successful liberation struggles in Mozambique and Angola in 1975 and their emergence as independent states with revolutionary governments. The tide was turning our way.

In keeping with the increased openness on the island, we now had our own cinema. Almost every week, we watched films on a sheet in a large room adjacent to our corridor. Later, we had a proper screen. The films were a wonderful diversion, a vivid escape from the bleakness of prison life.

The first films we saw were silent, black-and-white Hollywood action movies and westerns that were even before my time. I recall one of the first ones was *The Mark of Zorro*, with the swash-buckling Douglas Fairbanks, a movie that was made in 1920. The authorities seemed to have a weakness for historical films, particularly ones with a stern moral message. Among the early films we saw — now in color, with dialogue — were *The Ten Commandments* with Charlton Heston as Moses, *The King and I*, with Yul Brynner, and *Cleopatra*, with Richard Burton and Elizabeth Taylor.

We were intrigued by *The King and I*, for to us it depicted the clash between the values of East and West, and seemed to suggest that the West had much to learn from the East. *Cleopatra* proved controversial; many of my comrades took exception to the fact that the queen of Egypt was depicted by a raven-haired, violet-eyed American actress, however beautiful. The detractors asserted that the movie was an example of Western propaganda that sought to erase the fact that Cleopatra was an African woman. I related how on my trip to Egypt I saw a splendid sculpture of a young, ebony-skinned Cleopatra.

Later, we also saw local South African films with black stars whom we all knew from the old days. On those nights, our little makeshift theater echoed with the shouts, whistles, and cheers that greeted the appearance of an old friend on screen. Later, we were permitted to select documentaries — a form that I preferred — and I began to skip the conventional films. (Although I would never miss a movie with Sophia Loren in it.) The documentaries were ordered from the state library and usually selected by Ahmed Kathrada, who was our section's librarian. I was particularly affected by a documentary we saw about the great naval battles of World War II, which showed newsreel footage of the sinking of the H.M.S. *Prince of Wales* by the Japanese. What moved me most was a brief image of Winston Churchill weeping after he heard the news of the loss of the British vessel. The image stayed in my memory a long time, and demonstrated to me that there are times when a leader can show sorrow in public, and that it will not diminish him in the eyes of his people.

One of the documentaries we watched concerned a controversial American motorcycle group, the Hell's Angels. The film depicted the Hell's Angels as reckless, violent, and antisocial, and the police as decent, upstanding, and trustworthy. When the film ended, we immediately began to discuss its meaning. Almost without exception the men criticized the Hell's Angels for their lawless ways. But then Strini Moodley, a bright, young Black Consciousness member, stood up and accused the assembled group of being out of touch with the times, for the bikers represented the equivalent of the Soweto students of 1976 who rebelled against the authorities. He reproached us for being elderly middle-class intellectuals who identified with the movie's right-wing authorities instead of with the bikers.

Strini's accusations caused a furor, and a number of men rose to speak against him, saying the Hell's Angels were indefensible and it was an insult to compare our struggle with this band of amoral sociopaths. But I considered what Strini said, and while I did not agree with him, I came to his defense. Even though the Hell's Angels were unsympathetic, they were the rebels against the authorities, unsavory rebels though they were.

I was not interested in the Hell's Angels, but the larger question that concerned me was whether we had, as Strini suggested, become stuck in a mind-set that was no longer revolutionary. We had been in prison for more than fifteen years; I had been in prison for nearly eighteen. The world that we left was long gone. The danger was that our ideas had become frozen in time. Prison is a still point in a turning world, and it is very easy to remain in the same place in jail while the world moves on.

I had always attempted to remain open to new ideas, not to reject a position because it was new or different. During our years on the island we kept up a continuing dialogue about our beliefs and ideas; we debated them, questioned them, and thereby refined them. I did not think we had stayed in one place; I believe we had evolved.

Although Robben Island was becoming more open, there was as yet still no sign that the state was reforming its views. Even so, I did not doubt that I would someday be a free man. We may have been stuck in one place, but I was confident the world was moving toward our position, not away from it. The movie reminded me once again that on the day I did walk out of prison, I did not want to appear to be a political fossil from an age long past.

It took fifteen years, but in 1979, the authorities announced over the intercom system that the diet for African, Coloured, and Indian prisoners would henceforth be the same. But just as justice delayed is justice denied, a reform so long postponed and so grudgingly enacted was hardly worth celebrating.

All prisoners were to receive the same amount of sugar in the morning: a spoonful and a half. But instead of simply increasing the African quota, the authorities reduced the amount of sugar that Coloured and Indian prisoners received by half a spoonful, while adding that amount for African prisoners. A while before, African prisoners had begun to receive bread in the morning, but that made little difference. We had been pooling bread for years.

Our food had already improved in the previous two years, but not because of the authorities. In the wake of the Soweto uprising, the authorities had decided that the island would become the exclusive home of South Africa's "security prisoners." The number of general prisoners had been drastically reduced. As a result, political prisoners were recruited to work in the kitchen for the first time.

Once political prisoners were in the kitchen, our diet improved dramatically. This was not because they were better chefs, but because the smuggling of food immediately stopped. Instead of siphoning off food for themselves or to bribe the warders, the new cooks used all the food allotted us. Vegetables became more abundant, and chunks of meat began to appear in our soups and stews. Only then did we realize we should have been eating such food for years.

# 85

IN THE SUMMER OF 1979, I was playing tennis in the courtyard, when my opponent hit a cross-court shot that I strained to reach. As I ran across the court, I felt a pain in my right heel that was so intense I had to stop playing. For the next few days I walked with a severe limp.

I was examined by a doctor on the island who decided I should go to Cape Town to see a specialist. The authorities had become more solicitous of our health, afraid that if we died in prison they would be condemned by the international community.

Although under normal circumstances I and the other men would relish a visit to Cape Town, going as a prisoner was altogether different. I was handcuffed and kept in a remote corner of the boat surrounded by five armed warders. The sea was rough that day, and the boat shuddered at every wave. About midway between the island and Cape Town, I thought we were in danger of capsizing. I spied a lifejacket behind two warders young enough to be my grandsons. I said to myself, "If this boat goes under, I will commit my last sin on earth and run over those two boys to get that lifejacket." But in the end, it was unnecessary.

On the docks, we were met by more armed guards and a small crowd. It is a humiliating experience to watch the fear and disgust on ordinary citizens' faces when they watch a convict go by. My inclination was to duck down and hide, but one could not do that.

I was examined by a young surgeon who asked if I had ever before injured my heel. In fact, I had when I was at Fort Hare. One afternoon, I was playing soccer when I attempted to steal the ball and felt a searing pain in my heel. I was taken to the local hospital, the first time in my life I had ever been to a hospital or seen a doctor. Where I grew up, there was no such thing as an African doctor, and going to see a white doctor was unheard of.

The Fort Hare doctor examined my heel and said he would need to operate. The diagnosis alarmed me, and I abruptly told him that I did not want him to touch me. At that stage in my life I regarded seeing a doctor as unmanly and having a medical procedure seemed even worse. "Suit yourself," he said, "but when you are old this thing will worry you."

The Cape Town surgeon X-rayed my heel and discovered bone fragments that had probably been there since Fort Hare. He said he could remove them in a procedure that could be performed with a local anesthetic right in his office. I immediately agreed.

The surgery went well, and when it was over, the doctor was explaining to me how to care for my heel. He was abruptly interrupted by the head warder, who said that I had to return immediately to Robben Island. The surgeon was incensed by this and in his most authoritative manner said that it was necessary for Mr. Mandela to remain in hospital overnight and that he would not release me under any circumstances. The warder was intimidated and acquiesced.

My first night in a proper hospital turned out to be quite pleasant. The nurses fussed over me a good deal. I slept very well, and in the morning, a group of nurses came in and said that I should keep the pajamas and dressing gown that I had been given. I thanked them and told them that I would be the envy of all my comrades.

I found the trip instructive in another way because in that hospital I sensed a thawing in the relationship between black and white. The doctor and nurses had treated me in a natural way as though they had been dealing with blacks on a basis of equality all their lives. This was something new and different to me, and an encouraging sign. It reaffirmed my long-held belief that education was the enemy of prejudice. These were men and women of science, and science had no room for racism.

My only regret was that I did not have the opportunity to contact Winnie before I went into hospital. Rumors had appeared in newspapers that I was at death's door and she had become quite concerned. But when I returned, I wrote to her to dispel her fears.

*          *          *

In 1980, we were granted the right to buy newspapers. This was a victory, but as always, each new privilege contained within it a catch. The new regulation stated that A Group prisoners were granted the right to buy one English-language newspaper and one Afrikaans newspaper a day. But the annoying caveat was that any A Group prisoner found sharing his newspaper with a non–A Group prisoner would lose his newspaper privileges. We protested against this restriction, but to no avail.

We received two daily newspapers: the *Cape Times* and *Die Burger*. Both were conservative papers, especially the latter. Yet prison censors went through each of those newspapers every day with scissors, clipping articles that they deemed unsafe for us to see. By the time we received them, they were filled with holes. We were soon able to supplement these papers with copies of the *Star*, the *Rand Daily Mail*, and the Sunday *Times*, but these papers were even more heavily censored.

One story I was certainly not able to read was in the *Johannesburg Sunday Post* in March 1980. The headline was "FREE MANDELA!" Inside was a petition that people could sign to ask for my release and that of my fellow political prisoners. While newspapers were still barred from printing my picture or any words I had ever said or written, the *Post*'s campaign ignited a public discussion of our release.

The idea had been conceived in Lusaka by Oliver and the ANC, and the campaign was the cornerstone of a new strategy that would put our cause in the forefront of people's minds. The ANC had decided to personalize the quest for our release by centering the campaign on a single figure. There is no doubt that the millions of people who subsequently became supporters of this campaign had no idea of precisely who Nelson Mandela was. (I am told that when "Free Mandela" posters went up in London, most young people thought my Christian name was Free.) There were a handful of dissenting voices on the island who felt that personalizing the campaign was a betrayal of the collectivity of the organization, but most people realized that it was a technique to rouse the people.

The previous year I had been awarded the Jawaharlal Nehru Human Rights Award in India, another bit of evidence of the resurgence of the struggle. I was of course refused permission to attend the ceremony, as was Winnie, but Oliver accepted the award in my absence. We had a sense of a reviving ANC. Umkhonto we Sizwe was stepping up its sabotage campaign, which had become far more sophisticated. In June, MK set off bombs at the vast Sasolburg refinery just south of Johannesburg. MK was orchestrating an explosion a week at some strategic site or another. Bombs exploded at power stations in the eastern Transvaal, at police stations in Germiston, Daveyton, New Brighton, and elsewhere, and at the Voortrekkerhoogte military base outside Pretoria. These were all strategically significant locations, places that would attract attention and worry the state. The defense minister, General Magnus Malan, backed by P. W. Botha, introduced a policy known as "total onslaught," which was a militarization of the country to combat the liberation struggle.

The Free Mandela campaign had its lighter side as well. In 1981, I learned that the students at the University of London had nominated me as a candidate for the honorific post of university chancellor. This was a wonderful honor, to be sure, and my rivals were none other than Princess Anne and the trade union leader Jack Jones. In the end, I polled 7,199 votes and lost to the daughter of the queen. I wrote to Winnie in Brandfort that I hoped the voting might have for a moment turned her humble shack into a castle, making its tiny rooms as grand as the ballroom at Windsor.

The campaign for our release rekindled our hopes. During the harsh days of the early 1970s, when the ANC seemed to sink into the shadows, we had to force ourselves not to give in to despair. In many ways, we had miscalculated; we had thought that by the 1970s we would be living in a democratic, nonracial South Africa. Yet as we entered the new decade my hopes for that South Africa rose once again. Some mornings I walked out into the courtyard and every living thing there, the seagulls and wagtails, the small trees, and even the stray blades of grass, seemed to smile and shine in the sun. It was at such times when I perceived the beauty of even this small, closed-in corner of the world, that I knew that someday my people and I would be free.

# 86

LIKE MY FATHER BEFORE ME, I had been groomed to be a counselor to the king of the Thembu. Although I had chosen a different path, I tried in my own fashion to live up to the responsibilities of the role for which I had been schooled. From prison, I did my best to remain in contact with the king and advise him as best I could. As I grew older, my thoughts turned more and more often to the green hills of the Transkei. Although I would never move there under the government's auspices, I dreamed of one day returning to a free Transkei. Thus, it was with great dismay that I learned in 1980 that the king, Sabata Dalindyebo, the paramount chief of the Thembu, had been deposed by my nephew, K. D. Matanzima, the prime minister of the Transkei.

A group of Thembu chiefs requested an urgent visit with me, which was approved by the authorities, who were usually willing to countenance visits by traditional leaders — believing that the more involved I was in tribal and Transkei matters, the less committed I would be to the struggle.

The government promoted the power of traditional leaders as a counterpoint to the ANC. While many of my comrades thought we should disavow those leaders, my inclination was to reach out to them. There is no contradiction between being a traditional leader and a member of the ANC. This spurred one of the longest and most delicate debates we had on the island: whether or not the ANC should participate in government-sponsored institutions. Many of the men considered this collaborationist. Once again, I thought it necessary to draw a distinction between principle and tactics. To me, the critical question was a tactical one: Will our organization emerge stronger through participating in these organizations or by boycotting them? In this case, I thought we would emerge stronger by participating.

I met with the chiefs in a large room in the visiting area, and they explained their dilemma. Although their hearts were with Sabata, they feared Matanzima. After listening to their presentation, I advised them to throw their support to Sabata against Matanzima, who was illegally and shamefully usurping power from the king. I sympathized with their situation, but I could not condone Matanzima's actions. I asked them to convey my support to Sabata and my disapproval to Matanzima.

Matanzima had also proposed a visit to discuss Sabata and family matters. As my nephew, he had actually been requesting such a visit for a number of years. Although Matanzima claimed to want to discuss family matters, such a visit would have political consequences. From the moment of Matanzima's first request, I referred the matter to the High Organ and the ANC men in our section. Some simply shrugged their shoulders and said, "He's your nephew; he has a right to visit." Raymond, Govan, and Kathy, however, insisted that although such a visit could be explained away as a family matter, it would be interpreted by many people inside and outside as a sign of my endorsement of the man and his policies. That was the reason why Matanzima wanted to visit, and the reason such a visit was unacceptable.

I understood and in large part agreed with their arguments, but I wanted to meet with my nephew. I have always had perhaps too high a regard for the importance of face-to-face meetings and of my own ability in such a meeting to persuade men to change their views. I was hoping I could convince Matanzima to modify his policies.

Eventually, the ANC men in our section decided not to object to a visit. In the interests of democracy, we then consulted with our men in F and G on the matter, and they were adamantly opposed. Steve Tshwete, who was one of the leading ANC figures in the general section, said such a visit would help Matanzima politically and was therefore out of the question. Many of them noted that Matanzima had already tried to coopt my approval by making Winnie's father, Columbus Madikizela, the minister of agriculture in his government. This was bad enough, they said, without Madiba agreeing to see him. I bowed to the views of the membership in the general section and regretfully informed the authorities that I would not accept a visit from my nephew.

In March of 1982, I was told by the prison authorities that my wife had been in a car accident, and that she was in hospital. They had very little information, and I had no idea of her condition or what her circumstances were. I accused the authorities of holding back information, and I made an urgent application for my attorney to visit me. The authorities used information as a weapon, and it was a successful one. I was preoccupied with my wife's health until I was visited on March 31 by Winnie's attorney and my friend Dullah Omar.

Dullah quickly eased my mind about Winnie. She had been in a car that overturned but she was all right. Our visit was brief, and as I was led back to Section B my mind was still dwelling on Winnie, and I was plagued by the feeling of powerlessness and my inability to help her.

I had not been in my cell long when I was visited by the commanding officer and a number of other prison officials. This was highly unusual; the commanding officer did not generally pay calls on prisoners in their cells. I stood up when they arrived, and the commander actually entered my cell. There was barely room for the two of us.

"Mandela," he said, "I want you to pack up your things."

I asked him why.

"We are transferring you," he said simply.

Where?

"I cannot say," he replied.

I demanded to know why. He told me only that he had received instructions from Pretoria that I was to be transferred off the island immediately. The commanding officer left and went in turn to the cells of Walter, Raymond Mhlaba, and Andrew Mlangeni and gave them the same order.

I was disturbed and unsettled. What did it mean? Where were we going? In prison, one can only question and resist an order to a certain point, then one must succumb. We had no warning, no preparation. I had been on the island for over eighteen years, and to leave so abruptly?

We were each given several large cardboard boxes in which to pack our things. Everything that I had accumulated in nearly two decades could fit in these few boxes. We packed in little more than half an hour.

There was a commotion in the corridor when the other men learned we were leaving, but we had no time to say a proper goodbye to our comrades of many years. This is another one of the indignities of prison. The bonds of friendship and loyalty with other prisoners count for nothing with the authorities.

Within minutes we were on board the ferry headed for Cape Town. I looked back at the island as the light was fading, not knowing whether or not I would ever see it again. A man can get used to anything, and I had grown used to Robben Island. I had lived there for almost two decades and while it was never a home — my home was in Johannesburg — it had become a place where I felt comfortable. I have always found change difficult, and leaving Robben Island, however grim it had been at times, was no exception. I had no idea what to look forward to.

At the docks, surrounded by armed guards, we were hustled into a windowless truck. The four of us stood in the dark while the truck drove for what seemed considerably longer than an hour. We passed through various checkpoints, and finally came to a stop. The back doors swung open, and in the dark we were marched up some concrete steps and through metal doors into another security facility. I managed to ask a guard where we were.

"Pollsmoor Prison," he said.

*Part Ten*

———

# TALKING WITH
# THE ENEMY

# 87

POLLSMOOR MAXIMUM SECURITY PRISON is located on the edge of a prosperous white suburb of green lawns and tidy houses called Tokai, a few miles southeast of Cape Town. The prison itself is set amidst the strikingly beautiful scenery of the Cape, between the mountains of Constantiaberge to the north and hundreds of acres of vineyards to the south. But this natural beauty was invisible to us behind Pollsmoor's high concrete walls. At Pollsmoor I first understood the truth of Oscar Wilde's haunting line about the tent of blue that prisoners call the sky.

Pollsmoor had a modern face but a primitive heart. The buildings, particularly the ones for the prison staff, were clean and contemporary; but the housing for the prisoners was archaic and dirty. With the exception of ourselves, all men at Pollsmoor were common-law prisoners, and their treatment was backward. We were kept separately from them and treated differently.

It was not until the next morning that we got a proper sense of our surroundings. The four of us had been given what was in effect the prison's penthouse: a spacious room on the third and topmost floor of the prison. We were the only prisoners on the entire floor. The main room was clean, modern, and rectangular, about fifty feet by thirty, and had a separate section with a toilet, urinal, two sinks, and two showers. There were four proper beds, with sheets, and towels, a great luxury for men who had spent much of the last eighteen years sleeping on thin mats on a stone floor. Compared to Robben Island, we were in a five-star hotel.

We also had our own L-shaped terrace, an open, outdoor section that was as long as half a soccer field, where we were allowed out during the day. It had white concrete walls about twelve feet high, so that we could see only the sky, except in one corner where we could make out the ridges of the Constantiaberge mountains, in particular a section known as the Elephant's Eye. I sometimes thought of this bit of mountain as the tip of the iceberg of the rest of the world.

It was greatly disorienting to be uprooted so suddenly and

LONG WALK TO FREEDOM

without explanation. One must be prepared for precipitate movements in prison, but one does not ever get used to them. Though we were now on the mainland, we felt more isolated. For us, the island had become the locus of the struggle. We took solace in each other's company, and spent those early weeks speculating on why we had been transferred. We knew the authorities had long resented and feared the influence we had on younger prisoners. But the reason seemed to be more strategic: we believed the authorities were attempting to cut off the head of the ANC on the island by removing its leadership. Robben Island itself was becoming a sustaining myth in the struggle, and they wanted to rob it of some of its symbolic import by removing us. Walter, Raymond, and I were members of the High Organ, but the one piece that did not fit was the presence of Mlangeni. Andrew was not a member of the High Organ and had not been in the forefront of the island leadership, although we considered the possibility that the authorities did not know this. Their intelligence about the organization was often inexact.

One of our hypotheses seemed to be confirmed a few months later when we were joined by Kathy, who had indeed been a member of the High Organ. More important, Kathy had been our chief of communications, and it was because of his work that we were able to communicate with new young prisoners.

A few weeks after Kathy arrived, we were also joined by a man we did not know who had not even come from Robben Island. Patrick Maqubela was a young lawyer and ANC member from the eastern Cape. He had been articled to Griffiths Mxenge, a highly respected attorney who had appeared for many detained ANC men and who had been assassinated near Durban the year before. Maqubela was serving a twenty-year sentence for treason and had been transferred to Pollsmoor from Diepkloof in Johannesburg, where he had made waves by organizing prisoners.

At first, we were skeptical of this new arrival, and wondered if he could perhaps be a security plant by the authorities. But we soon saw that this was not the case. Patrick was a bright, amiable, undaunted fellow with whom we got along very well. It could not have been easy for him bunking in with a group of old men set in their ways who had been together for the previous two decades.

\*       \*       \*

We were now in a world of concrete. I missed the natural splendor of Robben Island. But our new home had many consolations. For one thing, the food at Pollsmoor was far superior; after years of eating pap three meals a day, Pollsmoor's dinners of proper meat and vegetables were like a feast. We were permitted a fairly wide range of newspapers and magazines, and could receive such previously contraband publications as *Time* magazine and *The Guardian* weekly from London. This gave us a window on the wider world. We also had a radio, but one that received only local stations, not what we really wanted: the BBC World Service. We were allowed out on our terrace all day long, except between twelve and two when the warders had their lunch. There was not even a pretense that we had to work. I had a small cell near our large one that functioned as a study, with a chair, desk, and bookshelves, where I could read and write during the day.

On Robben Island I would do my exercises in my own cramped cell, but now I had room to stretch out. At Pollsmoor, I would wake up at five and do an hour and a half of exercise in our communal cell. I did my usual regimen of stationary running, skipping rope, sit-ups, and fingertip press-ups. My comrades were not early risers and my program soon made me a very unpopular fellow in our cell.

I was visited by Winnie shortly after arriving at Pollsmoor and was pleased to find that the visiting area was far better and more modern than the one on Robben Island. We had a large glass barrier through which one could see the visitor from the waist up and far more sophisticated microphones so that we did not have to strain to hear. The window gave at least the illusion of greater intimacy, and in prison, illusions can offer comfort.

It was far easier for my wife and family to get to Pollsmoor than Robben Island, and this made a tremendous difference. The supervision of visits also became more humane. Often, Winnie's visits were overseen by Warrant Officer James Gregory, who had been a censor on Robben Island. I had not known him terribly well, but he knew us, because he had been responsible for reviewing our incoming and outgoing mail.

At Pollsmoor I got to know Gregory better and found him a welcome contrast to the typical warder. He was polished and soft-spoken, and treated Winnie with courtesy and deference. Instead of barking, "Time up!" he would say, "Mrs. Mandela, you have five more minutes."

The Bible tells us that gardens preceded gardeners, but that was not the case at Pollsmoor, where I cultivated a garden that became one of my happiest diversions. It was my way of escaping from the monolithic concrete world that surrounded us. Within a few weeks of surveying all the empty space we had on the building's roof and how it was bathed in sun the whole day, I decided to start a garden and received permission to do so from the commanding officer. I requested that the prison service supply me with sixteen 44-gallon oil drums that I had them slice in half. The authorities then filled each half with rich, moist soil, creating in effect thirty-two giant flowerpots.

I grew onions, eggplant, cabbage, cauliflower, beans, spinach, carrots, cucumbers, broccoli, beetroot, lettuce, tomatoes, peppers, strawberries, and much more. At its height, I had a small farm with nearly nine hundred plants; a garden far grander than the one I had on Robben Island.

Some of the seeds I purchased and some — for example, broccoli and carrots — were given to me by the commanding officer, Brigadier Munro, who was particularly fond of these vegetables. Warders also gave me seeds of vegetables they liked, and I was supplied with excellent manure to use as fertilizer.

Each morning, I put on a straw hat and rough gloves and worked in the garden for two hours. Every Sunday, I would supply vegetables to the kitchen so that they could cook a special meal for the common-law prisoners. I also gave quite a lot of my harvest to the warders, who used to bring satchels to take away their fresh vegetables.

At Pollsmoor, our problems tended to be less consequential than those we experienced on Robben Island. Brigadier Munro was a decent, helpful man, who took extra pains to make sure we had what we wanted. Nevertheless, small problems sometimes got blown out of proportion. In 1983, during a visit with Winnie and Zindzi, I mentioned to my wife that I had been given shoes that were a size too small and were pinching my toe. Winnie was concerned, and I soon learned that there were press reports that I was having a toe amputated. Because of the difficulty of communication, information from prison often becomes exaggerated in the outside world. If I had simply been able to telephone my wife and tell her that my foot was fine, such confusion would not have happened. A short while later, Helen Suzman was permitted to visit, and she inquired about my toe. I thought the best answer was a demonstration: I took off my socks, held my bare foot up to the glass, and wiggled my toes.

We complained about the dampness in our cell, which was causing us to catch colds. Later, I heard reports that South African newspapers were writing that our cell was flooded. We asked for contact with other prisoners, and in general made the same basic complaint that we always had: to be treated as political prisoners.

In May of 1984, I found some consolation that seemed to make up for all the discomforts. At a scheduled visit from Winnie, Zeni, and her youngest daughter, I was escorted down to the visiting area by Sergeant Gregory, who instead of taking me to the normal visiting area, ushered me into a separate room where there was only a small table, and no dividers of any kind. He very softly said to me that the authorities had made a change. That day was the beginning of what were known as "contact" visits.

He then went outside to see my wife and daughter and asked to speak to Winnie privately. Winnie actually got a fright when Gregory took her aside, thinking that I was perhaps ill. But Gregory escorted her around the door and before either of us knew it, we were in the same room and in each other's arms. I kissed and held my wife for the first time in all these many years. It was a moment I had dreamed about a thousand times. It was as if I were still dreaming. I held her to me for what seemed like an eternity. We were still and silent except for the sound of our hearts. I did not want to let go of her at all, but I broke free and embraced my daughter and then took her child into my lap. It had been twenty-one years since I had even touched my wife's hand.

# 88

AT POLLSMOOR, we were more connected to outside events. We were aware that the struggle was intensifying, and that the efforts of the enemy were similarly increasing. In 1981, the South African

Defense Force launched a raid on ANC offices in Maputo, Mozambique, killing thirteen of our people, including women and children. In December 1982, MK set off explosions at the unfinished Koeberg nuclear power plant outside Cape Town and placed bombs at many other military and apartheid targets around the country. That same month, the South African military again attacked an ANC outpost in Maseru, Lesotho, killing forty-two people, including a dozen women and children.

In August of 1982, activist Ruth First was opening her mail in Maputo, where she was living in exile, when she was murdered by a letter bomb. Ruth, the wife of Joe Slovo, was a brave anti-apartheid activist who had spent a number of months in prison. She was a forceful, engaging woman whom I first met when I was studying at Wits, and her death revealed the extent of the state's cruelty in combating our struggle.

MK's first car bomb attack took place in May of 1983, and was aimed at an air force and military intelligence office in the heart of Pretoria. This was an effort to retaliate for the unprovoked attacks the military had launched on the ANC in Maseru and elsewhere and was a clear escalation of the armed struggle. Nineteen people were killed and more than two hundred injured.

The killing of civilians was a tragic accident, and I felt a profound horror at the death toll. But as disturbed as I was by these casualties, I knew that such accidents were the inevitable consequence of the decision to embark on a military struggle. Human fallibility is always a part of war, and the price for it is always high. It was precisely because we knew that such incidents would occur that our decision to take up arms had been so grave and reluctant. But as Oliver said at the time of the bombing, the armed struggle was imposed upon us by the violence of the apartheid regime.

Both the government and the ANC were working on two tracks: military and political. On the political front, the government was pursuing its standard divide-and-rule strategy in attempting to separate Africans from Coloureds and Indians. In a referendum of November 1983, the white electorate endorsed P. W. Botha's plan to create a so-called tricameral Parliament, with Indian and Coloured chambers in addition to the white Parliament. This was an effort to lure Indians and Coloureds into the system, and divide them from Africans. But the offer was merely a "toy telephone," as all parliamentary action by Indians and Coloureds was subject to a white veto. It was also a way of fooling the outside world into thinking that the government was reforming apartheid. Botha's ruse did not fool the people, as more than 80 percent of eligible Indian and Coloured voters boycotted the election to the new houses of Parliament in 1984.

Powerful grassroots political movements were being formed inside the country that had firm links to the ANC, the principal one being the United Democratic Front, of which I was named a patron. The UDF had been created to coordinate protest against the new apartheid constitution in 1983, and the first elections to the segregated tricameral Parliament in 1984. The UDF soon blossomed into a powerful organization that united over six hundred anti-apartheid organizations — trade unions, community groups, church groups, student associations.

The ANC was experiencing a new birth of popularity. Opinion polls showed that the Congress was far and away the most popular political organization among Africans even though it had been banned for a quarter of a century. The anti-apartheid struggle as a whole had captured the attention of the world; in 1984, Bishop Desmond Tutu was awarded the Nobel Peace Prize. (The authorities refused to send Bishop Tutu my letter of congratulations.) The South African government was under growing international pressure, as nations all across the globe began to impose economic sanctions on Pretoria.

The government had sent "feelers" to me over the years, beginning with Minister Kruger's efforts to persuade me to move to the Transkei. These were not efforts to negotiate, but attempts to isolate me from my organization. On several other occasions, Kruger said to me: "Mandela, we can work with you, but not your colleagues. Be reasonable." Although I did not respond to these overtures, the mere fact that they were talking rather than attacking could be seen as a prelude to genuine negotiations.

The government was testing the waters. In late 1984 and early 1985, I had visits from two prominent Western statesmen, Lord Nicholas Bethell, a member of the British House of Lords and the European Parliament, and Samuel Dash, a professor of law at Georgetown University and a former counsel to the U.S. Senate

Watergate Committee. Both visits were authorized by the new minister of justice, Kobie Coetsee, who appeared to be a new sort of Afrikaner leader.

I met Lord Bethell in the prison commander's office, which was dominated by a large photograph of a glowering President Botha. Bethell was a jovial, rotund man and when I first met him, I teased him about his stoutness. "You look like you are related to Winston Churchill," I said as we shook hands, and he laughed.

Lord Bethell wanted to know about our conditions at Pollsmoor and I told him. We discussed the armed struggle and I explained to him it was not up to us to renounce violence, but the government. I reaffirmed that we aimed for hard military targets, not people. "I would not want our men to assassinate, for instance, the major here," I said, pointing to Major Fritz van Sittert, who was monitoring the talks. Van Sittert was a good-natured fellow who did not say much, but he started at my remark.

In my visit with Professor Dash, which quickly followed that of Lord Bethell, I laid out what I saw as the minimum for a future nonracial South Africa: a unitary state without homelands; nonracial elections for the central Parliament; and one-person-one-vote. Professor Dash asked me whether I took any encouragement from the government's stated intention of repealing the mixed-marriage laws and certain other apartheid statutes. "This is a pinprick," I said. "It is not my ambition to marry a white woman or swim in a white pool. It is political equality that we want." I told Dash quite candidly that at the moment we could not defeat the government on the battlefield, but could make governing difficult for them.

I had one not-so-pleasant visit from two Americans, editors of the conservative newspaper the *Washington Times*. They seemed less intent on finding out my views than on proving that I was a Communist and a terrorist. All of their questions were slanted in that direction, and when I reiterated that I was neither a Communist nor a terrorist, they attempted to show that I was not a Christian either by asserting that the Reverend Martin Luther King never resorted to violence. I told them that the conditions in which Martin Luther King struggled were totally different from my own: the United States was a democracy with constitutional guarantees of equal rights that protected nonviolent protest (though there was still prejudice against blacks); South Africa was a police state with a constitution that enshrined inequality and an army that responded to nonviolence with force. I told them that I was a Christian and had always been a Christian. Even Christ, I said, when he was left with no alternative, used force to expel the moneylenders from the temple. He was not a man of violence, but had no choice but to use force against evil. I do not think I persuaded them.

Faced with trouble at home and pressure from abroad, P. W. Botha offered a tepid, halfway measure. On January 31, 1985, in a debate in Parliament, the state president publicly offered me my freedom if I "unconditionally rejected violence as a political instrument." This offer was extended to all political prisoners. Then, as if he were staking me to a public challenge, he added, "It is therefore not the South Africa government which now stands in the way of Mr. Mandela's freedom. It is he himself."

I had been warned by the authorities that the government was going to make a proposal involving my freedom, but I had not been prepared for the fact that it would be made in Parliament by the state president. By my reckoning, it was the sixth conditional offer the government had made for my release in the past ten years. After I listened to the speech on radio, I made a request to the commander of the prison for an urgent visit by my wife and my lawyer, Ismail Ayob, so that I could dictate my response to the state president's offer.

Winnie and Ismail were not given permission to visit for a week, and in the meantime I wrote a letter to the foreign minister, Pik Botha, rejecting the conditions for my release, while also preparing a public response. I was keen to do a number of things in this response, because Botha's offer was an attempt to drive a wedge between me and my colleagues by tempting me to accept a policy the ANC rejected. I wanted to reassure the ANC in general and Oliver in particular that my loyalty to the organization was beyond question. I also wished to send a message to the government that while I rejected its offer because of the conditions attached to it, I nevertheless thought negotiation, not war, was the path to a solution.

Botha wanted the onus of violence to rest on my shoulders and I wanted to reaffirm to the world that we were only responding to the violence done to us. I intended to make it clear that if I emerged from prison into the same circumstances in which I was arrested, I would be forced to resume the same activities for which I was arrested.

I met with Winnie and Ismail on a Friday; on Sunday, a UDF rally was to be held in Soweto's Jabulani Stadium, where my response would be made public. Some guards with whom I was not familiar supervised the visit, and as we began discussing my response to the state president, one of the warders, a relatively young fellow, interrupted to say that only family matters were permitted to be discussed. I ignored him, and he returned minutes later with a senior warder whom I barely knew. This warder said that I must cease discussing politics, and I told him that I was dealing with a matter of national importance involving an offer from the state president. I warned him that if he wanted to halt the discussion he must get direct orders from the state president himself. "If you are not willing to telephone the state president to get those orders," I said coldly, "then kindly do not interrupt us again." He did not.

I gave Ismail and Winnie the speech I had prepared. In addition to responding to the government, I wanted to thank publicly the UDF for its fine work and to congratulate Bishop Tutu on his prize, adding that his award belonged to all the people. On Sunday, February 10, 1985, my daughter Zindzi read my response to a cheering crowd of people who had not been able to hear my words legally anywhere in South Africa for more than twenty years.

Zindzi was a dynamic speaker like her mother, and said that her father should be at the stadium to speak the words himself. I was proud to know that it was she who spoke my words.

I am a member of the African National Congress. I have always been a member of the African National Congress and I will remain a member of the African National Congress until the day I die. Oliver Tambo is more than a brother to me. He is my greatest friend and comrade for nearly fifty years. If there is any one amongst you who cherishes my freedom, Oliver Tambo cherishes it more, and I know that he would give his life to see me free. . . .

I am surprised at the conditions that the government wants to impose on me. I am not a violent man. . . . It was only then, when all other forms of resistance were no longer open to us, that we turned to armed struggle. Let Botha show that he is different to Malan, Strijdom and Verwoerd. Let him renounce violence. Let him say that he will dismantle apartheid. Let him unban the people's organization, the African National Congress. Let him free all who have been imprisoned, banished or exiled for their opposition to apartheid. Let him guarantee free political activity so that people may decide who will govern them.

I cherish my own freedom dearly, but I care even more for your freedom. Too many have died since I went to prison. Too many have suffered for the love of freedom. I owe it to their widows, to their orphans, to their mothers, and to their fathers who have grieved and wept for them. Not only I have suffered during these long, lonely, wasted years. I am not less life-loving than you are. But I cannot sell my birthright, nor am I prepared to sell the birthright of the people to be free. . . .

What freedom am I being offered while the organization of the people remains banned? What freedom am I being offered when I may be arrested on a pass offense? What freedom am I being offered to live my life as a family with my dear wife who remains in banishment in Brandfort? What freedom am I being offered when I must ask for permission to live in an urban area? . . . What freedom am I being offered when my very South African citizenship is not respected?

Only free men can negotiate. Prisoners cannot enter into contracts. . . . I cannot and will not give any undertaking at a time when I and you, the people, are not free. Your freedom and mine cannot be separated. I will return.

# 89

IN 1985 after a routine medical examination with the prison doctor, I was referred to a urologist, who diagnosed an enlarged prostate gland and recommended surgery. He said the procedure was routine. I consulted with my family and decided to go ahead with the operation.

I was taken to Volks Hospital in Cape Town, under heavy security. Winnie flew down and was able to see me prior to the surgery. But I had another visitor, a surprising and unexpected one: Kobie Coetsee, the minister of justice. Not long before, I had written to Coetsee pressing him for a meeting to discuss talks between the ANC and the government. He did not respond. But that morning, the minister dropped by the hospital unannounced as if he were visiting an old friend who was laid up for a few days. He was altogether gracious and cordial, and for the most part we simply made pleasantries. Though I acted as though this was the most normal thing in the world, I was amazed. The government, in its slow and tentative way, was reckoning that they had to come to some accommodation with the ANC. Coetsee's visit was an olive branch.

Although we did not discuss politics, I did bring up one sensitive issue, and that was the status of my wife. In August, shortly before I entered the hospital, Winnie had gone to Johannesburg to receive medical treatment. The only trips she was permitted from Brandfort were to visit either me or her doctor. While in Johannesburg, her house in Brandfort and the clinic behind it were firebombed and destroyed. Winnie had no place in which to reside, and she decided to remain in Johannesburg despite the fact that the city was off-limits to her. Nothing happened for a few weeks, and then the security police wrote to inform her that the house in Brandfort had been repaired and she must return. But she refused to do so. I asked Coetsee to allow Winnie to remain in Johannesburg and not force her to return to Brandfort. He said he could promise nothing, but he would indeed look into it. I thanked him.

I spent several days in hospital recuperating from the surgery. When I was discharged, I was fetched at the hospital by Brigadier Munro. Commanding officers do not usually pick up prisoners at the hospital, so my suspicions were immediately aroused.

On the ride back, Brigadier Munro said to me in a casual way, as though he were simply making conversation, "Mandela, we are not taking you back to your friends now." I asked him what he meant. "From now on, you are going to be alone." I asked him why. He shook his head. "I don't know. I've just been given these instructions from headquarters." Once again, there was no warning and no explanation.

Upon my return to Pollsmoor I was taken to a new cell on the ground floor of the prison, three floors below and in an entirely different wing. I was given three rooms, and a separate toilet, with one room to be used for sleeping, one across the hall for studying, and another for exercise. By prison standards, this was palatial, but the rooms were damp and musty and received very little natural light. I said nothing to the brigadier, for I knew the decision had not been his. I wanted time to consider the ramifications of the move. Why had the state taken this step?

It would be too strong to call it a revelation, but over the next few days and weeks I came to a realization about my new circumstances. The change, I decided, was not a liability but an opportunity. I was not happy to be separated from my colleagues and I missed my garden and the sunny terrace on the third floor. But my solitude gave me a certain liberty, and I resolved to use it to do something I had been pondering for a long while: begin discussions with the government. I had concluded that the time had come when the struggle could best be pushed forward through negotiations. If we did not start a dialogue soon, both sides would be plunged into a dark night of oppression, violence, and war. My solitude would give me an opportunity to take the first steps in that direction, without the kind of scrutiny that might destroy such efforts.

We had been fighting against white minority rule for three-quarters of a century. We had been engaged in the armed struggle for more than two decades. Many people on both sides had already died. The enemy was strong and resolute. Yet even with all their bombers and tanks, they must have sensed they were on the wrong side of history. We had right on our side, but not yet might. It was clear to me that a military victory was a distant if not impossible dream. It simply did not make sense for both sides to lose thousands if not millions of lives in a conflict that was unnecessary. They must have known this as well. It was time to talk.

This would be extremely sensitive. Both sides regarded discussions as a sign of weakness and betrayal. Neither would come to the table until the other made significant concessions. The government asserted over and over that we were a terrorist organization of Communists, and that they would never talk to terrorists or Communists. This was National Party dogma. The ANC asserted over and over that the government was fascistic and racist and that there was nothing to talk about until they unbanned the ANC, unconditionally released all political prisoners, and removed the troops from the townships.

A decision to talk to the government was of such import that it should only have been made in Lusaka. But I felt that the process needed to begin, and that I had neither the time nor the means to communicate fully with Oliver. Someone from our side needed to

take the first step, and my new isolation gave me both the freedom
to do so and the assurance, at least for a while, of the confidentiality
of my efforts.

I was now in a kind of splendid isolation. Though my colleagues
were only three floors above me, they might as well have been in
Johannesburg. In order to see them, I had to put in a formal request
for a visit, which had to be approved by the Head Office in Pretoria.
It often took weeks to receive a response. If it was approved, I would
then meet them in the visiting area. This was a novel experience:
my comrades and fellow prisoners were now official visitors. For
years, we had been able to talk for hours a day; now we had to
make official requests and appointments, and our conversations were
monitored.

     After I had been in my new cell for a few days, I asked the
commanding officer to arrange such a meeting. He did so, and the
four of us discussed the issue of my transfer. Walter, Kathy, and
Ray were angry that we had been separated. They wanted to lodge
a strong protest, and demand that we be reunited. My response was
not what they expected. "Look, chaps," I said, "I don't think we
should oppose this thing." I mentioned that my new accommoda-
tions were superior, and maybe this would set a precedent for all
political prisoners. I then added somewhat ambiguously, "Perhaps something good will come of this. I'm now in a position
where the government can make an approach to us." They did not
care too much for this latter explanation, as I knew they would not.

     I chose to tell no one of what I was about to do. Not my col-
leagues upstairs or those in Lusaka. The ANC is a collective, but
the government had made collectivity in this case impossible. I did
not have the security or the time to discuss these issues with my
organization. I knew that my colleagues upstairs would condemn
my proposal, and that would kill my initiative even before it was
born. There are times when a leader must move out ahead of the
flock, go off in a new direction, confident that he is leading his
people the right way. Finally, my isolation furnished my organization with an excuse in case matters went awry: the old man was
alone and completely cut off, and his actions were taken by him as
an individual, not a representative of the ANC.

# 90

WITHIN A FEW WEEKS of my move, I wrote to Kobie Coetsee to propose talks about talks. As before, I received no response. I wrote once more, and again there was no response. I found this peculiar and demoralizing, and I realized I had to look for another opportunity to be heard. That came in early 1986.

At a meeting of the British Commonwealth in Nassau in October 1985, the leaders could not reach agreement on whether to participate in international sanctions against South Africa. This was mainly because British Prime Minister Margaret Thatcher was adamantly opposed. To resolve the deadlock, the assembled nations agreed that a delegation of "eminent persons" would visit South Africa and report back on whether sanctions were the appropriate tool to help bring about the end of apartheid. In early 1986, the seven-member Eminent Persons Group, led by General Olusegun Obasanjo, the former military leader of Nigeria, and former Australian Prime Minister Malcolm Fraser, arrived in South Africa on their fact-finding mission.

In February, I was visited by General Obasanjo to discuss the nature of the delegation's brief. He was eager to facilitate a meeting between me and the full group. With the government's permission, such a meeting was scheduled for May. The group would be talking with the cabinet after they saw me, and I viewed this as a chance to raise the subject of negotiations.

The government regarded my session with the group as something extraordinary. Two days before the meeting I was visited by Brigadier Munro, who had brought along a tailor. "Mandela," the commander said, "we want you to see these people on an equal footing. We don't want you to wear those old prison clothes, so this tailor will take your measurements and outfit you with a proper suit." The tailor must have been some kind of wizard, for the very next day I tried on a pinstriped suit that fit me like a glove. I was also given a shirt, tie, shoes, socks, and underwear. The commander admired my new attire. "Mandela, you look like a prime minister now, not a prisoner," he said and smiled.

\*          \*          \*

At the meeting between myself and the Eminent Persons Group, we were joined by two significant observers: Kobie Coetsee and Lieutenant General W. H. Willemse, the commissioner of prisons. Like the tailor, these two men were there to take my measure. But, curiously, they left shortly after the session started. I pressed them to remain, saying I had nothing to hide, but they left anyway. Before they took their leave, I told them the time had come for negotiations, not fighting, and that the government and the ANC should sit down and talk.

The Eminent Persons Group had come with many questions involving the issues of violence, negotiations, and international sanctions. At the outset, I set the ground rules for our discussions. "I am not the head of the movement," I told them. "The head of the movement is Oliver Tambo in Lusaka. You must go and see him. You can tell him what my views are, but they are my personal views alone. They don't even represent the views of my colleagues here in prison. All that being said, I favor the ANC beginning discussions with the government."

Various members of the group had concerns about my political ideology and what a South Africa under ANC leadership might look like. I told them I was a South African nationalist, not a Communist, that nationalists came in every hue and color, and that I was firmly committed to a nonracial society. I told them I believed in the Freedom Charter, that the charter embodied principles of democracy and human rights, and that it was not a blueprint for socialism. I spoke of my concern that the white minority feel a sense of security in any new South Africa. I told them I thought many of our problems were a result of lack of communication between the government and the ANC and that some of these could be resolved through actual talks.

They questioned me extensively on the issue of violence, and while I was not yet willing to renounce violence, I affirmed in the strongest possible terms that violence could never be the ultimate solution to the situation in South Africa and that men and women by their very nature required some kind of negotiated understanding. While I once again reiterated that these were my views and not those of the ANC, I suggested that if the government withdrew the army and the police from the townships, the ANC might agree to a suspension of the armed struggle as a prelude to talks. I told them that my release alone would not stem the violence in the country or stimulate negotiations.

After the group finished with me, they planned to see both Oliver in Lusaka and government officials in Pretoria. In my remarks, I had sent messages to both places. I wanted the government to see that under the right circumstances we would talk and I wanted Oliver to know that my position and his were the same.

In May, the Eminent Persons Group was scheduled to see me one last time. I was optimistic as they had been to both Lusaka and Pretoria, and I hoped that the seed of negotiations had been planted. But the day before we were to meet, the South African government took a step that sabotaged whatever goodwill had been engendered by the Commonwealth visitors. On the day the Eminent Persons Group was scheduled to meet with cabinet ministers, the South African Defense Force, under the orders of President Botha, launched air raids and commando attacks on ANC bases in Botswana, Zambia, and Zimbabwe. This utterly poisoned the talks, and the Eminent Persons Group immediately left South Africa. Once again, I felt my efforts to move negotiations forward had stalled.

Oliver Tambo and the ANC had called for the people of South Africa to render the country ungovernable, and the people were obliging. The state of unrest and political violence was reaching new heights. The anger of the masses was unrestrained; the townships were in upheaval. International pressure was growing stronger every day. On June 12, 1986, the government imposed a State of Emergency in an attempt to keep a lid on protest. In every outward way, the time seemed inauspicious for negotiations. But often, the most discouraging moments are precisely the time to launch an initiative. At such times people are searching for a way out of their dilemma. That month I wrote a very simple letter to General Willemse, the commissioner of prisons. In it, I merely said, "I wish to see you on a matter of national importance." I handed the letter to Brigadier Munro on a Wednesday.

That weekend, I was told by the commanding officer to be prepared to see General Willemse, who was coming down from

Pretoria. This meeting was not treated in the usual fashion. Instead of conferring with the general in the visiting area, I was taken to his residence on the grounds of Pollsmoor itself.

Willemse is a direct fellow and we got down to business immediately. I told him I wanted to see Kobie Coetsee, the minister of justice. He asked me why. I hesitated for a moment, reluctant to discuss political matters with a prison official. But I responded with frankness: "I want to see the minister in order to raise the question of talks between the government and the ANC."

He pondered this for a moment, and then said, "Mandela, as you know, I am not a politician. I cannot discuss such issues myself, for they are beyond my authority." He then paused, as if something had just occurred to him. "It just so happens," he said, "that the minister of justice is in Cape Town. Perhaps you can see him. I will find out."

The general then telephoned the minister and the two spoke for a few moments. After putting down the phone, the general turned to me and said, "The minister said, 'Bring him round.' " Minutes later, we left the general's residence in his car bound for the minister's house in Cape Town. Security was light; only one other car accompanied the general's vehicle. The ease and rapidity with which this meeting was set up made me suspect that the government might have planned this rendezvous ahead of time. Whether they had or not was immaterial; it was an opportunity to take the first step toward negotiations.

At his official residence in the city, Coetsee greeted me warmly and we settled down on comfortable chairs in his lounge. He apologized that I had not had a chance to change out of my prison clothes. I spent three hours in conversation with him and was struck by his sophistication and willingness to listen. He asked knowledgeable and relevant questions — questions that reflected a familiarity with the issues that divided the government and the ANC. He asked me under what circumstances would we suspend the armed struggle; whether or not I spoke for the ANC as a whole; whether I envisioned any constitutional guarantees for minorities in a new South Africa. His questions went to the heart of the issues dividing the government and the ANC.

After responding in much the same way as I did to the Eminent

Persons Group, I sensed that Coetsee wanted some resolution. What is the next step? he asked. I told him I wanted to see the state president and the foreign minister, Pik Botha. Coetsee noted this on a small pad he had kept beside him, and said he would send my request through the proper channels. We then shook hands, and I was driven back to my solitary cell on the ground floor of Pollsmoor Prison.

I was greatly encouraged. I sensed the government was anxious to overcome the impasse in the country, that they were now convinced they had to depart from their old positions. In ghostly outline, I saw the beginnings of a compromise.

I told no one of my encounter. I wanted the process to be under way before I informed anyone. Sometimes it is necessary to present one's colleagues with a policy that is already a fait accompli. I knew that once they examined the situation carefully, my colleagues at Pollsmoor and in Lusaka would support me. But again, after this promising start, nothing happened. Weeks and then months passed without a word from Coetsee. In some frustration, I wrote him another letter.

# 91

ALTHOUGH I DID NOT GET a direct response from Kobie Coetsee, there were other signs that the government was preparing me for a different kind of existence. On the day before Christmas, Lieutenant Colonel Gawie Marx, the deputy commander of Pollsmoor, wandered by my cell after breakfast and said quite casually, "Mandela, would you like to see the city?" I was not exactly certain what he had in mind, but I thought there was no harm in saying yes. Good, he said, come along. I walked with the colonel through the fifteen locked metal doors between my cell and the entrance, and when we emerged, I found his car waiting for us.

We drove into Cape Town along the lovely road that runs parallel to the coast. He had no destination in mind and simply meandered around the city in a leisurely fashion. It was absolutely riveting to watch the simple activities of people out in the world: old men sitting in the sun, women doing their shopping, people walking their dogs. It is precisely those mundane activities of daily life that one misses most in prison. I felt like a curious tourist in a strange and remarkable land.

After an hour or so, Colonel Marx stopped the car in front of a small shop on a quiet street. "Would you like a cold drink?" he asked me. I nodded, and he disappeared inside the shop. I sat there alone. For the first few moments, I did not think about my situation, but as the seconds ticked away, I became more and more agitated. For the first time in twenty-two years, I was out in the world and unguarded. I had a vision of opening the door, jumping out, and then running and running until I was out of sight. Something inside was urging me to do just that. I noticed a wooded area near the road where I could hide. I was extremely tense and began to perspire. Where was the colonel? But then I took control of myself; such an action would be unwise and irresponsible, not to mention dangerous. It was possible that the whole situation was contrived to try to get me to escape, though I do not think that was the case. I was greatly relieved a few moments later when I saw the colonel walking back to the car with two cans of Coca-Cola.

As it turned out, that day in Cape Town was the first of many excursions. Over the next few months, I went out again with the colonel not only to Cape Town but to some of the sights around the city, its beautiful beaches and lovely cool mountains. Soon, more junior officers were permitted to take me around. One of the places I regularly visited with these junior officers was known as the "gardens," a series of smallholdings on the edge of the prison grounds where crops were grown for the prison's kitchen. I enjoyed being out in nature, being able to see the horizon and feel the sun on my shoulders.

One day I went to the gardens with a captain, and after walking in the fields we strolled over to the stables. There were two young white men in overalls working with the horses. I walked over to them, praised one of the animals, and said to the fellow, "Now, what is this horse's name?" The young man seemed quite nervous and did not look at me. He then mumbled the name of the horse, but to the captain, not me. I then asked the other fellow in turn what the name of his horse was, and he had precisely the same reaction.

As I was walking back to the prison with the captain, I commented on what I thought was the curious behavior of the two young men. The captain laughed. "Mandela, don't you know what those two chaps were?" I said I did not. "They were white prisoners. They had never been questioned by a native prisoner in the presence of a white officer before."

Some of the younger warders took me quite far afield, and we would walk on the beach and even stop at a café and have tea. At such places, I often tried to see if people recognized me, but no one ever did; the last published picture of me had been taken in 1962.

These trips were instructive on a number of levels. I saw how life had changed in the time I had been away, and because we mainly went to white areas, I saw the extraordinary wealth and ease that whites enjoyed. Though the country was in upheaval and the townships were on the brink of open warfare, white life went on placidly and undisturbed. Their lives were unaffected. Once, one of the warders, a very pleasant young man named Warrant Officer Brand, actually took me to his family's flat and introduced me to his wife and children. From then on, I sent his children Christmas cards every year.

As much as I enjoyed these little adventures, I well knew that the authorities had a motive other than keeping me diverted. I sensed that they wanted to acclimatize me to life in South Africa and perhaps at the same time, get me so used to the pleasures of small freedoms that I might be willing to compromise in order to have complete freedom.

# 92

IN 1987, I RESUMED CONTACT with Kobie Coetsee. I had several private meetings with him at his residence, and later that year the government made its first concrete proposal. Coetsee said the government would like to appoint a committee of senior officials to conduct private discussions with me. This would be done with the full knowledge of the state president, Coetsee said. Coetsee himself would be head of the committee, and it would include General Willemse, the commissioner of prisons; Fanie van der Merwe, the director general of the Prisons Department; and Dr. Niel Barnard, a former academic who was then head of the National

Intelligence Service. The first three individuals were associated with the prison system, so if talks foundered or were leaked to the press, both sides would be able to cover up and say we were discussing prison conditions and nothing more.

The presence of Dr. Barnard, however, disturbed me. He was the head of South Africa's equivalent of the CIA, and was also involved with military intelligence. I could justify to my organization discussions with the other officials, but not Barnard. His presence made the talks more problematic and suggested a larger agenda. I told Coetsee that I would like to think about the proposal overnight.

That night I considered all the ramifications. I knew that P. W. Botha had created something called the State Security Council, a shadowy secretariat of security experts and intelligence officials. He had done this, according to the press, to circumvent the authority of the cabinet and increase his own power. Dr. Barnard was a key player in this inner council and was said to be a protégé of the president. I thought that my refusing Barnard would alienate Botha, and I decided that such a tack was too risky. If the state president was not brought on board, nothing would happen. In the morning, I sent word to Coetsee that I accepted his offer.

I knew that I had three crucial matters that I needed to address: first, I wanted to sound out my colleagues on the third floor before I proceeded any further; second, it was essential to communicate with Oliver in Lusaka about what was occurring; and finally, I intended to draft a memorandum to P. W. Botha laying out my views and those of the ANC on the vital issues before the country. This memorandum would create talking points for any future discussion.

I requested a meeting with my colleagues, and to my surprise, the authorities summarily refused. This was remarkable, and I assumed it reflected a great deal of nervousness about the prospect of secret talks between myself and the government. I took my complaints to more senior officials. Finally, the request was approved, with the proviso that I could see my colleagues one by one, not together.

I met them in the visiting area. I had resolved to leave out a few details; I would seek their counsel about the idea of having talks with the government without mentioning that an actual committee had been formed. Walter was first. I told him about my letter to the commissioner of prisons and my meeting with Coetsee. I said that I had discussed with Coetsee the idea of beginning talks with the government and that the government seemed interested. What were his views on the matter?

I have been through thick and thin with Walter. He was a man of reason and wisdom, and no man knew me better than he did. There was no one whose opinion I trusted or valued more. Walter considered what I told him. I could see he was uncomfortable, and at best, lukewarm. "In principle," he said, "I am not against negotiations. But I would have wished that the government initiated talks with us rather than us initiating talks with them."

I replied that if he was not against negotiations in principle, what did it matter who initiated them? What mattered was what they achieved, not how they started. I told Walter that I thought we should move forward with negotiations and not worry about who knocked on the door first. Walter saw that my mind was made up and he said he would not stop me, but that he hoped I knew what I was doing.

Next was Raymond Mhlaba. I explained the entire situation to him as I had to Walter. Ray was always a man of few words, and for several moments he digested what I had said. He then looked at me and said, "Madiba, what have you been waiting for? We should have started this years ago." Andrew Mlangeni's reaction was virtually the same as Ray's. The last man was Kathy. His response was negative; he was as resolutely against what I was suggesting as Raymond and Andrew were in favor. Even more strongly than Walter, he felt that by initiating talks it would appear that we were capitulating. Like Walter, he said he was not in principle against negotiations, and I responded exactly as I had with Walter. But Kathy was adamant; he felt I was going down the wrong path. But, despite his misgivings, he said he would not stand in my way.

Not long after this I received a note from Oliver Tambo that was smuggled in to me by one of my lawyers. He had heard reports that I was having secret discussions with the government and he was concerned. He said he knew I had been alone for some time and separated from my colleagues. He must have been wondering: What is going on with Mandela? Oliver's note was brief and to the point: What, he wanted to know, was I discussing with the government?

Oliver could not have believed that I was selling out, but he might have thought I was making an error in judgment. In fact, the tenor of his note suggested that.

I replied to Oliver in a very terse letter saying that I was talking to the government about one thing and one thing only: a meeting between the National Executive Committee of the ANC and the South African government. I would not spell out the details, for I could not trust the confidentiality of the communication. I simply said the time had come for such talks and that I would not compromise the organization in any way.

Although the ANC had called for talks with the government for decades, we had never been confronted with the actual prospect of such talks. It is one thing to consider them in theory, and quite another to engage in them. As I was writing my response to Oliver, I was also beginning to draft my memorandum to P. W. Botha. I would make sure that Oliver saw this as well. I knew that when Oliver and the National Executive read my memo, their fears that I had gone off the road would be allayed.

# 93

THE FIRST FORMAL MEETING of the secret working group took place in May 1988, at a posh officers' club within the precincts of Pollsmoor. While I knew both Coetsee and Willemse, I had never before met van der Merwe and Dr. Barnard. Van der Merwe was a quiet, levelheaded man who spoke only when he had something important to say. Dr. Barnard was in his mid-thirties and was exceedingly bright, a man of controlled intelligence and self-discipline.

The initial meeting was quite stiff, but in subsequent sessions we were able to talk more freely and directly. I met with them almost every week for a few months, and then the meetings occurred at irregular intervals, sometimes not for a month, and then suddenly every week. The meetings were usually scheduled by the government, but sometimes I would request a session.

During our early meetings, I discovered that my new colleagues, with the exception of Dr. Barnard, knew little about the ANC. They were all sophisticated Afrikaners, and far more open-minded than nearly all of their brethren. But they were the victims of so much propaganda that it was necessary to straighten them out about certain facts. Even Dr. Barnard, who had made a study of the ANC, had received most of his information from police and intelligence files, which were in the main inaccurate and sullied by the prejudices of the men who had gathered them. He could not help but be infected by the same biases.

I spent some time in the beginning sketching out the history of the ANC and then explaining our positions on the primary issues that divided the organization from the government. After these preliminaries, we focused on the critical issues: the armed struggle, the ANC's alliance with the Communist Party, the goal of majority rule, and the idea of racial reconciliation.

The first issue to arise was in many ways the most crucial, and that was the armed struggle. We spent a number of months discussing it. They insisted that the ANC must renounce violence and give up the armed struggle before the government would agree to negotiations — and before I could meet President Botha. Their contention was that violence was nothing more than criminal behavior that could not be tolerated by the state.

I responded that the state was responsible for the violence and that it is always the oppressor, not the oppressed, who dictates the form of the struggle. If the oppressor uses violence, the oppressed have no alternative but to respond violently. In our case it was simply a legitimate form of self-defense. I ventured that if the state decided to use peaceful methods, the ANC would also use peaceful means. "It is up to you," I said, "not us, to renounce violence."

I think I advanced their understanding on this point, but the issue soon moved from a philosophical question to a practical one. As Minister Coetsee and Dr. Barnard pointed out, the National Party had repeatedly stated that it would not negotiate with any organization that advocated violence: therefore, how could it suddenly announce talks with the ANC without losing its credibility? In order for us to begin talks, they said, the ANC must make some compromise so that the government would not lose face with its own people.

It was a fair point and one that I could well understand, but I would not offer them a way out. "Gentlemen," I said, "it is not my job to resolve your dilemma for you." I simply told them that they must tell their people that there can be no peace and no solution to the situation in South Africa without sitting down with the ANC. People will understand, I said.

The ANC's alliance with the Communist Party seemed to trouble them almost as much as the armed struggle. The National Party accepted the most hidebound of 1950s cold war ideology and regarded the Soviet Union as the evil empire and communism as the work of the devil. There was nothing that one could do to disabuse them of this notion. They maintained that the Communist Party dominated and controlled the ANC and that in order for negotiations to begin we must break with the party.

First of all, I said, no self-respecting freedom fighter would take orders from the government he is fighting against or jettison a longtime ally in the interest of pleasing an antagonist. I then explained at great length that the party and the ANC were separate and distinct organizations that shared the same short-term objectives, the overthrow of racial oppression and the birth of a nonracial South Africa, but that our long-term interests were not the same.

This discussion went on for months. Like most Afrikaners, they thought that because many of the Communists in the ANC were white or Indian, they were controlling the blacks in the ANC. I cited many occasions when the ANC and the CP had differed on policy and the ANC had prevailed, but this did not seem to impress them. Finally, in exasperation, I said to them, "You gentlemen consider yourselves intelligent, do you not? You consider yourselves forceful and persuasive, do you not? Well, there are four of you and only one of me, and you cannot control me or get me to change my mind. What makes you think the Communists can succeed where you have failed?"

They were also concerned about the idea of nationalization, insisting that the ANC and the Freedom Charter supported blanket nationalization for the South African economy. I explained that we were for a more even distribution of the rewards of certain industries, industries that were already monopolies, and that nationalization might occur in some of those areas. But I referred them to an article I wrote in 1956 for *Liberation* in which I said that the Freedom Charter was not a blueprint for socialism but for African-style capitalism. I told them I had not changed my mind since then.

The other main area of discussion was the issue of majority rule. They felt that if there was majority rule, the rights of minorities would be trampled. How would the ANC protect the rights of the white minority? they wanted to know. I said that there was no organization in the history of South Africa to compare with the ANC in terms of trying to unite all the people and races of South Africa. I referred them to the preamble of the Freedom Charter: "South Africa belongs to all who live in it, black and white." I told them that whites were Africans as well, and that in any future dispensation the majority would need the minority. We do not want to drive you into the sea, I said.

# 94

THE MEETINGS had a positive effect: I was told in the winter of 1988 that President Botha was planning to see me before the end of August. The country was still in turmoil. The government had reimposed a State of Emergency in both 1987 and 1988. International pressure mounted. More companies left South Africa. The American Congress had passed a sweeping sanctions bill.

In 1987, the ANC celebrated its seventy-fifth anniversary and held a conference at the end of the year in Tanzania attended by delegates from more than fifty nations. Oliver declared that the armed struggle would intensify until the government was prepared to negotiate the abolition of apartheid. Two years before, at the ANC's Kabwe conference in Zambia marking the thirtieth anniversary of the Freedom Charter, members of other races were elected to the National Executive Committee for the first time, and the NEC pledged that no discussions with the government could be held until all ANC leaders were released from prison.

Although violence was still pervasive, the National Party had never been stronger. In the white general election of May 1987, the Nationalists won an overwhelming majority. Worse still, the liberal Progressive Federal Party had been replaced as the official opposition by the Conservative Party, which was to the right of the Nationalists and campaigned on the theme that the government was too lenient with the black opposition.

Despite my optimism about the secret talks, it was a difficult time. I had recently had a visit from Winnie and I learned that 8115 Orlando West, the house in which we had been married and which I considered home, had been burned down by arsonists. We had lost invaluable family records, photographs, and keepsakes — even the slice of wedding cake Winnie was saving for my release. I had always thought that someday when I left prison I would be able to recapture the past when looking over those pictures and letters, and now they were gone. Prison had robbed me of my freedom but not my memories, and now I felt some enemies of the struggle had tried to rob me of even those.

I was also suffering from a bad cough that I could not seem to shake, and I often felt too weak to exercise. I had continued to complain about the dampness of my cell, but nothing had been done about it. One day, during a meeting in the visiting area with my attorney, Ismail Ayob, I felt ill and vomited. I was taken back to my cell, examined by a doctor, and I soon recovered. A few days later, however, I was in my cell after dinner when a number of warders and a doctor arrived. The physician gave me a cursory examination, and then one of the warders told me to get dressed. "We are taking you to hospital in Cape Town," I was told. Security was tight; I went in a convoy of cars and military vehicles accompanied by at least a dozen warders.

I was taken to Tygerberg Hospital, on the campus of the University of Stellenbosch, in a rich and verdant area of the Cape. As I later discovered, they had nearly chosen a different facility because the authorities feared I might attract sympathetic attention at a university hospital. The warders went in first and cleared everyone out of the entrance area. I was then escorted up to a floor that had been entirely emptied. The hall of the floor was lined with more than a dozen armed guards.

While sitting on a table in the examining room, I was looked at by a young and amiable doctor who was also a professor at the university medical school. He inspected my throat, tapped my chest, took some cultures, and in no time pronounced me fit. "There is nothing wrong with you," he said with a smile. "We should be able to release you tomorrow." I was anxious not to be diverted from my talks with the government, so I was pleased with his diagnosis.

After the examination, the doctor asked me if I would like some tea. I said I would and a few minutes later, a tall young Coloured nurse came in with a tray. The presence of all the armed guards and warders so frightened her that she dropped the tray on my bed, spilling the tea, before rushing out.

I spent the night in the empty ward under heavy guard. The first thing the next morning, even before I had breakfast, I was visited by an older doctor who was head of internal medicine at the hospital. He was a no-nonsense fellow and had far less of a bedside manner than the cordial young physician of the night before. Without any preliminaries, he tapped me roughly on my chest and then said gruffly, "There is water in your lung." I told him that the previous doctor had done tests and said I was fine. With a hint of annoyance, he said, "Mandela, take a look at your chest." He pointed out that one side of my chest was actually larger than the other, and said that it was probably filled with water.

He asked a nurse to bring him a syringe, and without further ado he poked it into my chest and drew out some brownish liquid. "Have you had breakfast?" he said. No, I replied. "Good," he said, "we are taking you to the operating theater immediately." He told me I had a great deal of water on my lung and he wanted to draw it out right away.

In the operating room I was given anesthesia, and the next thing I recalled was waking up in a room with the doctor present. I was groggy, but I concentrated on what he said: he had removed two liters of water from my chest and when the liquid was analyzed, a tuberculosis germ had been discovered. He said it was in the very early stages of the illness, and that the germ had done no damage to the lung. While full-blown tuberculosis normally took six months to cure, he said, I should be better in two months. The doctor agreed that it was probably the damp cell that had helped cause my illness.

I spent the next six weeks at Tygerberg recuperating and receiving treatment. In December, I was moved to the Constantiaberge Clinic, a luxurious facility near Pollsmoor that had never had a black patient before. My first morning there, I had an early visit from Kobie

Coetsee, who was accompanied by Major Marais, a deputy commander responsible for looking after me. We had barely exchanged greetings when the orderly brought in my breakfast.

Because of my recent illness and my history of high blood pressure, I had been put on a strict low-cholesterol diet. That order had apparently not yet been conveyed to the clinic's kitchen, for the breakfast tray contained scrambled eggs, three rashers of bacon, and several pieces of buttered toast. I could not remember the last time I had tasted bacon and eggs, and I was ravenous. Just as I was about to take a delicious forkful of egg, Major Marais said, "No, Mandela, that is against the orders of your physician," and he reached over to take the tray. I held it tightly, and said, "Major, I am sorry. If this breakfast will kill me, then today I am prepared to die."

Once I was ensconced at Constantiaberge, I again began to meet with Kobie Coetsee and the secret committee. While I was still at the clinic Coetsee said he wanted to put me in a situation that was halfway between confinement and freedom. While he did not spell out what this meant, I had a notion of what he was talking about, and I merely nodded. I would not be so naïve as to consider his proposal to be freedom, but I knew that it was a step in that direction.

In the meantime, the clinic was extremely comfortable and for the first time I actually enjoyed a hospital convalescence. The nurses — who were white or Coloured, no black nurses were permitted — spoiled me; they brought extra desserts and pillows and were constantly visiting, even during their time off.

One day, one of the nurses came to me and said, "Mr. Mandela, we are having a party tonight and we would like you to come." I said I'd be honored to attend, but that the authorities would undoubtedly have something to say about it. The prison authorities refused permission for me to go, which nettled the nurses, and as a result, they decided to hold their party in my room, insisting they could not have their party without me.

That night, a dozen or so of these young ladies in party frocks descended on my room with cake and punch and gifts. The guards seemed befuddled, but they could hardly consider these vivacious young girls a security risk. In fact, when one of the guards attempted to prevent some of the nurses from entering my room, I jestingly accused him of being jealous of an old man receiving so much attention from such beautiful young ladies.

# 95

IN EARLY DECEMBER 1988, security on my ward was tightened and the officers on duty were more alert than usual. Some change was imminent. On the evening of December 9, Major Marais came into my room, and told me to prepare myself to leave. Where to? I asked him. He could not say. I packed my things and looked around for some of my loyal nurses; I was disappointed at not being able to thank them and bid them farewell.

We left in a rush, and after about an hour on the road we entered a prison whose name I recognized: Victor Verster. Located in the lovely old Cape Dutch town of Paarl, Victor Verster is thirty-five miles northeast of Cape Town in the province's wine-growing region. The prison had the reputation of being a model facility. We drove through the entire length of the prison, and then along a winding dirt road through a rather wild, wooded area at the rear of the property. At the end of the road we came to an isolated, whitewashed one-story cottage set behind a concrete wall and shaded by tall fir trees.

I was ushered into the house by Major Marais and found a spacious lounge, next to a large kitchen, with an even larger bedroom at the back of the house. The place was sparsely but comfortably furnished. It had not been cleaned or swept before my arrival, and the bedroom and living room were teeming with all kinds of exotic insects, centipedes, monkey spiders, and the like, some of which I had never seen before. That night, I swept the insects off my bed and windowsill and slept extremely well in what was to be my new home.

The next morning I surveyed my new abode and discovered a swimming pool in the backyard, and two smaller bedrooms. I walked outside and admired the trees that shaded the house and kept it cool. The entire place felt removed, isolated. The only thing spoiling the idyllic picture was that the walls were topped with razor wire, and there were guards at the entrance to the house. Even so, it was a lovely place and situation; a halfway house between prison and freedom.

That afternoon I was visited by Kobie Coetsee, who brought a case of Cape wine as a housewarming gift. The irony of a jailer bringing his prisoner such a gift was not lost on either of us. He was extremely solicitous and wanted to make sure that I liked my new home. He surveyed the house himself, and the only thing he recommended was that the walls outside the house be raised — for my privacy, he said. He told me that the cottage at Victor Verster would be my last home before becoming a free man. The reason behind this move, he said, was that I should have a place where I could hold discussions in privacy and comfort.

The cottage did in fact give one the illusion of freedom. I could go to sleep and wake up as I pleased, swim whenever I wanted, eat when I was hungry — all were delicious sensations. Simply to be able to go outside during the day and take a walk when I desired was a moment of private glory. There were no bars on the windows, no jangling keys, no doors to lock or unlock. It was altogether pleasant, but I never forgot that it was a gilded cage.

The prison service provided me with a cook, Warrant Officer Swart, a tall, quiet Afrikaner who had once been a warder on Robben Island. I did not remember him, but he said he sometimes drove us to the quarry and purposely steered the truck over bumps to give us a rocky ride. "I did that to you," he said sheepishly, and I laughed. He was a decent, sweet-tempered fellow without any prejudice and he became like a younger brother to me.

He arrived at seven in the morning and left at four, and would make my breakfast, lunch, and dinner. I had a diet outlined by my physician and he would follow it in his preparations. He was a lovely cook, and when he went home at four, he would leave me supper to heat up in the microwave oven, a device that was new to me.

Warrant Officer Swart baked bread, made home-brewed ginger beer and assorted other delicacies. When I had visitors, which was increasingly often, he would prepare gourmet meals. They always praised the food and I daresay my chef was the envy of all my visitors. When the authorities began to permit some of my ANC comrades and members of the United Democratic Front (UDF) and the Mass Democratic Movement (MDM) to visit me, I accused them of coming only for the food.

One day, after a delicious meal prepared by Mr. Swart, I went into the kitchen to wash the dishes. "No," he said, "that is my duty. You must return to the sitting room." I insisted that I had to do something, and that if he cooked, it was only fair for me to do the dishes. Mr. Swart protested, but finally gave in. He also objected to the fact that I would make my bed in the morning, saying it was his responsibility to do so. But I had been making my own bed for so long it had become a reflex.

We also traded off in another respect. Like many Afrikaans-speaking warders, he was keen to improve his English. I was always looking for ways to improve my Afrikaans. We made an agreement: he would speak to me in English and I would answer in Afrikaans, and in that way we both practiced the language at which we were weakest.

I would occasionally ask him to make certain dishes for me. I sometimes requested samp and beans, which I used to eat as a boy. One day, I said to him, "You know, I would like you to cook me some brown rice." To my astonishment, he said, "What is brown rice?" Swart was a young man, and I explained to him that brown rice was the unrefined rice kernel, and we used to eat it during the war when white rice was unavailable. I said it was far healthier than white rice. He was skeptical, but managed to find me some. He cooked it and I enjoyed it very much. But Mr. Swart could not abide the taste and vowed that if I ever wanted it again, I would have to cook it myself.

Even though I was not a drinker, I wanted to be a proper host and serve wine to my guests. I would occasionally take a sip of wine in order to make my guests feel comfortable, but the only wine I can stomach is a South African semisweet wine, which is actually very sweet.

Before my guests came I would ask Mr. Swart to get a certain type of Nederburg wine, which I had tasted before and knew was a semisweet. One day, I was expecting my friends and lawyers for lunch, Dullah Omar, George Bizos, and Ismail Ayob, and asked Mr.

Swart to purchase some Nederburg wine should George Bizos, not a Muslim, want some with his meal. I noticed that he grimaced when I said this, and asked him what was wrong.

"Mr. Mandela," he said. "I always buy that wine for you because you ask me to, but it is cheap stuff and not very nice." I reminded him that I did not like dry wines and I was sure George could not tell the difference anyway. Mr. Swart smiled at this and proposed a compromise: he would go out and buy two bottles, a dry wine and my Nederburg, and then he would ask my guest which wine he preferred. "Fine," I said, "let us try your experiment."

When all four of us were seated for lunch, Swart came out holding the two bottles and turned to the guests and said, "Gentlemen, which wine would you like?" Without even looking at me, George pointed to the bottle of dry white. Warrant Officer Swart just smiled.

# 96

THE MEETINGS with the committee continued, and we stalled on the same issues that had always prevented us from moving forward: the armed struggle, the Communist Party, and majority rule. I was still pressing Coetsee for a meeting with P. W. Botha. By this time, the authorities permitted me to have rudimentary communications with my comrades at Pollsmoor and Robben Island and also the ANC in Lusaka. Although I knew I was going out ahead of my colleagues, I did not want to go too far ahead and find that I was all alone.

In January 1989, I was visited by my four comrades from Pollsmoor and we discussed the memorandum I was planning to send to the state president. The memorandum reiterated most of the points I had made in our secret committee meetings, but I wanted to make sure the state president heard them directly from me. He would see that we were not wild-eyed terrorists, but reasonable men.

"I am disturbed," I wrote to Mr. Botha in the memorandum, sent to him in March, "as many other South Africans no doubt are, by the specter of a South Africa split into two hostile camps — blacks on one side . . . and whites on the other, slaughtering one another." To avert this and prepare the groundwork for negotiations, I proposed to deal with the three demands made of the ANC by the government as a precondition to negotiations: renouncing violence; breaking with the SACP; and abandoning the call for majority rule.

On the question of violence I wrote that the refusal of the ANC to renounce violence was not the problem: "The truth is that the government is not yet ready . . . for the sharing of political power with blacks." I explained our unwillingness to cast aside the SACP, and reiterated that we were not under its control. "Which man of honour," I wrote, "will desert a lifelong friend at the insistence of a common opponent and still retain a measure of credibility with his people?" I said the rejection of majority rule by the government was a poorly disguised attempt to preserve power. I suggested he must face reality. "Majority rule and internal peace are like the two sides of a single coin, and white South Africa simply has to accept that there will never be peace and stability in this country until the principle is fully applied."

At the end of the letter, I offered a very rough framework for negotiations.

> Two political issues will have to be addressed; firstly, the demand for majority rule in a unitary state, secondly, the concern of white South Africa over this demand, as well as the insistence of whites on structural guarantees that majority rule will not mean domination of the white minority by blacks. The most crucial tasks which will face the government and the ANC will be to reconcile these two positions.

I proposed that this be done in two stages, the first being a discussion to create the proper conditions for negotiations, the second being the actual negotiations themselves. "I must point out that the move I have taken provides you with the opportunity to overcome the current deadlock, and to normalize the country's political situation. I hope you will seize it without delay."

But delay there was. In January, P. W. Botha suffered a stroke. While it did not incapacitate the president, it did weaken him and, according to his cabinet, made him even more irascible. In February, Botha unexpectedly resigned as head of the National Party, but kept his position as state president. This was an unparalleled situation in the country's history: in the South African parliamentary system, the leader of the majority party becomes the head of state. President

Botha was now head of state but not of his own party. Some saw this as a positive development: that Botha wanted to be "above party politics" in order to bring about true change in South Africa.

Political violence and international pressure continued to intensify. Political detainees all across the country had held a successful hunger strike, persuading the minister of law and order to release over nine hundred of them. In 1989, the UDF formed an alliance with the Congress of South African Trade Unions (COSATU) to form the Mass Democratic Movement (MDM), which then began organizing a countrywide "defiance campaign" of civil disobedience to challenge apartheid institutions. On the international front, Oliver held talks with the governments of Great Britain and the Soviet Union, and in January 1987 met with the U.S. secretary of state, George Shultz, in Washington. The Americans recognized the ANC as an indispensable element of any solution in South Africa. Sanctions against South Africa remained in force and even increased.

Political violence also had its tragic side. As the violence in Soweto intensified, my wife permitted a group of young men to act as her bodyguards as she moved around the township. These young men were untrained and undisciplined and became involved in activities that were unbecoming to a liberation struggle. Winnie subsequently became legally entangled in the trial of one of her bodyguards who was convicted of murdering a young comrade. This situation was deeply disconcerting to me, for such a scandal only served to divide the movement at a time when unity was essential. I wholly supported my wife and maintained that while she had shown poor judgment, she was innocent of any serious charges.

That July, for my seventy-first birthday, I was visited at the cottage at Victor Verster by nearly my entire family. It was the first time I had ever had my wife and children and grandchildren all in one place, and it was a grand and happy occasion. Warrant Officer Swart outdid himself in preparing a feast, and he did not even get upset when I permitted some of the grandchildren to eat their sweets before their main course. After the meal, the grandchildren went into my bedroom to watch a video of a horror movie while the adults stayed outside gossiping in the lounge. It was a deep, deep pleasure to have my whole family around me, and the only pain was the knowledge that I had missed such occasions for so many years.

# 97

ON JULY 4, I was visited by General Willemse, who informed me that I was being taken to see President Botha the following day. He described the visit as a "courtesy call," and I was told to be ready to leave at 5:30 A.M. I told the general that while I was looking forward to the meeting, I thought it appropriate that I have a suit and tie in which to see Mr. Botha. (The suit from the visit of the Eminent Persons Group had long since vanished.) The general agreed, and a short while later, a tailor appeared to take my measurements. That afternoon I was delivered a new suit, tie, shirt, and shoes. Before leaving, the general also asked me my blood type, just in case anything untoward should happen the following day.

I prepared as best I could for the meeting. I reviewed my memo and the extensive notes I had made for it. I looked at as many newspapers and publications as I could to make sure I was up to date. After President Botha's resignation as head of the National Party, F. W. de Klerk had been elected in his place, and there was said to be considerable jockeying between the two men. Some might interpret Botha's willingness to meet me as his way of stealing thunder from his rival, but that did not concern me. I rehearsed the arguments that the state president might make and the ones I would put in return. In every meeting with an adversary, one must make sure one has conveyed precisely the impression one intends to.

I was tense about seeing Mr. Botha. He was known as *die Groot Krokodil* — the Great Crocodile — and I had heard many accounts of his ferocious temper. He seemed to me to be the very model of the old-fashioned, stiff-necked, stubborn Afrikaner who did not so much discuss matters with black leaders as dictate to them. His recent stroke had apparently only exacerbated this tendency. I resolved that if he acted in that finger-wagging fashion with me I would have to inform him that I found such behavior unacceptable, and I would then stand up and adjourn the meeting.

*          *          *

At precisely 5:30 in the morning, Major Marais, the commander of Victor Verster, arrived at my cottage. He came into the lounge where I stood in front of him in my new suit for inspection. He walked around me, and then shook his head from side to side.

"No, Mandela, your tie," he said. One did not have much use for ties in prison, and I realized that morning when I was putting it on that I had forgotten how to tie it properly. I made a knot as best I could and hoped no one would notice. Major Marais unbuttoned my collar, loosened and then removed my tie, and then, standing behind me, tied it in a double Windsor knot. He then stood back to admire his handiwork. "Much better," he said.

We drove from Victor Verster to Pollsmoor, to the residence of General Willemse, where we were served breakfast by the general's wife. After breakfast, in a small convoy, we drove to Tuynhuys, the official presidential office, and parked in an underground garage where we would not be seen. Tuynhuys is a graceful, nineteenth-century Cape Dutch-style building, but I did not get a proper look at it that day. I was essentially smuggled into the presidential suite.

We took an elevator to the ground floor and emerged in a grand, wood-paneled lobby in front of the president's office. There we were met by Kobie Coetsee and Niel Barnard, and a retinue of prison officials. I had spoken extensively with both Coetsee and Dr. Barnard about this meeting, and they had always advised me to avoid controversial issues with the president. While we were waiting, Dr. Barnard looked down and noticed that my shoelaces were not properly tied and he quickly kneeled down to tie them for me. I realized just how nervous they were, and that did not make me any calmer. The door then opened and I walked in expecting the worst.

From the opposite side of his grand office, P. W. Botha walked toward me. He had planned his march perfectly, for we met exactly halfway. He had his hand out and was smiling broadly, and in fact, from that very first moment, he completely disarmed me. He was unfailingly courteous, deferential, and friendly.

We very quickly posed for a photograph of the two of us shaking hands, and then were joined at a long table by Kobie Coetsee, General Willemse, and Dr. Barnard. Tea was served and we began to talk. From the first, it was not as though we were engaged in tense political arguments but a lively and interesting tutorial. We did not discuss substantive issues, so much as history and South African culture. I mentioned that I had recently read an article in an Afrikaans magazine about the 1914 Afrikaner Rebellion, and I mentioned how they had occupied towns in the Free State. I said I saw our struggle as parallel to this famous rebellion, and we discussed this historical episode for quite a while. South African history, of course, looks very different to the black man than to the white man. Their view was that the rebellion had been a quarrel between brothers, whereas my struggle was a revolutionary one. I said that it could also be seen as a struggle between brothers who happen to be different colors.

The meeting was not even half an hour, and was friendly and breezy until the end. It was then that I raised a serious issue. I asked Mr. Botha to release unconditionally all political prisoners, including myself. That was the only tense moment in the meeting, and Mr. Botha said that he was afraid that he could not do that.

There was then a brief discussion as to what we should say if news of the meeting leaked out. We very quickly drafted a bland statement saying that we had met for tea in an effort to promote peace in the country. When this was agreed upon, Mr. Botha rose and shook my hand, saying what a pleasure it had been. Indeed, it had been. I thanked him, and left the way we had come.

While the meeting was not a breakthrough in terms of negotiations, it was one in another sense. Mr. Botha had long talked about the need to cross the Rubicon, but he never did it himself until that morning at Tuynhuys. Now, I felt, there was no turning back.

A little more than a month later, in August 1989, P. W. Botha went on national television to announce his resignation as state president. In a curiously rambling farewell address, he accused cabinet members of a breach of trust, of ignoring him and of playing into the hands of the African National Congress. The following day, F. W. de Klerk was sworn in as acting president and affirmed his commitment to change and reform.

To us, Mr. de Klerk was a cipher. When he became head of the National Party, he seemed to be the quintessential party man, nothing more and nothing less. Nothing in his past seemed to hint at a spirit of reform. As education minister, he had attempted to keep black students out of white universities. But as soon as he took over the National Party, I began to follow him closely. I read all of his speeches, listened to what he said, and began to see that he represented a genuine departure from his predecessor. He was not an ideologue, but a pragmatist, a man who saw change as necessary and inevitable. On the day he was sworn in, I wrote him a letter requesting a meeting.

In his inaugural address, Mr. de Klerk said his government was committed to peace and that it would negotiate with any other group committed to peace. But his commitment to a new order was demonstrated only after his inauguration when a march was planned in Cape Town to protest police brutality. It was to be led by Archbishop Tutu and the Reverend Allan Boesak. Under President Botha, the march would have been banned, marchers would have defied that ban, and violence would have resulted. The new president lived up to his promise to ease restrictions on political gatherings and permitted the march to take place, only asking that the demonstrators remain peaceful. A new and different hand was on the tiller.

# 98

EVEN AS DE KLERK became president, I continued to meet with the secret negotiating committee. We were joined by Gerrit Viljoen, the minister of constitutional development, a brilliant man with a doctorate in classics, whose role was to bring our discussions into a constitutional framework. I pressed the government to display evidence of its good intentions, urging the state to show its bona fides by releasing my fellow political prisoners at Pollsmoor and Robben Island. While I told the committee that my colleagues had to be released unconditionally, I said the government could expect disciplined behavior from them after their release. That was demonstrated by the conduct of Govan Mbeki, who had been unconditionally released at the end of 1987.

On October 10, 1989, President de Klerk announced that Walter Sisulu and seven of my former Robben Island comrades, Raymond Mhlaba, Ahmed Kathrada, Andrew Mlangeni, Elias Motsoaledi, Jeff Masemola, Wilton Mkwayi, and Oscar Mpetha, were to be released. That morning, I had been visited by Walter, Kathy, Ray, and Andrew, who were still at Pollsmoor, and I was able to say good-bye. It was an emotional moment, but I knew I would not be too far behind. The men were released five days later from Johannesburg Prison. It was an action that rightly evoked praise here and abroad, and I conveyed my appreciation to Mr. de Klerk.

But my gratitude paled compared to my unalloyed joy that Walter and the others were free. It was a day we had yearned for and fought for over so many years. De Klerk had lived up to his promise, and the men were released under no bans; they could speak in the name of the ANC. It was clear that the ban on the organization had effectively expired, a vindication of our long struggle and our resolute adherence to principle.

De Klerk began a systematic dismantling of many of the building blocks of apartheid. He opened South African beaches to people of all colors, and stated that the Reservation of Separate Amenities Act would soon be repealed. Since 1953 this act had enforced what was known as "petty apartheid," segregating parks, theaters, restaurants, buses, libraries, toilets, and other public facilities, according to race. In November, he announced that the National Security Management System, a secret structure set up under P. W. Botha to combat anti-apartheid forces, would be dissolved.

In early December, I was informed that a meeting with de Klerk was set for the twelfth of that month. By this time I was able to consult with my colleagues new and old, and I had meetings at the cottage with my old colleagues, and the leaders of the Mass Democratic Movement and the UDF. I received ANC people from all of the regions, as well as delegates from the UDF and COSATU. One of these young men was Cyril Ramaphosa, the general secretary of the National Union of Mine Workers and one of the ablest of the new generation of leadership. I also had visits from colleagues of mine from Robben Island, including Terror Lekota and Tokyo Sexwale, who stayed to lunch. They are both men with large appetites, and the only complaint I heard about them was from Warrant Officer Swart, who said, "Those fellows will eat us out of house and home!"

With guidance from a number of colleagues, I then drafted a letter to de Klerk not unlike the one I had sent to P. W. Botha. The subject was talks between the government and the ANC. I told the president that the current conflict was draining South Africa's lifeblood and talks were the only solution. I said the ANC would accept no preconditions to talks, especially not the precondition that the government wanted: the suspension of the armed struggle. The government asked for an "honest commitment to peace" and I pointed out that our readiness to negotiate was exactly that.

I told Mr. de Klerk how impressed I was by his emphasis on reconciliation, enunciated in his inaugural address. His words had imbued millions of South Africans and people around the world with the hope that a new South Africa was about to be born. The very first step on the road to reconciliation, I said, was the complete dismantling of apartheid and all the measures used to enforce it.

But I said that the spirit of that speech had not been much in evidence of late. The government's policies were perceived by many as a continuation of apartheid by other means. The government, I said, had spent too much time talking with black homeland leaders and others coopted by the system; these men, I asserted, were the agents of an oppressive past that the mass of black South Africans rejected.

I reiterated my proposal that talks take place in two stages. I told him I fully supported the guidelines the ANC had adopted in the Harare Declaration of 1989, which put the onus on the government to eliminate the obstacles to negotiations that the state itself had created. Those demands included the release of all political prisoners, the lifting of all bans on restricted organizations and persons, the end to the State of Emergency, and the removal of all troops from the townships. I stressed that a mutually agreed-upon cease-fire to end hostilities ought to be the first order of business, for without that, no business could be conducted. The day before our meeting the letter was delivered to Mr. de Klerk.

On the morning of December 13, I was again taken to Tuynhuys. I met de Klerk in the same room where I had had tea with his predecessor. Mr. de Klerk was accompanied by Kobie Coetsee, General Willemse, Dr. Barnard, and his colleague Mike Louw. I congratulated Mr. de Klerk on becoming president and expressed the hope that we would be able to work together. He was extremely cordial and reciprocated these sentiments.

From the first I noticed that Mr. de Klerk listened to what I had to say. This was a novel experience. National Party leaders generally heard what they wanted to hear in discussions with black leaders, but Mr. de Klerk seemed to be making an attempt to truly understand.

One of the issues I emphasized that day was the National Party's recently introduced five-year plan, which contained the concept of "group rights." The idea of "group rights" was that no racial or ethnic group could take precedence over any other. Although they defined "group rights" as a way of protecting the freedom of minorities in a new South Africa, in fact their proposal was a means of preserving white domination. I told Mr. de Klerk that this was unacceptable to the ANC.

I added that it was not in his interest to retain this concept, for it gave the impression that he wanted to modernize apartheid without abandoning it; this was damaging his image and that of the National Party in the eyes of the progressive forces in this country and around the world. An oppressive system cannot be reformed, I said, it must be entirely cast aside. I mentioned an editorial that I had recently read in *Die Burger*, the mouthpiece of the National Party in the Cape, implying that the group rights concept was conceived as an attempt to bring back apartheid through the back door. I told Mr. de Klerk that if that was how his party's paper perceived group rights, how did he think we regarded it? I added that the ANC had not struggled against apartheid for seventy-five years only to yield to a disguised form of it and that if it was his true intention to preserve apartheid through the Trojan horse of group rights, then he did not truly believe in ending apartheid.

Mr. de Klerk, I saw that day, does not react quickly to things. It was a mark of the man that he listened to what I had to say and did not argue with me. "You know," he said, "my aim is no different than yours. Your memo to P. W. Botha said the ANC and the government should work together to deal with white fears of black domination, and the idea of 'group rights' is how we propose to deal with it." I was impressed with this response, but said that the idea of "group rights" did more to increase black fears than allay white ones. De Klerk then said, "We will have to change it, then."

I then brought up the question of my freedom and said that if he expected me to go out to pasture upon my release he was greatly mistaken. I reaffirmed that if I was released into the same conditions under which I had been arrested I would go back to doing precisely those things for which I had been imprisoned. I made the case to him that the best way to move forward was to unban the ANC and all other political organizations, to lift the State of Emergency, to release political prisoners, and to allow the exiles to return. If the government did not unban the ANC, as soon as I was out of prison I would be working for an illegal organization. "Then," I said, "you must simply rearrest me after I walk through those gates."

Again, he listened carefully to what I had to say. My suggestions certainly came as no surprise to him. He said he would take all that I said under consideration, but that he would make no promises. The meeting was an exploratory one and I understood that nothing was going to be resolved that day. But it was extremely useful, for I had taken the measure of Mr. de Klerk just as I did with new prison commanders when I was on Robben Island. I was able to write to our people in Lusaka that Mr. de Klerk seemed to represent a true departure from the National Party politicians of the past. Mr. de Klerk, I said, echoing Mrs. Thatcher's famous description of Mr. Gorbachev, was a man we could do business with.

# 99

ON FEBRUARY 2, 1990, F. W. de Klerk stood before Parliament to make the traditional opening speech and did something no other South African head of state had ever done: he truly began to dismantle the apartheid system and lay the groundwork for a democratic South Africa. In dramatic fashion, Mr. de Klerk announced the lifting of the bans on the ANC, the PAC, the South African Communist Party, and thirty-one other illegal organizations; the freeing of political prisoners incarcerated for nonviolent activities; the suspension of capital punishment; and the lifting of various restrictions imposed by the State of Emergency. "The time for negotiation has arrived," he said.

It was a breathtaking moment, for in one sweeping action he had virtually normalized the situation in South Africa. Our world had changed overnight. After forty years of persecution and banishment, the ANC was now a legal organization. I and all my comrades could no longer be arrested for being a member of the ANC, for carrying its green, yellow, and black banner, for speaking its name. For the first time in almost thirty years, my picture and my words, and those of all my banned comrades, could freely appear in South African newspapers. The international community applauded de Klerk's bold actions. Amidst all the good news, however, the ANC objected to the fact that Mr. de Klerk had not completely lifted the State of Emergency or ordered the troops out of the townships.

On February 9, seven days after Mr. de Klerk's speech opening Parliament, I was informed that I was again going to Tuynhuys. I arrived at six o'clock in the evening. I met a smiling Mr. de Klerk in his office and as we shook hands, he informed me that he was going to release me from prison the following day. Although the press in South Africa and around the world had been speculating for weeks that my release was imminent, Mr. de Klerk's announcement nevertheless came as a surprise to me. I had not been told that the reason Mr. de Klerk wanted to see me was to tell me that he was making me a free man.

I felt a conflict between my blood and my brain. I deeply wanted to leave prison as soon as I could, but to do so on such short notice would not be wise. I thanked Mr. de Klerk, and then said that at the risk of appearing ungrateful I would prefer to have a week's notice in order that my family and my organization could be prepared for my release. Simply to walk out tomorrow, I said, would cause chaos. I asked Mr. de Klerk to release me a week from that day. After waiting twenty-seven years, I could certainly wait another seven days.

De Klerk was taken aback by my response. Instead of replying, he continued to relate the plan for my release. He said that the government would fly me to Johannesburg and officially release me there. Before he went any further, I told him that I strongly objected to that. I wanted to walk out of the gates of Victor Verster and be able to thank those who looked after me and greet the people of Cape Town. Though I was from Johannesburg, Cape Town had been my home for nearly three decades. I would make my way back to Johannesburg, but when I chose to, not when the government wanted me to. "Once I am free," I said, "I will look after myself."

De Klerk was again nonplused. But this time my objections caused a reaction. He excused himself and left his office to consult with others. After ten minutes he returned with a rather long face

and said, "Mr. Mandela, it is too late to change the plan now." I
replied that the plan was unacceptable and that I wanted to be
released a week hence and at Victor Verster, not Johannesburg. It
was a tense moment and, at the time, neither of us saw any irony
in a prisoner asking not to be released and his jailer attempting to
release him.

De Klerk again excused himself and left the room. After ten
minutes he returned with a compromise: yes, I could be released at
Victor Verster, but, no, the release could not be postponed. The
government had already informed the foreign press that I was to
be set free tomorrow and felt they could not renege on that statement. I felt I could not argue with that. In the end, we agreed on
the compromise, and Mr. de Klerk poured a tumbler of whisky for
each of us to drink in celebration. I raised the glass in a toast, but
only pretended to drink; such spirits are too strong for me.

I did not get back to my cottage until shortly before midnight,
whereupon I immediately sent word to my colleagues in Cape Town
that I was to be released the following day. I managed to get a
message to Winnie and I telephoned Walter in Johannesburg. They
would all fly in on a chartered plane the next day. That evening, a
number of ANC people on what was known as the National Reception Committee came to the cottage to draft a statement that I
would make the following day. They left in the early hours of the
morning, and despite my excitement, I had no trouble falling asleep.

*Part Eleven*

———

# FREEDOM

# 100

I AWOKE ON THE DAY of my release after only a few hours' sleep at 4:30 A.M. February 11 was a cloudless, end-of-summer Cape Town day. I did a shortened version of my usual exercise regimen, washed, and ate breakfast. I then telephoned a number of people from the ANC and the UDF in Cape Town to come to the cottage to prepare for my release and work on my speech. The prison doctor came by to give me a brief checkup. I did not dwell on the prospect of my release, but on all the many things I had to do before then. As so often happens in life, the momentousness of an occasion is lost in the welter of a thousand details.

There were numerous matters that had to be discussed and resolved with very little time to do so. A number of comrades from the reception committee, including Cyril Ramaphosa and Trevor Manuel, were at the house bright and early. I wanted initially to address the people of Paarl, who had been very kind to me during my incarceration, but the reception committee was adamant that that would not be a good idea: it would look curious if I gave my first speech to the prosperous white burghers of Paarl. Instead, as planned, I would speak first to the people of Cape Town at the Grand Parade in Cape Town.

One of the first questions to be resolved was where I would spend my first night of freedom. My inclination was to spend the night in the Cape Flats, the bustling black and Coloured townships of Cape Town, in order to show my solidarity with the people. But my colleagues and, later, my wife argued that for security reasons I should stay with Archbishop Desmond Tutu in Bishop's Court, a plush residence in a white suburb. It was not an area where I would have been permitted to live before I went to prison, and I thought it would send the wrong signal to spend my first night of freedom in a posh white area. But the members of the committee explained that Bishop's Court had become multiracial under Tutu's tenure, and symbolized an open, generous nonracialism.

The prison service supplied me with boxes and crates for packing. During my first twenty or so years in prison, I accumulated very few possessions, but in the last few years I had amassed enough property — mainly books and papers — to make up for previous decades. I filled over a dozen crates and boxes.

My actual release time was set for 3 P.M., but Winnie and Walter and the other passengers from the chartered flight from Johannesburg did not arrive until after two. There were already dozens of people at the house, and the entire scene took on the aspect of a celebration. Warrant Officer Swart prepared a final meal for all of us, and I thanked him not only for the food he had provided for the last two years but the companionship. Warrant Officer James Gregory was also there at the house, and I embraced him warmly. In the years that he had looked after me from Pollsmoor through Victor Verster, we had never discussed politics, but our bond was an unspoken one and I would miss his soothing presence. Men like Swart, Gregory, and Warrant Officer Brand reinforced my belief in the essential humanity even of those who had kept me behind bars for the previous twenty-seven and a half years.

There was little time for lengthy farewells. The plan was that Winnie and I would be driven in a car to the front gate of the prison. I had told the authorities that I wanted to be able to say good-bye to the guards and warders who had looked after me and I asked that they and their families wait for me at the front gate, where I would be able to thank them individually.

At a few minutes after three, I was telephoned by a well-known SABC presenter who requested that I get out of the car a few hundred feet before the gate so that they could film me walking toward freedom. This seemed reasonable, and I agreed to do it. This was my first inkling that things might not go as calmly as I had imagined.

By 3:30, I began to get restless, as we were already behind schedule. I told the members of the reception committee that my people had been waiting for me for twenty-seven years and I did not want to keep them waiting any longer. Shortly before four, we left in a small motorcade from the cottage. About a quarter of a mile in front of the gate, the car slowed to a stop and Winnie and I got out and began to walk toward the prison gate.

At first, I could not really make out what was going on in front of us, but when I was within one hundred fifty feet or so, I saw a tremendous commotion and a great crowd of people: hundreds of photographers and television cameras and newspeople as well as several thousand well-wishers. I was astounded and a little bit alarmed. I had truly not expected such a scene; at most, I had imagined that there would be several dozen people, mainly the warders and their families. But this proved to be only the beginning; I realized we had not thoroughly prepared for all that was about to happen.

Within twenty feet or so of the gate, the cameras started clicking, a noise that sounded like some great herd of metallic beasts. Reporters started shouting questions; television crews began crowding in; ANC supporters were yelling and cheering. It was a happy, if slightly disorienting chaos. When a television crew thrust a long, dark, furry object at me, I recoiled slightly, wondering if it were some newfangled weapon developed while I was in prison. Winnie informed me that it was a microphone.

When I was among the crowd I raised my right fist and there was a roar. I had not been able to do that for twenty-seven years and it gave me a surge of strength and joy. We stayed among the crowd for only a few minutes before jumping back into the car for the drive to Cape Town. Although I was pleased to have such a reception, I was greatly vexed by the fact that I did not have a chance to say good-bye to the prison staff. As I finally walked through those gates to enter a car on the other side, I felt — even at the age of seventy-one — that my life was beginning anew. My ten thousand days of imprisonment were over.

Cape Town was thirty-five miles to the southwest, but because of the unexpected crowds at the gate, the driver elected to take a different path to the city. We drove round to the back of the prison, and our convoy took small roads and byways into town. We drove through beautiful green vineyards and manicured farms, and I relished the scenery around me.

The countryside was lush and well cared for, but what surprised me was how many white families were standing beside the road to get a glimpse of our motorcade. They had heard on the radio that we were taking an alternate route. Some, perhaps a dozen, even raised their clenched right fists in what had become the ANC power salute. This astonished me; I was tremendously encouraged by these few brave souls from a conservative farming area who expressed their solidarity. At one point, I stopped and got out of the car to greet and thank one such white family and tell them how inspired I was by their support. It made me think that the South Africa I was returning to was far different from the one I had left.

As we entered the outskirts of the city, I could see people streaming toward the center. The reception committee had organized a rally at the Grand Parade in Cape Town, a great open square that stretched out in front of the old City Hall. I would speak to the crowd from the balcony of that building, which overlooked the entire area. We heard sketchy reports that a great sea of people had been waiting there since morning. The plan was for our motorcade to avoid the crowd and drive around to the back of City Hall, where I would quietly enter the building.

The drive to Cape Town took forty-five minutes, and as we neared the Grand Parade we could see an enormous crowd. The driver was meant to turn right and skirt its edges, but instead, he inexplicably plunged straight into the sea of people. Immediately the crowd surged forward and enveloped the car. We inched forward for a minute or two but were then forced to stop by the sheer press of bodies. People began knocking on the windows, and then on the boot and the bonnet. Inside it sounded like a massive hailstorm. Then people began to jump on the car in their excitement. Others began to shake it and at that moment I began to worry. I felt as though the crowd might very well kill us with their love.

The driver was even more anxious than Winnie and I, and he was clamoring to jump out of the car. I told him to stay calm and remain inside, that others from the cars behind us would come to our rescue. Allan Boesak and others began to attempt to clear a way for our vehicle and push the people off the car, but with little success. We sat inside — it would have been futile to even attempt to open the door, so many people were pressing on it — for more than an hour, imprisoned by thousands of our own supporters. The scheduled beginning of the speech had long passed.

Several dozen marshals eventually came to the rescue and managed slowly to clear an exit path. When we finally broke free, the driver set off at great speed in the opposite direction from City Hall. "Man, where are you going?" I asked him in some agitation. "I don't know!" he said, his voice tense with anxiety. "I've never experienced anything like that before," he said, and then continued driving without any destination in mind.

When he began to calm down I gave him directions to the house of my friend and attorney Dullah Omar, who lived in the Indian area of the city. We could go there, I said, and relax for a few minutes. This appealed to him. Fortunately, Dullah and his family were home, but they were more than a bit surprised to see us. I was a free man for the first time in twenty-seven years, but instead of greeting me, they said with some concern, "Aren't you meant to be at the Grand Parade?"

We were able to sip some cold drinks at Dullah's, but we had only been there a few minutes when Archbishop Tutu telephoned. How he knew we were there I do not know. He was quite distressed and said, "Nelson, you must come back to the Grand Parade immediately. The people are growing restless. If you do not return straightaway I cannot vouch for what will happen. I think there might be an uprising!" I said I would return at once.

Our problem was the driver: he was deeply reluctant to return to the Grand Parade. But I remonstrated with him and soon we were on our way back to City Hall. The building was surrounded by people on all sides, but it was not as dense in the back, and the driver managed to make his way through to the rear entrance. It was almost dusk when I was led up to the top floor of this stately building whose halls had always been filled with shuffling white functionaries. I walked out onto the balcony and saw a boundless sea of people cheering, holding flags and banners, clapping, and laughing.

I raised my fist to the crowd and the crowd responded with an enormous cheer. Those cheers fired me anew with the spirit of the struggle. *"Amandla!"* I called out. *"Ngawethu!"* they responded. *"iAfrika!"* I yelled; *"Mayibuye!"* they answered. Finally, when the crowd had settled down a bit, I took out my speech and then reached into my breast pocket for my glasses. They were not there; I had left them at Victor Verster. I knew Winnie's glasses were a similar prescription and I borrowed hers.

Friends, comrades and fellow South Africans. I greet you all in the name of peace, democracy and freedom for all! I stand here before you not as a prophet but as a humble servant of you, the people. Your tireless and heroic sacrifices have made it possible for me to be here today. I therefore place the remaining years of my life in your hands.

I spoke from the heart. I wanted first of all to tell the people that I was not a messiah, but an ordinary man who had became a leader because of extraordinary circumstances. I wanted immediately to thank the people all over the world who had campaigned for my release. I thanked the people of Cape Town, and I saluted Oliver Tambo and the African National Congress, Umkhonto we Sizwe, the South African Communist Party, the UDF, the South African Youth Congress, COSATU, the Mass Democratic Movement, the National Union of South African Students, and the Black Sash, a group formed by women that had long been a voice of conscience. I also publicly expressed my gratitude to my wife and family, saying, "I am convinced that [their] pain and suffering was far greater than my own."

I told the crowd in no uncertain terms that apartheid had no future in South Africa, and that the people must not let up their campaign of mass action. "The sight of freedom looming on the horizon should encourage us to redouble our efforts." I felt it was important publicly to explain my talks with the government. "Today," I said, "I wish to report to you that my talks with the government have been aimed at normalizing the political situation in the country. I wish to stress that I myself have at no time entered into negotiations about the future of our country except to insist on a meeting between the ANC and the government."

I said I hoped that a climate conducive to a negotiated settlement could soon be achieved, ending the need for the armed struggle. The steps to achieving such a climate, I said, had been outlined in the ANC's 1989 Harare Declaration. As a condition to real negotiations, I said, the government must immediately end the State of Emergency and free all political prisoners.

I told the people that de Klerk had gone further than any other Nationalist leader to normalize the situation and then, in words that came back to haunt me, I called Mr. de Klerk "a man of integrity." These words were flung back at me many times when Mr. de Klerk seemed not to live up to them.

It was vital for me to show my people and the government that I was unbroken and unbowed, and that the struggle was not over for me but beginning anew in a different form. I affirmed that I was "a loyal and disciplined member of the African National Congress." I encouraged the people to return to the barricades, to intensify the struggle, and we would walk the last mile together.

It was evening by the time my speech was finished, and we were hustled back into our cars for the trip to Bishop's Court. As we entered its pristine environs, I saw hundreds of black faces waiting to greet me. When they saw us, the people burst into song. When I greeted Archbishop Tutu, I enveloped him in a great hug; here was a man who had inspired an entire nation with his words and his courage, who had revived the people's hope during the darkest of times. We were led inside the house where more family and friends met us, but for me, the most wonderful moment was when I was told that I had a telephone call from Stockholm. I knew immediately who it was. Oliver's voice was weak, but unmistakable, and to hear him after all those years filled me with great joy. Oliver was in Sweden recuperating from a debilitating stroke he had suffered in August 1989. We agreed that we would meet as soon as possible.

My dream upon leaving prison was to take a leisurely drive down to the Transkei, and visit my birthplace, the hills and streams where I had played as a boy, and the burial ground of my mother, which I had never seen. But my dream had to be deferred, for I learned very quickly of the extensive plans that the ANC had for me, and none of them involved a relaxing journey to the Transkei.

# 101

I WAS SCHEDULED to hold a press conference the afternoon after my release, and in the morning I met with a number of my colleagues to talk about scheduling and strategy. A small mountain of telegrams and messages of congratulations had arrived, and I tried to review as many of these as possible. There were telegrams from all around the world, from presidents and prime ministers, but I remember one in particular from a white Cape Town housewife that amused me greatly. It read: "I am very glad that you are free, and that you are back among your friends and family, but your speech yesterday was very boring."

Before I went to prison I never held such a press conference as I did that day. In the old days there were no television cameras, and most ANC press conferences were conducted clandestinely. That afternoon, there were so many journalists, from so many different countries, I did not know whom to speak with. I was pleased to see a high percentage of black journalists among the throng. At the press conference I was once again keen to reassert a number of themes: first, that I was a loyal and disciplined member of the ANC. I was mindful of the fact that the most senior ANC people would be watching my release from abroad, and attempting to gauge my fidelity from a distance. I was aware that they had heard rumors that I had strayed from the organization, that I was compromised, so at every turn I sought to reassure them. When asked what role I would play in the organization, I told the press that I would play whatever role the ANC ordered.

I told the reporters that there was no contradiction between my continuing support for the armed struggle and my advocating negotiations. It was the reality and the threat of the armed struggle that had brought the government to the verge of negotiations. I added that when the state stopped inflicting violence on the ANC, the ANC would reciprocate with peace. Asked about sanctions, I said the ANC could not yet call for the relaxation of sanctions, because the situation that caused sanctions in the first place — the absence of political rights for blacks — was still the status quo. I might be out of jail, I said, but I was not yet free.

I was asked as well about the fears of whites. I knew that people expected me to harbor anger toward whites. But I had none. In prison, my anger toward whites decreased, but my hatred for the system grew. I wanted South Africa to see that I loved even my enemies while I hated the system that turned us against one another.

I wanted to impress upon the reporters the critical role of whites in any new dispensation. I have tried never to lose sight of this. We did not want to destroy the country before we freed it, and to drive the whites away would devastate the nation. I said that there was a middle ground between white fears and black hopes, and we in the ANC would find it. "Whites are fellow South Africans," I said, "and we want them to feel safe and to know that we appreciate the contribution that they have made toward the development of this country." Any man or woman who abandons apartheid will be embraced in our struggle for a democratic, nonracial South Africa; we must do everything we can to persuade our white compatriots that a new, nonracial South Africa will be a better place for all.

From my very first press conference I noticed that journalists were as eager to learn about my personal feelings and relationships as my political thoughts. This was new to me; when I went to prison, a journalist would never have thought of asking questions about one's wife and family, one's emotions, one's most intimate moments. While it was understandable that the press might be interested in these things, I nevertheless found their curiosity difficult to satisfy. I am not and never have been a man who finds it easy to talk about his feelings in public. I was often asked by reporters how it felt to be free, and I did my best to describe the indescribable, and usually failed.

After the press conference, Archbishop Tutu's wife telephoned us from Johannesburg to say that we must fly there straightaway. Winnie and I had hoped to spend a few days in Cape Town relaxing, but the message we were getting was that the people of Johannesburg were getting restless and there might be chaos if I did not return directly. We flew to Johannesburg that evening, but I was informed that there were thousands of people surrounding our old home, 8115 Orlando West, which had been reconstructed, and that it would be unwise to go there. I reluctantly acceded; I yearned to spend my second night of freedom under my own roof. Instead, Winnie and I stayed in the northern suburbs at the home of an ANC supporter.

The following morning we flew by helicopter to the First National Bank Stadium in Soweto. We were able to make an aerial tour of Soweto, the teeming metropolis of matchbox houses, tin shanties, and dirt roads, the mother city of black urban South Africa, the only home I ever knew as a man before I went to prison. While Soweto had grown, and in some places prospered, the overwhelming majority of the people remained dreadfully poor, without electricity or running water, eking out an existence that was shameful in a nation as wealthy as South Africa. In many places, the poverty was far worse than when I went to prison.

\*　　\*　　\*

We circled over the stadium, overflowing with 120,000 people, and landed in the center. The stadium was so crowded, with people sitting or standing in every inch of space, that it looked as though it would burst. I expressed my delight to be back among them, but I then scolded the people for some of the crippling problems of urban black life. Students, I said, must return to school. Crime must be brought under control. I told them that I had heard of criminals masquerading as freedom fighters, harassing innocent people and setting alight vehicles; these rogues had no place in the struggle. Freedom without civility, freedom without the ability to live in peace, was not true freedom at all.

> Today, my return to Soweto fills my heart with joy. At the same time I also return with a deep sense of sadness. Sadness to learn that you are still suffering under an inhuman system. The housing shortage, the schools crisis, unemployment and the crime rate still remain. . . . As proud as I am to be part of the Soweto community, I have been greatly disturbed by the statistics of crime that I read in the newspapers. Although I understand the deprivations our people suffer I must make it clear that the level of crime in the township is unhealthy and must be eliminated as a matter of urgency.

I ended by opening my arms to all South Africans of goodwill and good intentions, saying that "no man or woman who has abandoned apartheid will be excluded from our movement toward a nonracial, united and democratic South Africa based on one-person one-vote on a common voters' roll." That was the ANC's mission, the goal that I had always kept before me during the many lonely years in prison, the goal that I would work toward during the remaining years of my life. It was the dream I cherished when I entered prison at the age of forty-four, but I was no longer a young man, I was seventy-one, and I could not afford to waste any time.

That night, I returned with Winnie to number 8115 in Orlando West. It was only then that I knew in my heart that I had left prison. For me, 8115 was the centerpoint of my world, the place marked with an X in my mental geography. The house had been soundly rebuilt after the fire. When I saw the four-roomed house, I was surprised by how much smaller and humbler it was than I remembered it being. Compared to my cottage at Victor Verster, number 8115 could have been the servants' quarters at the back. But any house in which a man is free is a castle when compared to even the plushest prison.

That night, as happy as I was to be home, I had a sense that what I most wanted and longed for was going to be denied me. I yearned to resume a normal and ordinary life, to pick up some of the old threads from my life as a young man, to be able to go to my office in the morning and return to my family in the evening, to be able to pop out and buy some toothpaste at the pharmacy, to visit in the evening with old friends. These ordinary things are what one misses most in prison, and dreams about doing when one is free. But I quickly realized that such things were not going to be possible. That night, and every night for the next weeks and months, the house was surrounded by hundreds of well-wishers. People sang and danced and called out, and their joy was infectious. These were my people, and I had no right and no desire to deny myself to them. But in giving myself to my people I could see that I was once again taking myself away from my family.

We did not sleep much that night, as the singing continued until the early hours, when members of the ANC and UDF who were guarding the house begged the crowd to remain quiet and allow us to rest. There were many in the ANC who advised me to move to the home a few blocks distant, in Diepkloof extension, that Winnie had built while I was in prison. It was a grand place by Soweto standards, but it was a house that held no meaning or memories for me. Moreover, it was a house that because of its size and expense seemed somehow inappropriate for a leader of the people. I rejected that advice for as long as I could. I wanted not only to live among my people, but like them.

# 102

MY FIRST RESPONSIBILITY was to report to the leadership of the ANC, and on February 27, when I had been out of prison a little over two weeks, I flew to Lusaka for a meeting of the National Executive Committee. It was a wonderful reunion to be with old comrades whom I had not seen in decades. A number of African heads of state were also in attendance, and I had brief talks with

Robert Mugabe of Zimbabwe, Kenneth Kaunda of Zambia, José Eduardo Dos Santos of Angola, Quett Masire of Botswana, Joaquim Chissano of Mozambique, and Yoweri Museveni of Uganda.

While the members of the executive were pleased that I had been freed, they were also eager to evaluate the man who had been released. I could see the questions in their eyes. Was Mandela the same man who went to prison twenty-seven years before, or was this a different Mandela, a reformed Mandela? Had he survived or had he been broken? They had heard reports of my conversations with the government and they were rightly concerned. I had not only been out of touch with the situation on the ground — since 1984 I had not even been able to communicate with my colleagues in prison.

I carefully and soberly explained the nature of my talks with the government. I described the demands I had made, and the progress that had been achieved. They had seen the memoranda I had written to Botha and de Klerk, and knew that these documents adhered to ANC policy. I knew that over the previous few years some of the men who had been released had gone to Lusaka and whispered, "Madiba has become soft. He has been bought off by the authorities. He is wearing three-piece suits, drinking wine, and eating fine food." I knew of these whispers, and I intended to refute them. I knew that the best way to disprove them was simply to be direct and honest about everything that I had done.

At that session of the NEC I was elected deputy president of the organization while Alfred Nzo, the organization's secretary-general, was named acting president while Oliver was recuperating. At a press conference after our meeting, I was asked about a suggestion made by Dr. Kaunda, the president of Zambia and a longtime supporter of the Congress, that the ANC should suspend armed operations inside South Africa now that I had been released. I replied that while we valued Mr. Kaunda's wisdom and support, it was too soon to suspend the armed struggle, for we had not yet achieved the goal for which we took up arms; it was not the ANC's job, I said, to help Mr. de Klerk placate his right-wing supporters.

I began a tour of Africa, which included many countries. During the first six months after my release, I spent more time abroad than at home. Nearly everywhere I went there were great enthusiastic crowds so that even if I felt weary the people buoyed me. In Dar es Salaam I was met by a crowd estimated at half a million.

I enjoyed my travels immensely. I wanted to see new — and old — sights, taste different foods, speak with all manner of people. I very quickly had to acclimatize myself to a world radically different from the one I had left. With changes in travel, communication, and mass media, the world had accelerated; things now happened so fast it was sometimes difficult to keep up with them. Winnie tried to get me to slow down, but there was simply too much to do; the organization wanted to make sure we took advantage of the euphoria generated by my release.

In Cairo, the day after a private meeting with the Egyptian president, Hosni Mubarak, I was scheduled to address a large meeting in a local hall. When I arrived, the crowd seemed to be spilling out of the building and there was precious little security. I mentioned to a policeman that I thought he needed reinforcements but he merely shrugged. Winnie and I waited in a room behind the hall, and at the appointed hour, a policeman motioned for me to go in. I told him to escort the rest of my delegation in first because I feared that when I went in there would be pandemonium and they would be cut off. But the policeman urged me to go first, and indeed as soon as I was in the hall, the crowd surged forward and overcame the cordon of policemen. In their enthusiasm, I was jostled and a bit shaken, and at one point I lost my shoe in the general confusion. When things began to calm down a few minutes later, I found that neither my shoe nor my wife could be located. Finally, after nearly half an hour, Winnie was brought onto the stage with me, quite cross that she had been lost. I was not able to even address the crowd, for they were shouting "Mandela! Mandela!" so furiously that I could not be heard above the din, and finally I left, without my shoe and with an uncharacteristically silent wife.

While in Cairo I held a press conference at which I said the ANC was "prepared to consider a cessation of hostilities." This was a signal to the government. Both the ANC and the government were engaged in creating a climate whereby negotiations would succeed. While the ANC was demanding that the government normalize the situation in the country by ending the State of Emergency, releasing all political prisoners, and repealing all apartheid laws, the government was intent on first persuading the ANC to suspend the armed struggle. While we were not yet ready to announce such a suspension, we wanted to provide Mr. de Klerk with enough encouragement to pursue his reformist strategies. We knew that we would eventually suspend the armed struggle, in part to facilitate more serious negotiations and in part to allow Mr. de Klerk to go to his own constituency, the white voters of South Africa, and say, "Look, here are the fruits of my policy."

After my last stop in Africa, I flew to Stockholm to visit Oliver. Seeing my old friend and law partner was the reunion I most looked forward to. Oliver was not well, but when we met we were like two young boys in the veld who took strength from our love for each other. We began by talking of old times, but when we were alone, the first subject he raised was the leadership of the organization. "Nelson," he said, "you must now take over as president of the ANC. I have been merely keeping the job warm for you." I refused, telling him that he had led the organization in exile far better than I ever could have. It was neither fair nor democratic for a transfer to occur in such a manner. "You have been elected by the organization as the president," I said. "Let us wait for an election; then the organization can decide." Oliver protested, but I would not budge. It was a sign of his humility and selflessness that he wanted to appoint me president, but it was not in keeping with the principles of the ANC.

In April 1990, I flew to London to attend a concert at Wembley, held in my honor. Many international artists, most of whom I never knew, were performing and the event was to be televised worldwide. I took advantage of this to thank the world's anti-apartheid forces for the tremendous work they had done in pressing for sanctions, for the release of myself and fellow political prisoners, and for the genuine support and solidarity they had shown the oppressed people of my country.

# 103

WHEN I EMERGED from prison, Chief Mangosuthu Buthelezi, the head of the Inkatha Freedom Party and the chief minister of KwaZulu, was one of the premier players on the South African political stage. But within ANC circles, he was a far from popular figure. Chief Buthelezi was descended from the great Zulu king Cetywayo, who had defeated the British at the Battle of Isandhlwana in 1879. As a young man, he attended Fort Hare and then joined the ANC Youth League. I saw him as one of the movement's up-coming young leaders. He had become chief minister of the KwaZulu homeland with the tacit support of the ANC, and even his launching of Inkatha as a Zulu cultural organization was un-opposed by the organization. But over the years, Chief Buthelezi drifted away from the ANC. Though he resolutely opposed apart-heid and refused to allow KwaZulu to become an "independent" homeland as the government wished, he was a thorn in the side of the democratic movement. He opposed the armed struggle. He criticized the 1976 Soweto uprising. He campaigned against inter-national sanctions. He challenged the idea of a unitary state of South Africa. Yet, Chief Buthelezi had consistently called for my release and refused to negotiate with the government until I and other political prisoners were liberated.

Chief Buthelezi was one of the first people I telephoned after my release to thank him for his long-standing support. My inclination was to meet with the chief as soon as possible to try to resolve our differences. During my initial visit to Lusaka, I brought up the idea of such a meeting and it was voted down. While I was at Victor Verster, Walter had been invited by the Zulu king, Goodwill Zweli-thini, to visit him in Ulundi, KwaZulu's capital, and I urged him to accept. I thought it was an excellent opportunity to influence the head of one of the most respected and powerful royal families in the country. The visit was tentatively approved by the NEC provided Walter went to the king's palace in Nongoma; it was thought that going to Ulundi would suggest recognition of the authority of the homeland.

When I returned from Lusaka I telephoned both Chief Buthelezi and the king, and explained that Walter would be coming to see the king, not in Ulundi but at Nongoma. The king said he would not accept Walter coming to see him anywhere else but in the capital. "I am the king," he said. "I have invited him to see me in Ulundi, and he has no right to say I will see you elsewhere." "Your Majesty," I said, "we are facing a wall of opposition from our membership who did not want Mr. Sisulu to go to KwaZulu at all. We managed to get this compromise approved, surely you can bend as well." But he could not, and he refused to see Walter.

Relations deteriorated after this, and in May, I persuaded the ANC of the need for me to make a visit to the king and Buthelezi. The king approved, but a week or so before the visit I received a letter from him saying I must come alone. This proved to be the last straw, and the NEC would not give in to such a demand. I told the king that I could not come unless I was accompanied by my colleagues; the king regarded this as another slight and canceled the visit.

My goal was to forge an independent relationship with the king, separate from my relationship with Chief Buthelezi. The king was the true hereditary leader of the Zulus, who loved and respected him. Fidelity to the king was far more widespread in KwaZulu than allegiance to Inkatha.

In the meantime, Natal became a killing ground. Heavily armed Inkatha supporters had in effect declared war on ANC strongholds across the Natal Midlands region and around Pietermaritzburg. Entire villages were set alight, dozens of people were killed, hundreds were wounded, and thousands became refugees. In March 1990 alone, 230 people lost their lives in this internecine violence. In Natal, Zulu was murdering Zulu, for Inkatha members and ANC partisans are Zulus. In February, only two weeks after my release, I went to Durban and spoke to a crowd of over 100,000 people at King's Park, almost all of whom were Zulus. I pleaded with them to lay down their arms, to take each other's hands in peace: "Take your guns, your knives, and your pangas, and throw them into the sea! Close down the death factories. End this war now!" But my call fell on deaf ears. The fighting and dying continued.

I was so concerned that I was willing to go to great lengths to meet Chief Buthelezi. In March, after one particularly horrifying spasm of violence, I announced on my own that I would meet Chief Buthelezi at a mountain hamlet outside of Pietermaritzburg. On a personal level, my relations with Chief Buthelezi were close and respectful, and I hoped to capitalize on that. But I found that such a meeting was anathema to ANC leaders in Natal. They considered it dangerous and vetoed my meeting. I did go to Pietermaritzburg, where I saw the burned remains of ANC supporters and tried to comfort their grieving families, but I did not see Chief Buthelezi.

# 104

IN MARCH, after much negotiation within our respective parties, we scheduled our first face-to-face meeting with Mr. de Klerk and the government. These were to be "talks about talks," and the meetings were to begin in early April. But on March 26, in Sebokeng Township, about thirty miles south of Johannesburg, the police opened fire without warning on a crowd of ANC demonstrators, killing twelve and wounding hundreds more, most of them shot in the back as they were fleeing. Police had used live ammunition in dealing with the demonstrators, which was intolerable. The police claimed that their lives were endangered, but many demonstrators were shot in the back and had no weapons. You cannot be in danger from an unarmed man who is running away from you. The right to assemble and demonstrate in support of our just demands was not a favor to be granted by the government at its discretion. This sort of action angered me like no other, and I told the press that every white policeman in South Africa regarded every black person as a military target. After consultation with the NEC, I announced the suspension of our talks and warned Mr. de Klerk that he could not "talk about negotiations on the one hand and murder our people on the other."

But despite the suspension of our official talks, with the approval of the leadership, I met privately with Mr. de Klerk in Cape Town in order to keep up the momentum for negotiations. Our discussions centered primarily on a new date, and we agreed on early May. I brought up the appalling behavior at Sebokeng and the police's unequal treatment of blacks and whites; police used live ammunition with black demonstrators, while they never unsheathed their guns at white right-wing protests.

The government was in no great rush to begin negotiations; they were counting on the euphoria that greeted my release to die down. They wanted to allow time for me to fall on my face and show that the former prisoner hailed as a savior was a highly fallible man who had lost touch with the present situation.

Despite his seemingly progressive actions, Mr. de Klerk was by no means the great emancipator. He was a gradualist, a careful pragmatist. He did not make any of his reforms with the intention of putting himself out of power. He made them for precisely the opposite reason: to ensure power for the Afrikaner in a new dispensation. He was not yet prepared to negotiate the end of white rule.

His goal was to create a system of power-sharing based on group rights, which would preserve a modified form of minority power in South Africa. He was decidedly opposed to majority rule, or "simple majoritarianism" as he sometimes called it, because that would end white domination in a single stroke. We knew early on that the government was fiercely opposed to a winner-takes-all Westminster parliamentary system, and advocated instead a system of proportional representation with built-in structural guarantees for the white minority. Although he was prepared to allow the black majority to vote and create legislation, he wanted to retain a minority veto. From the start I would have no truck with this plan. I described it to Mr. de Klerk as apartheid in disguise, a "loser-takes-all" system.

The Nationalists' long-term strategy to overcome our strength was to build an anti-ANC alliance with the Inkatha Freedom Party and to lure the Coloured Afrikaans-speaking voters of the Cape to a new National Party. From the moment of my release, they began wooing both Buthelezi and the Coloured voters of the Cape. The government attempted to scare the Coloured population into thinking the ANC was anti-Coloured. They supported Chief Buthelezi's desire to retain Zulu power and identity in a new South Africa by preaching to him the doctrine of group rights and federalism.

The first round of talks with the government was held over three days in early May. Our delegation consisted of Walter Sisulu, Joe Slovo, Alfred Nzo, Thabo Mbeki, Ahmed Kathrada, Joe Modise, Ruth Mompati, Archie Gumede, Reverend Beyers Naude, Cheryl Carolus, and myself. The setting was Groote Schuur, the Cape Dutch-style mansion that was the residence of South Africa's first colonial governors, among them Cecil Rhodes. Some of our delegation joked that we were being led into an ambush on the enemy's ground.

But the talks, contrary to expectation, were conducted with seriousness and good humor. Historic enemies who had been fighting each other for three centuries met and shook hands. Many wondered out loud why such discussions had not taken place long before. The government had granted temporary indemnities to Joe Slovo, the general secretary of the Communist Party, and Joe Modise, the commander of MK, and to see these two men shaking hands with the National Party leaders who had demonized them for decades was extraordinary. As Thabo Mbeki later said to reporters, each side had discovered that the other did not have horns.

The very fact of the talks themselves was a significant milestone in the history of our country; as I pointed out, the meeting represented not only what the ANC had been seeking for so many years, but an end to the master/servant relationship that characterized black and white relations in South Africa. We had not come to the meeting as supplicants or petitioners, but as fellow South Africans who merited an equal place at the table.

The first day was more or less a history lesson. I explained to our counterparts that the ANC from its inception in 1912 had always sought negotiations with the government in power. Mr. de Klerk, for his part, suggested that the system of separate development had been conceived as a benign idea, but had not worked in practice. For that, he said, he was sorry, and hoped the negotiations would make amends. It was not an apology for apartheid, but it went further than any other National Party leader ever had.

The primary issue discussed was the definition of political prisoners and political exiles. The government argued for a narrow definition, wanting to restrict the number of our people who would qualify for an indemnity. We argued for the broadest possible definition and said that any person who was convicted of an offense that was politically motivated should qualify for an indemnity. We could not agree on a mutually satisfactory definition of "politically motivated" crimes, and this would be an issue that would bedevil us for quite a while to come.

At the end of the three-day meeting, we agreed on what became known as the Groote Schuur Minute, pledging both sides to a peaceful process of negotiations and committing the government to lifting the State of Emergency, which they shortly did everywhere except for the violence-ridden province of Natal. We agreed to set up a joint working group to resolve the many obstacles that still stood in our way.

When it came to constitutional issues, we told the government we were demanding an elected constituent assembly to draw up a new constitution; we believed that the men and women creating the constitution should be the choice of the people themselves. But before the election of an assembly, it was necessary to have an interim government that could oversee the transition until a new government was elected. The government could not be both player and referee, as it was now. We advocated the creation of a multiparty negotiating conference to set up the interim government and set out the guiding principles for the functioning of a constituent assembly.

# 105

ALTHOUGH I HAD WANTED to journey to Qunu immediately after my release from prison, it was not until April that I was able to go. I could not pick up and leave whenever I wanted; security had to be arranged, as well as speeches prepared for local organizations. By April, the ANC and General Bantu Holomisa, the military leader of the Transkei and an ANC loyalist, had arranged for a visit. But what was foremost in my mind and heart was paying my respects to my mother's grave.

I went first to Qunu and the site where my mother was buried. Her grave was simple and unadorned, covered only by a few stones and some upturned bricks, no different from the other graves at Qunu. I find it difficult to describe my feelings: I felt regret that I had been unable to be with her when she died, remorse that I had not been able to look after her properly during her life, and a longing for what might have been had I chosen to live my life differently.

In seeing my village again after so many years, I was greatly struck by what had changed and what had not. When I had been young, the people of Qunu were not political at all; they were unaware of the struggle for African rights. People accepted life as it was and did not dream of changing it. But when I returned I heard the schoolchildren of Qunu singing songs about Oliver Tambo and Umkhonto we Sizwe, and I marveled at how knowledge of the struggle had by then seeped into every corner of African society.

What had endured was the warmth and simplicity of the community, which took me back to my days as a boy. But what disturbed me was that the villagers seemed as poor if not poorer than they had been then. Most people still lived in simple huts with dirt floors, with no electricity and no running water. When I was young, the village was tidy, the water pure, and the grass green and unsullied as far as the eye could see. Kraals were swept, the topsoil was conserved, fields were neatly divided. But now the village was unswept, the water polluted, and the countryside littered with plastic bags and wrappers. We had not known of plastic when I was a boy, and though it surely improved life in some ways, its presence in Qunu appeared to me to be a kind of blight. Pride in the community seemed to have vanished.

That month, I had another homecoming: I returned to Robben Island in order to persuade twenty-five MK political prisoners to accept the government's offer of amnesty and leave the island. Though I had left the island eight years before, my memories of prison were still fresh and untinged by nostalgia. After all the years of being visited by others, it was a curious sensation to be a visitor on Robben Island.

But that day, I did not have much opportunity to sight-see for I met immediately with the men protesting the government offer of amnesty. They maintained that they would leave only after a victory on the battlefield, not the negotiating table. They were fiercely opposed to this particular settlement, in which they had to enumerate their crimes before receiving indemnity. They accused the ANC of retreating from the Harare Declaration demand for an unconditional, blanket amnesty covering political prisoners and exiles. One man said, "Madiba, I have been fighting the government all my life, and now I have to ask for a pardon from them."

I could sympathize with their arguments, but they were being unrealistic. Every soldier would like to defeat his enemy on the field, but in this case, such a victory was out of reach. The struggle was now at the negotiating table. I argued that they were not advancing the cause by remaining in jail. They could be of greater service outside than inside. In the end, they agreed to accept the government's offer.

\*　　　\*　　　\*

In early June, I was scheduled to leave on a six-week tour of Europe and North America. Before going, I met privately with Mr. de Klerk, who wanted to discuss the issue of sanctions. Based on the changes he had made in South Africa, he asked me to mute the call for the continuation of international sanctions. While we were mindful of what Mr. de Klerk had done, in our view sanctions remained the best lever to force him to do more. I was aware that the European Community and the States were inclined to relax sanctions based on Mr. de Klerk's reforms. I explained to Mr. de Klerk that we could not tell our supporters to relax sanctions until he had completely dismantled apartheid and a transitional government was in place. While he was disappointed at my response, he was not surprised.

The first leg of the trip took Winnie and me to Paris, where we were treated in very grand style by François Mitterrand and his charming wife, Danielle, a longtime ANC supporter. This was not my first trip to the European mainland, but I was still entranced by the beauties of the Old World. Although I do not want to stint on the loveliness of the City of Light, the most important event that occurred while I was in France was that the government announced the suspension of the State of Emergency. I was pleased, but well aware that they had taken this action while I was in Europe in order to undermine my call for sanctions.

After stops in Switzerland, Italy, and the Netherlands, I went to England, where I spent two days visiting with Oliver and Adelaide. My next stop was the United States, but I would be returning to England on my way back to South Africa, which is when I was scheduled to meet with Mrs. Thatcher. As a courtesy, however, I phoned her before I left, and Mrs. Thatcher proceeded to give me a stern but well-meaning lecture: she said she had been following my travels and noting how many events I attended each day. "Mr. Mandela, before we discuss any issues," she said, "I must warn you that your schedule is too heavy. You must cut it in half. Even a man half your age would have trouble meeting the demands that are being made on you. If you keep this up, you will not come out of America alive. That is my advice to you."

I had read about New York City since I was a young man, and finally to see it from the bottom of its great glass-and-concrete canyons while millions upon millions of pieces of ticker tape came floating down was a breathtaking experience. It was reported that as many as a million people personally witnessed our procession through the city, and to see the support and enthusiasm they gave to the anti-apartheid struggle was truly humbling. I had always read that New York was a hard-hearted place, but I felt the very opposite of that on my first full day in the city.

The following day I went up to Harlem, an area that had assumed legendary proportions in my mind since the 1950s when I watched young men in Soweto emulate the fashions of Harlem dandies. Harlem, as my wife said, was the Soweto of America. I spoke to a great crowd at Yankee Stadium, telling them that an unbreakable umbilical cord connected black South Africans and black Americans, for we were together children of Africa. There was a kinship between the two, I said, that had been inspired by such great Americans as W. E. B. Du Bois, Marcus Garvey, and Martin Luther King Jr. As a young man, I idolized the Brown Bomber, Joe Louis, who took on not only his opponents in the ring but racists outside of it. In prison, I followed the struggle of black Americans against racism, discrimination, and economic inequality. To us, Harlem symbolized the strength of resistance and the beauty of black pride. This was brought home to me by a young man I had seen the previous day who wore a T-shirt that read, "BLACK BY NATURE, PROUD BY CHOICE." We were linked by nature, I said, but we were proud of each other by choice.

After journeying to Memphis and Boston, I went to Washington to address a joint session of Congress and attend a private meeting with President Bush. I thanked the U.S. Congress for its anti-apartheid legislation and said the new South Africa hoped to live up to the values that created the two chambers before which I spoke. I said that as freedom fighters we could not have known of such men as George Washington, Abraham Lincoln, and Thomas Jefferson "and not been moved to act as they were moved to act." I also delivered a strong message on sanctions, for I knew that the Bush administration felt it was time to loosen them. I urged Congress not to do so.

Even before meeting Mr. Bush, I had formed a positive impression of him, for he was the first world leader to telephone me with congratulations after I left prison. From that point on, President Bush included me on his short list of world leaders whom he briefed on important issues. In person, he was just as warm and thoughtful, though we differed markedly on the issues of the armed struggle and sanctions. He was a man with whom one could disagree and then shake hands.

From the United States I proceeded to Canada, where I had a meeting with Prime Minister Mulroney and also addressed their Parliament. We were due to go to Ireland next, and before crossing the Atlantic, our plane, a small jet, stopped for refueling in a remote place above the Arctic Circle called Goose Bay. I felt like having a walk in the brisk air, and as I was strolling on the tarmac, I noticed some people standing by the airport fence. I asked a Canadian official who they were. Eskimos, he said.

In my seventy-two years on earth I had never met an Innuit and never imagined that I would. I headed over to that fence and found a dozen or so young people, in their late teens, who had come out to the airport because they had heard our plane was going to stop there. I had read about the Innuit (the name "Eskimo" was given to them by the colonists) as a boy, and the impression I received from the racist colonialist texts was that they were a backward culture.

But in talking with these bright young people, I learned that they had watched my release on television and were familiar with events in South Africa. "Viva ANC!" one of them said. The Innuit are an aboriginal people historically mistreated by a white settler population; there were parallels between the plights of black South Africans and the Innuit people. What struck me so forcefully was how small the planet had become during my decades in prison; it was amazing to me that a teenaged Innuit living at the roof of the world could watch the release of a political prisoner on the southern tip of Africa. Television had shrunk the world, and had in the process become a great weapon for eradicating ignorance and promoting democracy.

After Dublin, I went to London, where I had a three-hour meeting with Mrs. Thatcher. Standing out in the cold talking with the young Innuits had given me a chill. On the day I was to see Mrs. Thatcher it was wintry and raining, and as we were leaving, Winnie told me I must take a raincoat. We were already in the lobby of the hotel, and if I went back for my coat we would be late. I am a stickler about punctuality, not only because I think it is a sign of respect to the person you are meeting but in order to combat the Western stereotype of Africans as being notoriously tardy. I told Winnie we did not have time, and instead I stood out in the rain signing autographs for some children. By the time I got to Mrs. Thatcher I was feeling poorly, and I was later diagnosed as having a mild case of pneumonia.

But it did not interfere with our meeting, except that she chided me like a schoolmarm for not taking her advice and cutting down on my schedule. Even though Mrs. Thatcher was on the opposite side of the ANC on many issues, such as sanctions, she was always a forthright and solicitous lady. In our meeting that day, though, I could not make the slightest bit of headway with her on the question of sanctions.

# 106

WHEN I RETURNED to South Africa in July, after brief trips to Uganda, Kenya, and Mozambique, I requested a meeting with Mr. de Klerk. Violence in the country was worsening; the death toll of 1990 was already over fifteen hundred, more than all the political deaths of the previous year. After conferring with my colleagues, I felt it necessary to speed up the process of normalization. Our country was bleeding to death, and we had to move ahead faster.

Mr. de Klerk's lifting the State of Emergency in June seemed to set the stage for a resumption of talks, but in July, government security forces arrested about forty members of the ANC, including Mac Maharaj, Pravin Gordhan, Siphiwe Nyanda, and Billy Nair, claiming that they were part of a Communist Party plot called Operation Vula to overthrow the government. De Klerk called for an urgent meeting with me and read to me from documents he claimed had been confiscated in the raid. I was taken aback because I knew nothing about it.

After the meeting I wanted an explanation and called Joe Slovo. Joe explained that the passages read by Mr. de Klerk had been taken out of context and that Vula was a moribund operation. But the government was intent on using this discovery to try to pry the ANC from the SACP and keep Joe Slovo out of the negotiations. I went back to Mr. de Klerk and told him that he had been misled by his own police and that we had no intention of parting ways with the SACP or dropping Joe Slovo from our negotiating team.

In the middle of July, shortly before a scheduled meeting of the National Executive Committee, Joe Slovo came to me privately with a proposition. He suggested we voluntarily suspend the armed struggle in order to create the right climate to move the negotiation process forward. Mr. de Klerk, he said, needed to show his supporters that his policy had brought benefits to the country. My first reaction was negative; I did not think the time was ripe.

But the more I thought about it, the more I realized that we had to take the initiative and this was the best way to do it. I also recognized that Joe, whose credentials as a radical were above dispute, was precisely the right person to make the proposal. He could not be accused of being a dupe of the government or of having gone soft. The following day I told Joe that if he brought up the idea in the NEC, I would support him.

When Joe raised the idea in the NEC the next day there were some who firmly objected, claiming that we were giving de Klerk's supporters a reward but not our own people. But I defended the proposal, saying the purpose of the armed struggle was always to bring the government to the negotiating table, and now we had done so. I argued that the suspension could always be withdrawn, but it was necessary to show our good faith. After several hours, our view prevailed.

This was a controversial move within the ANC. Although MK was not active, the aura of the armed struggle had great meaning for many people. Even when cited merely as a rhetorical device, the armed struggle was a sign that we were actively fighting the enemy. As a result, it had a popularity out of proportion to what it had achieved on the ground.

On August 6, in Pretoria, the ANC and the government signed what became known as the Pretoria Minute, in which we agreed to suspend the armed struggle. As I was to say over and over to our followers: we suspended armed action, we did not terminate the armed struggle. The agreement also set forth target dates for the release of political prisoners and the granting of certain types of indemnity. The process of indemnity was scheduled to be completed by May 1991, and the government also agreed to review the Internal Security Act.

*          *          *

Of all the issues that hindered the peace process, none was more devastating and frustrating than the escalation of violence in the country. We had all hoped that as negotiations got under way, violence would decrease. But in fact the opposite happened. The police and security forces were making very few arrests. People in the townships were accusing them of aiding and abetting the violence. It was becoming more and more clear to me that there was connivance on the part of the security forces. Many of the incidents indicated to me that the police, rather than quelling violence, were fomenting it.

Over the next few months, I visited townships all across the violence-racked Vaal Triangle south of Johannesburg, comforting wounded people and grieving families. Over and over again, I heard the same story: the police and the defense force were destabilizing the area. I was told of the police confiscating weapons one day in one area, and then Inkatha forces attacking our people with those stolen weapons the next day. We heard stories of the police escorting Inkatha members to meetings and on their attacks.

In September, I gave a speech in which I said there was a hidden hand behind the violence and suggested that there was a mysterious "Third Force," which consisted of renegade men from the security forces who were attempting to disrupt the negotiations. I could not say who the members of the Third Force were, for I did not know them myself, but I was certain that they existed and that they were murderously effective in their targeting of the ANC and the liberation struggle.

I came to this conclusion after becoming personally involved in two specific incidents. In July of 1990, the ANC received information that hostel dwellers belonging to the Inkatha Freedom Party were planning a major attack on ANC members in Sebokeng Township in the Vaal Triangle on July 22. Through our attorneys, we notified the minister of law and order, the commissioner of police, and the regional commissioner, warning them of the impending attacks and urging them to take the proper action. We asked the police to prevent armed Inkatha members from entering the township to attend an Inkatha rally.

On July 22, busloads of armed Inkatha members, escorted by

police vehicles, entered Sebokeng in broad daylight. A rally was held, after which the armed men went on a rampage, murdering approximately thirty people in a dreadful and grisly attack. I visited the area the next day and witnessed scenes I have never before seen and never hope to see again. At the morgue were bodies of people who had been hacked to death; a woman had both her breasts cut off with a machete. Whoever these killers were, they were animals.

I requested a meeting with Mr. de Klerk the following day. When I saw him, I angrily demanded an explanation. "You were warned in advance," I told him, "and yet did nothing. Why is that? Why is it that there have been no arrests? Why have the police sat on their hands?" I then told him that in any other nation where there was a tragedy of this magnitude, when more than thirty people were slain, the head of state would make some statement of condolence, yet he had not uttered a word. He had no reply to what I said. I asked de Klerk to furnish me with an explanation, and he never did.

The second incident occurred in November, when a group of Inkatha members entered a squatter camp known as Zonkizizwe (Zulu for "the place where all nations are welcome") outside the city of Germiston, east of Johannesburg, and drove ANC people out, killing a number of them in the process. Inkatha members then proceeded to occupy the abandoned shacks and confiscate all the property. Residents of the area said that the Inkatha members were accompanied by the police. Once again, in the wake of this tragedy, the police and the government took no action. Black life in South Africa had never been so cheap.

Again, I met with Mr. de Klerk and his minister of law and order, Adriaan Vlok. Again, I asked Mr. de Klerk why no action by the police had been taken in the aftermath of these crimes. I said the attackers could easily be found because they were now occupying the shacks of the people they had killed. Mr. de Klerk asked Mr. Vlok for an explanation and then Vlok, in a rather rude tone, asked me on whose property the shacks were located, the implication being that these people were squatters and therefore had no rights. In fact, I told him, the land had been made available to these people by the local authorities. His attitude was like that of many Afrikaners who simply believed that black tribes had been killing each other since time immemorial. Mr. de Klerk again told me he would investigate and respond, but never did.

During this time, the government took another action that added fuel to the flames. It introduced a regulation permitting Zulus to carry so-called traditional weapons to political rallies and meetings in Natal and elsewhere. These weapons, assegais, which are spears, and knobkerries, wooden sticks with a heavy wooden head, are actual weapons with which Inkatha members killed ANC members. This gave me grave doubts about Mr. de Klerk's peaceful intentions.

Those opposed to negotiations benefited from the violence, which always seemed to flare up when the government and the ANC were moving toward an agreement. These forces sought to ignite a war between the ANC and Inkatha, and I believe many members of Inkatha connived at this as well. Many in the government, including Mr. de Klerk, chose to look the other way or ignore what they knew was going on under their noses. We had no doubts that men at the highest levels of the police and the security forces were aiding the Third Force. These suspicions were later confirmed by newspaper reports disclosing that the South African police had secretly funded Inkatha.

As the violence continued to spiral, I began to have second thoughts about the suspension of the armed struggle. Many of the people in the ANC were restive, and in September, at a press conference, I said that the continuing violence might necessitate taking up arms once more. The situation looked very grim, and any understanding that had been achieved with the government seemed lost.

# 107

IN DECEMBER OF 1990 Oliver returned to South Africa after being in exile from his native land for three decades. It was wonderful to have him near. He returned for an ANC consultative conference in Johannesburg, which was attended by over fifteen hundred delegates from forty-five different regions, home and abroad.

At the meeting, I spoke in tribute to Oliver as the man who had led the ANC during its darkest hours and never let the flame go out. Now, he had ushered us to the brink of a future that looked bright and hopeful. During the twenty-seven years that I was in prison, it was Oliver who saved the ANC, and then built it into an international organization with power and influence. He took up the reins when most of its leaders were either in prison or in exile. He was a soldier, a diplomat, a statesman.

Although I criticized the government for its orchestrated campaign of counterrevolutionary activities, it was Oliver's address that created a storm. He opened the meeting with a controversial speech in which he called for our sanctions policy to be reevaluated. The ANC, he maintained, faced "international marginalization" unless it took the initiative to deescalate sanctions. The European Community had already begun to scale back sanctions. The countries in the West, particularly the United Kingdom and the United States, wanted to reward Mr. de Klerk for his reforms, believing that this would encourage him to go further. We felt this was the wrong strategy, but we had to recognize international realities.

Although Oliver's speech had been discussed and approved by the NEC, his proposal was met with indignation by ANC militants, who insisted that sanctions must be maintained unchanged. The conference decided to retain the sanctions policy as it was.

I myself was the target of complaints by those who charged that the negotiators were out of touch with the grass roots and that we spent more time with National Party leaders than our own people. I was also criticized at the conference for engaging in "personal diplomacy" and not keeping the rank-and-file of the organization informed. As a leader of a mass organization, one must listen to the people, and I agreed that we had been remiss in keeping the entire organization informed about the course of the negotiations. But I also knew the delicacy of our talks with the government; any agreements that we arrived at depended in part on their confidentiality. Although I accepted the criticism, I believed we had no alternative but to proceed on the same course. I knew that I had to be more inclusive, brief more people as to our progress, and I proceeded with that in mind.

Each day, each weekend, the newspapers were filled with fresh reports of new and bloody violence in our communities and townships. It was clear that violence was the number one issue in the country.

In many communities in Natal and on the Reef around Johannesburg, a poisonous mixture of crime, political rivalries, police brutality, and shadowy death squads made life brutish and untenable. As long as the violence was not dealt with, the progress to a new dispensation would remain uneven and uncertain.

To try to arrest the spiral of violence, I contacted Chief Buthelezi to arrange a meeting. We met at Durban's Royal Hotel in January. Chief Buthelezi spoke first to assembled delegates and media and in the process opened old wounds rather than healing them. He catalogued the verbal attacks the ANC had made on him and criticized the ANC's negotiating demands. When it was my turn to speak, I chose not to respond to his remarks but to thank him for his efforts over many years to secure my release from prison. I cited our long relationship and underlined the many matters that united our two organizations rather than divided us.

Progress was made during our private talks, and Chief Buthelezi and I signed an agreement that contained a code of conduct covering the behavior of our two organizations. It was a fair accord, and I suspect that if it had been implemented it would indeed have helped to staunch the bloodletting. But as far as I could tell, Inkatha never made any effort to implement the accord, and there were violations as well on our own side.

The violence continued between our two organizations. Each month people were dying by the hundreds. In March, Inkatha members launched an attack in Alexandra Township north of Johannesburg in which forty-five people were killed over three days of fighting. Again, no one was arrested.

I could not sit idly by as the violence continued, and I sought another meeting with Chief Buthelezi. In April I went down to Durban and we again made strong statements and signed another agreement. But again, the ink was no sooner dry than it was drenched in blood. I was more convinced than ever that the government was behind much of the violence and the violence was impeding the negotiations. Mr. de Klerk's failure to respond put our own relationship in jeopardy.

In April, at a two-day meeting of the National Executive Committee, I discussed my doubts about Mr. de Klerk. The NEC believed that the government was behind the violence and that the violence was upsetting the climate for negotiations. In an open letter to the government, we called for the dismissal of Magnus Malan, the minister of defense, and Adriaan Vlok, the minister of law and order; the banning of the carrying of traditional weapons in public; the phasing out of the migrant-worker hostels, where so many Inkatha members lived in the townships around Johannesburg; the dismantling of secret government counterinsurgency units; and the appointment of an independent commission to probe complaints of misconduct on the part of the security forces.

We gave the government until May to meet our demands. Mr. de Klerk responded by calling for a multiparty conference on violence to be held in May, but I replied that this was pointless since the government knew precisely what it had to do to end the violence. In May, we announced the suspension of talks with the government.

In July 1991, the ANC held its first annual conference inside South Africa in thirty years. The conference was attended by 2,244 voting delegates who were democratically elected at ANC branches at home and abroad. At the conference I was elected president of the ANC without opposition. Cyril Ramaphosa was elected secretary-general, evidence that the torch was being passed from an older generation of leadership to a younger one. Cyril, whom I met only upon my release from prison, was a worthy successor to a long line of notable ANC leaders. He was probably the most accomplished negotiator in the ranks of the ANC, a skill he honed as secretary-general of the National Union of Mine Workers.

In my speech I expressed my appreciation for the great honor that had been bestowed on me, and spoke of how difficult it would be to follow in the large footsteps of my predecessor, Oliver Tambo. Though we were then at loggerheads with the government, negotiations in and of themselves, I said, constituted a victory. The mere fact that the government was engaged in negotiations at all was a sign that they did not have the strength to sustain apartheid. I reiterated that the process would not be smooth, as we were dealing with politicians who do not want to negotiate themselves out of power. "The point which must be clearly understood is that the struggle is not over, and negotiations themselves are a theater of struggle, subject to advances and reverses as any other form of struggle."

But negotiations could not wait. It was never in our interest to prolong the agony of apartheid for any reason. It was necessary, I said, to create a transitional government as soon as possible.

The conference underlined one of the most important and demanding tasks before the ANC: to transform an illegal underground liberation movement to a legal mass political party. For thirty years, the ANC had functioned clandestinely in South Africa; those habits and techniques were deeply ingrained. We had to reconstruct an entire organization, from the smallest local branch to the national executive. And we had to do so in a matter of months during a period of extraordinary change.

A large part of the ANC and Communist Party leadership had been in exile. Most of them had returned for the conference in July. They were unfamiliar with present-day South Africa; it was a newfound land for them as well as me. There was, however, an extraordinary crop of young leaders of the United Democratic Front and COSATU who had remained in the country, who knew the political situation in a way that we did not. These organizations had in some measure been surrogates for the ANC inside South Africa during the 1980s. The ANC had to integrate these men and women into the organization as well.

We faced not only logistical problems but philosophical ones. It is a relatively simple proposition to keep a movement together when you are fighting against a common enemy. But creating a policy when that enemy is across the negotiating table is another matter altogether. In the new ANC, we had to integrate not only many different groups, but many different points of view. We needed to unite the organization around the idea of the negotiations.

In the first seventeen months of legal activity, the ANC had recruited 700,000 members. This was an impressive number, but there was no room for complacency. A proportionately low number of these members were from the rural areas, the regions where the ANC had historically been weakest. At the same time, the National Party was throwing open its doors to nonwhites and was busily recruiting disaffected Coloureds and Indians.

Ever since my release from prison, the state had continued its campaign to discredit my wife. After the alleged kidnapping of four youths who were staying in the Diepkloof house and the death of one of them, Winnie had first been vilified by a whispering campaign and was then charged with four counts of kidnapping and one of assault. The continuing aspersions cast on her character were such that both Winnie and I were eager for her to have her day in court and prove her innocence of the charges.

My wife's formal trial began in February in the Rand Supreme Court in Johannesburg. I attended the trial on the first day, as did many senior figures in the ANC, and I continued to attend as often as I could. I did this both to support my wife and to show my belief in her innocence. She was ably defended by George Bizos, who attempted to demonstrate that Winnie had no involvement with either the kidnappings or the beatings.

After three and a half months, the court found her guilty of kidnapping charges and being an accessory to assault. The judge, however, acknowledged that she had not taken part in any assault herself. She was sentenced to six years in prison, but was released on bail pending her appeal. As far as I was concerned, verdict or no verdict, her innocence was not in doubt.

# 108

ON DECEMBER 20, 1991, after more than a year and a half of talks about talks, the real talks began: CODESA — the Convention for a Democratic South Africa — represented the first formal negotiations forum between the government, the ANC, and other South African parties. All of our previous bilateral discussions had been laying the groundwork for these talks, which took place at the World Trade Centre, a modern exhibition center near Jan Smuts Airport in Johannesburg. CODESA comprised eighteen delegations covering the gamut of South African politics, plus observers from the United Nations, the Commonwealth, the European Community, and the Organization of African Unity. It was the widest cross section of political groups ever gathered in one place in South Africa.

The opening of such talks was an historic occasion, certainly the most important constitutional convention since that of 1909 when the British colonies of the Cape and Natal and the former Boer republics of the Transvaal and the Orange Free State agreed to form a single union. Of course, that convention was not a tribute to democracy but a betrayal of it, for none of the representatives there that day were black. In 1991, the majority of them were.

Our planning delegation, led by Cyril Ramaphosa, and including Joe Slovo and Valli Moosa, had been engaged in weekly discussions with the government on the issues of elections, the constitution, a constituent assembly, and a transitional government. Delegates from twenty different parties including the homeland governments had already agreed on the ground rules for the convention.

The optimism at the opening of the talks could not be dampened even by a few spoilers. The PAC decided to boycott the talks, accusing the ANC and the National Party of conspiring together to set up a multiracial government. This occurred despite the formation, a month before, of the Patriotic Front, an alliance of the ANC, the PAC, and the Azanian People's Organization around a declaration of common goals. The PAC feared democratic elections because they knew such a vote would expose their meager popular support. Chief Buthelezi also boycotted the talks on the grounds that he was not permitted three delegations: for Inkatha, the KwaZulu government, and King Zwelithini. We argued that the king should be above politics, and that if he were included then every tribe in South Africa should be able to send their paramount chief.

There was not only a sense of history at the World Trade Centre, but of self-reliance. Unlike the negotiations preceding new dispensations in African states like Zimbabwe and Angola, which required outside mediators, we in South Africa were settling our differences among ourselves. Mr. de Klerk talked about the need for a transitional, "power-sharing" government on a democratic basis. The National Party's chief delegate to the talks, Dawie de Villiers, even offered an apology for apartheid.

In my own opening remarks, I said that with the dawn of CODESA, progress in South Africa had at last become irreversible. Governments, I said, derive their authority and legitimacy from the consent of the governed, and we had assembled to create such a legitimate authority. I said that CODESA marked the beginning of the road to an elected assembly that would write a new constitution, and I did not see any reason why an election for such a constituent assembly could not occur in 1992. I called on the government to usher in an interim government of national unity to supervise such an election, control the state media and the military, and generally oversee the transition to a new, nonracial, democratic South Africa.

On the convention's first day, the lion's share of the participating parties, including the National Party and the ANC, endorsed a Declaration of Intent, which committed all parties to support an undivided South Africa whose supreme law would be a constitution safeguarded by an independent judiciary. The country's legal system would guarantee equality before the law, and a bill of rights would be drawn up to protect civil liberties. In short, there would be a multiparty democracy based on universal adult suffrage on a common voters' roll. As far as we were concerned, this was the minimum acceptable constitutional threshold for a new South Africa. Inkatha refused to sign on the grounds that the phrase an "undivided" South Africa implied that a federal system was off-limits.

The convention created five working groups that would meet in early 1992 to prepare the way for the second round of CODESA scheduled for May 1992. The groups would explore the question of creating a free political climate, the future of the homelands, the restructuring of the South African Broadcasting Corporation, the examination of various constitutional principles such as federalism, and the creation and installation of an interim government. The parties agreed that decisions would be taken by "sufficient consensus," which was never defined, but in practice meant an agreement between the government and the ANC and a majority of the other parties.

The first day of CODESA 1 was uneventful, until it came to a close. The night before the convention I had been negotiating with Mr. de Klerk on the telephone until after eight in the evening. Mr. de Klerk asked me whether I would agree to permit him to be the final speaker the next day. Though I was scheduled to give the concluding remarks, I told him that I would take up the matter with our National Executive Committee. I did so that evening, and despite their misgivings, I persuaded them to permit Mr. de Klerk to have the last word. I did not see the issue as a vital one, and I was prepared to do Mr. de Klerk the favor.

At the end of the session, all seemed well; I spoke about the importance of the talks and I was followed by Mr. de Klerk. He proceeded to underline the historic significance of the occasion and discuss the need for overcoming mutual distrust. But then Mr. de

Klerk did a curious thing. He began to attack the ANC for not adhering to the agreements that we had made with the government. He began to speak to us like a schoolmaster admonishing a naughty child. He berated the ANC for failing to disclose the location of arms caches and then rebuked us for maintaining a "private army," Umkhonto we Sizwe, in violation of the National Peace Accord of September 1991. In intemperate language, he questioned whether the ANC was honorable enough to abide by any agreements it signed.

This was more than I could tolerate and I would now be damned if I would permit Mr. de Klerk to have the last word. When he finished, the meeting was meant to be over. But the room had grown very quiet; instead of allowing the session to end, I walked to the podium. I could not let his remarks go unchallenged. My voice betrayed my anger.

> I am gravely concerned about the behavior of Mr. de Klerk today. He has launched an attack on the ANC and in doing so he has been less than frank. Even the head of an illegitimate, discredited minority regime, as his is, has certain moral standards to uphold. He has no excuse just because he is the head of such a discredited regime not to uphold moral standards. . . . If a man can come to a conference of this nature and play the type of politics he has played — very few people would like to deal with such a man.
>
> The members of the government persuaded us to allow them to speak last. They were very keen to say the last word here. It is now clear why they did so. He has abused his position, because he hoped that I would not respond. He was completely mistaken. I respond now.

I said it was unacceptable for Mr. de Klerk to speak to us in such language. I reiterated that it was the ANC, not the government, that started the initiative of peace discussions, and it was the government, not the ANC, that time and again failed to live up to its agreements. I had told Mr. de Klerk before that it served no useful purpose to attack the ANC publicly, yet he continued to do so. I noted that we had suspended our armed struggle to show our commitment to peace, yet the government was still colluding with those waging war. We told him that we would turn in our weapons only when we were a part of the government collecting those weapons.

I added that it was apparent the government had a double agenda. They were using the negotiations not to achieve peace, but to score their own petty political gains. Even while negotiating, they were secretly funding covert organizations that committed violence against us. I mentioned the recent revelations about million-rand payoffs to Inkatha that Mr. de Klerk claimed not to have known about. I stated that if a man in his position "doesn't know about such things, then he is not fit to be the head of government."

I knew I had been harsh, but I did not want to capsize the whole ship of negotiations, and I ended on a more conciliatory note.

> I ask him to place his cards on the table face upwards. Let us work together openly. Let there be no secret agendas. Let him not persuade us that he would be the last speaker because he wants to abuse that privilege and attack us in the hope that we won't respond. I am prepared to work with him in spite of all his mistakes.

CODESA convened the following day for its final session, and both Mr. de Klerk and I took pains to show that no irreparable harm had been done. At the beginning of the session, he and I publicly shook hands and said we would work together. But much trust had been lost, and the negotiations were now in a state of disarray.

Six weeks after the opening of CODESA 1, the National Party contested an important by-election in Potchefstroom, a conservative university town in the Transvaal, traditionally the party's stronghold. In a stunning upset, the Nationalists were defeated by the candidate of the right-wing Conservative Party. The Conservatives resolutely opposed the government's policy of negotiations with the ANC, and were composed mainly of Afrikaners who felt that Mr. de Klerk was giving away the store. The election result seemed to cast doubt on Mr. de Klerk's policy of reform and negotiations. The National Party was alarmed; these were their own voters in their own heartland rejecting their policies.

Mr. de Klerk decided to gamble. He announced that as a result of the by-election in Potchefstroom he would call a nationwide referendum for March 17 so that the white people of South Africa could vote on his reform policy and on negotiations with the ANC. He stated that if the referendum was defeated, he would resign from office. The referendum asked a plain and direct question of all white voters over the age of eighteen: "Do you support the continuation of the reform process which the state president began on 2 February 1990 which is aimed at a new constitution through negotiation?"

The ANC opposed the referendum on the principle that it was a vote that excluded all nonwhites. At the same time, we were realistic: we certainly did not want white voters to rebuff Mr. de Klerk's efforts to pursue negotiations. Though we disdained the election on principle, we urged whites to vote yes. We saw such a vote as a signal of support for negotiations, not necessarily for de Klerk.

We watched Mr. de Klerk's campaign with interest and some consternation. He and the National Party conducted a sophisticated, expensive, American-style political campaign accompanied by extensive newspaper and television advertisements, bumper stickers, and colorful rallies. We saw this as a dress rehearsal for the campaign Mr. de Klerk would wage against us.

In the end, 69 percent of the white voters supported negotiations, giving de Klerk a great victory. He felt vindicated; I think the margin even swelled his head a bit. His hand was strengthened, and as a result, the Nationalists toughened their negotiating positions. This was a dangerous strategy.

# 109

ON APRIL 13, 1992, at a press conference in Johannesburg, flanked by my two oldest friends and comrades, Walter and Oliver, I announced my separation from my wife. The situation had grown so difficult that I felt that it was in the best interests of all concerned — the ANC, the family, and Winnie — that we part. Although I discussed the matter with the ANC, the separation itself was made for personal reasons.

I read the following statement.

The relationship between myself and my wife, Comrade Nomzamo Winnie Mandela, has become the subject of much media speculation. I am issuing this statement to clarify the position and in the hope that it will bring an end to further conjecture.

Comrade Nomzamo and myself contracted our marriage at a critical time in the struggle for liberation in our country. Owing to the pressures of our shared commitment to the ANC and the struggle to end apartheid, we were unable to enjoy a normal family life. Despite these pressures our love for each other and our devotion to our marriage grew and intensified. . . .

During the two decades I spent on Robben Island she was an indispensable pillar of support and comfort to myself personally. . . . Comrade Nomzamo accepted the onerous burden of raising our children on her own. . . . She endured the persecutions heaped upon her by the Government with exemplary fortitude and never wavered from her commitment to the freedom struggle. Her tenacity reinforced my personal respect, love and growing affection. It also attracted the admiration of the world at large. My love for her remains undiminished.

However, in view of the tensions that have arisen owing to differences between ourselves on a number of issues in recent months, we have mutually agreed that a separation would be best for each of us. My action was not prompted by the current allegations being made against her in the media. . . . Comrade Nomzamo has and can continue to rely on my unstinting support during these trying moments in her life.

I shall personally never regret the life Comrade Nomzamo and I tried to share together. Circumstances beyond our control however dictated it should be otherwise. I part from my wife with no recriminations. I embrace her with all the love and affection I have nursed for her inside and outside prison from the moment I first met her. Ladies and gentlemen, I hope you will appreciate the pain I have gone through.

Perhaps I was blinded to certain things because of the pain I felt for not being able to fulfill my role as a husband to my wife and a father to my children. But just as I am convinced that my wife's life while I was in prison was more difficult than mine, my own return was also more difficult for her than it was for me. She married a man who soon left her; that man became a myth; and then that myth returned home and proved to be just a man after all.

As I later said at my daughter Zindzi's wedding, it seems to be the destiny of freedom fighters to have unstable personal lives. When your life is the struggle, as mine was, there is little room left for family. That has always been my greatest regret, and the most painful aspect of the choice I made.

"We watched our children growing without our guidance," I said at the wedding, "and when we did come out [of prison], my children said, 'We thought we had a father and one day he'd come back. But to our dismay, our father came back and he left us alone because he has now become the father of the nation.'" To be the father of a nation is a great honor, but to be the father of a family is a greater joy. But it was a joy I had far too little of.

# 110

IN MAY OF 1992, after a four-month interruption, the multiparty conference held its second plenary session at the World Trade Centre. Known as CODESA 2, the talks had been prepared by secret meetings between negotiators from both the ANC and the government as well as talks between the ANC and other parties. These meetings culminated in a final session between me and Mr. de Klerk the day before the opening of CODESA 2, the first time the two of us had met since before CODESA 1.

Only days before CODESA 2 was to begin, the government was hit by two scandals. The first involved the revelation of massive corruption and bribery at the Department of Development Aid, which was responsible for improving black life in the homelands, and the second was the implication of high government security officials in the 1985 murder of four UDF activists, the best known of whom was Matthew Goniwe. These revelations were added to the recent evidence implicating the police in murders in Natal and suspicions that the Department of Military Intelligence was conducting covert operations against the ANC. These two scandals coming together undermined the credibility of the government and strengthened our hand.

Over the previous months, the government had made numerous proposals that fell by the wayside. Most of them, like the idea of a rotating presidency, sought to preserve their power. But through negotiations over the past months, the ANC and government teams had put together a tentative agreement involving a two-stage transitional period to a fully democratic South Africa. In the first stage, a multiparty "transitional executive council" would be appointed from the CODESA delegations to function as a temporary government in order to "level the playing field" for all parties and create an interim constitution. In the second stage, general elections would be held for a constituent assembly and legislature in which all political parties winning 5 percent or more of the vote would participate in the cabinet. Half the members of the assembly would be elected on a national basis and half on a regional one, and the assembly would be empowered both to write a new constitution and to pass legislation. An independent commission would preside over the election and make sure it was free and fair.

Yet there were many matters on which the ANC and the government could not reach agreement, such as the percentage of voting necessary in the assembly to decide constitutional issues and to agree on a bill of rights. Only days before CODESA 2, the government proposed a second body, a senate, composed of regional representatives, as a way of ensuring a minority veto. They also proposed that before all this, CODESA 2 first agree on an interim constitution, which would take months to draw up.

All of this bargaining was going on behind the scenes and by the time CODESA 2 opened on May 15, 1992, prospects for agreement looked bleak. What we disagreed about was threatening all that we had agreed upon. Mr. de Klerk and I had not managed to find a consensus on most of the outstanding issues. The government seemed prepared to wait indefinitely; their thinking was that the longer we waited, the more support we would lose.

The convention was deadlocked at the end of the first day. At that time, the two judges presiding over the talks told Mr. de Klerk and me to meet that evening to attempt to find a compromise. We did meet that night over coffee, and though we did not find a way out of the impasse, we agreed that the negotiations must not founder. "The whole of South Africa and the world is looking at you and me," I told Mr. de Klerk. "Let us save the peace process. Let us reach some kind of agreement. Let us at least fix a date for the next round of talks." We decided that we would each speak the following day in a spirit of constructive compromise.

The next afternoon we spoke in the reverse order that we had agreed to at CODESA 1: Mr. de Klerk first and I last. In his remarks, Mr. de Klerk insisted that the National Party did not seek a "minority veto," but that he did want a system of "checks and balances" so that the majority would not be able "to misuse its power." Although this certainly sounded to me like outright opposition to the idea of majority rule, when I spoke after Mr. de Klerk, I merely said we needed to work in a constructive manner and dispel the tensions around the negotiations.

Despite our attempts to put a positive face on the matter, the convention ended the second day in a stalemate. The impasse, as I saw it, was caused by the National Party's continuing reluctance to submit their fate to the will of the majority. They simply could not cross that hurdle.

Ultimately, CODESA 2 broke down on four fundamental issues: the government's insistence on an unacceptably high percentage of votes in the assembly to approve the constitution (essentially a back-door veto); entrenched regional powers that would be binding on a future constitution; an undemocratic and unelected senate that had veto power over legislation from the main chamber; and a determination to make an interim constitution negotiated by the convention into a permanent constitution.

These were all difficult issues, but not insoluble ones, and I was determined not to let the deadlock at CODESA 2 subvert the negotiation process. The government and the ANC agreed to continue bilateral talks to work toward a solution. But, then, other matters intruded to render this impossible.

With negotiations stalled, the ANC and its allies agreed on a policy of "rolling mass action," which would display to the government the extent of our support around the country and show that the people of South Africa were not prepared to wait forever for their freedom. The mass action consisted of strikes, demonstrations, and boycotts. The date chosen for the start of mass action was June 16, 1992, the anniversary of the 1976 Soweto revolt, and the campaign was meant to culminate in a two-day national strike set for August 3 and 4.

But before that happened, another event occurred that drove the ANC and the government even further apart. On the night of June 17, 1992, a heavily armed force of Inkatha members secretly raided the Vaal township of Boipatong and killed forty-six people. Most of the dead were women and children. It was the fourth mass killing of ANC people that week. People across the country were horrified by the violence and charged the government with complicity. The police did nothing to stop the criminals and nothing to find them; no arrests were made, no investigation begun. Mr. de Klerk said nothing. I found this to be the last straw, and my patience snapped. The government was blocking the negotiations and at the same time waging a covert war against our people. Why then were we continuing to talk with them?

Four days after the murders, I addressed a crowd of twenty thousand angry ANC supporters and told them I had instructed ANC secretary-general Cyril Ramaphosa to suspend direct dealings with the government. I also announced an urgent meeting of the National Executive Committee to examine our options. It was as if we had returned to the dark days of Sharpeville. I likened the behavior of the National Party to the Nazis in Germany, and publicly warned de Klerk that if he sought to impose new measures to restrict demonstrations or free expression, the ANC would launch a nationwide defiance campaign with myself as the first volunteer.

At the rally, I saw signs that read, "MANDELA, GIVE US GUNS" and "VICTORY THROUGH BATTLE NOT TALK." I understood such sentiments; the people were frustrated. They saw no positive results of the negotiations. They were beginning to think that the only way to overthrow apartheid was through the barrel of a gun. After Boipatong, there were those in the NEC who said, "Why did we abandon the armed struggle? We should abandon negotiations instead; they will never advance us to our goal." I was initially sympathetic to this group of hardliners, but gradually realized that there was no alternative to the process. It was what I had been urging for so many years, and I would not turn my back on negotiations. But it was time to cool things down. Mass action in this case was a middle course between armed struggle and negotiations. The people must have an outlet for their anger and frustration, and a mass action campaign was the best way to channel those emotions.

When we informed the government that we were suspending talks, we sent Mr. de Klerk a memo outlining the reasons for our withdrawal. In addition to resolving the constitutional deadlocks at CODESA 2, we demanded that the people responsible for the violence be tracked down and brought to justice and that some mechanism be found for fencing in and policing the hostels, the seedbeds of so much violence. Mr. de Klerk sent us back a memo asking for a face-to-face meeting with me, which we rebuffed. I felt such a meeting would suggest that we had something to talk about, and at the time we did not.

*          *          *

The mass action campaign culminated in a general strike on August 3 and 4 in support of the ANC's negotiation demands and in protest against state-supported violence. More than four million workers stayed home in what was the largest political strike in South African history. The centerpiece of the strike was a march of one hundred thousand people to the Union Buildings in Pretoria, the imposing seat of the South African government, where we held an enormous outdoor rally on the great lawn in front of the buildings. I told the crowd that we one day would occupy these buildings as the first democratically elected government of South Africa.

In the face of this mass action, Mr. de Klerk said that if the ANC made the country ungovernable, the government might be forced to consider some unpleasant options. I warned Mr. de Klerk that any antidemocratic actions would have serious repercussions. It was because of such threats, I said, that it was absolutely critical to set up a transitional government.

Inspired by the success of the mass action campaign, a group within the ANC decided to march on Bisho, the capital of the Ciskei homeland in the eastern Cape, a bantustan led by Brigadier Oupa Gqozo. The Ciskei had a history of repression against the ANC and in 1991 Brigadier Gqozo had declared a State of Emergency in the Ciskei to curtail what he called ANC-sponsored terrorism. On the morning of September 7, 1992, seventy thousand protesters set out on a march to Bisho's main stadium. When a group of marchers attempted to run through an opening in a fence and take a different path to town, the poorly trained homeland troops opened fire on the marchers and killed twenty-nine people, wounding over two hundred. Now Bisho joined Boipatong as a byword for brutality.

Like the old proverb that says that the darkest hour is before the dawn, the tragedy of Bisho led to a new opening in the negotiations. I met with Mr. de Klerk in order to find common ground and avoid a repetition of another tragedy like Bisho. Our respective negotiators began meeting regularly. Both sides were making a good-faith effort to get the negotiations back on track, and on September 26, Mr. de Klerk and I met for an official summit.

On that day, Mr. de Klerk and I signed the Record of Understanding, an agreement which set the mold for all the negotiations that followed. The agreement established an independent body to review police actions, created a mechanism to fence in the hostels, and banned the display of "traditional weapons" at rallies. But the real importance of the Record of Understanding was that it broke the constitutional deadlock of CODESA 2. The government finally agreed to accept a single, elected constitutional assembly, which would adopt a new constitution and serve as a transitional legislature for the new government. All that was left to negotiate was a date for the election of the assembly and the percentage of majorities necessary for it to reach its decisions. We were now aligned on the basic framework that would take the country into a democratic future.

The Record of Understanding prompted Inkatha to announce its withdrawal from all negotiations involving the government and the ANC. The agreement infuriated Chief Buthelezi, who severed relations with the NP and formed an alliance with a group of discredited homeland leaders and white right-wing parties solely concerned with obtaining an Afrikaner homeland. Chief Buthelezi called for the abolition of the Record of Understanding, the ending of CODESA, and the disbanding of Umkhonto we Sizwe.

Just as Joe Slovo had taken the initiative concerning the suspension of the armed struggle, he again took the lead in making another controversial proposal: a government of national unity. In October, Joe published a paper in which he wrote that negotiations with the government were not armistice talks in which we could dictate terms to a defeated enemy. It would probably take years for the ANC to control the levers of government, even after an election. An ANC government would still require much of the present civil service to run the country. Joe proposed a "sunset clause" providing for a government of national unity that would include power-sharing with the National Party for a fixed period of time, an amnesty for security officers, and the honoring of contracts of civil servants. "Power-sharing" was a debased term within the ANC, considered a code-phrase for the government's quest for a minority veto. But in this context it merely meant that the National Party would be part of any popularly elected government provided it polled enough votes.

After much discussion, I supported Joe's proposal and it was endorsed by the National Executive Committee on November 18. The NEC agreed to support power-sharing, provided the minority parties did not have a veto. In December, we began a new round of secret bilateral talks with the government. These were held over a five-day period at a game lodge in the bush. The talks proved to be critical, for they built on the foundation established in the Record of Understanding. At this bush meeting we agreed in principle on a five-year government of national unity in which all parties polling over 5 percent in a general election would be proportionally represented in the cabinet. After five years, the government of national unity would become a simple majority-rule government. In February, the ANC and the government announced an agreement in principle on the five-year government of national unity, a multiparty cabinet, and the creation of a transitional executive council. Elections would be held as early as the end of 1993.

# 111

I HAVE ALWAYS BELIEVED that a man should have a home within sight of the house where he was born. After being released from prison, I set about plans to build a country house for myself in Qunu. By the fall of 1993, the house was complete. It was based on the floor plan of the house I lived in at Victor Verster. People often commented on this, but the answer was simple: the Victor Verster house was the first spacious and comfortable home I ever stayed in, and I liked it very much. I was familiar with its dimensions, so at Qunu I would not have to wander in the night looking for the kitchen.

In April, I was at my house in the Transkei on a brief holiday. On the morning of April 10, I had just gone outside to greet some members of the Transkei police rugby team when my housekeeper ran out and informed me of an urgent telephone call. She was weeping. I excused myself from the young men and learned from a colleague that Chris Hani, the secretary-general of the SACP, the former chief of staff of MK, and one of the most popular figures in the ANC, had been shot at point-blank range in front of his home in Boksburg, Johannesburg, a mostly white working-class suburb that Chris was seeking to integrate.

Chris's death was a blow to me personally and to the movement. He was a soldier and patriot, for whom no task was too small. He was a great hero among the youth of South Africa; a man who spoke their language and to whom they listened. If anyone could mobilize the unruly youth behind a negotiated solution, it was Chris. South Africa was now deprived of one of its greatest sons, a man who would have been invaluable in transforming the country into a new nation.

The country was fragile. There were concerns that Hani's death might trigger a racial war, with the youth deciding that their hero should become a martyr for whom they would lay down their own lives. I first flew via helicopter to pay my respects to Chris's eighty-two-year-old father in Sabalele, a tiny, dusty town in the Cofimvaba district in the Transkei, a place well known to me because it was the home region of the Matanzima family. As I arrived in this village with no running water or electricity, I marveled at how this poor and tiny village could produce a man like Chris Hani, a man who stirred the entire nation with his passion and ability. His concern for the rural poor came from his childhood in Sabalele, for his roots were deep and true, and he never lost them. Chris's father spoke eloquently of the pain of losing a son, but with satisfaction that he had died in the struggle.

Upon my return to Johannesburg I learned that the police had arrested a member of the militant right-wing Afrikaner Weerstandsbeweging (AWB), a Polish immigrant to South Africa who had been captured after a courageous Afrikaner woman had phoned the police with the killer's license plate number. The murder was an act of mad desperation, an attempt to derail the negotiations process. I was asked to speak on the SABC that night to address the nation. In this instance, it was the ANC, not the government, that sought to calm the nation.

I said that the process of peace and negotiations could not be halted. With all the authority at my command, I said, "I appeal to all our people to remain calm and to honor the memory of Chris Hani by remaining a disciplined force for peace."

> Tonight I am reaching out to every single South African, black and white, from the very depths of my being. A white man, full of prejudice and hate, came to our country and committed a deed so foul that our whole nation now teeters on the brink of disaster. A white woman, of Afrikaner origin, risked her life so that we may know, and bring to justice this assassin. . . . Now is the time for all South Africans to stand together against those who, from any quarter, wish to destroy what Chris Hani gave his life for — the freedom of all of us.

The assassination of Chris was an attempt by white supremacists to arrest the inevitable. They preferred that the country descend into civil war rather than have majority rule by peaceful means.

We adopted a strategy to deal with our own constituency in the ANC. In order to forestall outbreaks of retaliatory violence, we arranged a week-long series of mass rallies and demonstrations throughout the country. This would give people a means of expressing their frustration without resorting to violence. Mr. de Klerk and I spoke privately and agreed that we would not let Hani's murder derail the negotiations.

We learned within days that a member of the Conservative Party, Clive Derby-Lewis, had been arrested in connection with the murder. More confirmation of a Third Force. It was Chris himself who had criticized a recent theft of weapons from an air force base; preliminary police reports suggested that the gun that killed him had come from that stockpile.

Exactly two weeks later, there was another significant passing. This one did not shake the nation as Chris's had, but it shook me. Oliver had not been well for a long time, but the stroke that killed him occurred suddenly and without warning. His wife, Adelaide, phoned me early in the morning and I rushed to Oliver's bedside. I did not have a chance to say a proper good-bye, for he was already gone.

In Plato's allegory of the metals, the philosopher classifies men into groups of gold, silver, and lead. Oliver was pure gold; there was gold in his intellectual brilliance, gold in his warmth and humanity, gold in his tolerance and generosity, gold in his unfailing loyalty and self-sacrifice. As much as I respected him as a leader, that is how much I loved him as a man.

Though we had been apart for all the years that I was in prison, Oliver was never far from my thoughts. In many ways, even though we were separated, I kept up a lifelong conversation with him in my head. Perhaps that is why I felt so bereft when he died. I felt, as I told one colleague, like the loneliest man in the world. It was as though he had been snatched away from me just as we had finally been reunited. When I looked at him in his casket, it was as if a part of myself had died.

Though we were not yet in power, I wanted Oliver to have a state funeral, and that is what the ANC gave him. At a mass rally at a stadium in Soweto, hundreds of dignitaries from foreign governments gathered to pay their respects to the man who kept the ANC alive during its years of exile. MK troops marched in his honor and a twenty-one-gun salute was given at his graveside. Oliver had lived to see the prisoners released and the exiles return, but he had not lived to cast his vote in a free and democratic South Africa. That was what remained to be accomplished.

# 112

ALTHOUGH FEW PEOPLE will remember June 3, 1993, it was a landmark in South African history. On that day, after months of negotiations at the World Trade Centre, the multiparty forum voted to set a date for the country's first national, nonracial, one-person-one-vote election: April 27, 1994. For the first time in South African history, the black majority would go to the polls to elect their own leaders. The agreement was that voters would elect four hundred representatives to a constituent assembly, which would both write a new constitution and serve as a parliament. After convening, the first order of business for the assembly would be to elect a president.

The talks had reconvened in April. This time, the twenty-six parties included Inkatha, the Pan Africanist Congress, and the Conservative Party. We had been pressing the government to establish a date for months, and they had been stalling. But now the date was written in stone.

A month later, in July, the multiparty forum agreed on a first draft of an interim constitution. It provided for a bicameral parliament with a four-hundred-member national assembly elected by proportional representation from national and regional party lists and a senate elected indirectly by regional legislatures. Elections to regional legislatures would take place at the same time as national elections, and the regional bodies could draw up their own constitutions consistent with the national constitution.

Chief Buthelezi wanted a constitution drawn up before the election and walked out in protest against the setting of an election date before a constitution was finalized. A second draft interim constitution in August gave greater powers to the regions, but this did not placate either Chief Buthelezi or the Conservative Party. The

Conservative Party described the resolutions as hostile to Afrikaner interests. A group called the Afrikaner Volksfront, led by General Constand Viljoen, a former chief of the South African Defense Force, was formed to unite conservative white organizations around the idea of a *volkstaat,* a white homeland.

Just after midnight on November 18, an interim constitution was approved by a plenary session of the multiparty conference. The government and the ANC had cleared the remaining hurdles. The new cabinet would be composed of those winning more than 5 percent of the vote and would make decisions by consensus, rather than the two-thirds majority proposed by the government; national elections would not take place until 1999, so that the government of national unity would serve for five years; and finally, the government gave way on our insistence on a single ballot paper for the election, rather than separate ballots for national and provincial legislatures. Two ballot papers would only confuse a majority of voters, most of whom would be voting for the first time in their lives. In the period leading up to the election, a Transitional Executive Council with members from each party would ensure the right climate for the elections. In effect, the TEC would be the government between December 22 and the election on April 27. An Independent Electoral Commission with extensive powers would be responsible for the administration of the election. We were truly on the threshold of a new era.

I have never cared very much for personal prizes. A man does not become a freedom fighter in the hope of winning awards, but when I was notified that I had won the 1993 Nobel Peace Prize jointly with Mr. de Klerk, I was deeply moved. The Nobel Peace Prize had a special meaning to me because of its involvement with South African history.

I was the third South African since the end of the Second World War to be so honored by the Nobel committee. Chief Albert Luthuli was awarded the prize in 1960. The second was Archbishop Desmond Tutu, who selflessly fought the evils of racism during the most terrible days of apartheid.

The award was a tribute to all South Africans and especially to those who had fought in the struggle; I would accept the award on their behalf. But the Nobel award was one I never thought about.

Even during the bleakest years on Robben Island, Amnesty International would not campaign for us on the grounds that we had pursued an armed struggle, and their organization would not represent anyone who had embraced violence. It was for that reason that I assumed the Nobel committee would never consider the man who had started Umkhonto we Sizwe for the peace prize.

I had tremendous respect for the nations of Norway and Sweden. In the 1950s and 1960s, when we went to Western governments seeking contributions to the ANC, we were turned down flat. But in Norway and Sweden, we were greeted with open arms, and given assistance and scholarships and money for legal defense and humanitarian aid for political prisoners.

I used my speech in Norway not only to thank the Nobel committee and sketch out a vision of a future South Africa that was just and equitable, but to pay tribute to my fellow laureate, Mr. F. W. de Klerk.

> He had the courage to admit that a terrible wrong had been done to our country and people through the imposition of the system of apartheid. He had the foresight to understand and accept that all the people of South Africa must, through negotiations and as equal participants in the process, together determine what they want to make of their future.

I was often asked how could I accept the award jointly with Mr. de Klerk after I had criticized him so severely. Although I would not take back my criticisms, I could say that he had made a genuine and indispensable contribution to the peace process. I never sought to undermine Mr. de Klerk, for the practical reason that the weaker he was, the weaker the negotiations process. To make peace with an enemy one must work with that enemy, and that enemy becomes one's partner.

Although the official campaign for the national assembly was not scheduled to begin until February 1994, we started to campaign in earnest after the new constitution was ratified. That did not give us a head start; the National Party began its campaign the day they released me from prison.

Although the polls showed the ANC with a healthy margin, we never took victory for granted. I counseled everyone against over-optimism. We had all read dozens of accounts of parties favored to win who came in second. We faced an experienced, well-organized, and well-financed rival.

Our campaign was under the capable leadership of Popo Molefe, Terror Lekota, and Ketso Gordhan, all veteran UDF activists adept at mass mobilization. The task was a formidable one. We estimated that there would be over twenty million people going to the polls, most of them voting for the first time. Many of our voters were illiterate, and were likely to be intimidated by the mere idea of voting. According to the Independent Electoral Commission, there would be ten thousand polling stations around the country. We sought to train over one hundred thousand people to assist with voter education.

The first stage of our election effort was what was known as People's Forums. ANC candidates would travel all over the country and hold meetings in towns and villages in order to listen to the hopes and fears, the ideas and complaints, of our people. The People's Forums were similar to the town meetings that candidate Bill Clinton held in America on his way to the presidency. The forums were parliaments of the people, not unlike the meetings of chiefs at the Great Place that I witnessed as a boy.

I reveled in the People's Forums. I began in Natal in November, and then went to the PWV area, the northern Transvaal, and the Orange Free State. I attended as many as three or four forums in a day. The people themselves enjoyed them immensely. No one had ever come to solicit their opinion on what should be done in their own country.

After incorporating the suggestions from the forums, we traveled the country delivering our message to the people. Some in the ANC wanted to make the campaign simply a liberation election, and tell the people: Vote for us because we set you free. We decided instead to offer them a vision of the South Africa we hoped to create. We wanted people to vote for the ANC not just because we had fought apartheid for eighty years, but because we were best qualified to bring about the kind of South Africa they hoped to live in. I felt that our campaign should be about the future, not the past.

The ANC drafted a 150-page document known as the Reconstruction and Development Program, which outlined our plan to create jobs through public works; to build a million new houses with electricity and flush toilets; to extend primary health care and ten years of free education to all South Africans; to redistribute land through a land claims court; and to end the value-added tax on basic foodstuffs. We were also committed to extensive affirmative action measures in both the private and public sectors. This document was translated into a simpler manifesto called "A Better Life for All," which in turn became the ANC's campaign slogan.

Just as we told the people what we would do, I felt we must also tell them what we could not do. Many people felt life would change overnight after a free and democratic election, but that would be far from the case. Often, I said to crowds, "Do not expect to be driving a Mercedes the day after the election or swimming in your own backyard pool." I told our supporters, "Life will not change dramatically, except that you will have increased your self-esteem and become a citizen in your own land. You must have patience. You might have to wait five years for results to show." I challenged them; I did not patronize them: "If you want to continue living in poverty without clothes and food," I told them, "then go and drink in the shebeens. But if you want better things, you must work hard. We cannot do it all for you; you must do it yourselves."

I told white audiences that we needed them and did not want them to leave the country. They were South Africans just like ourselves and this was their land, too. I would not mince words about the horrors of apartheid, but I said, over and over, that we should forget the past and concentrate on building a better future for all.

Each rally was also designed to teach people how to vote. The ballot itself was a long, narrow piece of paper with the parties listed in descending order to the left, and then the symbol of the party and a picture of its leader to the right. Voters were to place an X in the box next to the party of their choice. I would tell audiences, "On election day, look down your ballot and when you see the face of a young and handsome man, mark an X."

# 113

THE ROAD TO FREEDOM was far from smooth. Although the Transitional Executive Council began functioning in the new year, some parties opted out. Inkatha rejected participation in the election and gave itself over to the politics of resistance. King Zwelithini, supported by Chief Buthelezi, called for an autonomous and sovereign KwaZulu, and discouraged everyone in his province from voting. The white right called the elections a betrayal and clamored for a *volkstaat,* yet they still had not proposed where it would be located or how it would work. There was no magisterial district in all of South Africa where whites constituted a majority of residents.

February 12, 1994, was the deadline for registration of all parties, and on that day, Inkatha, the Conservative Party, and the Afrikaner Volksfront failed to sign. The government of the Bophuthatswana homeland also refused to participate and resisted reincorporation into a united South Africa. I was disturbed that these important groups were choosing not to participate. To bring them on board, we proposed certain significant compromises: we agreed to the use of double ballots for provincial and national legislatures; guarantees of greater provincial powers; the renaming of Natal province as KwaZulu/Natal; and the affirmation that a principle of "internal" self-determination would be included in the constitution for groups sharing a common cultural and language heritage.

I arranged to meet Chief Buthelezi in Durban on March 1. "I will go down on my knees to beg those who want to drag our country into bloodshed," I told a rally before this meeting. Chief Buthelezi agreed to provisionally register for the elections in exchange for a promise to subject our differences over constitutional issues to international mediation. To this I gladly assented. Before the final registration deadline, General Viljoen also registered under a new party known as the Freedom Front.

Though Lucas Mangope, the president of Bophuthatswana, had chosen to keep his homeland out of the election, the tide of events soon altered the situation. I spoke to him on a number of occasions urging him to let his people decide, but he would not listen. Those who wanted to participate launched mass demonstrations and strikes, which soon spread to the Bophuthatswana civil service. The radio and television networks went off the air. On the streets of Mafikeng, battles broke out between the homeland police and striking workers and students. Mangope called in military help from his white right-wing allies. Soon, his own forces deserted him and he was ousted in a coup in early March. A few weeks later, Brigadier Gqozo in the Ciskei capitulated and asked South Africa to take over the homeland.

Violence in Natal worsened. Inkatha supporters were blocking our efforts to campaign in Natal. Fifteen ANC election workers were shot and hacked to death after putting up ANC posters. In March, Judge Johann Kriegler reported to me and Mr. de Klerk that because of the lack of cooperation from the KwaZulu government, free elections could not be held there without direct political intervention. To demonstrate our strength in Natal, the ANC held a mass march through the center of Durban. Then Inkatha attempted to do the same in Johannesburg, with dire results.

On March 28, thousands of Inkatha members, brandishing spears and knobkerries, marched through Johannesburg to a rally in the center of town. At the same time, an armed Inkatha group attempted to enter Shell House, the ANC headquarters, but were repulsed by armed guards. Shots by unidentified gunmen were also fired in the city center, and altogether fifty-three people died. It was a grisly spectacle that made South Africa appear as if it was on the brink of internal war. Inkatha was attempting to postpone the election, but neither Mr. de Klerk nor I would budge. That day was sacrosanct.

I had agreed to international mediation, and on April 13 a delegation arrived led by Lord Carrington, the former British foreign secretary, and Henry Kissinger, the former American secretary of state. But when Inkatha was informed that the election date was not subject to mediation, they refused to see the mediators, who left without talking to anyone. Now Chief Buthelezi knew the election would take place no matter what. On April 19, barely a week before the election, Chief Buthelezi accepted the offer of a constitutional role for the Zulu monarchy and agreed to participate.

Ten days before the vote, Mr. de Klerk and I held our single television debate. I had been a fair debater at Fort Hare, and in my early years in the organization I had engaged in many impassioned debates on the platform. On Robben Island, we had honed our debating skills while we chipped away at limestone. I was confident, but the day before, we held a mock debate in which the journalist Allister Sparks ably performed as Mr. de Klerk. Too ably, according to my campaign advisers, for they chided me for speaking too slowly and not aggressively enough.

When the time came for the actual debate, however, I attacked the National Party quite firmly. I accused the National Party of

fanning race hatred between Coloureds and Africans in the Cape
by distributing an inflammatory comic book that said the ANC's
slogan was "Kill a Coloured, kill a farmer." "There is no organization
in this country as divisive as the new National Party," I declared.
When Mr. de Klerk criticized the ANC's plan to spend billions of
dollars on housing and social programs, I scolded him, saying he
was alarmed that we would have to devote so many of our resources
to blacks.

But as the debate was nearing an end, I felt I had been too harsh
with the man who would be my partner in a government of national
unity. In summation, I said, "The exchanges between Mr. de Klerk
and me should not obscure one important fact. I think we are a
shining example to the entire world of people drawn from different
racial groups who have a common loyalty, a common love, to their
common country. . . . In spite of criticism of Mr. de Klerk," I said,
and then looked over at him, "sir, you are one of those I rely upon.
We are going to face the problem of this country together." At
which point I reached over to take his hand and said, "I am proud
to hold your hand for us to go forward." Mr. de Klerk seemed
surprised, but pleased.

# 114

I VOTED ON APRIL 27, the second of the four days of voting,
and I chose to vote in Natal to show the people in that divided
province that there was no danger in going to the polling stations.
I voted at Ohlange High School in Inanda, a green and hilly township just north of Durban, for it was there that John Dube, the first
president of the ANC, was buried. This African patriot had helped
found the organization in 1912, and casting my vote near his grave
site brought history full circle, for the mission he began eighty-two
years before was about to be achieved.

As I stood over his grave, on a rise above the small school below,
I thought not of the present but of the past. When I walked to the
voting station, my mind dwelt on the heroes who had fallen so that
I might be where I was that day, the men and women who had
made the ultimate sacrifice for a cause that was now finally succeeding. I thought of Oliver Tambo, and Chris Hani, and Chief

Luthuli, and Bram Fischer. I thought of our great African heroes, who had sacrificed so that millions of South Africans could be voting on that very day; I thought of Josiah Gumede, G. M. Naicker, Dr. Abdullah Abdurahman, Lilian Ngoyi, Helen Joseph, Yusuf Dadoo, Moses Kotane. I did not go into that voting station alone on April 27; I was casting my vote with all of them.

Before I entered the polling station, an irreverent member of the press called out, "Mr. Mandela, who are you voting for?" I laughed. "You know," I said, "I have been agonizing over that choice all morning." I marked an X in the box next to the letters ANC and then slipped my folded ballot paper into a simple wooden box; I had cast the first vote of my life.

The images of South Africans going to the polls that day are burned in my memory. Great lines of patient people snaking through the dirt roads and streets of towns and cities; old women who had waited half a century to cast their first vote saying that they felt like human beings for the first time in their lives; white men and women saying they were proud to live in a free country at last. The mood of the nation during those days of voting was buoyant. The violence and bombings ceased, and it was as if we were a nation reborn. Even the logistical difficulties of the voting, misplaced ballots, pirate voting stations, and rumors of fraud in certain places could not dim the overwhelming victory for democracy and justice.

It took several days for the results to be counted. We polled 62.6 percent of the national vote, slightly short of the two-thirds needed had we wished to push through a final constitution without support from other parties. That percentage qualified us for 252 of 400 seats in the national assembly. The ANC thoroughly dominated the northern and eastern Transvaal, the northwest, the eastern Cape and the Free State. We won 33 percent of the vote in the western Cape, which was won by the National Party, which did extremely well among Coloured voters. We captured 32 percent in KwaZulu/Natal, which was won by Inkatha. In Natal, fear of violence and intimidation kept many of our voters at home. There were charges, as well, of vote fraud and vote rigging. But in the end, that did not matter. We had underestimated Inkatha's strength in KwaZulu, and they had demonstrated it on election day.

Some in the ANC were disappointed that we did not cross the

two-thirds threshold, but I was not one of them. In fact I was relieved; had we won two-thirds of the vote and been able to write a constitution unfettered by input from others, people would argue that we had created an ANC constitution, not a South African constitution. I wanted a true government of national unity.

On the evening of May 2, Mr. de Klerk made a gracious concession speech. After more than three centuries of rule, the white minority was conceding defeat and turning over power to the black majority. That evening, the ANC was planning a victory celebration at the ballroom of the Carlton Hotel in downtown Johannesburg. I was suffering from a bad case of the flu and my doctors ordered me to remain at home. But there was nothing that could keep me away from that party. I went onstage at about nine o'clock and faced a crowd of happy, smiling, cheering faces.

I explained to the crowd that my voice was hoarse from a cold and that my physician had advised me not to attend. "I hope that you will not disclose to him that I have violated his instructions," I told them. I congratulated Mr. de Klerk for his strong showing. I thanked all those in the ANC and the democratic movement who had worked so hard for so long. Mrs. Coretta Scott King, the wife of the great freedom fighter Martin Luther King Jr., was on the podium that night, and I looked over to her as I made reference to her husband's immortal words.

> This is one of the most important moments in the life of our country. I stand here before you filled with deep pride and joy — pride in the ordinary, humble people of this country. You have shown such a calm, patient determination to reclaim this country as your own, and now the joy that we can loudly proclaim from the rooftops — Free at last! Free at last! I stand before you humbled by your courage, with a heart full of love for all of you. I regard it as the highest honor to lead the ANC at this moment in our history. I am your servant. . . . It is not the individuals that matter, but the collective. . . . This is a time to heal the old wounds and build a new South Africa.

From the moment the results were in and it was apparent that the ANC was to form the government, I saw my mission as one of preaching reconciliation, of binding the wounds of the country, of engendering trust and confidence. I knew that many people, particularly the minorities, whites, Coloureds, and Indians, would be feeling anxious about the future, and I wanted them to feel secure. I reminded people again and again that the liberation struggle was not a battle against any one group or color, but a fight against a system of repression. At every opportunity, I said all South Africans must now unite and join hands and say we are one country, one nation, one people, marching together into the future.

# 115

MAY 10 DAWNED bright and clear. For the past few days, I had been pleasantly besieged by arriving dignitaries and world leaders who were coming to pay their respects before the inauguration. The inauguration would be the largest gathering ever of international leaders on South African soil.

The ceremonies took place in the lovely sandstone amphitheater formed by the Union Buildings in Pretoria. For decades, this had been the seat of white supremacy, and now it was the site of a rainbow gathering of different colors and nations for the installation of South Africa's first democratic, nonracial government.

On that lovely autumn day I was accompanied by my daughter Zenani. On the podium, Mr. de Klerk was first sworn in as second deputy president. Then Thabo Mbeki was sworn in as first deputy president. When it was my turn, I pledged to obey and uphold the constitution and to devote myself to the well-being of the republic and its people. To the assembled guests and the watching world, I said:

> Today, all of us do, by our presence here . . . confer glory and hope to newborn liberty. Out of the experience of an extraordinary human disaster that lasted too long, must be born a society of which all humanity will be proud.
>
> . . . We, who were outlaws not so long ago, have today been given the rare privilege to be host to the nations of the world on our own soil. We thank all of our distinguished international guests for having come to take possession with the people of our country of what is, after all, a common victory for justice, for peace, for human dignity.
>
> We have, at last, achieved our political emancipation. We pledge

ourselves to liberate all our people from the continuing bondage of poverty, deprivation, suffering, gender, and other discrimination.

Never, never, and never again shall it be that this beautiful land will again experience the oppression of one by another. . . . The sun shall never set on so glorious a human achievement.

Let freedom reign. God bless Africa!

A few moments later we all lifted our eyes in awe as a spectacular array of South African jets, helicopters, and troop carriers roared in perfect formation over the Union Buildings. It was not only a display of pinpoint precision and military force, but a demonstration of the military's loyalty to democracy, to a new government that had been freely and fairly elected. Only moments before, the highest generals of the South African Defense Force and police, their chests bedecked with ribbons and medals from days gone by, saluted me and pledged their loyalty. I was not unmindful of the fact that not so many years before they would not have saluted but arrested me. Finally a chevron of Impala jets left a smoke trail of the black, red, green, blue, white, and gold of the new South African flag.

The day was symbolized for me by the playing of our two national anthems, and the vision of whites singing *"Nkosi Sikelel' iAfrika"* and blacks singing *"Die Stem,"* the old anthem of the republic. Although that day, neither group knew the lyrics of the anthem they once despised, they would soon know the words by heart.

On the day of the inauguration, I was overwhelmed with a sense of history. In the first decade of the twentieth century, a few years after the bitter Anglo-Boer War and before my own birth, the white-skinned peoples of South Africa patched up their differences and erected a system of racial domination against the dark-skinned peoples of their own land. The structure they created formed the basis of one of the harshest, most inhumane societies the world has ever known. Now, in the last decade of the twentieth century, and my own eighth decade as a man, that system had been overturned forever and replaced by one that recognized the rights and freedoms of all peoples regardless of the color of their skin.

That day had come about through the unimaginable sacrifices of thousands of my people, people whose suffering and courage can never be counted or repaid. I felt that day, as I have on so many other days, that I was simply the sum of all those African patriots who had gone before me. That long and noble line ended and now began again with me. I was pained that I was not able to thank them and that they were not able to see what their sacrifices had wrought.

The policy of apartheid created a deep and lasting wound in my country and my people. All of us will spend many years, if not generations, recovering from that profound hurt. But the decades of oppression and brutality had another, unintended effect, and that was that it produced the Oliver Tambos, the Walter Sisulus, the Chief Luthulis, the Yusuf Dadoos, the Bram Fischers, the Robert Sobukwes of our time — men of such extraordinary courage, wisdom, and generosity that their like may never be known again. Perhaps it requires such depth of oppression to create such heights of character. My country is rich in the minerals and gems that lie beneath its soil, but I have always known that its greatest wealth is its people, finer and truer than the purest diamonds.

It is from these comrades in the struggle that I learned the meaning of courage. Time and again, I have seen men and women risk and give their lives for an idea. I have seen men stand up to attacks and torture without breaking, showing a strength and resiliency that defies the imagination. I learned that courage was not the absence of fear, but the triumph over it. I felt fear myself more times than I can remember, but I hid it behind a mask of boldness. The brave man is not he who does not feel afraid, but he who conquers that fear.

I never lost hope that this great transformation would occur. Not only because of the great heroes I have already cited, but because of the courage of the ordinary men and women of my country. I always knew that deep down in every human heart, there is mercy and generosity. No one is born hating another person because of the color of his skin, or his background, or his religion. People must learn to hate, and if they can learn to hate, they can be taught to love, for love comes more naturally to the human heart than its opposite. Even in the grimmest times in prison, when my comrades and I were pushed to our limits, I would see a glimmer of humanity in one of the guards, perhaps just for a second, but it was enough to reassure me and keep me going. Man's goodness is a flame that can be hidden but never extinguished.

We took up the struggle with our eyes wide open, under no illusion that the path would be an easy one. As a young man, when I joined the African National Congress, I saw the price my comrades paid for their beliefs, and it was high. For myself, I have never regretted my commitment to the struggle, and I was always prepared to face the hardships that affected me personally. But my family paid a terrible price, perhaps too dear a price for my commitment.

In life, every man has twin obligations — obligations to his family, to his parents, to his wife and children; and he has an obligation to his people, his community, his country. In a civil and humane society, each man is able to fulfill those obligations according to his own inclinations and abilities. But in a country like South Africa, it was almost impossible for a man of my birth and color to fulfill both of those obligations. In South Africa, a man of color who attempted to live as a human being was punished and isolated. In South Africa, a man who tried to fulfill his duty to his people was inevitably ripped from his family and his home and was forced to live a life apart, a twilight existence of secrecy and rebellion. I did not in the beginning choose to place my people above my family, but in attempting to serve my people, I found that I was prevented from fulfilling my obligations as a son, a brother, a father, and a husband.

In that way, my commitment to my people, to the millions of South Africans I would never know or meet, was at the expense of the people I knew best and loved most. It was as simple and yet as incomprehensible as the moment a small child asks her father, "Why can you not be with us?" And the father must utter the terrible words: "There are other children like you, a great many of them . . ." and then one's voice trails off.

I was not born with a hunger to be free. I was born free — free in every way that I could know. Free to run in the fields near my mother's hut, free to swim in the clear stream that ran through my village, free to roast mealies under the stars and ride the broad backs of slow-moving bulls. As long as I obeyed my father and abided by the customs of my tribe, I was not troubled by the laws of man or God.

It was only when I began to learn that my boyhood freedom was an illusion, when I discovered as a young man that my freedom had already been taken from me, that I began to hunger for it. At first, as a student, I wanted freedom only for myself, the transitory freedoms of being able to stay out at night, read what I pleased, and go where I chose. Later, as a young man in Johannesburg, I yearned for the basic and honorable freedoms of achieving my potential, of earning my keep, of marrying and having a family — the freedom not to be obstructed in a lawful life.

But then I slowly saw that not only was I not free, but my brothers and sisters were not free. I saw that it was not just my freedom that was curtailed, but the freedom of everyone who looked like I did. That is when I joined the African National Congress, and that is when the hunger for my own freedom became the greater hunger for the freedom of my people. It was this desire for the freedom of my people to live their lives with dignity and self-respect that animated my life, that transformed a frightened young man into a bold one, that drove a law-abiding attorney to become a criminal, that turned a family-loving husband into a man without a home, that forced a life-loving man to live like a monk. I am no more virtuous or self-sacrificing than the next man, but I found that I could not even enjoy the poor and limited freedoms I was allowed when I knew my people were not free. Freedom is indivisible; the chains on any one of my people were the chains on all of them, the chains on all of my people were the chains on me.

It was during those long and lonely years that my hunger for the freedom of my own people became a hunger for the freedom of all people, white and black. I knew as well as I knew anything that the oppressor must be liberated just as surely as the oppressed. A man who takes away another man's freedom is a prisoner of hatred, he is locked behind the bars of prejudice and narrow-mindedness. I am not truly free if I am taking away someone else's freedom, just as surely as I am not free when my freedom is taken from me. The oppressed and the oppressor alike are robbed of their humanity.

When I walked out of prison, that was my mission, to liberate the oppressed and the oppressor both. Some say that has now been achieved. But I know that that is not the case. The truth is that we are not yet free; we have merely achieved the freedom to be free, the right not to be oppressed. We have not taken the final step of our journey, but the first step on a longer and even more difficult road. For to be free is not merely to cast off one's chains, but to live in a way that respects and enhances the freedom of others. The true test of our devotion to freedom is just beginning.

I have walked that long road to freedom. I have tried not to falter; I have made missteps along the way. But I have discovered the secret that after climbing a great hill, one only finds that there are many more hills to climb. I have taken a moment here to rest, to steal a view of the glorious vista that surrounds me, to look back on the distance I have come. But I can rest only for a moment, for with freedom come responsibilities, and I dare not linger, for my long walk is not yet ended.

# Index

Abdurahman, Abdullah, 618
abeSotho, 4
abeThembu. See Thembuland/Thembu people
Adams, Farid, 247–250
Addis Ababa, 287, 288, 293, 304–305
African Mine Workers Union (AMWU), 102
African National Congress (ANC), 3, 49, 65, 73, 159, 227, 283, 368, 518–519; Action Committee, 130; annual conferences, 236, 337; armed protest, violence policy, 270–274, 303–304, 528, 537–538, 546, 572, 585–586, 588–589; arrest and imprisonment of members, 200, 239–241, 422, 436, 438, 442–443; bail issue, 321; ban against, 486, 519, 556; branches, 97–98, 107; civil disobedience activities, 123–124, 126–131, 133, 138–140, 157–158; Congress of the People, 170–174; External Mission, 438; government of South Africa and, 144, 231, 243; international activities, 287–307; leadership, 429–430, 436, 442–443; membership, 132, 134, 139, 366; mobilization/mass action, 113–115, 117–119; National Executive Committee, 116–118, 123, 135, 143, 144, 158, 168–169, 172, 254, 337–338, 539, 575, 576, 577, 591–592, 606; negotiations with government of South Africa, 528–531, 534–536, 539, 553, 594–599, 601–607; NM as deputy president, 572; NM as president, 135–136, 161–162, 592–593; NM's early activities, 95–97, 330; nonviolence policy, 234, 235–236, 253, 254, 256, 259, 270–274, 273–274, 364; release of imprisoned members, 552–553; release of NM and, 571–572; removal schemes and, 155, 164–165; Robben Island activities, 442–443, 451, 467–468, 486–488, 508, 514; terrorism against, 518, 529, 587–589, 603–604; voting campaign, 109; white influence on, 108. See also ANC and; communism/Communist Party; Freedom Charter; MK; Women's League; Youth League

African People's Party (APO), 109, 115, 117
Afrikaner Rebellion, 551
Afrikaner Volksfront, 611, 615
Afrikaner Weerstandsbeweging (AWB), 607
Alexander, Neville, 385, 411, 440, 442
Alexandra Township, 68, 69, 76–77, 79, 86
Algeria, 298–299
All-African Convention, 44, 114
All-in Conference, 256, 257
amaBaca, 4
amaBomvana, 4
amaGcaleka, 4
amaMfengu, 4, 12
amaMpemvu, 6
amaMpodomis, 4
amaMpondo, 4, 37
amaNgutyana, 214
Amnesty International, 612
Angola, 439, 484, 500, 595
anti-ANC alliance, 578
apartheid, 111, 133, 205, 267, 338, 518–519, 566; education and, 166–167; grand, 190, 230, 431–432; legislation, 121–122, 520; regulations, 383; struggle against, 143, 176, 189–190, 518–519, 548; treason trial and, 247, 249; treatment of prisoners, 243–245
April, Jimmy, 464
Aronsohn, William, 163
Asiatic Land Tenure Act, 103
assassinations, 431–432
Astor, David, 303
Atlantic Charter, 95–96
Aucamp, Brigadier, 416, 446
Aucamp, Colonel, 321, 381
Autshumao, 340
Ayob, Ismail, 521, 522, 545
Azanian People's Organization, 595

Baard, Frances, 186, 220
Badenhorst, Piet, 458–459, 460–462
Bam, Fikile, 385, 433, 442, 476

Terblanche, Lieutenant, 466
Terblanche & Briggish law firm, 147
terrorism, 282, 283, 338, 506, 605
Terrorism Act, 445
Thatcher, Margaret, 527, 556, 582, 585–586
Thema, Selope, 135
Thembuland/Thembu people, 3–4, 6, 7, 21, 23, 36, 82, 85, 184, 231, 507
Theron, Captain, 345–346
Theron, M. E., 461
Thumbumuzi, Prince, 494–496
Thumbumuzi, Zaziwe (NM's grand-daughter), 495–496, 517
Tighy, Sarel, 90
Tloome, Dan, 99, 102, 218, 311
Toivo ja Toivo, Andimba, 459–460
Tomlinson Commission for the Socio-Economic Development of the Bantu Areas, 190, 191
Transkei, 3, 4, 176–184, 189, 190, 191, 231, 338, 507, 580
Transvaal Executive Committee, 108–110, 129
Transvaal Indian Congress (TIC), 91, 103, 104, 109, 116, 129, 137, 155
Transvaal Indian Youth Congress, 319
Transvaal Law Society, 426–427
travel documents, 57. See also pass system
Treason Trial, 199–205, 209–213, 217, 223–225, 231–236, 242–261, 362
Treason Trial Defense Fund, 205, 214
Trengove, Advocate, 236
tribal solidarity, 12, 23–24, 38, 79–80
Truter, Warrant Officer, 314
Tshabalala, Simon, 194
Tshwete, Steve, 508
Tubman, William, 300
Tuli, Jake, 195
Tutu, Desmond, 519, 522, 552, 561, 565, 567, 611
Tyamzashe, Victor, 216
Tyesi, Barrett, 169
Tyhalarha, 26

Umkhonto we Sizwe. See MK
unions, 87, 113. See also Congress of South African Trade Unions; strikes
United Democratic Front (UDF), 519, 522, 545, 548, 553, 566, 571, 593, 601, 613
United Jewish Reformed Congregation, 168
United National Independence Party (UNIP), 295–296
United Nations, 328, 593. See also sanctions, international

United Party, 110, 135, 166, 260
United States, 229, 238, 319–320, 539, 548, 582–584, 590
Unity Movement, 412, 442
University of South Africa (UNISA), 69, 71, 77, 88
University of the Witwatersrand, 89–92
Urban Areas Act, 99–100, 151, 154

Vabaza, Gamaliel, 45
Van Aarde, Colonel, 458
van der Merwe, Fanie, 533, 536
Van Heerden, Magistrate, 325
Van Niekerk, Prosecutor, 204–205
Van Rensburg, Warder, 432–438, 451
Van Riebeeck, Jan, 124
Van Sittert, Fritz, 520
Versailles peace conference (1918), 3
Verwoerd, Hendrik F., 167, 169, 190, 230, 258, 338, 377; 1961 strike and, 269; assassination, 431–432
Victor Verster prison, 543–546, 548, 607
Viljoen, Constand, 611, 615
Viljoen, Gerrit, 552
Vlok, Adriaan, 588, 592
Vorster, B. J., 163
Vorster, John, 338–339, 374, 499–500
Vorster, Sargeant, 314
Votes for All, 109, 110
voting rights, 100, 109, 110, 113, 171, 172, 252, 518–519

Washington, Booker T., 44
Wellbeloved, Mr., 65–66, 70
Wellington, Arthur, 37, 38, 39, 40–41
Welsh, Rex, 224
Wesleyan Church, 168, 187
Wessel, F. C., 203–204, 212
Wessels, Colonel, 403, 422
Western Areas townships, 153–154
Western Native Township, 68, 73
whites, 23–24, 30, 103, 108, 111–112, 113, 124, 387, 504
Willemse, W. H., 462–464, 528, 529–530, 533, 536, 549, 550, 554
Williams, Cecil, 307, 311, 312–315
Witkin, Sidelsky and Eidelman law firm, 70–74, 106, 147
Witwatersrand Native Labor Association (WNLA), 82, 83
Wolpe, Harold, 91, 224, 316, 348–349, 352, 359, 369
Women's League, 220, 222, 254
World Festival of Youth and Students for Peace and Friendship, 159